W9-ABP-047

A WOMAN OF HER TIMES

A Woman of Her Times

G.J. Scrimgeour

G.P. PUTNAM'S SONS
NEW YORK

Published simultaneously in Canada by General Publishing Co. Limited, Toronto.

PRINTED IN THE UNITED STATES OF AMERICA

For Norman Collins,
who first gave me London,

and for all the other writers
who made their worlds belong to me.

"I should like you also to reflect that its events could have taken place only in a world where man considers himself superior to woman. In what the Americans call 'a man's world.' That is, a world governed by brute force, humourless arrogance, illusory prestige, and primeval stupidity. . . . Men love war because it allows them to look serious. Because they imagine it is the one thing that stops women laughing at them. In it they can reduce women to the status of objects. That is the great distinction between the sexes. Men see objects, women see the relationship between objects. Whether the objects need each other, love each other, match each other. It is an extra dimension of feeling we men are without and one that makes war abhorrent to all real women–and absurd. I will tell you what war is. War is a psychosis caused by an inability to see relationships. Our relationship with our fellow men. Our relationship with our economic and historical situation. And above all our relationship to nothingness. To death."

–John Fowles, *The Magus*

PART I

Before the First War

1

February 1914

Elizabeth Wingate was not beautiful, but manners, grooming, and voice made her seem so. She was a woman of her times. Or at least we now see such women–long hair pinned by amber combs to the back of the head, skirts falling in folds to just above the ankle, ruched white blouse clasped at the throat with ivory brooch bestowed by Victorian mother–we see them as the women of their time, as though everyone then belonged to the upper middle class, even shop-girls and tweenies and the chimney sweep's common-law wife, as though the richly feminine were the times' emblem, and Einstein had not had his bright idea a decade before, and there never would be a war, never a *real* war.

Elizabeth's Irish skin was still brushed with natural pink despite years of Ceylon's tropical sun and the growing fashion for rouge in the evenings. Her hair, touched with auburn as though she were eighteen rather than thirty-two, was full and gleaming, to make one think of riches and the bedroom. Her eyes were almost greenish, and because she did not wear glasses though a trifle short of sight, seemed more than ordinarily languid. As she leaned over the packing case in her room, one's eyes were drawn to her full lips, to the line of chin and throat, to the full bosom modestly concealed by pleated lawn but thrust forward by the boned corset beneath, so that even her seductiveness was ladylike, as though those women of her times waited, sheathed and pliable, for men to bring them to life.

That year before the war, she had servants, more servants than any woman in England, because native labor was cheap. Her own work was clean and passive: this slow, graceful unpacking, the writing of letters, the quietening of squabbles. She had leisure and did not realize that a life spent in morning visits, shopping, reading, playing bridge, accompanying one's husband, was not only idle but antique. She danced, always, the waltz, for the two-step and the bunny hop had caught on only among the younger set, and she imitated youth only in allowing herself as the hot evening wore on to discard the long white gloves which she had been brought up to believe obligatory. Her education had been better than her mother's, but her mind as yet remained superior to any use she had made of it; she preferred Rudyard Kipling to Joseph Conrad, Elinor Glyn to H. G. Wells, and Somerset Maugham to George Bernard Shaw. Her habits of thought were those of Society, for she disciplined her ideas under good manners very much as she confined her flesh under the right clothes.

She revealed her times (here in this colonial mansion, pausing in a shaft of sunlight to lift personal articles from the wooden packing case) but she was not typical of them, for only the dully anonymous are typical, and she had too much character to be dull, too much wit to be anonymous, too much imaginativeness to be as smug as wealth, station, and the color of her skin would have allowed her to be. She would have been a success in London, even, and out here in the crown colony she had become the best friend of the Governor's wife.

Because it was 1914, there were occasions lately when, having read the newspaper to induce sleep, she lay open-eyed under the mosquito netting and canopy of her double bed and heard the wash of the great ocean upon the fragile eternal beach a hundred yards away and thought that she and her world were drifting, not sailing. But at thirty-two one clings to belief in purpose. One believes that the destiny of life is to triumph, not just to survive. And to be British in 1914, to be wealthy, to belong to the ruling class in a crown colony, to have just moved into a house that England would have called a mansion, to have a husband successful and handsome, and a new and long-awaited baby girl—surely this was triumph.

Ceylon is the land of Serendib, called the island of treasures. A lush green teardrop separated from the brash tumult of India by a channel even narrower than that which protects England from the Continent, Ceylon was in 1914 peacefully Buddhist under the distant Christian monarch and spent its time producing what one would expect of the fabled Orient: pearls and emeralds, spices and tea. There was, of course, the heat to put up with: the damnable burning heat of the dry season, the suffocating prickly heat of the twice-yearly monsoons, and the unexpected warm bad breath of occasional typhoons swiping the island. There were, of course, malaria, cholera, dengue, suppurating ulcers, as well as the more usual English ills of measles and diphtheria and consumption and scarlet fever and infantile paralysis. But in Ceylon peace had lasted so long that it was easy now to pretend that life was threatened by nothing more than—as at this moment of Elizabeth lifting her head to listen—the wretched monkeys screeching in attack upon the fruit trees.

Elizabeth could hear the monkeys' cries through the open windows as she knelt on the carpet in front of her armoire, fussing at the creases in garments which had been packed inevitably dampish, and she could hear the shrieks of the native army she had deployed in counterattack. She could also hear baby Jennifer wailing in the great bare nursery at the southern end of the corridor. The child-raising theories of the day demanded that she pay instant attention, but Elizabeth ignored the cry; the ayah would return in a moment and attend to whatever was the matter. But then she heard a third sound, which made her clasp with unfortunate strength the linen skirt which happened to be in her hands. It was the sound of boot heels clacking on the staircase from the main floor. Elizabeth's expression became one of irritation tinged with guilt. Charles had returned early from his morning ride, and it was too bad that he should have found her ignoring Jennifer. His voice came to her, almost shouting, as male as the sound of his boots, "And where the devil is the mem? I've told you—I don't care about the bloody monkeys in the bloody fruit trees—I've told you the baby is not to be left alone for a minute, and I come back to hear that!"

Poor Nona, thought Elizabeth, and set aside the white linen skirt with its fresh creases and rose from her knees and tucked a wisp of hair back into place and moved quickly toward the emergency.

The tall teak double doors of the nursery had been flung open, and the room stretched to the view: huge white walls and curtains, red tile floor. It was destined to become the dining room once they had settled in, but at the moment its only contents were a large wooden crate near the door, twin to that which Elizabeth had been emptying in her bedroom, and dead center of the floor a bassinet draped with white cretonne and mosquito net, standing so alone in stripes of sunlight that it resembled a throne or perhaps a shrine. Just inside the doorway stood a proud native woman, gold jewelry shining against her dark skin, her sari the room's only touch of color. She flashed a look at Elizabeth, encoded but indignant.

Charles had almost reached the bassinet. Babies two months old measure the world by the extent of the attention they get, and this girl child's voice rose against her bare surrounds: a demand, a fear, a grief, a rage. And so Charles Wingate, a handsome man in the prime of life and pique, was all masculine solicitude as he bent over the cradle and lifted up his daughter, trailing lacy swaddling clothes.

"Did they leave her all alone, poor pet?" he cooed. "There, there, Daddy's little princess . . . There, there, now . . ." Well, what's done is done, thought Elizabeth, and was suddenly struck by the contrast: this most male of men in this most female of postures. At her elbow, Nona jangled golden bangles and muttered, probably of the injustices which fatherhood levies on servants. Clutched to her father's chest, the baby stopped her wail and lifted her head up to make sure who held her. Wobbly-necked, she seemed reassured. What might have been a smile came over her face, and she let the tiresome head fall against his shoulder.

As Charles turned toward Elizabeth, she cannily preempted his complaint by speaking first, "You will really spoil her, Charles." Her tone was firm but light, and she let an edge of irritation show. Her voice was Elizabeth's great distinction. It was low, mannish, variable as a musical instrument, and instantly attractive. Whenever she spoke, one listened to more than her words.

"But look at her, Elizabeth!" Preempted, he had now been made to seem querulous. "Her face is flushed. She could have a fever. God knows how long she's been crying while these bloody monkeys chase their friends in the garden." The two parents stared at the baby in his arms, as though posing for a portrait of the perfect couple. Both were aware that he had gone too far.

"It's too bloody hot in this room," he grumbled.

The point was beyond dispute. Lying only a few degrees north of the equator, Ceylon is not as hot as India, but it will cause northern Europeans, like their flowers, to wilt. Its heat is of the kind in which the chatter of monkeys or the irregular clanging of a far-off Buddhist bell can produce an instant anger out of nowhere, which is then allayed as quickly by lassitude.

"*I* told the ayah to get rid of the monkeys," said Elizabeth, pressing her attack. "Last evening you complained. The outside servants had not noticed. . . ." The outside servants were Charles' responsibility. Quickly she smiled, lightening both tone and manner. "Our precious Jennifer seems to have fallen asleep again. You must have given her exactly what she wanted. Let me check her temperature."

It was her concession to save his face. She took the baby, cupped a hand on its forehead, then handed it to the ayah with a glance at

Charles. "You know as well as I do that the natives worship babies! Put her down again, will you, Nona? She's wet, but leave her for now. Put the netting down again." The women's eyes met in small conspiracy. Elizabeth looked at Charles, and since he had not accepted her hint that an apology was due the ayah, she chose to drive her point home, "The danger is in spoiling her, not neglecting her. These things are really better left to us."

She was being unusually firm. She regarded Charles' behavior as an intrusion into her domain. But Charles heard the remonstrance as no more than a wheedle, and (husband, father) he let himself be wheedled.

"A night nurse and a day nurse, and I come back from riding to find her left alone! I'll be glad when that nanny arrives. How else are we going to free you to go out during Colombo Week?"

Soft, this confrontation between husband and wife, in a time when softness was valued and when the woman, having won, made the man the victor. She moved toward him, becoming winsome and somehow shorter, and she took his left arm with the lightest, firmest weight of both her linked hands, and turned him, by means of this weight and the momentum of his own politeness, toward the door, the exit from argument, the breakfast that awaited them downstairs.

"She'll be here on the *Oronsay* on Tuesday, rain or shine. Are you ready for breakfast, or do you want to bathe first?" She watched him give baby and ayah one last inspection from the door, and thought, studying his face: You'd really be a bit of a stick if it weren't for those eyes.

Their unusual gray made Charles' eyes the focal point of his face. His features were regular, and although the tropical sun and forty-two years of life had removed the blandness of youth, they had not yet laid bare the revelations of middle age. His chin and jaw were too Victorianly resolute, but the disreputably high arch of his eyebrows and the curve of his full lips gave him a usual expression of good temper. His brown hair was suppressed by brilliantine. The mustache was thick, but short-clipped to fit respectability. Thus, as with all products of mannered generations, one could see even on Charles' surface the conflicts that lay within. He was a middle-aged man, tall, handsome, well-muscled, confident—but not as inalterable nor as immaculate as he looked. Elizabeth tugged gently at his elbow to make him lead her out of the room and down the wide staircase.

"Shall we have the carpeting tomorrow?" Her inquiry had a touch of feigned breathlessness and she did not pause for answer. "This place is so enormous! It's just as well that silly man put electric wiring in only half of it." She gestured at a loop of wires festooned over the balustrade. "We have to do something about that! I don't think we can fill the east wing with our belongings anyway, and except for the morning room, we *could* close it off, I suppose. . . ."

Amused by her girlishness, he accepted the bait. "The east wing?" He smiled. "You make us sound like bluebloods instead of Johnny-come-latelies!"

"You know what I mean." She almost pouted. "Without new furniture we shall rattle around like peas in a pod."

A traditional gambit, it might seem, but Elizabeth was a trifle overwhelmed by the big house into which they had moved this very week. In the newly fashionable suburb of Mount Lavinia, a discreet distance from the old Barnes mansion, which had recently been turned into a busy family hotel, the house lay back from low cliffs fronting a crescent of golden beach, palm trees, and blue ocean that brought a healthy breeze. Mosquitoes were rare here, and the natives' fishing village was just remote enough to make the scene exotic. It was only that Elizabeth was not quite used to it; new furnishings from England would make it less Eastern.

The Wingates had abandoned their Colombo house, scarcely more than a bungalow really, because it was too unhealthy for the baby and too small—far too small—for Charles Wingate's status and income. At the moment they had a sense of living up to the new home: three solid stories of imposing stone, verandaed, balconied, shuttered, porticoed, even balustraded. Separate buildings housed the servants' quarters, the laundry, the stables, the garage, and the kitchens. The rooms offered frightening vacancies, but there would come a time when the Wingates would occupy them like conquerors. Grounds and rooms would slowly surrender. Over there would be a court for lawn tennis, and those palms would give way (salt air permitting) to a croquet lawn of imported turf, and just this side of the kitchen garden would be the spot for Jennifer's playing, and once the purple waterfalls made by the jacarandas were tamed, there would be room for rosebushes.

Charles and Elizabeth both caught the foretaste of permanence as they sat to breakfast on the sun-screened south veranda in rattan chairs while their Sinhalese head boy, Abbuhamy, a man of some fifty years, many grandchildren, and the dignity brought by long and successful service, laid before them a breakfast of kippers, eggs, toast, curried kidney, tomato, and fried potato. Elizabeth poured tea with the delicate wrist of wifely deference. Charles thanked her as he took cup and saucer.

Like many men, Charles tended to see his wife less as the Elizabeth Malloy he had courted and captured than as Mrs. Charles Wingate. He behaved toward her as he believed Mr. Charles Wingate should, and because this made him susceptible to whatever small wiles she chose to use, it amused Elizabeth. She could reduce him to generic propriety in an instant.

"Peace at last," she sighed, sipping her tea and not seeming to look at him. They sat in contented silence as Elizabeth thought out her next small plan of campaign and Charles' mind began to turn to the office. Elizabeth's present dilemma was brought about by a slight touch of guilt. She was well aware that her concern for Jennifer's well-being was not as overwhelming as Charles would have liked. This baby had been long awaited, and at thirty-two she had felt too old to be a mother for the first time, but to her surprise, the coming of Jennifer had been untraumatic. She floated through pregnancy and confinement with an ease which belied the general belief that Nature and the angry God of Eden had decreed childbirth the sole but murderous route from femaleness to womanhood, and now she saw Charles' paternalism as both temporary and exaggerated. Since the image of proprietous motherhood was at least as important as the reality, however, she could not simply tell him that he fussed too much. He might think she fussed too little. There has to be, she thought, a gentler way, a safer way. She also thought: I should have guessed he might come home early from riding. I brought this on myself. I shouldn't have given him occasion to get angry.

But guilt was not enough quite to stifle her irritation at his trampling over her domestic boundaries, and now (after an unconscious sigh) she began carefully to restore them. "I know Nona irritates you, dear, and I'm sorry."

"Not important," he said.

"Perhaps," she continued after a measuring pause, "it would be easier if you left her to me. After all, she was only doing what I had told her to do, and I'd hate to have her start not doing things on the excuse that you'd told her something different." Charles did not seem to be listening, which meant that he was attending, so she continued. "You've got the office and the plantation and all the stables to worry about already, so perhaps it might be easier just to let me know if something upsets you, and I'll attend to it. We do have a new nanny coming, and I'll have to get on with her, too, won't I?"

"If you let the beggars take an inch," suddenly replied Charles, "they'll take a mile." They had a staff of more than twenty, mostly new, and to Charles there seemed always to be a scurrying of small relatives with dark faces, white eyeballs, ingratiating smiles, and mangled English politenesses. "You have to be firm with them. If you let them chase monkeys, that's all they'll do."

Elizabeth glanced apprehensively at the dignified Abbuhamy, who happened at that moment to be clearing their plates. Charles really ought to be more discreet, she thought. But it sounded as though Charles were delegating his authority to her, which was exactly what she wanted, so she sacrificed Abbuhamy's feelings and proceeded with her main objective. "It's just a matter of convenience, really, isn't it? A woman having to have the authority in the household? I'd never thought of it in those terms, but . . ."

She let the sentence trail off as though the idea were too energetic for her powers of pursuit. She had chosen her moment very well, just as Charles had lit the first pipe of his day, so he surrendered without thinking about it. As he settled back into the creaking chair, he stretched a jovial arm to rub her shoulder. It was his usual sign of truce.

"Shall you come with me to meet the nanny on Tuesday morning?" It was his way of signaling acknowledgment of her rights as mother and wife.

"Oh, I should love to," she said a trifle too effusively, flushed by the ease of her victory. "But I do hope she disembarks well before the gymkhana, or it'll be such a busy day, getting her settled."

"Hours before," said Charles confidently. "She'll be with us by nine at the latest. We'll both go, then?" He stood up and kissed the top of her head. "I'm going to change. Anything you need in the city? I'll send a boy down to see about that carpeting, but I can't imagine there'll be any problem. Too big an order to ignore, what?"

"Can you send the motor back? I have a fitting at Thresher and Glenny's, and it's so much faster than the carriage. I might drop in at Cargill's about the new stuff for curtains."

"Joe Plunkett's back in town, and I'm asking him for dinner tonight. Tell Abbuhamy, would you? I'll bring him home around teatime, so send Tara Singh back around four, will you?" Tara Singh, a Sikh with full beard and enormous dignity, was their chauffeur and tended to intimidate them as much by mechanical competence as by his turbaned and towering stature. He and his family shared a special bungalow on the grounds with the motorcar, an object even more awesome than he to both Elizabeth and Charles.

"Of course, dear," replied Elizabeth, and placed herself, and smiled so, that Charles gave her a husbandly embrace and walked inside with her tucked under his arm.

The affairs of the world thus disposed to everyone's satisfaction, Abbuhamy was left to clear the table, which he did with an expression less than veiled and a clatter more than accidental. From the servants' quarters rose the sudden shrill of a domestic squabble, suddenly stilled. In front of the house a Tamil clad only in loincloth chopped clumsily at the coarse dhoab grass overgrowing the edges of the flowerbeds, and the gatekeeper squatted in the shade to watch. A great bird or animal screamed in the broadleafed trees at the bottom of the garden, but the shrill of the insects and the rhythm of the ocean were uninterrupted. Upstairs Nona sat cross-legged on the floor beside the cradle, fanning herself and her boredom. Jennifer, feverless, slept steadily on in the quiet, white-walled room. The Wingate family was in order and at peace.

2

Men like Charles Wingate are at their worst when playing husband and father. They perform self-consciously. They speak the lines and seem stuffy. They feel awkward and act poorly. But Charles Wingate's fault was not so much stuffiness as complacency. From men like Charles, the times expected not kindness, only benevolence; not truthfulness, only earnestness; not sensitivity, but work; not perceptiveness, but duty. He had done well indeed at what the age had told him a man should do. He did not yet know what more he could do.

In 1914 Charles (like the Empire which sheltered him) saw no need for change. Those changes which he had just endured—the new home, fatherhood—were such as he had anticipated, caused. At forty-two he was reaching the apex of his career, and his rise, like that of the Empire, originated from ability and resulted in complacence. The British Empire believed that it set the norm of civilized behavior for the world, and Charles Wingate thought almost as highly of his marriage. The least that Empire and husband expected was civility; the most they needed was obedience. They called deeds of emotion bad form, thereby refusing to anticipate the novelties which others' passions bring, and Charles Wingate dressing for the office that morning worried about nothing more than a nick on his chin caused by the straight-edge razor. Safety razors, like wristwatches, he vaguely regarded as effeminate, and that was enough to make him hurt himself rather than change.

Charles Wingate came from the Hampshire gentry, which meant that his family was well enough bred to receive invitations to every ball in the county and too poor to reciprocate. The family funds went to education rather than entertainment, and Charles, having shown himself dutiful enough to benefit from the education, was also fit enough to find his own entertainment. In 1889, two years after the Empire celebrated Victoria's fiftieth year on the throne, three years before the first Socialists took their seats in Parliament, when he was just eighteen, he sailed for the Orient with a job obtained through the good offices of a friend's father. Ceylon was not India, and a broker's clerk was no Bengal lancer, but Charles had a nose for opportunity, and all the spices of the East smelled fine to him. Younger sons of country gentry did not find opportunity knocking at the door.

His family was sad to see him go, but understanding. The Lord knows what the lad will get up to overseas, thought his father privately, but at least his mother won't find out. Charles was already a full-grown man, displaying as in a shop window that intense and spontaneous sexuality which stimulates the envy of friends and the suspicions of mothers. Had his family not taught him the pleasures of industry rather than idleness, he might have turned out badly, but through their discipline he had grown into one of those handsome men who so lack vanity that they earn our admiration rather than our envy. Success seems to be their very nature. They do not exploit. Things are given to them. Even now as he stood in full-length underwear of fine wool before the tall mirror to survey the curve of his stomach and adjust his genitals, that carnal energy was still apparent. He knew women found him attractive.

It had not always been so. When Charles first came to Colombo, he had seen no connection between his popularity in the drawing room and his unusually rapid acceptance in the Polo Club, the Cricket Club, and the Army and Navy Club. In rooms where satin swayed to the triple-time of the Viennese waltz, where bare white shoulders gleamed and floral essences excited with mock innocence, he at first never noticed the occasions on which some young lady ignored the other name scrawled on her dance card. He did not think of himself as a good catch. Penniless, though of good family, he lacked the glamour of the military and the cachet of the civil service, and although cosmopolitan and polyglot Colombo was infinitely less snobbish than nervous India, when it came down to it, he was only in commerce, one shallow step above trade. If he became a planter, then of course!

So Charles had begun a long career as the lover of married women. Their husbands liked him. He was free to come and go. Good fellow, Wingate. In the Edwardian colonies, the Victorian art form of flirtation had become so indistinguishable from good manners that the innocent could not tell where social intercourse gave way to sexual. "Picnics and adultery," said the Europeans of their summer retreats to cool, mountained Kandy, and copied the Anglo-Indians by installing in each large house a *kala jugga,* or dark place, where stays creaked and starched shirtfronts gleamed among the potted ferns. Picnics and adultery, the youthful Charles thought with a smile: That's life! But he learned discretion through dining with the men he cuckolded, and it helped his business dealings greatly. At the age of thirty he told Joe Plunkett, who had become his closest friend, that business excited him just about as much as sex.

The job that brought him to Ceylon had been that of under-manager with Clarkson and Son, a hodgepodge business shackled together in an old warehouse by one of the old-timers: import and export, brokerage, storage and transshipment. Old man Clarkson knew everyone and ran the business out of his hip pocket, planning for his son (a man of Charles' age) to take over. Charles rather overwhelmed the old man with his efficiency and imaginativeness. In his sixth year with the firm, his advice to purchase a bankrupt international chain of warehouses brought in quick and enormous profits. In the same year, young Clarkson died of cholera in Calcutta. Old Clarkson made Charles a partner at the age of thirty and then completed his generosity by dying two years later. Thus Charles became a man of property, and during the next decade a man of wealth. At thirty-three he owned a tea plantation and needed a wife, whom he had sought during a visit home to Hampshire but met—in the person of Elizabeth—on the voyage back to Colombo. His possession of such an attractive hostess and companion greatly broadened the social circles into which he was accepted.

As Charles now tugged his waistcoat smooth and looped his fob watch and chain into place, he could smile at his image in the mirror with good reason. By 1914 his life lacked nothing. He stood for something. Polo, cricket, snooker, politics, brandy. Last night at the dinner party he had heard the Colonial Secretary himself recommend him as "a good chap with a steady head." Those dinners were boring enough by now, but they meant he had what he wanted: money, the ear of the government, and more to come in the future. He was a good businessman, modern, the first in Colombo to install typing machines and adding machines, the first to have his own telegraph and telephone wires. Those dinners might be boring, but he enjoyed them anyway: the searching for advantage, the competition, the winning men over and the winning over them. Briefly he smoothed the fine alpaca of his suit coat with the palm of his hand, then called out to Abbuhamy, waiting as usual beyond the door, "You can tell Tara Singh to crank up the car."

His good mood continued as he descended the staircase, admiring its magnitude. Yes, he thought, boring these dinners may be, but he could always enjoy his own private joke: when the host inevitably said, "Shall we join the ladies, gentlemen?"

As Tara Singh negotiated the usual stream of bullock carts and pedestrians on their way to market, Charles leaned comfortably back against the Napier's cushions. A spilled load of bamboo stopped the car's progress briefly next to a small palm-thatched shrine for a stone Buddha who obscurely smiled over offerings of fruit and flowers at the human chaos before him, but Charles paid no more attention to the Buddha's smile than to the hot sun, the violent tropical smells, the natives' color and anxiety. He had as yet experienced few of life's more foolish emotions: the conflict of irreconcilable impulses, the logic of the incomprehensible. He knew the ways of the world very well; the universe could take care of itself. Though churchy, he was not religious; though shrewd, not subtle; and though well-informed, he read to confirm not to shake his beliefs. Because he could not see the future, he would not examine purpose, and he therefore had found no need to study his soul.

The motorcar at last trundled on, and soon its warm jostling stirred his genitals into life and slipped him into lustful reverie. Only the need to raise his hat to the Methodist missionary's wife when they drove past her pony trap brought him back to reality, and as they proceeded into Colombo's steaming, shouting city life, he pondered the new contract for hemp and what might be done to get around Portugal's Goan tariffs. By the time they reached the hot stone building on Galle Face Road which held the offices of Clarkson and Son, he was ready for another day that would contain just enough familiarity to keep him calm, just enough variety to give him ginger. He gave his orders to Tara Singh, he climbed the stairs and greeted his hovering chief clerk, he took his seat at his gleaming mahogany desk under the gentle stir of the ceiling fan and reached for his morning's correspondence.

An hour later Elizabeth followed Charles' route from Mount Lavinia to Colombo. Tara Singh had put up the side windows to keep her free of dust, and she opened her parasol against the sun, and she felt not quite as much contentment as had her husband. When the motor drove sedately past the Buddha's shrine, she promised herself that one day soon she would order a stop so that she might inspect it.

The impulse toward respect was probably a vestige of her Roman Catholic upbringing. Though she was now eight years away from being Elizabeth Malloy and a decade from Dublin, and scarcely more religious than Charles, she was much less sure than he of the permanence of success. He was just as aware as she of the currently troubled state of the world–the headlines about Ireland, London's suffragettes, Field Marshal Roberts' latest warning about the deplorable condition of the army–but where he scanned the news for its offerings of business opportunity, she lacked the illusion that anything she did would make a difference.

Her father was a solicitor and that nineteenth-century rarity, an Irish Catholic who had become successful, moderately wealthy, and international in habits. As a man who specialized in representing English and Continental businesses through the tangle of Irish politics, he had come to love both London and Paris and eventually to marry a Parisienne. He had encouraged Irishness in his family only for the sake of social disguise, and as the tide of hatred rose in Dublin during the 1890's, he had sought to protect his family from embroilment by sending Elizabeth to a Protestant boarding school in London. The experience had proved a worse shock to Elizabeth, aged ten, than either of her parents realized. Set among enemies at an age where belonging is the greatest need one feels, she had to make deliberate choices of the kind which children are not supposed to comprehend. Within a day she realized that to be Irish was to be scorned. Within a week she had abandoned her Dublin accent and manners. After a month of acute misery, she had transformed herself into a haphazard but skillful imitation of the upper-class English girls who had pulled her hair, kicked her ankles, and called her Paddy. The imitation amused her father; he never realized that he had doomed his daughter forever to live between identities.

In Dublin Elizabeth had learned the art of confronting oppression with words, and words with dreams. But her mind also belonged to her mother: her French mother, who had that quality of compact energy by which Parisiennes seduce or frighten the world. Convinced as only a Parisienne can be that beauty lies not in the eye of the beholder but in the being of a woman, and that, whatever else, one must have strength, Henriette Malloy had taught Elizabeth to stand firm though not alone. She had taught pride and culture and manners and made her daughter into a lady, and these qualities had won Elizabeth acceptance in circles far beyond the station of life to which she had been born. She had proved adept at adjusting to her husband's rise through the interlocking circles of Colombo society, seen never as a climber but as someone floating naturally to her proper place. During the years of their marriage there had been only occasional bitter moments–and not even Charles knew about them–to remind her of the price she paid. The English had a habit. "Tell me about yourself," they would invite, full of friendliness. And if she then made the mistake of saying she came from Dublin, their tone would instantly change: "Oh, you're Irish, are you? How very interesting." And that tone, flat as tundra, would freeze and burn Elizabeth with the freshened sense of her own failure to belong.

Her husband was by far the most important person in her life. She was sure of their relationship, sure of him, sure of her feelings, sure of their lovemaking. They were unquestioned allies against the world, their domesticity the reason for their existence. Nothing much else and nobody much else really counted, and she had come to feel so comfortable in the domestic womb that their marriage had functioned with a strength and calm that others regarded as extraordinary.

It had not occurred to Elizabeth that she now saw Charles more as her husband than as an individual. He made a charming, admirable, thoughtful husband. He was a man who went out and did the things men do, then returned to her and treated her very well. They were very close, she might have said, possessiveness having crept upon her. If, unlike other wives, she was unconcerned about women starting to work in the office as typists, she thought it was because she was less petty, because she knew Charles very well, because he loved her.

She did not know what to blame for the irritability that plagued her today as the Napier rolled along the narrow road to the city, skirted by ricefields on the right and the bright ocean blue on the left. When the motorcar plunged into a channel of village walls filled with squawking chickens and yapping dogs, she glimpsed small dark women bent over domestic labor and scolded herself for restlessness. Why, sometimes and for no reason, should she have this absurd feeling of futility? Why, every now and then, should she feel as though one lived in a bubble of space and a tick of time? And that she was wasting both. She pulled her gloves tighter and rearranged her skirts and thought about the purchase she needed to make at Thresher and Glenny's. It must be the start of my period, she told herself, and began counting days.

Thresher and Glenny's was in the heart of the European business district near the Old Clock Tower and the heavy government buildings. Tara Singh's route skirted the thronged Pettah bazaar, where cries from children and vendors wrapped the crowd, wooden houses and booths elbowed the pedestrians, and the chickens and dogs treated the automobile as though it did not exist. They were held up briefly by a two-wheeled wagon thatched with palm leaves and drawn by a humpbacked and nervous bullock. Motionless as they waited for the road to clear, Elizabeth found herself staring directly into the curiously loving eyes of a young Buddhist priest with saffron robe and shaved head, who stood equally motionless and much more serene by the side of the road, his begging bowl held modestly a few inches from his chest. He was the image of passivity; he would not gesture even for sustenance. The slightest shape of a smile lay on his clear features.

His expression and the directness of his gaze made Elizabeth suddenly, almost desperately uneasy. Amidst the demands of this native color, and the about-to-be fitting of a corset that did not seem right, she fumbled hastily in her purse for coins, but the balky bullock surrendered and cleared the pathway, the car lurched forward into the Galle Road, leaving the Buddhist face behind, and she was again in the midst of cleanliness, order, and the stone and brick and glass which the seventeenth-century Portuguese and the eighteenth-century Dutch and the nineteenth-century English had gathered firmly into their final statement of permanence. A cooling breeze swept up from the harbor, bringing the perfume of cinnamon and the stench of copra from the waterfront warehouses. Elizabeth shook her head once, sharply, and settled her gaze firmly on the back of Tara Singh's white turban.

3

In front of the neat facade of Thresher and Glenny, Merchants and Haberdashers, Ladies' Apparel Our Specialty, another motorcar was parked. The sash across the chest of the turbaned driver dozing in its front seat told her it was from Government House. As she approached, the shop door opened with a loud jangle of its bell, and a bowing Indian in European dress welcomed her by name. His greetings were cut short by a rotund Englishman, dapper as a piece of painted wood. "That'll do, Hamid. Good morning, Mrs. Wingate. Beautiful morning, isn't it? We do get such nice weather in February, even down here. I hope you are finding it agreeable in Mount Lavinia?"

"Good morning, Mr. Batterson. Yes, thank you."

They went through the greeting ritual as conducted by a man who knew that women had nothing to do but spend time, and Elizabeth, lacking patience, began to remove her gloves and unpin her hat. Mr. Batterson, still chatting, led her to the tiring-rooms at the rear, murmuring that the fitter would be with her momentarily. There was a tap at the door of the little room and Mrs. Bodley entered, a pigeon-breasted woman in her forties, pins and needles stuck in her bodice, like some self-punishing Spanish saint.

"Good morning, madam. How are you this morning? Lady Pearsall inquires whether you would be kind enough to join her?"

A thin hand became visible, waving over the mahogany partition between this room and the next, and Mrs. Bodley held the door in readiness. A stage whisper floated over the partition: "Do come, Elizabeth. This process is so tedious. Mrs. Bodley can do for us both at the same time."

Elizabeth gathered her belongings and moved next door. "Genevieve, good morning!"

The two women embraced, a peck in the general area of the other's cheek.

"Just look at this thing, will you?" Lady Pearsall, wife of the Colonial Governor, was draped in something that looked vaguely like a kimono. "It seems so frightfully shapeless. What am I to do about it? These new fashions! Shall I help you with the hooks and eyes . . . oh, thank you, Mrs. Bodley. Take these things away, will you, and bring another chair."

Mrs. Bodley vanished with purses, gloves, and hats, then reappeared carrying a strange shape made of bone, cloth, and rubber and a plain cotton gown.

"And what, pray, is that?" asked Lady Pearsall antiquely, as though through a lorgnette.

"I'm having them make a copy of the new Twilfit. My shape has so changed that it is the only thing I can get into. Thank you, Mrs. Bodley."

Elizabeth struggled out of her clothing: skirts, petticoats, high-necked blouse, boots, cotton stockings, corset. Clad only in undergarments, she was faintly embarrassed as Lady Pearsall inspected her figure, and relieved to cover herself with the gown, under which Mrs. Bodley discreetly placed the new corset around her body.

Lady Pearsall was a thin but not vinegary woman of some fifty years. Her hair was a gray bird's nest perched on too thin a neck, but she was oddly attractive nonetheless, something of the gamine. Her face was long, pale, impeccably aristocratic: long nose, hooded eyes, crisp little jaw. Caesar's wife, as she liked to call herself, beyond fear or reproach, a formidable woman widely criticized for being too "informal" and a trifle "strange." The informality was easy to see. She regarded her husband's current post as faintly beneath her, a duty rather than privilege, and therefore she refused to behave as people erroneously believed royalty behaved. This was Sir Reginald Pearsall's second tour as Governor. He had retired gratefully five years earlier, after eight years in office, but his successor proving too feeble to survive tropical onslaughts on his gout, rheumatism, and blood pressure, Sir Reginald had returned with the understanding that he was rendering a particular service to his monarch. Lady Pearsall, who had earlier found Ceylon stifling, had come back to enjoy herself, and she did, and the gossips had come to accept her as a favorite topic and an agreeable-enough woman.

She and Elizabeth had first met in 1906, shortly after Elizabeth's marriage and on the occasion of her first major ball at Government House. Her white skin luminous against the pale mauve of her ball gown, Elizabeth had dropped into a graceful curtsy as she was presented.

"*Who* is this attractive gel?" Lady Pearsall said rather loudly as Elizabeth straightened.

"Mrs. Charles Wingate," murmured an embarrassed aide. Lady Pearsall stepped back to stare rudely at Elizabeth, who felt a hot blush flooding face, neck, and bosom. She felt, she told an amused

Lady Pearsall years later, exactly like a china teapot which *might* be purchased.

"And this is the husband?" said Lady Pearsall to her companion in fact but to the air in appearance. Charles repeated his bow.

"So glad," said Lady Pearsall abstractedly, "that you enjoy Ceylon." Her sudden nod of dismissal snapped a clasp on the imaginary conversation. With an offended Charles at her elbow, Elizabeth had begun to move on when unexpectedly Lady Pearsall's hand, in long white glove, tapped her shoulder, and without turning her head—so that she seemed to be speaking to the bewildered couple next in line—Lady Pearsall said, "We shall see you again."

Elizabeth thought the Governor's wife either profoundly stupid or drunk. "It could have been laudanum," Lady Pearsall confessed. "One needs something to get through those occasions, my dear. How amusing!"

Lady Pearsall had sensed something about the Wingates, and the encounter had been the start of what Elizabeth mockingly used to call My Success. The Governor's wife took her up, and she became part of the Set. Even as a bride she spent whole days at Government House, and like a lady-in-waiting she accompanied Lady Pearsall on various official occasions, one of a string of women who sailed in plumed hats between rows of outsiders, as sedate as swans through reeds. From then on, engraved cards fluttered onto the Wingates' silver tray bearing invitations to tea, to bridge, to dinner, to musical soirees, to balls, and they moved quickly into social circles which they would not normally have entered for years.

Friendship with her patroness had come later, when a much less formal Lady Pearsall had returned to Ceylon and chosen to reveal a woman who knew a world of vastly greater dimensions than this Ceylon of heat, pomp, and social climbers.

"Well," said the new Lady Pearsall. "I warned Reggie that things would be different if he accepted the job again. I mean, we are doing them a favor by coming back—or at least we have made them think so—and they will have to take whatever they get, won't they? I am too old to care. One is brought up for a job like this, you know. I might even say bred to it. But I am too old to work all the time. Would you care for a little brandy?"

Friendship had flowered quickly. Lady Pearsall sent for Elizabeth the day after her return. They walked in the gardens of the sprawling Government House as Elizabeth brought her up-to-date on gossip. A heavy rain shower sent them fleeing to a door in a far wing of the mansion, where no servants lurked. They came to a corridor, turned left, turned right, then left again, and then all of a sudden Lady Pearsall stopped short and said, "Where the *devil* am I?" They had broken into helpless laughter, retraced their steps, and to the amazement of servants hastening with umbrellas, walked arm-in-arm through the heavy warm rain back to the main entrance, where Lady Pearsall gave orders for them to be wrapped in towels. After that it was as though she had unwrapped heart as well as body.

"I can't imagine," she now said, watching Elizabeth squirm inside the elastic and bone of the new corset, "why we do that sort of thing to ourselves."

"My figure seems to have altered . . . inalterably," replied Elizabeth as Mrs. Bodley tugged at her. "I feel like a bucket of suet."

Her enlarged breasts fell awkwardly. She tussled with them as though they were small animals.

"I have lived more than fifty years," said Lady Pearsall, "and I have yet to make up my mind whether women dress for men or for other women. It is obviously not for the sake of comfort. If the Middle Ages had invented corsets, they would have used them for torture. I used to have one that stood up all by itself. I believe, if you kicked it, it kicked back."

"Be a Mrs. Pankhurst. She wears no corset, they say. I wonder what she looks like?"

"The natural woman, my dear. Perhaps I shall give up wearing them. But how disturbing if nobody noticed! I shall wear my shimmy to a reception, and bare feet, like that mad American dancer woman in Paris."

"You must admit she probably has more fun than do we. You could cut off all your hair, too, like Irene Castle."

"My crowning glory? Never! Reggie would shoot himself."

"Then we know you dress for men."

"What don't we do for men, my dear? What don't we all do for men?" Lady Pearsall's tone was suddenly serious. She looked at the floor as though on it lay something peculiarly disgusting. "Is your staff sufficiently unhysterical to provide the Governor's wife with morning tea?"

"Of course, as long as you don't expect too much. The place is absolutely bare."

"I shall see what you need and send something over. It all belongs to the government, of course, but they will never know if it goes on a brief vacation."

The fittings over, the two women rejoined their chauffeurs, and the stately automobiles moved processionally south to the Wingate home. Lady Pearsall admired the baby, wide-awake and happy under the supervision of a less languid Nona. Elizabeth ordered tea to be served in the summerhouse.

A square white structure with embrasures and latticework instead of windows, the summerhouse stood several feet off the ground, surrounded by white splashes of quicklime to ward off termites. Placed on the low cliffs to catch the ocean breeze, with sky and sea for backdrop, it looked demanding rather than neglected, an alternative rather than an afterthought to the large mansion, and the two women in white moved softly within it, as though exploring an empty stage. They chatted about nothing while the bearer boiled water on a small kerosene stove, heated pot and cups, and set the tea to brew. Discarding the excess hot water, he aimed the splash at a small lizard, which went rigid, writhed, and fled under the steps. Elizabeth dismissed him with a flash of irritation.

"The sanctity of life under Buddhism?" she commented sourly after the man had left.

"On the whole I find them less hypocritical than we," replied Lady Pearsall with a touch of rue. "They don't pretend that what they inflict on other beings is good for them."

She took her tea and sipped it, looking placidly enough with hooded eyes at the golden beach and blue ocean. Sea gulls squawked above them.

"Will you have a biscuit, Ginny?" Elizabeth offered. "They're Carr's, and quite fresh. We opened a new tin this morning."

Lady Pearsall politely accepted a biscuit, and Elizabeth, catching her quietness, turned to admire the view of the high mountains to the east, green, hazy, soft of edge.

"We seem very close to the plantation here," she said.

Lady Pearsall nodded. Her face was pale and today seemed thin, the skin pouchy and tired. Colombo Week was an endless round of informal but mandatory appearances. She did not look forward to it. It was more penance than pleasure—as was, she reminded herself, the present occasion. She unpinned her hat, placed it fussily on the window seat beside her, then abruptly stood and spread her arms wide as though she had just pushed away something suffocating.

"Ah!" The exclamation was a gasp of exasperation. "I am faced with a scene, Elizabeth, and I don't know how to handle it or even if I want to."

Elizabeth, taken by surprise, was immediately all alertness, her mind racing to conclusions as though the next few sentences had already been spoken. It was a moment of pure intuition. Lady Pearsall moved to the railing and seemed to peer intently through the lattice at a brace of gardeners chopping haphazardly at the elephant grass. A tumble of brilliant flowers obscured the view of them. "And it is such a *conventional* scene. I abhor feeling that I am reciting lines from some cheap drama." She looked at Elizabeth, her eyes for once fully open, their bright blue shrewd and contemplative. "How well do I know her?" she interrogated the air. Elizabeth gave her no help, looking at her steadily, taking a sip from a steady teacup. "Well, perhaps if I began by saying, 'Elizabeth, you know I am your friend . . .' "

As though she had at last heard what she wanted, Elizabeth placed her cup and saucer sharply on the table and spoke even as she straightened her back. "Then I should immediately assume that you have something unpleasant to tell me about my husband."

It was Lady Pearsall's turn to be surprised.

"How very clever of you, my dear," she said, as though absent-minded. "How much more should I say?" Her tone was almost indignant, but cautious.

Elizabeth replied without hesitation, "All of it. Everything. If I am to suffer, I shan't settle for less than everything." And she gave a small smile, her low voice ironic.

Lady Pearsall studied her for a moment, a little shocked. "You seem so very calm. You knew already?"

Again Elizabeth smiled, picking up her cup and saucer. "No I did not know—do not know—anything. But my husband's attractiveness to other women is something with which I am familiar, Ginny. He is attractive to me, I would be a fool to assume that other women failed to find him appealing, especially out here." She waved at her surroundings, turning them into a backdrop. "This is an extraordinarily personal conversation, Ginny. Forgive me."

"Forgive you? You speak as though you, not Charles, were at fault!"

"Well." There was a long pause as Elizabeth drew a considering breath. "I hadn't thought of it that way, but I expect you are right. I suppose I see Charles as prey, not predator. It has suddenly occurred to me that—it may seem extraordinary to say this at this particular moment—in my own maidenly way I knew what Charles was like when I married him. . . . I am *not* naive."

Elizabeth, in fact, was recalling with total intensity her first encounters with Charles. At this moment, naive was precisely what they seemed. She had followed a porter on board the SS *Soudan* at Tilbury through the clatter and confusion of a stormy winter afternoon, rain drumming on her umbrella, mud and straw splashing onto her boots and skirts, not a soul to see her off or greet her, and yet she had been undaunted. Like every twenty-two-year-old in 1904 who feared spinsterhood, she faced a single task: finding a husband. She had become one of the famous "fishing fleet": girls in search of husbands among men in search of empire. The P. and O. liner was fluffy with them; all mahogany elegance and deferential service, it had the air of an arena full of performers waiting for the show to start.

Elizabeth was a good sailor, which made her future husband's first sight of her as romantic as one could wish. On the chill first morning after departure, as he took his brisk constitutional on the boat deck, he came across Elizabeth's dramatic figure tucked into a corner next to the rail, the wind whipping loose strands of her dark hair, an air of courage lent by the cold gray-and-white loom of the waves. They nodded, laughed. Her throat gleamed white as she lifted her head and her scarf fought free. They were now comrades of the unseasick, and though he had lifted his hat and walked by, they were irretrievably impressed with each other.

During the four-week journey between Home and Colombo, Charles enjoyed great popularity among the girls of the fishing fleet—the prize catch—while Elizabeth, free from the conventions of Home, also played the field as far as she was capable. They laughed together at quoits, sang duets in the evening concerts, and often were in the same clique for beef tea in the morning and Ceylon tea in the afternoon.

Elizabeth was well aware of Charles' attractiveness and amused rather than shocked when, escaping one night into the fresh air of the boat deck, she interrupted a flurry of moans and sighs that accompanied his seduction of one of the sillier girls. That, she thought instantly, is not the way to his heart. And she held herself aloof, even though she enjoyed the sight and feel of his body: when he did his early-morning calisthenics in pajamas and robe on deck, when he lifted her from gangway to launch for the shore trip at Port Said, when, once, her long skirts tripping her in the egg-and-spoon race, he helped her to her feet with a mildly salacious comment about her legs.

Charles found her attractive and, more important, sensible. On

Baggage Day, when all the trunks marked "Cabin" were sent below in exchange for other trunks marked "Wanted on Voyage" containing the tropical gear which custom forbade before Port Said and mandated thereafter, most ladies became helpless in the face of their own belongings, but Elizabeth emerged early and serene in a long white linen dress, light cashmere jacket, and sensibly narrow-brimmed pith helmet of white felt, as though she had done this all a hundred times before. As they waited for the shore boats, he admired her open banter with the gully-gully men who squatted half-naked on the deck to conjure with live chickens, flattering the women into parting with coins by calling them all alike "Lillie Langtry." They saw the pyramids and the sphinx, and for the rest of the voyage through the blazing heat of the Red Sea and the Indian Ocean, they fell into the habit of sitting together, in the middle of the hot nights, at the very bow of the ship where dark humps of equipment were the sole eavesdroppers.

Charles did most of the talking, and he talked of himself as he had never talked to anyone in his life, about his ambitions, his successes. His main interest then was his plantation in the mountains some thirty miles west of Colombo, and in great detail he told of supervising his manager's experiments with cross-fertilization, with picking and drying the tea. "One doesn't like to boast," he said, "but in terms of profits per acre, my little place is second only to Lipton's, and of course his show is much larger." He lectured her on colonial administration: "It's so obvious that the plantations need decent roads. The money's there. The military budget could be cut–the Colonial Secretary could transfer sums internally–but nothing can be done without Whitehall, and you know what they're like." Elizabeth listened, and Charles found her very intelligent. He attempted no familiarity, not even verbal, and thus she knew he was interested in her. It was as though neither had dared touch the other, lest a beginning be made. It might not (thought Elizabeth now) have been very romantic. But I was *not* naive.

"Then am I to believe," said Lady Pearsall, "that you already knew what it has taken me a great deal of effort to decide to tell you? I can't believe it! Well, at least we shan't play a stale scene! But I cannot see you as a complaisant wife. If you were older, perhaps. There are so many things which old women learn to tolerate. After all, if men take good care of us, what right do we have to object to the fact that they are no longer our exclusive possessions?" It was a bitter remark, and Lady Pearsall clipped it off with pinched lips. "*Did* you know?"

"Know? Even 'suspect' is too strong a word, Ginny. But I'm still capable of adding two and two together. Or one and one." For a third time she smiled.

The suspicion entered Lady Pearsall's mind that Elizabeth was rather more of a cold fish than she had realized.

"You can smile at a time like this?"

"This pregnancy," said Elizabeth. "Isn't this one of the main reasons we worry about pregnancy, what it can do to a marriage? Did I really think that Charles could go for six months without . . . entertainment?" She put her hand on the older woman's arm. "Don't think me unfeeling, Ginny. I've seen this happen to other women. I don't have any right to think it wouldn't happen to me. We've had eight years of fidelity. And I have always been realistic, have I not?"

There was a sudden clatter of surprised bird wings in the trees. At Elizabeth's words Lady Pearsall realized that Elizabeth thought Charles' infidelity was recent, emerged out of a temporary need. She grew suddenly greedy about the Carr's biscuits.

"I am trying to imagine what you are thinking," she said after a long pause. "I had the same problem with Reginald once, when we were both much younger. We have rubbed along together very well for thirty years despite it, and I have all sorts of reassuring advice to offer if you should need it."

Elizabeth looked at her. "Am I the last to know?" For the first time there was a hard tone in her voice.

"That's the worst part, is it not? In a way. But I think I can reassure you on that point." She wondered if this was a lie. "Your husband is very discreet. It was merely a chain of circumstances that brought it to my attention, and I think you need not fear public humiliation." Not exactly a lie, anyway. "Do you know, I find you are right, calling men the prey? I remember distinctly I was furious at the woman with whom Reginald . . . became involved, and I thought of him as merely unwise, poor lamb. So unwise. And he had been so very pleased with himself. Perky as a schoolboy. Perhaps that is what alerted me. Men are such boys, such boys."

She shook her head gently, her expression reminiscent, cold.

"I remember I thought for a time that Reggie was unclean. I could not bear the thought of his . . . his *touching* me. I forbade him the bedroom. I was very foolish. Yet what *does* one do? There is one thing I find it difficult to understand: how do men not see that their

. . . their infidelity humiliates the woman whom they say they love? It is as though it all had nothing to do with wives and children and real life. I do not think that women separate passion from its environment so easily."

"You give advice so very gently, Ginny," said Elizabeth.

Lady Pearsall looked vaguely pleased. "You are not supposed to notice. But it would be better to take things calmly. I must say you show no signs of behaving stupidly, anyway. But one never knows—"

Elizabeth cut across her words. "Who is she?"

Lady Pearsall rose from her wrought-iron chair and walked slowly to stand beside Elizabeth at the balustrade. "I would rather not," she said. To her, this was the moment of truth she had earlier avoided.

"I understand that, but I think you wouldn't have told me part of the story without having decided to tell me the rest."

"Do you really," and Lady Pearsall made her decision in mid-breath, "want to know their names?" There, it was done.

"*Their* names?"

To Elizabeth the summerhouse suddenly seemed airless, as though something tumescent were about to burst, pushing against her. For a second she wanted to cry out. Something in Lady Pearsall's voice sounded like grief, and it found a bodily echo in her of a kind she had never before felt, as though she were immeasurably older than Charles, as though she labored along some ancient track while he did no more than tug at wayside grasses. There was a brief but profound pause before she spoke again, and her voice was deeper and harsher than before. "So this has been going on for some time, then?"

This time it was Lady Pearsall who sought forgiveness by placing her hand on the other woman's arm. "Perhaps I should have told you before, my dear, but really . . . it never seemed the right time—this is not an easy task. I'm sorry."

"I realize that. I'm grateful, I suppose." Elizabeth walked to the table, seated herself, poured a cup of tea with steady hand, then placed it untasted on the table. "I suppose I'm angry. I must be. I'm sorry. I don't know quite what I feel. What am I supposed to feel?"

"May I give you some very temporary advice?"

"Of course."

"Perhaps if we just stay here for a while, quietly, without saying anything. I think half an hour or so might make a difference, and I shall sit here very comfortably. You have things you need to sort out by yourself."

4

Elizabeth accepted the offer without remark. She rose to gain the privacy of pacing, the boards of the summerhouse floor giving her a pattern on which her mind and body could organize themselves. Genevieve Pearsall turned her head toward the view of the ocean, as still as a graven image moving down some broad river in grand processional.

The wooden floor was gouged with the tracks of some vanished implement, and Elizabeth stared at the scar. Flashes of emotion were chasing themselves through her mind: gibbering little creatures that fled down long corridors. She could not seize and name them. What did she feel? Elizabeth had been accustomed to thinking quickly rather than deeply, with moments of perception that gained her a reputation for acuteness she did not fully deserve. She had spent no hours, days, weeks, months, thinking things through, feeling pain, and while she was far from obtuse about life's uglinesses, she had never as yet had to view them. Now? She found herself distracted by a column of ants heading for the sugar bowl. How had they known it was there? She frowned at her own waywardness of mind, hugged herself, resumed the burden which she felt belonged properly to someone else, anyone else.

Images confused her thoughts: Charles' penis drawn erect and wet with juices from some other woman's body; bared white buttocks, the hair of genitals dark and evil; Charles again naked, cowering before her. She shook the images from her head, growling slightly both at and because of their presence. She felt anger. No! Humiliation. Had he talked to those other women about *her?* What did they think of her?

The unfortunate truth was that Elizabeth could not tell what she felt. Designed for peace, her mind was not trained to cope with the unexpected. The Victorian ideals of perfect permanent marriage and the wronged wife had dissipated a generation ago; on the other hand, the Equal Property Act still existed only in the minds of the poets of politics. The solutions to problems are limited by time and place, and Elizabeth, unfortunately, was caught between, in a time when no clear lead was offered her. Instead of feeling, she only sought a way out.

Anger, she knew, would bring a moment as irretrievable as the splintering of vase on marble. Was she willing to risk that much? But say-nothing acceptance? Darby and Joan indeed: locked forever in irritation bred of self-interest. He had started a war. He had turned what is into what was. Not even her victory would bring *back*. She watched a fly scuttle across Lady Pearsall's cheek and forehead, searching for protein and water. She heard a combat of gulls screaming over torn fishy flesh. Her underarms itched in the growing heat. And her blank mind again took revenge on her—again the image of Charles' penis, reddened, veined, erect, wet. She staggered in her pacing, banged against the table, and set the teacups rattling. Genevieve glanced and reached forward, but Elizabeth straightened the china herself, though for a moment she was tempted to crush the cup between her fingers.

Lady Pearsall was looking at her inquiringly. "You know, of course, that divorce is out of the question? Had *you* committed adultery, my dear, that would be one thing." Elizabeth stared at her, startled by the acerbic note in her voice. "An adulteress risks everything, no defense at all. But an adulterer? No, according to the law, Charles must do something a great deal worse than this . . . this peccadillo of infidelity." She was staring at the ocean rather than Elizabeth, and her voice was brittle. "Perhaps we could encourage him to commit bigamy? That would do it. Desertion for at least two years? Not out here—they would merely say he is a busy man! Are you willing to say he beats you regularly?" She reached for her teacup, sipped, and looked at Elizabeth unsmilingly. "A little incest on his part would help, of course. But infidelity? The law pays attention to adultery only when committed by wives."

"Of course I know the divorce laws," claimed Elizabeth falsely. "I had not thought of divorce in any case."

"Of course not," replied Ginny. "I can see that it will take more to make an equal suffragist of you than this. You do realize that in my circle back in London you would be regarded as a ninny for bothering yourself about such a trifle as your husband's infidelity?"

"We're not in London."

"And it is not a trifle to you. I knew it would not be. But how nice if you could just take a lover yourself. You would be the perfect modern couple."

"I don't find it very amusing."

"Nor should you, my dear, but in these circumstances one needs a sense of humor. It is so easy to be married to the same man for far too long."

Elizabeth, irritated, did not reply. With her handkerchief she dabbed at the slight sheen of sweat on her forehead. It was time to go inside. Her bladder was full and she wanted to bathe her hands and feet. Lady Pearsall rose to her feet, gathering handbag, gloves, hat, and umbrella in neat order.

"You need more time, my dear, and you do not need me right now."

Elizabeth accompanied her to the motorcar, in which she departed without further discussion of the subject. As Elizabeth used the earth closet, and then bathed her face, she realized that she had forgotten to obtain the women's names from her. Later, she thought. Tomorrow. It is not important who they are. The problem is not them but me; I have to decide what I am going to do.

She spent some time with Nona and baby, ate a dispirited light lunch, and tried to work out exactly how she would deal with Charles when he came home this evening. It was all too soon, too fast. When the afternoon sun began to shine through the louvers on the western windows, she disrobed for her nap and fell asleep with unexpected ease in her shift on top of the flowered coverlet of her marriage bed. She slept long, and when Charles arrived home, she had still not thought through how she would feel toward him.

Thus she was relieved to find him in the company of Captain Joseph Plunkett, his closest friend, having totally forgotten that he had said he would bring Joe home for dinner. Plunkett had been absent from Colombo for many weeks, and there was a great amount of gossip to be exchanged. The two men left few conversational gaps.

Plunkett was much more Charles' friend than hers, and an odd choice. Their shared love of horses had established the friendship. Plunkett was an officer in the Ceylon Mounted Rifles, in charge of purchasing their horseflesh. He supervised the regimental stables and traveled widely, playing polo everywhere. He was a small, thin man with the wiry strength of the expert horseman and a rich, plummy manner of speech. His black hair was held in place with macassar oil thick as glue. His gingery mustache was trimmed every morning by the old and arthritic Indian bearer who naggingly accompanied him everywhere. His uniforms were immaculate: creases like knife edges, tunics starched flat then damped slightly to fit their curves to his shoulders, boots upon which no speck of dust lingered. He had never married–and no wonder, thought the women, who found themselves placed on so high a pedestal by phrases and gestures from the etiquette books that no feeling was possible.

Nona was ordered to bring out Jennifer for inspection. She was wide-awake and ready to smile, lying in Plunkett's lap and studying his face with open-eyed absorption while Plunkett made himself slightly ridiculous with tummy-pokings and baby-fascinating noises.

"Jolly good things, babies!" He smiled at Elizabeth, who made him slightly nervous, as she handed the baby back to the ayah. "Don't know where the world would be without them, what?"

Elizabeth smiled back a trifle wanly. "Why not have some of your own, Joe?"

"Oh, I will, I will. Can't find the woman who'll have me, don't you know? Too smart, too smart. See through me right away."

"Don't you ever get lonely for a wife and family?"

"I rub along, I rub along. Plenty to do, plenty to do. Travel all the time. Not a good idea for the wife, eh?"

Elizabeth never minded Joe Plunkett's presence, but she had not been able to take him seriously since, one evening, Lady Pearsall had expressed her opinion: "The man's an embarrassment! So small! So smug! A parody of a man, a parody of the great British Army officer! On one of those endless trips of his, I believe, the headhunters must have shrunk him. If he's the best the army can do, then we had better give up."

Since then Joe Plunkett always made Elizabeth think of diminution, helping her shrink the British. Bachelor heroes had won England its Empire, which in exchange for their deaths gave their relatives the Victoria Cross, but by 1914 all that—the faces darkened by berry juice, the regimental messes, the weaponry on the walls—seemed faintly absurd. Neither Elizabeth Wingate nor Lady Pearsall could know that Plunkett had spent his leave in the mountains of Central Asia traveling alone by pony, mule, bullock cart, sleigh, eventually on foot, nor that even his apparent mania for hunting was a cover for collecting military intelligence. He told Elizabeth that he had bagged a tiger and a snow leopard. She thought him ridiculously boyish.

Having dined, the three Europeans took coffee and sweet biscuits on the same veranda where Elizabeth and Charles had breakfasted, watching the great sun set over the ocean, catching a breeze strong enough here to rattle the palm leaves. Captain Plunkett sat neatly, square and stiff. Charles sprawled like a youth, his thighs apart, head tilted to catch sounds. After the morning's contretemps he had ordered two small children stationed in the orchard, and now he listened for the clatter of their wooden rattles as they defended the house. Two bearers stood against the wall ready to serve, the sinking sun burnishing their blue-black hair and dark faces. The conversation was as soft as a boll of cotton, ordinary as a cup of tea, and Elizabeth was amazed to find herself sinking into misery. Charles spoke of the house: its cost, their plans. The gravel had been raked and the edge of the driveway trimmed, the flowerbeds weeded.

"But inside!" He smiled at Joe Plunkett. "Wait till you see what we have planned for that! There's my Elizabeth's domain–right, my dear?"

And to emphasize the echo of the morning's conversation, he laid his arm along the back of her chair and touched her shoulder.

"More coffee, Joe?" said Elizabeth, jerking abruptly forward in her chair, so that Charles withdrew his arm.

Plunkett began to gossip about polo ponies and the best source of feed. Charles wandered into a lecture on the poundage of spices exported to France each month and the precise number of plants needed to produce a peck of pepper. Elizabeth sat calmly between the two men, looking content.

In fact, she was possessed by fury at the two men: the small stiff one to her left as much as the great lax one to her right. Furious and despairing, so that the scene's calm was something all her senses smashed against. She felt outwitted by the ordinary, as though wrapped in tight blankets: the house, her baby, her husband. Like a giant fruit bat flapping soundlessly through the dark, the thought came to her: There is *nothing* I can do.

And as the sudden setting of the tropical sun turned them all into a glimmer of whites and a haze of darks, she felt as though her peace, her past, had vanished. Her past gone, the present intolerable, the future unthinkable; she felt not just alone but suspended.

She heard Charles inquire, "Did the chap come about the carpeting, dear?"

"The carpeting?" she said.

He laughed gently. "Go back to sleep," he said. "We'll worry about the carpeting tomorrow."

"Yes," she said. "We'll worry about the carpeting tomorrow."

5

On the following Tuesday, Charles and Elizabeth met the *Oronsay* with the mild trepidation proper to the arrival of an unknown woman sent by a mother-in-law to bring the benefits of civilization to a child in the tropics. Charles went to discover her among the confusion of porters, customs officers, health officials, and slack-jawed bystanders at the wharf, leaving Elizabeth under her umbrella in the Napier stranded among the crowd. Natives eddied around the motorcar: Sinhalese, Tamils, Malays, Chinese, slender Filipinos, Indians, bright in colored cloths, selling, begging, carrying, barefoot, talking and shouting, spitting streams of red betel juice from between blackened teeth, infallibly polite to the memsahib. They battered her only with their noise and smell and strangeness. Bicyclists pushed through the crowd clanging their tinny bells. Battered rickshas stood like wet birds' nests in autumn. A few carriages of Europeans were islanded like the Napier. A horse-drawn omnibus stood ready to take to the railway station those tourists intent on speeding to cooler and more picturesque Kandy.

At last Elizabeth glimpsed Charles ferrying a pert young woman through the crowd, saw the whole scene briefly through the stranger's eyes, and thought: Poor girl! The only thing familiar will be the umbrellas, and here they are used against sun, not rain!

The new nanny, however, proved unalarmed. Clad formally for this first meeting in the uniform and composure of her profession, she said her how-do-you-dos with confidence. A woman pretty because of youth rather than bone structure, with dark hair, bright brown eyes, and sturdy deportment, she was some dozen years junior to Elizabeth but nonetheless mature. Elizabeth's mother had found her at Ravenscroft, a well-known Roman Catholic girls' school outside London, which she had entered years before as an orphaned charity pupil. Her name was Mabel Greggs. She was a Londoner of the uncertain lower middle class, precisely right for a nanny: subservient, but likely to cause no social anxiety. In the opinion of the nuns, she was both clever and discreet, and there were no ties back home to make her restless. She greeted Elizabeth with a light handclasp and a direct gaze, and Elizabeth liked her at once–for the simple reason that she was undismayed and neat. She saw in Mabel something of herself arriving at this same bright wharf a decade ago from that great gray city.

With the three Europeans safely boarded, Tara Singh forced the Napier to lumber some hundred yards through the crowd to the steps of the Grand Oriental Hotel. A cup of tea seemed in order, and on the great veranda of that majestic place, peering over the hibiscus as though at an opera from the dress circle, they began to size up each other.

"A lovely trip, thank you, Mrs. Wingate. Very comfortable, really. Scarcely a wave all the way. Though it was awfully hot in the Red Sea."

"Oh, you must have been on the starboard side, poor creature! Do you know that's where the word 'posh' came from?" Elizabeth was finding herself inclined to nervous chatter. "Port Out, Starboard Home–you know, to avoid the sun?"

"Yes, how interesting," replied Miss Greggs rather flatly. "Yes, I will have another cup of tea, if you don't mind, thank you, sir."

Elizabeth found herself snatching for conversational topics. One could scarcely *interrogate* the poor girl the moment she set foot on dry land. She was grateful when Charles leaned over the balcony to order Tara Singh to send his dog Peter up for a biscuit. Peter was an overweight and aging white fox terrier who regarded himself as supremely privileged. Released from the Napier, he waddled toward the hotel steps, where, as the Wingates and Miss Greggs watched, he paused to lift his leg and piss against the skirt of a middle-aged Sinhalese man standing near the curb. As a healthy yellow stream soiled the white cloth of the man's dhoti, Elizabeth and Mabel caught each other's eye. And suddenly both women burst into most unladylike laughter. It was one of those moments which sweep barriers away. Their giggling sealed a bond; in this world they were more alike than unalike, and the stiffness which can endure for years between Englishwomen living even in the same house had vanished once and for all between these two. Charles immediately relaxed and rewarded Peter with an affectionate tousling.

Back at Mount Lavinia, Jennifer was brought forth in lace and ribbons and Mabel Greggs marveled at her appropriately, and when the baby was placed in her lap for the first time, to play solemnly with the silver buttons of her cape, the second great acceptance quietly took place; Mabel became Nanny. Installed in her own room and the nursery without fuss, she assured the Wingates that she was not in the least fatigued and would prefer to begin her duties at once, with the result that Elizabeth and Charles were able to set about enjoying Colombo Week with the sense of liberation that only the parents of young children can experience.

What with one thing and another, the Wingates did not arrive at the club until nearly four o'clock, to find the informal gymkhana already under way. Charles, clad in riding gear, went immediately to the maidan for the day's first round of polo, and Elizabeth walked alone across the rough lawn to where bystanders gathered around folding wooden chairs and tables in the shade of the giant fig trees.

Elizabeth had passed the four days since Lady Pearsall had told her of Charles' infidelity in a state of suspension which only this morning's events had interrupted. She had planned nothing. She had looked at Charles and felt nothing, as though he had become furniture that needed to be moved but could not be attended to right now. She was displeased with him, but this was a marital sensation she had had over more trivial matters, and she felt vaguely puzzled that she had no real sense of crisis.

When she arrived at the gymkhana, elegant, rhythmic in walk and dress, smiling, many of her acquaintance had not seen her for weeks, and they welcomed her back with prattle of babies and houses and Colombo Week and how well she looked. A little village of chairs grew around her in the shade of the trees at the edge of the playing field, and she found herself dispensing lemonade from a doilied jug. There were no natives visible; the men, in whites and blazers, acted gallantly as bearers, some hatless and collarless. People carried badminton and tennis rackets or bounced balls against the clumps of turf. Moments of total languor were followed by vivacity as small groups raised their energy and departed for the courts. It was hot, but the air was comparatively dry, and the breeze rustled steadily in the broad leaves above their heads.

Not quite sad, vaguely restless, Elizabeth felt as though she should be elsewhere doing something else. Under the guise of repinning her boater to her hair, she looked around the group beneath the trees: so genteel in white, so calm at play, so comfortable with each other. They were a party to which she had come uninvited, a game for which she did not know the rules. Head down, pretending to struggle with hairpins, she was suddenly close to tears. I can't live like this, she thought, I simply can't. I have to do something, anything. She chatted servants and house-moving and child care while the day gave way to golden evening, the children were sent home, and men finished with polo strolled over to the shade of the trees to drink in lemonade or tea or women.

Charles arrived from polo and kissed her on the brow, smelling of sweat and horse and bay rum and the whiskey sneaked from silver flasks that was already making some of the men loud and relaxed. He'd been behind the stables watching the enlisted men wrestle, he said. He did not tell her that watching their handholds slip on sweaty, muscled flesh had made him feel like a youth again, that the smack and rub and grunt of male hand-to-hand had sent the brute surge of blood to his own head and limbs, that he had only just avoided making a fool of himself by trying to join in. Instead, the maleness stoppered in his body made him lean to whisper a gently obscene suggestion in her ear.

"I imagine you say that to all the girls," she replied flatly.

Well, he thought, not all of them . . .

Soon the quick sunset was upon them, flaring red, saffron, and purple like an explosion, and the Governor and his lady arrived, informal for the occasion. The porticoed veranda of the club was lit by strings of colored electric lights, and oil-rag torches flamed and smoked from poles hammered into the ground. The club secretary, Tony Jephson, a beefy, red-faced man with waxed mustaches and an accent which turned vulgar around the edges, marshaled everyone into seated rows on the broad flight of steps that led from veranda to maidan, and a platoon of blue-capped, barefoot bearers slipped deftly through the assemblage with tall glasses of iced gin or whiskey, and punch secretly supplemented with brandy by Jephson to "jolly up the girls a bit." The printed slips announcing the evening's program fluttered in the breeze, and laughter began to rise as the younger people anticipated excitements. Elizabeth sat with Charles near the front, and under the influence of two cups of punch she found herself becoming giggly. Charles was delighted to see her enjoying herself at last, and felt another spasm of sexual interest.

Jephson first shepherded a group of volunteers off to the right, where the torches lit several identical groups of inverted clay flowerpots. A single anna piece had been hidden under one of the pots in each group. The task was to find that anna while walking on top of the other pots. Neither foot nor hand might touch the ground. Gentlemen and ladies competed in separate heats, and there were screams of delight and much horseplay. Emily Wade, waving an anna in her fingers, managed to fall to the ground with legs in the air, flashing stockings and undergarments and claiming victory. The women would not acknowledge her claim, but a gentleman ceded her his place in the semifinals, winning in return an exaggerated kiss on the cheek.

The larger share of the crowd now moved out onto the maidan itself, where a circular course had been laid out, consisting of a series of shoulder-high poles on each of which teetered a polo ball. Near each pole Jephson posted a lady, giving her a galvanized iron bucket full of whitewashed tennis balls. Selected men were given long, ill-fitting overcoats, all black. Their task was to cover the course on horseback, picking up the polo balls while the ladies pelted them with tennis balls. Competitors won a point for every polo ball carried back to the judges and lost a point for every circle of whitewash visible on the black coat. Bullied by Jephson into taking part, Elizabeth found exuberant satisfaction in scoring no fewer than three hits on Charles. His horse shied under her onslaught and danced away from the next pole, giving a clear win to the jubilant Julian Wade.

The next event took place on the long veranda, where an enormous row of chairs had been laid out for a game of musical chairs played to the accompaniment of march music from a scratchy gramophone. Everyone participated and no chivalry was permitted. Male and female bottoms bounced each other out of chairs, and roaring girls collapsed in flurries of underskirts into the laps of grinning men. Lady Pearsall miraculously won by taking every advantage of her rank, sex, and age.

"None of us gets enough exercise!" she exclaimed to Elizabeth. "To think, when I was a gel I played hockey and walked three miles to church! These days the only exercise I have is walking from the steps to the motor. Really! Oh, my old bones will ache tomorrow! Elizabeth, you look marvelous."

"I feel marvelous. Perhaps it's the punch," replied Elizabeth.

On the grass in front of the veranda, a troop of lancers and the regimental band, all scarlet and brass, assembled. The torches were beginning to flare out against the gloom, and a frond of smoke set both women to coughing and waving.

"Quickly," said Lady Pearsall, "let's move inside. They haven't changed a step in this musical ride since the Mutiny, and sometimes I think I must have been watching them then."

"Let's walk on the driveway. The air will be fresher there."

The two women picked their way unobtrusively through guests still disorderly and ribald from their games, and as they emerged in front of the club, dimly lit by electric bulbs and the afterglow of the night sky, they escaped into peacefulness. Elizabeth realized that, once alone, they would have to continue their conversation about Charles, but it was seemingly on another subject that Lady Pearsall began.

"We are all so staid, normally," she said, "and then we revert to all this childish horseplay. Simla is exactly the same, and Kandy–all very proper for afternoon tea, and then high jinks after dinner, and at least once a year everything breaks loose. It seems very Mediterranean of us."

"I feel much more comfortable with the English in this mood than when they are all being genteel," replied Elizabeth.

Night hawks swooped at insects, brushing past the women like memories. "We normally avoid all sign of conflict, do we not?" said Lady Pearsall. "And here in these silly games it all comes out rather more directly than usual, but still not very directly. We stay true to ourselves after all."

The crunch of their footsteps on the gravel was a leisurely sound, and the only noise of animation came from the band, muted by the club building and the dark trees. Lady Pearsall brought their stroll to a stop and dug the toe of her shoe into the gravel.

"Unless, of course, your apparently high spirits are completely assumed?" she said.

Elizabeth felt reluctant to surrender her good mood to Lady Pearsall's cool blue eyes. "No, I'm not playing the hypocrite," she said. "I really have felt better today, and tonight. I cannot imagine why, for I haven't yet spoken to Charles, and I haven't decided what to do about anything."

There was a silence, in which the women did not look at each other.

Lady Pearsall spoke. "Perhaps you would prefer to do nothing, say nothing?"

"Oh, no. No!" exclaimed Elizabeth. In that single instant she made up her mind. "I don't want to become bitter, Ginny, and for that reason alone I am going to do *something* about it. Is it vulgar to say, 'I have my pride'?" She paused. "I shall do something." Lady Pearsall nodded her head, not just with agreement but as though with relief. "It's really a matter of deciding *what*. Everything I think of has drawbacks."

"Indirection is often a virtue," said Lady Pearsall lightly. "You've heard the story about Lady Blandford?"

"A little before my time. . . ."

"A marvelous woman, quite mad, of course, but resolute. She put up with Lord Blandford for years without, one supposes, saying a word, and then she heard that he had gotten his latest mistress, Lady Aylesford, with child, which was really quite unnecessary. There are limits, after all. But she solved it rather beautifully, I thought. Never said a word about it to him. For months! And then, the morning after the child was born, she had the butler put one of those awful celluloid dolls in the covered dish where Lord Blandford expected his usual bacon and eggs." Lady Pearsall laughed.

"Are you recommending something to me?" inquired Elizabeth dryly.

"Oh, the times aren't right for that sort of thing anymore," said Lady Pearsall airily. "Your generation are such a solemn lot. No, I just found the deed imaginative." She paused. "Personally, I have always thought that the most gratifying power of the imagination was its ability to conceive of the death or suffering of those one loves. So helpful when they . . . er, misbehave. I don't know how I should have survived Reggie and the children without it."

"Yes, I've done plenty of daydreaming." Elizabeth laughed, and the two women resumed their stroll. "I've imagined myself at least whipping Charles, if not quite murdering him! I suppose best of all I would like to see him thoroughly repentant, telling me that nothing is as important to his life as I." They reached the shrubbery at the end of the drive, where shoals of fireflies danced in the dark, and turned back. "But I don't think that's at all likely, I'm afraid."

"How would he behave if you were to confront him?"

"I imagine he would deny everything. Or worse, justify it. He would have the cheek to be indignant." She paused and said in a very thoughtful tone, "He would never feel safe with me again."

"Irritational, is it not?" Lady Pearsall's voice had a touch of rue. "I think men find it very difficult to have consciences. It doesn't seem to bother them to do things, just to be caught. My mother used to say we owed our vacations in the south of France and our trips to Switzerland to a chorus girl with brown eyes."

"I may be angry with Charles," replied Elizabeth. "But I have no wish to rule the roost. I suppose I must still love him." She brushed her skirt as abruptly as though beating a carpet. "I know I should like to save our marriage, and that is scarcely the way to do it, is it? But then, what is?" She paused, and when she spoke again, she found she had made a decision. "Emily Wade is one of his women, isn't she?"

Lady Pearsall stopped, leaned forward with one hand massaging her knee, and stared ahead at the club's lighted entrance. "I think," she said, "that I have banged my knee playing that silly game."

Elizabeth stood still, willing the other woman to reply. Further knowledge would be her goad to action. During these past days she had been avoiding Ginny precisely because she would have to push her for that further knowledge.

Lady Pearsall straightened. On her thin face in the glimmer of light there was an almost malevolent expression. "You must understand, my dear," she said, "that I did not tell you about Charles' . . . about Charles without thinking about the repercussions. What you do inside your own family is entirely your own affair, but I cannot, I really cannot let you know anybody's name until you have decided exactly what you intend to do outside your family. You have behaved magnificently tonight, but would you have been able to do so if you . . . ? Though I am not surprised that you have guessed Emily Wade. She is, after all, one of your closest friends."

The bitterness of this last remark was so pronounced that Elizabeth recoiled. "Do you dislike women so much?"

"I do not think well of them," said Lady Pearsall in a manner both clipped and starched. "It seems to me absolutely ridiculous that a woman would have an affair with a friend's husband–with any husband at all, for that matter–and yet they do, don't they? And I cannot believe that such women are swept off their feet." She was now speaking in all seriousness, as though addressing herself. "Men–one cannot blame men in such situations, can one? They are led by their silly desires. They are like children who will cast aside all thought of risk or rules to get whatever it is they want. They have no control, no restraints. *Much* more emotional than we, which is why we forgive them, no? But we women, what is to excuse us? Who is to forgive us? Women take aim, Elizabeth. Surely even you know this by now."

They were nearing the steps once more, and Lady Pearsall's hand grasped Elizabeth's arm to bring them to a stop. Elizabeth found her perceptions crystal clear, but momentary, as though nothing had a particular continuity. She was conscious of a horrible odor of decaying flesh where some small animal had died and rotted unfound beneath the ornamental plants, and of the sound of the tuba from the other side of the building patiently providing the bass continuum for the band. She felt Ginny Pearsall's hand as a clutching.

"Have you yourself," continued Lady Pearsall, peering into Elizabeth's withdrawn features, "never found a man attractive to you, other than Charles? wondered what it would be like to sleep with him? wondered how you would set about getting him? Did you give a hoot about his wife when you looked at his back and his thighs and his hands and his jaw and his mouth? Even here, in public?"

"Ginny, I . . ." She had nothing with which to complete the sentence. Lady Pearsall's thin figure was charged with a tension that was almost a visible force and felt almost a blow.

"They say," continued Lady Pearsall, at last releasing her arm, "that women are more emotional because we weep and faint and love and are sentimental. But you yourself are a woman, Elizabeth, and have you not held yourself under such intense control these last few days that Charles has no idea whatsoever that his entire future—and that of his family—depends on you at this moment? Men are simple, simple. They don't even know when they are the victims of their own emotions. They think that whatever they do is pure reason, or at very least"—and her tone became bitterly scornful—"at very least understandable."

Elizabeth was repulsed. She had never dreamed that such savagery of scorn lay within the cool and aristocratic Ginny Pearsall. She was frightened by the outburst, and she turned to reenter the club, but again Lady Pearsall seized her forearm with fingers of steel.

"Do you think Emily Wade showed the world her underwear by chance? Do you imagine that all the hustle and bustle in that silly musical chairs was caused by the men? Do you think for a moment that one male hand brushed against one bosom without the woman's consent? Oh, Elizabeth . . ." She turned abruptly away, turning her back, slightly bent as though she were leaning to look at a stone. "Oh, don't, please, make yourself out to be more innocent than I! You *must* know better than to trust other women. You *ought* not to trust them, not even your closest friends . . ."

Her voice trailed off, and her back straightened as she turned to face Elizabeth again, and her expression was bleak and hurt. Elizabeth was filled with a cold and brilliant certainty as to what this woman was about to say.

"You cannot trust Emily Wade, Elizabeth, and you cannot, the Lord forgive me, trust me."

Her shoulders were clenched tight to her body, her features floating like some mask suspended from a blank wall, and she stared directly into Elizabeth's eyes with a glimmer of tears veiling her own. Then she took in a breath that was almost a shudder, turned, and walked, shoulders straight, up the steps and into the clubhouse. At the top of the steps the hem of her skirt knocked over a punch glass, which rolled bumping down the steps to Elizabeth's feet. Elizabeth stared at it, completely still, then lifted one foot and brought it down, hard, so that the glass shattered into fragments on the gravel.

6

An hour or so later, Elizabeth drove home with her husband through the damp heat of the tropical night. She sat apart from Charles, for he was drunk.

Her first reaction to Ginny's confession had been in her own judgment nothing but vulgar. She had thought: But you are so old, Ginny? So plain? What on earth could he see in you? It was a stupid reaction, as though the whole thing had happened to someone else, and its very inappropriateness had startled her. Surprised to find that she felt no anger toward either husband or friend, during the half-hour of solitude before departing partygoers disturbed her, she slowly realized something else: that Ginny's betrayal was less important than her confession. Elizabeth was an intelligent woman. Her mind might be sluggish when faced with the unexpected, but she could, if the issue were important enough, think brilliantly, and if she had some basis on which to stand, think decisively. In this situation, that basis was the value she placed on friendship, and the knowledge that Ginny Pearsall had risked not just her friendship and reputation, but her self-esteem. This made her treachery a dim glimmer. Elizabeth knew what conscience was all about, and she knew that only conscience could have forced Ginny to break silence. She quickly realized that Ginny's honesty had caused something more important than adultery to happen–she was not quite sure what, but she could see a sapphire glint in the mud.

As she had sat alone in the veranda's darkness, she made herself admit the difference between her and the older woman and felt shame. When faced with risk, Ginny but not she had found the courage to act, thereby winning whatever gain honesty and the confessional offered. And by overcoming her own fears of action, Ginny Pearsall had almost compelled Elizabeth Wingate to do the same. Reluctantly Elizabeth had come to an acknowledgment: the past never just fades away. She had no choice *except* as to what action she should take. Whatever the consequence, feeling and deed must unite.

So great was the pressure of that realization that she almost confronted Charles there in the motor in the privacy of the sweet-smelling night–but he was drunk, and she was tired, and Tara Singh might overhear, and they had to face Nanny when they got home, and the habits of peace are hard to shake. And once at home–the servants shepherding them into the house, hot water waiting in their rooms, the dinner table gleaming with expectancy–Elizabeth found herself pleading headache as excuse for taking a tray in her room.

There in solitude she forced herself to avoid all sense of drama and sat still in the armchair near the full-length windows onto the veranda. Forget, she ordered herself, what I feel or do not feel. What can I do? I love Charles, don't I? And if I leave him, what on earth will I do? And if I stay, how will I live with him?

A bearer knocked at the door, and she bid him enter through the dark to take the tray of spoiled and untouched food. She heard Charles come late to bed, thumping about in the dressing room that joined their bedrooms, dismissing his valet. Once he opened the connecting door, but he failed to see her in the armchair by the windows and retreated softly. He wanted her, she knew. She could not tolerate him, she knew.

Because Elizabeth understood the power of sexual arousal, she could not wholeheartedly condemn Charles for feeling it toward other women. Their own appeal for each other was not as great as it had been in the early days of their marriage, when each body was as ripe fruit to the other's hunger and thirst, but it was still alive. There had been no sexual attachment between them before their marriage until an evening party some weeks after her arrival in Colombo. Charles was an excellent dancer. Skilled, athletic, his hands light on her back and palm, he had steered through the intricate patterns of the waltz with speed and felicity. They danced close and joked about why they, of all couples, should never need hesitation or apology. Elizabeth loved the male smell that rose from Charles' body as the evening wore on; he was a dashing, reassuring man.

They sought air on the veranda, escaping with laughter from the hot ballroom into moonlight shadowed by tamarisk and rhododendron, scented by cinnamon and gravid frangipani and night-blooming exotics. Elizabeth's shoulders were bare, their powder interrupted by runnels of perspiration. Her hair was piled high, revealing her neck, and her throat rose white and vulnerable. She was, Charles thought, an extraordinarily lovely woman; ripe, moist. She turned suddenly to lean back against the balustrade, head and eyes lowered, and he—too close—caught the perfume of her hair and body, and he seized her, lifting her face with strong fingers, and he kissed her, his mouth loose and urgent, his hips pushing her against the stone. To his surprise her mouth opened under his and her tongue returned his kiss. Her stomach moved restlessly against the hardness of his swiftly risen member, and he felt passion catch in his stomach with a force he experienced rarely enough to recognize its worth. Both of them discovered in that moment that Elizabeth was no lady. Neither of them wanted her to be.

Over a decade of marriage they of course had grown calmer, but even now in the night-quiet solitude of her bedroom Elizabeth found herself greatly tempted to bury her knowledge in Charles' arms, to erase her fears of his infidelity against the hard, hot surface of his body. She saw herself walking into his room, removing her gown, sliding under the mosquito net and into the bed, awakening him to musky lust. As the images seduced her mind, her body shuddered her into movement; she started up from the chair and began pacing as though some jungle beast had roared.

It was not so much her powerlessness that now perturbed her. She had power—oh, indeed she had the power. To act a drama, look a fool, wreck a family, lose the man she still—she did, didn't she?—she still loved. Yes, she had the power and the responsibility; yes, she could act. Or—and in the heat of the night and her body a core of coldness began to grow—or not act. Her only avenue, her only *real* choice—granted the marriage, granted their love, granted the existence of Jennifer, granted her own desire not to give up what she had—the only avenue into which she might channel that power was self-restraint. To preserve pride, admit nothing. To preserve marriage, take no revenge. To preserve love, allow no anger. To preserve herself, put up with it.

She walked to her large teak vanity table. Opening the top drawer, she took out a small box made of scented cedarwood and ivory inlay, and with a key that hung next to the locket around her neck she opened it and removed a diary with a calfskin cover and brass edgings. Tucked inside was a piece of writing paper neatly folded and slightly worn. She held the paper between her fingers for a moment; then, carrying it toward the armchair by the window, she opened it slowly and studied it carefully, as though it were a text or a love letter, and as she read, the glow of lamplight revealed on her lips the beginning of a smile which was almost mischievous.

7

Lady Pearsall required small daily disciplines of herself, as both her upbringing and the tropics demanded. Each day at first light she descended to the side garden of Government House, where she had cherished into bright life the semblance of an English garden. The task brought endless small victories, preserving English delicacy against the humidity, the heat, the drought, and she liked it as metaphor. This was also the time in which she sorted out her private thoughts, and on the morning after her confession to Elizabeth Wingate she clipped dead marigolds with more decisiveness than usual.

All in all, Lady Pearsall felt she had arranged matters tactfully. Elizabeth would probably do nothing, which was sensible, and say nothing, which was better for everyone. It was as she had hoped. But somehow disappointing. There came the sound of a motorcar in the driveway. Trowel and secateurs in her canvas-gloved hands, she straightened. The Wingate Napier. Lady Pearsall dreaded scenes which she did not control.

Elizabeth stepped out of the motorcar without waiting for Tara Singh's ministrations and almost ran across the dried grass of the lawn. To the wary Ginny Pearsall's astonishment her face was alight and smiling, her gaze open, and her embrace so intense that it conveyed much more than forgiveness. Lady Pearsall held her at arm's length to take in her smiling face.

"I should betray my friends more often," she said.

"Oh, Ginny, Ginny!" laughed Elizabeth. "I'm sorry!"

"Sorry?" queried Lady Pearsall, taken back. "*You* are sorry?" She started a flurry of laughter. "Life is full of the most extraordinary surprises. I think you mean *I* am sorry."

"Well, I don't exactly know what I mean, but you know what I mean–I have the most marvelous idea, and I need your help. Will you . . ." For a moment her face was serious. ". . . an alliance?"

"Against?"

"Charles. The others. You yourself, in a way."

"Ah! Penitence! Embarrassing?"

"Yes."

"Good. Yes. Whatever it is! It's a bargain. My soul will undoubtedly benefit. What is it? No, wait. Some coffee? Breakfast?"

"I have the appetite of the proverbial horse."

They walked toward the stairs of the house, skirts trailing across the dusty grass. Lady Pearsall surrendered gloves and implements to a hastening servant and ordered breakfast to be served on her private balcony. As they drank coffee, she brought them to the point. "And now the bargain?"

"It's very simple, really." Elizabeth was smiling again, with mischievous amusement. "I'll ask you to a dinner party, and you'll give me the guests' names."

Lady Pearsall looked hard at Elizabeth, then placed her cup and saucer loudly on the table, threw back her head, and let loose a peal of laughter that no finishing school could ever have forgiven.

"Elizabeth!" she gasped. "It's the Irish in you. No Englishwoman would dare! All of us? At the same time?"

"Unless"—Elizabeth smiled dryly—"there are too many for table."

"Oh, I think not! Not that I know, anyway." Lady Pearsall laughed again. "When?"

"Before the dance on Saturday. I know it's short notice, but I'd like to do it quickly. They will come if you will."

"Oh, poor Charles, I do feel sorry for the poor man," sighed Lady Pearsall, and laughed again. "What a magnificent revenge!"

The two women found it surprisingly easy to identify others with whom Charles had been romantically engaged. When one thought about it, his discretion was not enough to make him a good dissembler. They did not trouble as to whether or not he had actually slept with all the wives, since good sense demanded that they assume the worst, and because no woman would know why she had been invited, no innocent could be offended. Sipping coffee at the white-painted wrought-iron table on the side veranda of the Governor's residence in the heat of the morning, they had soon selected the nine women who seemed most likely. The process was a trifle grim, but there was also laughter, and as the two women set down names as though for execution, Elizabeth had at last a sense of power.

Sir Reginald tried to discover what they were up to. Waved off, he shied away, as nervous as most men when women form alliances. Something's up, he thought, seeing their flushed faces, hearing their shared laughter. And whatever it is, God knows the women out here need each other. As he walked downstairs to public life, he felt a touch of envy, of nostalgia for friendship. Which (he thought) only work or war bring us men.

"Permit me to be astonished," said Lady Pearsall later, "that you have not erupted in fury or tears at me. There must surely be some unhappiness in you, about me?"

"There was." Elizabeth's tone was direct. "Not anymore. I think I know how it could happen." She paused, and Lady Pearsall did not take advantage of the opening. "But I should have thought you were too much the . . . well . . ."

"The lady? *I* should have thought I was too old." Lady Pearsall's voice was at once bitter, humorous, and tired. "And perhaps that is the real problem." She gestured at her chin, where flesh sagged despite her thinness, and at her eyes, where nests of lines grew. "I cannot any longer *expect* to be found attractive, can I? One takes so much for granted when one is young. One does not know what one has until one has lost it, and one wants it back again suddenly, as though one could use it properly now." She was very still, speaking softly. "One comes to feel that one has foolishly missed what others took, and for what reason? One comes to believe in the last chance. This sounds terribly immoral, does it not, and may God forgive me for it, but it is so very, very nice to be found attractive, and Charles, to be brutally frank, *did* find me attractive, at least for that single occasion." Her voice trailed off, and her bright blue eyes were briefly those of an old woman.

"You regret it, then," said Elizabeth.

"It is all so frightfully undignified, Elizabeth. Of course I regret *almost* everything about it. To the point–and I hope very much that you know this–that an apology to you would be obscene. But it *is* only 'almost everything.' That 'almost' must stay where it is. I do not, even now, regret everything about it. Does that offend you?" Alliances between women are individual, not indiscriminate. Ginny had asked for forgiveness. Repentance was the issue to Elizabeth, not sin.

"Strangely enough, no," Elizabeth said eventually.

"It shall not happen again, I think," said Lady Pearsall firmly. "Not with Charles. Not with anyone. I am, to say the least, no hoyden." Wry amusement had returned to her face and voice. "But you haven't answered my question."

"Why am I not more indignant? Well, I think the less of Charles, of course, much less, but even now I don't think he can be blamed too much. Oh, he is *such* a reckless fool!" She spoke with a firmness that would have graced a nanny. "But I expect I agree with my mother. She always said that one could do one of two things with broken eggs: throw them out or make an omelet. And without an omelet one might well go hungry."

The shadows of the veranda fretwork had moved so that they fell across both women's faces, and as the two sat silent for a few moments, eyes lowered, postures unconsciously identical, the mixed light was that used by artists to make femininity mysterious. Lady Pearsall broke the moment by dabbing her lips with a napkin and raising her eyes to Elizabeth's face.

"I fear," she said, drawing a breath, "that you have been forced into the kind of bargain which all of us seem to have to make at some time or another." Elizabeth remained motionless. "Marriage is comfortable, you know, especially when you consider the alternative, but it has always surprised me how much of the comfort depends on the wife. I think most men have not the slightest notion of what to do with marriage. Perhaps Mrs. Pankhurst is right–they think a wife is some kind of superior household convenience!"

"But Charles is very kind to me," protested Elizabeth, laughing.

"And Reggie to me, my dear," agreed Lady Pearsall. "He is a very nice man, and he treats me very well, but as far as knowing what marriage is all about? My dear, ask him about horses, or natives, or politics, but do not ask him to explain me or us. The poor boy, if you had known his mother! She waited hand and foot on him and his father, and she died in dreadful pain within a week of being hostess for the Hunt Ball–hunting was her husband's passion, after all! Nobody knew, says Reggie, how ill she was."

"One could say that was her own fault," said Elizabeth cautiously. "Perhaps wives protect husbands too much, perhaps we keep them *too* sheltered."

Lady Pearsall snorted. "They need all the shelter we can give them in this world. That, my dear, is the marriage bargain."

"I suppose you are right." Elizabeth seemed reluctant still. "My mother has always said that a woman should never be too serious with her husband." Both women sipped coffee in silence; then Elizabeth took from her handbag the folded piece of paper which she had last night removed from its hiding place. "Let me show you this. It's something I wrote on the boat the first night out of London all those years ago. A kind of inventory of myself. I can't remember exactly why I wrote it, but whenever I look at it again, it surprises me." She handed the paper to Lady Pearsall. In Elizabeth's neat handwriting, it read:

Virtues	*Vices*
1. An attractive appearance	1. Vanity
2. New dresses	2. Poverty (genteel)
3. Domestic experience	3. A preference for idleness
4. Sense of humor	4. Giggling
5. A pleasing voice	5. A slight brogue
6. Popularity as a dancing partner	6. The unmarried state
7. Good education	7. A lazy mind
8. A desire to please God	8. Dislike for the Church
9. Love of children	9. The unmarried state

Holding the list at arm's length to accommodate her long-sightedness, Lady Pearsall read it slowly and at last commented, "It is quite amazing how much we know about ourselves when we are young. Do we forget it, or prefer not to think about it? How clever of you to make a list."

"It has come in handy. Last night it reminded me of why I came to Ceylon–the fishing fleet . . . finding a husband . . . some freedom. I certainly found what I wanted, did I not? Listing the unmarried state twice as a vice! I think I believed that when one got married, all life's problems stopped. There one was, forever after. I mean, what could be a problem compared to not having a husband?"

"And this inventory, as you call it, reminded you of your good fortune in getting not only a husband but one as good as Charles."

"Perhaps," said Elizabeth, staring at the piece of paper in her hand. "But I think this wretched list reminds me always to keep my sense of humor. We need a sense of humor, don't we? Wives? To survive?"

"It is included in the bargain, I believe," replied Ginny, and they laughed.

Elizabeth had herself driven home to a light lunch, gave final meditation to her course while nursing Jennifer, and then at last, committed herself to action. She painstakingly wrote out invitations on linen writing paper and sent Tara Singh to deliver them. It would take him all afternoon and deprive Charles of the motor, but she didn't care. That evening she told him of the coming dinner party but remained vague about the guest list. He made no inquiries, pleased enough to be playing host to the Governor at the end of Colombo Week, proud that his clever wife had found such an obvious seal for their respectability. On the next morning, the formal and elegantly written acceptances returned. The dinner party would proceed.

During the hectic days that followed, Elizabeth was secretly glad that she could use Jennifer as the excuse for avoiding several of the social events that filled the week. Having chosen her cast, she had no desire to meet them again until they were onstage. Instead she turned her own attention to the huge and poorly tended house. She deployed echelons of servants with zinc buckets and straw brooms, so that by the evening of the dinner nobody would see her establishment as less than complete. The occasion came to be generally thought of as a housewarming.

On the evening itself, Elizabeth was in a state of high but controlled excitement which made her look her best. Laced for the first time into the new Twilfit corset which restored her slender waist and erect carriage, she wore a stately evening gown of dark blue satin, low-cut and flattering to her white skin, bringing out the auburn in her hair and the green of her eyes. She armed herself with the diamond necklace and teardrop earrings which Charles had presented her as reward for Jennifer's birth, and sailed downstairs to greet the first arrivals. It was as though now she were fighting the battle to capture Charles that she had never had to fight before their marriage. She was committed, and whatever happened, she could handle it, and in the drawing room before dinner Charles looked at her with surprised admiration.

8

Travelers remarked upon the strangeness of colonial dinner parties. Some claimed that it was merely the effect of the environs: temperature, humidity, decor, odd blossoms in conventional vases, the noises of strange nights through open windows, the brown or yellow faces that watched and waited. Others blamed the social mixture among the guests, where the claims of birth and breeding gave way to those of job title or wealth and created a disconcerting confusion of accent, origin, and interest. The hosts, however, felt anything but alien. They felt very English, very hospitable, and very up-to-date.

They were all British together. The world of the Empire was huge and exotic; that of the diners was small and cousinly, not very different after all from Home.

Elizabeth, however, felt the stranger at her own dinner party, alienated from the women, from her husband. Inevitably she watched the couples for clues to herself and Charles. Her role, she intended, would be only that of watcher.

"One cannot know what might happen, can one?" murmured Lady Pearsall as they had sherry in the drawing room while the guests gathered. She had raised her eyebrows and hooded her eyes. "One cannot help but hope that for some of them at least things might be a trifle sticky."

"Only for Charles," Elizabeth replied shortly. "And that is precisely what I want."

"Shall you say nothing to him?"

"I cannot imagine what."

"You look like one of the Furies, however, when you say that."

"A very timid Fury."

Elizabeth's objective for the evening was no more than that Charles should suspect that she knew about his affairs. This was the compromise between silence and speech which suited her: a signal, to be read. Convinced that she had the most to lose from frankness, she sought victory through stimulating her husband's better nature by diplomatic understatement. She watched him move among the guests in the drawing room, his grace as winning as his manners, the women looking up to him, the men leaning toward him, and because he seemed at ease she was sure that the special nature of the guest list had not yet registered. Even when he led the guests upstairs to the dining room, the penny had not dropped, but Elizabeth was sure that it would and that she would know precisely when it did.

She was quite wrong. As the guests arrived, Charles had recorded every woman (with one exception) as one with whom he had slept. He assumed it was coincidence, and it was half the charm of the evening. The guilt about his affairs through which Elizabeth had hoped to reach his heart did not exist, and indeed on occasions like this, while remaining shrewd enough to keep up his own guard, he also tended to keep an eye on the other men's conduct with his own wife, since one never knew. . . .

From the walls of the great dining room upstairs, photographs of Wingates and Malloys looked down on crystal, silver, flowers, mahogany. The shadows of the white-gloved bearers shifted with the candle flames. Elizabeth, he thought, has done a magnificent job. And looks her best. Things have started very well indeed, he thought, and bent his head to listen smiling to Vicky Bellingham at his side.

Everything was going so smoothly that Elizabeth was amazed to find herself looking at Charles down the length of the table and shivering with tension. His courteous touch on Emily Wade's plump elbow, followed immediately by his whispering something to Ruth Anscombe and her apparently witty response, briefly and simply infuriated her. As Sir Reginald placed her chair for her, she was so discombobulated that she failed to thank him and then felt irrationally resentful that it should be she rather than Charles who had been put off-key. Nothing, she felt, could be less appropriate than anger at this moment, and she ordered Abbuhamy to begin serving the soup. She watched Charles sit back in his chair, such a handsome man, one hand lightly on the table, toying with a napkin half out of its silver ring, superintending the serving of Lady Pearsall's soup; she saw for the first time in years how Charles looked to others: his smile, his wealth, his force, that curious lithe quality that he had kept even into middle age. She looked at him in that moment of the first lifting of the spoons, that bowing of the heads over food, as though he were an animal and his appearance a pelt. She found herself appraising him and did not enjoy the sensation.

The other nine couples between hostess and host were seated in a priority determined mostly by consultation with the Civil List. At least Charles' taste is catholic, thought Elizabeth. What did the plump and very Scottish Jean McDonald, wife of an engineer, have in common with the pompous Vicky Bellingham, loaded with jewels, affectations, and the arrogance given by her husband's high rank in the civil service? Or with thin young Mary Williams, too pallid to melt butter should anyone ever care enough to place it in her mouth? They all seemed unlikely as lovers, and her thoughts shied rapidly away from the subject. At that moment the Governor spoke to her. He was a small man, with quick, neat gestures and a face too large for his body: roundish, dominated by a large forehead and bushy eyebrows, a clown's face had it not been forceful, saved from ugliness only by lips so elegantly defined that they seemed borrowed.

"You and my good wife have been extraordinarily busy this week, Elizabeth, my dear," said Sir Reginald, "and I see that all your plotting has had its usual felicitous result."

Elizabeth was flustered into thinking that Ginny had told her husband what was afoot, until she realized that he was merely complimenting her powers as hostess.

"Thank you, Sir Reginald, but I shall be much happier if you can still say that after we've seen what the cook does to the fish." She found herself giving him a soulful glance, wildly inappropriate but as usual effective.

"You always set a magnificent table, my dear, but I was referring to your guests." He gestured with his left hand. "You always manage to assemble a group of people I wouldn't have thought possible."

Elizabeth smiled. "You give me too much credit," she said. "You might say the guests selected themselves."

"Returning obligations, eh?" said the Governor.

"Or favors, perhaps."

The bearers cleared away the soup plates and under close supervision from Abbuhamy served flounder steamed in spicy herbs which inspired Sir Reginald to send his compliments to the cook.

At the other end of the table, Charles had come upon a thought. Men compete; women satisfy. The thought had come partly from admiration of his wife's achievement this evening, more perhaps from his swift glances at the individuality of flesh: lips, shoulders, breasts, wrists. It was a jungle out there, but one had women to come home to. He found himself watching plump Emily Wade, who had a trick of licking wine from her lips. He did not know which pleased him more: his silver or his women. Both were riches. Watching Emily's mouth close around the spoon, he felt his member swell slightly against the cloth of his trousers. He cleared his throat and paid attention to the conversation.

The conversation was going so well that Elizabeth had no need to exercise her skills as hostess. Vicky Bellingham, the slightly blowsy and very wealthy wife of the Deputy Colonial Secretary, joined with her husband in a long duet about their recent visit to the Temple of the Tooth in Kandy, and the drollness of her snobbery engaged the entire table's attention. Peter Williams alone took her seriously. Something of a hobbyist in Buddhism, he tried unsuccessfully to draw the Bellingham woman out on the subject of reincarnation. Elizabeth was amused. Only he, she thought, would expect something worthwhile of her.

She had seated Peter to her left because she liked him. A handsome, fair man in his mid-thirties who looked more like a don than the planter he tried to be, he had been the Wingates' friend for years. He had sought Charles' advice about some disastrous Tolstoyan experiment with his labor force, and the advice had proven unkind but good. Since then, he would appear unannounced, offer up his practicalities for solution, hand over an idea or two in exchange, then vanish back into the hinterland. Charles owed him his introduction to his favorite novel: Lawrence's *Sons and Lovers.* At Elizabeth's bedside currently sat his personal copy of Chesterton's essays. Charles found him naive but intriguing: the colony's only intellectual. Elizabeth regarded him as one would a younger brother.

While Peter met frustration at the hands of the Bellinghams, Elizabeth watched his wife, Mary, who was staring at her husband as though she were enraged. What on earth did Peter see in her? She was a pale woman beginning to look younger than her years, as though experience were passing her by. When younger, she had been pliant, lissome, graced by melancholy. Of late she was rarely seen and seemed a trifle mad. People did not know what to say to her intensity and fumbled with politenesses. And what, frowned Elizabeth, did Charles see in her? She tugged herself back to listening.

"And that wretched priest," drawled Vicky Bellingham, reaching at last the point of her long anecdote, "had the unmitigated gall to commiserate with me for having been born English and wished me better luck next time around! Can you *imagine?*"

"But my dear," urged her husband, "you haven't told the best." He paused for the audience. "He said you might even be fortunate enough next time to be born a man!"

The table dissolved in amusement.

"Kandy contains at least one priest," murmured Peter to Elizabeth, "who can recognize a leg ripe for the pulling."

The dry-frost voice of the police magistrate, Archie Lord, captured the table. "Evidently," he said, "we should send that priest chappie to London. Put all those suffragettes in their place by turning them into good little Buddhists, what? After all, while they're chained to the railings of Buckingham Palace, they'll have to listen!"

Again the laughter was general, but Lady Pearsall cut across it. "Now, now! I shan't have the suffragists laughed at."

There was a moment of embarrassment. Lady Pearsall had a reputation as something of a bluestocking, and people could not tell, sometimes, whether she was serious or not. In another time and place, she might have been one of those aristocrats with a cause, and therefore comfortably boring, but in this time and role she had always to hesitate in front of others' expectations, with the result that one could not tell whether she was being acid or tactful.

"They say you know Mrs. Pankhurst, my lady," said Emily Wade.

"They do, do they?" parried Lady Pearsall. "Thank you, yes," she said to Charles, who was offering mutton, "but no beef."

"May I ask, is that true?" spoke up Mary Williams, surprising even herself.

"My dear, who doesn't know Emmeline Pankhurst? Emmeline Pankhurst has made it her business to see that everyone who is anyone knows Emmeline Pankhurst."

"What is she really like?" said Emily Wade.

Lady Pearsall studied Emily: dark, embonpoint, little-puss manner. "As you would expect, my dear," she said. "A remarkable woman. Remarkable." She stared Emily Wade down. "Very direct. Courageous. I like her very much."

"And her ideas?" shot back Emily with a disarming giggle.

"You probably are as familiar with her ideas as am I, Mrs. Wade," said Lady Pearsall. "What do you think of them?"

"I?" Emily blushed. "I should certainly not go to jail or get trampled by a horse for the sake of a vote!"

"I had not expected you would," replied Lady Pearsall. "Nor I, obviously. That, one assumes, is what makes the Pankhursts remarkable women."

"'That house,'" interpolated Ruth Anscombe with unexpected loudness, "'doth every day more wretched grow, where the hen louder than the cock doth crow!'"

"Frankly," said Vicky Bellingham, "I think that any woman who needs a vote to get what she wants, *I* think is no sort of woman at all."

Lady Pearsall looked at neither woman. The contest was unworthy as well as perilous.

"It'll come," said the glossy-surfaced Mallory-Watson gloomily. "It'll come, mark my words. They've got that damned socialist Keir Hardie on their side, and now Lloyd George."

"Parliament is far too busy worrying about Ireland," drawled Vicky Bellingham. "I say, why not give Ireland to the suffragettes and let them chop at each other?"

Next to Elizabeth, Peter Williams groaned softly. "Why you should have invited the Bellingham woman, I cannot imagine," he murmured. "She hates everyone."

Elizabeth laughed. "She was not exactly my choice," she said, staring at Charles down the length of the table. Peter followed her glance.

"Why do I get the feeling there's more going on tonight than I know?"

Elizabeth was innocent as a lamb. "Your imagination, as usual, and after all, you should know better than to draw out the Bellinghams."

"I know, but one of those priests at Kandy said the most extraordinary thing to me once. I've always remembered it. I asked him whether he believed in God, you see, because the Buddhists don't, you know, not the way we do, and he said, 'I don't believe. I know.' Extraordinary thing to say. I envy the blighters."

"Dear Peter, you should really stop adopting the cause of the unfortunate. You are such an idealist."

"Me?" laughed Peter. "Colombo's pet anarchist?" He laughed, then gave a quick, serious glance in turn at Elizabeth, Vicky Bellingham, and his wife. "Though I shouldn't mind adopting a suffragette if I could find one. *That* would make life more interesting." Then he smiled again. "Why don't you become a suffragette, an Irish suffragette, then I could fight the Bellinghams on your behalf."

"I can take care of my own fights, thank you very much."

"Precisely why I admire you," he said, and raised a glass of wine in tribute.

Charles at the same moment had been distracted by his bank manager, Mallory-Watson. "Scheduled your leave Home yet, old man?"

"Haven't had time to think about it," said Charles. "I shouldn't think we'll make it this summer, with the baby so small."

"Your parents will want to see their grandchild," Lady Pearsall addressed the air between the men.

"And me, I hope." Charles smiled. "It's been, what, almost ten years. We should have gone back for the coronation, I suppose, but we chose the Durbar instead, and there just hasn't been time since. Trouble is, I can't see spending the winter back Home, can you?"

"As long as we don't have a war with Kaiser Bill," said Mallory-Watson lugubriously.

"War?" said Lady Pearsall, her voice rising. "There's no danger of war!"

Mallory-Watson quailed. "I wasn't suggesting we *should* have one," he said defensively. "Just that we *might.*"

Emily Wade's high sweet voice jumped across the table, as though she had been a leopard lurking for opportunity. "I must know what you all think of Major Marsh's sudden departure for Home!" she exclaimed.

"Emily, really!" protested her husband, knowing he was already defeated.

"Do be quiet, Julian. There's not a military man here. We can gossip as we like!" She giggled prettily.

The Governor, the Deputy Colonial Secretary, and the Police Magistrate looked each according to his character: amused, shocked, watchful.

"I think we all know what everyone thinks," said Priscilla Lord, seeking to clip off the subject and Emily Wade with thin lips.

"But after all," said Ruth Anscombe with a dry glance at Emily, "he has made an honest woman out of her!" She raised some laughter with the sally.

Major Marsh had for years been faithful to a Sinhalese mistress who had grown from graceful youth to (reputedly) fat middle age in the course of bearing him several children. A bluff but quiet military man, the major was in his family life simply old-fashioned, and his discretion had long protected him. His quiet announcement of forthcoming marriage, however, set the bridge tables in a roar. The players would be forced to receive a Mrs. Marsh in their homes: a mistress, with bastards, a native who scarcely spoke the language, Lord knows, probably with a diamond in her nose and a red spot on her forehead. The major had disappointed them by sailing unannounced for England, having resigned his commission, two days previous.

"One wonders," said Lady Pearsall across the laughter, "what they call the children. Charles the Second, I believe, named all his little by-blows Fitzroy, did he not? Should it be, then, Fitzmarsh? Or perhaps Fitzmajor?"

Again the laughter was general, and Elizabeth was plunged into despair: back in the playground of that school for English young ladies, back being alien, lost, angry.

"Dear God!" she exclaimed, her voice raised. "I should think that we of all people should be ashamed to cast the first stone!"

Lady Pearsall lifted her head sharply to look at her. Peter Williams gave her a swift glance, as did one or two of the women.

"Ah, the ice cream!" said Charles hastily into the silence. "Now, you must let me boast at great length about at least one modern invention: the refrigerator!"

And as Abbuhamy hastily marshaled the bearers into carrying in dishes of the menu's *pièce de résistance,* the conversation again grew general.

Lady Pearsall turned to Charles. "You seem in very good temper tonight, Charles," she said sweetly. "I hope that means you find your guests agreeable?"

"Very," said Charles with a polite smile. "Indeed! Very agreeable." His wife had surprised and irritated him. What on earth was wrong with her?

"As on previous occasions?" continued Lady Pearsall sweetly.

"Indeed, indeed," he replied, then faltered. Just what did that remark mean? The damned woman kept staring at him. His smile felt as though there were something wrong with his mouth.

"But then," she said, "we all know each other so well here, don't we?"

He was saved by Abbuhamy, who bent to ask whether he should serve the champagne to go with the ice cream. That damned Ginny Pearsall, thought Charles. She made him nervous. But if she did know anything about the other women present, surely to Christ she wouldn't say anything to Elizabeth. Just as well he *had* slept with her. And what the devil was wrong with Elizabeth?

He let his eyes roam the table again. Now, that Emily Wade . . . a regular romp, she was, and for all her chatter, as discreet as the night was long. Or Jean McDonald, plain perhaps, but kindly as a warm kitchen. And Priscilla, Priscilla Lord, cool as ice in public. Charles felt his loins stir again, and he leaned forward to offer Vicky Bellingham grapes, staring at her breasts. Suddenly he laughed. What if women ever compared notes? Ah well, he sighed, toying with the stem of his champagne glass, that's one thing he could say for Elizabeth. She was no hypocrite, like these other women. She spoke her mind.

He felt suddenly tired, drained, exhausted for no reason, and when he looked around the table this time, he drew back in his chair and his expression became bleak, dry. His eyes rested on woman after woman until at last they arrived at his wife. She was staring at him, an odd expression on her face, as though she expected something from him. He raised his glass to her in a private toast. Well, old girl, he was thinking, that's at least one of the ways you're better than the others–you'd never even think to make a fool of your husband. He smiled ruefully at her, and toasted her again.

To Elizabeth's ears, her outburst had sounded like an open accusation; she had said nothing more because it sounded to her that she had said it all. She was appalled at her directness. She watched Charles' face when Ginny engaged him in conversation, and by its blankness knew that he was distracted, thinking. She watched his face when Ginny released him in favor of ice cream and saw him look at three women in particular and then slowly, as though reluctantly, at her. As their eyes met, she felt a moment of terrible suspense: what would be in his? And when she saw regret there, and when he raised his glass to her, not once but twice, she was flooded with relief.

Thank God! she thought. He has understood, and he is *not* a bad man.

She raised her glass to him. One *can* put the past behind, she thought. One *can* start over without pain.

9

Elizabeth spent the rest of the evening edgy with excitement. When silken pairs of women drifted off to the earth closets, she and Ginny Pearsall had a moment of privacy.

"What happens next?" she asked. "Do I say something or does he?"

Ginny, powdering her nose, paused for a moment to stare at their combined reflection in the mirror, expressionless. "Perhaps neither of you need say anything," she said finally, and Elizabeth welcomed the idea.

Gaiety carried her through the ball to which the party moved as a group. She and Charles treated each other with a brilliant politeness that could have been interpreted as any emotion based on goodwill, and they were not alone until, very late, with coffee as a nightcap, he began to undress in her room, the old signal of desire.

She took off gown and corset quickly, put her evening slippers on their forms, and sat in front of the mirror in shift and stockings, shedding her jewelry item by item in a delicate, careful manner that he always found intensely sensual. He struggled with cummerbund and shoelaces, and she watched him in reflection, letting her hair loose into a cascade that shone warmly in the soft lighting.

"Did you enjoy the dinner, dear?" she asked.

"The fish was a great success. The mutton was good–bit spicy perhaps–but you'll never find a native who can master beef Wellington, my sweet."

A before-dawn breeze from the ocean stirred the curtains at the window, and for once the tropical night seemed completely quiet: no chirruping or squawking or drum-banging, just the slightest dry rustle of palm fronds against the roof's overhang.

She moved to the bed, brushing her hair, and he took her place in front of the mirror to struggle with cufflinks and studs.

"I meant the people, not the food," she said after a pause.

"Strange group, dear." He shrugged and plucked at the back of his black tie. "Were we clearing up obligations? I don't remember ever dining with the McDonalds."

"No, dear," she replied quickly, setting down her brush. "A little more purposeful than that." She looked at him, thinking calmly that they were going to have it out after all.

"Oh?" he said inquiringly.

If any single moment could be chosen as the point at which the vitality began to drain out of the Wingate marriage, it was now, this moment of casual domesticity in the quiet night. Elizabeth splayfooted at bedside, Charles with flushed face in front of the mirror wrestling with a collar stud.

Had he in that moment asked what she meant, the obvious question, then she–flushed with the evening's excitement, sure of their affection for each other, certain that his question meant that he wanted to admit the truth–she would have spoken. But he–occupied with the discomfort at his throat and unaware that his conscience should be bothering him, blurred by alcohol, fully engaged as one can be only in a temporary fight (that obdurate, inanimate, tiny stud)–he said nothing, so that she, unable to take a risk unforced, made the error of leaping forward to forgiveness.

"Can I help, dear?" she said. "Come over here and let me do that for you."

Fingers probing between throat and collar, he moved toward her and then, oddly, knelt in front of her at the bedside so that he was between her knees. The posture almost made him recognize what was happening; something flickered in his intuition. A sensation of being trapped was brought on by both the collar and the wifeliness, so that he bowed his head. She saw it as apology. She took his face between her hands as though he were a fretful boy and lifted his head. His neck hurt. Forced to look into her face, he felt the choking sensation redoubled. He knew very clearly that he did not want to be caught and held, and with brute anger he ripped at the stiff collar and stubborn stud at his throat.

"Oh, my poor Charles," she laughed gently. "How uncomfortable you have made yourself! How you hate to be hemmed in!"

Accusation and forgiveness. But the moment for metaphor was over.

She leaned forward to kiss him sensually on the mouth. Her hand slid down his neck behind his ear, and she loosened the stud from his collar and his collar from his shirt. He stayed still, and her hands slid down his chest and began to tug at the studs, ties, and snaps of his starched shirtfront and soft lawn shirt, pulling them down from his shoulders. Within moments they were stretched on the bed together, she underneath him, spread wide, he arching his back to pull off his clothes without ceasing to hold her, and soon they made quick love with limbs as loose and heads as empty as of old.

Of course they should have talked, but to act is to risk blame, dismay. Failing to act is much easier; it involves only the slow rubbing away of the moral by the temporal. And so the Wingates could let the evening sink into the course of their lives like an alligator under the waters of a pond. Elizabeth could think of nothing that could be said without their both paying a price she did not want to exact. Charles never realized that anything remained unsaid. It would take years for the bill for this night's sin to come due.

Curiously, in later years Charles' main recollection of the evening was a brief conversation with Peter Williams. After dinner, he had led the grateful and hasty gentlemen downstairs into the garden, where they formed a ragged row to urinate onto lawn and flowerbed with various sounds of satisfaction or discomfort. As Charles buttoned his flies, Peter Williams, clipping a cigar in the dim light, addressed him. "Sad that we don't take this Buddhism business more seriously, don't you think? In this day and age, it seems more than a little antique to be thinking of them as just heathens."

Charles grinned at him. "Most of us don't think of Buddhism at all."

"You're right, of course," Williams agreed amiably. "But they do have some fascinating ideas as to why we are here."

"Not a subject that grabs me much, I must say," said Charles genially. "We're here for business, aren't we?"

"And saving pagans." Williams grinned. "And bearing the white man's burden, yes, and spreading the virtues of the parliamentary system, and teaching that cleanliness is next to godliness. And making a quid or two for the sake of the descendants, yes." He paused to puff his cigar alight, the flame of the match showing him looking solemnly up at Charles. "I suppose you're right, you know. The Empire doesn't have an ideology, does it? It's no more than an idea, really."

Charles took his arm to lead him back into the house. "And not a bad idea at that, old chap! Freedom to make a quid or two for the descendants? Keeps us out of mischief, doesn't it?"

"I suppose so," said Williams, shaking his head slowly. "But it's a meager sort of idea, isn't it, old chap? I mean, if that's the only reason for our being here, well."

Charles stopped and looked at him. The others having gone inside, only the chugging of the generator interrupted the sounds of the night and the sea. They could have been in some jungle clearing. "I don't like to think of that sort of thing too much, as you know." He was unexpectedly solemn. "Me? I'll take the path of least resistance, thank you."

"You should have had a Methodist for a father," said Williams with a small dry laugh. "The path of least resistance, my father was given to saying, leads only to the depths of despair."

Had Elizabeth challenged Charles, he might have discovered what he really wanted. He was neither stupid nor thoughtless. Though his feelings were often secondhand, he was not callous, not foolishly romantic, not casually cynical. He took no favors from those unready to give them, even his wife. He did not knowingly relinquish his closeness to Elizabeth; he did so because the alternatives were easier.

When, some months later, he again began to be unfaithful to her, it was less because he was dishonest with his wife than because he was dishonest with himself, less because of what he was than because he could find no reason to be otherwise. Sometimes with her the curiously boyish feeling he had experienced when kneeling between her knees that night returned briefly. He did not enjoy it, and it was enough to shift the balance of their relationship. Uncomfortable, he grew more polite, as though within her there was a power which he would not chance evoking.

So a domain grew which they both unspokenly agreed to skirt: a mutual mute deceit. Slowly, by a thousand tiny choices to do and not to do, to say and not to say, the ties between them eroded as minutely as they had previously grown. Instead of being secure in each other, they sought security in their separate selves, though not so far as to feel lonely. They were still an alliance but no longer a union.

Charles eventually began a discreet but long association with the wife of an officer absent overseas, a woman to whom he gave small gifts instead of himself. When he came home, the household still centered upon him, and baby Jennifer became a growing, charming child.

And Elizabeth? She put away the evening and Charles' infidelity as one would a letter to be read later. Part of her knew what she had failed to do; but she had done enough to feel comfortable. Half-knowingly she avoided the knowledge of solitude in favor of the illusion of love. She saw Charles' infidelity as an interruption of the normal, and when the dinner party offered her enough to believe that the normal had resumed, the world had lived up to what she expected from it. It was a fault she shared with her times: the belief that no matter how things changed, the more they would remain the same.

Not that she was quite as comfortable as before. Unlike Charles, she was nervous about the politeness which now separated them. But it was to be expected, she told herself, after years of marriage, and she had Jennifer to distract her. Early that summer an accidental exchange with Ginny Pearsall brought her close to understanding what made her keep silent. They were seated on the same veranda where they had assembled the list of Charles' women. Desultorily they had been discussing war—one did not know whether it would come, let alone between which European powers. A cat fossicked in Ginny's English garden beneath them, exploring nervously, and suddenly one of the Government House cats raced to interrogate it. Elizabeth and Ginny watched the encounter: freeze, pricking sniff, stare, circle, the reluctance to fight or disengage, the slow blinking.

Elizabeth was reminded of herself and Charles, but Ginny broke into the embryonic idea wryly. "The Czar and the Kaiser," she said. "One assumes that they know what they are saying to each other even if it all seems incomprehensible to outsiders."

"And what if they don't?" replied Elizabeth. "What if they are stupid? Perhaps it is all chance or accident or misunderstanding that decides whether or not they fight. One silly wrong move."

Ginny laughed. "I'm sure they have rules which they understand."

"We all have rules," said Elizabeth briskly, "and we're very stupid about them. When I was a girl, I hated peas, and I've always remembered one night when I refused to eat them. Maman gave me such a look of astonishment. 'But one *always* eats one's peas!' she said, and I did, and I still do, even though I still hate them."

"It's so much more comfortable to stay with things as one knows them," sighed Ginny. Beneath the veranda, the Government House cat crouched blinking, and the stranger slowly picked its track away. "There, you see, the Czar and the Kaiser have worked it all out. They will not fight. It is too hot to bother."

"But perhaps they ought," Elizabeth said slowly. "Or at least do *something* different."

Ginny gave her a quizzical look, then leaned forward to pat her forearm. "Eat your peas like a good girl, Elizabeth. Eat your peas. . . ."

PART II

The First War

10

1915

During the next eighteen months, the mansion in Mount Lavinia grew tidier, Jennifer bigger, and Charles busier. Europe went to war, taking the Empire with it and forcing the Wingates to postpone their trip Home. On the third day of mobilization, Captain Joseph Plunkett obeyed regulations laid down a century previous by parading with the other officers to have his sword sharpened at the armorer's shop.

"I've never used the damned thing except to salute," he apologized to Charles that evening. "Bloody nuisance it'd be in battle, I imagine. Except to cut kindling wood."

Charles laughed.

"And what do you think of this war, Abbuhamy?" he asked of his head bearer in exchange for a whiskey. Even Tamils and Sinhalese were English at this hour.

"Ah, sir, very exciting!" Abbuhamy was solemn. "Maybe I go off soon. Men tell us that the Germans have took Berlin."

"Oh, they did, did they?" said Charles, straight-faced. "Very good. Carry on, then."

"H.Q. could use him," said Plunkett dryly. "Hot to trot. Well informed."

So the first war began with laughter, and when the regiment sailed for France with guns and grins equally on display, the children's band from Dr. Barnardo's Home for Orphans played "Hold Your Hand Out, Naughty Boy," and baby Jennifer, lifted high to see, closed her eyes against the sunlight glinting off their instruments. One really did think, then, of war as some kind of greater sport, and one sent the German consul to Coventry as though he had said something unpardonably rude to one's daughter. So far, death was no more than the game's final score. It was all very far from Ceylon.

Very quickly, however, the war became a trench-bound stalemate, and one had to pay more serious attention. Joe Plunkett did not sail with the regiment. Rumor said his job was to ferret out spies rather than horses, and Charles was amused to find his small, immaculate friend turned into the club's resident expert on tactics, strategy, ordnance, and supply. Charles himself was plunged into heavy work when both the Legislative Council and the Governor called upon him for advice. He appointed his former chief clerk, Arthur Barker, to be undermanager of Clarkson and Son, knowing that Barker's gimpy leg prevented him from volunteering, but even with his help Charles was away from home in the evening more often than not, dining at the club or the half-deserted mess.

One evening he and Joe attended a formal dinner of balding, bellied men of affairs, from which they escaped into the quiet of the veranda at the mess.

"God," groaned Charles. "It used to be we were all glad to get to the toast to His Majesty because we could all have a smoke or a pee. Since the war started, we're all as solemn as though we were about to march off to battle, patent-leather shoes and all."

"I don't see any of that lot volunteering," said Joe.

"Well, we all have to make a living." Charles sighed. "Thank God I'm too old–the desire but not the capacity. Or, frankly, the time."

"Business still in chaos?" Agriculture, shipping, storage–they were all battlefronts now. The question was not idle.

"If we could get an answer from Whitehall about neutral ships," Charles said grumpily. "But at least the markets have settled down."

The price of commodities having skyrocketed, Charles had made a great deal of money by coercing the nervous Mallory-Watson into making his bank lend sums that would have terrified them both a few months ago. His warehouses bulged. Charles had joined the board of the Widows and Orphans League and vowed not to complain publicly about the hugely increased taxation.

"No hurry, anyway," said Joe. "Wasn't over by Christmas like everyone predicted. Last another two years, shouldn't be surprised."

"Ah, yes, you and your theory about trenches and machine guns."

There was a long pause.

"Know who's trying to join up?" said Joe. "Williams. Your friend Peter Williams."

"At his age? Well, I suppose he's younger than me."

"And in worse shape," said Joe. "They won't take him. But I would have thought the feller'd turn out to be a conscientious objector, frankly."

"Never can tell what anybody will feel these days."

"Weren't you worried one time about him and, you know, Elizabeth?"

Charles grinned. "Was I?" He shook his head in wonderment. These last few months he had drifted away from all things feminine with surprising ease. "Must have had nothing better to worry about. Williams? He's too much of a fool to please Elizabeth."

To her duties as wife, mother, and housekeeper, Elizabeth that year added work with all the patriotic women's organizations and spent hours rolling bandages, knitting socks, writing letters to men at the front, going to rallies, and running a booth at bazaars. Ginny Pearsall, frantically busy as the Governor's wife and the mother of two sons in the army, made Elizabeth her deputy as morale officer for the Mothers' Union. They were in attendance at the weekly meeting precisely one year after the declaration of war, seated in the St. Mark's assembly hall before some fifty women who nodded hats like offerings of fruits and flowers and parts of birds.

The president of the union, Mrs. Barrington, occupied the chair as firmly as usual. She was a large iron-gray woman with an icily commanding manner. The meeting's main business, she had announced, was the reading of a pamphlet sent by the government. "Not enough mothers," declared the pamphlet, "say to their sons, as one did lately, 'My boy, I don't want you to go, but if I were you, I should go.'" By the time Mrs. Barrington's authoritative sonority had finished the long prayer for survival with which the pamphlet ended, many laced handkerchiefs were damp, and gloved applause pattered gently among the dust motes.

"Now," she said, "I think you will agree that every British mother in Ceylon should read this leaflet." The consensus was stately, Mrs. Barrington satisfied. "The distribution committee will have bundles delivered to your homes, and I expect by Saturday to see it everywhere I go, absolutely everywhere!"

Near the rear and the side of the crowd, a hand rose to the surface.

"Yes, Mrs. Beardsley?"

"But I mean *are* there that many British mothers, I mean, who are the British mothers out here, I mean, *are* we to consider the *natives* are British mothers?"

"Any lady who is a mother, any lady who is a wife, is a British mother, Mrs. Beardsley. Any woman who can send a man to war."

Another round of applause.

"Oh, I say, thank you," said Mrs. Beardsley.

"But who are all these *loungers* I see everywhere?" protested Lady Gerrard in the ancient high voice which, some believed, had killed her husband twenty years ago. "I see them *every*where. Perfectly able-bodied, *healthy* men of all classes, wherever I go, just lounging about with cigarettes or filthy pipes in their mouths. They must be slackers! Who are they?"

"If we see a gentleman, any gentleman, whom we suspect of being a slacker, Lady Gerrard," replied Mrs. Barrington, "then he is our *target*. We must *address* him."

"I?" said Lady Gerrard.

Another hand arose, from a small lady with flat gray hair seated immediately behind Lady Gerrard, who now nervously half-rose to speak. "I find it frightfully easy with this," she said, indicating a scarlet-and-blue rosette pinned to her bosom bearing the inscription in golden letters: "ENLIST NOW." "I go and stand near them, you see, and I sort of point it at them, and I can see that it affects them, I really can. One doesn't have to actually speak to them, you know."

Lady Gerrard turned to scrutinize the rosette.

"Give her one quickly," murmured Lady Pearsall to Elizabeth. They sat at the end of the front row near a pile of assorted boxes, in one of which Elizabeth rummaged for a rosette. It was passed hastily down the row to Lady Gerrard, who said in a loud voice, "May I have another for Chuckles?" Her pug dog panted in her lap, half-buried by knitting.

"We cannot afford to be *timid,*" Mrs. Barrington was saying. "May I remind you, once again, that His Majesty has officially requested the help of the Mothers' Union in this matter, and that it is our *duty.*"

Another pattering of applause.

"Find another for Chuckles, will you, dear?" Mrs. Roundtree leaned forward to give the order to Elizabeth across Ginny. "Or the old girl will never let us have peace."

Mrs. Barrington and Priscilla Lord were now distributing pledge cards, and there was a great search for pencils in handbags. Each signer pledged to "persuade every man I know to offer his services to the country" and "never to be seen in public with a man who refused to respond to his country's call." The only objection came from someone who pointed out that the cards came not from the headquarters of the Mothers' Union but from the Women's Service League, which, she understood, was founded by the Baroness Orczy, who was, she believed, a foreigner, and whose novels, she had been told, were scandalous, though, she was sure, the lady herself was perfectly respectable.

Mrs. Barrington had further announcements. Thresher and Glenny's had agreed to withdraw their corsets from sale since, as had been suspected, though made in Birmingham, they did use German steel for the busks and steels.

"We shall just have to make do, shan't we?" said Mrs. Barrington in reply to a flurry of anxiety.

"We shall just have to have a quiet word with Mr. Batterson," muttered Ginny to Elizabeth. "I hope the fool doesn't throw them out."

"Finally," said Mrs. Barrington, "ladies have been heard complaining about such things as the shortages of hairpins and lucifers, although we have agreed this sort of thing is not good for the morale. If Government House can agree to us giving up our long white gloves"–a nod and smile to Lady Pearsall–"then we can all make our sacrifices without complaint, I believe? The enemy has ears, remember!"

Another pattering of applause.

"Now I shall ask the head of our Morale Committee to speak to us. Lady Pearsall?"

Ginny rose to her feet and turned to the rows of women fanning themselves with pamphlets in the August heat. After a full year of war, morale was more of a problem than it had been. The ladies had been upset last week to learn that the Polo Club intended to resume the matches which last season had been suspended for the duration, and it had taken all of Lady Pearsall's authority to convince them that they too should not slacken off. But, she thought today, looking at the rows of gray hair and steeled figures, they'll keep working; they've been given one more motherly mission much later in life than they could have expected.

"You will be glad to know," she began, "that in response to a member's request we have clarified the position of the Women's Social and Political Union. Mrs. Emmeline Pankhurst continues to endorse the war wholeheartedly, as does the whole WSPU. The only dissent comes from Miss Sylvia Pankhurst, who is *not* a member of the union at this time."

The ladies seemed a little bewildered until Mrs. Barrington exclaimed that this was smashing news because it meant that all women, even the suffragists, supported the war.

Lady Pearsall resumed. She had acquired a new poster, which she unrolled. Peering shortsightedly, the ladies read: "If your young man does not think that you and your country are worth fighting for, do you think he is *worthy* of you? If your young man neglects his duty to his King and Country, the time may come when he will *neglect you.* Think it over, then ask him to JOIN THE ARMY TODAY." While these posters would be distributed by the Junior Service League, ladies with daughters might also care to have their own copy. Mrs. Wingate would be glad to supply them.

"I admire the *sentiment,*" said Lady Gerrard. "One cannot trust a *shirker,* whoever he may be." Chuckles' rosette was now pinned to his collar.

"Concerning the problem of native recruits," continued Lady Pearsall, "I do have a suggestion to overcome the language problem. We may not know many natives, and few of them may read, but we do know our own servants." The ladies rustled with unease. "Every one of us has a butler, a groom, a chauffeur, a valet, even a gardener who one knows would make a good soldier because he has been exposed to the British way of doing things."

"I can't *imagine,*" said Lady Gerrard loudly to Mrs. Roundtree, "that any natives make good fighters."

Elizabeth detected a glint of amusement on Ginny's features as she continued. "One can always replace them from the civilian population and do one's bit by undertaking a little extra training."

The silence was broken only by the sound of faster fanning, and as Ginny sat down Mrs. Barrington moved quickly: "And now I think in this heat we are all a little fatigued, and if Mrs. Higham-Smith doesn't mind"—an interrogatory command, an acquiescent nod—"we will postpone our discussion of the rummage sale until next week. Shall we all now join in singing 'Your King and Country Need You'?"

Soprano voices trembled into the air, bouncing against the corrugated iron roof like birds seeking escape:

Oh, we don't want to lose you
But we think you ought to go,
For your King and your Country
Both need you so. . . .

Elizabeth leaned forward to rummage in the boxes, and Ginny, singing, gave her an amused glance.

> We shall want you, and miss you,
> But with all our might and m-a-i-n,
> We shall CHEER you, THANK you, KIIISS you—
> When you come back again.

"Fortunate that we have all trained in church," said Elizabeth quietly as the ladies applauded themselves.

They all stood to serenade God on behalf of the King-Emperor, Lady Gerrard dropping her ball of knitting wool, Elizabeth rescuing it from Chuckles.

The five of them took tea during the committee meeting which followed, tea from chipped china mugs provided by the church, made by Elizabeth while the others finished their executive tasks. Ginny gave her unnecessary help in order to speak discreetly.

"I think Mrs. Barrington noted that your singing lacked fervor," she said lightly.

"I *am* Irish," replied Elizabeth quickly, rattling the mugs with irritation. "I grew up listening to drunken men carry on like this."

"There has been a little talk about your Irishness," replied Ginny.

"Oh, dear," said Elizabeth, and stared at the big tin teapot. "Well, I shall do my best to blast the roof off next time. If I knew why we were fighting this wretched war, perhaps it would be easier."

She lifted the tray of white mugs, and they joined the other women in time to hear Mrs. Barrington complain. "Well, apparently we've all received one. Though why anyone should have the impudence to send one to me, of all people, I simply cannot imagine."

"They probably don't know what the Mothers' Union *is,*" said Mrs. Higham-Smith.

"Are we discussing the mysterious leaflet again?" inquired Ginny as she helped Elizabeth distribute tea. During the previous fortnight or so the postman had agitated many ladies by delivering rich linen envelopes addressed in block letters and containing a leaflet headed in bold type: "THE WOMEN'S PARTY. VICTORY, NATIONAL SECURITY, AND PROGRESS." The text called not just for "war till victory" but also for "equal pay for equal work" and "full suffrage for women." It was signed by the leaders of the Women's Social and Political Union: Emmeline and Christabel Pankhurst, Annie Kenney, and Flora Drummond.

Mrs. Higham-Smith regarded Ginny sternly. "And I'm not at all sure, Genevieve, that you were wise to try to clear up the matter today. Better, much better, if we had no association at all with those wretched suffragettes."

"I don't see why we should be so upset by it," said Priscilla Lord, leaning back from jotting notes in the minutes. "If they have seen the error of their ways, think of the satisfaction we can get from treating them as fallen sisters redeemed." She smiled cheerily.

"Redeemed my foot!" snorted Mrs. Higham-Smith. "Unsexed, brick-throwing Bolsheviks! One can't be respectable and a suffragette."

"But, after all," said Ginny quietly, sipping her tea, "women are staffing the munitions factories, we are told. Without women, there would be no war, would there?"

"You might be surprised at who supports them these days," said Priscilla Lord calmly. "One hears from London that they have made a deal with Lloyd George: their efforts at recruitment in exchange for the vote."

"Oh, my Lord," said Mrs. Barrington. "Shall we see that awful Mrs. Pankhurst invited into Parliament instead of thrown out of it? And surely, Priscilla, you yourself don't . . ."

"Indeed I don't," replied Priscilla hastily. "But we do have to face facts."

"Well, I'm sure that despite what Genevieve tells us, the Pankhurst woman is really opposed to the war. I wouldn't trust her for a minute."

"That's Sylvia Pankhurst, the younger daughter," replied Priscilla. "She has split with her formidable mother, I believe, and dashed off to the East End, where she is begging milk and clothes for layabouts. Mrs. Pankhurst is said to be quite annoyed with her and sent her a cable saying she strongly disapproved. It was all in the newspapers."

"Where these women find the time!" wondered Mrs. Higham-Smith. "If any of them had husbands and families, it would be a different kettle of fish, I can tell you." She clasped a small padlock onto the cashbox. "There, that's one chore finished."

"Perhaps we should pay attention to this Mrs. Pankhurst," said Ginny quietly. "You must admit that if women are doing all that munitions work, then probably they should get equal pay for it."

"Munitions are different, of course," said Mrs. Barrington, deferring to the Governor's wife. She removed her glasses and let them hang from their chain across her generous chest. "Though why they should expect to be paid bonuses for doing patriotic work, I cannot imagine. We do it for nothing at all."

"Of course, they do it for a living," said Elizabeth.

"And should be grateful for the opportunity," snapped Mrs. Higham-Smith. "What were they telling us before the war but that they could not get work at all?"

"There is that, of course," said Ginny.

"Anyway, I cannot for the life of me see what equal pay has to do with the vote," said Mrs. Barrington. "If we give the vote to women, we may as well give it to everyone."

"You are quite right, of course," said Ginny. "And Elizabeth? Would you like the vote?"

"Me? I don't understand things like that. I haven't the slightest idea what I would do with it if they gave it to me."

"Ask your husband, I should hope," said Mrs. Higham-Smith.

"But if we all do that," said Elizabeth, "then what is the point of giving women the vote?"

"Precisely," said Mrs. Barrington.

"Well," said Priscilla Lord, "all that aside, I would still like to know who is sending out those leaflets. I suppose they are not subversive really, but I think I shall ask Archie to have his men investigate anyway."

"Good thinking, Priscilla," said Lady Pearsall. "In wartime it is just as well to know who one's friends are, is it not?" She smiled at Elizabeth.

Later, after the tea things and the boxes had been cleared away and the other women had departed, Elizabeth and Ginny sat on a bench in the vestibule of the church hall. Both were sweating slightly in the hottest part of the afternoon. The doors were open upon a street shaded by great green leaves that hung motionless, and heat waves from the iron roofs of the bungalows made the air shimmer.

"Are you sure I can't take you with me?" inquired Ginny. "It is far too hot to wait."

"Peter is usually late." Elizabeth smiled. "Please don't bother waiting." More often in town since the war, Peter had become the sort of single-male friend that happily married couples attract, as though he were a bachelor.

Ginny shook her head. "I sometimes think you need a chaperon, my dear Elizabeth. Tongues do wag, you know. They'll give you Mr. Williams as a lover whether you want him or not."

"Because that is what they'd expect of an Irishwoman?" said Elizabeth with some asperity.

"Because, as you should know, they will see you as having what they want. Discretion is the better part of respectability, you know."

Elizabeth laughed. "And do you too think I am having an affair with Peter? I'm not, you know. He is just a very good friend."

"I do not think you are. I do think you should."

"Ginny!"

"Oh, well," laughed Ginny. "There is a war on, you know. We do have to change with the times."

At that moment, Peter's figure appeared dark against the bright light outside, wiping his forehead with a handkerchief and peering into the gloom of the vestibule. "Ah!" he said. "I take it the harpies have all gone."

They left the church hall, Ginny for her motorcar parked in the shade, the chauffeur sound asleep with his head on the edge of the window, Elizabeth and Peter for a canopied surrey, into whose backseat Peter piled several of the boxes which Elizabeth had superintended at the meeting. As he chucked the tired horse into activity, he grinned at Elizabeth. "And what did we accomplish today?" he asked with a grin.

"As usual, nothing."

"Tsk, tsk," he said. "All that time wasted when you could have been rolling bandages."

They moved steadily through the neat streets of the European district. In this heat they were deserted except for an occasional native, a panting pariah dog. The smell of rotting vegetation hung heavy in the air, even here, and they were glad to get out onto the main road, where despite the humidity given off by the rice paddies a small breeze from the ocean cooled their faces. Elizabeth opened her parasol against the slant of the sun.

"My mother writes that she has been back and forth to London working with the Belgian refugees," said Elizabeth. "She worries that they left their homes and have been sent to Dublin without warm coats. It seems absurd out here, doesn't it?"

"But that's what it's all about, isn't it?" said Peter. "Warm coats? You have plenty of them: money, Charles, Ceylon."

In silence, she studied his profile: the firm mouth and prominent nose, the high brow with fair and unruly hair, the amused blue eyes.

"Then why do I feel like a Belgian refugee among those women?"

"Well, whatever the reason for that is, you can't blame them.

They're merely doing what they were brought up to do. They send their sons off to the war just the way they used to stop them dirtying their nappies or biting their nails or climbing too high or talking to naughty girls."

"You know that poster, the one with the girl saying to the man, 'Will you go? or must I?' Well, if these women went instead of their men, I should feel sorry for the Hun," said Elizabeth.

"Don't worry," he said, "your Captain Plunkett has a nice expression. He likes to say war'll last longer than the patriotism."

"I don't want to talk about war. I don't want to talk about those women. I don't want to *think* about war or those wretched women."

"Charles says to tell you he'll be home about four. Do you think he's giving you fair warning, that he thinks we are lovers?"

Elizabeth looked briefly shocked. "I was going to say that you mustn't say such things, but perhaps it wouldn't hurt Charles if he did think that."

"Ah," sighed Peter melodramatically. "Would that you would give him reason to tear me limb from limb!"

They ate a very light lunch with cool drinks and separated for their afternoon naps. Elizabeth fell heavily asleep, and when she arose she found Peter and Nanny on the veranda laughing over a batch of newly arrived magazines which fluttered and skidded in the breeze.

"I like this one," Peter was saying. "Look, 'Stirring Times,' with a picture of a nurse's hands stirring the Fry's Cocoa."

"How about this one, then?" said Mabel, handing a copy of the *Tatler* to Peter.

" 'Sanatogen in a Service Pack'?" he read incredulously. " 'With unequaled potential for the maintaining of health and powers of resistance'? No thank you." He handed the magazine back and waved *Queen* in its place. "I bet it doesn't work as well as the Dayfield Body Shield, which, it says here, is 'proof against bayonet, sword, lance, bullets, shrapnel, shell splinters, *and* grenades.' Equal that potential if you can, Sanatogen!"

"What on earth are you two doing?" interjected Elizabeth into their laughter.

"Just reading the ads," laughed Peter back at her. "Look here, is there nobody at the front you would know who would like a portable Decca gramophone? It says here that they could use it 'on the wayside, in dugout, camp, or billet'! On the wayside!" Suddenly he grew serious. "Good Lord . . ."

Nanny, sobered, rose to her feet. "Shall I order tea now, Mrs. Wingate?"

"No, Nanny. We are expecting Mr. Wingate any minute. Sit down and relax, please."

"Yes, Nanny, sit down and tell us what you think about the war."

"I think about all that just as little as I can," said Nanny staunchly. "I have better things to occupy my mind with, thank you. I've no time for men when they don't show the sense God gave them when they were born."

"Aha! You'd agree with the New York *Times,* then: 'the least justified of all wars since man emerged from barbarism.'"

"I don't know about that," said Nanny. "I imagine all that means is that America will join in as soon as it can."

"If anyone could tell me," said Elizabeth, "why men like to fight wars, I might be more interested in this one. Nanny and I are doing our best to ignore it."

"Why do men fight?" said Peter with a touch of melancholy. "Because they enjoy it. Why do women–normal women–like war? Because it's exciting. It's not very hard to understand the beginning of any war, really. If peace lasts long enough, we lose our taste for it. So we start belting each other about the ears and cheering from the sidelines."

Elizabeth gestured at the back page of the Colombo *Times,* which lay on the table in the breeze, trapped by a vase. On its front page a photograph had caught her eye: a grainy photograph of the aftermath of the shelling of a British dugout, a dozen or so men slumped or spread-eagled casually about, spattered with mud and shrapnel, discarded, as it were, on the edges of the shell hole, disarranged but unmussed, as though they could if they would stand up to fight again. They did not seem dead until one saw that they were not fat, but distended; not shadowed, but headless or legless.

"And why," said Elizabeth softly as they stared at the photograph, "do they choose this rather than being alive?"

"Well, they can't stop once they've started, can they?" said Mabel, disturbed by the picture.

"So you tell me that we fight because we have started fighting," said Elizabeth coolly to Nanny. Then, turning to Peter, "And you say that the passion for war is the reason for war. Not very satisfactory explanations, are they?"

Mabel stood and shook out her skirts. "I'd better see if Jennifer is stirring yet. Are you sure you wouldn't like your tea now?"

Elizabeth shook her head slowly, and after Nanny's departure she and Peter fell quiet, looking out toward the ocean.

"If I were a proper socialist," said Peter slowly, "I would blame war on historical necessity, I suppose, but there is a nice quotation from Thucydides which says more or less that it is a law of nature—for both men and gods—that they rule where they can. Ask Charles, if you don't believe me!"

"Let's talk about something else, shall we?" said Elizabeth wearily.

"Which reminds me," continued Peter, "that I have a little gift for you."

"Peter! How nice! In honor of anything special?"

"Special but not particular—just something which I have enjoyed long enough to want you to have it now. Stay there a sec."

He unlimbered himself from the rattan chair and went quickly into the house, from where he soon returned carrying a milliner's box, all silly ribbons.

Elizabeth, pleased and amused, took the box and scrabbled to untie the ribbons. "Of all things, a hat?"

"Not exactly."

And from the ribbons and tissue paper emerged a clay figure some eighteen inches high: an ancient model of the Buddha. The clay was red, hollow, fragile. The Buddha's features were of fading paint. He was large-bellied and long-eared and chipped, but the artist had managed to capture the elusive expression that was and was not a smile.

"Oh, how very beautiful," exclaimed Elizabeth softly. "Peter, how perfect."

"It's something I picked up a long time ago in the north." He was pleased, embarrassed.

"But I can't accept it," said Elizabeth. "It must be very valuable. And precious to you."

"I think this little chap goes wherever he is most needed. It occurred to me he might help you survive Higham-Smith, Barrington, and Mars." He looked at her very seriously as she turned the figurine in her hands, and he seemed to be hoping for something from her—or perhaps for her. "This is one god," he said slowly, "whose nature it is *not* to rule where he can. One needs the freedom, I think, these days."

Whether the thought was Peter's general wish for womankind, or his personal wish for Elizabeth, not even Peter could know. Elizabeth did not ponder. She saw the Buddha as a gift, not a message.

"They say if you rub his belly, it brings you luck," she said girlishly, and proceeded to do so.

"Yes," said Peter, "they do say that." And his tone was disappointment.

It was at this moment that Charles arrived upon the balcony, to see the couple admiring the figurine. The pleasure on Elizabeth's face made him feel a flash of jealousy: something shared with someone else by her who should share all things with him. Because the other man was Peter, the feeling vanished immediately.

Elizabeth looked up. "Charles!" she exclaimed, the figurine in her hands, the light on her features fading. "It must be time for afternoon tea!"

11

May 1916

Nineteen-sixteen was the year of Verdun, the year of the Somme, the year of killing. The Germans invented the *Trommelfeuer,* a creeping barrage from hundreds of cannon that could be heard as far away as London. The British gave orders that shellshock no longer warranted even a temporary absence from the line. The Germans used a seventeen-inch howitzer firing a shell which weighed more than a ton and stood as tall as a man. The British, with Winston Churchill's help, invented the tank. Inventions were many that year: against tanks, the land mine; against poison gas, the respirator; against U-boats, the depth charge; against the artillery barrages, the cave. Endurance came to be called heroism, and Great Britain became the last civilized nation to introduce conscription.

The great leaves of the trees protecting the ugly brick bungalow drooped in the noon heat, and when Joe Plunkett and Charles handed their horses to the groom, their hooves kicked up sprays of dust. The wind had dropped away entirely. The northeast of Ceylon is arid, and eerie with ancient relics: temples and fortresses conquered by vegetation, reed-filled lakes and streamlets remaining from a long-dead civilization's triumphant irrigation. The army encampment sat in the middle of a flat plain surrounded by mirage, and the bungalow sat in the middle of a camp so abandoned that the only signs of life at this hour were a high buzzard and the two men wiping their necks and faces free of sweat.

"For a military man, Joe, you're just too damned cynical." Charles was irritable, and this was the end of a long discussion.

Plunkett blinked and thumped dust from his uniform. Under this sun, not even he was immaculate, nor placid. "We military chaps tend to leave the idealism to the civilians, old bean," he said firmly, daring offensiveness.

They had been too much together the last few weeks. It had started as a lark, this census of horses and other livestock in the region, a break for Charles from the grind of the office.

"Man'd be a fool," continued Plunkett, "to think either headquarters or Whitehall know what they're about. But that ain't, like you suggest, to cast aspersions on the courage of the men that do the fighting and the dying."

"Well, leave it be, leave it be," said Charles, his armpits chafed, his mouth and eyes dry with dust. "Come in and have a peg of whiskey."

"Not now, thanks all the same," said Joe. It had started as an adventure, a sort of camping trip, they'd get some good hunting in. He marked its decline from the arrival of Elizabeth, intending to do her wifely duty but soon crushed into moodiness. "All the best to the wife," he said in farewell. "Feeling better, is she?"

"God knows," said Charles with a sigh. "She's over the Dublin business, if that's what you mean."

When she had arrived, Elizabeth had been filled with concern over the Easter uprising in the streets of Dublin, bullets chipping the cobblestones of her childhood, fighting around the post office where she had been lifted to put the letters in the big brass slot.

"Well, all the best, then," said Plunkett, and trudged off down the street of dust toward the tattered bachelor officers' quarters. Charles half-raised a hand in farewell, then turned and stomped up the steps, crossed the rickety porch, and pushed his way through the curtain of beaded strips into the interior's darkness and comparative cool, loosening his tie and collar.

"Elizabeth?" he called.

"In here," answered her low voice.

She was in their bedroom, motionless in the rocking chair. The room was spotless and homey and dim, so that the glow of her white dress belonged.

"What's the matter?" he said, seeing her expression.

"You'd better read this."

He was grateful for the stir of air created by the punkah overhead. Outside a boy dozed in the shade, tugging on its cord. Charles undid the buttons of his jacket, staring at his wife, before taking the two pages of handwriting she held out to him.

"From your mother?" he said. "Why don't you read it to me? Ah, you've had my bath drawn for me. Marvelous!"

To one side of the room stood a large zinc hip tub.

"And how about a whiskey?"

The hand holding the letter fell back into her lap; then she pushed herself wordlessly from the rocking chair and went into the dining room to make his drink while he took off his riding boots and started on the buttons of his shirt. Returned, she handed him his whiskey, then picked up the jacket he had thrown on the bed and took it to the wardrobe for a hanger.

"I don't have to read it to you," she said. "I can tell you the news."

But she spoke no further as he removed trousers, shirt, and underwear, taking them from him one by one and putting them in their proper places.

"Ahhh!" he sighed, lowering himself into the tepid water.

She stood over him until he was comfortably lying back waist-deep, then handed him his glass a second time. Then she spoke, staring at him. "My parents have moved to London."

"Oh?" he said, closing his eyes. "That's a bit of a turn-up, isn't it?"

"They have to," she said, turning away. "My father has been accused of being a traitor to the Irish republic."

"What?" said Charles, opening his eyes upon her back.

"They say he had dealings with the English during the uprising this Easter. They say he is an informer. My father a traitor." She was folding and refolding his sweat-wet shirt, as though it should be put away in a drawer.

"That's a bit of a facer," said Charles, squeezing cool water from the sponge over his chest. His knees stuck out of the water, showing the firm muscles of his thighs and the hairiness of his legs. His shoulders, arms, and chest were all muscular. "Well, so long as he's not a traitor to the English."

"My father has never been a traitor to anyone!" she said, turning on him, low but angry. He looked up at her, startled. He had encountered the passion of war in the voice of his wife. He did not know what to do about it, there in his own house.

"Of course not," he reassured, then went back to the squeezing of water he had interrupted. She moved behind him and picked up a copper ladle that hung from the edge of his tub. "And I'm sure they'll be better off in London. They've both been back and forth for years, and you've said yourself your mother hates the Irish."

"Oh, they'll be all right in London," she said, bending to scoop cool water with the ladle. "Maman says he already has joined a firm of solicitors. They've taken a house in Wimbledon. Wimbledon!" She poured the water over his back. He bent his head, baring the nape of his neck to her as she dipped more water.

"You don't know Dublin in the spring," she said slowly, dribbling water on his neck. "It's so peaceful then, so clean. It's full spring, and everyone goes to church." She forgot to pour, and her face grew young with memory. "Whatever church. There is sunshine and dresses and new hats."

"Well, I'm sure they'll be all right," he said.

She stooped to her task again. "Oh, I'm sure they'll be all right," she said briskly. "You English can't kill off all your enemies that easily, I think."

"Hang it, Elizabeth, wait a minute, you can't use the English as whipping boys in this one." He turned to glare at her. "And the Irish are using German arms. We know. We've captured them."

He pushed himself to his feet, dripping, naked, and turned to face her. She stood there holding a towel, and his anger hesitated. She was his wife.

"I wish it were that simple," she said, and handed him the towel. He started to dry his hair, then his genitals. "God knows," he said, "if you are in one of your Irish moods, it's probably just as well you're away from Colombo."

She gave him a small grim smile, then turned away and sat again in the rocking chair, watching him towel himself, a very handsome man.

"That's just where I think I shall go on this Friday's train. I feel so useless here. I have no purpose here." She had felt this way ever since she left the house at Mount Lavinia, ever since she had given Jennifer into Nanny's charge.

"Whatever you want," he said, raising his eyebrows at her as he stepped from the tub, dropping the towel onto the floor.

"Don't worry," she said. "I shan't argue Irish politics. The English can't understand the Irish, anyway." She rose and stooped to pick up the towel as he went to the chest of drawers and took out a pair of loose cotton pajamas. "Which doesn't prevent me from blaming them. Do you want another whiskey before lunch? I think I'll have one too."

"So long as you don't blame *me,*" he said, bending to get into the bottoms of the pajamas.

"Ah you . . ." she sighed, and went to stand beside him, placing one hand lightly on his smooth and naked back. "How could anyone blame you? What on earth could you do about it?"

Elizabeth had been back in Mount Lavinia for four days when Peter rang up and cadged an invitation to dinner. Vicky Bellingham had been unpleasant that afternoon about her Irishness, and she felt she needed the understanding that Peter always brought. Abbuhamy served them quietly at the table in the big dining room. A rain shower had made the noise of the ocean clearer and driven the scent of wet earth and vegetation in through the big windows, overcoming the perfume of flowers on the table. She told him of her parents, but he was little interested. They talked desultorily of Mary Williams, of Vicky Bellingham, of war, of Gandhi, their shared hero.

"They feed the suffragettes in jail," said Elizabeth, "by pushing stomach tubes down their throats. They don't do it to Gandhi. Why not? Passive resistance was his idea originally, not theirs."

Peter was revolted and would not answer. Peter tonight was nervous for some reason, and spilled his wine. Abbuhamy seemed disapproving. By the time he served them ice cream with sliced mangoes and left them alone with the cheese and coffee, they had reached the second level of discussion; facts had given way to a search for meaning.

"It's not that I mind losing my ties to Ireland," said Elizabeth, running her finger around the rim of her wineglass. "The whole thing just seems the most awful *intrusion.* I don't want any kind of fighting to have anything to do with me."

Peter laughed. "You sit in the middle of a worldwide war and expect to remain untouched?"

"Not untouched. Intact."

"Delusion."

"It is not. Yes, I suppose it is now. But to have gotten at me through my Irishness when I had least expected it. . . . I feel exactly as I did at school, when those wretched English girls pulled my hair and called me Paddy."

"You can't blame the English."

"You and Charles would agree."

"Nor can you blame us men. In fact, why blame anybody? If you are not doing as well out of all this as most women, then who's to blame but yourself?"

"What do you mean?"

"I mean that the war has been good for women, good to women. It's given them an interest, moved them out of their homes and their megrims. It isn't just the parlormaids making more money in the factories, you know. People all over are beginning to treat women as though they were people—you're important now. And what I mean is that if you haven't found something useful to do, then that is probably the problem, and it's your problem, not anyone else's. You could be a Mrs. Barrington if you wished. Or a Mrs. Pankhurst, for that matter."

"What nonsense! Out here? Anyway, I'm neither a Pankhurst nor a Barrington. I just don't fit, Peter. I'd thought that once Jennifer came along, I'd be content, and I'm not, you know. I just feel that I don't belong anywhere."

And suddenly Peter exploded with anger. "I *hate* it when you whine like that, and I mean it when I say it's your own problem. There's nothing stopping you from doing something about it at all. You have the education, the money, the social position, the time. I hate it when women complain about having nothing to do. For God's sake, everyone nowadays knows that they have the intelligence, the ability. And now they have the opportunity. Only you and Mary still doubt it, don't you? If the doctor tells you to spend the first day of your monthlies in bed, you will, won't you, with cologne on your temples, even if you feel perfectly fine?"

A stunned silence fell between them. White-faced, Elizabeth folded her napkin and started to rise. "I think perhaps I shall go to bed early."

Flushed of face, Peter let her get almost to the door of the dining room before speaking. "You'll have to make up your mind who you are, Elizabeth. Sometime."

She turned at the door, dim and distant in the candlelight. "I'm neither English nor Irish, neither Catholic nor Protestant, neither pacifist nor warmonger, not old but outmoded—and all you can do to help is bully."

Peter was suddenly embarrassed at his anger. "All I mean is," he stumbled, "that if what you feel and what you do–if they are out of kilter, then you ruin both. You sabotage the value of feeling. You doubt the value of doing. Elizabeth! I know this so well myself." It was almost a plea.

Buoyed by anger, she was about to snap good night and leave him, but he had tried to understand, so she left the door and came back to him standing by the table.

"Give me a cigarette, will you?"

He took out his cigarette case and matches, offering. "Nobody would mind if you were a raving Irish patriot, you know, nor if you went to Mass every morning like Nanny. People would know where you stood, and they wouldn't really mind."

She smoked the cigarette smoothly.

"You inhale now?" he said, raising his eyebrows.

"I never smoke in public."

"There you are again!" laughed Peter. "Are you a modern woman or not?"

She looked at him very seriously. "In this awful world, who knows where they are anymore?"

He reached forward awkwardly, with one hand, half-patting her arm, as though to reassure without condescension, finally deciding on a light grip of her upper arm. "If it's any consolation," he said, "it's not the world I grew up in either."

Elizabeth sought the security of the nursery. There lay Jennifer, rosily asleep under the mosquito netting, thumb in mouth, her dark red curls in papers. There sat Nanny reading *The Mother's Companion* by lamplight, her uniform crisp, a cup of tea and digestive biscuits at her side.

"The world has gone mad, Nanny."

"Well, it does that four times a week, doesn't it?" said Nanny calmly.

"I don't understand war, and I don't understand men. What do they want of me?"

"If I could answer that, I would be a bright one, wouldn't I?" Nanny gave her a shrewd look, all Londoner suddenly. And with equal suddenness she measured her opportunity and took a risk. "All men need a bit of mothering, that's all."

"You've never been married. You can't know how difficult it all is."

"I grew up in an orphanage. You'd be surprised what that will teach you about men." She was no more sympathetic than Charles or Peter had been. Was there never to be sympathy in the world again? Elizabeth turned from her impatiently to fuss at Jennifer's coverings. "I *used* to know what to do," she said quietly.

Nanny came and stood at her shoulder, and the two looked down at the little sleeping girl.

"All Mr. Wingate wants is for you to be his wife," said Nanny sturdily. "What that Mr. Williams wants, well, who knows?"

"Peter is not in love with me, Nanny."

"Well, there, there, your heart's in the right place, bless you. We must only do what we can, no less and no more, is how I was brought up to think." She picked up the coverlet from Jennifer's bed and started to fold it away. "About men, about war, about . . . Well, you tell me! I'll say a prayer for you tonight. Fat lot of good that'll do, I expect, but it's what I *can* do."

"Nanny!"

"Religion's a great consolation, though. I never said it was realistic." Nanny grinned, and Elizabeth felt better.

12

November 1916

One bright morning of the following November, the Wingates accompanied the Pearsalls to Communion at St. Mark's. The big stone church was cool, but stuffy for all its high ceilings, and plagued today by the smell of something vile burning in the distance. The dean gave a remarkably boring sermon on the virtues of sacrifice in time of war, and as they shook his limp and charitable hand at the door and headed down the steps to their motorcars, all four people had a sense of release.

"What's Newcombe doing here?" snapped Sir Reginald, pausing halfway down the steps. "Something's up. Wait here, will you, my dear?"

The Governor's aide-de-camp, a youthful captain, stood in full uniform near their car, fingering his gloves and looking apprehensive. Sir Reginald descended the steps toward him while Lady Pearsall looked at the departing churchgoers with composure. The men's conversation was brief. Captain Newcombe did most of the talking. They could see only the Governor's back. He said something to Newcombe, who cast one glance in their direction and then walked up the steps toward them, while Sir Reginald remained standing near the car with his back turned. Newcombe glanced at Lady Pearsall as though about to speak, then instead addressed Elizabeth: "The Governor says . . . would you and Mr. Wingate . . . would you mind accompanying us to Government House, ma'am?" he stammered.

Without further word, Lady Pearsall started off down the steps, intent on her husband. Newcombe touched both Charles and Elizabeth lightly to hold them back. They looked down at him from the steps above.

"It's their . . ." he stammered again. "There's death in the family," he said grotesquely, his face twisted.

A few steps away, Lady Pearsall clearly overheard his words. She paused and gathered herself and looked at her husband, whose face was now partly visible to her. The Wingates heard her say, too loud but in her usual dry, astonished tone, "The man's distraught. Should get hold of himself."

Then she proceeded down the steps more slowly, and they followed even more slowly. They watched her lift one hand to her husband's arm as he turned toward her, and when she spoke again, they heard her voice a full octave lower and cracking in the middle of a word: "Is it Henry? Or Edgar?"

The Governor looked at her as though she had done something terrible. His bushy brows were gathered in cartoon anger, and his fine lips thin-drawn. As he spoke, he reached out for his wife. "Both."

With her left hand, she struck him, slashed at his supporting arm to knock it away. Elizabeth could not see her face. She watched her back in the white lace dress bow as she leaned forward over her parasol, her big netted and feathered hat stooping and trembling to bare the unsheltered neck. For a moment an old, old woman stood in Ginny Pearsall's place, and Sir Reginald's expression softened from shock to pity. Then she straightened bone by bone, took her husband's arm, and without a backward glance climbed into the motorcar in a manner as stately and elegant as a departure from a garden party.

The Wingates followed the Governor's car in their own, with the tongue-tied Captain Newcombe sitting in the jump seat. Like a procession they swept by the park, where the Europeans were already at their golf, their cricket, their lawn tennis, as Newcombe stumblingly explained the morning's events. News of the completely unrelated deaths of Harry and Edgar Pearsall–Harry at the River Ancre near the Somme, and Edgar during a skirmish with Lettow-Vorbeck's patrols near Maliwa in Tanganyika–had reached Government House by cables arriving within ten minutes of each other. At first the staff thought there had been a mistake, but then the ghastly coincidence sent them into a loud-voiced panic which quickly communicated itself to the whole household. When the Wingates arrived at Government House they found the Pearsalls still in the lobby, taking off gloves and hats and giving starchy orders that would settle everyone down.

"Will you go with Genevieve?" demanded the Governor peremptorily of Elizabeth. "I have something to attend to. Make yourself comfortable, will you, Wingate?"

Lady Pearsall led Elizabeth abruptly toward the private quarters on the first floor, leaving Charles to fend for himself. The corridors seemed full of scurrying natives, their expressions compassionate, and Lady Pearsall closed the doors of her private sitting room on them sharply.

This drawing room was the most agreeable of the mansion's many rooms. Its large shuttered windows overlooked on two sides the quiet of formal gardens. It was furnished in dark wood and dusky rose, emanating the same restrained elegance as Lady Pearsall herself. The walls were covered with portraits and photographs, and every surface had its ornament in the old Victorian style, but the room was too large to seem crowded, and the effect was that of intimacy and light.

Lady Pearsall paused in the middle of the room as if to survey for interlopers. She turned to Elizabeth and spoke, her face white and puffy, as though she had a severe cold, "Stay with me, please."

Elizabeth nodded and murmured her assent. She was terrified of grief, and so she watched Ginny intently. Lady Pearsall's face was slowly growing ugly, her eyes darting from corner to corner, object to object, her hands beginning to twist each other more and more forcefully until they were wringing each other as though each held energy which the other must annihilate. They seemed boneless. Suddenly Ginny burst into motion. With rapid steps she crossed the space between the sofas in front of the ornate chimneypiece, reached down, drew a shiny brass poker from among the fire irons as cleanly as a sword from its scabbard, and turned in a half-circle, holding it in both hands. Her face was now not just white but livid, her eyes narrowed, and Elizabeth had a sudden fear that she might strike at her.

But she turned again, and with a great cry from her belly Lady Pearsall struck at the mantel, from where a collection of vases, small porcelain objects, and photographs in silver frames flew crashing to the sides of the room. This was not just a gesture; she cleared the mantel with two sweeps of the arm, so that only a Staffordshire figurine remained: a cheery redcoat stepping out with rifle held loosely in hand, a form as resolute as it was delicate. Lady Pearsall drew the poker straight back over her head with both arms, the lace of her dress ripping as she stretched back, and brought it down with tremendous force on the figurine. It was crushed to powder, and a crack appeared in the marble mantel.

Elizabeth was appalled; the force of that blow must have hurt Ginny's whole frame, but she turned from that destruction without pause, and lashed out at a small table covered with neat feminine objects near the sofa. The table's spindly legs disintegrated even as its top split, and a piece of flying wood knocked over the fire irons with a tremendous crash. Ginny looked at them rolling over the floor, as though they were an attack, and lashed out at them with her feet, stamping and kicking as they rolled onto the carpet and the brilliant parquet floor. Her graying hair came loose from its pinnings.

There was a great thumping at the room's double doors, which then flew open to reveal the frightened brown faces of a gaggle of servants, their eyes showing white. Lady Pearsall turned toward them across the room and suddenly rushed past Elizabeth at them with her poker raised. "Get out! Get away! Leave me alone!" she screamed. "I don't owe you anything anymore. Leave me alone!" She slammed the door in their faces, so hard that it bounced back open again, but she turned and fled across the room.

Elizabeth, moving for the first time, closed the doors on the servants quietly. Ginny now stood in front of her desk, looking at the wax-polished surface, at the neat piles of papers, at the carefully arranged oddments of her days and ways. She stood quite still a moment, then crooked her head curiously to stare at Elizabeth, who saw that her face was mad, grim. She turned her head again toward the desk, and her left hand trembled forward in the direction of a small row of photographs that faced her when she wrote at that desk.

"They tell us we are good at creating," she said, quite loud, but with a throat so full of phlegm that it was hoarse and low and virulent. Slowly she raised the poker above her head. "But I can destroy, too." There was a moment of pause. "I too can *destroy*."

And on that last word, with terrible strength again she brought the poker down, smashed it down onto the desk, scattering a stack of correspondence awaiting answer, sending the appointments book flying, breaking the pen set in two, crushing the frames and glass of photographs, finally smashing into the wood of the desk itself and leaving scar after scar after scar as her slender body heaved and panted and hoarsely expelled each breath until she stood exhausted, gasping, her hair in strands, sweat running down her face, the floor around her covered with debris. She stood a moment, still, then staggered a few steps, shaking involuntarily, collapsed facedown onto a prim couch, buried her face in its cushions, and began such a heaving weeping as Elizabeth had never thought to hear.

Elizabeth stood looking at her a moment, then turned and opened one of the doors near which she was still standing, and addressed the nearest of the alarmed servants. "Bring us brandy," she commanded. "And sandwiches. Then leave us alone. Get away from here. I'll ring when I want you."

As the morning wore on, Ginny Pearsall continued her weeping, wiping mucus onto velvet cushions. Her sobs came continuous and uncontrollable as though she had been taken over by something. Elizabeth made Ginny drink: a glass, a second glass of brandy. She let her refuse food. Mostly she sat at the other end of the sofa, one hand resting limply on Ginny's twisted rump to let her know she was there, sipping occasionally from her own glass of brandy.

Ginny's violence, the crushing annihilation of beautiful cherished things, had at first shocked and then appealed to Elizabeth. It was so intent, so purposeful, thorough, perfect unto itself. Ginny Pearsall was not a sweet-tempered woman. Logically her grief would allow her no collapse into sodden little handkerchiefs. She *would* lash out if the time was right. And Elizabeth found herself very tentatively enjoying this lashing-out. It was the opposite of everything to which she had been trained and for which she stood. And yet in these last few years, some small fetus of violence had grown in her, so that some little face within her sniggered as pretty things crumpled.

Eventually she grew hungry and stirred herself to bite at a drying sandwich. Her movements roused Lady Pearsall, who at first slowly and then with a laboriousness that betrayed the ache of muscles began to bring some order to her person. Her lowered eyelids were red, her face puffed and white, her dress torn, her hair messily down, but the slow habit of tucking and pinning and adjusting brought her back to an approximation of normality, as though she had glued herself together. She stood up and brushed slivers of glass from the folds of her skirt, and still without looking at Elizabeth, spoke for the first time. "I must go to Reggie. He *may* need me." Her voice was a little hoarse but her tone almost normal, and the wry emphasis on the word "may" announced the return of pride. "Will you wait for me? I'll send luncheon." She looked around the room. "And someone to clean up." Without further apology, she left the room. Shortly the butler arrived to ask if Mrs. Wingate would prefer tea or coffee with her luncheon. "No food," said Mrs. Wingate. "Coffee. A glass of sherry." The dark-skinned butler nodded with British impassivity and announced that he would return immediately to clean the room.

"Just bring me a brush and pan," said Elizabeth.

"Madam?"

"I'll do it myself," said Elizabeth firmly. "At least the worst. I want something to do."

The butler bowed slightly, left, and returned almost at once to hand her, with slight distaste, the cleaning implements. She had already assembled a pile of splintered wood on the fireplace. Wilted flowers lay in a pool of water on the floor. She took her time clearing the debris, inspecting each piece for damage and significance. The desk was the worst, its rosewood surface and mementos damaged beyond restoration. She collected all the scattered papers, sat on the slender chair, and began to sort as well as she could without prying.

Looking for a cloth with which to wipe up a small pool of congealing ink, she opened the desk drawers: orderly, feminine, perfumed by a box of violet cachous. Two things surprised her. In the top drawer was an opened packet of De Reszke cigarettes. She had not known Ginny smoked. And in the bottom drawer was a neat stack of pamphlets. They were the pamphlets from the Women's Social and Political Union which had been sent out anonymously more than a year ago in hand-addressed cream-laid envelopes. Elizabeth heard Mrs. Higham-Smith's voice again: "It's bad enough for a woman to work! But one simply cannot be both respectable and a suffragette!"

Of course the woman had been wrong. Suffragism was now an idea whose time had come. There were no more marches, no more starvings and forced feedings, no more chaining to the rails of Buckingham Palace and 10 Downing Street. Parliament even had taken up the issue, and woman suffrage, they said, would soon be the law of the realm. Emmeline Pankhurst's deal with Lloyd George had brought her what she wanted. Forget Lysistrata. Suffragism and militarism went now hand in glove. But the stack of pamphlets was still a shock to Elizabeth Wingate, like the package of cigarettes. Ginny Pearsall had been their anonymous distributor? Lady Pearsall, patroness of the Mothers' Union, honorary chairman of the Bond Fund, president of the women's division of the Widows and Orphans Society, wife to the royal governor of the crown colony? It seemed as improbable as finding under her pillow some blue-covered French book of naughty drawings. It seemed incomprehensible.

13

"It seems rather a dead issue at this moment." It was Ginny Pearsall's voice.

Startled, Elizabeth looked up from the pamphlet to see her standing with her hand on the doorknob. She was dressed in high-necked black and her face was powdered and rouged. She seemed so composed that Elizabeth, caught with her private papers in hand, was embarrassed. She rose hastily, stuffing the stack of pamphlets back into the drawer like a guilty child, and some skidded to the floor.

"I'm sorry . . ." she began.

Ginny Pearsall stooped to pick up a pamphlet from the floor. " 'The Women's Party,' " she read from it with a trace of mockery, " 'calls upon all British women to join its ranks and work for the achievement of its objects in order to defend the great heritage that has been handed down to us, and to hand it on enriched and glorified to the generations to come.' Ah, yes, the generations to come. . . ."

She stared at the paper a moment, released it to drift to the floor, and said, "Well, it seemed the right compromise at the time."

She took the remaining few pamphlets from Elizabeth and placed them facedown on the top of the desk, then reached into the open drawer and took out the packet of cigarettes.

"Would you care for a De Reszke?" she offered calmly.

"Why, yes. I would. Thank you. I didn't know you smoked."

"Nor I, you," said Lady Pearsall with another small smile. And the lighting of the cigarettes created a small conspiracy between them that salved Elizabeth's embarrassment.

"Reggie says he detests the smell," said Lady Pearsall. "But I rather imagine it's the idea he dislikes. And so I compromise. I do it only in private, and suck peppermints like a naughty child." She looked squarely at Elizabeth. "As with these." She poked the pamphlets with a forefinger. "You seemed so surprised, looking at them."

Elizabeth said nothing, even more confused by her friend's composure than by the discovery of her prying.

"They're perfectly respectable, you know," continued Ginny, holding her gaze. "But Reggie would not like the governor's wife to be a suffragist, would he? And so I compromised. It seemed so harmless at the time. Do my bit for the vote while I did my bit for war."

"I had no idea you supported the suffragists," said Elizabeth. The conversation sounded irredeemably askew to her.

"Oh, of course you did," said Ginny impatiently. "You know what kind of person I am. And you certainly know the meaning of wifely compromise, do you not?" She looked sharply at Elizabeth, and then let her gaze drift over the wreckage of the room. Her face grew bleak. "Though it all seems a trifle antique at the moment."

Her voice trailed off, and this weakening made Elizabeth feel that she had her footing for the first time since Ginny had reentered the room. "Is Sir Reginald . . . ?" she began.

"Sir Reginald is doing as well as can be expected," replied Ginny, starch and a trace of mockery again in her voice. "Sir Reginald is not a demonstrative man. We spoke. He is very quiet. He is making arrangements. I shall leave them to him." Compassion crept into her last sentence, distant compassion of the kind which one uses for a bereaved friend. She was not behaving as one would expect, and Elizabeth found herself the victim of so many conflicting expectations that she was reduced again to dumbness.

"To be frank," resumed Ginny, "I think you may be the only person whose company I could abide today, and I do not want to be alone. You are not a silly woman, Elizabeth, and you won't give me sentiments, consolations, will you?"

Elizabeth felt enormously flattered. "I *have* no sentiments to offer," she said. "What is there to say that would help?"

"Ah, that good common sense again," replied Ginny almost cheerfully. "I think at heart you are ruthless, you know, and I like it." She paused. "And you never have approved of the war or any of its products, have you? That, in itself, is very consoling."

Elizabeth found herself forced again onto the defensive. Ginny seemed as willing to tear aside the veils of social intercourse as she had been to smash the room. "What do you know of my feelings about the war? I've done nothing to make you think that–"

"Yes, you have been just as discreet as I," interrupted Lady Pearsall. "Let us just say that your bandage-rolling lacks a little in enthusiasm, shall we? Were I in your position, free of claims, I should be even less enthusiastic. Disliking war is only common sense."

"If you are opposed to war," Elizabeth challenged, "then why have you never said so?"

"And why have you never said so?"

"But I have no influence," protested Elizabeth. "Who would listen to me? I'm a private citizen. A nobody. I'm Irish. Nobody would pay attention to me. But you, you are Lady Pearsall."

"Yes, of course. Lady Pearsall. . . ."

"Forgive me, but I don't wholly believe you. I cannot believe that you of all people would be so much the hypocrite."

"Hypocrite?" Lady Pearsall repeated the word wanly. "It is not the word I would have used. Perhaps 'hypocrisy' is another word for 'duty.' You must have known that I was amused at the Mothers' Union, that I despise those women. Why else would I have taken you, but for friendship, but to have someone who might understand?" She grew softer in expression, and a new thought brought the old veil over the aristocratic face. She spoke to the air: "What *would* she have me do?" She turned to Elizabeth: "What *would* you have me do? What would *you* have done if you were Lady Pearsall and did not believe in this war?"

"I should have said what I believed," replied Elizabeth without hesitation.

"Oh, don't be so sanctimonious," snapped Ginny. She stubbed her cigarette out on a piece of broken china, then moved to the window to dispose of the ashes from the balcony. "And just because you were Mrs. Wingate, a woman of no account, you were free not to say what you believed? How very easy."

She sat on the edge of the desk and poked the pamphlets again with her forefinger. "What should a woman do in face of war, Elizabeth? Emmeline Pankhurst had no doubts. She set about getting women equal pay. The war was such a good *opportunity* for her, you see? I know Emmeline, and I'm sure she hasn't had the slightest doubt about supporting the war if it would suit her purposes. She knew what she wanted. I know Emmeline, and I don't like her. I like Sylvia. Who hates war and says it's caused by male oppression and then dashes off doing the sorts of thing women are supposed to do, starting restaurants and day-care centers and buying milk for widows whose men died too soon to qualify for a pension, and generally tidying things up. Both of them are absurd."

She stood up and rested one hand on the back of Elizabeth's chair.

"My heart is with Sylvia, but I am so very tired of women being *ineffectual.*" She walked restlessly over to the window. "And so I compromised. I may not have known how I felt, but I knew what Lady Pearsall had to do, I thought. So I sat here and addressed many envelopes in block letters."

She stared at the garden outside. Masses of bougainvillea bloomed in the sunlight, and a flight of butterflies surrounded them, and when after a minute or so Ginny spoke again, her voice was flat, dry, hard. "I have been waiting two years for this day. Two years. Day after day. Night after night. Waiting to hear, ever since the boys volunteered. That's what a woman does in face of war." She paused, staring at the garden's life. "They had lives stretching out before them. . . ." She turned and looked at Elizabeth from the open window space, the light blazing around her thin black-clad body. "I have no more sons to worry about," she said. "Can you *ever* have doubted how I felt about the war?"

And suddenly she was angry with Elizabeth, who had lost no sons, and her voice was thin as a whip. "Did you say what you believed when Charles was unfaithful to you?"

Elizabeth looked away. She briskly stubbed out her cigarette in the bottom of the destroyed lamp base.

"Or did other things interfere?" continued Lady Pearsall. "Was it easier to say nothing, though you knew you ought? Did you think about consequences? Your own future perhaps? Your duty to Jennifer? Did you want to keep your money and your peace of mind?"

Each question was a cut to Elizabeth's cheek. Flayed, she grew angry. "That was just personal! Being angry with one's husband is not a *conviction!*"

"I'm sure you had *convictions* about adultery," sneered Ginny. She laughed bitterly. "And what did you do after Charles had bolted —lock the stable door?" She gestured again at the pamphlets. "Be clever and deceitful?"

"I was not *clever* about Charles!" protested Elizabeth. "There was so little I *could* do. You said it at the time: I stood to do less harm by being indirect."

"You put it so well, my dear." Sneering again, but the sneer at herself this time. "We know what we feel, but what should we do? We have such nets around us, such webs. . . ."

She had turned her back again to stare out the bright window, and Elizabeth used indignation. It was as though she had to make Ginny lose this argument so that she herself might change.

"It is not right to avoid saying what you passionately believe just because society has rules about what a governor's wife should and should not do, not when it's something as important as war."

Ginny turned like a flash. "*You* dismiss those rules? You who came here a nobody, married our most eligible bachelor, became the best friend of that governor's wife you now lecture?" She was as hard as the light behind her. "You of all people should know what one gains from playing by the rules."

A moment sparked like electricity. Elizabeth tried and failed to stifle anger. "Friendship seems to matter very little to you today."

"And what should? Today." Ginny's voice became brittle, light. "The greatest good of the greatest number? What should I do today, Mrs. Wingate–rush out and tell the Mothers' Union to stop rolling bandages? Get Reggie to telegraph the king that he believes the war should end now?" The bitter laugh again. "I can see myself telling Reggie: our boys' deaths were as meaningless as their lives, I was wrong about the war." Another change of voice: gentler, but shaking with anger. "It is *precisely* like you with Charles. There is no alternative to what we choose, and once we have chosen, we cannot unchoose."

The two women were face to face, glaring at each other. Suddenly Ginny picked up the box of cigarettes and thrust it at Elizabeth. "Have another cigarette," she ordered.

Elizabeth glared a moment longer, then sank back. "In exchange for a brandy," she said.

Ginny fumbled over matches, and Elizabeth splashed brandy, but anger faded.

"When did grief or disgust ever stop a war?" said Ginny mournfully. "Women are good at feeling things, my dear, but when it comes to getting something done, they are not worth a brass farthing." She dropped the box of matches onto the desktop. "What we feel *is* purely personal. One doesn't *use* grief." She smiled and placed her hand on Elizabeth's. "Not even against husbands."

She straightened, bracing for the world.

"I have always done what was expected of me, as have you." She had wrenched composure back on. "And we have received the right rewards, have we not? Why should we turn against the rules just because they don't suit us at this moment? One can at least have *their* power, if not one's own."

She gave Elizabeth the smile of a victor across graves.

And, smiling this way, all composure, she ground out her cigarette on the rosewood surface of the desk.

A few days later, while sewing Belgian lace on a new set of nightgowns for Jennifer, Elizabeth asked Nanny's opinion about obeying society's rules.

"Rules?" said Nanny. "I'm not sure what you mean, Mrs. Wingate. You mean laws? Manners? Manners are very important. I've always told Jennifer she should do what people expect. That's the way to be liked."

"Do you think she ever gets angry at them?"

"I should think she does! You saw her tantrum the other day, or the start of it, over that silly doll, if you recall. And what does she do about that but what all grown-ups have to learn to do–stop the anger right then and there! I ask you! Be very nice if we all just set out to get whatever we wanted, wouldn't it!"

"Has she learned that going by the rules will get her what she wants?" inquired Elizabeth, aware of her daughter's transparent skill at manipulating parental rules to her own advantage.

Nanny laughed. "Now, that's a thought, isn't it?" She thought a moment. "Yes, of course she has. I should hope so, clever little minx that she is. Don't we all do the same, Mrs. Wingate?" She looked at Elizabeth wryly, all London shrewdness for a moment. "I shouldn't have thought a girl would let the rules stop her from getting what she wants, good or bad. She knows how to take care of herself."

"And you, Nanny?"

Again Nanny was amused. "Ask me no questions, and I'll tell you no lies! I learned to look out for myself when I was knee-high to a grasshopper. Had to. And stayed respectable, mind you. I've never worried much about what you call the rules. Come in quite handy, as a matter of fact, when a gentleman has his hand on your knee."

"Nanny!"

"Well, you did ask, and I'm sure you've done the same thing. What woman hasn't? I mean, it's our only weapon, when you think of it. If some rule, as you call it, will stop a man in his tracks, well then . . ."

This time both women laughed, but Elizabeth was left contemplative. She thought she understood Nanny, who tamed ideas by tethering them to her own experience, but she did not understand Ginny, or herself, who, in trying to turn experience into ideas, showed themselves only to be clumsy. The subject of their conversation on the day of Ginny's mourning irritated her; she had ended up knowing there was something important there but not what it was. I am not good at thinking things through, she scolded herself. I must learn to do better, she commanded.

14

1917

Thanks to the war, she had plenty to think about. These days people were all saying that war was terrible, but she could see the truth all around her: war enhances life. It gave people the excuse for escaping whatever they needed to escape. It allowed them to stop being what they had been or planning what they would be. Time had shrunk. To hell with yesterday's wisdom, tomorrow's constraint, they said. Everybody's doing it. There's a war on, you know. You have to change with the times.

But she could not make any sense of all that because it was less idea than mood. As she commented to Charles, people laughed at the wrong things these days. When George the Fifth changed the family name to Windsor, gossip said that his cousin Kaiser Wilhelm joked that he would look forward to the next performance of *The Merry Wives of Saxe-Coburg-Gotha.* She laughed with the others when she heard the gossip; then she swallowed her laughter. One cannot be amused, she thought, when a world crumbles. One *should* not be amused. Should one?

Laughter became rarer in 1917, after a full year of killing men by hundreds of thousands found those still alive in the same trenches from which they had started. What does one *think* in the face of that? She asked herself: does it matter anymore what one person thinks? A president elected to keep the United States at peace led it into a war which he could tolerate only by declaring it the war to end wars, and a prime minister who had come to office refusing to act like "a butcher's boy driving cattle to the slaughter" authorized the bloodiest battles in human history. Londoners were growing gloomy now, according to her mother. The bombing, wrote Henriette Malloy, and all the streetlights painted half-blue, and the pubs ordered to keep shorter hours, and shortages of everything from soap to sugar to coffee to safety pins, and the bread as gray as the weather, and the Wimbledon house warm only because Bernard had bought coal on the black market, the miners being still on strike. Is victory, wondered Elizabeth, what generals offer in lieu of peace? I used to think that life would always be the same, more or less. What if I am left with only one sameness: change?

We absorb great change by shrinking it to our own size. The ladies of Colombo, rolling bandages a trifle grimly now, were fascinated to learn that at the front the nurses used them instead of washable rags for menstruation. No more pinkish embarrassment boiling in the copper? How marvelous! Colombo acquired its first cinema at the beginning of the year, and the Americans became real through newsreels. The ladies watched President Wilson's eyeglasses flash and did not like his thin mouth. It's all very well, they said, to make the world safe for democracy, but does he think the Empire isn't more than democratic enough already? "We shall fight," said the President, "for the right of those who submit to authority to have a voice in their own governments." The ladies of the crown colony eyed their servants speculatively. They did not want to say a permanent farewell to anything, except those menstrual rags.

Unnoticed by Elizabeth, Charles too was doing some thinking of his own. One evening he and Joe Plunkett attended a memorial service for the club's vulgar but popular Tony Jephson. He had drowned some months before on the way to his first battle when the cross-channel steamer *Sussex* was torpedoed, and it had taken some time for the news to reach his friends because the government would no longer allow publication of casualty lists.

"Always thought of him as the complete civilian," said Joe as they descended the steps of the church. "Never thought he'd catch a packet."

"Apoplexy more like it," agreed Charles, pulling on his formal black gloves. "All that fat, all that booze."

"A bit grotesque, isn't it?" said Joe. "The *Sussex?* Those old channel tubs. . . . They seem so . . . so . . ."

"Feminine!" completed Charles, smiling. "Little old ladies in holiday gear, eh? Ribbons and picnic hampers."

Shaking their heads, they moved on to the mess for a drink in Jephson's honor, and there they were joined by Major Talbot, a portly elderly man who carried his spine straight, his huge belly in front of him, and his patriotism like a flag. Charles, in mourning mood, said something which made Talbot think he was less than ardent in support of war. He berated Charles for betraying the boys at the front and departed shaking his head.

Joe eventually broke the silence. "The problem is those men in the front line, isn't it? The one thing you can't question is their courage."

Charles sipped his whiskey and stared into the darkness of the parade ground. "I think I was brought up to believe that's what war was for," he said slowly. "To give a man a chance to show his courage, test himself. I'm not sure that's true anymore."

Joe sucked in a breath through pursed lips and shook his head. "Courage never was a reason for war, and it certainly isn't now."

Silence settled over the pair. Charles was thinking that he had always been progressive because he had always assumed that the future would be better than the past. At the moment the future offered losses, and it instilled an uneasiness he was reluctant to label fright. It was death that worried him: his own death. Jephson was his stand-in.

Joe Plunkett was thinking that he had never seen Wingate so subdued. He listened to the peepers shrill into the hot and bottomless night and thought he knew why.

"How's the wife?" he asked.

"Elizabeth?" said Charles, shifting himself back into the present. "Fine, fine. Been giving me a bit of trouble lately. This war upsets everyone, and she's been taking it out on me, I expect. What the devil I'm supposed to do about it, I don't know."

The peepers made themselves heard again until Charles this time pulled them out of their brown study. "At least business is going well. Practically runs itself these days, with a little help from Arthur Barker."

"Still losing many shipments?"

"We've been concerned in about eleven this year, I think. It's the bloody Bay of Biscay that gets them. I hate to think of all that stuff going to the bottom. Total waste, total waste. God knows where the government's getting the money to reimburse us–out of these fierce damn surtaxes, I suppose." He paused. "But I can't complain from the money viewpoint."

The cane chair creaked as he leaned forward. Joe struck a match and held it for him to light his cigar.

"Though I tell you, Joe, that's another game that isn't what it used to be. It's all paperwork now. Once you fill out the import forms and the tax reports, and the manifests and the storage lists for the embargo, and you collect all the affidavits to prove the cargo's innocent and the bills of lading to prove it fits government priorities, and all the rest of the rubbish, you've got a mountain of paper and nothing much else. I don't know, I seem to have lost that sense of building things up that I used to have. We work harder—God knows I told Barker to get himself an undermanager, caught him working Sundays —but it's all quite extraordinarily dull."

Joe cautiously said nothing. He had always seen the ebullient Charles as invulnerable to the small doubts that gnawed one's edges ragged.

"What do you see yourself doing when this war is over, Joe?" inquired Charles with more energy.

"After the war?" Plunkett was surprised by the question. "I don't know. Going to offer me a job?" He smiled to show he was not serious. "I've got another good ten years to retirement. Then I suppose I'd better find myself a wife to take care of my old age and settle down in some godforsaken hole like Cheltenham or Brighton." He ashed his cigar carefully. "Might stay here. Seems a long way off still. Why do you ask?"

"No reason," said Charles. "Just wondering. I can't see any of us quietly going back to the old way of life, and I'm not sure I like what I see happening to business, but what the hell else is there? I suppose I am really getting to be just another middle-aged duffer."

"I'll drink to that." Plunkett grinned. "Another?"

"Another."

Because she and Charles spoke now only of the practical, never the personal, Elizabeth did not see change in her husband. Change came to her instead through her mother's increasingly frequent letters. For a while after her work with Belgian refugees had run down, Henriette's letters were filled with complaints that seemed trivial to Elizabeth: allowed only a single bun with her tea at Atkinson's, no meat for sale in the whole of Wimbledon, no chocolates, no toffee, not even any cut flowers. "Is there anything I can send?" replied Elizabeth. "I think I should work," wrote Henriette, "perhaps as a Red Cross tea lady in a canteen at one of the railway stations."

Then the government issued a call for ladies of education to give working-class women some rest by taking over their jobs at weekends, and Henriette Malloy thought this a kindly and delightful idea. To Henriette, change meant freedom. "I love the work!" she wrote. "You cannot imagine the foolish thrill I get with the pay envelope!" Those first weeks she set off by the tube before daylight with men carrying billy-cans and girls in straw hats.

"But she's sixty, Charles!" complained Elizabeth. "She'll wear herself out, and then where will she and Father be? She's always been a dogged little woman, of course, but this is too much."

"You might make a few tactful inquiries about the family finances, old girl," suggested Charles. "Perhaps it's time we were supplementing their budget a bit?"

"I hadn't thought of that," said Elizabeth, startled. "But no, it couldn't be that, could it?"

She wrote; and awaited a reply; and took to hating her own activities: reading in the cool of the evening, listening to the chug-chug of the generator, waiting for her husband to come home.

"Frankly, I think it's rather shocking, a woman of her years," drawled Vicky Bellingham when Elizabeth shared the news with her in Daubeny's Emporium. Elizabeth was not an intimate of the ripe Mrs. Bellingham, but inevitably they saw each other now and again, as on this occasion when both were beginning the search for Christmas presents. "I hope only that she doesn't *enjoy* it." She dismissed a saleslady bearing an armful of chiffon scarves. "Too démodé! Of course I can understand all this . . . this enthusiasm back Home these days, poor dears. I suppose they're all very brave with their sacrifices and things. But there has to be *some* limit, don't you agree? At your mother's *age,* to give up all her *privacy*. It's not something *I* would do. Would you?"

Elizabeth merely smiled. Mrs. Bellingham looked at her coldly, the gleam of intelligence under her fat. "It may be a hard saying," she resumed, "but the world is here for us to *enjoy, not* the other way around, and we shouldn't *forget* it. There can be too much sacrifice, can there not? And I personally draw the line at giving up one's class, even for one's country. What would be the point, don't you agree? What would be left?"

She turned away from Elizabeth toward the counter of stuffs upon which her handbag lay.

Elizabeth had to admit that the woman had put her own feelings in a nutshell.

Mrs. Bellingham lifted her generous figure from the stoollike chair against which she had been leaning, accepted her tumbled parasol from Elizabeth, and stared wryly at her gloves as she tugged them straight on her fingers. "I sometimes *wonder,"* she concluded, "what it would feel like actually to have to take a pay envelope from someone? What an *amusing* idea. I shall have to ask Norman to give me my pin money in an envelope!" She sailed away with laughter.

Ginny Pearsall's attitude was the reverse. "That nonsense about class!" she exploded when Elizabeth recounted Vicky Bellingham's words. "If this war has shown us one thing, it is how out-of-date that sort of nonsense is. How typical of that silly woman!"

Elizabeth enjoyed Ginny's outrage. "But Mother's age!" she protested.

"Be tactful, my dear Elizabeth. Be tactful, you wretched girl. . . . Do you want to put her away in a Bath chair with a hearing trumpet, and wheel her out when Jennifer comes to tea? You should be glad she has an interest in life!" Her eyes focused on the ceiling. "Lord God, make this girl grateful!"

As the year wore on, the tone of Henriette's letters changed. It seemed the working classes wanted cash more than rest. The educated ladies, they said, did more harm than good and drove everyone up the wall, and Henriette did not know how to react to being cheeked by a foreman. Later the bad news grew more serious. "This week," wrote Henriette, "my face and hands are a bright yellow. They had us pouring TNT and nitrates into canisters all weekend, and it seems they forgot to give us the mask and gloves to avoid the fumes. I should have known, of course, because the stuff makes one cough so, and sometimes I feel quite unwell."

Elizabeth wrote her an angry letter insisting that she stop endangering her health. It crossed with one from Henriette about working conditions. The water closets were few and always left filthy, and one could use them only at stated periods four times a day. There was no canteen. One ate sitting on the machinery with hands bitter from nitrate salts. "I had no idea the working classes put up with this sort of thing," wrote Henriette. They were supposed to stop work at six-thirty, but the foremen made the women stay late to clean up the shop floor, which meant a twelve-hour day. "And I have found out that they pay men seven shillings a day while the women get only three and sixpence. I shall write to the editor of *The Women's Dreadnought,*" she wrote. "They warned us when we signed up, and I paid no attention. I had not imagined war and work were like this."

On the evening this letter arrived, Nanny was hand-stitching a pinafore for Jennifer in the chair by the tall windows in Elizabeth's room.

"I should have thought your mother would know better," she said. "Who'd want to work in some nasty factory where you might get blown up any moment, I ask you. If she wants to work, why doesn't she get a good job in an office?"

Elizabeth sat in front of the mirror at her dressing table, idly trying on necklaces to match a new blouse. The necklaces were looped around the neck of the clay Buddha which Peter had given her. Its dignity survived even the baubles.

"I wonder how the sisters are getting on at Ravenscroft," said Nanny meditatively. "Of course, they're used to doing their own work." She bent over her sewing, and the sounds of the ocean and the wind in the palm trees filled the silence. "No lights in London either, she says? What's the point of it all, then?"

"You're getting to like it better here than Home." Elizabeth smiled in the mirror.

"I should say I do like it better here than Home!" Nanny cast an almost scornful look at Elizabeth. "Of course the Home you and your mother come from, and the Home I come from, well, they might be two different countries really. I'm only glad I didn't have to spend the rest of my life there. I was one of the lucky ones. I got out." She let the sewing fall into her lap, dark eyes chasing memory. "Cold, dirty." She shuddered and brought herself back to the present. "Well, what you don't know won't hurt you, Mrs. Wingate."

Nanny had never mentioned before her childhood in the slums. Elizabeth, in front of the mirror with her jewels, had no response beyond stillness, and Nanny's glance was ironic. "*I* shouldn't mind," she continued, "if those bombing planes burned up the whole East End. I'd call it a good spring cleaning."

"That's not a very Christian thought, Nanny."

"That's not a very Christian world," replied Nanny, brusquely nodding to indicate the world outside the open window.

"But the government is doing something about it."

"And the poor will always be with us, Mrs. Wingate, and a hundred years from now it will be the same. Mind you, they'd better do something about it or they'll go the way of that Czar!"

Silence fell on the pair again. Elizabeth fiddled with the electric light and studied Nanny in the mirror. Eventually she spoke. "Should you mind going back, then? Home, I mean?"

"To London, you mean?" Nanny paused and gave Elizabeth a measuring look. "Are you and Mr. Wingate thinking of going back, then?"

"We haven't talked about it, but of course we shall go back at least for a visit after this war is over. We should like you to come with us."

"Well," said Nanny, "I shouldn't mind *that,* I expect. It's all very warm and nice here, but it isn't Blighty, is it, with all these black people around? Mind you, it'll cost a lot more to live there. You won't have all this there, will you?" Her gesture took in the mansion, its grounds, the chatter of servants preparing dinner, even the sound of the ocean.

Elizabeth turned from the mirror to face Nanny. "I think there may be other things there that I want more."

Nanny gave her a glance quick but shrewd. "I shouldn't mind going back to Ravenscroft, you know. When I left, they were thinking of keeping me on as a lay teacher. Imagine that? Of course it would only be something like domestic science, but imagine me a teacher! It's a nice place. Healthy. You could do worse than send young Jennifer there."

Silence fell as she resumed her sewing. Elizabeth rose from her dressing table and walked over to her armoire to take out clothes for dinner. The breeze brought a sudden wave of heavy floral perfume to them, and the clatter of the kitchen.

"I suppose it's all right to say the government will do something about it. Those slums, I mean," said Nanny. "But the more they do, the more people'll want. That's Labor Party, that, and I think the Lord helps those who help themselves, thank you very much. I got out of there thanks to Ravenscroft. But I would have gotten out of there all by myself if had to. I was that determined. I would have."

Her spirit lay between them like a bolt of cloth upon whose price they could not agree.

"It sounds to me that you will head for America one of these days, Nanny." Elizabeth was smiling. "That's the land of opportunity."

"And that's all a person worth her salt needs, isn't it?"

"You sound exactly like my mother."

"Your mother?"

"You both expect to earn your own way. You both seem eager for change."

"I shouldn't worry too much about it, your mother taking this job." Nanny's tone was very matter-of-fact, almost crisp. "It's not as though she needs it. Rich people are different from the rest of us. Not better, not worse, just different. I mean, she can give it up if things don't work out right, can't she?"

She rose to her feet, folding the pinafore, snapping her sewing basket closed. Elizabeth, an evening dress in her hands, advanced slowly toward her.

"You both of you, you make *me* feel as though I lived my life in a display case afraid someone may break the glass."

Nanny studied her unsympathetically. "Well, *I* shan't break it," she said shortly. "Don't worry about that. I'd only have to clean it up, wouldn't I?"

A few weeks later Nanny was proven right in one respect; Henriette gave up her job when she needed to. The bronchitis brought on by the TNT fumes persisted, and the doctor ordered her to stop. After she felt better, she wrote, she would find work as a practical nurse, and thank you, but she and Bernard were not short of money. Thank God, thought Elizabeth. I don't have to worry about that anymore! But she knew that her mother's courage had changed her, and waited to find out how.

15

December 1917

"If I finish my peas, will you read right to the end of the story?"

"No bargaining, thank you, miss. Waste not, want not."

The peas lay on the plate, relics in congealing butter. The evening sun reddened the white of the nursery. The breeze had dropped, and the shrill of frogs and insects rose to drown out the sound of waves on the beach. Elizabeth entered the room, a glass of whiskey in her hand, dressed for the evening, fiddling awkwardly with one diamond earring.

"Mummy! If I finish all my peas, will you tell Nanny to read right to the very end of the story?"

"Yes, dear, of course. Nanny, could I have a word with you?"

Nanny in white, Elizabeth in evening green, the two women walked the length of the room, bars of light from the shutters making them flicker like a moving-picture show. Elizabeth led the way onto the balcony, leaving Jennifer to face the peas alone.

"You just bribed young miss, Mrs. Wingate." Nanny was indignant. "If we aren't careful, we'll be bribing her to clean her teeth next, I shouldn't wonder."

"I'm sorry, Nanny. I wasn't thinking. I knew she was going to ask about Charles again. He disappoints her so often."

"Little girls have to learn they are not the apple of their father's eye *all* the time."

"They enjoy each other so much when he does get home in time for the story. I hate to disappoint her. I don't like spoiling things."

"Spoiling's the word, in any case," sniffed Nanny.

It was an old argument. Kept out late with business, Charles had taken to upsetting the routine of the nursery. Nanny had patiently laid out three sets of rules simple enough for a young lady going on four, or even for her parents. There were Safety Rules, which demanded total, instant, and unwavering obedience. There were Health and Hygiene Rules, almost as commanding, which the child had originally accepted without demur but recently showed signs of entering the arena of negotiation.

"I don't like to be an ogre to the child, Mrs. Wingate, but if I send her to bed, and she gets all settled down, and then Mr. Charles comes in and wakes her up to play with her, and I'm in charge of getting her settled down again . . . !"

Then there were Comfort and Convenience Rules, such as not speaking until spoken to, always telling the truth, not bothering Mummy when she is in bed, curtsying when offering the plate of cakes to guests at tea, and a myriad of other character-building matters.

"I understand, Nanny, and I'll speak to Mr. Charles again, but it *is* very difficult for him."

Then, outside the pale, Daddy's Rules had grown up. These were to be obeyed by Nanny and Elizabeth as well as Jennifer.

"Mr. Wingate thinks he is the exception that proves the rule."

"And so he is, I suppose, Nanny." She gave up the attempt to fix her earring. "Can you see what's wrong with this blessed hoop? My eyes! I shall have to get spectacles for close work."

Nanny took the glittering diamond and peered at it in the crimson light.

Elizabeth, made imperious by gown, station, and pose, stood sipping her drink. "I sometimes think," she said meditatively, "that we ought *not* to teach her all these rules. I sometimes think we would all be better off without them, if we had never learned them."

"I learned a long time ago that to get what you want, you'd better be either very pretty or a lady, and preferably both."

"Perhaps the war is sending ladies out of style."

"Jennifer's clever enough at getting her own way already, without encouragement," said Nanny. A pretty enough young woman, growing a little staunch as her twenties and her profession wore on, Nanny had an air of compact toughness about her, as though there were more she could have said. In this mood she intimidated Elizabeth and felt it right to do so. Ravenscroft had given her six months' training at the brand-new and up-to-date Norland Institute. When armed with the Norland *Quarterly* (full of tips from nannies all over the world), she did not hesitate to assert her authority.

Elizabeth now eyed her a trifle sourly. "We ladies seem to get our own way only in things that don't matter very much," she said.

The earring hoop reshaped, Nanny handed it back with a level look. She was about to reply when Jennifer in nightgown appeared at the door of the balcony. "I've finished my peas, Nanny!" The evening light made her glow. Her coloring was angelic. Her face was still baby-shaped, but she had beautiful gray-green eyes and a well-formed chin, and her hair was thick and curly and tinged with red.

"Of course you have," said Nanny.

"Now may I have my story?"

Nanny looked stolidly at her. Elizabeth shifted nervously. "Yes, dear, but not right to the end. Just as far as Nanny promised you before."

The beautiful eyes filled with disappointment. "But you promised!"

"Did I, dear? Well, I don't remember. Now, we must both do what Nanny wants–"

She was interrupted by a sob.

A few minutes later, Elizabeth joined Peter Williams downstairs to await the belated Charles. They were all dining out together tonight, though as usual Mary Williams had declined. In evening dress, Williams looked younger than his forty-odd years. Recently lines had stretched from the base of his nose to the corners of his mouth, making him look severe, but his smile brought back the fine-drawn whimsy of his expression, the brilliant blue eyes dominant, the lips mobile. As she entered the drawing room, he was standing at the sideboard, from which he turned with a whiskey and soda to offer her.

"You shall make me drunk," she protested.

He shrugged. "I heard Jennifer wailing," he said dourly.

"A little problem. Nanny and I are trying to keep her orderly,"

Elizabeth murmured discontent. "It's hard when Charles fails to show up for bedtime."

"What monsters children are! She's acting just like the little princess he always calls her, I imagine."

"I've told you many a time you wouldn't feel that way if you had children of your own."

"God forbid!" said Williams. "I know what the routine is. 'Down the throat!' That's the motto, isn't it? Every blasted morning: down the throat with that awful treacly fishy Kepler's stuff. Every blasted afternoon: down the throat with Parrish's Chemical Food, and don't let the straw slip or you'll get black teeth! Oh, how well I remember! Every night at bedtime: California Syrup of Figs, so good for the b-o-o-o-w-els." He mimicked a nanny of monstrous sweetness, a child cringing in horror. "Am I right?"

Elizabeth laughed. "Remarkably!"

"Do we do it for their health or their character?"

"Both."

"If I were a parent, I shouldn't have the least idea why I did whatever I did. I should simply do it because my own nanny did it or my mother said so."

"One tries to avoid the worst sufferings of one's own childhood, but then one has to realize that some of them are caused by the things–California Syrup of Figs–that are best for the child. Health and character–" she tried to anticipate him, but he interrupted:

"A terribly modern parent?"

"Terribly modern."

"And then out it comes: 'We don't do that in public, Jennifer!'" Williams' voice was parody. "God will *die* if you don't eat your dessert! Terribly modern, isn't it?"

"You're wicked, Peter." She smiled.

"Perhaps it would be easier if you had some idea of what sort of person you wanted her to become. Or better still, what you wanted her to do."

"What will Jennifer *do?*"

"Do you really want her to live, if she can, the kind of life you and Mary lead?"

"I have a good life! So does your wife!"

"Boring, Elizabeth, and you know it. She's a bright child. There should be more to life for her than a husband and tea cakes and a dozen screaming Jennifers of her own." He had grown gloomy, what she called his failed-schoolmaster mood.

"I don't think she'll win the Nobel Prize." Elizabeth was a little miffed with Peter, who sometimes went too far. Who often, now she thought of it, went too far. She walked away from him to end the conversation, and then perversely returned. "She's a beautiful child. She'll have no trouble making her way in the world."

"Not with that temper, she won't! I should give anything to keep quiet a child of mine wailing like that: toffee? ice cream? toys? diamonds? here, what would you like, little princess!"

"I must admit I feel like that sometimes. Sometimes I think that I do not *like* my daughter very much. Of course I love her, dearly. But I'm not positive that I like her. Is that inhuman?"

"It's unlikely to be inhuman. Nothing is to be unexpected among humans. You ask, rather, isn't it wrong? I have not the slightest idea. It seems very difficult to control one's likes and dislikes." Williams had grown as serious as if the topic were of personal concern to him, dealing with more than a child.

"Jennifer is so likable, so charming."

"From what I've seen of her, Jennifer puts herself out to be charming."

"She's a child. She could not be as calculating as you imply."

"My dear Elizabeth, children calculate incessantly. They have to, to survive. They study the terrain better than the front-line troops, I imagine, making fierce little maps in their horrid little minds. Watch them push *us* to the very limit before they yield an inch of ground! Not calculating, indeed!"

Elizabeth was laughing again. "I will admit only that she goes after what she wants."

Williams was still serious. He sat forward on a cane chair, studying Elizabeth from under his brows. He had the air of a missionary looking for sin. "Perhaps that's why you dislike her."

There was a sudden stillness.

Elizabeth looked away. "You're very shrewd," she murmured.

"Or are you jealous?"

"Of Jennifer?"

"Of Jennifer and Charles."

Elizabeth dropped her chin, shielding her face from light and interrogator. In a low voice she said, "Sometimes. Disgusting, is it not?"

"Because he treats her the way you would want him to treat you?"

"I'm not a child."

"As regards Charles' affections, would you like to be?"

She turned away from him as though afraid of hurt, and her low voice made the confession: "Sometimes I wish it could be that way. That love, it's so uncontaminated. But that's not what I really want. It's just that we've been married a long time. We've grown apart. Charles is so busy these days. He is my husband. I have a right—"

Williams interrupted, speaking sharply. "He is your husband. You have *no* rights."

She looked at him, startled.

"You must find them for yourself," he continued, still staring intently at her. "Charles can make you comfortable. Charles can make you miserable. Charles can't make you happy." He stopped his flow of words, drew in a deep breath, and looked away. "You can only do that for yourself."

Elizabeth finished half her glass in a single draft.

"You're telling me," she said, "that I must be more like Jennifer."

"Just don't wail." He put one hand on her knee, leaning toward her. She drew back sharply. There was a moment of time's suspension. Then Williams stood up, and with that motion released the tension in the room as though it had been strands he held in his hands. "I'm not making advances," he said unexpectedly.

"Charles is very well, thank you." She smiled. "And how is Mary?"

"I shall telephone Charles, if I may, to see if he has left the office yet."

"Please."

His departure left her free to compose herself. Peter had this effect on her too often. She liked him because he was the only man who talked to her as though she could understand ideas, but sometimes he expected too much of her. Charles was at least predictable.

When Peter reentered the drawing room with the news that Charles had left the office and would be home any minute, she deliberately turned the conversation to the trivia of war and society. One result was an invitation—uncharacteristically given and accepted—to accompany her and Charles to the Christmas fancy-dress party that was the Mothers' Union's main activity for this year.

"As long as I may leave before the stirring speeches," he said. "I can stand a four-year-old singing 'Keep the Home Fires Burning,' but not a forty-year-old telling me to give my all for the men at the front."

* * *

When the Wingates returned fairly late from that evening's dinner party, they had a tired squabble over the head of the sleeping Jennifer. As she did now and then pursuant to Elizabeth's instructions, Nanny had tied the child's hands to the bed rails with soft cloths. The practice irritated Charles, who had previously said he did not think it mattered that the child liked to play with her genitals as she fell asleep, drowsy-eyed and dreamy. "She doesn't know what she's doing, dammit!" he fumed. "She's a child, and it's simply dirty-minded to think she knows anything about sex."

"You'd be surprised," snapped Elizabeth.

"I want you to speak to Nanny tomorrow morning," said Charles, loosening the bonds. "I won't have any more of it."

"Would you care to speak to her yourself?"

"It's hardly a matter that . . . Oh, just take care of it, will you?" He stumped off to bed, boiled-faced.

So Nanny and Elizabeth talked about the problem next morning, standing on the balcony again, Jennifer spreading water paints happily over newspapers in the nursery.

"I think the real problem is her imagination, Mrs. Wingate," said Nanny with serious concern. "She has a very active fancy, too much for a child her age. You know the stories she makes up, quite shocking, really. I know she gets them from the servants. It's only a blessing she doesn't understand what she's saying."

"Can't you read her Bible stories, then?" Elizabeth suggested. "I thought she loved them."

"Not when she has a tale of her own to tell. They all end up with the heroine full of happiness and victory and the man of her choice which is often enough her own daddy."

"That does sound rather adult, doesn't it?" said Elizabeth, flinching. "Well, try the Bible stories and I'll see what else we have. You might see what the library has to suggest. In the meantime, let us not tie her hands anymore. We shall just have to keep a better watch and gently take her hands away. I see no point in making a fuss."

"They say it brings on insanity."

"Yes, they do."

Both women smiled, still sane. Eventually Jennifer stopped "touching herself," and Nanny was gratified. She had pinned a quotation clipped from *Childlife* to her mirror: "The nurse should not strive for victory over the child but rather get the child to see its own interests by winning victory over itself."

* * *

"Come, come, Williams!" chided Charles quietly at the back of the hall. "You made the promise while of sound mind. How could you think of giving up all this just for a drink?"

"All this?" said Williams with a reciprocating smile and a pained survey of the church hall. "Ah, what a sacrifice that would be!"

Rows of folding chairs stretched in front of them, facing a wooden stage and makeshift curtains of dark blue velvet. Women and children (and a few men, clumpy as toadstools) filled the seats with clamor, and the women's hats dipped and swayed in response to infantile restlessness like dahlias to a fitful breeze. Every now and again a single child broke free, running up an aisle with heavy tread. Charles stood legs apart and hands behind his back, refusing the wall which supported Peter Williams. The collar of his white suit was too tight. Middle age was making him soft as a golden retriever, while it stripped the flesh from Williams, like a whippet.

"Think Jennifer's up next," grunted Charles, folding his arms across his chest in expectation of embarrassment. He lowered at the rainbows of women. "Can't stand this gushing!"

In answer to his stare, the curtains gave a sudden twitch on their rings, and a tall, thin woman with a large bosom slipped onstage. Edith Taverner burned her fat in community activities. Once champion at tennis, she was now forever damned as a thoroughly good sort. Her maidenhood seemed to bewilder her like a heel caught in a hem, but she stayed hearty and invaluable. She now raised her hands in a hushing flutter, and the audience began to still. "Now, before the third act of our little drama . . . Now, *before the third* . . . thank you so much . . . act of our pantomime . . ." A burst of thumping came from behind the curtain, which billowed dangerously close to her. "Before our next act, a little song from a *very* charming little newcomer . . ."

"Here comes yours," muttered Williams.

"In her first appearance on any stage . . ."—nervous giggle—"Miss Jennifer Wingate, four years of age, to sing for us, 'Little Bo-Peep.'" Miss Taverner held the curtain open, and Jennifer appeared.

"Done a damn fine job, your wife, I'll give you that!" exclaimed Williams.

Especially in the midst of wartime drabness, Jennifer was a magic of flowing velvets and creaming laces and ribbons and bows: a dress of sprigged muslin, with a green velvet overskirt and jacket with gold frogging, layers of petticoats trimmed with lace, tiny boots gleaming with brass buttons, and a tiny hat perched on her curls. In one gloved hand she held a posy of white flowers, in the other a shepherd's crook decorated with white ribbons. For a moment she posed as still as a doll, one foot placed elegantly in front of the other, her chin raised high enough so that extraordinary gray-green eyes were half-visible beneath exquisite lashes. She had that beauty of which most pretty children only remind us.

She stood center stage, securely balanced, as though she waited for the audience to get their fill of her before she began. The pianist to the left of the stage interrupted the polite smattering of applause with a chord. Jennifer turned her head sideways coquettishly and bobbed a curtsy, one forefinger to the side of her chin. Charming! murmured the mothers. She rose from the curtsy. The pianist began the first chords of the familiar melody.

Then, nothing. Jennifer simply stood there, facing the audience, posy in one hand, crook in the other, her face expressionless. "Oh, Lord, stage fright," muttered Charles.

The pianist repeated the opening chords. The audience was politely still. Jennifer maintained her silence. The expression on her face became one of hauteur, as though she waited for ortolans or poodles or a limousine. Again the opening chords sprang forth. They bounced off the hall's corrugated iron roof and into tension.

"Why doesn't she sing?" piped a child's voice.

One glance in that direction from Jennifer. She would speak volumes if she could. Meanwhile, she waited. Edith Taverner's voice became audible behind the curtain, crooning in large, squeaky syllables, "*Little* Bo-Peep has *lost* . . ." Again the pianist struck the opening chords.

And then Jennifer moved. Raising her head slowly, she cast a withering glance in Edith Taverner's direction. She shook her shoulders slightly and moved forward two paces. She raised her crook to silence the pianist with imperious negligence, surveyed the audience, allowed a sunburst smile to spread across her face, and finally she spoke.

"I shall now recite–*not* sing–'Little Bo-Peep.'" Which she proceeded to do with absolute assurance, each syllable crystal clear, no unnecessary or mother-trained gesture, her face a play of changing if childish emotions to fit the old tale, the audience in startlement resting in the palm of her hand. She finished. The audience began to applaud. She curtsied, not a waver in her tiny legs, and at the very moment before the applause began to die, she turned and slid between the curtains.

* * *

That evening Charles found himself especially pleased with life. The contract with Felspar International had at last been signed, the London price of tea was rising sharply, and now that his new office building was complete, he could tell Arthur Barker that he could have the partnership he had earned by stumping the floor so resolutely with his gimpy leg and tugging at his thinning hair in a more enduring fret about submarines than even Charles himself. His little daughter had been a great success. It had been a good day. He had had a peg of whiskey with Williams, then another by himself, and he had brought a third to take into the bath with him. The great zinc tub with its sponges and brushes and headrest was luxurious, the water cool, soapy, and sympathetic. House and garden were quiet, save for the chattering of birds. The overhead fan stirred air that caressed his head and shoulders.

Charles soaped his penis absentmindedly, affectionately bringing it to half-arousal, and closed his eyes, half-smiling, a state of content from which he was suddenly shaken when Jennifer burst through the door, all bows and pink nightgown and ready for her evening playtime with Daddy. Smoothly he moved the washcloth to cover his privates. They chatted and he teased. She perched backwards on the edge of the tub, making the zinc resound with idle heel beats, and he splashed her to make her stop. She giggled, tried to splash back, and tumbled into the water, delighted. Placing the whiskey glass out of harm's way, Charles, charmed, gave permission for her to climb into the tub with him and take another bath. He watched her little girl's body wiggle out of the nightgown: frog, fish, naiad. They played for a while with suds and water and slippery soap, Charles tactfully and cautiously warding her lunges away from his genitals. Elizabeth stuck her head in to see what all the noise was about, scolded mildly, said not to be too long, and went to her own room to dress for dinner. They sang foolish songs together, Jennifer big-eyed and squeezing the washcloth between her fingers to drip water on Daddy's chest hairs, and as the songs grew gentler and she a little sleepy, she slid onto her back and laid her head on his chest and floated softly, light as silk, on top of him.

Her little body felt tight and warm against him, no holding back of body space. Bony and tender, smooth, gentling toward drowsiness. He sang lullabies from his own childhood, let his head fall back against the wooden rest, and separated his knees to hold them both firm in place against the sides of the tub. Her little bottom slid slowly across his genitals as she relaxed, and he, placid, felt the half-arousal return. His fingertips had been dabbling the water, and now the dreamy rhythms of the lullabies made them softly stroke her chest and torso and limbs. The stroke turned into a caress, and father and daughter lay afloat in the water, no scene so innocent, their eyes closed, crooning separate soft half-melodies, lost among half-dreams of golden afternoons and spires and princesses and handsome lovers. Incurious but not unconscious of her father's stiffened penis thrusting along her small backside, Jennifer drowsed in some place of perfect bliss. Charles lost thought and stroked her thighs and let his thumb trace down the unbudded crevice of her genitals, lightly, gently, placidly, in one of those most precious moments when lust is reverie, when nothing fills the mind but the erotic itself, no implications, no thought of consequence or rule, when lust itself is rendered innocent.

Nothing more than that happened. Charles' sense of the proper stirred, or the water became too cool, and he wakened them both with a kiss and a "That's enough, now. Off with you to bed!" and shuffled her out of the tub and himself into a seated position that discreetly hid under the suds the tumescent penis, crimson with full veins. Nothing happened, yet for both it was a moment of the perfect, which for the rest of their lives neither was completely to forget or fully to remember.

That day's events left Elizabeth far less content than Charles, closed in by envy. She hated her daughter's self-assurance. She disliked her husband's smug pride. She resented Peter's praise. She lay that night in the naked dark and thought: I am trapped.

Charles had made love to her despite the stifling heat. Though he had been as thoughtful as usual, she had eventually been forced to feign satisfaction and had turned away her head afterward and pretended to sleep, though her leg muscles twitched. Before leaving her bed, he had kissed her lightly on the temple and replaced the mosquito netting. It formed a cocoon she did not want. She lay under a single sheet, her eyes on the glitter of the necklaces around the neck of Peter's Buddha.

Not Charles' fault, she thought. Mine.

She pushed the sheet down to her hips to let what air the netting permitted cool her breasts, which felt swollen. In her head she made a list of Jennifer's virtues: brave, generous, intelligent, observant, well-mannered, precocious, beautiful.

Her hands strayed over her body, and she shifted tautly, smoothing flank and thigh with her palms, pushing up the flesh of her breasts from the side. She made a list of the ways in which Jennifer was deprived: an only child; too few friends; a father too much absent; no grandparents, aunts, uncles. She caught a memory: Jennifer after a visit to ladies come for afternoon tea, looking up with frightened eyes to say, "Did I get it right?" Did that explain her today—exquisite, triumphant? "I shall recite—*not* sing—'Little Bo-Peep'!"

Guilt turned Elizabeth's head from side to side. Joined, her hands pushed down hard on the mound of flesh at the meeting of her thighs.

She already has the spirit I need, she thought with despair. And I am trying to train it out of her. I must stop that.

Her hands relaxed, a middle finger resting in the crevice of her flesh, and she tightened her thighs around it, moving with slight tight squeezes. She thought: Jennifer is only trying to become what I am.

Her flesh began to move against itself in small quick thrusts. She thought: I'm intelligent; Jennifer shrewd. I stand up to Charles; she stands alone. I want; she acts. She gets what she wants, wants, wants.

And it was not the climax she wanted so much as the feeling of surcease, of languor that flowed from her center to her limbs, warm instead of hot. She turned her head sideways on the pillow and let the muscles of her legs relax. She pulled the sheet over the top of her body and closed her eyes. She thought: Peter is right. She is already more modern than I. I really ought to fight.

She was drowsing off to sleep, wishing this war was over.

16

1918

Death by fire came to Charles. The heat and roaring of the flames was inconceivable: their red and yellow billowing, that they should trap him. He was pinned by the legs, and when he looked down the length of his body, he could see his legs aflame, twisting as they charred, bubbling under the flames. He could move his head, and he lifted it up and away, and his being sought to flee through his mouth in a soundless scream of agony. But death, not rescue, faced him. Death unfair, death with nothing, *nothing* to be done.

He knew it was a dream, part of him. Even in the dream, he knew he was not on the torpedoed *Sussex,* not with fat, vulgar, dying Tony Jephson. That part of him fought for consciousness, but he was drugged and could not push the dream away, and he lost faith that it was a dream, and the loss of faith brought a terror greater than the flames.

He, or part of his brain and will, forced his eyelids open. They opened onto blackness; and supine, held by nightmare, he did not know that he was alive. Naked will moved one hand. He was alive. Gratitude closed his eyes, and the dream of flames came back, and the terror with it.

He forced his eyes open again, ordered them to see. He could feel: his heart racing, the blood thudding in his head. He could hear: panting. As though an animal panted on his pillow, and he was filled with terror again even with his eyes open. Then the world tilted back into meaning. I am here, in my bed, in my room.

Charles cleared his throat and tried to turn his panting into one long inhalation. He half-lifted himself from the pillow and shook his head to batter it free of images. He pushed his legs from under the coverlet and groped for the familiar opening in the mosquito netting. He stood, and his knees trembled. He was embarrassed, shamed, afraid to lie down again. They came every few weeks like snapshots in the mail, these dreams of the manner in which he would die, snapshots of the moment the wound gaped, the flesh tore, the breath would not draw. And the Charles caught in that snapshot of the indelible future was a Charles he hated.

He could see clearly now, and without turning on a light, he walked the familiar route to the bathroom and urinated, and as he watched the stream he also watched the folio of snapshots in his mind. One part of him said: It has to be one or the other of them. The other part said: None, ever. There must be something wrong with him. As long as no one else ever realizes. He shook the last drops from his penis and looked at the face which the night light and the mirror reflected. He found it hard to believe it remained unmarked, and touched it with his hand.

During all those months of 1918, Elizabeth led a normal life in Mount Lavinia. She smiled, she entertained, she shopped in town, she danced to "Alexander's Ragtime Band," she wrote many letters and read late at night. She spent hours with Jennifer, chatted with Nanny, enjoyed Ginny Pearsall, laughed at Peter's sense of humor, and got on well enough with Charles. She went riding three times a week for her figure's sake, brushed her hair a hundred times a night and found the first gray in it, stared overlong into the mirror. Why, she asked her image, should I ever have expected more? She had not peace but armistice. She had no right to complain. She could still not put a name to much that she felt. During those months she noticed that Charles had let youth slip. Suddenly his waistline was thicker, his hair thinner, his dignity more pronounced. He seemed lonely after Joe Plunkett was summoned to London, but business seemed to keep him happy. He was out many evenings and he had grown very wealthy.

Charles' life remained private. The officer's wife with whom he had enjoyed a long and comfortable affair became a widow early in the year, and he encouraged her to go home to her husband's family. They needed her, he said. He rented a suite of rooms in a dusty hotel run by Indians on the Galle Face Road, where he would sit alone of an afternoon and sip whiskey in a seedy armchair. Occasionally he would have a girl up for company. The new breed of wartime girls was racier than his generation, their skin unmarked. He mused much about himself and Elizabeth, though he never told her so. He wondered how things had gone wrong between them. Mostly he thought that whatever had happened in their marriage was normal. He regretted that.

At home sometimes, with a few drinks in him, he mused about Nanny, Mabel Greggs, now filling out with her mid-twenties and experience. There was something about her mouth, the sparkle in her eyes, the unconventual shifting of her hips inside her dress as she walked down the corridor. He liked her. He was tempted into making a sally or two in her direction. Though neither spoke of it, both Nanny and Elizabeth noticed. As Charles suspected, Nanny was no more innocent than a child of the slums can be, but she was continent, canny, and attracted to men younger than Charles. Elizabeth had come to find Charles' enthusiasm about other women as familiar as his catarrhal cough in the mornings, and it interested her as little. Once she overheard one of Charles' bolder gallantries and Nanny's firm reply. She thought she ought to say something but decided it was better to let sleeping dogs lie.

Henriette wrote regularly, but her letters were full of fatigue. She had taken up nursing, but it was too much for her. The food was appalling, the queuing exhausting, the coal unburnable. When the Great Flu Epidemic began that summer, Henriette and Bernard were too old and tired to risk getting about. Both gave up work and stayed at home. Temporarily, of course, wrote Henriette. Elizabeth spoke to Charles, and he insisted on sending them regular bank drafts. "Your father," wrote Henriette, "has become impossible."

Elizabeth preferred the letters she got from a young officer serving in France. His name was Anthony James. Their correspondence had begun accidentally, their words striking some spark not produced by the other stranger-correspondents which duty had given her. He seemed young and sensitive. She asked him the impossible question: What is war really like? He answered: Not much different from peace. He declined to describe battles. He wrote about the other ranks: "Beautiful lads, grand chaps." He wrote: "I think sometimes if we all went home, would it make any difference?"

He wrote again: "I remember vividly what old Grimsby, my house-master, said when I told him I was leaving school. 'Leaving?' he said. 'Why on earth should you do that?' 'To join up, sir,' I replied. 'Idiot!' he snorted. 'You'll be no use in the war, but you could serve some purpose on the school Eleven.' "

He wrote later: "Today one of the lads asked me to translate the old Horatian slogan *'Dulce et decorum est, Pro Patria mori.'* He'd seen it on his brother's grave. When I translated it, he looked a bit thoughtful. 'Nice little poem, that,' he said, then looked me straght in the eye. 'For an officer's grave.' That was enough of a stopper right there, but he went on: 'But I can't go on much longer with *this* bloody business,' he said, and walked away."

He wrote of going on leave in London. He had breakfasted in the trenches and dined at the Savoy. He had not gone home to see his parents: "Too wrenching for all concerned, the other chaps tell me." The last night of leave he had taken a friend to see *Chu Chin Chow*. "Everybody here," he wrote, "talks quite rationally in terms of two insanely contrasting beliefs: that the war will never end, and how soon we will win it."

Some weeks before the Armistice, coincident with the great battles fought by exhausted armies whose outcome none could predict, his letters ceased coming. Elizabeth wrote once or twice without a reply before she realized that he must have been killed. But she kept his letters, putting them in the same drawer as her diary and the list of her qualities she had drawn up when she had set out from England and a small collection of photographs and clippings from the newspapers. She had liked him. She had been real to him.

* * *

On January 10, 1918, the House of Lords agreed that respectable women over thirty-five should be allowed to vote. During the war, said former Prime Minister Asquith, the women had earned it. "What use is a vote among these shortages?" wrote Henriette Malloy. On November 11, the war itself ended. Darkness fell early in London, for there was a heavy rain, and all over the great city people flung back curtains to let the lights shine upon the crowds. Drunken celebrations lasted three whole days, the bobbies discreet among the waving Union Jacks and searchlights probing safe skies. In Trafalgar Square Nelson looked even more like Napoleon, and the boys yelling from the smooth backs of Landseer's lions made the pigeons on the wire-netted windowsills of the War Office puff their chests with indignation.

"What are you celebrating?" asked a shuffling man in gray of the revelers, peering into their faces, holding them by the arm.

"What?" they shouted. "War's over, isn't it?"

He nodded slowly and released them.

"What's the matter with him, then?" they asked each other, and blew into paper squeakers.

After the Armistice and despite the Flu, the politicians went to Paris to redraw the map of the world while their wives went shopping. They kept millions of young men under arms just in case. "They are really much better off where they are!" rumbled Winston Churchill, who was staying at the Hotel Georges Cinq: the budget would be out of whack if they all went on poor relief; there would be no jobs until the factories could get rid of all those women; the world wondered how you created wealth if not by war. The soldiers clung to the guy ropes of tents in the cold winter rain and found the dead landscape better than their nightmares. Hope, not imagination, enables us to survive war. Imagination, not hope, helps us survive peace. Having felt no joy at the ending of war, Elizabeth and Charles, unknown to each other, both felt like the soldiers looking at the cold winter rain. Each faced a private war now, and neither could imagine what its ending would be.

17

April 1919

Elizabeth's effort to define herself began with events in a city in the far northwest of India whose name she barely knew. She had heard of Amritsar only because Tara Singh made a pilgrimage there upon his retirement as their chauffeur. To the Sikhs it is a holy city. The gold-leafed dome of their Golden Temple dominates the cascade of its whitewashed buildings and the bountiful gardens for which it is famous. The Sikhs were popular with the British. They look magnificent—beards, turbans, fierce pride—and they had behaved even in the Great Mutiny like Imperial India's boy scouts: trustworthy, obedient, efficient. On the evening of April 13, 1919, when the Wingates sat as usual in the late-afternoon gold on the veranda sipping drinks before dinner while Nanny bathed Jennifer, Elizabeth had no reason at all to think that the holy city of the Sikhs would become important on the map of her life.

"Well, I'm glad to see that!" exclaimed Charles, breaking a long silence with a sudden waving of the newspaper.

"What's that, dear?" asked Elizabeth, looking at him over the top of the spectacles she now used for close work.

"What it says in the paper: 'The train is just escaped from a collusion.' "

"A what? What on earth are you talking about?"

"Tonight's program for the Bioscope. It all happens in a thrilling detective drama called *The Golden Beetle,* in three parts and apparently Babu English."

Elizabeth did not respond. Silence fell again.

"Poor George!" sighed Charles.

"George? Who's George?"

"The hero, of course. It says here: 'He is tied merciless on the railroad. An express train crossing over his body and with many other thrilling and sensational scenes, which makes the audience to stand their hairs on end!' " Charles laughed. "Shall we go?"

"I think not," said Elizabeth. "I have this to finish." She gestured at her sewing. "Have Abbuhamy fix me another pink gin, would you, dear?"

"But we could do with a sensational scene or two."

"You can't be restless again. We've been out three nights already this week!" protested Elizabeth.

Six months of peace had been enough to make Charles bored. The importances of business were not enough compared with those of war, and though Clarkson and Son had even prospered through the general slump in world trade which followed the Armistice, the effort of supervising the business's move into a brand-new building of its own had not been enough to satisfy him. Elizabeth liked to keep him more at home, where she could to some extent manage his drinking, but she thought sometimes that it was as though he were fleeing something.

"But soon we shall be out of town for four weeks," he now complained, then, hearing his own tone, sought to retrieve himself by ponderous humor. "I shall miss the glories of the cinema."

In fact, he would miss the Bioscope. Everyone in Colombo would, even though the moving pictures had been with them only since the war. An ambitious draper from Bombay owned the Bioscope, screening films made in a score of countries without understanding either their logic or the mechanical and electrical processes that set their mysteries flickering on the whitewashed wall. None of the audience understood those mysteries either; they just accepted them as a modern miracle. But worship at that altar had become important to natives and Europeans alike. Already some people thought them more real than real life.

Elizabeth continued sewing silently for a moment or two. She enjoyed the cinema herself, and she resented equally either prospect which her refusal would bring: his going out to the club, or his prowling and growling until he went to bed half-drunk.

"There are two newsreels, it says," Charles resumed. "You might even see your beloved Gandhi."

It had become a bone of contention between them, this interest in politics which she had developed since the Easter rebellion in Dublin in 1916. He didn't mind all the League of Nations nonsense so much, but he did deeply resent her growing obsession with this wretched little creature Gandhi, whose scrawny dhoti-clad, barefoot little figure obsessed the natives. Wherever he went, and he went everywhere, he walked unprotected, confident, penitential. The crowds that gathered to see him grew calm, because they called him the man of peace, and this infuriated the Raj, who, having forgotten during the last five years how to deal with war made up of peace, fumed that his doctrine of "freedom through noncooperation" was not only childish but blasphemous.

Elizabeth and Charles had actually had words about him just the day before. Gandhi had declared a *hartal,* or day of mourning, to protest new legislation by the British Parliament to suppress Indian agitation for freedom, and starting on April 7 the great subcontinent and the wheels of Empire ground slowly to a halt. The Raj was powerless not just to stop things but even to start them. Charles was furious, Elizabeth defiantly supportive of Gandhi, and they had argued. But she was too smart to pick up such an obvious gauntlet as that which he had just now flung before her.

"Well," she simply said, resting her sewing in her lap, "I shall ring up Ginny and see if they would like to go. They prefer to pop in late and sit discreetly at the back, but we could meet them there, I suppose."

The Pearsalls were agreeable, for even regality has its domesticity, and so the Wingates said good night to Nanny and Jennifer, dressed for public, and had a light meal.

"Ginny did seem a trifle worried about going into a crowd in case of the flu," commented Elizabeth.

"I didn't think of that," said Charles, a little taken aback.

"We haven't had a case among the Europeans for three weeks, and she seemed as bored as we, so we decided to take the risk."

"I didn't think of it," repeated Charles. "Perhaps she's right. Perhaps it would be better not."

Elizabeth looked at him across the table, amused. The flu epidemic which had started in Europe in the spring of 1918 and reached Ceylon the previous October, thereby ruining the Armistice festivities, was by now, April, almost over. Though still killing hundreds of natives in the back country, in Colombo it seemed to have run itself out. And one can be afraid of death for only so long; after a while it becomes commonplace. The epidemic was the only thing Elizabeth had ever known Charles to fear. As it struck down their acquaintances week after week, he insisted upon their living as if under siege: no visitors, no playmates for Jennifer, and no festive public occasions (which had ruined Christmas and New Year).

"You can wear your little gauze mask," said Elizabeth unkindly.

"Sarcasm!" Charles grumbled. "I suppose it will be all right by now."

And so they clambered into the aging Napier, driven by the eldest son of the august Tara Singh, who held himself as bearded and erect as had his father. At the Bioscope they were greeted with nervous amiability by the proprietor, who sent his children scurrying to place their folding wooden chairs precisely where they wanted them. The Bioscope was a long, narrow shed of corrugated iron. For five nights a week it was jammed with natives, the men hunkering on the concrete floor, their wives and children quieter on a carpeted segment toward the rear, but on Thursdays and Fridays the theater transformed itself magically for European audiences. Potted palms appeared. The floor was swept and washed with a carbolic mixture whose acrid smell became associated with the moving pictures for a generation of colonials. Prices went up tenfold. Portraits of King George and Queen Mary were hung on nails in the lobby, along with an oil painting of an overripe, flimsily clad woman advertising Turkish cigarettes.

The Wingates ordered their chairs placed toward the rear and on the side, where a youth crouched near an open door, rising at unpredictable intervals to drive away native children who tried to stick their heads under the foot-wide gap between walls and floor. The Bioscope's atmosphere was like that of a picnic, and discomfort was a small price for the pleasures of the flickering screen.

The newsreel proved unexciting: Clemenceau and Lloyd George looking self-satisfied in top hats at some meeting in Paris; President Wilson waving jerkily from a large motorcar in front of some giant American building, his wife buried in a fur collar; bathing beauties simpering on a chill English beach; a troop ship filled with riotous Anzacs docking in Sydney; a queue of refugees in Budapest, each with a little metal pail in hand, waiting for food.

"Aha!" exclaimed Charles. "You see, I promised you! Your hero!" There was Gandhi, a shrunken figure among the Bombay crowds that surrounded him near the Victorian arch called the Gateway to India. "HEAD OF CONGRESS PARTY ASKS PEACE," read the title, and Gandhi moved his lips soundlessly while the Bioscope pianist played neutrally. Immediately after the newsreel, they were joined by Joe Plunkett, now a colonel, to whom they chatted while the reels were changed. He was angry at the filmed reminders of the peace conference.

"Seems a rather dangerous illusion to feed the sheep, don't you think?" he said sourly. "Peace, I mean. Never has been a time of peace throughout the world. Never will be. This man Wilson's an ass."

"You've grown so cynical, Joe," replied Elizabeth crossly.

Since his visit to London and then to various European capitals, he had become bitter about politics, disillusioned by the mysterious military mission that had meant promotion to him. "When they find out you've fed them dreams, that's when you'll get the real cynicism. Ask your husband where the smart money is going these days."

"Now, come on, you two, with your blessed politics!" protested Charles.

"Now, Charles, answer his question," probed Elizabeth. "Where *is* the smart money going these days?"

"Well," said her husband reluctantly, "it's not as bad as Joe says, but the insiders are picking up the shares of the arms manufacturers on the cheap. Steel companies, that sort of thing. For the long run, they are considered a good buy, I'll give you that," he addressed Joe. "By the smart money."

"Ours?" said Elizabeth.

"I have picked up a few shares here and there."

"I can't accuse money of being cynical, can I?" said Elizabeth sharply. "Clearly it is only realistic. And you say, Joe, that it says we'll forever have a world of soldiers?"

Plunkett was by now embarrassed. Elizabeth had taken him deeper into the worlds of both domestic and international dispute than he cared to blunder, and he was relieved when Charles groaned, "Enough is enough." Conveniently, the projector and the pianist at that moment flickered into life again.

The rest of the program was a hodgepodge: a western from America, with horses like marionettes and guns exploding like milkweed pods; a Hungarian fantasy of Arabia, all dark eyes, low necklines, and clumsy sword fights; the promised *Golden Beetle,* with a train so dim it could scarcely be seen, certainly not as clearly as the chalk-white face of handsome George. The Pearsalls arrived just before this three-reeler began, and after a few minutes of it, Elizabeth and Ginny agreed to withdraw, pleading that the constant flicker made their eyes ache. Leaving the men grateful to light up cigars, they retreated to a room at one side of the lobby marked with a hand-painted sign reading "LADDIES ONLY." There, among the potted palms and the strong smell of carbolic, they smoked a surreptitious cigarette and gossiped.

Ginny Pearsall had aged a little of late, but her spirit was unchanged. Not so her plans. With the war over, there was a surplus of distinguished gentlemen needing royal appointments, and Sir Reginald's replacement as governor was already on the way to Ceylon. To everyone's surprise, perhaps even Ginny's, the Pearsalls had decided to return Home rather than stay overseas permanently.

Ginny sat and fanned herself rapidly with a bamboo fan. "Whew!" she said comically. "This change of life! I suppose I shall be glad of it during a London winter, but in this heat it is a bore!"

"May I long avoid both," said Elizabeth. "London winters and hot flashes, I mean!"

"We seem to be part of the general longing to see London again," said Ginny. "Everyone wants to go back this summer. Perhaps we need to make sure it is still there."

Indeed London was to be flooded by colonials that summer, free at last from exile by submarine and shortage. The Wingates themselves had their cabins reserved for June on the *Oronsay,* the trip postponed since the summer of 1914.

"Shall you be ready in time?"

"Oh, yes, people are only too eager to help, you know. Perhaps rather too eager." Ginny smiled. "Never mind, we shall see those whom we want to see quite soon, and in rather more civilized circumstances."

"Are you eager to go yet?"

"Not eager, I think, but we do recognize that the time has come. Reggie has never been quite the same since the boys passed on, and that wretched National Congress last December took it out of him." He was proud of Ceylon's reasonability and peacefulness, and he believed it ready for the evolution which had freed many of the Empire's white colonies during the previous generation.

"We are very lucky we did not get the flu," said Ginny. "We had dinner with the Bellinghams, you know, the very day before they went down with it. When Mrs. Bellingham died, I was sure that we would catch the wretched thing. But what could one do? I seem to have spent my life worrying about things I could do nothing else about."

There was a pause in their conversation. Then Ginny continued. "You shall visit your friend Peter Williams during your trip, of course. I am told nobody has seen him since his wife's funeral."

"Charles has seen him. He's leaving too, you know, or at least selling up. Charles is arranging the sale of the plantation for him."

"And you? You haven't seen him?"

"No," she said firmly. "And I'm looking forward to it."

"I see," said Lady Pearsall. She lifted her nose as though to avoid the carbolic odor, and under her hooding eyelids addressed, it seemed, the lighted end of her cigarette. "The girl has an open field. But will she run?"

"What did you think of his wife?" asked Elizabeth directly.

"Mary Williams?" inquired Lady Pearsall of her cigarette. "I should have written to him personally, I know, but he's too intelligent to need the sort of letter one usually writes on these occasions." She looked queerly at the cigarette end and then addressed Elizabeth. "I did not like his wife, though I scarcely knew her. She had the composure of a fish. Perhaps you should ask Charles about her less discernible charms."

Elizabeth was amused. "I do not think it was a happy marriage," she said.

"You still expect far, far too much from marriage, Elizabeth," replied Lady Pearsall. "Idealism is as dangerous to marriage as it is to peace. I should introduce you to Beatrice Webb when you come to London. I remember her once describing marriage as a 'waste pipe' for emotion. An image perhaps a trifle biological for me, but nonetheless apropos. At its worst, familiarity breeding contempt. At its best, friendship, I think. Romance of the kind you expect does not exist in marriage. I daresay an old family servant would do as well as a spouse."

"Peter Williams would make a much more interesting husband than does Charles," replied Elizabeth flatly.

"Such illusions, child!" mocked Ginny Pearsall. "What you mean is that you now find Peter as interesting as you once found Charles, which puts the responsibility where it ought to be."

"Charles is duller than he used to be. We are duller."

"Perhaps you are right," ceded Lady Pearsall. "But then, none of us is what we used to be, are we? Undoubtedly," she laughed, "that is why we are all carrying on about the decline of the West. But I shall say it only one last time, and that very quietly, you could have your cake and eat it too." An impudent look came upon her face. "Experience makes me recommend it."

At that moment there was a knock at the door, followed by Sir Reginald's voice: "Would you join us, dear? There's a bit of a flap on, and I shall have to get back to the office."

Sir Reginald in the brighter light did indeed look tired, older, his fine mouth now drooping at the corners with the weight of his cheeks, his hair as well as his eyebrows completely white.

"I've asked Charles to join me, my dear," he said to Elizabeth. "So perhaps you would like to keep Genevieve company?"

"May we know what this 'flap' is?" inquired Lady Pearsall with some irritation.

"The Punjab," he answered shortly. "Amritsar. An uprising of some kind. This nonsense started by Gandhi. Not to worry, but we've been put on alert."

They slipped quietly out the door of the theater, thereby devastating the morale of the proprietor, who followed them to the Governor's Rolls-Royce with apologies for a hundred unknown sins.

"Have your driver follow us, will you, Wingate?" said the Governor, glancing at Tara Singh's son, alert and impassive by the door of the Wingates' Napier. "Better to be discreet, I think. We can all fit in."

Charles and the aide-de-camp who had brought the news to the Governor sat on the jump seats, and this hasty arrangement brought Elizabeth for the second time in her life to hear bad news from the lips of an insipid young officer in a motorcar speeding toward Government House through the streets of Colombo. The aide was full of incident, bright with eager anxiety: threatened Europeans, incipient revolution in the Punjab, an uprising among the Sikhs, armed attacks on the barracks in Amritsar.

Government House was full of comings and goings, and Ginny and Elizabeth retreated to the private drawing room upstairs, where Charles joined them an hour or so later.

"Nothing to get alarmed about," he reassured them. "Bit of a set-to in Amritsar, apparently caused by the followers of that Gandhi chap, and the Viceroy's ordered all the provinces—and suggested to us—to be on the lookout. No news of its spreading, and we shan't have any trouble here. Just a few precautions."

"What's all this about a massacre?" demanded Lady Pearsall implacably.

"Nothing to worry about," said Charles patronizingly.

"A massacre is nothing to worry about?" intervened Elizabeth.

"A massacre of *Indians,* dear, not British," he said.

"Thank God!" exclaimed Lady Pearsall.

"Thank God?" echoed Elizabeth, looking shocked at both her husband and her friend.

They looked back at her as though she were an ill-behaved child, lacking comprehension.

"Now, Elizabeth—" began Charles.

"Don't you 'now, Elizabeth' me!" she snapped, quiet but angry. "Who are you British killing this time?"

Charles, embarrassed, said nothing, while Elizabeth glared back at him.

Ginny studied Elizabeth's face steadily for a moment, then turned to Charles and spoke quickly. "You say there'll be no trouble here?"

"We don't think so. There seems to have been some excitement in the Moslem quarter, but we're not sure it has anything to do with this." Charles spoke to Lady Pearsall as though Elizabeth were not present, and Elizabeth sat back on the sofa, her face flushed. "Your husband's done such a good job, you know, I doubt we shall ever have any trouble here."

It was not a good evening for Charles, for now Lady Pearsall snapped at him: "With a new constitution being negotiated right now? With the Hindus and the Moslems ready to slit each other's throats at the drop of a pin in that awful native quarter?" She gestured toward the windows, where the tropic night stretched placid as usual, and as usual vaguely threatening, as though it lurked. "I've told Reggie before, they're *not* ready for independence." Now she turned on Elizabeth. "And your wretched little Gandhi stirring up trouble wherever he goes. I shall be glad when we can get out of here. The sooner the better."

Elizabeth said nothing, though she was obviously holding back.

Charles spoke placatingly again. "We've had no troubles since 1915."

Lady Pearsall unexpectedly looked at her wristwatch. "I shall have to convince the Governor that the Empire will survive if he gets a few hours' rest. I shall order rooms readied for you, if you'll excuse me."

But the Wingates politely declined her hospitality. On the drive along the winding road to Mount Lavinia, Charles found himself scanning the roadside, dimly visible in the headlamps, for bands of enemies. Elizabeth spoke not at all, staring straight ahead at the back of the young Sikh chauffeur's spotless turban and taking pains to thank him warmly as he held the door open for them at the bottom of the steps of their house.

During the next few days, accurate news of events at Amritsar trickled in. For the most part the British always had shown restraint when faced with the prospect of rebellion, but in Amritsar a brigadier general named Dyer declared martial law, and on April 13—the day on which the Wingates went to the Bioscope—the citizens of that white and gleaming city attempted a second day of *hartal*, or mourning. By thousands they gathered in a place where many meetings were held, the Jallianwalla Bagh, a great stony field surrounded by the walls of houses and gardens, on an afternoon hot and plagued by flies. It was, no doubt, a dangerous situation, though witnesses later said it had the atmosphere of a racetrack.

The single major entry to the stony field was by means of a rough and narrow alleyway between buildings. Down that narrow alleyway marched Brigadier General Dyer, leading fifty British soldiers. At the gateway to the field, he ordered his men, properly shielded by pillars, to set up machine guns. Some say he warned the gathering. It seems unlikely. With an economical 1,650 rounds the machine guns slew or wounded 1,516 people within ten minutes. The gouts of blood, the stink of death, the screams of fear, the gyre of vultures in the blue April sky–none of this mattered to Dyer. He had the peace he sought. Some Britons demanded investigations and a court-martial, but as weeks passed with the memsahibs continuing to sleep safe under their mosquito nets, most agreed that Dyer's firmness had been right, and when he resigned on request, the gentlemen in clubs and messes all over the country contributed twenty-six thousand pounds to supplement his pension.

During these weeks Peter Williams' eroded statue of the Buddha preserved Elizabeth's marriage. The day following the evening at the Bioscope, she ordered a special table built and had the little statue placed under the shelter of the summerhouse at the bottom of the garden. It was her move in the marital game they seemed to be playing. She wondered whether she still loved Charles, whether she could again forgive him. She stood in front of the Buddha. His ear and elbow were chipped, a finger missing, his colors much paler but more powerful than the flowers before him. His eyes were not blind, but to him she was no more than vapor. She knew it, but spoke to him nonetheless. "I hate men for their hatred," she said.

Like all Buddhas, this Buddha smiled the kind of smile that is gentle but not compassionate, all-comprehending but not understanding.

"And I love men for their love," she said, without the illusion that he heard. Around them the day sparkled, and she could hear the noises of life from the garden and the house. She could sense a million million marriages at her back. And suddenly she felt surprise.

"That is something that *I* know, isn't it?" she said to him, and for some reason felt suddenly relieved. No flowers grew nearby, so she took a handful of grasses and tugged them from the earth, laying them roots and all upon his lap.

Many days after that she visited this shrine, and she brought from her garden flowers with soft and softly colored petals to which his hand seemed indifferent. But she did not fight with Charles. She replayed over and over the words that had come to her on that first visit, varying them like a musical phrase: "That is something that *I* know," she said. "That is *something* that I know," she said. "That is something that I *know.*" She also knew now that whatever battle was to be fought was hers, not theirs.

18

May 1919

This knowledge that she had a mind of her own produced no deed from her until some three weeks after the Amritsar massacre, during a cricket match on a Saturday afternoon. The Pearsalls, now within days of departure from office, had invited the Wingates to join them for afternoon tea in the members' tent, where they sat at a round table covered with green crepe paper which happened to be next to a table of officers singing the praises of their comrade Dyer. Looking forward to her own imminent trip to the mountain country, Elizabeth was cheerful and fetching in white lace.

Charles was also in good temper. They chatted about gardening back Home. At the neighboring table, however, spirits of another kind were taking charge. The officers were loud with liquor. Elizabeth, seated nearest them, was disturbed by both the noise and the subject of their conversation, and quietly asked Charles to request them to be a little less loud. Charles approached the table of men with brusque good humor. They were abashed and insisted on sending Colonel Talbot as emissary of apology.

Colonel George Talbot was not the humble type. Well over six feet and broad-shouldered, he had chest, belly, and voice better suited to the parade ground than the tea table. Bachelordom and thirty years of service in the tropics had given his face the brilliance his intellect lacked and graced him with no understanding whatsoever of the female sex. Elizabeth felt that she had accidentally invoked the devil. He gripped the back of Elizabeth's chair with chunky, hairy hands and leaned over her shoulder to boom waves of whiskey at the company: "Apologies, apologies, apologies, dear ladies! Terribly sorry and all that, my lady, Mrs. Wingate, madam! Quite right of you to complain at us! Forget where we are, you see, when we get in a group of all soldiers. Quite right not to want to hear the gory details! Apologies most gladly given, reform immediate! But you'll have to admit Dyer showed the blighters what's what, eh?"

He leered at the table group. Elizabeth, who would have had to crick her neck to look at him, ignored his presence entirely. Lady Pearsall nodded coolly in dismissal. An uncomfortable silence took over until Charles, now embarrassed by either side, sought to retrieve the situation. "Certainly seems to have quieted things down, George," he said.

Talbot laughed. "Quiet a few more of the beggars down too, anytime they ask for it!" he chortled. Retaining his grip on the back of Elizabeth's chair, he leaned forward to address the Governor directly, thus brushing the back of her hat with his chest and forcing her to shift forward. She picked up her teacup, which revealed her hand to be trembling.

"With all due respect, Governor, killing a few of the blighters now and then is better than negotiating, what? You'd find it a lot faster, hah, hah!"

In so referring to Sir Reginald's support for the Ceylon National Congress, Talbot was openly expressing opinions possessed by many of the British in Ceylon, especially the military, but which he would never have dared had he not been drunk and had Sir Reginald not been about to leave his post. The Governor now found himself in a classic situation for diplomacy, but he too knew that his term of service was coming to an end, and for once he chose not to exercise the talent natural to his breeding and profession. Looking directly at the large colonel, he said in a tone muted but icy, "I can't agree, of course. Dyer's policy is as foolish as it is inhumane."

His wife gave him a look of startlement, Elizabeth one of gratitude.

Disagreement with a royal governor is no mean matter and never one for public display, but Talbot seemed driven to folly. "Foolish!" he exclaimed, thereby attracting alarmed looks from his table of fellow officers. "Dyer's a bl . . . Dyer's a hero to every man in this country, or should be! Showed us the right way, dash it!"

Lady Pearsall took alarm at her husband. Though Sir Reginald's eyes were now cast down as though to avoid dispute, the skin of his neck had turned bright red, infallible sign of anger. She quickly intervened. "I'm sure you may be right, Colonel," she said hastily, drawing his gaze. "But we women can't help seeing it from a different viewpoint. We can't help but feel very sorry for the families of all those poor dead natives. You understand, I'm sure?" The ploy was as sentimentally feminine as a mother bird trailing a wing to distract predator from nest, but this particular beast was not misled.

"What they need is a good sharp knock on the head," he continued, "instead of mollycoddling. Give them an inch, and they'll take a mile."

Nobody interrupted. By now Sir Reginald's head was almost bowed, and Genevieve had surreptitiously laid her hand on his knee under cover of the table.

Talbot leaned forward, bringing his belly to press against Elizabeth's shoulder. "Better to teach them to keep to their place, and we'll keep to ours!" he concluded with a boozy, triumphant grin.

Now it was that Elizabeth acted. Straightening her back, she forced Talbot off her shoulder. Standing, she forced him to release the back of her chair. Turning to face him, she made him step back a pace, he staring at her as though she had materialized from nowhere. Looking him straight in the eye, she spoke, her low voice throbbing with strength. "We were discussing gardening, Colonel Talbot, not killing. But you are quite right, I expect. Indeed it would be better if we all learned to keep our proper place. Now, would you be so kind as to return to yours?"

It would be hard indeed to tell who in the group was most surprised. Talbot backed toward his comrades, goggling. Stunned, Charles turned his gaze on his wife as though he too had never seen her before. Admiring, Sir Reginald let his face light up.

"Oh, well played, Elizabeth!" exclaimed Ginny Pearsall, and everyone except Charles laughed aloud as Colonel Talbot fled to the haven of his fellow officers, they suddenly not eager to welcome him.

Elizabeth did not laugh, nor even smile. She turned instead to look at Charles. "They offer us a Gandhi," she said quietly, with as little emotional weight as possible. "We give them a Talbot in return."

Charles protested, "That's scarcely fair, Elizabeth. Talbot can scarcely be said to be typical." He cast a quick glance at the table of his friends in search of support. For all its public nature, their exchange had become completely personal. "It's simply a matter of styles of administration, after all," he continued.

Elizabeth now looked at her husband as cool and direct as she had at Talbot. "It is a matter," she said, "of ethics."

"Ethics?" said Charles, his voice rising.

Glancing at husband and wife, Ginny Pearsall hastily intervened. "Perhaps it is time we all left," she said, rising from her chair.

Elizabeth turned to look levelly at her. "Ceylon?" she asked. A moment of silence hung there as the two women looked at each other, leaving the men out of it.

"The tent," said Ginny. "For the moment."

The party gathered their belongings, left the hot members' tent, and returned to the makeshift seating to watch the remainder of the cricket match. Looking at the game but thinking of Amritsar and Colonel Talbot, Elizabeth commented to Genevieve, "As we feared, men find their old lives too dull after war."

"They'll lose the habit, given time."

"I doubt it, Genevieve. We have changed, you know. Whether the war changed us, or whether we changed and caused the war, we have changed. I think I am not looking forward to going back to England as much as I had expected. It will be nice to see my mother and father, of course, though Maman warns me they are grown quite old, but I don't look forward to rationing and train strikes and dimming the lights to save coal–six months after the war is over!"

"You will enjoy a visit to London, you know," said Lady Pearsall seriously. "I know you didn't like it before, but it will do you good, brace you. It makes one use one's mind more, if only to feel secretly superior, and as one grows older, one needs to do that. As I've said to Reggie, it's the only thing one *can* do more of as one grows older."

"You won't miss Colombo?"

"The recollection more than the reality, I fancy."

"I shall miss you when we return, a great deal. Ceylon will not be the same."

"And I you, my dear." Ginny was looking at the game in progress. "Oh, I say, look at Julian Wade showing off with only one arm! What a lovely stroke." She leaned forward and poked her husband in the ribs discreetly. "Call out 'Well played,' Reginald!" Her husband did her bidding, and she returned to Elizabeth. "But perhaps you can visit Home every season, as we did in the civilized days."

"I had rather give Colombo up altogether."

"Oh?"

"I've had enough of bridging two worlds in my life, Ginny. I think it makes one not care about anything enough. I wish I could commit myself to something . . . anything, really. I think now that I would have done better to commit myself on the side of the war."

"What nonsense!"

"Because now the peace is here, it simply does not seem to offer much that one can commit oneself to. Sometimes I wish that the old laws of life held good: a husband, house, servants, establishments. . . ."

"Honestly, Elizabeth," said Ginny Pearsall sternly, "I cannot believe this is you speaking."

"There seems so much disturbance these days, so many leave-takings and packings-up and that sort of thing."

"Is this the same woman who put that brute Talbot in his place half an hour ago?"

"That was unexpected, wasn't it? Somehow I'd just had enough. I just couldn't take any more of that man and what he stands for."

"You gave Charles a surprise, I imagine. He's been eyeing you as we sit here, you know. I fancy he thinks rather differently of you as a result of that little bit of courage."

"Yes, but do I care anymore?" said Elizabeth, looking at her sleek husband. Nineteen-nineteen was a year of dislocation, wherein nobody knew her or his proper place.

19

Two days after the cricket match, Charles and Elizabeth set off on their tour of the back country. Charles wanted to delay the journey because of the danger of flu, but there was really little choice: he had to attend to the plantation, whose manager was finding difficulty in replacing the workers who had died; he wanted to get in some hunting in Wilpattu before the monsoon started; and the date for their trip Home was close. They set off without too much pleasure in each other's company and headed east by rail, up into the mountain country toward Kandy. The train ran through rice paddies waiting for the rains, then alongside the slow and muddy Kelani River, where loud-colored birds flashed from tree to tree, then up into tropical jungle where great vines pushed against the sides of the puffing engine and the heat became stifling, then through foothills, the blue and green terraces of tea shrubs dotted with the bright saris of workers, and finally into the cool, clean, cloud-shrouded mountains themselves. Elizabeth felt released by the ascent, as though she were climbing above not just Colombo but also her life.

Their first stay was in Nuwara Eliya, long a favorite mountain resort and center of the tea-garden district. Safe among its neat Victorian houses with names like Glenloch or Sweetbriar Cottage, its gardens full of temperate English blooms, its Anglican church, Charles deposited Elizabeth and departed to spend several days at his own plantation. Elizabeth stayed at the august Hill Club: magnificent mountain views, immaculate service and bathrooms. But the day after Charles left, she did something unusual. She took a side trip which she arranged herself and of which she had not informed Charles. The trip had been suggested by Peter Williams, who assured her that it would be one of the finer experiences of her life.

It was a kind of pilgrimage she took, to a place known as Adam's Peak, a cone-shaped mountain a few miles to the southwest that was an object of respect to all the island's major religions. Her professional guide was a balding Sinhalese who wore European dress and, for propriety, brought along his sari-clad young wife, who spoke no English.

"My name," he said, "is Kulasinghe Buddararichchi. It is such a long journey, that name! Please, the British call me Mr. Rich." He smiled. "Perhaps it will bring me good fortune?"

They set off by chauffeured motor early in the afternoon, along a narrow earth road clinging to the hillsides and interrupted now and again by small villages of native huts and booths festooned with bunches of coconuts or bananas or piles of mangoes and papaws.

At one of these shops, Mr. Rich suggested a stop. "He is, I confess, a cousin," he said, with smile and gentle charm. "He will make tea for you, or perhaps you would prefer fresh coconut milk?" Mr. Rich's cousin fiercely chopped the green coconut with a machete, so that it became a cup, and she drank thus, realizing with surprise that it was the first time she had done so since she had come to Ceylon, though coconut palms surrounded her house.

"The people eat the meat of this fruit, you see," said Mr. Rich. "The coconut, it is their stable–staple!–food in the country. They use it for everything. Everything, you see?"

Elizabeth nodded sympathetically, unable to think of a response, feeling stupid about poverty, as though she had never seen it before.

"A European friend is joking with me once," continued Mr. Rich. "In his country, he is saying, a child asks, 'Mother, what are we having for dinner?' But in this country, he is saying, a child asks, 'Mother, are we *having* dinner?' "

Elizabeth smiled, embarrassed. "And yet they seem very happy," she said.

"Very content, very content," agreed Mr. Rich.

Elizabeth insisted on paying for her sustenance with such unknowing generosity of rupee that Mr. Rich's cousin smiled to split his face, murmuring over and over, *"Ayubowan. Ayubowan."*

As they reentered the motor, Elizabeth said, "I've heard that many times, of course, but what does he mean by it precisely? And why does he say it so *often?"*

"The exact translation is, 'May you live long,' " replied Mr. Rich in the manner of a schoolmaster. "It is like you say, 'God be with you,' which is precise meaning of 'good-bye.' It is a good omen for our trip, no? He knows we go on pilgrimage."

Arriving near Adam's Peak, Elizabeth was given simple accommodations in the government resthouse set among the forested foothills. She sat in the sunlight, watching dozens of hummingbirds whir and squeak at rhododendron blossoms. She dined and retired early because, at midnight, there was to be a knock at the door and tea to wake her for the beginning of her pilgrimage.

Adam's Peak is a modest but prominent mountain of perfect triangular shape among others more clumsily chopped. Near its summit is a depression in the rock shaped precisely like that of a bare foot, and the footprint is variously attributed: by the Christians to St. Thomas, by the Moslems to Adam, by the Hindus to Siva, and by the Buddhists to the Buddha himself. There are other such footprints in the world, other such places where all religions agree some vortex exists where man and god make contact, holy places where the infinite was in time and left its mark on space.

At Adam's Peak, pilgrims climb by night, for it is the dawn they await. Elizabeth found herself surrounded by a crowd of natives at the foot of a long flight of steps curling around and up the mountainside. The stone steps were narrow but well-lit by coconut-oil torches stuck in crevices or held by motionless, shaven, gentle-eyed monks in saffron robes who reminded her for some reason of a young monk who had once looked into her eyes while she was seated in the Napier—ah, yes, the day Ginny had first told her of Charles' infidelity.

The chain of pilgrims created a mood such as Elizabeth had never known. They started fatigued and overexcited, separate groups and individuals. Then the climb through the dark splashed by torchlight tamed and joined them all, and her to them. At resting places there were little shrines, and from their clothing the pilgrims tugged flowers to leave as offerings. Elizabeth wished for blossoms to strew, and other pilgrims gave them to her without her asking. She felt strangely exhilarated. A sense of order came upon her, of the kind that had ceased to exist in that world below.

All the talk was quiet, the faces gentle. As they neared the top, they could look down to see the winding chain of torches beginning to gutter back along their way. Here, at a height that began to seem enormous, the air was chill and clear. At the very top, on the shoulder of the triangular peak, everyone admired the footprint and then sat down. There were men selling tea that steamed, and the women wrapped their saris around their heads and their fingers around the brass cups. There were cool fruit and small cooked bananas and compact charcoal fires. Mr. Rich seated Elizabeth near one of the small fires and brought her refreshment.

To the east, dawn began, and as people watched, all of them in rows turning eastward, color grew in them, that of their exotic clothing, that of their burnished brown faces, and Elizabeth all in white with a dark gray cloak felt pale, not knowing that the firelit shining of the auburn in her hair was a thing of great beauty to them. To the east, dawn began, and all the people watched the world begin–the rose and gray and gold washing the sky toward blue, the stretch of land beneath, still dark, then dark blue, then green, and then suddenly, as the very tip of the sun's first rays began to reach the higher eastern hills, all tipped with gold, the crowd gave a great sigh and brought forth the sun, and some covered their eyes against the blinding, and others smiled.

"Turn now!" said Mr. Rich.

And with the rest of the crowd, as one being, she and Mr. Rich turned sharp round to look out due west, its visibility unexpected, the stars and the dark vanished unnoticed. Immediately beneath their mountain the land was still dark, with lights of houses glimmering. A little further and higher was the soft blue-gray of the mist, and then the hills, and then the sky, together making a spectrum of blues and grays and palest white. And there, cast against the backdrop of the mists, was a great, precisely pyramidal shadow, floating as solid as reality.

"It's the shadow of this mountain," said Elizabeth aloud. "Of Adam's Peak, where we are!"

She felt her breath short, and with the others she heard herself cry out, a small cry of the heart, and as the cry ran through the crowd, the shadow suddenly seemed to bob, once, twice, as though in reverence, so that one could not tell whether the crowd worshiped the shadow or the shadow them. And then it vanished.

The descent was easy and gentle. Mr. Rich remained silent. Elizabeth, who had felt transcendent, came down to earth. Once in the motorcar back to Nuwara Eliya, she dozed. At the entrance to the Hill Club, she thanked Mr. Rich quietly.

"It is, of course, a simple atmospheric trick." He paused, and in the dhoti which he had worn for the climb suddenly looked very un-English. "But we say the mountain pays homage in gratitude to God."

Elizabeth put her hand upon his arm, and there was that moment of closeness that exists between people who have shared.

"Ayubowan," she said, smiling, bobbing her head, fingertips touching in front of her chest.

"Ayubowan," replied Mr. Rich. "May you live long."

He turned to clamber back into the motorcar, and she to enter the open glass doors of the club, and then she heard his voice agitated and turned again to see him gesturing at her. "Ah, Mrs. Wingate! Mrs. Wingate! We are forgetting! Sorry, this bad manners. My tip? If you would be so kind, to tell Mr. Ashburn, the Secretary, don't you know, how much?"

Elizabeth told nothing of her adventure on Adam's Peak when Charles returned from the plantation. He was all talk of costs and hiring and the interruption to the tea picking and the lateness of shipments and the loss of whole families, indeed an entire small village, to the flu. When they motored north from Kandy and then down, down from the mountains to the flatlands and the ancient Ceylonese capital Anuradhapura, they passed funeral party after funeral party walking along the roadside, the monks in saffron robes beating drums, the reed flutes weeping, the women stoic. In the midst of all this, Elizabeth found that whatever she had experienced on Adam's Peak was too difficult to explain to Charles, no matter how important it might have been to her. One cannot make others, she realized, understand an experience. Charles, on the other hand, refrained from talking to her about the shudder that those funerals made his body and heart surrender.

To take in the sights of Anuradhapura, they spent several days.

Centuries ago, this had been the ancient capital of Ceylon, a city of some million people. Today's inhabitants were few, and most of the capital's domain was crumbling monument and jungle. Huge structures rose from the plain, earth and plants having turned them into hills. Blocks of hewn granite lay where they had fallen, deep in dried grasses. The former inner city was more intact. Domes still stood, Buddhas smiled, flowers were fresh on altars, monks filed quietly toward reliquaries, and one might still, as did the Wingates, turn a corner and find before them the huge stone trough from which thousands of monks had once taken their communal rice, now solitary, with only birdcalls to keep it company. Elizabeth saw the city not as time past, nor as time present, but as time future, and she hated it. One cannot make oneself, she thought, understand another's experience.

Only in one spot did she take pleasure. The heart of Anuradhapura was a bo tree, indeed the oldest tree in existence whose origin is known, for it grew from a slip planted by monks in the third century B.C., and that slip had been taken from the tree in northern India under which the Buddha had achieved enlightenment. The tree was enormous and alive. People came to it, and monkeys and birds were in it, and because it was the time of migrations, a spiral of yellow butterflies alighted on it for rest, and because it was cool in the heat of the day, ugly dogs panted in its shade. But it did not need animal life, for it had its own. At the slightest breeze the broad leaves of a bo tree, hanging lightly on long stems, rustle against each other, so that the bo tree is in soft and constant song. One cannot be unhappy near a bo tree, no matter how huge and ancient. Even Charles sat on the ground and enjoyed. Some of the monks sit there day after day after day (they say, year after year after year) learning to meditate upon the nothing that lies at the heart of the bo tree and of all living things.

For the journey into the heart of Wilpattu, the jungle where Charles was to hunt, the Wingates had to transfer first to a shooting brake and then to a bullock cart, for here were tracks, not roads. Jungle alternated with savanna, and there was no habitation, and whether the great canopy of trees screened out both sun and air or whether the water meadows let in sun and steam, one felt breathless and endangered. On the carpeting in the back of the bullock cart, the Wingates were jolted every moment. They sweated, and watched the water buffalo wallow in reed-filled lakes, the thick air making them feel that they too waded in water. They wiped their necks and faces with handkerchiefs and watched peacocks preen in clearings. For rest, they walked, stumbling in the rutted mud, and fled back to the cart and Charles' guns when a sudden leopard appeared on the trail and looked at them and walked away with the peculiar hunching gait of great cats.

In the evening light, they paused by a riverbank and watched a group of elephants which had carted lumber all day cumbersomely play as their mahouts washed them. Without remark, whatever breach had been between them so far on this journey healed itself, and they became companions.

The government resthouse lay beyond the jungle and near the ocean at the edge of dry scrub country. It sat on a lagoon where heron fished, surrounded by tall coconut palms, and morning and evening the breeze cooled them on its way to and from the sea. Elizabeth rested and read, enjoying the slow routine of the servants. Charles, each morning, went hunting with a paid guide and returned insect-bitten, filthy, exhausted, and laden with trophies. The district game warden, a Dane by the name of Carlson, lived near enough to visit for a drink. He had lived in Wilpattu doing one job or the other for nearly thirty years. His hair was bleached gray by sun and age and his face was a seamy yellow-brown. Tall, with old stringy muscles, he was thin with past malarial fevers. He showed Elizabeth the way to spot lagoon life by sitting motionless–the life in roots, water, and sand. He loved this kind of life, it seemed, without sentiment, sometimes crouching to enjoy it, other times wrenching it from hiding to display it for her interest and then discard it. There was something of the animal about him, thought Elizabeth, or of God.

The monsoon season was growing closer, and sometimes on the southeast horizon Elizabeth could see the giant tumbles of blue-black and white thunderheads gather in brilliant sunlight. They would draw closer during the day, stretching out a thin gray cover of humidity for the sky, but then they would draw back and sky and horizon would be blue again. They gave the sense of mild foreboding which the days before monsoon always bring, when one cannot tell whether one wishes or avoids the coming ruthlessness of rain. Charles fretted that the season was early and would ruin his hunting.

Carlson would not reassure him. "The natives say that the monsoon's like death." He laughed. "It'll come in its own good time, not yours, but it'll come!"

One morning shortly after Charles set out, Carlson arrived at the resthouse leading a string of ponies and accompanied by a handful of native assistants to invite Elizabeth to see a strange occurrence a few miles north along the coast.

"May be nothing much," he said curtly, "but I thought you might enjoy the ride. These things upset the natives, but they usually have some simple explanation. It's some kind of cave-in, or water hole, I can't quite make out which from what they say. But they say it's big and getting bigger, so I'd better take a look at it and let the office wallahs know before the bush telegraph has the natives here in thousands saying it's a sign of the power of God or the devil or something else. When something like this happens, they seem to come out of the ground!"

So the party set off northward through the dry scrub country, Carlson in the lead, Elizabeth sidesaddle, the native assistants strung out behind, the ponies head-down and chopping at the sandy earth with their hooves. Their route led them along the inland side of coastal bluffs which hid them from the cooling breeze of the ocean, and by ten o'clock, when they finally broke from the bluffs above their destination, Elizabeth thoroughly regretted the expedition. It felt more like a penance.

The sky was the color of staled milk after rotting cream has been scraped off: neither gray nor white nor blue, but something livid and sick. The little party seemed to have been placed inside an upturned bowl, damned to trace its circumference endlessly. They stood above a peninsula of land that stretched due west, low and flat, from the coastal escarpment. Under the grayish sky, the ocean was a plain gray sheet, a hospital corpse cover. Huge swells moved it sluggishly from the southwest and broke in long, elephantine combers on the beaches to the north and south as though the ocean were breathing, expelling. The peninsula was featureless save for the perfectly circular pond which was the object of their journey and lay directly ahead. It seemed a small and meaningless objective. One saw first the small clots of natives gathered around it, perhaps some fifty people in all, standing out like black sticks against the gray plain of sand and the gray loom of sea and sky. They too seemed small, or everything around them seemed larger and more ominous because of them, and Elizabeth shuddered with distaste. The whole expedition seemed pointless.

Down the sandy bluffs slid the ponies in showers of grit, but at least here there was a breeze to dry face and neck. The peninsula was more than a mile wide and so low that after leaving the escarpment one could neither see nor hear the ocean. There were the creaking and jangle of gear. There was the buzz of flies disturbed from the sand and seeking horse sweat. There was the hissing of sand grains lifted by the ponies' hooves and the low but steady wind. There was the crackling of dry leaves from trampled shrubs. No tracks led here, for there was need of none, and so each man made his own way toward whatever thing he sought on the featureless plain. Not all the ground was sand. The peninsula was a spit torn and worn from the escarpment over the centuries, with enough soil to give hold to the taproots of the scrub. The scrub itself seemed aged, crouched, watchful—a sacrificial vanguard sent to test, not to guarantee, the permanence of land. Sand flies crawled everywhere, seeking moisture in eye holes, ear holes, nose holes, mouth, as though the body were a keep for some treasure which the flies sought. They were the only living things the land produced. There was no reason for living things to be here under this wasteland sky, on this stale-milk earth.

The party on horseback dismounted at Carlson's command some hundred yards away from the nearest people in the circle around the water hole, next to a low small ridge topped with scrub to which the ponies could be tethered. From here they could see the edge of the hole—a side of sandy earth—but no water within it, and Carlson led Elizabeth nearer on foot. Suddenly a moan arose from the entire ring of natives, and those immediately in front started into life, some pointing, some stepping back, all with mouths open. Not a sigh, not a groan, not quite a word they uttered, this sound, and yet one could almost understand it, and it startled Carlson and Elizabeth, and they strode forward, and then, into the silence that followed the moan, Elizabeth spoke in a voice not loud but clear: "Name of God!" She had caught her first glimpse of the water.

The pond was by now much larger than when first reported to Carlson. Some hundred yards in diameter, it was an almost perfect circle, and it had been expanding steadily by eating away at the rim of sandy earth that confined it. As Elizabeth and Carlson drew near, the water surged up as from the bottom of a well or a blowhole in ocean rock, upward more forcibly at the center than at the sides, so that the water spread out in a wave pushing toward the sandy edges, which, when struck by the wave, were undermined and crumbled and collapsed into the water. The pond enlarged itself by some two feet all around while they watched, but did not overflow its banks, though flattened sand and the shape of runnels near them showed that it had done so previously. Very shortly the water subsided as silently as it had risen.

Carlson and Elizabeth moved closer, and even as they covered the few hundred feet between them and the hole, the water welled again, and this time the water at the center was or seemed briefly higher than the land, which unnerved the nearby Tamils enough to send them back toward the Europeans. Carlson, talking to them in their own tongue, turned back with them toward the ponies, so Elizabeth went on alone. She stopped some thirty feet from the edge, able to see the bottom of the hole for the first time, just as another welling took place. It was like a breathing, as quick down as up.

The great welling and unwelling of the leaden water made her aware of the fragility of the solid earth. Here at its center, the land was crumbling, undermined by some mysterious force so powerful that it could not be conceived. She looked down at the ground before she stepped on it, conscious of the soles of her feet, as though crumbling might begin around her any minute. It made one sense one's own solitariness; there could be no shelter.

The Tamils around the well shared Elizabeth's sense of the ominous. Very clearly the well inspired in them an awe which they were neither ashamed nor unaccustomed to showing, an excited awe, full of expectation. They knew the mysterious welling of the gray waters was alien and dangerous, but they accepted it, they even saluted it with their breath, as though it were another manifestation of something they had sought and seen before. Almost, it seemed to Elizabeth, their expressions said that this was another proof, and whatever the meaning of that strange "a-i-y-a-a-o-o-m-m" which their breaths sounded, she was religious enough to recognize it as something to do with God, even though she knew the Buddhists did not believe in God.

Nor did she, in any thoughtful way, believe in God, though at this moment the great well of water—which, even as she watched and thought and felt the low wind pluck the skirt at her ankles, now rose to consume still more circular feet of sandy soil and sank again—inspired her with a shudder at her own disbelief, which she recognized as superstition. It was not awe she felt. She sensed neither God nor the devil here. Rather, a metaphor. The sky, the earth, the welling of the waters to the upper air, there was something intellectual not emotional for her here. She felt puzzled, as though she had been given a picture which she had to study to understand.

Carlson was still busy giving orders to his assistants. Elizabeth realized that she had wandered a considerable distance from the low ridge, where natives were now moving among the scrub seeking sticks straight enough to use as markers by which to measure the hole's expanding width. She found her only remaining companion to be an aged, white-bearded, almost naked man with skin black as mahogany. He was a goatherd, perhaps a permanent wanderer in this wasteland, and his small collection of scrawny, dirty, fly-plagued beasts coughed around him, unalarmed, foraging with yellow teeth. Elizabeth turned away from him. She distrusted and detested goats, and so she began to return to her party on the ridge.

She had taken a single meditative step when a series of rapid events took place. First, there was a sharp, single shout from behind her, from some native on the other side of the hole. The cry had in it enough startlement to make her lift her head, giving her a glimpse of Carlson and his group frozen into alarm, turned toward her. Her head turned sharply, and her gaze caught on the face of the old goatherd some five yards to her right and facing the hole, and even as she looked, his expression changed from curiosity to wonder. At that same instant, as her heart gave its first adrenaline thump, she also heard something–something not loud but big. She knew at once what it was and turned to face it. A great hump of water had risen in the well, a hump so large that the center of the water was already higher than the edges of its well.

Her first glimpse froze it only in her mind. In reality, the water moved quickly, spreading outward as it mounted, blocking her view of the people on the other side as they turned to run, covering the lower portion of the sky. Before even she had time to feel terror, she too had turned to run, glimpsing again the old goatherd frozen motionless and somehow glad to face the great mound of water spreading with oily speed toward, up, and over the lip of land, inches, then more inches, then feet of water over the soil, a wave, waist-high, which caught Elizabeth in mid-stride, thumped the breath out of her and the legs from under her, and flung her forward and facedown into its own mass, tumbling her forward at its fringe as though she were flotsam at the very edge of the tide. Under the water her shoulder hit the ground harder than she had ever hit anything before. Her legs were twisted apart as if for rape, and sharp sand scraped into the left side of her face. She felt totally physically powerless for the first time in her life. She had no strength, no force, no breath–only the blazing of her mind with which to fight the water lifting, tumbling her, rolling her sideways.

Then the direction of her motion changed abruptly. There was a split second when the water hung suspended, she moving through it.

Her face was briefly uncovered to the gray sky, its eyes and mouth closed. Then the flow turned back, its recession as sudden and strong as its progress, as though it had been sucked from underground, its drag vicious and swift toward the great hole. Elizabeth felt the turn and the danger, and her arms reached out. And her hands did clutch something, something that she rolled over, something hairy and vile, something so vile that her hands would have recoiled had instinct not made them grasp it, so that she dug her fingers in and, because it did not move, found herself jerked violently around, so that now she faced the water streaming past her, and she lowered her face into the vile hairy mass, that she might not drown. At last the water vanished from her head and shoulders, that she might draw in a gasp of air before her head fell forward again, even as the water left her chest, her hips, her thighs, her draggled legs, rejecting her as too slow for its mad rush back into its hole.

They reached her within a few seconds, splashing from dry land in great leaps across the flooded plain. From their viewpoint, a great wave of water had spread from the hole across the flatland equally in all directions and then been gulped back as quickly as hounds to hell. The whole event had been a matter of seconds, and the water's residue was already vanishing into the thirsty earth as they reached her body. She was lying half on top of a clump of spiky, stubborn shrubs. Their roots had been bared by the flood, but they still clung, and their branches had ripped into Elizabeth's clothing with such force that the men could scarcely loose them and eventually tore off her skirt. She lay prone, head lower than waist, and face still buried in what had saved her: a goat whose dead body (its head grotesquely angled) had caught around the shrubs and in turn been caught by her. On the surface of that well of water another goat was briefly visible, drowning, and that was all.

Around the well the people began to reshape their broken circle, some stopping in their flight, some picking themselves up from where they had been flung, all beginning to move away from the sudden might. Quickly Carlson lifted Elizabeth and carried her at a stumbling run back to the safety of the ridge. One of his assistants ran behind, carrying the remnants of her skirt. She regained consciousness, and they began the hasty motions of comfort: the chatter, the flask of brandy, the smoothing back of tangled hair from face and forehead, as though they had seen such scenes in moving pictures and learned the role.

Elizabeth's neck was sore. Her left cheek was scraped raw. A large bruise was already coming visible on her right shoulder. There were no spare clothes and no blanket. Carlson collected a sari from one of the native women and his own shirt stinking with sweat and wrapped her in them. Already shivering with shock, she could not stay here even to rest, and so Carlson loaded her onto a pony and headed back toward the resthouse.

Elizabeth did not begin to think or feel until they were once more at the top of the slope leading from the peninsula, concealed from the blank indifference of the bowl of gray ocean and land. The first emotion to absorb her was plain social embarrassment stemming from the awareness that she was riding half-naked between Carlson's hairy arms with his bare chest pressed against her to hold her up. Impropriety and vulgarity were the newborn's first concepts. She thought: I have made a complete fool of myself! She thought of the goatherd who had stood even nearer than her to the water, and only when she told Carlson did he realize that the old man had vanished with the wave.

"They will have to stay there until we get a fence put up, a guard." Carlson could not recollect the goatherd, but it was he who delivered the old man's eulogy: "I knew something like this would happen."

20

At the resthouse they put her to bed with hot tea and stationed a native on the veranda to move the old-fashioned punkah in her bedroom, so that the sluggish air stirred the spiderwebs in slow waves. Elizabeth lay still and watched a gecko flicker its tongue along the walls. She appraised her accident. Bruised and sore, she also felt calm, as though something long awaited had at last arrived and was over: the impending, having happened, has no more strength to terrify. Survival brings its own strength: consciousness of the presence of existence. Her mind, restless as the little lizard on the wall, insisted on the mundane rather than the transcendent, until she rose and dressed and ordered that fresh fruit and tea be brought upon the veranda, then found that in her freshness even the food and drink seemed images of God.

She watched piles of monsoon clouds at the horizon rise and shift. She needed someone to talk to. She wished she had not dismissed Carlson, who had reluctantly set off to inform the district officer of the danger of the hole. Civilization has its uses, she thought. It would put a fence around the danger. It would keep people away from risk.

The day burned toward sunset, and Elizabeth ordered an oil lamp lit early, for Charles was almost late enough to create anxiety. He appeared out of the jungle, however, before the edge of night. He was miserable. His clothes were bloodied by his kill, and great red welts and a fierce itch wrought upon his arms by some tropic nettle made him so uncomfortable that even as he marveled at Elizabeth's wounds and listened to her story he was demanding calamine lotion and a cool bath. On the veranda at last with whiskey, they did without lamps, to avoid insects, and Charles' arms and hands glimmered white like those of a ghost. Elizabeth's shoulder grew painful with the night, and she took to stroking herself softly.

"I think we should leave tomorrow," she said. "If you've had enough of hunting, I would rather be back in civilization."

"Of course," murmured Charles, thinking she meant they ought both see a doctor.

His mood was strange. On the one hand he wanted to be practical and sensible and reassuring. On the other his remarkably unpleasant day left his mind uneasy at depths greater than those of the proper husband. One cannot hunt in the jungle for days on end without paying some price: its great silences and shriekings, its tricks with direction, the hold of its upper net upon the sun, its offer of aid and hindrance to hunter and hunted alike, as though both were equal. The wound it had given him today, a poison in its and his system, had made him feel too old for it.

"Actually," he said, "I've had enough of this trip altogether. Shall we cut it a bit short? Go home?"

"I would like that," said Elizabeth. "That's what I had in mind. I thought we might still visit Peter–he won't mind if we are a day or two early–but then I should rather like to get back."

They sipped their drinks in silence. The giant monsoon clouds were closer tonight, spread across half the western horizon and lit by huge sheets of lightning. For the first time they could dimly hear their thunder, a faint sound that reminded Elizabeth of the sound the natives had made around the hole: "a-a-a-i-y-o-o-m-m!" The palm fronds stirred in bursts as though someone shook them in the darkness.

The Wingates had been fortunate, living without serious illness in a land where almost everyone contracted at least malaria or typhoid or a brush with something more exotic: smallpox, sandfly fever, dhobie itch, dengue. The soldiers called cholera "Corporal Forbes" familiarly and to stop all diarrhea drank a mixture of opium and chloroform bottled by the Army and Navy Cooperative Society. Housewives consulted Dr. Moore's *Family Medicine,* first published in 1874, and did whatever it recommended, even if they knew better. Officialdom would keep them safe from risk. One did not feel a right to life there, especially after the Great Flu.

Out of the human silence, Charles spoke softly. "I don't want you to die."

Elizabeth was startled. Death was not a subject Charles ever discussed.

"And I don't want you to die, my dear," she replied, placing her hand on Charles' arm, then quickly removing it as he winced. "But it's not something I like to think about often. It seems so long we've been together now."

"I do," said Charles quietly. "Think about it, I mean. My own, mostly."

Elizabeth was surprised enough to lack immediate response. She could not very well gather him to her bosom murmuring, "There, there," and yet, she knew, the statement was extraordinary for Charles: a confession.

Charles thought of the folio of dyings which plagued his sleep, and he stood on the verge of admitting his terror. But Elizabeth spoke hastily. "There's no point in worrying about it. It'll come in its own good time." She was trying to shield him from embarrassment. It showed how far they had grown apart: that tendril of communication from him, that snip of truism from her.

She sensed what she had done and tried to retrieve affection. "They say it all gets easier when one is older. I never thought of it at all, when I was younger. They say you don't think about it when you get nearer to it."

To reveal himself, Charles needed more coaxing than that, and yet he persisted after a silence, "I know it's an extraordinary thing to say." He paused for a suck at his pipe, which had gone out. "But do you believe in God, the afterlife, all that sort of thing?"

The chair creaked as he wrestled for matches in his pocket.

"That certainly is an extraordinary question for a husband to ask a wife," said Elizabeth, embarrassed. "Surely after all these years one should know."

"Anyway," said Charles. She watched his face in the light of the flaring match, eyes cast down toward the bowl of his pipe and therefore hidden from her.

"I suppose I do," she replied.

"I saw a baby drown a couple of years ago, in Jaffna. Slipped off the boat in the surf." He drew on his pipe again. "Parents made no attempt to save it, just let it go. The ADM was so angry he wanted to have them up on a murder charge. They said its time had come. I suppose they grieved, but they didn't do anything."

"Nobody worried about the goatherd," said Elizabeth suddenly.

A long silence fell between the two. Charles interrupted it: "I hope you won't go first, I hope I won't go first."

Elizabeth started to her feet. "Shall we dress for dinner?" she said abruptly. "There's no sense dwelling upon it."

They went inside and gave orders for a meal and changed into clothes uncomfortable enough to impress the servants and the jungle, and they spoke of other things and slept soundly that night, because they were both very tired. The next day they gave orders for the bullock cart, said farewell to a sympathetic Carlson, and repeated the trek through the jungle, arriving at the railroad line in time to take the evening train to Negombo, where they stayed overnight, feeling comfortably surrounded. Charles' arms were furiously itchy, and Elizabeth's face blue with bruise, so after breakfasting in their room they visited the doctor, who was Dutch and gave them heartiness and embrocations. They wandered through the town, one of the early Portuguese settlements, and they sought shelter from the sun inside a Catholic church, which lay within yards of the mangrove-fringed lagoon, convenient for worshipers who arrived by fishing boat: solid, old, dusty, very large, very European, except for the sand on its floors. As usual when with Charles, Elizabeth made no devotions, and they sat to rest in a pew and admired the carvings and the crucifix. The confessionals stood empty.

From this haven too, Elizabeth started, as she had from that offered her by Charles the night before. It has, she thought to herself, too much of the relic about it. And they returned to the hotel and waited in their room until informed that the motor had arrived. Carried to Williams' plantation, they offered their consolations afresh to the new widower, told their own tales of adventure, and for that evening skittered across the surface of things comfortably enough.

Elizabeth did only one odd thing. Williams found her in the study before dinner, a copy of D. H. Lawrence's *New Poems* in her hand.

"I thought I lent that to you last month, did I not?"

"I remembered something from it. I was thinking of my adventure, yesterday. Listen: 'Are you willing to be made nothing?/dipped into oblivion?/If not, you will never really change.'"

"A very proper Christian sentiment."

"That's what it felt like, being dipped into oblivion. Exactly."

"And now you wonder if you have changed."

"And now I hope that I have changed." She smiled.

21

Next morning, in distress from the stinging of his arms, Charles decided to drive to Colombo for the day so that he might see his own doctor. He would not go on to Mount Lavinia, he would return that night, and Elizabeth was to stay with Peter Williams, resting for the day from her own wounds. After Charles' departure, she and Williams strolled in the cool clean air of the foothills. His bungalow was on the side of a hill, facing a spur that overhung the flatlands to the sea, and they walked across the dried golden grasses to see the view. It was the site of Mary's grave, a drying mound of earth.

"Mary liked to walk here," he said. "If she left the house."

"Did she suffer greatly, when she was ill?"

He gave her an inappropriate smile. "No more than usual, I think. She died three days after getting sick. Half the house servants were down with it. She felt a little dizzy, she said, that evening, and woke up to be sick in the night and had a fever, and then she just grew worse. I took care of her. She just stopped breathing. I was sitting there across the room. She just stopped. She never tried, I think." He shuddered. "I have no *time* for death just now."

He spoke flatly. Elizabeth saw asceticism in his face. He seemed not to need sympathy, and she was glad of that. Their exchanges had always tended to be bone-bare; pretense bored them both.

"You seem more tired than mournful," she said.

"I'm not mournful," he agreed. Then he looked up from the grave at her. "I'm free." He laughed. "I'm better off without her."

As though he had splashed water in her face, she withdrew her arm from his and looked at him. "You didn't love her."

"There are circumstances in which love is present but irrelevant. I took care of her. I cared for her. We had not really liked each other for years."

"One never knew."

"Why should one? It was nobody's business but our own. I stuck by her. I did my duty. She was my wife."

He paused and they walked on again. He watched the grass beneath his feet, and spoke his thoughts: "I think now that was wrong. I should have left her years ago." The words were relentless but scarcely cold. "With most people one can live because one knows they will change. One knows they may be irritable this week, but not next, in a bad mood this month, but better next. But not Mary. She never changed. She never would have changed. Nothing would change her."

"We haven't seen much of her in recent years, but I had no idea . . . You make her sound terrifying. I never realized. She didn't look terrifying."

"Because she was small and quiet, and lately grew fat. She never attacked, you see. She drained." He gave his usual laugh in the face of seriousness.

"You mean boredom?"

"The boredom was bad enough, but one gets used to that. I had my books." They had wandered without thinking away from the grave and stood to admire the view, but Williams' eyes saw elsewhere. "The fear was worse," he said softly. "The fear of being drained. We scarcely spoke of late."

"We heard rumors."

"Mary gave up. She gave up getting angry. She gave up going out. She gave up reading even. She gave up everything except sitting there, and sometimes she would cry. It used to be when she cried I could always do something about it. But not lately. I used to sit there across the room, reading, and she would sit there with tears in her eyes, looking at me, and I just fought to keep my mind on the page. She blamed me. She thought there was still something I could do. But not anymore. No matter what I did for her, it was never enough. She became like a bottomless well. I could have thrown myself into it and it would not have been enough. There are some people you can never do enough for. You have to stop sometime or they'll drag you down."

"You sound ruthless."

"I don't think you really mean that." He turned and looked at her with sharp blue eyes, seeing the sky beyond her. "You must realize that I didn't know any of this to start with. Mary and I married in the spirit of gentleness." He barked a laugh. "Like two silly children, to shield each other from the world! She knew I was different. I knew she was . . . melancholy. We began with a lot of tenderness, even some joy that first year." He shrugged and turned toward the bungalow. "Then it all went away. You try all the little things you think will make a difference, you know–trips, and treats, little things. Just as though we were children. But it didn't make any difference. She wouldn't change. Ruthless?" Again he turned to face Elizabeth, and this time his short laugh was bitter. "Do you think a man weeps willingly? I wept those years ago. And that didn't *change* things. It didn't make Mary a survivor. She didn't die of flu really. She died because she just gave up living."

There was silence between the two of them.

"Ruthless?" said Williams again. He sounded angry. "You haven't seen a ruthless person until you've seen someone who simply wills herself to sit there. I sometimes think she was very, very angry with the world for not being the way she wanted it to be and that she took all that anger and just poured it into sitting there, just as a child will." He paused again, looking at the ground. "But perhaps you understand. There's some of that in you, too."

"In me!"

"I suppose in all of us." He looked at her casually. "You know that Charles carries on with other women, don't you?"

Surprised into truth, she nodded.

"I thought so," he said. "And yet you do nothing about it, do you? You just sit there and feel miserable with the world."

Now Elizabeth was angry and therefore stiff. "You have no right to discuss my marriage like that!"

"I suppose not," he said indifferently. "And yet it's not all that important, you know." He gave her an amused glance. "You make a great deal of your marriage, as though it were bedrock. But it isn't. A husband and a wife are no more than incidents in each other's lives."

"What am I expected to reply to remarks like that?"

"Nothing." Suddenly Peter looked extremely tired, his face down and drawn, his voice softer. "Someday you will have to face the fact that you cannot simply turn your life over to another for safekeeping, as Mary did. You know I want you, don't you? That I'd take you on almost any terms? But not for safekeeping, not so you can hide, not till you face the real cause of whatever's wrong in your so-called life." Again he was angry.

"And that is?" asked Elizabeth icily. She had no rules for responding to a declaration of love like this one.

"You know that as well as I do." His tone was near contempt. "It's in the Confession, isn't it? You say it every Sunday: 'We have left undone those things which we ought to have done. And we have done those things which we ought not to have done. And there is no health in us.' It's not that hard to understand. You're a woman of enough beauty, sufficient wealth, and unusual intelligence. What do you do with your days?"

"I do what every normal woman does."

"You wait for your husband to come home."

"That's not true!"

"What else?" Now he mocked her. "Sew? Complete your butterfly collection? Borrow books from me which you then insist were not as good as you had hoped? You're worth more than that, and you know it."

"I'm an ordinary woman! I have no special talents. I—"

He interrupted. "I'm not going to be trapped again into arguing a woman into thinking better of herself than she wants to."

"I asked for no such argument."

"You didn't?"

He was weary again. They began to stroll back toward the bungalow, to let their passions lie and cool. The thin dry grass stretched around them.

"What will *you* do now?" She meant the question as a challenge, for she was now angry with him.

But he had done with passion and used the statement to bring them back to the mundane. "After the plantation?" He looked around him. "There are a dozen things I'd rather do than this. I've never been free till now." Then he laughed at himself. "You see, the original sin is in us all—the power to make excuses. Perhaps I'll become a boarder at the Buddhist monastery."

She stopped walking and looked at him. "I believe you may," she said.

"I haven't decided yet whether to stay in Colombo or to go Home. It would be very different, being Home. One shouldn't refuse the world, at least until one has grappled with it." He laughed again. "There is a quotation famous in the Fabian Society, you know. I don't know who said it first—either the Webbs seriously or Shaw in fun, I should imagine. 'A railway guard is the most enviable of men. He has authority, and he is responsible to a government.' That's it, I shall become a railway guard."

"On the Brighton line?"

What could be so funny about the Brighton line, neither knew, but they broke into peals of laughter and took each other's arms as they walked on to the bungalow. They were taking afternoon tea when Williams' motor returned with a message from Charles: that the doctor required him to stay in town for treatment, that he would expect her in Mount Lavinia tomorrow, that he sent his apologies to Peter.

Peter and Elizabeth seemed unable to look at each other. Attuned, they made their faces blank. He would not choose for her; she gave no sign either way.

He left her alone after tea on the excuse of work. She thought: to give me time to make up my mind. Such a minor thing to Charles, she thought. Fidelity. And yet I can't, can I? She thought: I am not myself today after my accident. But I welcomed that, I wanted change. In the back of her mind: I want love. She sat in the shade and looked down the spur to Mary Williams' grave across the wind-combed grasses. We could make it up to each other for what we have lost. If he says he needs me, she thought, and did not complete the thought, feeling grief either for him or herself or for what was past or passing.

They were both quiet at dinner, sensing the tremor of sensual expectation. When she glanced at Peter, Elizabeth thought: This is the first man other than Charles.

Eventually she looked up to find him motionless, looking at her with an air of great fatigue. "Has it occurred to you that Charles left us here alone so that you would choose?"

She put her knife and fork down carefully, and for a moment did not reply. "Charles does not decide whether or what I will choose."

He drank slowly but deep from his wineglass, looking at her.

"It is not the right time, is it? Or place."

In agreement, she shook her head. "No," she said very quietly.

22

Epiphanies, by definition, are rare. Elizabeth and Charles knew that they had changed without having much idea as to when. Each blamed the other a little, but in fact they had changed so much that they found blame no longer important. And because they were civilized, they could proceed to admit the breakdown of their marriage without anger. Instead, they parleyed.

Abbuhamy unwittingly began the parley. Abbuhamy was now a rich man by native standards, and since the coming absence of the Wingates in England offered him the chance at one last skim off the household accounts, he had decided to retire. He would like to leave, he told Elizabeth, upon their return from Great Britain.

"We shall be very sorry to lose you, Abbuhamy," she said graciously, for one does not reveal surprise to the servants. "Mr. Charles will be most distressed. Leave it to me to break the news to him, will you?"

Alone, Elizabeth walked backward and forward across the carpet of her bedroom, thinking rapidly. Her steamship tickets lay in the glove drawer, and she took them out for study. Then she rang the bell and asked Abbuhamy to send Nanny to her.

"Do you think Ravenscroft would accept Jennifer a year earlier than planned, Nanny? Should we be able to get her in?"

"She's not six, Mrs. Wingate!"

"I know she's not six. Will they take her anyway?"

London's quick wits stood Mabel Greggs in good stead. She guessed at once that a permanent move from Ceylon was in the wind.

"It depends," she said cautiously. Her forehead and cheeks turned red with the strain of thinking fast.

"On what?"

"If I were to say a word . . ."

"Of course you will. We're thinking of staying longer in England, you see. I would of course see that you are well settled."

"Or better still," Nanny said slowly, "if I were to stay on with Jennifer at Ravenscroft . . . So that she wouldn't be a bother, you see, because I'd be there if she needed me." She looked at Elizabeth shrewdly. "If you were to say a word, I'm sure they'd give me my old job back."

Elizabeth recognized bargaining when she saw it. "We could even keep on your salary."

Mabel looked discomfited.

"As a teacher, of course, not just a nanny."

Mabel's brow cleared. "I think we might be able to arrange something," she said. "Jennifer'll not be that much younger, after all, only a year and a bit. And with me to take care of her, well then?"

"Shall I write to the headmistress?"

"I should leave it till we get there, if I were you. Better done face-to-face, things like that, aren't they?"

The two women smiled at each other.

"Leave it to me to tell Mr. Wingate," said Elizabeth, and they proceeded to discuss the complexities of getting completely packed up in the remaining three weeks. The new plans had to be explained to Jennifer, who accepted them without demur once told she could take all her doll collection with her, this way, instead of leaving most of it behind.

"But don't say anything to Daddy," adjured Elizabeth. "It's my surprise, and I must tell him myself."

She summoned Abbuhamy again and spoke to him standing near the window against the sunlight, where he could not see her face. "How long would it take, do you think, to pack up everything in this house?"

Abbuhamy was a Londoner too. "Three month," came his unhesitating answer.

"If you do it in three," said Elizabeth, who understood native promises well, "you shall have a bonus. In two, a bigger bonus. In four, smaller. If I tell you exactly what to do before I leave, can you get it done?"

Abbuhamy was all smiles. "Very well indeed, madam, very well!"

"With Mr. Charles to supervise you."

Abbuhamy's expression faltered, but the deal was struck. "Mr. Charles is staying behind for a while?"

"Mr. Charles will be staying behind for a while."

Chance and will combine; we act and are acted upon, we ignore some opportunities but seize others. Whatever web of circumstance from the past few weeks had brought Elizabeth to decisiveness, the choice as to what she was about to do was hers alone.

The house already seemed empty. The rooms were beautiful, but this, and this, could be sold, and that could go to the Hilliards, and young Prentice would probably be glad to take the bedroom suite. English servants again! She sighed with relief, surprising herself by the first burst of excitement at the prospect of going Home. She wandered down to the summerhouse to visit her Buddha. The old, deep scar was still in the surface of the floor, and the quicklime needed freshening. How different gardening will be in England, she thought.

She remembered very well that other day in the summerhouse when Ginny had first angered her with Charles' infidelity. Today she felt sad that she would make him pay for what he could not help. She shrugged and planned her strategy. He would give up Ceylon: his boredom, Jennifer's well-being. But she must ease into the subject, get him to think that her idea was his brilliant solution.

However, it is not easy to be new overnight. Because they still did not know each other, Elizabeth and Charles could still exchange the gift of surprise. That evening after dinner when they sat in the drawing room to coffee and brandy, he was in a subdued mood and wanted to read. He had removed his jacket and folded back his shirtsleeves, for his arms still itched unendurably at the contact of cloth. But even vulgar as this, she thought, he is a handsome man. His hands were as powerful as ever, though the skin had aged to show the veins underneath. His habits—that way of stuffing the pipe, even the catarrhal cough—were familiar enough.

She began her campaign. "I've been thinking about whether it would be a good thing to start Jennifer in school a little earlier than we had planned," she said.

"Oh?" he said. "Isn't she a bit young to worry about that yet?"

"The Warrens have sent young Arthur off, and he's not much older than Jennifer."

Charles looked at her steadily over the top of his spectacles. "He's a good six, isn't he?" he asked. "And will be seven soon enough. Almost a full year older than she, isn't he?"

"Ten months," she said reluctantly. "It's just that there isn't much left for her in Ceylon. We shall have to go to the bother of finding a governess for her out here for just a year. I thought it might be better . . ."

Charles was still looking at her expressionlessly, and she listened to herself trail off. There was a moment's silence.

"You want to stay in England," he said factually. "Sell up here and not come back." As so often before, she had underestimated him.

"Yes," she said, her hands open and helpless on her lap, surprised into the truth as simply as she had been by Peter Williams.

As Charles cared less about Elizabeth, he also cared less about being the ideal husband, and so he was more often right about her. He had tried at the resthouse to reestablish some recognition of closeness, but now he did not care enough to persevere. "Does Williams have anything to do with this?"

"No," she said, as simply as she had said yes. And then she saw passivity falling upon her again and stood to shake it off. "Give me a cigarette." He offered her a Sobranie. She took it and the matches and lit it for herself.

"Would you like a whiskey?" he asked.

"Yes," she said, and walked over to the sideboard to pour for herself a glass of Glenlivet Malt, which went smoothly down her throat.

Having half-risen to get her the drink, Charles sank back and watched her silently. Other friends than the Pearsalls had left permanently for Home, and the subject had been at the edges of their conversation since November. He had no reluctance, one way or the other. There would do him as well as here. He did not believe her about Williams, but that was another matter for another time. He was tired, listless. He felt besieged: by the plantation, his sore arms, his wife, his life. He was reading Tolstoy in search of companionship, and he wanted to get back to his reading. "It will take me too long for us to leave at once," he said quietly. "Six months, perhaps. I shall have to come back in the autumn. I shall have to tell Mallory-Watson. We have to find someone who can afford to buy the telephone company."

It was her turn to look steadily at him. She spoke from across the room, looking unusually desirable in green satin, high color, and lamplight. "I want to go by myself," she said. "With Jennifer and Nanny."

"I see," he said gently.

"Williams has nothing to do with it."

"I have booked a suite."

"I shall move Nanny in with us."

"You've spoken to Nanny?"

"It's all arranged. She will be at Ravenscroft to take such care of Jennifer as is needed. At our expense."

"It's all arranged," he said, and lifted a smile and eyebrow in ironic tribute. He was forty-seven, she thirty-seven. They had been married for fourteen years.

"Would you like a whiskey?" she asked, and poured a glass for him and brought it over.

"I suppose it will be better for Jennifer," he said.

"It won't be a long separation—six months, you say?"

"Yes, at most." He was surprised. Moments before, he had faced the end of his marriage and felt blank. He did not now feel relieved to know he had misunderstood.

Her hands, against her will, began to shake, and she placed her glass of whiskey carefully on the table. She felt a need to weep but would not. "Much has happened in the last five years," she exclaimed, and walked away from him toward the windows, where the dark stretched from the veranda. The room was stifling despite the ceiling fans. "I need time, Charles. I *can't* stay here. I *have* to get away, from everything."

He looked at her back, knowing she was about to cry.

"Surprisingly enough, I understand," he said cheerfully.

"Then leave me alone, would you?" she said roughly.

"I should rather like to continue with my Tolstoy," he said.

"Then please excuse me," she replied, and left the drawing room without looking at him.

That night both lay sleepless in their beds. Charles read Tolstoy and sipped his whiskey and rubbed his eyes under his spectacles. Elizabeth sat by her window, watching the fantastic display of lightning from the nearing clouds, their thunder now bold as artillery across the ocean water. She went to look again at the steamship tickets, tapping them slowly against the back of her hand and staring at her reflection in the mirror. It is Charles' money that paid for them, she was thinking.

Once asleep, they both slept soundly. They did not hear the monsoon's arrival, sweeping across the ocean like a waterfall, crashing onto the beach, the summerhouse, the palm trees, Jennifer's tricycle left outside, the tiles of the mansion roof. The sun did not shine next morning, and the rain brought the illusion of coolness, and so one felt relief. They sat to breakfast as they had these many years of residence in the Wingate home, served by a placid Abbuhamy, watching the heavy rain trail its folds across the ocean and the garden. The sky but not the light was gray. The world was full of motion, shoots of fresh green already visible in the muddy garden, a quickening upon the world. They felt no boredom today, and little soothing from custom. They felt the need to talk even while they wished they did not have to.

Charles twice sent Abbuhamy to the kitchen to have it produce bacon correctly cooked. Then he abruptly dismissed him, and even before the servant had left the veranda, he spoke to Elizabeth hastily, as though he had to seize the single moment or lose the time and courage together–a timidity of marriage, when he knew how to hurt and did not do so. "What are your plans?" he said, and cleared his throat. "In London, I mean."

Looking out upon the grounds, the summerhouse, the rain, Elizabeth seemed to be trying to hear the ocean. "We shall stay with my parents, I imagine," she said coolly.

"I shall have Mallory-Watson place a thousand pounds in our account at Coutts for you to draw on."

"You are very generous."

"We have more money than we need."

"I can't imagine what I shall spend it on."

"Having your hair cut? Paris fashions?"

She scrutinized him for sarcasm, but he was ingenuous and nervous and seemed of goodwill. "There will be Jennifer's school fees, her uniforms, whatever," she said.

He nodded, and they sat musing as on quiet mornings past.

"It will be such a very new world to go back to," she said, and then, seizing a moment as hastily as had he, "Do you still care for me?"

He looked not at her but at his pipe, and took in a deep breath through his nostrils as his face expressed–doubt? surprise? the need to disappoint, regretfully? "I don't know," he said slowly. "We shall have to see, shan't we?"

She might then have spoken hastily, but did not. She might have wept, but this was not a moment for high emotion. Neither she nor Charles imagined that her question had offered the prospect of reconciliation; it had been a factual inquiry, such as a police detective might have made, and his answer mirrored it in truthfulness.

He continued when she stayed silent, "We seem to have reached a pause. In our marriage, I mean. Between the acts, sort of. Of course I care for you. You are my wife and always will be."

"There is that," she said, and one could not tell whether her tone was that of rue or amusement.

"Apart from love," he said, "one gets used to each other."

"Is that enough?"

"Williams would give you more–"

"It isn't a matter of Peter Williams."

"I couldn't very well blame you, if it is."

"It isn't." She spoke harshly, and this brought a pause which might have ended it, had she not spoken again. "I've become greedy, like everyone else. It's the modern way. There has to be more to life, and to me, than I will ever find out this way." She gestured around her at rich and tropic comfort.

Their conversation took on irony, of which both were vaguely aware. As their marriage broke, they were for the first time communicating each to each as adults: hesitant, staccato, but truthful, as though there were no more roles to play and the rules had let them down.

With the sensation that hidden wings beat the air around his ears, Charles asked, "And you? Do you still care for me?"

She looked at him. His face was for a moment terrifyingly young and open, and what she felt was a rush of maternal caring with which she would at some other time have found it easy to blind herself and him, and for a moment she was tempted. But there was bleakness in her. Like the waters which had overwhelmed her on the peninsula, there was an indifference to individuality brought on by her pursuit of some greater goal.

"It's no use," she said, and turned her eyes away, leaving his face to reassemble itself in privacy. She had the courage to cease. She could not fill him up with explanation.

"You want simply to postpone everything," he said roughly.

"Everything about us. An armistice."

"Life doesn't allow postponements." His voice began to rise, reflecting the rising anger within him. "You can't put me on the shelf."

She rose from her chair, not looking at him. "If we are going to trade truisms about Life!"

He reached up and seized her by the arm. "Sarcasm is not right, you fool. Sit down!"

She jerked her arm away and stepped out of reach, to stand rubbing the forearm where he had grabbed her, and to stare at him. "I shall do what I like," she said, her voice low with fury.

"With my money," he counterattacked.

She left the veranda. Both right, each felt the other wrong. They did not speak intimately again before the ship sailed. For now, there was nothing more to say.

23

June 1919

A little less than three weeks later, it was raining again when Charles came to see them off on the *Oronsay*. He looked small and very wet under the umbrella far below them. The many-colored streamers were quickly soaked and broke in sodden clumps of each other's weight, long before the line of water between hull and dock began to widen. Jennifer saved Charles and Elizabeth embarrassment by refusing to let them share a single strand alone. The final bells rang. The ship's whistle blew. The last gangplank rattled down onto the dock. The engines rumbled into life to help the tugs. The gap widened. Charles looked forlorn, waving and smiling to his wife and daughter. Elizabeth fled to their cabin in tears.

That night Nanny took Jennifer to the first sitting, while Elizabeth dressed with special care, applying cosmetics. Nanny and Jennifer arrived back shortly before she finished, and to avoid their company she went to the lounge for a drink before the chimes sounded. The doors were open to a hot, damp breeze which fluttered the leaves of the potted palms and dulled the gilt of the mirrors but smelled salty and bracing. She was acquainted with some of the other passengers in the lounge, but she merely nodded politely and kept her eyes to her drink and the table. She was thus taken by surprise when Peter Williams stood in front of her. "Good evening, Elizabeth."

"Peter! What are you doing here?"

He in turn was taken by surprise. "I managed a booking. I told Charles. A fortnight ago. Surely he told you?"

"I hadn't seen you . . . You told Charles?"

"He did not mention it?"

They looked at each other in search of implications.

Williams gave his short, barking laugh. "Have I underestimated the husband?" he said lightly. "And may I sit down?"

She did not reply, and he stood with his hand on the back of a chair while they looked at each other. She grew flustered. "I'm not sure."

"So far I am guilty only in intent–not the public eye." Amused, he gestured at the quiet lounge. She gave a nod which he took as assent and sat down. Her color heightened.

"What did you think when I didn't appear to say good-bye?"

"I didn't think about it."

"You thought about it."

"I thought . . . you had said . . . you would leave it up to me."

"Not entirely. That's not how the war between the sexes works."

"Charles . . ."

"I'm not interested in Charles. Or what Charles did, or why he did it."

"I want to stay your friend."

"That's not possible. Not yet."

"You'll have to excuse me . . ." She gestured as if to leave.

"A coward as well as a liar?"

"You choose the strangest words to woo a woman."

"I'm not wooing. I'm not an infant. Nor are you."

She looked at him in panic. They were so intent on each other that both were startled when someone addressed them. "Ah, these shipboard romances!" It was the voice of the witty Ruth Anscombe. "So quick to bloom, so soon to die! Elizabeth! Mr. Williams! How good to see friendly faces! Dick will be with us soon, but I couldn't wait for him. May I join you? Elizabeth, I've been to see the purser and we are seated at the same table, isn't that nice? And you are with us too, Mr. Williams, so you will have plenty of time to advance your cause!" She giggled with delight. "Just wait till I tell Charles!"

"Charles already knows," said Williams, standing to seat Mrs. Anscombe and waving to the waiter.

"Shocking thing!" protested Ruth. "These modern marriages! The war has made us all immoral and wicked!"

"There was wickedness before the war," said Elizabeth levelly.

"I expect you're right," said Ruth Anscombe, discomposed by memory. "But it wasn't such fun as now, was it?"

The waiter and Dick Anscombe arrived simultaneously, so that Elizabeth and Peter were drawn slowly into society. They dined seated next to each other and stayed with the party afterward, leaving Elizabeth briefly safe from decision. The presence of the Anscombes inevitably made her think back to the dinner party before the war, when she had tried to deal with Charles by indirection. She detested the Anscombes: the complacent husband, the wife on the prowl, stalking Peter right now, almost certainly. But she took their jokes about her solitariness with good humor.

Elizabeth's feelings during that dinner and its aftermath were those of high excitement. She had made her decision about herself and Peter, but she had not expected to be so soon in the conveying it. She accepted extra drinks and grew gay, and then, later, used the need for fresh air as excuse to walk alone upon the deck. The polished wood shone wet under the lights, as it had when she had left Tilbury in the face of a storm the night of her setting out, and now as then she took shelter in the lee, feeling the roll of the boat under her feet, the gusts of wind–cold that time, hot this–blow loose her hair and tug her clothing against her body.

Peter appeared in the lights at the other end of the deck and walked toward her as though he knew where she would be. He came to a stop a few feet away, his face good-tempered but serious, and she felt herself tremble with fear. He did not take those few steps that separated him from sweeping her off her feet. Instead he spoke. "My cabin is number forty-two."

He nodded at her, smiled with a lifted eyebrow, and permitted himself an irony: "My life is in your hands." Slightly he bowed and walked away, leaving her alone to her choice.

Elizabeth watched him go, his figure slender under the lights and so unlike that of Charles, and she remained standing there, feeling let down and almost angry. She knew her wish; she needed excuse for it. At the other end of the deck there was a small effusion of people. Among the laughing voices rose that of Ruth Anscombe, and as the group headed in her direction, Elizabeth fled, and in her mind as she fled toward Peter Williams' cabin was the excuse she needed: What's sauce for the gander is sauce for the goose.

She knocked lightly on the door of his cabin, and when he opened it, he seemed to try and fail to conceal the pleasure on his features. He took her gently by the hand to draw her in, but then, before the door quite closed, he frowned and held her hand with force. "I won't have you come to me with guilt," he said.

"No guilt," she said. "This has nothing to do with Charles."

She placed her hands on either side of his neck, and they kissed, and she was amazed at the feel of his lips. When they made love that first time, she felt passion, not guilt, her body like the earth to rain. Passion and embarrassment, because he was so very different from Charles and, a schoolgirl again, she could not anticipate him for their pleasure. His body was that of a stranger. She worried in case she had not pleased him; he was so much more gentle, subdued, than Charles.

Afterward they had to lie very close together on the narrow bunk, and his breath was warm on her cheek, and she found herself treasuring that warmth as though it were life, and tears came to her eyes. "I'm so amazed," she said softly to him in the dark, "that anyone finds me attractive."

During the weeks of the journey, Elizabeth and Peter were discreet, but scarcely enough so for shipboard eyes. Much of the day they were intentionally apart, Williams buried in a book on a deck chair, Elizabeth with Jennifer and Nanny or with friends. They were together inevitably at each meal, sometimes sitting next to each other, sometimes apart–taking pleasure in watching the other. Williams would not join in deck sports but sat to watch Elizabeth play.

At the breakfast table Elizabeth addressed him pointed good-mornings. If they were accidentally alone, people tended to leave them alone, and Ruth Anscombe dropped delighted hints both to them and, they suspected, in letters back to Colombo. Once, on the first fine night brought by the Arabian Ocean, they were seen kissing on the boat deck, but the unseen observer, a sensible girl, said nothing to anyone. At this stage in their relationship, surprised by pleasure, they spoke little to each other, for talk could do only harm. Peter made no attempt to get to know Jennifer, and she simply watched him, irritated at the distraction he caused in her mother.

They did not talk of the past or future until the night the *Oronsay* left Port Said. They had returned to the ship after an excursion to the pyramids, stumbling from lighters up the gangway onto a deck crowded with native hawkers still singing the praises of Lillie Langtry. They stayed with the group as the natives were driven off and the anchor chain rattled onto the bow and the ship boomed a farewell and began to etch its smoke against the first evening sky of the Mediterranean. There was a ceremony here. As the liner steamed northwest toward Europe, one came to the rail and cast one's topi overboard, leaving it behind. Some people came in great jolly parties and made the throwing a contest. Some came alone and quietly dropped the Raj's symbol into the nostalgic wake. Some then faced west from the bow, to where the sunset stretched out against the sky. Others lingered at the stern looking to where the darkness gathered in the east. It was a moment of hinge, duplicating in reverse the emotions of the voyage out.

Elizabeth and Peter watched a hearty group led by Ruth Anscombe fling their topis overboard in gales of laughter, but they reserved their own. They watched the wake gleam white and curved through the early dark. The ocean had a purple tinge.

"The wine-dark sea," said Williams. "I see what Homer meant."

Elizabeth made no reply, and they leaned on the rail directly above the ocean, looking down. Then she spoke. "I wish Charles would think like that."

"Charles and I are very different," he said. "You underestimate him. He will always be a success, and I don't intend to be. He set out to be a success. I never did, never could. I have more time than he."

"What do you intend to do now?"

He pondered a moment: not the answer so much as how to answer her. "I have the money from the sale of the plantation. It'll keep me awhile."

"But that's your capital, your future!"

"I intend not to worry about the future. I shall, perhaps, sit about and read a great deal for a while. I need rest. I need to look at the world again."

"Is this before or after you become a railway guard on the Brighton line?"

They laughed, for their mood was serious but not solemn.

"I intend to spend the summer with you," he said.

They touched hands, leaning heads together. The lights on deck came to life, and the ocean grew immediately darker.

"And then?"

"I shall worry about then when the time comes."

They pondered, looking out along the wake.

"Perhaps Charles and I are not as unalike as you think," he said.

"Oh?"

"We chose the same woman." He smiled. "And then gave her the same choice: him or me."

"You mean his not telling me that you were booked on the *Oronsay?* I can't imagine he cares, at least no more than I do. Indifference, more likely."

"I think not. I think he is calling your bluff. Perhaps we are both learning to admire a woman who stands on her own two feet."

"Charles' money pays for my standing on my own two feet," she said slowly. "I suppose I've earned it."

"One grows greedy when one starts to lust for life."

She looked at him beneath her shoulder, sideways. "You have your own money to live on," she said.

"You will have to come to an arrangement. Or earn your own living."

"I shan't divorce him," she said quietly.

He looked at her with a raised eyebrow and gave a short laugh. "I don't intend to make enough money to support you!"

"Then what shall we do?"

He looked at her seriously, turning to lean his back against the railing so that they faced each other.

"You know as much as I do, or as little. There isn't anybody to tell you what to do anymore." He shrugged. "Just take the future as it comes, I expect."

And with a burst of effort he turned and flung his topi violently out across the sea. It glimmered briefly and vanished into the dark before hitting the water.

Elizabeth watched it vanish. "Take the future as it comes," she echoed his phrase in a murmur, and then released her topi from her fingers, so that it fell straight and landed upside down in the white wake that stretched eastward upon the dark of night and ocean, where it bobbed a moment before the boil of water tipped and swallowed it.

PART III

Armistice

24

October and November 1919

If Elizabeth imagined that preference controls destiny, the next months disabused her. Aging and unwell, her parents shocked her with the unwilled changes of fifteen years. She had to use Charles' money rather than them for shelter; she had to make a flat, not a house, into a home. Encounter with Ravenscroft produced frustration rather than an acceptance of Jennifer, so she had to make that home a household and let freedom wait. Charles acted without consulting her. Instead of selling up their home in Mount Lavinia, he stayed there. It was to be three years before he visited England, thus setting her free where she had expected fret. Her wishes, her intentions, her hopes, her worries–now they had to become acts.

Only she herself was as she had expected: full of surprises. The rhythm of the new age was quick, chopped, syncopated, many-melodied. London was still a bit down-at-heel, but not for want of spirit. Famine in Germany? War in Russia? Fighting in Ireland? But you could tear up your ration book and buy Paris fashions, and the whole beat was American now. One had to move fast. Elizabeth found that she could move fast.

Great London was awash with people that year, jammed with motorcars, dusty with building, but what she loved was still there–those rows of brick houses cuddling the ground, those small square gardens keeping neatly to themselves, and those swatches of blue sky and gray clouds, softly eager to hurry on. They couldn't change that. Silvered by smoke from a million chimneys, by soft sunlight, suburban, civilized to the furthest outskirts' hem, great London was the most feminine of cities and still the center of the world. In London Elizabeth felt she had come Home–that great city offered settlement to strangers. Blowsy, tipsy, a trifle odd with old age, it still knew how to make a good cup of tea.

The first of many letters from Charles arrived within ten days. It was brief, but not cold:

> I shall not be coming to England for some time. I think it better that you—and I—have the experience of freedom for a while. I have arranged unlimited drawing privileges for you at Coutts, where you should visit a Mr. Blakeley as soon as possible. You should see, if you would, that Williams does not benefit from the independence I provide you. Please give my love to Jennifer and tell her a letter is on the way.

She appreciated what Charles offered: independence in both senses of the word. She rang up Mr. Blakeley at once and leased a flat in St. James's Mansions on his recommendation. She had expected to have to gird against Charles, but now she could put down her armor and look about awhile at peace. It felt right to get on with matters of life smaller and more important than marriage. For a while she had her freedom from the two-person of life.

Charles let impatience overcome regret. If freedom was what she thought she wanted, then let her try it. Alone in the big house in Mount Lavinia, half its rooms under dust sheets, he felt self-sufficient rather than abandoned, recognizing instantly the pleasure of being alone, comfortable as old slippers. He thought at this time very little about Elizabeth. If Williams appealed to her, then let her get her fill of him. He himself could scarcely throw the first stone. He stayed home most evenings, turning the pages of books by lamplight, a glass of whiskey at his elbow, the dim sound of the ocean his guarantee of domestic peace and quiet.

In London Peter Williams did not take advantage of his possession of the field. He rented a suite of rooms in Bloomsbury, on Gower Street, and hastened to the center of his universe: the Reading Room of the British Museum. Liking women without trusting them, he held Elizabeth at arm's length, clear that she must live her own life if she was to share his. His rooms became their place of rendezvous, but they never became home to Elizabeth, who did not let sensuality this time entrap her and never hung an extra frock in Peter's wardrobe. She might not be sure whether or not she was just taking a holiday from marriage, but she knew she did not want to settle down. She turned thirty-eight.

* * *

When the maid opened the drawing-room door to admit Genevieve Pearsall, Elizabeth was on her knees, half-naked.

"Ah! A penitent!" exclaimed Genevieve softly, pulling off her gloves.

Elizabeth smiled, rose to her feet, and went to kiss the older woman in greeting, adjusting the pins in her dress at the same time. The rose carpet had a surplus covering of soft fabrics and crisp white tissue paper.

"Penitent, no," she said. "Sorry, yes. I'm beginning to learn why one pays a hundred guineas for a Worth dress. Come in and sit down if you can find a seat." The October-afternoon sunlight shone full in the tall windows and Ginny picked her way across the carpet, swimming in the golden light, an elegant woman in a slim blue voile afternoon frock by Vionnet and a knitted overcoat with bright bands of pattern and huge lapels, and a Paris straw hat uplifted to show off softly waved gray hair.

Mabel Greggs, taking pins from her mouth, stood up from behind a low armchair that had screened her from view. She wore a white blouse, dark gray skirt, and gray cardigan rather than the uniform in which Ginny was accustomed to seeing her.

"It's this new cutting on the bias that's the problem," she said. "Shall I take that out to the sewing machine, then?" She gestured at the half-finished garment of green mousseline de soie, a calf-length tunic that hung from Elizabeth's shoulders.

"No. I'll wear it. Ginny won't mind. Tell the maid I'm not home to anyone else, will you?"

Nanny stood a moment, hands crossed in front of her, scrutinizing the dress and Elizabeth. "That chest still isn't flat enough. It's all very well our having a nice visit to Paris, but I will say, if Mr. Charles says you've got unlimited drawing privileges at Coutts, you should have used them and saved us the work. It's not as though we didn't have other things to do."

"You're quite right, Mabel, I expect," said Elizabeth meekly.

Lady Pearsall had been studying Mabel with surprise. "Would you see about tea, Nanny?" she said coolly.

"I'll see if Mrs. Hooker is ready," replied Mabel with equal coolness.

As soon as she had left the room, Lady Pearsall turned to Elizabeth and spoke sharply. "I realize there is the most dreadful servant shortage, Elizabeth, but to allow a nanny to speak of one's income!"

"I haven't told you, have I?" said Elizabeth a little guiltily. "We shall have to get used to calling her Miss Greggs. I've promoted her—after the disappointment about Ravenscroft—I've made her sort of housekeeper. She's very good, you know, terribly practical about money and making arrangements and dealing with people and all that sort of thing."

"Ah!" said Ginny, her eyebrows raised. "The transformation of Nanny. Quite miraculous, what the lower classes are up to these days!" Elizabeth realized that she was being teased. "And you, poor helpless thing, you couldn't cope with all this household by yourself, of course. Too confusing for you after Mount Lavinia, I'm sure."

Elizabeth laughed. Mr. Blakeley from Coutts had found her a flat with eleven rooms on the second floor in a highly fashionable location. Mabel had hired the maid from an agency and found the beefy cockney Mrs. Hooker in a huge block of nearby workers' flats. Ginny had found the governess.

"You see through me," said Elizabeth to Ginny. "But if I am to get rid of running a household, then who better than Mabel? It's a big step up for her, and she's very good. I think we can let her feel her oats for a while." She did not tell Ginny that she had doubled Mabel's wages immediately upon their return to London to compensate for the horrendous wartime inflation, nor that she had doubled them again to accompany promotion and given her a full one and a half days off.

"Always an intention beyond the visible with you." Ginny smiled and relaxed against the cushions, crossing her ankles neatly and tugging her dress down. "I cannot get used to these new girdles. I always feel half-naked." When she was seated, the dress came only to mid-calf. "I wish I had your ankles," she said, eyeing Elizabeth. "But I have a great deal less trouble with the bust-flattener, I can see."

"This whole thing was a mistake," replied Elizabeth, gesturing at the room spread with patterns and beautiful fabrics. "Nanny's right. Mabel's right. I should have bought those originals." The dispute had simmered during the whole of the four-day visit to Paris. While Ginny purchased at the showings and submitted to fittings, Elizabeth and Mabel had used their eyes and memories to duplicate and modify the couturier's models. "It's just that I'm not . . . or at least I wasn't comfortable with the idea of using those unlimited drawing privileges on clothes."

"As I have said before, my dear," said Ginny, "you should always take a man at his word about money."

"Well, Mr. Blakeley has solved the whole problem." The man at Coutts had turned out to be soft, fat, courteous, and as resolute as his striped trousers and tailcoat indicated he should be. "He insists that I have the bills sent to him, and he deals directly with Charles. I haven't an idea even how much we are paying for the lease on this place."

"You have done a beautiful job on this room. I shouldn't have believed it possible."

"It was so gloomy! I shall have to do the whole place eventually."

"You've caught Colombo, you know. The colors, the light."

The original Victorian room had been transformed, using the light pouring from the big windows as a basis. Oak paneling had been covered with dove-gray paint that picked up the rose of the carpet. Long curtains of pale buttercup satin framed the windows and the sky. The sofa and chairs, all depth and flow, were covered in a nubby pearl-gray woolen fabric, and the other furniture was of pale wood. Bowls of fresh flowers floated against the walls, and the room was lit by table lamps with pottery bases and large shades of some hand-woven stuff. The effect was that of a country house, informal and inviting, and of summer, as though the smell of new-mown grass would come in through the windows if they were opened.

"Give the credit to the decorator. And to Harrod's. I had only the idea."

"It must, as the vulgar say, have cost a fortune."

"But I had to have a base of some kind, and what else could I do? I haven't the time!"

"Oh, I quite understand," said Ginny with a moue. "I am after Georgian antiques, and that will take me years." The Pearsalls had returned to their family home in Kent, which Ginny was officially in London to rescue from a Victorian modernization. "Never mind, it gives me a marvelous excuse to have a flat in town. Reggie doesn't mind, in fact he is probably glad to have me out of the way during the week, and it's not as though I had anything else to do." Suddenly she looked sad, or discommoded. She sat up and straightened her back, and her gaze became vague and fled over Elizabeth's shoulder in the old manner. "I envy the woman," she said.

Elizabeth looked at the carpet to give Ginny time to recover. Ginny now spent most of her week in a small service flat in Belgravia, her weekends at the country houses of friends. She and Elizabeth knew that she was fighting retirement, far too young at fifty-five to relinquish power or fashion. Departure from Ceylon had cut her off as ruthlessly from her past as the death of her boys in 1916 had eliminated her future, but instead of complaining she had chosen resolutely to live in the present. She was always bright, always gay, busy, a chic, modern matron, everywhere, knowing everyone. She took out a cigarette and lit it, and Elizabeth handed her a huge orange ashtray.

"It is a vast improvement over Wimbledon, I must say," said Ginny, recovering.

The fortnight at her parents' home in Wimbledon had been as awkward a period of life as Elizabeth had known. Her father had not been able to decide whether to treat her as girl or stranger, and embarrassed her by rising whenever she entered the room, an effort in his state of health. Her mother had grown acidulous, with a nervous twitch in her chin.

Elizabeth shrugged. "They've grown so old. I expect I shall get used to it. It's rather odd to be a daughter again."

"The advantages brought by wealth are somehow much more obvious in England than in Colombo," said Ginny idly, surveying the rich room. "And very much more important."

"At least," laughed Elizabeth, "shopping on Bond Street, in Paris —I no longer feel behind the times!"

"If you have at last seen *Chu Chin Chow?* Did you enjoy it?"

The question made Elizabeth vaguely uneasy. Sitting in the dress circle with Peter Williams to watch the war's most famous musical, she had found herself thinking of Anthony James, the young officer with whom she had corresponded who had mentioned seeing the play while on leave. She had given a florin from her evening bag to a young man on crutches begging outside the theater exit.

"Not as much as *Male and Female,*" she said.

"Oh, you did go!" exclaimed Ginny. "And did you not like that little girl Gloria Swanson? Now, there's a figure! I must say these new cinema palaces are rather grander than the old Bioscope, let alone the films. Decadence has its charms."

The maid arrived with afternoon tea for two.

"You are not expecting anyone else?" asked Ginny. "I can really only stay a minute."

"I know so few people here. Perhaps one of the girls from school. But she said she would telephone first."

"And how do you find them, your schoolgirl friends?"

"Older than I had expected." Elizabeth smiled.

"And plainer."

"And much less successful than I had feared!"

Both women laughed, confederate.

"Which reminds me," said Elizabeth, pouring tea. "I must thank you for Peter's invitation to Fanny Chalmet's dinner party next week. Do you think people will realize we're a couple?"

"My dear! Since the war, men are in such short supply, I shouldn't think they'd care! Just mention Charles frequently and with wifely adoration. Does your, ahem, Miss Greggs know about you two?"

"I never stay overnight with him." Elizabeth paused, taking a long Egyptian cigarette from a wooden humidor on the table at her elbow. "To tell the truth, I'm sure she does, since the ship."

Mabel had known what was in the wind perhaps even before Elizabeth. She had kept mum. You never knew when something like that might prove useful.

"But it doesn't really matter," continued Elizabeth, adjusting the tunic's uncomfortable neckline. "To tell the truth, our relationship has changed, rather, and all because of that wretched telephone."

"Oh?" said Lady Pearsall, teacup suspended.

"She was out shopping last week, and the maid was busy with something or other, and I answered the phone myself." She had picked up the jangling instrument from the table in the dark hallway.

"Could I speak with Miss Greggs, please?" The voice was youthful, male, cultivated enough in an assumed sort of way.

"Who is speaking, please?" inquired Elizabeth with curiosity.

"Is she there, then?" said the voice sharply, more cockney. "Is that the maid? Look, I can't stay to talk, love, just give her the message that we can't meet her as planned this afternoon, be a good girl."

"Who is this?"

"Oh, Lord. . . . Look, it's her brother speaking." (Brother indeed, thought Elizabeth, amused.) "All on the up and up. Now, you give her the message, will you, I've got to go." He rang off.

Elizabeth teased Mabel when she gave her the message, but to her surprise, the expected blush became a bright red and Mabel had to sit down on the hall chair. "Well that's torn it," she said. "I told him never to ring me up here. Well, I suppose it's better that it come out now than later."

The caller, it seemed, was indeed her brother, her youngest

brother, Fred, aged fifteen, who lived–and how uneasily did the supposedly family-less Mabel admit this–who lived with their mother in a little house in Wapping. "There's only her and him and me left now," explained Mabel, accent and grammar slipping under stress. "My other brother, the older one, he was killed in France during the war. My two sisters, they went last year, in the flu."

"But *you* are an orphan!" protested Elizabeth.

"Well, I suppose it was a bit of a fraud, if you like," said Nanny, looking sideways. "But there wasn't a proper time to tell you, it just rolled on, it got started when my father died, there was my mother with a brand-new baby–that was Fred–she had to go to work, she couldn't feed all of us, could she?" She blazed from sullenness into resentment. "I was as good as an orphan, I was! It didn't do Ravenscroft any harm. But I can't tell them now, can I? If I want a job there? You people don't understand . . . ."

"But you never said anything to me. At all!"

A hard glint flashed in Mabel's eyes. "And what could you do about it? Did it matter? What if I did send my money home instead of sticking it under the mattress? There's never been any *need* for you to know."

Elizabeth could think of nothing to say.

Mabel did not ask for sympathy. She offered no road in. "I'd better get about my business, then. I'll see that Fred doesn't bother you again."

"What an amazing thing!" commented Ginny upon hearing the tale. "I shouldn't trust the woman for a moment after that!"

"I don't feel that way at all," responded Elizabeth. "In fact, I rather admire her. She has her way to make in the world, you know. Life can't be as easy for a woman like her as it is for us. I've always thought her a little too much the Miss Goody Twoshoes, church every morning and all that sort of thing."

"You Roman Catholics are never happy until you catch each other in a little sin, are you?" Ginny laughed. "She with her mum, you with your *homme bien aimé*."

"Ginny!" protested Elizabeth, laughing.

"Oh, don't misunderstand me, you know I adore the idea of your having a little affair with Peter Williams. It's all so delightfully *ancien régime*."

"I thought it was terribly modern."

"But then, you are so terribly young." She finished her cup of tea.

Mabel knocked at the door and entered, looking a trifle severe.

"Excuse me interrupting, Mrs. Wingate, but will we be continuing with the fitting or shall I tidy this up?"

"Oh, Mabel, would you mind?"

Mabel began to assemble the pieces of fabric and their associated patterns. Lady Pearsall stubbed out her cigarette and rose to her feet, gathering gloves and parasol, putting her arms in her bright coat.

"I really must be moving on. Would you believe, I'm going to a tea dance with cocktails? Perhaps I shall learn to do the shimmy."

She looked down at Mabel squatting awkwardly on the carpet to shuffle backward as she gathered strips of paper. "Watch out for that electric radiator behind you, Miss Greggs," she said, delight dancing in her blue eyes. "You may burn your bum."

Mabel looked up at her, startled, and Elizabeth laughed. "Ginny!"

"Just the new slang, my dears," she said gaily. "One must be modern, at all costs. Why, in my day, I don't think we even had bums!"

Smoothing the fabric of her coat to her backside coyly, she made an exit in the Gladys Cooper manner, the grande dame with sauce. After the door had closed behind her, Elizabeth said, "She's a brave woman, that one. It takes courage to live each day for itself."

From the floor Mabel looked speculatively at her mistress. "I didn't know you knew that," she said quietly.

Life's major discomfort that particularly cold autumn was the coal shortage, but people were so relieved to be free of the flu and the war that not even the dank and soot-filled winds blowing off the October Thames could quite dampen spirits. London seemed filled with former army officers, impoverished because they did not qualify for unemployment relief, who cadged threepences, spent the afternoons in the warm cinemas, clipped their cuffs and collars free of frayed strands, and remained cynical and gay about the government and their futures. Elizabeth had expected that Jennifer would be a bit of a nuisance. Indeed the little girl missed her father and waited twice a day at the front door for the mail to slide through the brass slot into the wire box, but once her classes started in the newly painted "schoolroom," she gave up the habit, and soon she had discovered with cheer the existence of other children tucked away around the carpeted corridors of the St. James's Mansions. She was fascinated by the spectacle of leaves deserting their trees. She was exhilarated by snowfall. She was absorbed by the spectacle of the streets: motorcars and buses and trams and trolleys, fruit carts and milk wagons, apple sellers and beggars, the swarming of bowler hats at the entrance to tube stations, the returned soldiers on crutches rattling their cups in sheltered corners with a touch of the cap to the little miss, the shopgirls eating fish and chips from newspaper cornets while staring in the windows of Selfridge's. They were all so much more exotic than the natives of Colombo.

Elizabeth felt crisp and brisk. She looked at the wash of humanity and thought how interesting they all were. She looked at the leaves and saw them not as torn from their last hold but as gaily setting forth—voluntarily, as it were—upon the winds of autumn.

25

One evening in late October she and Peter lay abed in his suite of rooms. The steam-heated radiators installed specially for colonials rattled under the windows, and in the grate a prodigal coal fire burned. All the chill was outside. Peter lay face in the pillow, and the firelight gave his naked body—where the sharp lines around wrist and neck dividing tan from untan were fading—the glow of oiled poplar wood. She traced the outline of his buttocks with a fingertip as she lay propped on her elbow beside him.

"Our coming together was so cold," she said slowly. "Our staying together grows so warm. . . ."

He turned his head to look at her and moved his knee to touch her belly. She seemed maturer now, capable of variety. Unpredictable perhaps? Not quite, not yet. But filled sometimes with the energy of the moment as she had never been before. He smiled at her gently, lovemaking having removed his own tenseness. "You will turn us from lovers into friends."

"We began as friends."

"And was our coming together really cold? or inevitable?"

She looked at him seriously. "Either of us could have chosen differently."

They lay quietly, he gazing at her, she resting the palm of her hand around the curve of his bottom. She was wondering whether she still loved Charles, and if so, what love meant. Finally she spoke. "Inevitability is the excuse lovers give for infidelity."

He raised his eyebrows. "You don't feel swept off your feet?" He gave a mock sigh. "Ah, well, perhaps neither of us believes in the Grand Passion." He rolled the words in his mouth, to mock them.

"It would be hard with you around," she retaliated. Her sigh was small but genuine. "No. We are old enough to know one chooses." But she did not want to think of middle age right now, and before he could reply, she raced on, sitting upright, poking him in the side. "Now can I tell you my news?"

He groaned.

She resumed the tale their passion had interrupted. "I'm going to Plymouth tomorrow. For two weeks."

"You're going where?"

"I've found something to do. Something useful."

That word had become her refrain, he thought. He approved her energy but worried that she wanted drama. Disillusionment would be inevitable when she found out that nothing one did mattered, and he could not deal again with disillusionment in a woman. He could not help her find a cause. Interesting though causes were, he had none of his own: amusement at human nature is lessened by partnership. He had been amused when Ginny Pearsall had laid low her earliest intention of linking up with the Women's Social and Political Union: "Afternoon teas, bazaars," drawled Ginny. "Boring meetings about civil-service grades and infant care? We are quite too late, my dear. The spirit has gone out of it, no doubt. It was all very much easier when we were attacking the men. We knew who the enemy was. Now we have to decide who to vote *for*. Of course there is always the Women's International League for Peace and Freedom, if you care to listen to bishops and Bolsheviks tell you one should not shoot people one had never dreamed of shooting in the first place. . . ."

Too late for suffragism, thought Williams. Too late for pacifism. In what cause might Elizabeth now appropriately burn? Equal Pay for Equal Work while she wore dresses by Lucile and Lanvin? But she had not been dismayed by his cynicism, and she had not only found a cause for herself, she had gone to get it for herself. Yesterday she had telephoned Ginny Pearsall with an idea.

"I know exactly the person to talk to!" Ginny had responded when Elizabeth telephoned. "She's full of good ideas and knows all the people I don't. Are you free tomorrow afternoon?"

And today she had taken Elizabeth to tea with Frances, Countess of Warwick. The fifth Earl of Warwick's wife was Lady Pearsall's girlhood acquaintance, though she seemed much older. Ginny was fashionable. Lady Warwick had the bustline of the previous decade, a high strong voice, very thin English lips, and silvered hair piled high. Perhaps, Elizabeth thought, it is not so much age as it is period.

For more than twenty years Lady Warwick had been one of the few aristocratic ornaments worn by the stripling Labour Party. Orphaned heiress to one of England's largest fortunes, she had declined marriage with the Queen's youngest son in the 1870's, become a famous beauty and confidante of the Prince of Wales in the 1880's, and converted to socialism in the 1890's when an editorial about her wastefulness led to her meeting Robert Blatchford, who told her about the world outside her gate. The country house within that gate was now the Labour Party's weekend retreat.

"Ginny tells me you are interested in political work," she said to Elizabeth with a touch too much politeness.

"Not paid work," said Elizabeth, "but useful work nonetheless. I thought political organizing?"

"I see," said Lady Warwick. "As though we were a charity." The Labour Party was at least this year becoming a real rival to the Liberals and Conservatives. "And what are your political views?"

"I can't be said to have any," said Elizabeth, and watched a flicker of disdain cross Lady Warwick's features. "Except," she continued firmly, "that politics are the only alternative I can see to war."

"I had thought of introducing Mrs. Wingate to Clemmie Churchill," said Ginny hastily, "to see what Winston might do for her, but she would have none of him. She is Irish, you see, and Roman Catholic, and sympathized with the suffragists."

"Our august Colonial Secretary," drawled Lady Warwick, "would have us at war in Ireland as soon as say good morning, and the only women he takes seriously are his mother and Clementine. He has never forgiven Connie Markievicz."

"Connie Markievicz?" said Elizabeth, to receive a glance of mild scorn in response.

"I can see that you are *not* politically experienced," said Lady Warwick. "The Countess Markievicz is a Sinn Feiner and the first woman elected to Parliament–last year. She was in jail at the time and refused to take her seat. I do not know whether Winston dislikes her more for that or for having led his defeat for the seat in Manchester in 1908." She spoke like a schoolteacher, uninterested, then reached for her cup of tea. "Had you thought of practical nursing?" she continued. "God knows the country needs nurses right now."

"Something a little more imaginative?" intervened Lady Pearsall, protecting her protégée.

"Perhaps you might try the London Society for Women's Service?

Mostly for the lower classes of course, and they are swamped, Beatrice tells me, with women who *need* jobs–war widows, for instance. But they do find the most imaginative placements on occasion. Or if you were willing to do some training–the Sex Disqualification Removal Act this year, I'm sure you've heard of it, makes it possible for one to become a solicitor or an accountant now, you know."

Elizabeth could see herself through the older women's eyes: colonial, wealthy, naive, in search of diversion. The degree of truth in that unstated accusation was enough to hurt, but for once she refused to question herself.

Ginny had told her that Lady Warwick liked to refer to her former self as having been "a waster of substance, a waster of opportunity."

"I do not want," she therefore said with a flash in her eye, "to be a waster of substance and opportunity." Lady Warwick stiffened. Lady Pearsall relaxed. "I have the substance. I need the opportunity."

For a moment it seemed that Lady Warwick might end the interview in frost, but suddenly she laughed and let her eyes sparkle. "I expect I deserved that," she said to Elizabeth, hands defensively busy with her pearls. She made a decision: "How can I help you?"

"Do you know Lady Astor?" Elizabeth asked coolly.

"Lady Astor? Oh, of course, Nancy! Ah, I see what you have in mind!"

The American-born millionaire William Waldorf Astor, first Viscount Astor, had died ten days ago, thus elevating his son Waldorf from the House of Commons to the House of Lords. He had been Conservative member for the working-class district of Sutton in Plymouth, and on the previous Sunday the local Conservative Association had asked his wife, Nancy, the new Lady Astor, to stand in her husband's place at the by-election scheduled for November 15. Nancy Astor was then forty years old. Born a Virginia aristocrat, she had been one of the three Langhorne sisters who gave the Gibson Girl her famous silhouette. Divorced from her first husband, she had married Waldorf Astor in 1906 and become a nervous, celebrated hostess, lavish with one of the world's greatest fortunes.

"To be quite frank, I thought you might be able to arrange for me to help with her campaign," continued Elizabeth with somewhat more warmth. "The newspaper says she is going down to Plymouth today. I thought that if I arrived tomorrow, there would quite likely be something for me to do."

Lady Warwick leaned back in her armchair. "I shouldn't think through the Conservative Association," she said briskly. "But if I get in touch with Nancy's political secretary . . . And Astor owes me a favor. Just a minute, would you?"

She rose briskly to her feet and went into the next room, where she could be heard telephoning. She came back smiling. "It is all arranged! You are to go straight to 3 Elliot Terrace when you arrive in Plymouth, and they will tell you what to do. I must say they seem frightfully well organized," she continued a little ruefully, "and they have bags of money, of course, but they still need people. You *have* timed things well."

She began writing a letter of introduction on cream-laid, coroneted stationery. Thanking her, Elizabeth asked what return she might make.

Lady Warwick waved the question aside. "This sort of little thing is the lifeblood of politics, my dear, as you will quickly discover. If you should choose to lend your new skills to the Labour Party a little later, then we should all be equal, shouldn't we?"

Nor, thought Lady Warwick, am I making a blind bargain. If this works out, then Nancy Astor will owe me a little something too.

"There!" She handed the envelope to Elizabeth and turned to Lady Pearsall. "Have I done right by you, Genevieve?"

"And what do *I* owe you, Frances?" inquired Lady Pearsall. "I must say you have become terribly quid pro quo. If that is what politics does to one's character, I am not at all sure I shall let Elizabeth go to Plymouth."

As Elizabeth and Ginny took their leave, Lady Warwick detained them at the door. "I have always remembered the young women of my generation who went out to South Africa during the Boer War, you know, to nurse the wounded. They came back saying they had had a simply marvelous time. The Prince of Wales said that if a sense of the fitness of things was not enough to prevent their stupidity, one would have thought a sense of humor would deter them. You are a wealthy woman, which is not always an advantage. I am sure you will forgive my caution."

"Of course," smiled Elizabeth, tucking the coroneted envelope in her bag.

Clad now only in a peignoir, Elizabeth took that envelope from her handbag on the chair and waved it over Peter's naked body. "Letters of introduction," she said. "What makes the world go round, no?"

"Poking handbills in letter boxes?" he mocked. "You're going to freeze, especially in Plymouth of all places." He was thinking: It's good to see her like this. He was thinking: She's enormously desirable to me. He thought: Any cause will do, so long as it makes her happy. "Ah, well," he sighed, "any port in a storm, even Plymouth, I suppose."

He reached up to pull her down to the bed again, but she would have none of it. She had to go home to arrange a household and send a telegram reserving rooms at the Devonport Hotel. She began to dress, turning her back to him, dim in the firelight as she took her clothes from the chair. He watched her tug the rubber girdle over her hips and fasten her stocking tops. His wife, he thought, had never let him watch her dress. She slipped the straps of a pink bust bodice made from heavy broché over her shoulders and began to fasten its snaps down the side from armpit to waist. As she struggled to tighten it, he groaned. "What a frightful waste."

She did not reply, concentrating on the snaps, then slipping a beautifully cut afternoon dress of blue crepe de chine over her head, from whose slender lines she rose like Venus to repin her hair. Not looking at him, she then said, "I wish you could see me as a person."

"Me?"

She paused again to slip on high-heeled blue shoes, to don her loose thigh-length matching jacket trimmed with fur. "You see me mainly as a woman, don't you?"

"You are mainly a woman, and I hope always will be," he protested, drawing the sheet over his chest as she pinned her feathered hat to her hair, looking at him in the mirror.

"But whether I'll always be the woman you want," she mocked, "now, that's another matter, isn't it?" Kid gloves, silk umbrella, leather handbag, woolen coat. She stood over him fully armored for the world.

"Ah, well," she said, bending to kiss his forehead. "You beggars can't be choosers, I suppose."

As she moved toward the door, leaving the taste of face powder and her light perfume behind, he pretended to throw the pillow at her. "Just remember it's cold out there!" he half-shouted at her vanishing back.

"I know!" she shouted gaily back. "But I have my warm coat. Shall I leave the downstairs door open? It would do you good, Your Stuffiness."

She spent the next fortnight in chill rooms, bleak halls, and cold streets, as though bathed in a rapid flow of iced water. Plymouth convinced her finally that she was in England. Salt winds blew in from the sound and cleaned the row of brick houses and the huge docks with sweeps of icy rain. She served behind tea urns. She spent hours checking lists of names with a little fat lady with a heavy Devon accent. With others in the cold mornings she was driven up the city hillsides to streets of neat Victorian homes to distribute handbills. It amused her that the driver was a woman, and it surprised her that women in the middle of doing their own housework answered her knock. She never met Lady Astor in person, though she saw her every day. She was sent to the meetings of the Liberal candidate and the Labour candidate to take notes on the themes that candidates, questioners, hecklers bounced at each other:

"The League of Nations . . ."

"The unemployed coalminers . . ."

"Ireland has never . . ."

"The Tories have never . . ."

"Problems of foreign exchange mean that we must . . ."

"If Lloyd George . . ."

"The Russian menace . . ."

Lady Astor seemed bright and hard as a jewel, fast-talking, uncompromising, ill-informed. Her husband was always at her side. She dressed superbly in furs and pearls, but if the voters held anything against her it was not that she was rich or American or female or aristocratic or divorced or Conservative, but that she was, they thought, prohibitionist. They harassed her about closing hours. She urged the women to vote, which was always good for a giggle from the rear of the hall. Ireland was in the news every day: ambushes and murders and attacks on police barracks and boycotts and security precautions to protect the Lord Lieutenant and searches for the escapees from the jails in Lincoln and Dublin and Manchester. Lady Astor was loud for law, order, and the Union; her listeners stood to cheer while Elizabeth counted heads from the back of the hall, rubbing a foot on which the man from the *Daily Express* had accidentally stepped, later favoring a knee skinned when she stepped too soon from a tram. Late at night in the Devonport Hotel she soaked in a hot tub, wearier and sorer than she had ever been except for the days after her inundation at the water hole.

Election day was November 15. November 11 was the first anniversary of the Armistice, a day given more to mourning than to parades because the people had not yet quite learned to coat their wounds with words. To avoid all speeches, Elizabeth set off in midmorning to put handbills in the letter boxes of a long street that curved along the brow of the eastern hills high above the city and harbor. It was a day of fine clean wind and pale sunlight, the gray clouds hasty and tattered, the brick houses and roadway shining with recent rain. A man busying himself in the back of an ancient lorry was the only visible person as Elizabeth patiently worked her way along the street, snipping each gate open and closed, snapping the letter-box lids on her offerings. A hundred yards beyond where he labored to lift and shift long wooden crates lay a row of shops: a greengrocer, a dairy, a stationer's, a cake shop offering, she hoped, cups of hot tea.

Just as she approached the houses abreast the lorry where the man worked, there was the sudden sound of engines roaring up the hilly side streets in front of and behind her. Both she and the man stopped to look. He wore the cloth cap and dark suit of the laboring classes, but he was young, and under the cap were a handsome face and bright, deep blue eyes, Irish eyes. She and he turned to look as though by concert at the police cars which debouched into the street two hundred yards behind them and fifty yards ahead of them. A second later, Elizabeth found him beside her touching his cap, taking the handbills from her hand, saying, "Let me help you with this, then."

For a moment she thought he had not even noticed the police cars and so parted with the handbills cooperatively. Then she drew back. "What are you doing?" she said at the start of surprise.

"You're Irish, aren't you?"

Yes, she nodded.

"For God's sake, then, act as though we belong together. Keep working. Shall we try this little household, then?" And with a smile and a bow he was opening the latch of a gate and handing her a leaflet, which she placed in the brass letter box, returning to him like a child, not looking at the police officers she could see over his shoulder, now gathered around a horse-drawn delivery van that stood ahead of them. She stared at him with solemn eyes and he laughed at her and chatted to her, companionlike, and they proceeded to the next gate and the next as though they were correctly mismatched. They were well away from his lorry when a sergeant came toward them.

"Say hello to the nice man, then," muttered her companion sardonically.

Obedient, she spoke as the sergeant neared them. "Are you looking for the escaped prisoners, Sergeant?" Her voice, she knew, was high and strained, but she sounded only businesslike. He saluted her politely, but walked past without replying, intent now on the lorry they had left. It was the first occasion in Elizabeth's life on which she felt a police officer was something other than a special kind of servant. The stranger held handbills in one hand, the tip of her elbow in the other. His face was composed but she could see the tension in his jaw and neck. Both of them stiffened when the sergeant now behind them called out to his men.

"Act normal, now," hissed the man at her elbow, and he forced her to stop and turn naturally to look at the lorry, where they could see the sergeant lifting sacking from the long wooden crates, his men tense and jubilant.

"So the bastards were tipped off, I thought so," said her companion quietly.

She turned to him, shocked. "You're a gun-runner!"

"I'm Irish, aren't I?" and he smiled as though with hatred and turned her toward the cake shop.

She stopped and looked at him. "With guns from Germany, for Dublin. As they say in the papers?"

"With French guns." He had clipped his accent into English to mock her. "Would you be enjoying a cup of tea, now? No? Then you'll walk me to the corner with an air of kindness, and I'll be about my business." He was nervous now, cold, using no charm. Elizabeth followed his tug at her elbow as though they were resuming a stroll. They rounded the corner past the shops and moved out of sight of the police. "Stupid!" was the gun-runner's word with his last look. "They could have had me." He released her arm. "I'll be off, then." He turned to Elizabeth, standing slightly below her because of the steep slope of the street. "With a thank-you and all, lady."

He turned to go, tipping his cap, but she seized him by the arm. "Wait," she said. "You'll need money."

He stopped, and she fumbled in her handbag for her purse.

"I have only coins," she said in agitation.

"So you *are* Irish," he said.

"You didn't know?"

"It was worth the chance," he said, and smiled, and put out his hand for the coins she put into it, and saluted with a touch of his cap again as though she had tipped him, and smiled, and strode off down the hilly street. Elizabeth returned to the cake shop and sat at its one small table over a mug of black, sweet tea.

No, she told herself. Politics are the *opposite* of war.

After polling day, there was a two-week delay while they waited for the votes from various armies around Europe and the Middle East to be received and counted. Elizabeth returned to London without waiting and got into a row with Mabel.

"Lady Bountiful," sneered Mabel at Lady Astor, angry at Elizabeth's anecdotes. "Playing at politics. More fool her, with all that money! What does a woman want to be in Parliament for, anyway? And what does she know about being poor and out of work, I ask you? Now, Queen Mary, she goes visiting the sick in the East End. She'll have some idea. But Lady Astor? And those fools that think she'll set things right?"

It was to the Labour-party not the Conservative-party headquarters that Elizabeth offered her permanent services after the results of the by-election in the Sutton division of Plymouth made Lady Astor the first female member of Parliament. All Elizabeth and Lady Astor had in common, it proved, were femaleness and an interest in politics.

Lady Astor made a good-enough M.P., but not good enough for Elizabeth, even if Winston Churchill, whom Elizabeth had loathed ever since he had caused the slaughter of the Gallipoli invasion during the war, did not speak to her for three whole years. Later, in the 1930's, the two Conservatives had a famous exchange while he was her guest at Cliveden. "If I were your wife," Lady Astor said, "I would give you poison." "And if I were your husband," he replied, "I would drink it." Though Churchill is generally credited with having won the exchange, one should note that Lady Astor would have won the event. She authored another witticism too. "I married beneath me," she said. "All women do."

Elizabeth had to admit that she admired the way Lady Astor's arrogance and outspokenness swiftly dissipated the gentleman's-club atmosphere of the House. But for what good? Her views on social problems were antediluvian. She was idiotic about the Irish problem. She was far too pro-war. Lady Pearsall disliked her because she was too American to be a lady. Elizabeth Wingate disliked her because she was too Conservative to be a woman. Is there any real difference, she asked, between an Astor and a Churchill?

26

The 1920's

Charles Wingate had allowed his wife to sail alone for England because he did not know how he felt about her. He stayed in Colombo without seeing her for three years because he did not understand himself. And when later he rejoined her, self-puzzlement had made him gentle; to his own surprise, he had grown more interested in relationships than norms. "I would prefer," he replied to one of her frequent factual letters, "that you worked for the Conservatives rather than the Socialists." But it was an observation, not a wish or a command. Time helped him to see her as separate from him, as more than his.

Their reunion took place in 1922, when the death of his elder brother made it mandatory for Charles to attend to the family estate. He found at first that separation had not made him uncomfortable with either England or his wife. Both were older, both more modern, the weather was too cool for more than a summer visit, and Elizabeth was still Elizabeth. Election night happened to come just before his planned return to Ceylon, and only then did he begin to admit the changes in her; she came home slightly drunk from a celebration honoring the seventeen women elected to the House of Commons, and he was irritated at her being so triumphant about femininity. But he held his tongue, separation having deprived him of the right to school her, temporariness of the obligation.

On his second visit the following year he found that both she and Mabel had learned to type. He gave her luxury: a month in Nice, the best restaurants. By the time of his 1924 visit, one room of the St. James' flat had become an office, and the sight of Elizabeth and Mabel hammering away at Remingtons amused him. Their hemlines were shorter every year. In 1925 Elizabeth met him at the boat train with her own little Austin and drove them skillfully through heavy traffic as though she were used to it, and they had to cut short their holiday in Biarritz so that she could be back in London for a by-election. She was organized, he realized, and the household organized itself around her the way it had once centered on him.

He did not begrudge his respect. If he could still not take her independence quite seriously, however, it was because she did not respect money. She was not spendthrift, but she showed no interest in where the money came from, and she forwarded bills to Mr. Blakeley of Coutts without even opening them. And if he could not approve of her independence, it was because neither he nor Jennifer came first in her life. He wondered what did, but in their new and nervous equality he dared not ask.

Only once in all these years did they speak of her relationship with Peter Williams, and that exchange occurred only because one afternoon during his first visit in 1922 he came home from his club earlier than expected. The maid politely opened the door to the drawing room for him—opened it upon the sight of Elizabeth and Peter standing before the fireplace in an embrace. More affection than passion, but Charles was sharply angry.

He pretended to have seen nothing until Williams had left. Then he turned on Elizabeth. "God knows I'm broad-minded," he said loudly, his face flushed, "but I do have the right to a little more discretion from you two. Why do that sort of thing in the house in front of the servants, let alone me? Thank God Jennifer isn't here!"

"We were merely being affectionate," replied Elizabeth stiffly, a great fear within her that the balance of three years was to be destroyed.

"You might try not to make me look an ass," retorted Charles. "God knows I can't object to a spot of infidelity, but I do draw the line at disloyalty."

"But I've never *been* unfaithful!" blurted Elizabeth, turning from the fireplace toward the windows, knowing exactly what she meant. It did not make sense, so she tried to explain: "Not to Peter and you, that is."

Where Peter would have laughed, Charles grew angrier. "Well, *I've* been unfaithful," he almost shouted. "But as you know very well, I've never been disloyal. And I never shall be."

He stormed out of the room, and their farewell two days later at the boat train was stiff, but he was no longer really angry. Both she and he knew that he had affirmed rather than threatened her relationship with Williams by what he had said and not said. Neither of them noticed till later that the subject of his infidelity, so carefully concealed in 1914, had now been taken for granted.

"Will you discuss things further with him?" asked Ginny over lunch next day at Fortnum and Mason's.

"I think we said more in those few words than we ever have before. Perhaps there's some use for anger after all."

"Charles is, after all, a very tactful man."

"And I appreciate his tact. Peter treats the whole thing as a joke. He wants to give Charles a copy of the new grounds for divorce that will probably get through Parliament next year—you know, the things that make it equal for wives and husbands—just to stop him taking me for granted, but I don't think Charles takes me for granted."

Elizabeth was uncomfortable with the discussion and ordered a glass of cordial.

"So you shan't bring it up."

"There's no need to. Better not, I think. He hasn't pushed himself on me. He's very good-tempered. He's spent much of the time with his family or with Jennifer or at his club. We're getting used to each other gradually. I imagine he has his other women . . ."

"Before the war," pressed Ginny, but rather awkwardly, "you never brought up his infidelity then and came to think that wrong. Putting it bluntly, are you not making the same mistake again?"

"With my own . . . ?" Elizabeth grew contemplative, pushing her food around the plate. "Perhaps it was a mistake then. Perhaps things would have been different if we had talked it out. But this time we've said all that needs to be said, for good or ill."

Charles would have agreed with every word Elizabeth said that day. Disengagement without declaring a winner and a loser was possible, even successful. He was now heavily engaged in business, for when recession followed war, he and Arthur Barker switched Clarkson and Son into local manufacture to avoid the new export competition from America. Then in 1923 Joe Plunkett led him in a new direction by retiring from the army to go into the business of trading armaments. Charles put up the money for the enterprise, of which he owned half, and he soon felt guilty about the size of the profits which Plunkett's skill generated. He did not mention the new trade to Elizabeth, and he even felt a little ashamed of it himself.

He grew conscious that despite his wealth there was something about him of the man who has not lived up to his early promise. For a while he blamed Elizabeth for having deprived him of a consort, himself for having grown middle-aged, and the times for no longer being what they ought, but it came to him one day quite suddenly that the true reason was his loss of interest in power—over commerce, competitors, and wife. He was amused by the realization. He could even put his finger on the cause. Those nightmares of dying had ceased long ago, but he remembered them all too clearly. He thought of that evening in the resthouse at Wilpattu when he had almost confided his terror of mortality to Elizabeth, and he thought how much he missed her. One morning in January 1926, Charles' chief clerk unlocked the quiet offices of Clarkson and Son and was surprised to find the lights still burning. Exploring, he found Arthur Barker–gimpy, reliable, younger Arthur Barker, Charles' partner and deputy–dead of a heart attack upon the shining floor of his office. The following week Charles cabled Elizabeth and asked her to come out and pack up the house at Mount Lavinia, which she did. He sold up everything in Ceylon and invested the proceeds in England. He left the mansion at Mount Lavinia with almost no nostalgia for the more than thirty years he had spent building his empire.

Elizabeth feared that Charles' permanent return would interfere with her routine, her life, her ideas. She was happy; she enjoyed her work. She liked the image she saw in the eyes of fellow passengers in trains to the provinces: a busy woman with papers to read, something to do. Even the chimneys of the houses by the railway line seemed to salute. She enjoyed the authority: making lists, telephoning volunteers, reserving meeting halls, arguing with printers and local political associations, holding the fort when the speaker was late, tabulating results for headquarters. She did not mind that she was not paid.

Now she knew the ugliness of poverty firsthand: the chill dirt of broken hallways, the stench of outdoor toilets, the sly anger at her accent or dress, the beer drunk to achieve insensibility or impudence, the fear that she was the government lady sent to take away the dole. She also knew its poetry: chapped red hands twisted inside morning aprons, skirt-clinging children with the faces of angels and the limbs of rickets, colored photographs of the king and queen on the mantelpiece next to the china souvenir of Blackpool. She had a sense of mission. The world needed technicians as good as her, and she would not let Charles deprive her.

She had to back him off, even as soon as the first day of their return from Ceylon in April 1926. They visited Elizabeth's parents at the Wimbledon house, which was full of too much heat and the smell of peppermint and invalidism. Bernard Malloy was pale, thin, and feeling brave at sitting up in the living-room armchair. A new wave of political murders in Ireland had upset Henriette, who was snarling again at the folly of the Irish and of men, and Elizabeth snapped at the whine in her mother's voice: "Can't you see you make Father miserable?" She fussed with the rug around his knees. He looked up at her, bewildered, his hair white, his skin translucent, a tremor in his hands.

Henriette responded like a little French terrier. "Don't tell me what to say about those Irish thugs . . . those Irish . . . *salauds!* Your father thinks no better of them than I do, do you, Bernard?"

"That's not the point!" retorted Elizabeth, her lips thin. "You upset him all the time. Can't you see these days you've become so filled with *hatred?*"

"Hatred!" exclaimed Henriette. "Hatred!" She drew herself up, trying to beat her daughter and her temper down. "And what is wrong with that if it is hatred? If *you* do not hate that which is monstrous, then there is something wrong with *you!*"

Elizabeth's low voice grew cold, and she stood up to her mother. "When you don't know what you are talking about, it's better to say nothing at all! Now be quiet!"

Shocked, Henriette sputtered, Bernard half-rose, and Charles intervened: "I say, Elizabeth, that's not the way to speak to your mother."

He was thinking that both of them were foolish, that neither of them knew what they were talking about. To his astonishment, Henriette burst into tears and Elizabeth rushed to put her arm around her mother, turning to glare at him. "You stay out of this!" she said angrily. "You don't understand me or my mother."

Charles was left with the burden of hidden anger in his chest and Elizabeth without the desire to relieve him of it.

They were still prickly with each other the following evening when Peter Williams came to visit. Conversational trios performed by this triangle were neither unusual nor unpleasant. Having been friends before Elizabeth, the men had maintained a truce after her. Privately Charles rejoiced that inflation had made Williams' decision to live off his capital a disaster, so that in 1925 he had to take a job at Foyle's bookstore in Charing Cross Road.

"How delightful!" Charles had said blandly. "Bit dusty, I should think, old chap, but I imagine you'll be as comfortable there as at the British Museum."

Peter Williams, in revenge, displayed an insouciance about his humble work, and a cheeriness about life in general, that made Charles sometimes wonder whether all his own work and worry was worth the money it brought. That was about as far into dispute as the pair had ever entered. Tonight, however, was different. The first general strike in England's history threatened, and everyone held strong opinions. Peter was on the side of the unions, and Charles planned to answer the government's call as a volunteer to keep the buses running. Both drank too much whiskey while Elizabeth dressed for dinner, which the trio planned to eat at the Savoy. By the time she returned to the softly lit drawing room, Peter was leaning forward in his armchair and Charles sitting back in his, while both tried to interrupt and trip each other's arguments. Their faces were flushed, their egos bruised.

As Elizabeth entered the room elegantly gowned, wearing the diamonds that Charles had given her to honor Jennifer's birth, feeling beautiful and feminine, she heard Charles' loud assertion: "He's got balls, and balls is what the country needs right now!"

She looked at him astonished, his face flushed and eyes flashing.

"Balls instead of brains!" retaliated Peter with equal loudness. His thin, paler face was also flushed at the cheekbone and forehead. She had never seen him so angry.

"What on earth are you two arguing about?" she said.

They both turned to stare at her.

"Churchill," said Peter, as though she were a stranger.

"And stay out of this," snapped Charles.

Churchill was in yet another heyday as the general strike neared. It would do him instead of war, and he was as jubilant as he was prominent. Scarcely a year after everyone had declared him politically dead after three successive defeats in by-elections, he was back in Parliament and in the Cabinet's second-most-important post, Chancellor of the Exchequer. Elizabeth disliked Churchill even more strongly than did Peter, but tonight she was quickly aware that Churchill was not the real cause of the argument. The two men were fighting less over politics than territory, and the territory was her.

Women are supposed to like this sort of thing, but Elizabeth found it the opposite of flattering because in the murky foundations of their combat lay the unstated assumption that she was a prize, a thing. And when once or twice she tried to join in the argument herself and found that they ignored her, a new realization arose in her. She had her own territory that she would defend against both of them. She rang the bell for the maid and ordered her to bring both the gentlemen's coats. The two gentlemen looked up at her, flushed and astonished.

"I shall not be dining out tonight," she said. "You will both be much happier in each other's company than I should be with either. Please. Do go. Now."

Like wayward boys they found themselves sheepish on the doorstep. They shuffled a little and shook hands and went their separate ways.

During the entire week that followed, Elizabeth guarded her boundaries with circumspection, and neither of the two men knew quite what she felt. Peter, deeply involved with one of the strike committees, seemed more anxious to recruit her than make love, but was too busy to trouble her greatly on either subject. Charles, following the news stories with a bitter joy she found insufferable, demanded stronger defenses from her, so on Thursday she told him that she intended to spend a week alone with Jennifer near Ravenscroft and that his company was not required. Abashed, he let her leave on Friday in a train filled with the usual weekenders. It was the weekend that the general strike began, so the three adults spent the next fortnight very much apart. Becalmed in a mediocre inn, Elizabeth pretended she could not get back to London. Peter, furiously involved in meetings and pamphlets, gave her scarcely a thought. Charles, at one stage recruited to drive a bus but for the most part as becalmed as she, spent most of the time at his club, and when he came home he chatted pleasantly to Mabel Greggs, who had no more time for the strikers than did he.

The two weeks were a curious period in Elizabeth's life. Though the strike had few direct effects on the countryside, the inn's private bar was nightly crowded with men listening to the BBC over pints of ale, and the regulars complained jokingly that they had to use the clock instead of the whistle of the ten-o'clock express to tell when it was closing time. Elizabeth hated their smugness.

"It's not as though the strikers want a war, after all," she argued to the publican. "Just justice after all these years of frightful inflation."

"That's as may be," said the innkeeper.

"We will have revolution," she reassured the publican's nervous wife, "only if the government provokes it. The strikers are completely peaceful."

"Well, I don't understand things like politics," murmured the innkeeper's wife. "I just don't want us all murdered in our beds by the Bolsheviks."

"As though," said Elizabeth sourly to farmers who did not look at her, "the law and Britain belong only to the rich. If Churchill had not put us back on the gold standard with the pound at its prewar value, then none of this need have happened."

"What would a woman," said the farmers straggling home, "know about all that?"

Three days into the strike, copies of the *British Gazette* began to arrive. It was the government's organ, printed on the usurped presses of the strikebound *Morning Post,* using paper illegally confiscated from the *Times.* Churchill was the editor, and in the paper as in Parliament, Churchill was the one who announced the government's policy toward the workers as that of "unconditional surrender." If previously he had been Elizabeth's *bête noire,* now he became her demon. She walked the springtime lanes and hedgerows with her daughter's hand in hers, singing childhood's small and silly songs, and thinking that Churchill, not she, was the traitor to her class. In May's long warm sunset hour she walked back to the inn, thinking that men were at their most disgusting when most sure they were right. She hated what they stood for: injustice; repression. Men like Churchill. Men like Charles.

In the middle of the second week of her stay, she had to take to her bed for a day because of cramps. The publican's wife became sympathetic and expressed wonder about the mysteries of the ailments brought about by the Change. At first Elizabeth thought she was using some new term for the strike, and then she realized: I'm forty-five! She dismissed the woman's reverential sympathy brusquely. It couldn't be menopause, it couldn't. She wept. Her bones ached and she felt the flesh draw down on her cheeks and neck and the painful stuffiness of her insides. If only I weren't so damnably weak, she thought.

The strike ended without violence and for no discernible reason. Thousands of strikers were refused their former jobs, and the miners, after staying out alone for long months, eventually went back to work for longer hours and less money. Churchill told Parliament that he had not enjoyed himself so much in years. Elizabeth came back to London to find Charles jaunty, Peter in gloom, but the two of them back to the stiff amiability of prestrike days. Filled with a nervous discontent, she was cool to them for weeks.

"Mars disguised as Cupid," was her only comment to Charles about Churchill.

One day when Charles was skylarking with Mabel in the kitchen, chatting about America, and listening to jazz, Elizabeth snapped off the wireless rudely. "When do we ever listen to the silence anymore?" she asked. They looked at her oddly.

When Charles and Peter began on political subjects, she put a stop to it. Charles praised America. "Americans have the virtue of single-mindedness."

"And the vice of simplemindedness," Peter replied smugly.

"Perhaps," snapped Elizabeth, "both of you should talk less about what neither of you know anything about."

Each year that Charles had visited London the flat in St. James's had changed a little: the kitchen suddenly all electricity and Formica, the bathroom sleek with new plumbing, carpeting in the hall, his own bedroom suddenly blossoming with a sporty motif. Though he knew in advance of the changes, their visual effect was so great that he had never felt the flat was his home even though he paid the rent. Now, therefore, he refurbished the suite of rooms which Clarkson and Son had maintained for years on Great Swan Alley in the City and replaced its male clerk with a secretary, an officer's widow named Mrs. Mountjoy who treated Charles' desk as though it were a shrine and he a convalescent come for cure. He would labor there each morning from nine-thirty till one o'clock. If he felt like more business, he would take a taxi to his club for luncheon, but more often than not he ate a solitary stand-up lunch at one of the pubs among the other men in bowler hats and striped pants, then left to pursue interests which his lookalikes did not share: Italian delicacies from the gold-lettered shops near Covent Garden. Hepplewhite chairs in the antique market near the Strand, old books from the cubbyholes on Charing Cross Road and Paternoster Row. Great London opened itself like a ripe fig to his gentle prodding, so that he did not notice that where his pleasures had once all been sociable, they were now mostly solitary.

He talked to strangers of the afternoon, in the giant Lyons Corner House near Marble Arch or on the benches that overlooked the Serpentine, where nannies sought to rout him with sharp looks in case he were not as innocent as he seemed. He became a target for beggars, and because he found them interesting, he would insist that they talk to him. Having learned tales and personality, he would give them money. He had more money than he could ever use, and his generosity came from curiosity at the effects on others of, for instance, a sovereign where a penny had been expected. They were idle fellows, he chided himself. But then, so was he.

And Elizabeth? He had not intended to let matters go this long, but there never seemed to have been the right moment to set things straight. Divorce was not in prospect, and he had never been serious about anyone else. He minded most the loss of her intimacy. His thoughts returned more often than he wished to the evening of the resthouse at Wilpattu, which he had come to think of as the last occasion on which they had been together. He wanted her, wanted someone who had known him. But from what he saw as a position of weakness, he could not beg. She would return to him because she wanted to or not at all, and there was no place to start.

Thus resolute, Charles accepted the truce represented by the solitary master bedroom in the St. James's flat. Mornings he was up early, and since Mabel no longer went to mass, he would enjoy her domesticity as she prepared breakfast wearing dressing gown and braids. She grew a bit cheeky with him sometimes, as though he were her son, and he found her charming. They shared a taste for things American and were discovered by Elizabeth one morning joining in a chorus of "California, Here I Come!"

Mabel did not much like Peter Williams. "Bit of a simp, that one, if you ask me," she said sturdily one morning. "Always talking to me about the plight of the working classes, I ask you, as though *I* were working-class."

Charles teased her about being a false orphan, and one morning she proudly introduced him to her brother, Fred, who had come to be a good-looking young chap, well-turned-out, with very few traces of the cockney accent that Wapping should have guaranteed. Mabel admitted that her savings had paid for what she called an "accent school," where he learned the speech of his betters. Charles thought there must be more to the lad than accent and offered to help him find a good position.

"He's got a job," said Mabel, looking surprised. "He's been working ever since he finished school. I don't know that it's much of a job, but it's what he wants, and with Fred you don't . . . you don't muck around with young Fred."

"Is he in a shop?"

Nanny looked indignant. "He's an actor."

"And what does your mother think of that?"

"Mum says he's gotten hoity-toity," said Mabel matter-of-factly. "He doesn't visit her much these days. But I say, what do you expect? Good on him, say I, to get away from all that as fast as he can. I'll help if he needs it."

"California, here I come," murmured Charles. "Go west, young man!"

Thus we assemble our values by stumbling over the people in our lives. With middle age, other people become less interesting in themselves than for what they tell us about ourselves.

27

Jennifer's task for this decade was easier than that of her parents: she had only to acquire experience, not understand it. "Human history becomes more and more a race between education and catastrophe," wrote H. G. Wells in 1920. That was the year in which Jennifer entered Ravenscroft, much younger and marginally prettier than any other pupil. Even the starched habits of the nuns bent to accommodate her, with the result that in her case it would be hard to tell whether education or catastrophe won.

A huge brick Victorianism sited in soft Hertfordshire countryside, the Ravenscroft School for Young Ladies was expensive, demure, austere. Old Girls remembered beeswax and the squeaking of shined linoleum. Bored under high ceilings, girls fiddled with inkwells and stared at portraits of saints and popes, discovering them eventually to be men. In each bedroom white curtains on brass rails sequestered four girls, and every night on each of four straight-backed chairs lay the day's soiled clothing folded for the maids to launder, covered by an embroidered linen square, purified by stockings laid in the form of a cross. Dark wood partitioned the Victorian bathrooms into cubicles, in each of which stood a cast-iron bathtub with claw-and-ball feet. Each girl wore a long white shift to bathe.

As schools will, Ravenscroft defined catastrophe as the failure to do what is right. As pupils will, the girls defined education as learning to keep Original Sin alive. The teachers would allow no crooked seam or unruly tie, no loose blouse or unpressed collar, no shoe less than fully black, shiny. The girls tilted their hats, shaped their hair, made the ornaments of piety those of vanity, and, later in the twenties, inched their hemlines upward. As Mabel Greggs had earlier hoped, their discipline came more from the inside than out. As Elizabeth had earlier expected, Jennifer proved adept at turning the act of doing the right thing to her own advantage.

In 1925, when Jennifer was eleven, a former pupil married to an

American millionaire presented the school with a life-size wax figurine of the Christ Child hand-painted by Ursuline sisters in Padua. Preparations for display in the Christmas creche were pregnant with religious adoration: the figure was child, divine, male. It was also bald, awaiting crowning glory from a worthy maiden. This was no small matter. The nuns remembered their shearing as novitiates: renunciation of worldly vanity. To the girls, the significance of cutting was other: a public affirmation of nearness to adulthood that frightened them. Even the mothers of girls were nervous. Irene Castle had bobbed in 1914, and Antoine de Paris had shingled in 1921. By 1925 a few mothers had shorn—to go with their Chanel No. 5 and cigarettes. But young ladies, no. To mothers, girls, and nuns, short hair was the whisper of glamour, and glamour (they all agreed) was for Gloria Swanson, not for schoolgirls, not for years. There was no plethora of maidens eager for sacrifice.

Saturday night was hair-wash night. The girls giggled down the stone stairs to the great laundry room, where they scrubbed their heads over big tubs with bars of yellow soap, rinsed them with ale whose smell made their noses wrinkle, toweled them with coarse cloth. Yelping, they unsnagged each other's tangles with thick brushes and then knelt awkwardly beside an ironing board so that the maids might dry their hair under heavy iron lids taken from the stoves. The nuns thought the girls looked like angels all pink and white in their gowns and slippers, but the angels hated the entire process. When they went upstairs to cocoa and bed, their faces blotched with heat, exertion, and the occasional small burn or scrape, they would rub their sore knees and crimped necks and hate life.

One Saturday night Jennifer, between the toweling and the ironing, announced to Sister Martha her reluctant willingness to give up her hair to the Christ Child.

"I wondered why you hadn't been yelping and squeaking tonight!" said Sister staunchly. "Been thinking it all over, have you?"

Jennifer looked at her innocently. "Actually, I was feeling sad. This could be the last time I'll wash my hair."

Sister Martha looked at the child, kneeling with the square of towel in her hands, her bright curls tumbling around her face, spun rather than grown, catching the room's ruddy light with gleams of dark gold and hints of auburn.

"It'll take a long time to grow back, you know," said Sister.

"Yes, Sister."

"Do you think you'll look better or worse without that lovely hair, young lady?" She ran her fingers gently through the child's damp curls.

"I don't know, Sister. The same?"

"I'm telling you you look better with it long than you will with it short. You won't look the same." Jennifer looked at her calmly. "Do you still have that picture of Mary Pickford on the door?"

"No, Sister." It was not a lie. Mary Pickford had yielded to Vilma Banky not long before.

"Hmph," said Sister Martha. "You're supposed to pay no attention at all to film stars, if you recall."

"Yes, Sister," said Jennifer, dropping her glance to the floor.

"I shouldn't count my chickens," said Sister sourly. "Many are called, but few are chosen."

Jennifer looked up at her, and for a moment the two stared into each other's eyes, and then the aging nun laughed and tousled the child's hair and stood up. "Well, you're going to be a beautiful woman someday," she said, "so run along with you and get your hair ironed. I'll put in a word for you with the Mother General."

The Mother General cabled the Wingates, who were then in Positano, and Elizabeth cabled permission, and on the next Saturday afternoon Jennifer was taken to the Mother General's private sitting room and seated in the Mother General's own armchair, where with little cries of grief a lady sent specially from Dabney's in London shaped the style which the child had whispered to her: the bingle, the season's most dramatic fashion, a cut halfway between bob and shingle. After, Jennifer received the consolation of buttered scones and tea made by the Mother General herself, then left the room, quietly, feeling the December cold on her bare neck.

Fortunately for the Mother General she did not see the novitiate arrive back in the room where the other girls waited. Carrying her head as a stalk does a flower, she threw the door open dramatically, hitched her skirt above her knees, placed one forefinger under her tilted chin, crooked one leg in front of the other, and smiled a bee-stung smile to the wild applause of her friends. "The flapper!" they cried. The Mother General was surprised, however, when one of those sudden madnesses to which institutions are prone took hold in the weeks immediately following. A dozen girls came back from Christmas vacation with short hair, and by spring it seemed that there was not one left with long.

Throughout her life, Jennifer was to have phases when her beauty caught fire and brought her favors: in infancy; now at adolescence, when she became suddenly the envy of other girls; then later in early womanhood, when she trailed sensuality like silk and grew irresistible to the touch and heat of males. This was unfortunate for her. Because our imaginations lend an accident of nature the force of the ideal, we treat the beautiful gently, lest it remove itself from our presence, and we grant good will. The beautiful does not have to earn anything. Jennifer's education led her to believe that she had a right to favors. She grew too used to success.

Charles thought her beauty was delightful. His daughter was a bright little thing and deserved the best he and the world could give her. In London he dutifully attended to her education. They had a game to play on the upstairs of the bus on the way to a gallery or Hamley's in Regent Street or London Zoo, when they would haul the stiff tarpaulin over their knees and hold hands underneath. Where will we find an eighteenth-century window? Which of us will find the oldest date above a doorway? What famous author lived on that street? When she was older he gave her books which he had read and they would talk about them. Older still, she fed the swans with him in St. James's Park and they talked of finishing schools abroad. He looked at her body, now barely disguised by puppy fat, and he wondered what young cub would first enjoy it.

Elizabeth worried about her daughter's character and was angry when Charles gave her a wireless or Mabel slipped her extra treats. "This way of life is a privilege, you know, not a right," she would say. When they took the train home from Ravenscroft, Elizabeth would point out the window at the lines of washing strung in London's filthy air. "Imagine washing that," she said. "And without hot water!" She told Jennifer about the children who froze to death in winter, about the whole families living in a single room, about the old people who could not afford sugar for their tea. She had her join an organization called the Sunbeams, whose rich young members sent letters, clothes, toys, and lies to pen friends in the slums. Jennifer wanted her mother to hire her pen friend as a tweeny to rescue her from the East End, and reluctantly Elizabeth agreed to a summer's experiment. The girl was fat, pasty, and adenoidal rather than thin and romantically pale, and she and Jennifer had nothing to say to each other. By the end of a week Mabel was reporting that the girl had cried herself to sleep, and she was sent home in a state of joy. Jennifer read in Mrs. Beeton's *Book of Household Management* that a tweeny deserves commiseration. "Her life is a solitary one," said Mrs. Beeton, "and in some places her work is never done." Perhaps that had been the trouble, suggested Jennifer. Perhaps, said Elizabeth.

Mostly Jennifer confined her experiments to her group of closest friends, a foursome known as "the Beauties" because in their beauty and self-assurance they all seemed lightly harnessed to the same carriage. There was Jill Knight, a tall and very English girl of the kind destined to become Head Girl: clear blue eyes, fair skin and thick hair, beautiful carriage, and an instinct for the proper thing. There was Fern Hardacre, another blond English beauty, but sloe-eyed and slow-minded, already sensual in body and gesture, destined to be men's prize and victim. There was the American rawboned Maureen O'Flynn, slightly too wild, often in trouble for no bad reason, the leader across stepping-stones. And there was Jennifer, younger and smaller than they, never their leader, but somehow, always and without trying, their star. An innocent group, all told, moving through childhood and puberty with the usual mistakes and fears and small contempts.

During the final spring which the four Beauties spent at Ravenscroft, 1928, when Jennifer was fourteen and the others fifteen, summer warmth came early. In May the budding was an act of violence, and spring perfumes forced themselves upon girls restless in their beds on long, sunlit evenings. The girls fell in love with each other, with a nun, with a poem, with a picture postcard, gravid with eroticism. The nuns watched the girls have crushes and spites and finger the petals of flowers as though they were the skin of lovers, and they knew that the message of the Church was necessary. Around the school's brick buildings the flowers spread across fields and under hedgerows, the animals gave birth, and the girls smelled the scent of new grass and farmyards as they read each other Chaucer and Keats.

On a Saturday evening in June the four Beauties lay upon their backs in the deep grass out of sight of the school. They watched the fleecy clouds sail, and they half-heard the song of birds and the distant drone of farm machinery and the questions of their own dreams. They had been to town, where they had seen—illegally, of course—Greta Garbo and John Gilbert in *Flesh and the Devil* at the Odeon, and they had walked back across the summer fields, idling, in love with Garbo, each girl trying to find out what she would be. They were slightly sticky with sweat and the juice of grasses, and Maureen carried her shoes and stockings, having stepped into an unexpected streamlet. Their ties were loose. Fern had looped her dirndl into its belt, so that her thighs gleamed pale above her black stockings. Jennifer wore a chain of daisies around her neck, Jill another chain in her hair, and their lips and chins were golden with splashes of buttercup pollen.

Stripping a long blade of grass between her teeth, Fern gently broke a long silence. "In Hollywood . . . they must do things that are really . . . wicked. I wonder what it's like."

Maureen snorted. "Great fun, I should expect!"

Fern continued, "When we leave school . . ." She paused so that they might all adjust to her. "What are you going to do about . . . sex?"

Flat on their backs, knees raised or apart, the girls studied the clouds. As though she heard Pan's flute, Maureen giggled, very softly, nervously. Jennifer watched Fern idly stroke with one fingertip the white flesh of the back of her thigh bared between stocking top and bloomers.

"No, I mean it!" protested Fern. "What shall you *do?*"

She looked at Maureen, who did not look at her, and it was Jennifer who unexpectedly replied: "I shall do it as soon as possible," she announced seriously.

All three of her friends looked toward her, and she sat up to study the ground between her feet. The girls' ideas came from books and films and from their modern parents' conversations, but their feelings had other sources.

"I shall find myself someone agreeable, and kind. Probably during my first Season, after finishing school, certainly before I am eighteen. And we shall do it together."

"Oh, Jennifer," said Jill, turning away in protest, "you don't know what you are talking about!"

But Fern sat up to look at Jennifer silhouetted against the bright blue and green of nature and took her seriously. "It sounds so mechanical. So planned." She paused, and a haunted look was on her soft face. "What about love, and marriage?"

"Well, of course it will be *romantic,*" said Jennifer scornfully. *"He* will be in love with *me,* and I—"

"I shan't wait till I get married either," interrupted Maureen. "I certainly shan't *marry* until I've established my career."

"You and your career!" Jill was always irritated with Maureen's ideas about work.

"It must be so exciting, don't you think?" said Fern dreamily. "To give oneself, to give one's all, to a man, just to melt, to do *anything* for him."

"This is a terrible conversation," said Jill flatly. "You're talking about *sin.*"

"Well, there's no need to get so cross," flared Maureen.

"Well, you know we'll all get married, and it's such a lot of nonsense talking love and sex and all that stuff."

"Don't be such a stick, Jill," said Jennifer. "Haven't you any romance in you?"

At that moment across the fields the sound of the bell for evening prayers reached them through the westering sunlight, and Jill rose and brushed off her skirt and said, "We shall be late."

"I'm not going," said Jennifer. "What can they do about it in our last week? Do you want to come, Maur?"

"Where to?"

"Anywhere."

The four Beauties separated, Jill marching off to the school with Fern docile in her wake, Jennifer and Maureen straggling down the slope toward the trees shielding the brick wall that marked the school's gate, where lay the small lake and the evening's ducks. The sun still warmed the skin. They walked slowly behind the stables and the greenhouses shimmering with heat. They had no goal and still were dreamy with the film and the talk. Ahead lay the thick hedge of yew that bordered the driveway to the school, and they wandered through scattered shrubbery toward the gatehouse, a brick cottage protected from view by both the hedge and an extra border of rhododendrons.

The gatehouse was the residence of the only male who lived on the school grounds. He was known only as Hugh and functioned as a general handyman and watchdog. Hugh was not a large man, but he awed the girls by strangeness. Slow-talking with a heavy Kentish accent, he spoke very seldom, and his remarks were often beside the point, so that he seemed dim-witted. He was shy and knew that his mind worked more slowly than it once had. Though he was very young, his hair was all gray. He had come to the school only a month before Jennifer, after his release from the military hospital where he had spent long months recuperating from shellshock. According to the doctors with whom the Mother General had spoken, one of Big Bertha's huge shells had passed completely through the French barn in which Hugh and his company were sheltering, in one wall and out the other. The pressure generated by its passage had been enough to crush the men inside, and rescuers found Hugh alone, among twenty-seven men, alive. The Mother General did not quite believe the story—one heard so many incredible tales about the war—but Hugh, now passively in need of shelter and guaranteed both strong and gentle, was the best choice among the veterans offered to her for employ.

Hugh owned two pairs of gray woolen combinations, both of which he meticulously washed on Saturday afternoon and hung on the hedge surrounding his cottage to sweeten the wool while he took his weekly bath in a tin tub on the kitchen floor. The two manlike shapes—baggy at elbow, knee, seat, and crotch—caused delight in giggling girls, who had been known to detour for a glimpse of them. Now Jennifer and Maureen wandering unbuttoned came upon them looking defenseless upon the hedge, and the same thought entered their two heads at the same instant.

Jennifer glanced wildly at Maureen. "I dare you!"

"I double-dare you!" said Maureen, her green eyes wide.

"Oh, I couldn't!" protested Jennifer in giggles.

"Couldn't you just, cowardy-custard! Watch me! I'll take one, if you take the other."

Tense as wires, the two girls crept Indian fashion up to the hedge, which was chest-high to them. Without pausing for breath, Maureen half stood up, reached over, seized one pair by the neck, ducked, clutched them to her breast, and turned to flee, all glee.

"Go on! Go on!" she urged Jennifer, who still crouched beneath the hedge, startled by the speed and daring of Maureen's act. Her breath stuck in her chest. She stared briefly at Maureen, now disappearing into the trees behind the toolshed, then suddenly rose and snatched at the second pair of combinations. They stuck firm on a twig. Jennifer might then gracefully have given up, but she suddenly found herself determined not to give in, and so she tugged harder, and then, because she needed all her height to reach the snag, stood boldly up.

Hugh had just finished his bath and was standing in the tub drying himself with a rough towel, staring idly out the open kitchen door into an evening free of people at this hour of prayers, when suddenly he saw the first pair of underwear vanish before his eyes. As Jennifer reached unseeing for the second pair, Hugh reacted automatically and raced from the cottage, forgetting entirely his nudity. He grasped the underwear's flaccid legs just as Jennifer rose from hiding to untangle their neck from the twig, so that the two were brought face to face across the low hedge, each grasping the gray wool from different ends, each so surprised that for seconds they stood still studying each other, she slight and flushed, a schoolgirl with a dawning glee, he a man whose diffident nature and lower class for once, in his muscled nudity and youthful shock, did not show.

He stared at her, appalled. Her amazed gaze traveled over his body, the hair on his pale chest, the white scar of a bullet-wound snaking across his belly, the large genitals dusky and slack and nested, the sturdy legs, the big feet planted as firmly on the grass as those of Pan. His face turned slowly red with embarrassment.

"N-o-o-o, miss, you mustn't," he said slowly, his big hands gripping the wool. Suddenly he closed his eyes. "You mustn't, miss! Turn your back, miss! Close your eyes!"

Jennifer looked directly at his face with its closed eyes, the remnants of shock on her own. Then a small smile curled the corners of her lips. Her eyes lit up, and for a moment she had the face of a cat: bright, cold. "I shall have them," she said calmly.

"No-o-o-o, miss," he said again slowly, his mouth stubborn.

She replied, "If you don't let go, I shall tell Mother General."

His eyes flew open. Hers flicked again over his nakedness. He was, perhaps, as stunned by beauty as by will, by daisies in her hair, by the buzzing of bees along the hedge. In his face, dismay supplanted will. He became slack-jawed and slack-fingered, and instantly she whipped the underwear across the hedge, flung them over her shoulder, and ran down the path, with one single look at the devastated man as he in turn retreated, covering his nakedness with his hands as best he might.

The acquisition of Hugh's combinations by Maureen and Jennifer, and the tale of Hugh's nakedness, became the great joys of the last week at Ravenscroft. Through all the ceremonies of farewell and all the ritual warnings of going into the world, the girls bubbled with the tale. Hugh, going about his usual work, was faced with groups of girls who giggled as they passed. Mortification sank into him, where it burned as fiercely as had the bullet wound years before. After a few days displaying the combinations to privileged viewers, Jennifer and Maureen wrapped them in brown paper and placed them secretly upon his doorstep. They were not hard of heart. But that summer Hugh resigned his post. The Mother General was disappointed; she had expected him to be steadier.

28

July 1928

"One would scarcely think," said Lady Pearsall, "that less than six months ago where we are sitting was under water. That . . . how many people drowned within yards of here? Fourteen?"

They were seated at a table on the terrace of the Houses of Parliament. The day's sun and mild air had created a crowd for luncheon, but the others had left in a rush when the House began its sitting. Charles, feeling stuffy with the weather and an extra glass of ale, had refused the invitation of Elizabeth's host–Labor M.P. for some Midlands district–to take seats in the Strangers' Gallery, and he had been surprised when Ginny Pearsall had chosen to remain with him. They had not had a private conversation in years.

"I see they're building the embankments higher," he said, looking across the Thames toward St. Thomas's Hospital. Giant machines were lugging mud and stones with great gruntings.

"The bounds of civilization, set against rude nature," said Ginny idly. She looked up-to-date, staring down at the white gloves on her hands, a trace of smeared lipstick visible on her mouth. She wore a light coat flung over her shoulders, but her arms were bare except for bangles. A cloche hat clung to sleekly waved hair that was completely gray going white. She has aged, he thought, and looks a little too modern for her own good, but then, these days everyone seems to prefer fashion to beauty.

"Will you have more tea? Coffee?" she said, touching each pot lightly.

"No, thank you."

The silence grew between them as they looked at the buildings across the river, at the trees heavily green in the light from the water. This was the very heart of Empire–seven hundred feet of heart closed off, with the Gothic windows of the Peers Library and the long facade of statues and coats of arms of all the English monarchs and the sound of Big Ben chiming, muffled but near.

"And has my cousin converted you to the compost theory of English history?" said Lady Pearsall politely. They had been joined at luncheon by a well-connected eccentric who believed that the use of chemicals in the soil was undermining the English character.

"Chemicals?" Charles spoke almost crossly. "I know nothing about chemicals. *Something's* undermining our character."

"You *are* grumpy today."

Mildly surprised by the criticism, he watched Lady Pearsall take a cigarette from her handbag. Women these days . . . She accepted the light he offered and settled back, pointedly not disturbing him. He had not thought about their past for years.

"What is it you want?" he said abruptly.

She turned her head toward him slowly, one eyebrow arched, the lids hooding her blue eyes, the skin twisting at her neck. She let him see that she was amused. "I've always thought you were more acute than you seemed," she said, and when he did not reply, she spoke again, her focus shifting to some point over her left shoulder. "The man will think me presumptuous. It has been such a very long time."

That old habit, he thought. Does she do it deliberately when she's in a tight spot? But he owed her something for the silence she had preserved to Elizabeth all these years.

"I think," she said calmly, "that it is time you spoke to Elizabeth."

"About what?"

She looked at him directly.

"She and Peter Williams have been together for nine, almost ten years. That is a very long time." Interference was not her métier. "I suppose I'm old-fashioned, but I can't help wishing you would go after her, pursue her, court her. I can't help wondering why you do not."

"You *are* getting old-fashioned," he said without kindness, so that she in her turn was surprised.

"In what way?"

"About people, marriage."

Few people contradicted Ginny Pearsall. She was nonplussed and shifted uneasily in a chair grown uncomfortable.

Charles lay back in his chair expansively, putting his head back to look at the blue sky as though he were a boy. He looked at her shrewdly. "For all your rebelliousness, Ginny, you have led a very proper life, have you not? Followed the prescribed route, done your duty, the right thing?"

She flushed, embarrassed that overconfidence had made her step into deep water. "I was brought up–"

"You were brought up," he interrupted roughly, "to another

world. You've never really had a life of your own apart from Reggie, have you? Marriage has made you what you are."

"I don't care much for theory. I know you still care for Elizabeth."

"Do I?"

"Of course you do."

"I suppose you're right," he said, interrogating his cigar tip. "I think well of her for the most part. She's an intelligent woman."

"You sound as though she were an acquaintance."

"I don't think," he said, "that one can both respect and love a woman."

Suddenly she was angry. "I've never heard such nonsense in my life."

"I can covet what I don't own. I can respect it. But not, I think, love it. You want me to tell you I still love Elizabeth. She has her independence, and don't worry, she hasn't lost me, but . . ."

Ginny Pearsall realized that her careful plan had gone badly awry. She blamed herself for not having known better. The afternoon had taken on a glazed and sullen quality, an intensity she had not expected because she had anticipated ruling by a nudge. Then Charles' expression softened and he looked at her once more as though she were a friend of twenty years.

"Perhaps it's all just a matter of age," he said. "I'm not sure I have a heart to lose anymore. I've retired from all that. I've made a truce with life, an armistice with my wife. Better to leave it at that, Ginny. Peace may be a trifle dull, but it's better than the alternative."

"Are you being intentionally pathetic?"

"Pathetic?" Now it was he who was startled. "No," he said.

"Then you must be a very lonely man." She took another cigarette from her purse and held it for him to light, which he did automatically. "Have you never understood what love is, built from a thousand, a hundred thousand daily things of no importance whatever?"

"Perhaps women have more chance to learn what that is all about," he said resentfully. He knew very well what she meant. He had often thought that women, because they mothered children, learned to cherish the banal, but any man who clung thus to the quotidian was, well, an old woman. "I prefer a little romance myself."

Suddenly Ginny rose from the table, turned, and walked to the stone balustrade, where she leaned over to stare at the riverbed. The mud revealed by low tide stank, jeweled only with detritus. Against a backdrop of sky and river and buildings and machinery, in the drape of her summer coat and the hood of the cloche hat, it was Lady Pearsall who looked pathetic. He remained seated, so she turned to speak to him across the distance, and he was aware that her face looked pale and weak. "You dismiss our lives." She spoke loud with accusation. "As though they were important only if they suit you."

He felt the flare of sexual antagonism surge in him. "And you use our lives," he said angrily. "As though we only lived to suit you."

She walked toward him, so that for a moment he thought, amazed, that she would strike him, her eyes ablaze, but she simply picked up her handbag. "I think we have said enough for one afternoon," she said, and turned to walk along the stone path to the door leading to the Strangers' Dining Room, where a waiter stood resolutely not eyeing them, the only couple left on the terrace. Then she stopped and turned back to look at him, her shoulders tense, her hands clutching the purse in front of her. "I want you to know I am most desperately *sorry* for you, Charles. That you must, every day, go back to that empty life."

She turned on her heel and walked rapidly to the doorway.

"Empty?" he said, astounded. "There's so much more to life than . . ."

She vanished through the door, bowed by the waiter. Furious, Charles cast his cigar fiercely to the ground.

Shortly after this conversation, Charles and Joe Plunkett pulled off a major deal, and Joe insisted that the entire firm, including Mrs. Mountjoy, celebrate over drinks and dinner. They left her at the front door of her flat near Notting Hill Gate to dress for dinner and see that her two growing boys were cared for, while they searched for an Indian restaurant and champagne.

Mrs. Mountjoy was quick rather than intelligent. Her mind focused narrowly and with good effect on anything familiar, but the men's conversation often left her slightly bewildered by speed or humor, so that she tended to gape at them with a vague smile. She had married young, become quickly a mother, and lost her husband to a land mine while the first bloom was still on their love, with the result that she remained inexperienced beyond her age. Tonight she wore an ill-cut but pretty jacket of Chinese fabric over a midnight-blue dress that suited her full figure well, and she had let her hair loose from its office net and pins to reveal herself a pretty blond. The men were jovial with success and champagne, to the point of boyishness. She laughed both at and with them, like a patient mother, and refused the extra glasses of wine. She had never tasted Indian food, so the men led her through its rituals and poured water into her when the burn of curry brought color to her cheeks and tears to her eyes.

"Woman adores you!" said Joe, during her brief absence from the table. "And you could do worse, if I do say so myself, old man."

"Who?" said Charles vaguely.

"This woman. Mrs. Mountjoy."

"Oh. Shouldn't think so. I've known her for years."

But when he took her home, Joe having taken a taxi to his club, she paused with her hand on the door frame, clutching a key. "Can I offer you a cup of coffee?" she said.

She seemed very young. The glow of a soft lamp inside her flat cast a nimbus around her fair hair, and the fall of her elbow in the gaudy fabric was sensual.

"I should like that," he replied.

She showed him in, then went to conduct a murmured conversation at the door of the next-door flat.

"The children," she said when she returned. "I've asked my neighbor to keep them overnight. She's very kind."

While she made coffee, he lit the gas fire, and they sat on a couch to stare together at its blue flame, an afghan over both their laps. They were still lighthearted and foolish with the remnants of celebration and the unusualness of his coming to her home. Charles was filled with the discovery of someone different in someone he had known well. When he reached to kiss her, it was in the spirit of fun, but the scent of the flesh of her neck and throat and some stupid little perfume she wore excited him, and the buttons of her dress unloosed easily. She gasped at the touch of his hand under her slip and brassiere, her flesh warm and generous to his hand. He felt himself stir with sexuality and tumbled upon her, almost laughing.

"You make my Oedipus complex raise its ugly head!" he exclaimed, with his lips at her throat.

She did not know what he meant and looked at him aghast. For a moment each had a separate obscene fantasy in mind to excite themselves. But they did not make love that night, and next day, in consequence, they were not embarrassed but gentle, each tending the other in their different ways. He remembered vividly the softness of her dusky flesh; she was soft with the promise of his manliness.

When some weeks later they did begin to make love, and when they continued, always it was in her small flat, always late at night with the two boys asleep in their own room at the other end of the corridor, and thus for both of them the flat and lovemaking became inextricable, as though one were a dimension or fulfillment of the other. When he was not there, she savored what he left behind—a handkerchief, a pipe, ticket stubs, coins on the bureau. He, not being there, thought of her before the gas fire with the curve of breast showing in the gap of her bathrobe; being there, he read the paper and helped the boys with their homework and did the washing up.

A mood came upon her. "I am your back-street wife."

"You are my Cleopatra."

"I could never marry you. I have lost a husband myself."

Over the months she took not a penny from him, not a gift, not a thing, at very most, and after much persuading, only the food and wine which they consumed together, presents for the boys at Christmas, and a pair of earrings which she had admired in a shop.

"I should think badly of myself," she repeated, shaking her head.

He came to know that her ethics were simple and very clear. Life was to her a corner in the world where she and her children would be safe. Her obligation was to keep that corner tidy. She was at once so defenseless before him, and yet so impregnable in her own sense of the rightness of things, that there would be no point in combat. She did not mind if he sat in sleeve garters and stocking feet on the top of the counterpane given her by her mother. He was amused to find that he enjoyed the smell of wax if, in a fit of energy, she decided to get the floor done. Perhaps this was what was meant to be: at home, but a visitor.

Elizabeth knew nothing of Charles' relationship with Mrs. Mountjoy and would have been annoyed at a tattletale. During one of the weekly luncheons at Fortnum's which had become a habit, Ginny asked her what she thought of her husband, puzzled still as to whether she or Charles had been closer to the truth in their exchange on the terrace at Parliament House.

"I think what's wrong with Charles," said Elizabeth, leaning back on the leather banquette, "is his wretched reasonableness."

The waitress served the game pie and watercress salad without overhearing; Fortnum and Mason were familiar with this kind of conversation between lunching older ladies.

"At least Peter has some passion for life," said Elizabeth. "Oh, I know he's terribly intellectual, but somehow he *cares,* and that's what I like about him. Charles is such a stick. He never does anything different."

Motes danced in the sunlight from the room's tall western windows which were open to the summer's airlessness.

"That is odd," said Lady Pearsall. "I myself find the exact opposite true. Forgive me, my dear, but Peter is a terrible bore, while Charles . . . well, I find Charles a very exciting man." She smiled with mischief. "As you know, I have for years."

"I don't mean sensually," said Elizabeth, who still remembered Charles' lovemaking.

"Nor do I," said Ginny. "But then, if you don't see it, I can scarcely argue you into feeling."

"You yourself," said Elizabeth, "used to recommend that I make the best of both worlds. I like Charles, but I cannot trust him. Not just with other women, but with me. Whereas Peter, I'm safe with Peter." She pushed her plate away. "And for God's sake don't ask me which of them I love. I'm fond of both of them in very different ways."

The waitress cleared away their plates and wheeled the dessert cart to their table. It was filled with delicacies: patisseries and gateaux, confections from Vienna and solid English puddings, whimsies all fruit and cream, uncrumbable cake. Ginny delightedly accepted a mound of meringue and strawberries, while Elizabeth finally refused anything.

"Sometimes," said Ginny, eyeing the richness on her plate, "I envy your talent for *not* choosing."

The two women laughed at each other.

But the dilemma, thought Elizabeth, could be neither wheeled nor laughed away. As fifty began to loom before her, she developed a certain nostalgia for the simplicity of the old days, when she had known where she stood. Even war had its appeal, in retrospect. All these bitterly antiwar memoirs now appearing, they reminded one of war's drama, war's clarity. The everyday, she sighed, has very little romance to it. She having thus diminished war, it gave her a personal reminder. During a spring weekend at the house of friends in the country, a perfectly strange young man introduced himself the moment she came down from her room. "I'm so glad you've arrived," he said. "I've been waiting rather eagerly since I heard you would be here. I don't know if you remember me. Anthony James. We've never met, but we corresponded during the war."

She was startled at first. Having long since declared him dead, she was not sure he had the right to be alive. She had buried his letters somewhere along with the other bric-a-brac of her life from Ceylon.

But he proved charming, and she asked him to dine at St. James's Mansions.

"Oxford? and then banking?" inquired Ginny Pearsall after meeting him. "How very suitable. And about thirty, wouldn't you say? Such a nice age for a man. You two go so well together."

Tall, thin, energetic, with an Anglo-Saxon's sculptured features and fair hair and skin, Anthony James was indeed a good-looking man. But Elizabeth laughed and demurred. When he asked her to attend a gallery opening, she accepted and paid special attention to her appearance. His hand strong on her arm disconcerted her. She found herself watching his legs and thighs as he bounded up a flight of stairs. So she refused his later invitation to a cocktail dance. After that, they saw each other only at other people's occasions. There was a tacit admission that in other circumstances . . .

In these later years of the decade, Elizabeth complained only that she had nothing justifiably to complain about. She felt neither old nor young, and that there should be more to her than there was. When Ginny blamed menopause for her fits of irritability, she agreed. When friends blamed years and husbands for their boredom, she nodded her head. When Jennifer, turning sixteen in a Paris finishing school, underwent a brief but savage religiosity involving all the normal follies, she was unmoved.

"It is perhaps a little extreme," wrote Madame Fenton from the Fenton École des Filles, "but quite usual among girls of her age. The French call it a *crise de mysticisme*. It will pass. Opposition is not wise."

Opposition! thought Elizabeth, looking at Charles somnolent with evening across the drawing room. I envy the girl!

And then the sudden stab—her husband so peaceable in front of the fire. Have I failed him? She remembered his confession at the resthouse in Wilpattu of his fear of dying, of his need to believe in God. And all I could think of was whether or not I should try to liven up Peter. Had she done them all an injustice? In a flash of horrid memory she was back at the water hole, sensing the waters gather at her back, looking across her shoulder at the face of the simple soul whose body was about to vanish from the earth. She looked across the drawing room at the statue of the Buddha which Peter had given her and which looked cheerful amid this warmth. Even goatherds have faith in their gods and their futures, she thought. Why have I none?

29

May 1931

In 1911, a decade after her death, they gave Queen Victoria new responsibilities. They placed her in white marble in front of Buckingham Palace to glumly guard her descendants. They gave her Motherhood, Truth, and Justice to help, with Victory in bronze above her, Courage and Constancy at her feet. Pools protected her from subjects who would clamber on her lap. Twenty years later she was still dutiful, her gaze pinning the flat extent of the Mall to the ground as far as Admiralty Arch, keeping order among the palisade of mansions to the left–Lancaster House, Clarence House, St. James's Palace, Marlborough House, the Carlton House Terrace–and forbidding them to decline to the people's pleasures in St. James's Park, to her right.

She stared down the traffic too, so that it must divide around her, and on this day she had reduced it to stationary obeisance. The black backs of Rolls-Royces and Daimlers lay motionless on the Mall's strand, stared at like a phenomenon of seals by the people on the pavement eight deep under the generous green flutter of May's leaves on the plane trees. In each black car sat a maiden in white, slightly damp with excitement, separated by glass from the mob and the chauffeur, impatient with the limousines inching toward the palace courtyard. For two hours or more the maidens fiddled with uncomfortable armholes and tried not to crease their evening gowns. Inside the cars the sunlight fell warmly, and warm maidens rolled down the windows an inch or so. They waved to each other. They chatted with their mothers, their maids.

Two mums from Golders Green carrying string shopping bags stooped to stare into the Wingates' rented Rolls, looking at the four occupants in turn, slowly. They stared at Mabel last, and their final comment was audible: "What's she doing there, then?"

Mabel, staring ahead at Queen Victoria, ignored them for a few moments; then she sniffed. "You'd think they'd find something better to do with their time."

"Better than this?" Elizabeth smiled. "For instance?"

They sat next to each other on the jump seats with their backs to the chauffeur, Elizabeth in full evening dress, both tucking their feet out of the way of the gowns worn by Jennifer and Maureen, opposite. They were on their way to the second of the four evening courts which bring London society into full heat. The Season, lasting from May until the end of August, consisted of the months of mating for the fox, the grouse, and the quail. During these months Englishmen could be forced to imitate rather than shoot their fellow creatures. Accordingly, on each of four spring evenings, six hundred maidens were offered up to Their Majesties King George the Fifth and Queen Mary. The debutantes came out.

Maureen adored the onlookers and took to imitating their cockney comments in her soft American voice. " 'Ear that, luv? I'm smashing, I am,' " she said, mock-preening. "But you're no better than a corker, Jenny."

" 'Jennifer,' please, Maureen," corrected Elizabeth.

"Jennifer," said Maureen hastily. "Sorry, Mrs. Wingate."

The girls deserved the crowd's compliments. Maureen O'Flynn had more than just a chronological year on Jennifer; she had an experiential year at home in Long Island. She was thinner, wore more makeup, and had smoked a cigarette even in the confines of the automobile. Charles had met her industrialist father during a visit to New York the previous December and spent a week at their home waiting out the crisis in international payments which followed the wave of bank closings begun by the crash of the Bank of the United States. In return he had offered his family's hospitality for Maureen's debut. The girls had gone together to Madame Vacani's to learn the proper manner of the curtsy and to Hartnell's and Harrod's and Bond Street for the six ball gowns, six day dresses, four (so far) of the six cocktail dresses and two (so far) of the four Ascot outfits which the Season demanded. Elizabeth was grateful that Maureen's presence had spared her all that, along with the hours of giggles over Lady Troubridge's *Book of Etiquette* and helping compose breathless little bread-and-butter notes for the previous night's food and music.

Mabel had continued to stare gloomily at the crowd. "A shabby lot, they are," she murmured with a jerk of her chin. "I hate all cloth caps."

Most of the onlookers were men wearing cloth caps and baggy woolen workclothes, but there were trilby hats and snap-brims and even a bowler or two, and there were women wearing new cloche hats and clutching neat handbags.

"Many of them are unemployed, Mabel," replied Elizabeth crisply. "Let's not be snobbish. There are many here from the depressed areas. They're still here after the march on Downing Street, you know."

"Snobbish!" protested Mabel. "If they didn't take it all lying down, I'd have more sympathy for them."

Maureen gave a sudden giggle.

"What are you laughing at?" said Jennifer, catching the giggle.

"I was wondering," Maureen whispered, "if the Depressed Areas are anywhere near the Erogenous Zones."

Mabel suppressed a smile at the girls' giggling. She liked anything American and forgave Maureen many sins. They sang "Yes, We Have No Bananas" at each other in the morning, played Mah-Jongg, and gossiped about film stars.

But Elizabeth was offended. She had taken a great deal of time from work for this debutante business, and she felt as much resentment as scorn for it. Ginny had arranged Elizabeth's own presentation at a royal garden party last summer. Miserable afternoon it had been, idiotic. Rich people stealing spoons as souvenirs, and Labour members of Parliament present, ministers of the second Labour government in history, now just as forgetful of the poor who had elected them as if they had been Tories.

And why had she done it? Friendship, of course, for a Lady Pearsall no longer rich. Sir Reginald had died in the autumn of 1929, within a month of Bernard Malloy's death, and he had held on far too long to investments in shipbuilding and iron. The land in Northumberland was sold for taxes, and the collapse of the American stock market took the house in Kent. Ginny was supposed to live off an annuity designed by Mr. Blakeley of Coutts, that sleek and successful man now too experienced to be perturbed by the destiny of widows, and she lived in a tiny flat in St. John's Wood, all chromium and glass and built-in furniture. But she liked the building full of architects and screenwriters and other young people, and she soon found a way to make a living. The English upper classes were selling themselves these years, and she became their broker–dinner with a duke, shooting grouse for a week, Society for the Season, Ginny would fix it for you. For a thousand pounds, your daughter's debut. Elizabeth had handed over herself, her daughter, Maureen.

So here I am, she thought grumpily. Dressed like a stuffed chicken on the road to nowhere. No wonder men think we are nothing but ornamental.

She looked at the girls opposite, all clear skin and shining eyes. Jennifer looks very like Charles, she thought–the same straight nose, the arch of eyebrow, the broad forehead. But she has my eyes—spaced well apart, large, greener than mine. And my mouth. The combination is really very attractive, she thought.

The car jerked forward a few feet and brought Elizabeth in sight of a small group of tourists talking to a policeman.

"Look, some of your countrymen, Maureen," she said. "Now, I wonder how one can tell?"

Maureen leaned forward to look. "Do I know them? No, I don't. Oh, you can tell because we're all so clean, so well-pressed. So fat."

"I suppose only the rich can come over this year, since the slump," said Elizabeth.

"Anthony says quite the opposite," said Jennifer. "Anthony says our deflation makes it cheaper for them to holiday here than at home, just like us and the Continent. Isn't that awful?"

"Anthony, Anthony, Anthony!" sighed her mother. "I suppose I should be grateful that at least you're getting an education in economics from someone."

"And he's right, Mrs. Wingate," interpolated Maureen. "If you have any money at all, of course. I couldn't *believe* the bread lines in Manhattan when I came through for the boat, and lots of our friends have lost everything. Well almost everything. You seem to be getting off much more lightly over here. I mean, it's scarcely changed at all, has it?"

"With nearly three million unemployed, we can scarcely say we're well-off," replied Elizabeth stiffly.

"Anthony says there are *eight* million, at least, unemployed in America, and they don't have anything nearly as good as our dole, he says."

"Well, that group certainly doesn't look as though they'll have to sell apples," said Elizabeth. "You see the way that woman is wearing her fur tippet, Maureen? with that length of dress? That's what I was warning you against the other day."

Jennifer would not be ignored. "Anthony says it will get worse here. He says the Americans calling in their loans brought down this bank in Vienna the other day and that may bring us all crashing, which is why he's off to Switzerland for a week."

Elizabeth settled back onto her jump seat without reply. Jennifer had a talent, she thought, for getting at her these days, as though she were angry at her. Daughters! She had introduced her wartime correspondent, Anthony James, to Jennifer and watched him fall in love with her daughter, just like that, in a single evening. She was not worried; he would get over it. Jennifer was far too young for love and marriage, not even eighteen. As an escort he was much better than most of the boys one called the "deb's delights," and since even they were rare because of the war, Jennifer was lucky to have a steady escort. But she couldn't help feeling his conversation was largely wasted on a seventeen-year-old. Elizabeth smoothed the fingers of her gloves and looked out the window at the people. The difference between the educated and the uneducated, she thought, is much greater than that between the classes. If Jennifer looked at a town crouching where rivers met, she would see the site as beautiful perhaps; she would not see the routes of commerce that brought that town into existence, nor the misery under those calm roofs.

Late afternoon had become early evening. The crowd thickened as people flowed from Trafalgar Square, where they had bought pigeon food from the lady to whom Charles liked to talk, and from Leicester Square and Piccadilly Circus, where the huge tea shops fed them before they went to the cinema. They carried copies of the *Evening Standard* folded to the race results, or they munched fish and chips pulled from greasy paper cones. The car lurched ahead feet at a time now, and they left behind a lamplighter touching the gas lamps to life. Elizabeth looked across at the statue of Queen Victoria and wondered whether she had been any happier as a mother.

Inside the palace, the debutantes were in chaos, the staff calm, used to shepherding some fifteen thousand people a year up these stairs and through these halls. The women descended from their cars with fussing and brushing and straightening of seams and scared searches for small items. Mabel watched them critically, then ordered the chauffeur to drive her to a cinema. It was no small matter, this costume they all wore. Court rules and the king's affection for breasts prescribed its generals and its particulars. A low-cut white evening gown, this year clinging and satiny rather than full-skirted. A jeweled headband holding three white ostrich feathers arranged in the manner of the Prince of Wales's *Ich Dien* emblem, upright, but slightly to the left and slightly to the rear of the head. Attached to the back of the headband, a veil of white net or lace, no longer than twenty-seven inches. A train from the shoulders, no more than two and a half yards, stretching no more than eighteen inches back from the heel. (The king had personally ordered shorter trains, they said, disgusted by the lengths sported by the *nouveaux riches* after the war, and by the length of time for each presentation which the length of fabric necessitated.) And then the paraphernalia: the long white gloves, the fan, or the small bouquet of fresh flowers, the evening bag to be handed to mother or friend before entry to the throne room, the single strand of pearls.

The costume was a nuisance in the ladies' room, to which the women fled after their long confinement. It was a huge tiled room with gray metal stalls, filled with girls waiting, primping, fidgeting, squawking.

"Have you ever seen anything so sordid!" exclaimed Jennifer.

"God, where did they copy it from? The Piccadilly Underground?"

"Have you seen Jill yet?"

"She must be still ahead of us."

Tile and girls made the room noisy. One pale blond creature without eyelashes wailed like a child. She had emerged from a W.C. with her dress in total disarrangement, utterly baffled by her clothing. The weight of the train had to be distributed to underwear and stocking tops by an engineering fantasy of shoulder hooks, net corselet, and garters. Such engineering made the girls well-nigh impenetrable even to themselves.

"Oh, help, help, I'll wet myself!" cried the pale girl.

A harassed maid ran to her aid. Another handed out towels like an automaton—and pins, and hairpins, and needle and thread, and cough lozenges, and safety pins. In the pocket of her apron rested a diamond brooch worth some sixteen hundred pounds which a panicky maiden, discovering that girls this year were not wearing jewels for the presentation, had thrust at her for safekeeping. At her elbow rested a china dish containing a few pennies and threepences.

"In the palace? Isn't that vulgar!" said one girl to Jennifer.

"They probably don't pay them anything," hissed Jennifer back.

In the corridors and on the staircases, jammed with girls and their mothers, there was nowhere to sit. Jennifer took Maureen in search of friends and found Fern Hardacre of the liquid brown eyes and breasts so fair and firm they seemed covered with silk, busy now coquetting with a young footman in scarlet and gold braid.

"He never *moves,*" whispered Fern. "He just stares straight ahead. Isn't he beautiful! Doesn't he look just like Ronald Colman! Oh, God, isn't this *exciting!*"

The air was filled with the perfumes and powders of sweet girls, and the occasional mustiness of ostrich feathers handed down from grandmother.

"Not that he's really my *type,*" said Fern, with a mad roll of her eye. "I'm in love with that James Cagney! Have you seen *Public Enemy* yet? I thought I'd die when he squashed that grapefruit right in that woman's face! Oh, *God!*"

They found Elizabeth clinging to the corner of an oak bench. "I'm very happy that you do this but once in a lifetime," she said.

"Oh, Mummy, it's so glamorous!" protested Jennifer.

"It's too crowded to be anything but quite mad," said Elizabeth. "And have you girls seen Lady Pearsall?"

"She'll be waiting at the anteroom, she said, with her other debs," said Maureen.

Elizabeth surveyed the lines and clumps of maidens in white and was profoundly bored. Maureen chattered about the Prince of Wales, whom someone claimed to have seen, just back from the South American trip, in a side corridor. Would he be in the throne room? The girls were excited. From what they say, thought Elizabeth with a private smile, I don't think he cares for this kind of duty any more than I. People say he's democratic. Or are we both spoiled?

Her mind wandered to her work, planning tomorrow's schedule of visits to the administrators of the poor relief in Southwark. I'm out of sorts tonight, she blamed herself. I wonder how Peter is? Malaria again after all these years–it seems very unfair. I must not spoil Jennifer's big night. Think of motherhood. Think of Queen Victoria.

At last the feathers ahead began to move up the stairs and to wave through furlongs of corridors. A quarter of a mile from kitchen to dining room! No wonder the royals all hate the place! The girls donned sophistication to stalk past footmen in scarlet and gold with powdered hair. They arrived at the anteroom to the throne room, where there was quiet and order and a fine mist of hysteria. Elizabeth could not get out of her head the opening notes of "Poor Butterfly," whose aptness to her frame of mind was as irritating as sand. There was Ginny, checking her charges.

"Stiff upper lip and all that sort of thing," she murmured to Elizabeth. She looked soigné in brocade, emeralds, and orders, thin, stately. "The worst will soon be over."

They moved toward the entrance of the throne room, at last able to drop their trains from their arms, allowing an august uniformed attendant to settle them in place with a long ivory pole. Everyone took aim at dignity, hating their gowns and feathers for trembling.

"Over the top, girls," said Lady Pearsall cheerfully, stepping back as a footman gestured them into the mighty presence of the usher, an enormously tall man in gold braid and the demeanor of a duke who expressionlessly took the card from Elizabeth's hand and, as she led the way into the throne room with the two girls in row behind her, announced their names: "Mrs. Charles Wingate." Pause. "And to be presented." Pause. "Miss Jennifer Wingate." Pause. "Miss Maureen O'Flynn."

Elizabeth moved steadily up the long space of polished floor toward the dais on which the royal party was assembled. A chain of girls and women floated in advance of her like blossoms carried slowly downstream. The Wingate party was among the last to be presented, so the room was lined with people to watch them.

Jennifer held her head up to show off her neck and chin, her eyes down to reveal her lashes and draw attention to her high cheekbones. One quick glance showed her that the Prince of Wales was not among the royals. I'll get someone to take us to the KitKat or the Embassy. They say he's always there. Keep steps small, slow, pause. Watch Mother's back. If you step on my train, Maureen, I swear I'll kill you. Madame Vacani's voice in her head: "Slowly, girls, slowly! We are not catching a tram! *Step* and glide, *step* and glide!" She watched her mother reach the first throne and stoop into her curtsy, back straight, head bowed. The king nodded and smiled. Stiff, bearded, just like the sailor on the packet of Player's Navy Cut, small square hands on the arms of the great throne, eyes glittering, courtiers like a tapestry behind him. How*ever* can Mummy be anti-royalist! Elizabeth rose, stood aside, and Jennifer moved forward into her curtsy, feeling the veil and feathers tug at her hair. Thank God they warned us against diamanté buckles. Madame Vacani: "Left leg *behind* the right leg! Left foot to the *right* of the right foot! Now *bend* the knees, bend them all the way, and *lock!* Back *straight,* girls, back straight, fan across the *right* knee, bow the head only, *bow* the head. Be careful of that train! Watch that left shoe! Now *lift* the head . . . smile . . . upright . . . smooth . . . smooth . . . a little smile, you are not in the motion pictures—oh so pretty!—feet together! Good, good!" Piercing blue eyes, strangely human in that kingly face. Three steps sideways. Queen Mary.

A second curtsy. The queen looking so much more a queen than the king looks a king. Perched on the very edge of her throne, back rigid as a tent pole. God what training they had in her day! Feet crossed just so. Gown: rich, pale fabric like a treasure from the

Orient, gored, looped, cap-sleeved, gusseted, beaded and embroidered with seed pearls and real jewels in a flower pattern. Encrusted. Hands: neatly folded in the lap, fan, *five* strands of pearls around each wrist! The broad blue ribbon of the Order of the Garter off one shoulder and down the chest to the waist, dark and brilliant jewels, cascade, God they must be rich. Bosom: stately, built to take that order; that fine old-fashioned white skin, décolletage rather much, gold necklace of roped pearls, *six* strands around that aging neck. Ruby-and-diamond earrings, diamond-and-pearl coronet, that antique hairdo, little gray bangs like sausages. Face: strong features, long upper lip, looks just like her photographs, forthright nose, staunch chin held up, eyes direct, kindly, blue. A nod, a smile with real warmth. Asking a courtier. She's asked my name!

Jennifer suddenly felt light as light, so that when she turned to face the room of people her eyelashes were uplifted and her green eyes ablaze, and under the polish of her gown and ornaments something of the real and sensual animal flashed out, the little diamond cross drawing eyes to her cleavage. She held forth her arm so that the usher might loop her train over it. She and Elizabeth stood together side by side, waiting for Maureen.

A reception followed in state rooms filled with gilt and glitter. The punch was dull, the champagne mediocre, but the food (catered by Lyons) hearty, pretty, and abundant. The girls swirled about their business, Maureen stuffing chocolates between the flowers of her bouquet to take home. Elizabeth took her gold-edged plate and heavy silver fork into an alcove seat, where she was soon joined by Ginny rubbing a sore foot. "You must admit they do these things well," she said.

Elizabeth was still a trifle sour. "I can't help wondering how much," she said, "in this day and age, it all costs."

"I think it's the Joan Crawford principle," laughed Ginny. "If you have it, spend it. Do your bit to stimulate the economy. *Noblesse oblige.*"

"Now that's the kind of comparison I would make," laughed Elizabeth. "But I shouldn't have expected it of you."

"Between royalty and film stars? My dear! What else is the monarchy these days? We all serve to keep the natives from getting restless. I shouldn't be at all surprised if our little People's Prince, when he comes to the throne, doesn't make a sort of Douglas Fairbanks film of the whole thing, sliding down the banisters into the Coronation Coach, that sort of thing."

They laughed and tumbled into silence, gazing sideways at the room of women.

"Have you thought further about the coming-out ball for Jennifer? I still have another week before I *must* call the Dorchester to cancel, if cancel we must."

Elizabeth shook her head. "I'm not going to change my mind about that, Ginny. I simply can't agree to that kind of expense in times like these."

"With Searcy's doing the catering, it wouldn't cost that awfully much. I could do the whole thing for four hundred pounds, knocking off my commission?"

"It's the principle, not the money."

"There is an advantage to a ball late in the season, you know. It makes such a difference to the number of invitations one receives at this point. Though of course I could cancel just privately, which would mean the girls' names would still be on the list."

"Ginny, please."

"You really do feel very strongly about this, don't you? Rather different from Colombo days."

"With three million people living off a dole that won't buy them a roof over their heads?"

"I like to think of them as soldiers, you know," said Ginny, sitting back to survey the room. "We sent that many off to war, after all, and didn't mind *their* sacrifice."

Elizabeth could not tell from Ginny's tone whether she was being callous or ironic.

"I've changed since Colombo days," Elizabeth said soberly. "When I wear jewels like this, I feel disgustingly false to what I believe."

"They're the diamonds Charles gave you, aren't they?"

"Of course. But I haven't had them out of the bank for years. I can't buy a dress worth thirty pounds and wear jewels worth a thousand and then carry on about the people starving out there!" She gestured toward the alcove's window to their left. "Do you know what I spent this afternoon doing? Trying to convince the Council to deal with a family of six who'd had their light and gas cut off because they can't pay their arrears. And look at me now. Evenings like this make a farce of my days, and I'm not going to encourage Jennifer in this sort of thing."

Jennifer swirled out of the crowd in time to hear her last words and stood silent as Lady Pearsall, with her head turned away from her, spoke. "At least the Season will make her irretrievably a lady, whatever she does now. The ball would make the finishing touch to a very nice portrait—"

Jennifer interrupted, surprising both women. "Maureen and I can find someone else to share with. It wouldn't cost that much."

"Are you two in cahoots about this?" asked Elizabeth grimly, giving them a scrutiny a trifle too theatrical. "We've spent a fortune on your clothes, young lady. Eighteen pounds for a single cocktail dress! Three pounds a month for taxis and hairdressers! Plus whatever those pearls cost your father."

"Daddy says he doesn't mind," said Jennifer with the slightest touch of sulkiness.

"And I asked you not to talk to your father about it, young lady," replied Elizabeth with asperity. "If they put the moon up for sale, he'd buy it for you."

"Oh, Mother! If the Mystery Millionaire gave me the money, you wouldn't let me spend it!"

The Mystery Millionaire was everyone's dream. Tales had begun to circulate months ago about a well-dressed older man who gave out pound notes to poor individuals he spotted on the streets, in cafés, or even on soup lines. The press had counted his dividends as high as sixty pounds a day without finding who he was. He made the gray city a hopeful place. He stood for Luck, for God, for Goodwill. One had neither to earn nor deserve him.

"You're right about that," replied Elizabeth. "I've said over and over again that it's not a matter of whether we have the money but how we use it. I'd rather have you give it away than waste it on this sort of thing." With a wave she sought to turn the palace into folly.

"But it's once in a lifetime, Mother!" She too gestured at the room: countermagic. "And it's all worth it, isn't it, when you see this?"

Elizabeth wanted to make some scathing sociological comment, but it had all been said before, and when she looked at her daughter she did not really feel unkind, so she said rather gently, "The subject's closed, dear."

Jennifer started to protest, but Elizabeth spoke more sharply. "How much shall we be giving you for RADA?"

Jennifer surrendered and left. Having wanted to enroll at the Royal Academy of Dramatic Art, she had wheedled her mother until the payment of her fees turned into a victory of the kind which deprives children of lesser triumphs. Elizabeth had waited till now to make that point clear.

"Oh my, Elizabeth, you are becoming *grim* these days," said Ginny. "You espouse thrift the way others take up pacifism or antivivisection. I'm sure it's a terribly worthy cause, but somehow it doesn't seem my cup of tea, or yours."

"I know. I've become parsonical. But it really isn't the money. I suppose if Jennifer had any real plans, other than what dress she'll wear next Tuesday . . . But I can't, I really can't encourage her to be so desperately butterfly-ish."

"The child is only seventeen."

"Peter gave up criticizing me years ago over Jennifer, but I think he was right nonetheless. We've given her a superb education, but for what?"

"As I said before, a lady. And she'll make a good wife and mother when the time comes. She's a very intelligent girl, you know."

"She's educated to be all sorts of things, but to do nothing. I ask you: the Royal Academy of Dramatic Art with all the other debs, filling in the days while they wait for Prince Charming?"

"Which reminds me," said Ginny, rummaging in her reticule. "I have that list of mums I promised you."

"Mums?"

"Mums. Mothers of debs. Like you!" laughed Ginny, handing her a scrawled list. "Just think how many lists your own name is on these days. I've been frantically writing names down on the backs of envelopes and napkins for weeks, and now, voilà, some eighty suitable gels, I think."

"And what am I supposed to do with this list of mums?" Elizabeth regarded the list in her hand with the same suspicion she had shown of the Women's Party pamphlet she had found in Ginny's desk years ago.

"Telephone them, my dear. Visit them. Have a mum's luncheon for them. Wangle invitations, my dear, and names. Names of men!"

"White-slaving, in other words," grumbled Elizabeth. "Does the League of Nations suspect?"

"I must say I've worked harder at getting men's names this season than I ever did in the recruitment campaign for the War. You must not mock my efforts." Suddenly Ginny stood up, slipping her shoe back on. "Oh, dash it, wait a minute, there's Fiona in trouble again. I shall have to rescue the lump."

She sped off, leaving Elizabeth to put the folded list in her own evening bag. She craved a cigarette but had brought none. The alcove was separated by great velvet and corded draperies from the rest of the room, and by moving toward the window to her left, Elizabeth could make herself invisible. She did so, and found herself looking out the east front of the palace over the iron fences along the Mall toward the City. Here I am in the center's center at last, she thought, and I have just turned my back on it. Why should I never be content? Why should I not be like all those others and simply enjoy what money brings me? Ginny lunched at Lady Sybil Colefax's with Lady Castlerosse and Lady Diana Cooper and Lloyd George and Sir Oswald Mosley and H. G. Wells and Charles Chaplin and she says that there's no reason why I shouldn't do the same. She smiled grimly. They were able to agree, she says, that while it was nice to be famous, it was horrid to be recognized. I shall never be recognized. I am almost fifty years old. Where are my pleasures?

She looked down at the statue of Queen Victoria. And what are my proper responsibilities? To Peter, lying under covers with sweating and barley tea? To Maman, using a cane to take the weight off her arthritic hip, so much alone now? To Charles, probably out drinking despite his high blood pressure? There was a twist inside her like a pain. I'm becoming nothing but a nurse after all, taking care of everybody.

A burst of laughter came from the room behind her, and she was irritated all over again with Jennifer—the girl's sheer, narrow selfishness. Or do I worry about her triviality because I fear my own?

She could see her reflection in the window glass: gown, diamonds, headdress, lipstick. She focused her eyes beyond the window on the pavement at the other side of the railings where people drawn to revelry had washed up at the palace's foot to tease the guards. To the left under a streetlamp like a stage light stood a couple in tense conversation. They were middle-aged, he unshaven and down-at-heel, she shawled and thin, her face uplifted to him a white oval in the light. They were locked in some moment of intimate intensity that had seized them regardless of surrounding, she seeming to plead, he hunched but looming. As Elizabeth watched, he suddenly moved: swung back his arm as in a spasm, brought it forward swinging, crashed his closed fist into the side of her face so that she sprawled against the base of the streetlamp.

Appalled, Elizabeth stretched her palm against its reflection in the glass of the window, through which no sound came. No one out there had seen. Two policemen were walking couple-fashion in the opposite direction. The nearest tourist had turned and walked along the rails, as unnoticing as the statue of the Queen. The palace guard was required by duty to see nothing. The others were occupied. Elizabeth alone saw the man with total concentration haul back his booted foot and kick the woman in the ribs as she lay half-sitting, clinging to support. The woman lay still. Elizabeth's hand sought the latch of the window, then fell from it as though it burned. The woman stirred, sought to pull herself up the iron column.

Like a clockwork doll, Elizabeth turned her back, her face full of shock facing the room full of people. She took three steps and stood in the entry to the alcove, her hand still half-raised. There the girls still swirled and laughter ran up and down the scale. There were women her age there, old women. One with face painted a solid pink, one with a fright wig of gray hair and desperate eyes, one with skin white as marble and folded as curds, one gray as though gripped by cancer pain even as she nodded and talked and sought to charm. In front of Elizabeth now there were scarlet and gold diamonds where the virgins gossiped and the Queen strolled: a hieratic figure, her dress like lightning under the lights, her coronet a ring of fire, her face composed into benevolence.

There is nothing I can do about it, thought Elizabeth, letting her hand fall. Any of it.

PART IV

Between Wars

30

1931

Governments knew no better than Elizabeth what to do about any of it. Nineteen-thirty-one was the year when they learned that peace is not something that just happens in the absence of war. Economic crisis had cut the number of debutante dances by a third. "Better not to be too, too Tzarist!" said the girls. Since December the American banks had been collapsing at a great rate. In May the banks of Austria went, in July those of Germany. Mistaking strength for godliness, people began to seek heroes: Stalin, Mussolini, Hitler, Roosevelt. Would an increase in central authority, wondered the politicians, really mean a loss of individual freedom? If only it weren't for those muscular young men bashing innocent people's heads. . . . But someone has to get us out of this economic mess, they said. Someone has to take responsibility.

Responsibility was not Jennifer's concern during that summer of her eighteenth year, that season of her flesh. Hers was a glorious summer of first nights in borrowed white fox furs and parties mentioned in Marianne Mayfayre's column in the *Daily Telegraph;* of white organdy at Eton's Fourth of June and pink tulle at Claridge's and pale green silk at the Henley Regatta.

It was a summer of dancing the fox-trot cheek-to-cheek at the Coconut Grove and puffing on her escort's cigarette at Covent Garden during intervals from Colonel de Basil's Ballet de Monte Carlo and chattering with a flock of chums at a matinee of *Springtime for Henry* and humming "Where the Blue of the Night Meets the Gold of the Day" along with Ambrose and His Orchestra at the Embassy Club, where a dance hostess called Queenie Thompson told tales of the Prince of Wales and one actually *saw* him: shining hair and flashing smile and just tremendous sex appeal. It was up at midday and making Mabel help her dress so that she could be off for a fork lunch with the girls, whipping out engagement books to compare invitations, waving hello/good-bye to her parents before the cocktail party at six and the dinner at eight and the ball at ten.

"These young people are all so terribly witty," commented Lady Pearsall. "In my day we were happy enough to be up from the country."

"The twenties tried to be sophisticated," replied Elizabeth. "Perhaps the thirties *are.*"

It was being mentioned as a beauty in Lady Sibell Lygon's column in *Harper's Bazaar* and sneering at the brainy girls from Roedean who were on their way up to Oxford next term or at the Americans who—

"Like the poor," sighed Anthony James, "the Americans are always with us."

"No backgrounds, poor things," nodded Lady Pearsall. "Imagine having to be proud of being a daughter of their odd little revolution or confederacy or whatever it is!"

"Most extraordinary thing happened last night," said Anthony. "We were coming home in a taxi and Maureen insisted on stopping in Trafalgar Square to throw pennies in the fountain. 'Let's start a tradition,' she said. Imagine that: *start* a tradition!"

"But what else can they do? The American future is so impersonal!"

It was, in sum, a summer of dreams for Jennifer, where rich young women could ignore the crash of banks, the fall of governments, the inflation in Germany, the poor in Wales. "Let's drop from our conversation forever," resolved *Harper's Bazaar* for the new year, "the words 'crisis' and 'depression.'" "Let's," agreed *Queen.* "Let's this year be *grande dame* enough never to mention money at all!"

But the bank sent Anthony twice that summer to Austria and Germany.

"The money situation is serious," he said.

"My dear young man," laughed Ginny. "Money is never as serious as it seems! If Reggie were still alive, I should have him borrow enough to build a swimming pool and fill it with champagne and invite all the kinds of people Lady Londonderry loves and announce to the newspapers that I was doing my best for Britain. We do need to be more cheerful! I'm sure that while Rome burned, Nero spent."

Anthony shook his head and sighed, unconvinced. Lady Pearsall leaned forward and placed her hand on his arm. "I should let Jennifer have her fun, you know," she said seriously. "It's her time."

He looked startled. "I don't let Jennifer do or not do anything," he protested.

"You do intend to marry her, however?" she said directly.

Anthony was again taken aback, but he smiled. "You, Lady Pearsall, are presuming on your rank and years!"

"And what earthly use are they if I cannot?" she said, drawing back, amused, patting her neat gray hair. "You do mean to marry her, then?"

"I've said nothing to her, or to her parents."

"Her mother doesn't think Jennifer is old enough to marry."

"Jennifer thinks I am an old man."

"You would be very good for her after she has had this fling. Wait a little." She fussed with the interior of her handbag. "Of course, whether she would be good for you is another matter which I, being wise and foresightful, shall not go into."

Anthony tended to be poker-faced, the kind of man who prefers sherry to ale, but he had the fair skin that flushes easily, so his interest in Jennifer was never hard to detect. There was a touch of world-weariness about him this summer that could make him seem too controlled sometimes, at others truly disillusioned, and this charmed Jennifer. With him she felt mature. Slowly she began to use her guile on his behalf rather than against him, and the process of her falling in love was so steady that Elizabeth noticed far too late. At first it was because he had the money to take her for meals at Quag's and drinks at the Embassy and his own car, whereas youths came to dances for the sake of the free supper. Later he gave her conversation; she was bored with meeting only young people.

Jennifer was confident that summer, having discovered life. Her mother, she complained, thought of her as a child still. She had forgotten what it was like to have fun. Always down at the Council or off to Grandmother's or nursing that dim Peter Williams she's been in love with for years. Daddy approved of Anthony. Mother? Mother could be brought round. So she sought to push girlhood behind her that summer, dancing groin to groin, kissing soft-lipped in taxis, growing hot and moist when Anthony's hand rubbed the stiff fabric of her bra against her breast and she cupped her hand over the urgency in his trousers, until they reached that point where both knew they were in love, and love demanded life together forever and he proposed and she accepted.

Jennifer warned her father that Anthony wanted to make a formal proposal. Charles consulted Elizabeth. Elizabeth told him that Jennifer was far too young. Charles gently advised Jennifer that the formal visit should be postponed, that no marriage could take place until she was twenty, that certainly he had no objection to Anthony, just that she should have more experience of men. So by the end of this summer Jennifer could tell her girlfriends that she and Anthony were "sort of engaged," while the family still had not faced her growing up.

She grew thin that summer, through dancing too much and eating too little, so that her face rose like a bud from leaves, pale, with large green eyes set wide apart and high cheekbones in the manner of Garbo or Dietrich and lips that curled up at the corners with a challenge that made hot young men want to crush her for their victory and her father remember her as a bone-clad child.

In August, expecting galloping inflation, Great Britain sought loans from the United States. If you balance the budget, said the banks. Cut ten percent off everything. Including the dole. The Labour Party could not, but its leader Prime Minister Ramsay MacDonald could. On August 24 he went to the palace to resign and returned as head of a National Coalition Government made up mostly of Conservatives, thereby also replacing Winston Churchill (now out of office and powerless) as head of Elizabeth's pantheon of male perfidy. She stood on the verge of giving up her work for the Labour Party. On September 10 came the new budget. The King, not fearing starvation, gave up his ten percent gracefully. The fleet mutinied and won back their tithe. The unemployed demonstrated and were ignored. On October 6, MacDonald announced a general election for October 27; the National Coalition against the remnant. Grimly Elizabeth vowed to fight on the side of the remnant. It would be her hardest, best, last effort.

She also went into an irritable depression that made her impatient with Anthony because he seemed to know all the inside stories, with Peter because he could do nothing but expostulate, and with Jennifer because she was forced to chaperon her to parties abundant in smug Tories. It was a likely time for the Wingates to have the fight which they had amiably postponed for a decade, and Jennifer was the likely cause. The battle began with trivia.

Anthony had procured tickets for the opening night on October 13 of the new Noel Coward play, *Cavalcade,* and invited the Wingates to attend with Maureen as a sort of going-away present before her return to America. Having business in Rome, where he had to meet Joe Plunkett, Charles was unable to attend, but when the election announcement came just a week before and plunged Elizabeth into wild fits of organization for the two East End electorates where she was currently working for Labour members of Parliament, she asked him to postpone his trip and replace her as chaperon. He insisted that he could not do so, and that she should go, irritated by her habitual attitude that his business had no real significance. In passing he dismissed her political work as unimportant.

"Unimportant?" Elizabeth said, bridling. "Unimportant compared to what?"

If she had not been wearing the tailor-made suit which Charles loathed, if they had been seated elsewhere than the living room newly redecorated with glass and chromium and hard white lines in a style that Charles found hateful, he might not have replied as he did.

"Compared, my dear," he condescended, "to anything I might have to do to earn our income."

"In other words," said Elizabeth coldly, "nothing that I might do has anything like the importance of anything that you do."

He stared at her angrily. "So long as we have that straight at last."

"A doll in a doll's house."

"It's not a matter for sloganeering. You are Jennifer's mother. There can't be any conflict in obligations when it comes to matters like that. Get me a brandy and soda, would you?"

She moved to the wheeled drink cart automatically, but stood there thinking, then turned. "Do you really think that nothing I do with my own life is important?" She spoke slowly, as though with genuine curiosity.

"I've let you have your head in everything," he said with equal levelness. He had said the words often enough to himself. "You've had much more freedom than other women, perhaps more than is wise."

She picked up a glass automatically but stayed looking at him.

He continued speaking. "Mind you, it escapes me what happiness all this freedom brings you anyway. A lot of running around the country sleeping in third-rate railway hotels mixing with people you'd never give the time of day to normally. A lot of nonsensical political stuff . . ."

"Is that all you think I've been doing for the last ten years?"

"I don't mean to denigrate it. I say only that it has not brought you happiness."

The afternoon sun through the window was striking off a glass table surface into Elizabeth's eyes. Charles seemed blurred to her by that or rage, so she moved, dropping one hand on the crystal decanter of brandy as she did so. She waited for him to continue.

"I'm just saying that you . . . that *we* would be much happier if you didn't do all this running about. Jennifer would have a proper mother. Our life would have some shape to it. It would have some meaning. Which is more than it has had the last ten years."

She picked up the brandy decanter, finding with surprise that her hand shook with its weight so that she had to put it down again. She said, not looking at him, "Are you talking about Peter?"

Charles shifted in his armchair, surprised himself this time, eyebrows raised, glance shifting from her face to his own feet. Then he looked back at her speculatively. "Oddly enough, no. I've never criticized you about Williams, have I? And I must say you've behaved impeccably about him. No. Strangely enough, I think we could have survived Williams quite well." He smiled at her with broad impudence. "I suppose I've learned that sexual possessiveness is not the foundation of marriage." Then, serious again, very serious, he said, "But some greater fidelity *is.* You've betrayed me much worse with all this than you have with Williams. I can't *count* on you. As a man should be able to count on his wife." Again, the impudent smile. "I imagine Williams is even worse off."

Elizabeth picked up the brandy decanter and removed its stopper. "Would you mind not grinning at me like that?"

"There's no sense in getting angry."

"I'm not angry. I'm appalled. What on earth do you think my life is all about?"

"I have not the least idea," and suddenly *he* was angry. "I haven't exactly been privileged by admission to your confidence lately, have I? It used to be that you would do nothing without me, you used to care what I thought, but now? You're off here, off there, you don't even have time to chaperon your only daughter to a play! You're simply not the woman I married at all."

Elizabeth splashed brandy into the glass without measuring. "Of course I'm not. For God's sake, Charles, that's twenty-five years ago. Of course I'm not the girl you married."

She reached for the soda siphon, all bending anger and thin contempt, and her very efficiency, that damned masculine suit she wore, the tone of her voice, increased his anger, so that he sneered.

"You've had all the freedom a woman can want, and all you've shown by what you've done with it is that women don't know how to handle freedom. You were happier before the war, being a wife and mother. You don't know what to do with freedom!"

She banged the siphon down on the glass tabletop and turned on him. "By God, Charles, I've *acted,* I've *done.* When I think of the idle, trivial creature I was before the war, doing nothing but paying attention to you!" She picked up the siphon again and splashed soda into the brandy. "You talk as though you know better than I what makes me happy, and you don't." She looked into the brandy glass in her hand and laughed harshly. "You know a great deal, Charles, but all you know is what *you* know. You don't know what's right for me. You don't know what I need to know about life. You don't know what I need to find out–about myself, about people, about life. You have no idea what goes on in my head because you have never asked. Only what happens to *you* is important. Only if *you* are the center of the family does the family have a center. What I want is irrational, you say." She turned her back on him sharply. "But what you want isn't any more rational. It's just *usual.*"

She snapped the glass down onto the table, facing him with hands clasped in front of her. He looked at her for a moment, speculative again, then picked up not the last but the first words of her speech.

"You've *acted,* have you?" He half-laughed, dismissing her. "Women don't know what action is. You think it means fussing around in politics like some glorified housemaid. You're amateurs! There's a discipline to action that women never understand. Men learn that from the start! Only women can afford to be amateurs in life. We'd all have been better off if you'd had five children rather than one. It might have given you some sense of what life's proper obligations are. Men are not just some kind of drag, holding you women back from being your real selves." He sneered out the last words. She stood white and still, listening to him.

"I need that drink," he said, interrupting himself. She reached for the glass again, as he resumed with more calm, "Mabel knows what it's all about, earning a living, discipline. You've no sense of responsibility, Elizabeth." Now he leaned forward, wagging his finger magisterially. "You can afford not to, because I'm here, day after day, putting up with whatever you care to throw at me, giving you whatever you want, getting precious little in return. What does my world mean to you, eh?" He settled back in his chair, surveying her. "I go off to the office every day, and that's it. You don't even know how I earn my living, do you?"

She walked toward him, glass in hand, soda siphon in the other. "You spend a great deal of time wandering about the city talking to very strange people, I know that."

He ignored the wisecrack as beneath him. "You don't know what responsibility is. You women—you complain about belonging to us, but it's a pretty nice, safe way of going through life, isn't it? You don't stop to think what you may owe us in return, do you?"

She stood in front of him a few paces away. His face was suffused with blood, purplish, so that from the midst of shock she could worry about his blood pressure.

"I'd love you to have equality, real equality, without the damned privilege you want with it! Equality with earning the bloody money as well as spending it." He leaned forward, stretching his hand out for the glass, looking up at her. "You let me down, Elizabeth. You let me down all the time. You take and take and take, and you give nothing. All you've ever offered me in return was your body, and that's not enough. There are times when I loathe you. Really loathe you."

They stayed thus, glaring at each other for a moment that made them hear their heartbeats in their ears. Then she shoved the hand with the glass forward, and he took it and sat back in his chair, following her with his eyes as she turned, put down the siphon, and walked to the door. With her hand on the knob, she turned and looked sideways at him, feeling fear at his anger, and grief. "We've held each other off for ten years," she said quietly. "Why? What has it all accomplished? What does it all mean if after all that we can't be . . . friends?"

They had hurt each other badly, but what they had said was not the distortion of anger. Each knew what the other should hear, and for the first time in their lives they had said it loudly enough.

His words still divided them: "I loathe you. Really loathe you." How could he have said such a terrible thing? Feeling both angry and guilty, she could neither beat down those words nor ignore them. Husband and wife went about their business that day and the next, and before he went to Rome all she said to him was, "I shall go with Jennifer to the theater."

He gave her a nod in return. Not preoccupied, she thought. Indifferent. She felt as though he expected her to do something more. She was also angry at herself. She watched their fight over again in her mind, and saw herself: handing him his brandy and soda, the long years' habit of obedience even as he told her he loathed her.

When Peter telephoned, she said nothing to him about the combat. He in any case was too excited with his own news.

"I've taken a lease," he said, "on a cranny in Cecil Court. Can you see it? Peter Williams, Esquire. Used and Rare Books. Shall I collect Curiosa and Exotica as well? It seems the right area for it."

"Where did you get the money?"

"Last of the old capital, my beloved, and a little help from your fat friend Mr. Blakeley. It's all or nothing this time. Good-bye Foyle's, hello independence. Are you free tonight to celebrate?"

"No, not tonight. I have a meeting."

"Give me a ring when you have a moment, will you? I'm high as a kite."

She dressed and did a morning's business on the telephone, then left Mabel with instructions to hold the fort, changed into street clothes, and took a taxi for her regular weekly visit to her mother in Wimbledon. She was there often these days, worried about her mother's health and in search of something whose outlines she only sensed. Henriette Malloy in her mid-seventies had grown thin, stooped, and lamed by arthritis, but she was still her own person. The things of widowhood and modernity bothered her–taxes, vacuum cleaners, clogged gutters, airplane noise–but she was as keen as ever about ideas, moralities, people. She glinted through her ailments like the winter sun. For the last few years she had shared the Wimbledon house with a live-in maid. She saw her priest regularly and treated him with genial contempt, as half a man. She respected only her doctor and Charles.

She was delighted and relieved when Elizabeth told her of their row. *"Enfin!"* she exclaimed. "And not before time!"

The reward was her daughter's astonishment. "But it's the first real quarrel we've ever had!" protested Elizabeth. "And after all these years, it seemed so final. He said he loathed me."

Henriette sat in her armchair, a book open in her lap, her cane near her knees. For her comfort, the house was uncomfortably hot and close. "And did you think this polite truce would continue all your lives? But how *dead* that would be! I have warned you how often that one pays a terrible price for trying to balance between things. But now. What will you do, eh?"

"Do?" Elizabeth did not yet know whether her mother too was betraying her. "I hadn't planned to do anything. I haven't even had time to think about what it all means. The way he sees me–I don't even recognize myself."

"And if for once you did something without thinking about it endlessly, what would that be?"

"I'm so very angry with him. And he with me. I'd leave him, I suppose." She looked up at her mother under her eyelids, like a girl confessing guilt.

"Then leave him! You can come here."

"That's not what I expected you to say. You like Charles."

"I like Charles a great deal. He's a good man, a kind man. But what has that to do with anything? If you can't live with him, then you must leave him, no? Or stay with him if you will. But if you stay with him, you owe it to him to change." She poked a finger at Elizabeth's knee.

"Absolutely not! I'm not going to give up everything that makes me feel alive."

"After all these years, you owe him nothing?"

"Just precisely as much as he owes me."

"Ah!" said Henriette, throwing her head back, thoughtful. "I suppose you are right. But he won't see it that way, you know. Men don't. They give us money, which is more important to them than anything else, and what do we give them in return?" She put her head to one side, pursing her lips. "Faithfulness. Freedom from the battle. Just what you took away from him. The moment you took up with Mr. Williams, it would have been wiser to leave Charles. Your position since then has not been correct. Now you can remedy that."

Again Elizabeth was taken by surprise. "What do you know about me and Peter Williams?"

"My dear, a blind woman could have told about you and Peter Williams. And Charles cannot have liked it, no matter how broad-minded he pretends to be. So! There's nothing wrong with a woman taking a lover, but look at it from his viewpoint. You spend his money to look beautiful for Mr. Williams!"

"Money, money, money," exclaimed Elizabeth, rising from the footstool on which she had been seated. "The money situation won't change if I leave him. As he so kindly pointed out, I'm totally dependent on him."

"Then you must earn some money! You must get a job. Can you not get them to pay you for doing this political nonsense?"

"I doubt it," said Elizabeth, standing near the fireplace. "I work with the professionals, but I don't think I'm worth much to them. I'm fifty. There are no paid women except secretaries."

"Then you should take a job as a secretary. No! I am wrong. I dismiss this problem so easily! Money stopped *me* once. I wish it had not."

"What do you mean?" asked Elizabeth, turning toward her.

"Ah, why should you not know now? I almost left your father once, at the beginning of the war. I would have lived by myself when we came to London, but I was too old. I could not get a job that would pay enough. And he needed me, I thought. He relied on me because he'd lost everything else, he said. I owed it to him to stay." Her glance strayed to a photograph of Bernard on the table at her side. "He was such a fool, your father, such a romantic."

"But why?" said Elizabeth, absorbing yet another shock.

"Why did I want to leave him?" She shook her head. "I stayed with him and became a shrew. I was angry with him, of course, so very angry about his stupid politics. He did not deserve to keep me after losing us everything we had–just, for some silly reason of conscience, to betray the Republicans to the English." Henriette held her head down, lost for the moment in past passion.

"But Dad did not betray the Irish to the English!"

"I was there when he did," said Henriette grimly, looking at her daughter. "I argued against him." She shrugged. "It was not malice, just folly. He was caught between loyalties, just like you, Elizabeth, and of course by trying to please everybody, he ended up losing everything!"

Both women fell silent, Elizabeth forced to reassess the past, Henriette lost in it.

Then Henriette resumed. "But I think that was only the excuse for my anger. *Now* I think that. It went deeper, back to the beginnings, back when he took me from my beautiful Paris to that terrible Dublin, but I did not understand that for a long time, because I had made all those sacrifices willingly, out of love. I think love means becoming, for a while, what the other person wants you to be, and that is so foolish!"

She paused for a long time before resuming. "So! I grew angry because I loved him. Because he used my love to get him what he wanted and then took it for granted, as his right. No, *we* had used my love, because I was wrong too. I too thought that was the way a marriage should be. Until I got angry with him."

"You never said anything all these years."

"And why should I? Why should such matters concern a child? I speak to you now because you are a woman as well as my daughter, and because now you are angry with your husband because you have loved him."

"But Charles has always allowed me great freedom."

"And what kind of a word is that, this 'allowed'? A word for a child, a dog?"

"I said the same thing to him."

"There, you are showing some good sense." Henriette took her cane and leaned on it, putting one hand on Elizabeth's arm to ease the rising to her feet. "Now you must choose. Are you going to make each other's lives miserable? Or will you do something about it?"

She looked up into her daughter's eyes, her own tired but gleaming.

"But he doesn't have to choose," said Elizabeth. "Why should I?"

"Because it is a woman's choice, *ma petite,* not a man's. That is the way life is, no? And now, this is so tiring, we will have a *tisane,* eh, and talk about foolish matters?"

She picked a silver bell from her table and rang for the maid, looking exhausted. Her heart was bad, the doctor said. Then she shook her head. "There comes a time in life when we find out who we are. We have to swallow it, good or sour. It is time for you to choose, my dear." She patted her daughter on the cheek gently. "You should know, I think you are a very worthwhile woman." There were tears in the aging eyes. "What a pity Charles cannot feel affection for you. Affection undoes the damage we do by love." Elizabeth felt tears spring to her own eyes.

"All the good reasons . . ." said Henriette, wagging her head from side to side. "Generation to generation, all the good reasons . . . This is what I say: you can either be a good woman or a good wife. If you keep on finding reasons for doing nothing, you will be neither."

Elizabeth put her arms around her mother's thin shoulders and arms, and the two women, embracing, cried together a little.

31

On the day that Elizabeth was scheduled to see *Cavalcade* in the evening, she went to see Gandhi at six in the morning. He had come to London for the imperial conference on India's independence, staying at a cooperative hotel in Bow run by the Quakers for the East

End poor, where he slept on a thin mattress on a concrete floor. Elizabeth told herself it was a silly thing for her to do, but Gandhi had been her hero since the war, and she had never seen him except in newsreels, so now she stood in a nameless alley among clots of people who pretended to stop only for the circus of it, Londoners not easily admitting the charm of a black man. He appeared without making them wait, a little man with eyes gleaming behind thick lenses in gold-wire frames, a birdlike face, a white cloth and sandals his only clothing. He had met the King some time before. "The King wore enough for both of us," he had said.

Elizabeth stood out among this crowd, well-dressed, tall, and attractive, and because she was as out-of-place as he, Gandhi looked at her and smiled. Then he moved on while the crowd called out, "Watch 'er, Gandhi!" and " 'Ow's about a dance tonight, luv?" So she had her smile from Gandhi now, and what difference did that make? She sighed and set off for the tube station, regretting that not even he now had the force to lift her up. She thought of him during the day's meetings in chill little rooms, and it became clear to her that this was the end of something: she had had enough of politics.

The realization sent her back to the flat in midafternoon exhausted by the hope of Gandhi and the hopelessness of the election, by the fight with Charles and the prospect of *Cavalcade*'s rumored patriotism. The flat was full of Mabel and the maid and Jennifer and Maureen and Mrs. Hooker. Elizabeth bathed, dressed, and told the others she would have a sandwich and meet them at the theater.

Arriving very early, she handed her evening cloak to the uniformed maid in the cloakroom and ascended the ancient flight of marble stairs to the lobby of the grand tier. She saw her image in the landing's huge speckled mirror. Fatigue had made her interesting rather than ugly. She wore blue silk and her diamonds, with more makeup than usual and her nails red with the new polish borrowed from Maureen. There was a touch of drama about her, seated alone near the bar with a huge French-style ham sandwich and a glass of whiskey. She looked like a woman to whom things had happened. She smoked and had an unwise third drink that turned up the buzz of the beau monde the way static affects wireless, and she felt better.

Jennifer, Anthony, Maureen, and her young man arrived just ten minutes before curtain time. The floodlit facade of the ancient Drury Lane Theater towered like a reef above fish. Taxis pulled up, engines ticking, doors slamming. Crowds flowed up from the Strand, a cheerful lot in thick overcoats, and a file of buskers tootled and squeaked

"Singin' in the Rain," their impromptu band shuffling along under the eye of the law, one foot on the pavement, one on the street. The stalls and dress-circle crowd were all in evening dress and largely sheltered from the unwashed by ushers who sped them across the pavement and launched them through the glass doors into the lobby. But poverty stood among them like rocks in the floodtide: a man and a woman singing Victorian ballads; a dirty girl from Covent Garden selling flowers from a basket; a one-legged man pushing a little cart from which the smell of roasting chestnuts rose; a row of idlers leaning against the wall, faces expressionless, waiting for any chance to make a penny or a joke.

When Jennifer's taxi pulled up, one of these idlers leaped forward to open the door. Maureen and her young American exited from the jump seats. Anthony leaned forward to pass coins to the taxi driver through the sliding glass window, so that when Jennifer left the taxi she found herself standing next to this idler holding the door. He was a tall man in his mid-thirties, dressed in a gray flannel suit whose condition–damp, sagging, wrinkled, with baggy pockets–made her feel awkward with the realization that he was probably one of those respectable men whom the crisis had turned into unemployed drifters. His face was attractive; embarrassment made him look furtive. As Anthony stepped from the taxi, his opera hat hit the doorjamb and fell forward onto the pavement, so that both he and the idler moved to pick it up at the same time. There was recognition between them.

"Hello, old chap," said Anthony.

"How are you, old man?" muttered the stranger, his eyes hidden.

Anthony stayed half out of the taxi, coins in his hand. The stranger straightened jerkily, turned, walked away into the crowd. Anthony remained still a moment, looking after him, his expression unreadable. He took Jennifer brusquely by the arm and half-pushed her up the steps and into the lobby.

"What was all that about?" she asked as he helped her from her coat.

"That?" He looked down his nose at her, refocusing. "That," he said, "was John Keighley Truscott, DSO, M.C." His voice was flat. "I haven't seen him in years."

He had taken off topcoat and white scarf.

"Why didn't you speak to each other?"

For a moment he withheld his hat from the cloakroom attendant, balancing it on spread fingers, then suddenly collapsed it and handed it to the woman. "What is there to say?" He shrugged. " 'Let me lend you five quid'? The last I heard of him, he was selling cars. Obviously not anymore." He looked straight at Jennifer. "If you don't mind, I'd rather not talk about him. Especially here. He's not . . . an entertainment."

They caught up with Maureen and her companion at the foot of the staircase and moved upstairs to join Elizabeth, to whom Maureen presented her companion: "Mrs. Wingate. I should like you to meet Mr. Marvin Weidenbaum."

"Pleased to meet you," said Mr. Weidenbaum with an eager smile and a proffered hand.

"How kind," murmured Elizabeth, responding awkwardly to the smile and the unaccustomed handshake. "How do you do, Mr. Weidenbaum?"

"Please, call me Marvin."

"Oh," said Elizabeth.

"When you've been here longer, Mr. Weidenbaum," said Jennifer, "you'll realize that we English are terribly stuffy about getting to know people. Mother can't possibly call you 'Marvin' until she's known you for at least five years."

Elizabeth laughed good-naturedly. "I'm sorry, I am out-of-date with these young things."

Mr. Weidenbaum was apologetic and charming. One could dislike him only generically, not individually.

"I'm sorry Mr. Wingate isn't here," he continued, "to hear our good news."

"Which is?" said Elizabeth with a charming smile.

"Maureen has agreed to sign a contract to come to Hollywood!"

"But what on earth will your parents say?" said Elizabeth in tones of such Victorian astonishment that they all laughed. Mr. Weidenbaum was, it emerged, a talent scout for MGM. Having met Maureen on Long Island, he had looked her up in London. Upon her return to America, they would consult her parents, whose legal permission was necessary. Maureen anticipated no difficulties. "I'm too old, really, for them to interfere with what I want to do. It's just these silly rules," she said.

The bells for the performance had begun to jangle, and the group joined the crowd filing to seats. Noel Coward was popular as the author of a series of terribly sophisticated romantic comedies, never before of anything like *Cavalcade,* which was advertised as a panorama of English history from 1899 to date, a spectacle with a cast of some four hundred in twenty-two scenes. The gallery was jammed with young people who had been queuing, the newspapers said, for three days, and when the orchestra filed in, the hum of talk in the dress circle drowned out their tuning. A stir from the gallery, a few cheers, greeted the arrival in one of the boxes of the handsome and beautiful Mountbattens. To a great round of applause the conductor entered the orchestra pit, and as he nodded his gratitude, the curtains at the rear of a box on the right parted and the author's private party took their seats: Noel Coward, sleek, slender, beautiful, ushering his mother to the front seat. There was a swell of applause. He ignored it, hesitated, stood up, bowed jerkily with a modest smile, sat down. As the houselights dimmed, the excitement was electric.

At this very moment, Anthony suddenly leaned down to Jennifer, muttered that he would be back in a minute, and sped up the aisle. The conductor raised his arms, brought them down, and the overture began.

Jennifer could sit with eyes glued to the stage throughout an entire performance—any performance—as though the lights hypnotized her. Tonight, however, her enslavement was interrupted. She was irritated that Anthony should not be here for the curtain, and then during the overture she realized that her mother was only half-attending. The overture was a mélange of original music linking popular songs from the last fifty years. Elizabeth had been fussing with program, opera glasses, jewels, and shoe, and when the orchestra made "It's a Long, Long Way to Tipperary" slow and forlorn, a lament, she shook her head and asked.

"What's the matter?" hissed Jennifer.

Elizabeth looked at her startled. "Nothing," she said. "Don't worry about me. It's not a memory for you, is it?"

"Do sit still," said Jennifer.

Elizabeth seemed to settle down obediently for the first scene, but she was unhappy with the second: Boer War soldiers boarding a troop ship to go off to South Africa, sent off by a whole military band, an escort of real Guardsmen, a roar of applause from the audience, and, from the gallery, a few hat-waving huzzahs. During the third scene, played in front of the curtain, Anthony finally arrived back.

"Where have you been?" complained Jennifer in a whisper.

"I went to look for Truscott," he whispered back.

"Good Lord! Did you find him?"

"I'll tell you later."

With the fourth scene came a hitch. The orchestra played a pretty introductory waltz meant to raise the curtain, then they played it again, and yet again. In the audience there were mutters, then a wave of chatter, then a nervous laugh, then in the gallery the measured, heavy clap began, but just as disaster seemed likely, the curtain rose. First, to low musical accompaniment, came a single actor onto a bare and darkened stage. The news has just arrived, he announced, and the audience groaned in anticipation, that the siege of Mafeking had been broken! the British Army is victorious! the garrison is safe! For a moment the audience was confused by the dislocation of temporal reality–here or the Boer War–but before they could react the stage lights blazed to reveal, onstage, a full mock theater like a mirror to them, a theater filled with a real if Victorian audience, including whole tiers of boxes containing people on two enormous side wings that seemed almost to touch the real boxes.

The audience onstage went mad with joy–yelling, screaming, kissing, jumping up and down, and after a moment of pure stun, the real audience began to go mad too, as though by contagion. The gallery stamped and yelled, and cheers rose even from the stalls. Hats sailed across the footlights. People in the circle rose to their feet. A wave of patriotism as thick and full as arterial blood surged through the auditorium, and the audience's delirium became a roar which pulled Jennifer too to her feet, crying and laughing at the same time.

Elizabeth reached up and seized Jennifer's arm to pull her back into her seat. "Have you gone mad?" she said, furious.

Her daughter looked down at her, ravaged by patriotism. "Oh don't be such a *stick!*" she spat out.

Elizabeth withdrew her hand and sat motionless through the following scenes. At intermission the five members of the Wingate party crowded out to the lobby with everyone else, and the young people all smoked cigarettes and chatted about the play. Anthony was quiet, standing in Jennifer's background. When the bells to signal the end of intermission rang for the second time, Elizabeth spoke to him. "I wonder if you'll excuse me. The noise has given me the most terrific headache, and I should rather like to go home to bed. Will you see that Jennifer gets home at a reasonable hour?"

"Of course," he said. Jennifer was solicitous.

"Never mind, dear, I shall be quite all right," said Elizabeth. "You go along and enjoy yourselves. Now, hurry back or you'll miss the next scene."

During the rest of the play's too-great length, the audience remained like a duchess with her coronet askew, weeping and laughing as though on cue. *Cavalcade* was the hit of the season, the decade, and scene after scene gave birth to rapture: Victoria's funeral, the trains of war-wounded arriving at Victoria Station, peacetime at the seaside, the simple strength of the plain English soul in times of crisis. "Let's drink to the hope," said the heroine at the climax, "that one day this country of ours, which we love so much, will find dignity and greatness and peace again." The final scene seemed about to break the mood: the whine of "Twentieth-Century Blues," a nightclub on New Year's Eve in 1929, blank-faced couples with too much makeup dancing without souls, the stage darkening, sound effects of disintegration, a feeling of sourness in the audience. Then, rising out of the darkness to the strains of the national anthem, a giant Union Jack waving under soft lights, the stage slowly lightening, the entire cast assembling and facing the audience to sing "God Save the King!" The audience was on its feet, singing, many crying openly, and after endless curtain calls, Noel Coward, slender, small on the giant stage, flushed. "After all," he said, "it is a pretty exciting thing in these days to be English."

Afterward the two young couples took a taxi to Bond Street and the Embassy Club, where Anthony and Jennifer were able to sit in a discreet corner while Mr. Weidenbaum took Maureen to dance on the lower floor.

"You didn't really enjoy the play, did you?" said Jennifer as soon as they were alone.

"Not really."

"What didn't you like? I thought it was fabulous."

"Oh, I'm sure it was. Just not my cup of tea. You wouldn't understand."

"My darling, you will have to learn never to tell me I wouldn't understand."

"I'm just not one for much theatrical claptrap, I expect. Union Jack, God Save the Blessed King, that sort of thing."

"I suppose it was a bit much, but it was all so beautifully done, I really felt as though I were there. I wish I were *in* it."

"But that's rather the problem isn't it? You weren't there, and neither was Noel Coward, and I can't stand chaps who carry on about the glories of war when they couldn't even tell one end of a rifle from the other. I see something like that scene at Victoria Station, and it doesn't matter how good the actors are, they don't look exhausted enough, they're too fit." He shook his head. "It just wasn't like that.

Everyone was tired to the bone, and gray, and shabby. I was there once myself on leave, you know. I remember drinking tea at one of those Red Cross canteens on wheels and scalding my mouth because I'd forgotten tea could be hot, and the Red Cross ladies trying to find out where I wanted to go–I couldn't remember, all I wanted was a bed, but not at my club. And I was embarrassed about the lice, one had to scratch all the time, and the men didn't bathe, they had scabies, and the Red Cross ladies looked at us, well . . ."

"I understand," said Jennifer, placing a hand on his arm. "I know what you've gone through."

He looked at her with distance, her eyes liquid in the fresh face. "You mean you understand that I've gone through something, not what that something was. You couldn't be there. Women never will be there." He smiled slightly with recollection. "I went off with a tart, that leave. High heels and fox furs and face paint and all, called Dolores. She was very nice. She let me sleep. I paid her for two days' sleeping, and she made scrambled eggs and tomatoes and ghastly coffee for me and sat there knitting with her feet up. I think she enjoyed the rest. I took her to *Chu Chin Chow* before I went back. All dressed up. You wouldn't have known she wasn't my sister."

He looked around the room, quiet with subdued electric lights on each table. He listened to the orchestra playing downstairs: "Heartaches." He looked at Jennifer. "Well, it's a long way from now, and we shan't have to go through it again. But it wasn't at all like it was on the stage, I'm sorry."

"Did seeing your friend outside the theater upset you?"

"John Truscott?" He paused, looking down at the table, picking the label off a wine bottle. "Seeing him made me remember. I couldn't find him when I went to look for him." He shuddered and sighed away a feeling. "Look, Noel told me something interesting about putting on the play–maybe you can understand."

"Noel Coward told you? I didn't know you know Noel Coward!"

"That's who I got the tickets from. Anyway, I ran into him at the pub when he was starting rehearsals on this damn play, and he was all upset because of something that had happened. There were apparently hundreds, literally hundreds of actors looking for work, and they were good actors with real achievements in the theater, but now they'll take anything, even crowd scenes. They don't qualify for the dole, you see. And he had to turn lots of them down, and the budget wouldn't let him pay decent wages to the ones he hired, so Noel found the whole experience damned unpleasant. And in the middle of all this, three girls arrived, telling him Cochran had hired them for the crowd scenes, and they didn't need the money at all—just three deb types mad about the theater, rather like you I'm afraid, and he agreed to take them on, but only if he could hire two more regular actors as extras for each of those girls. It made him feel he'd done *something*, you see . . ." His voice trailed off.

"It was seeing your friend that upset you, then. I can understand that. A hero, catching pennies outside the theater."

"To tell the truth, he wasn't much to begin with. But he thought winning the DSO would make all the difference, and it hasn't, and I can't help feeling that's true about the whole blasted war. People don't care."

"Mother says that people are better off since the war, especially women. She says that—"

He was looking at her strangely. "You misunderstand," he interrupted. "I *miss* the war. I miss the good feelings we had for each other then."

His intensity brought them a period of awkward silence which Jennifer ended. "What do you think about Maureen's news?"

"About Hollywood? She's not serious, is she?"

"Oh, I think so. You know that film we were both in the crowd scene last spring at Elstree? As schoolgirls? Well, it was fun, and Maureen loved it, and when this Marvin person telephoned, well . . . It seems they're mad at the moment about anyone who can speak proper English since talkies came in, and she certainly has the looks. Did you hear Mr. Weidenbaum ask me if I'd be interested?" she laughed. "And I haven't even started at RADA!" At the Royal Academy of Dramatic Art on Gower Street she paid an exorbitant sum for a term of classes in walking and talking and for the chance of being admired in a student production.

"Would you go? To Hollywood?" Anthony smiled, sure of the answer.

"Not on your life! And leave you? No, my darling, you have the sole mortgage on my beautiful body."

"You do realize that if we wait as long as your mother wants, when you turn twenty, I shall be thirty-six? You could fit a whole career into that length of time! Perhaps your mother is right about the age difference being too much."

"You don't mean that."

"I suppose not, actually, but you're just starting your life."

"You're the only thing I want in my life." They made a pause for celebration of each other. Then Jennifer grew serious. "How soon would you like to get married, really?"

"There's no reason to wait at all, as far as I'm concerned. How long for the engagement? Till June?"

"I should rather like to be a June bride. Terribly corny, terribly romantic. Do you mean it, darling?"

"You sound as though I were the coy young maiden," he laughed. "I have an idea that we could manage it, you know."

"How? What are you scheming now?"

"Secrets, my dear. It's all between Mother and me, after all. Father will go along with whatever we decide. And I think I know how to get round Mother."

"You mustn't start to think of her as a dragon, you know. If I had a daughter your age–and God knows I'm almost old enough to–I should worry about her getting married, especially these days."

"Mummy thinks she's terribly modern, but when it comes to the jolly old brass tack, she's about caught up with the Boer War."

A horrible thought dawned on Anthony's face. "You're not going to try that stunt young Fern pulled, tell her you're pregnant! Are you?"

Jennifer laughed. "No."

"I shouldn't like her to know we've been . . . you know . . ."

"Now who's just catching up with the Boer War!"

"What is this great scheme, then?"

"Better you know nothing about it. A lady's secrets, after all . . ."

"And when does it start?"

Jennifer looked at him very seriously. "We shall be married in June? Are you serious?"

"Yes."

She gathered up her compact, her evening bag, her wrap. "Then if you'll drop me off at Bobby Page's, I think perhaps the sooner the better."

32

When Elizabeth left Drury Lane she had no plan in mind. She ordered the taxi to take her home, but she was too restless to spend the shank of the evening with Mabel. She would visit her mother. She sank back to enjoy the luxury of the ride to Wimbledon and thought about how grown-up her daughter was becoming, how bossy. The lights still shone in the windows of the Wimbledon bungalow, clearer because of autumn's trees. She paid the driver, watched the taxi swoosh away over the fallen leaves, shivering in a small breeze, walked up the wet path to the sound of her clicking heels, and pushed the doorbell. The door opened quickly and wide. Mabel stood there.

"What on earth are you doing here?" said Elizabeth. "What's wrong?"

"Thank God they reached you!" said Mabel simultaneously. "The news isn't good."

It was very late, and Elizabeth sat motionless by the bed. The figure under the coverlet hung on to life. Its breath rasped through nostrils and throat. Long, slow, embarrassing snores, fraying like old rope. Elizabeth's breath tried to keep time. Slowly, deeply in. A long, long pause. Then silently, slowly out. Then the long, slow inward rasp to tired lungs. In hope of dawn Elizabeth had drawn back the curtains and raised the blinds, but the window spaces stayed black. The night light behind marbled glass made shadows flicker. She could feel the slow thud of her heart so strongly that her crossed leg pumped to its beat and her ears heard its whir. She listened for any sound other than that breath. For the creak of old timber. For a cough or stir from Mabel, whom she had sent to bed hours ago. For the bark of morning's dog, the roar of the first lorry or the clang of the first tram.

A dozen, a score, a hundred Henriettes moved in this room. There was this slight figure on the bed, the body lumping the coverings Elizabeth had smoothed a dozen times, giving to the room a sweet-sour odor. The room gathered around it, the giant wardrobe gleaming, the glass bell filled with dried flowers catching a line of light with its curve, Bernard's photograph on the nightstand glinting with the movements of the candle flame. She had stilled the mantelpiece clock that had tick-tocked in her parents' bedroom since their wedding night, the clock which Henriette wound with a key on each of hundreds of Friday evenings before she unpinned her hair and turned to Bernard, the clock which Elizabeth had heard when in long fever she lay in her parents' bed, the clock which had stayed when she had left, the clock which knew them better than did she.

"There's nothing more we can do," the doctor had said. She had sat there, quiet, hands in her lap, listening to that breath draw slowly in, waiting for the clasp to loosen.

A dozen, a score, a hundred Henriettes moved in her mind. That staunch little woman had become a faery feint, laughing as she changed shape from girl to wife to mother to anger to love to old age and illness, a will-o'-the-wisp fleeing just ahead to remind of a shoelace tied, a dress sewed, a greeting given, always with some quick phrase, some gesture sharp as a bite to memory. Elizabeth's shoulders ached for the need of holding, her chest hollow with the melt of things not said. Oh, my mother . . . They had been so easy all the years that life was full: the anger, the indifference, the busyness. This stubborn little woman, poking her cane into the carpet as she fought her way alone along the corridor to see her daughter out the door, this fierce little woman who had her own life and never thought as well of her daughter as her daughter would have liked. In mind's eye Elizabeth saw her mother look away, chin up, head gesturing dismissal. Oh, my mother . . . my mother . . .

"Hail Mary, full of grace," she heard herself mumble. "The Lord is with thee. Blessed art thou among women."

She saw her mother as she had never seen her, as a bride, her eyes brilliant, laughing up at Bernard, full of future.

"And blessed is the fruit of thy womb, Jesus."

And me, Mother, and me! Almost aloud she cried it, as though there ought never have been anyone but her with her mother, with this figure quiet beneath the counterpane, strong in leaving her, object of her craving. Suddenly she saw her mother as she had stood that day she had left Dublin for the world, so clearly that it seemed not memory but fact, standing at the front door of the great rain-wet house draped with laburnum, one hand on the oval metal knob. She had been haloed by the door's colored glass, at the top of the steps leading to the path and the street, resolute in face of her daughter's farewell desire to weep.

"*Allons!*" she had said brusquely. "Get on with you now!" urging her down the rest of the steps to where Bernard waited with the hansom cab laden with her future, as though she would get this foolishness over and go about her business. Elizabeth had thought her unfeeling, but Henriette had written that night, "I filled your bedroom with flowers that I might not think you gone." Now the daughter would have reached up to the stern figure at the top of those steps and said: "I forgive you, I understand, I forgive you for being my mother."

"Holy Mary, mother of God. Holy Mary, mother of God. *Holy* Mary, mother of God." It ran inside her head as though threaded to the loops of the breath that shuddered from the dry lips of the figure on the bed where she would not look anymore. Still, on the chair in the darkened room, she waited once more for change. "*Holy* Mary, mother of God." Childish whimper against pain, incantation to ward off things evil, things inevitable. Stuck between ages, jammed as a river by blocks of ice, she could not remember what came next, the grief rising slowly through her body and spreading into limbs that began to tremble with the force of her life against that dying.

"*Holy* Mary, mother of God."

Life of its own, her body betraying her, suddenly her hands shot out in front of her, raised, rigid, their backs presented, their fingers spread. Though the candlelight softened their aging, she could see them still–that network of a thousand tiny creases, the brown spots and smears, the blemishes brought by living and dying, the veins like worms. They were not her hands–not mine, please, O Lord!–straining away from her, stranger hands betraying her, making her draw breath with disgust, the tension making the right hand set up a rhythmic spasming that made it seem a live and separate beast. "Mother, Mother." Not me, O Lord, not me, and not my mother, not me, her whole body starting to shake with the fear and mourning of it, and the hundred Henriettes and she fusing, crying for escape.

"*Pray* for us sinners!" exploded the words from her, as her hands let the fear loose. "*Now* and at the hour of our death, amen! *Pray* for us sinners."

And the tide of terror swept through her and from her, and her hands fell back into her lap and the tears welled yet once more, pushed by the hollow ache in her chest, and she sat at the bedside in the room with the long, slow rasp of breaths in the night's silence.

The priest had gone before she arrived, hastening to some other death with holy but no human consolation, the provisions for this mother's journey neatly made, the paraphernalia of crucifix and oil, the talismans of lemon and cotton wool placed in their proper compartments and carried on to the next needer in the cassock's falling folds.

She sat alone at the hour of her mother's death, no companion, no shelter. Mother's mother she had been in her mother's aging, she the grown, she the strong. Now mother alone would she be, she the next generation, she now rising to her generation's destiny unguarded, the forefront now, bared by this falling, she to sit alone forever now as she now sat alone in this room of her memories, none to remember her as she was and is, a girl inside this woman, a child, the youngest fears, the grandest triumphs, the rulings, the choices, the cherishings from which grows love. She did not like her mother; she loved her.

She found herself rocking lightly backward and forward at the edge of her chair–this comfort to herself now all the comfort she would have, oh, my mother. . . .

Slowly, grieving succumbed to life. She had to go to the bathroom. She rose from the hard chair. She straightened the coverlet one more time, brushed the sheet top. Her hand fluttered to the wisps of gray hair breaking the oval of gray face against white pillow, but she would not cry more. She walked out of the room hearing the susurrus of her blue silk gown, crossed the hall to the small bathroom quietly so as not to wake Mabel, and took her place on the stool. Her waters released in a stream as strong as life, but having finished, she stayed seated, her evening gown rucked over her hips, her lace and embroidered panties around her ankles, garter belt tight over her thighs, the shawl placed gently by Mabel round her shoulders, head bowed into her hands by a numbness that bent her neck as would another's hand. She sat for ten minutes or so, not so much reluctant as unable to move, to return.

In the corridor another night light burned, a candle making the mirror gleam, bringing up the oil shine on the teak blanket chest that Elizabeth had sent her mother twenty years ago, blocking the Axminster carpet into colorlessness, holding closed the doors of rooms. Outside it was the darkest of the night, where no birds sing. In the bedroom the breath rasped in, and the room waited for the exhalation. Waited.

Elizabeth tugged the chain to flush the toilet. She looked quickly at her face in the mirror. Drawn, tired, no longer elegant, suitable for the occasion. She tugged the diamonds from her ears as though they were shoddy and left them on the sink. She opened the door, snapped off the electric light, paused in that quiet corridor, heard nothing, heard nothing still, walked quickly to the bedroom. She switched on the light by the door and in its glare saw her mother's naked face, and a great surge came up from within her, heaving up from her diaphragm through her lungs, up her throat, into her face, and out of her open mouth as a rush of soundless air and tears. She stood with one hand on the light switch, and all her being cried, "Oh, Mother . . . oh, my mother . . ." As though her life would reach out and go, with the spirit and the life that had gone from the figure on that bed.

"E*ter*nal rest grant unto her, O Lord." Not her that spoke.

"And may the perpetual light shine upon her." The response from her, muttered. She walked toward the bed, where the coverlets seemed so brilliantly white that she had never before seen white.

"Upon her soul, and the souls of all the faithful departed."

Out went her hand to reach and touch the slack gray face, and as it touched, drawn back as though by a bolt of energy which surged through her to make her cry: Come back!

"Through the mercy of God," she said aloud.

"Rest in peace."

"Amen."

"Oh, my mother. . . ."

33

November 1931

The formal mourning which followed her mother's death allowed Elizabeth to release herself from obligations. She helped no more with the election campaign and cared little when the National Coalition's landslide victory swept even one of her candidates from office. She saw Peter scarcely at all for weeks. He came to the funeral, but she did not visit his new shop in Cecil Court. Jennifer went out almost every evening, but Elizabeth no longer accompanied her. Charles came back from Rome, arranged to postpone the legal matters arising from her mother's estate, went back to Rome having been gentle, reserved, solemn. Slowly she began to live with the having-died of life, grief retreating into pockets of the day. She spent much time alone in the bungalow at Wimbledon, ostensibly cleaning out her mother's things; they mostly remained unsorted though not untouched. She found comfort in that house; the milkman, the greengrocer, the baker, and the grocer continued their deliveries, and she cooked small meals for herself, occasionally staying the night alone, not morbid but at peace, testing her mother's space. Each morning she would take her mail to the bungalow in Wimbledon and sit at the table in the warm kitchen to read and answer it by hand.

Eventually, toward the end of November, it was the mail that pried her from shelter. She had read a long letter from Charles, now in Berlin. He wrote not at all of business but much of politics, for he was meeting many of the German leaders and thought better of them than he had expected. He would be home for Christmas—well before, if things went well. Next letter on the pile was different: a pale mauve envelope without return address, neatly block-lettered as by a meticulous schoolgirl, expensive. On the mauve paper inside, block letters: "YOUR DAUGHTER IS IN LOVE WITH AN ACTOR. ROBERT BRANDON. THEY PLAN TO ELOPE."

She held it in her hand and stared at the black on mauve, repulsed. What does one do? Talk to Jennifer? Hand the problem, if problem it is, to Charles when he returns? But indecision did not last; the letter was like a thing rotting at the bottom of a pond. The newspaper told her that a Robert Brandon was currently appearing in a supporting role at the Playhouse near Charing Cross Station.

Elizabeth knew the Playhouse only in its evening attire, all lights and taxis. In the morning it sat wallflower on the corner of Northumberland Avenue and the Embankment, shoved aside by traffic and pedestrians and shops with wire netting across their windows. The stage door was in an alleyway off a side street. She felt overdressed. The cubicle at the entrance was lit and heated by a crackling electric radiator but empty of stage-doorkeeper. She knocked on its glass, called, and peered along the corridor, where a bare electric bulb illuminated the top of a flight of stairs leading downward. She moved in search of people, her steps indicating that she did not mean to intrude. When she heard a man cough lightly she followed the sound down the stairs to another corridor lined with rooms whose doors were closed, all except one, where she could see the high back of an old armchair, the top of a man's head, his elbow, his lower legs and feet. He was reading, and turned a page.

Completely the stranger, she wished she had not approached so quietly. The room surprised her: a cubbyhole with brick walls from which layers of paint were peeling. There were two dressing tables, one chaotic, the other neat: two rows of cosmetic jars and implements, a set of brushes and combs properly stacked, two framed photos of glamorous young women, a yellow notepad on which two pencils lay in line. As Elizabeth's gaze went to the mirror above that table, the man in the armchair raised his eyes to it, so that they saw each other simultaneously. He wore glasses. For a moment studiousness clouded his features. Then he smiled. "I say!" He was mildly startled. "Are you a lost lamb? Can I help?" His was a tenor voice, its tone ironic and warm.

"I beg your pardon." Elizabeth was flustered. "I was looking for the, er, stage-doorkeeper?"

"Time for his elevenses, I should think," said the young man cheerfully, rising to his feet. "One would suspect he's toddled off to the local. Can I help?" He took off his glasses with one hand, set down his book with the other and Elizabeth was startled briefly by his handsomeness. His features were strong but irregular, his nose a little crooked and large, the lips beneath a small mustache full, the skin pale and blemished as though it were not quite finished with youth. He had vitality. He was tall and moved his body gracefully, though the pose of polite attentiveness was a little stagy. He wore a thick hand-knit sweater of dark green with a pale paisley ascot around his throat. His dark hair was disarranged into a cowlick. Very attractive. She had waited too long to reply. "Thank you, I think . . . Will he be back soon?"

"With Fred one never knows. At this hour?" He made it a conspiracy between them to be here in the deserted theater.

A kettle screamed a sudden whistle and made her jump. As he turned to attend to it, he gestured. "Do come in. You seem a damsel in distress, and both the kettle and I stand ready to offer rescue."

Really, he was very agreeable. He reminded her of someone. Charles? or Peter? Of course not. More likely Ronald Colman, that fashionable mustache. She found herself inside the room, accepting the proffered chair, indicating milk, no sugar. He was that kind of person, the air of a friendly doctor.

He chatted on about the day's hour, the coming matinee. "Have you seen the play? No? *The Painted Veil?* By Maugham himself, really, though the program says Cormack. Bit melodramatic, I suppose." A pose. "Gladys Cooper as Wife of Murderous Bacteriologist! I have a good scene or two, though. One in the midst of a Chinese cholera epidemic, can you imagine?"

She could only accept her cup of tea, assent to his boyish charm. Finally he seated himself on a straight-backed chair. "And now that we're all comfy, what can we do for you?"

She knew that he had taken charge but did not see how. She fought back. "Are you, by any chance, Mr. Robert Brandon?"

"Why, yes!" he said, all gladness, all open.

"I'm Mrs. Charles Wingate. Jennifer's mother."

"I say, how frightfully good to meet you!" All openness, all glad.

Elizabeth did not believe him for a moment. "I'm so glad I was at my most polite! I'm so sorry about this place, this mess. The old chap I share this room with, well, you know these old-timers, they sort of give up on tidiness–"

Elizabeth knew when she was being seduced. "I wanted to talk to you," she interrupted, feeling more in charge.

"Oh, yes?" he said coolly, and there was a flash beneath the surface of something darker than the bright youth he presently enacted. He was older than she had at first thought: twenty-five perhaps? Young enough to be her son. She had no idea how to say what she had to say next, and there was a moment's awkward silence, from which he rescued her by undergoing another change of personality. He put his tea mug down and leaned forward in the armchair, concern all over his face. "I've been wanting to meet you for weeks." His voice was baritone. "You must be terribly concerned, not knowing me." His dark eyes were locked sincerely into hers. "A girl like Jennifer. With me–an actor, an older man."

Suddenly Elizabeth laughed–a long laugh of genuine amusement that moved her head and body back in her armchair. He was, for the first time, discomposed.

"I'm sorry," she said, "but you're doing the what's-his-name, the country doctor in that Priestley play." She laughed again. "Aren't you? The pseudo-psychiatrist."

His concern vanished and he laughed with her. "I'm sorry," he said in his tenor voice. "We actors–you understand–it's terribly hard for us *not* to play roles. It's how we feel, you see."

She looked at him sharply, and when she spoke it was with the coolness of a door opening to the cold outside. "I hope that's not true."

He held her gaze for a moment, but this time he was really discomposed. "Oh, dear," he murmured. Then he rose from his chair and took the single step to the dressing table, where he opened a drawer and took out a packet of cigarettes, offering one, which she refused, lighting one for himself while she sat watching, giving him time to react. When he spoke, it was with one raised eyebrow, with an amused twist to the full lips. "Are we going to get on?" he said, the tenor voice dry, slightly breathless, Noel Coward to the life.

Was this the real Robert Brandon? she wondered. The man was a chameleon. "That depends very much on the issue of our present conversation," she said levelly.

And again she saw something flash beneath his surface, something as dark as anger, as he said, "Did you come here to beard me, specially?"

No, the man of the world was not the real Robert Brandon, she thought. Who he was, she must find out.

"Specially," she said.

He straightened, his bearing suddenly alert. "And what did you want to talk to me about?" The row of single syllables was like machine-gun fire.

"Jennifer, of course," she said, calmly sitting back in her chair, forcing a smile onto her face over the small burst of fear. "And I very much dislike being bullied. May I have that cigarette, please?"

Thus she forced him into the little subordinate ritual, tense, clicking a gold Dunhill lighter under her nose as though it were a trigger. But the ritual gave him time to think, and when he straightened he stood too close to her, legs apart, looking down at her so that she had to lift her head uncomfortably to look at him.

"Forgive me," he said, clipping the words. "But for a woman so extraordinarily attractive your manner is, how shall I say it, very masculine."

She flushed. It was an insult, but the tone was that of regret, almost of condescension. He sought to disarm her by surprise.

"Are we to fight?" she asked, sitting back.

"That rather depends on you."

"I shall fight you for my daughter."

For a moment he held his rigidity, then changed again, letting his body relax, moving sideways away from her, putting condescension into his expression and voice. "I can see in any case that you have a gift for the curtain line. *The Second Mrs. Tanqueray? Lady Windermere's Fan,* perhaps? *Mrs. Warren's Profession* at heart?"

Elizabeth was instantly furious. "I'm not in the least interested in cleverness. I should think it most unwise of you to speak that way to Jennifer's mother." Her tone was as harsh as she had ever used.

He hung for a moment like a strung wire humming with messages, white of face now, so that she feared his anger, but then his features dissolved and it was as though she were watching a watercolor bathed in rain, colors mixing and weakening until he stood before her, this time as he really was, she was sure: a young man, an unsure man, an actor caught in a gaffe that battered him into embarrassment and reality. He sat again on the chair and looked at her unhappily, the dark eyes beautiful and unguarded. She felt a spurt of gentleness, if not of motherliness. She had, she thought, overestimated the enemy.

"I can scarcely blame you," he said, "for thinking I'm a total cad. You know nothing about me, and this is scarcely the most respectable of professions, is it? You're probably sure I'm a most awful social climber. Jennifer is young, innocent, well-bred–I'm scarcely the man for her." He had read her thoughts exactly, and because of it he looked sad. He picked up his spectacles and put them on as though they were armor. "I'm sorry, but I knew all this, and I think perhaps that's why I've been avoiding meeting you. I can only ask you to understand."

"I understand only that you have been seeing a great deal of my daughter without her parents' knowledge. I want this to stop at once."

"You have spoken to Jennifer, then."

"I have not yet spoken to Jennifer. She's just a girl. But a girl who is promised to a man of whom we approve. If you are serious about Jennifer, then why all this hole-and-corner carrying-on?"

She had held his eyes. Now she leaned forward and placed her cup and saucer on the dressing table.

He stood up again with a gesture of exasperation. "But there it is, you see. Precisely. I'm *not* serious about Jennifer." Elizabeth felt relief like a shock. "The problem is, *she's* serious about *me,* and I don't really know quite what to do about it." He looked young and vulnerable behind the glasses, and for a moment she suspected him of acting again, but this, she concluded, was as real as he got.

"I should think it would be very easy to do the right thing."

"I had always thought so too." That tone of rue could not be feigned. "May I explain to you?"

She nodded consent.

"We met some months ago at a place called Bobby Page's. Do you know Bobby Page?"

"No."

"I thought not. Not your style, I expect. It's a bit of a dive, actually, a respectable dive, in a basement in Covent Garden."

Covent Garden basements were not the kind of place one expected an eighteen-year-old daughter to be.

Brandon saw her displeasure. "I'm putting this very badly, it's all very much on the up-and-up. A sort of private spot where friends, decent people go–theater people, a few RAF types, Guards officers, a lot of debs during the season. There's a gramophone and a room for dancing, and the other room has a sort of bar and a few tables and Bobby always keeps the fire going so it's a sort of homey atmosphere really, people know each other. The whole place is a bit nostalgic, a kind of hangover from the war, all sorts of cheery chaps, what-ho-remember-Arras, that sort of thing."

He was asking her approval. She gave it tentatively, for the time being, with a nod.

"Anyway, everyone sort of gets introduced, by Bobby mostly, and you sort of talk to each other, and that's how I met Jennifer. She came there with some chinless wonder, and he was a bit squiffy and I started to chat her up and ended up bringing her home, back to your place in St. James's Mansions, because this other bloke—well, they call them NST, don't they? Not Safe in Taxis?"

Elizabeth was beginning to feel an appalling guilt. Because she had not completely chaperoned the girl, she was sure that Jennifer could not know what she was doing.

"And then she came back the next night," he continued, unaware of her feelings. "Alone. Because I'd told her I'd be there after the show, I think. And so of course we had a couple of dances. She's a grand young lady, your daughter, very much the lady, but a spark, don't you know, a great spark. And then it was something of a medal for me, you see, with a girl as gorgeous as she is liking me? So it got to be a regular thing, our meeting there after she'd been to a dance and I'd done the show. I suppose we saw a lot of each other, but I didn't realize it at first, that it was too much. I didn't think of her as only seventeen, you know, until it was too late."

"Too late?"

He looked up at her, startled by her sharp interruption. "No, no, I've said it wrong again, not too late in the way you're thinking. I'm sure Jennifer . . . I mean, I've never thought of her that way. We were just having a marvelous time, you see, and then she told me, you see, that she loved me." He seemed, for a second, totally miserable, so that Elizabeth saw the scene, heard the confession, glimpsed her daughter's green eyes shining up at him. Unexpectedly, it was for him, not her daughter, that she felt sympathy.

"Well, that's it, really. That's where we are. I don't know what to do. I don't want to hurt her, she's the most terrific girl, I'm sure you know. I should have come to see you, I expect. I think I've imagined Mr. Wingate coming to see me!" He sat up in the chair and smiled broadly, becoming someone more assured. "With a horsewhip or something! What-are-your-intentions-toward-my-daughter-sir sort of thing. I suppose we're all still very Victorian at heart, you know, and being a parson's son and all that, one does want to do the right thing."

"You're a parson's son?"

"C. of E. Living in the country, all that sort of thing. Near Exeter when I was born. Of course the pater died some years ago. My mother, too. The flu, you know. I've made my own way in the world, of course, but those early days stick, don't they?"

He was so very, very different from anything she had expected an actor to be.

"How long have you been an actor?"

"Only a few years, really, but I'm serious about it. I'm twenty-seven now, and it hasn't been easy getting where I am. I'm no Gielgud, of course, but one can make a jolly fine career in the lighter theater, and I'm hoping for a part in the movies, which is where the real money is for chaps like me."

He seemed to indicate himself to be a tailor's dummy. He might be, she supposed, what they called photogenic, but he did not take his good looks seriously or seem to use them against women.

"Of course, British films aren't very good, are they?" he continued disarmingly. "I should like to try Hollywood if I could get there. Ronnie Colman started the trend. They like us because we speak the language, you know, now that talkies are here to stay. Apparently American actors don't speak English or something. Leslie Howard's made a lot of money over there. They say Ivor Novello's going to be a big star this time. Larry Olivier's going next year, he says, though he doesn't really want to. Everybody's off to the gold rush, and I have more experience than they, but–forgive the vulgarity–not the cash."

They chatted for minutes, the theater still quiet around them. She liked his frankness. "With me it's a matter of more money, less art," he laughed. Elizabeth saw why Jennifer should find him attractive. He was handsome, glib, charming, and straightforward. Love might be folly on her daughter's part, but not foolishness. The idea which now came to her made her feel pleasantly worldly. If he agreed, it would solve everyone's problems. How to put it to him?

"How much money does it take to get to Hollywood?"

"Not much, really," he demurred. "It's just that it's extremely difficult to save in this business. But I was talking to a chappie in Page's the other night, another actor, he's worked out the cheapest way. You go on an eight-day boat, second class, from Liverpool to

New York, then you transfer to the Clyde-Mallory Line to Miami, which is in Florida, and to Galveston, which is in Texas, where all the oil wells are, then you go by tram—can you imagine, a tram across the desert?—to another city called Houston, and there you get on a train called the Sunset Limited—isn't that beautiful? isn't that American?—and head off into the west for Sodom-by-the-sea. Takes days, they say, but sitting up you can do the whole trip for less than a hundred pounds. Then of course I'd need a bit of cash when I got to Hollywood, but there are a couple of chaps who'd put me up till I got on my feet—have you heard of a chap called Ray Milland, he's a friend of mine from Page's—and they say it's easy to get work. Ah, how near and yet so far!"

The sparkle in his eyes convinced Elizabeth. Animation had pulled him to his feet as he acted out the voyage in quick rhythms and postures.

"I can give you a hundred pounds," she said, rearranging her gloves.

He turned slowly toward her, and the change in his voice was the opposite of what she had expected. "And get rid of Jennifer's problem?" he said, icily baritone. "Surely there's a cheaper way. I'm disappointed in you."

She had offended him. Well, to coax him, she would be as feminine as she could. "I've offended you. I do apologize. I could have put it more tactfully." She looked up at him with wide eyes. "But I feel as though I know you. I certainly like you. It would serve both our purposes."

"It's very kind of you, I suppose," he said grudgingly. "What do I say: I'm not that kind of girl?"

"If you could think of it as a business loan. You could pay me back when you make good."

"A loan?" He turned his back on her. "What strings?"

"Only that you would not see Jennifer again."

"And you would take care of her?"

"Young hearts ache badly but not long. The man she is to marry knows nothing about this, I'm sure."

He stayed with his back turned, thoughtful. When he spoke, all ill-temper had gone. "We finish here in a fortnight. I could leave right after that. . . . The odd hundred quid, eh? My pride against my future. I don't like taking money from women." The touch of bitterness in his tone was a little theatrical. "One can afford pride when one has money. . . ."

He fell silent, but she was sure he had made up his mind to accept, and when he turned to face her, he was alight with decision. "Shall we shake on it? All right!"

She stood and they shook hands silently, both of them pleased.

"Will you tell Jennifer?" he asked.

"I think a note from you would be best, just telling her that you are going to Hollywood and wishing her the best."

"I can manage that."

"I'll have the bank send you a draft this afternoon."

"A loan only. I'll sign a note."

"A loan."

He took off his spectacles and ran his fingers through his hair, loosening again the boyish cowlick on his forehead. He looked as though he had regained health, and she was struck again by his handsomeness and vitality.

"I know this seems a little sordid," she said simply, restraining herself from touching his arm. "To me as well as you. But that sort of thing depends so much on one's intentions, doesn't it? It's a pleasure for me to be able to help your career, and I shall think of it that way. I hope we shall meet again under better circumstances."

He escorted her to the stage door saying farewells, exuberant. The doorkeeper was eating fish and chips inside his cubicle. As she walked back down the alley to the Embankment, she heard a single yell: "Whooopeee!"

She felt the same success in her own heart.

34

March–June 1932

Elizabeth immediately had Mr. Blakeley send a cash draft around to the Playhouse. She was pleased with her decisiveness. Without Charles' help she had used money purposefully to protect her family's interests. He would have done no better himself. She thought long about speaking to Jennifer, or even to Anthony, but decided that those tigers did not have to be ridden. She did not see Jennifer receive Brandon's promised letter. The girl seemed moody these days and looked at her mother speculatively now and then, but she spent most of her days at RADA or shopping for Christmas and most of her evenings with Anthony, so Elizabeth crossed her fingers. When Charles returned home, she told him that she had changed her mind, that as a Christmas present they might tell Jennifer that she could marry Anthony at the end of six months. Jennifer took the news with satisfaction rather than jubilation, but soon she was choosing silver and china patterns and collecting a trousseau for a June wedding. If there *is* any problem, thought Elizabeth, the process of the wedding will get her into the marriage.

Thus the whole incident might have passed from family memory, leaving only Elizabeth's pride at having taken action, if something quite unexpected had not taken place in March. Charles had the habit of distributing the morning's letters to his women-folk over the breakfast table in a little ceremony which, with his mild jokes about their correspondents, was one of the few relics of the *pater familias* he displayed. One day in March he feigned great astonishment. "I can't believe it!" he said, interrupting the sorting of the mail.

"What is it, Daddy?"

"Mabel! Come here!" he called to the kitchen. He was waving an envelope bright with American stamps. "We must all be here for this."

Mabel entered and stood patiently by the sideboard, a dishcloth in her hands, wearing an apron.

Charles put on mock solemnity. "Now . . ." He looked around his three women. "Who among us is likely to get a letter from America?"

"Oh, it's mine, Daddy," said Jennifer, reaching for the envelope. "It must be from Maureen."

"Aha!" he said. "But Maureen is not yet in Hollywood, is she?"

In the act of buttering toast, Elizabeth froze. Brandon? Had Brandon broken their bargain and written to Jennifer? What would he have to say, three months before the wedding?

But Jennifer lost interest. "If it's not Maureen, I don't know anyone in Hollywood. Not that I wouldn't like to."

"Well, I hate to disappoint you, princess," said Charles, "but it's not for you at all."

Elizabeth's alarm gave way to embarrassment. Could Brandon be writing to *her?* Surely it was too soon for him to pay off the loan. He couldn't know of this table ritual, of course, she'd have to warn him.

"Now," said Charles archly, looking alternately at Elizabeth and Mabel. "Who among us *never* gets letters?"

"Mabel?" exclaimed Elizabeth.

Mabel, startled, reached for the envelope. "Now, Mr. Charles, you give that here!"

Charles held it away from her laughingly. "But you must first tell us what it's all about, Mabel! Have you been writing fan letters to Ramon Novarro again? Or is this your MGM contract? I know! It's a love letter from Charlie Chaplin. I wondered what the real reason for his coming home last year was! Now we know–visiting his childhood sweetheart."

Mabel looked plump and flushed, as though delighted with the teasing.

"It's nothing of the sort, Mr. Wingate, and you give that letter right here. I bet it's from my brother Fred. I told you someone gave him the money to get to America! Look at the address on the back of the envelope."

Elizabeth relaxed. She knew nothing before this about Fred Greggs' going to America since Mabel rarely mentioned her family, but relief buried any surprise that news brought, relief that the letter had nothing to do with Brandon at all.

Charles made a great show of reading the back of the envelope through the bottom half of his spectacles, then shook his head in mock sadness. "Not good enough, Mabel. This says Robert Brandon."

"See, I told you!" crowed Mabel, snatching the envelope. "That's my brother Fred. His stage name."

A chasm opened in front of Elizabeth. Robert Brandon is Fred Greggs? For a moment she felt tied to the chair by webs, her mind flicking over its strands like a spider's sensors. Brandon: convicted instantly of fraud, and much worse, cruelty. Mabel: in the dock for collusion with her brother. Jennifer? She must have known Brandon was Greggs. Object: a hundred pounds from Mummy. There was a sense of hissing and laughing around her.

"Excuse me," she said, and went to her room.

Since Elizabeth did not know exactly who might have hoodwinked her, during the following days she was tied to silence. Brandon–that parson's son, that nice young man–she wasted little time on him. To plot with his sister against her, to lie directly to her for the sake of a hundred pounds? No innocent reason existed for hiding his identity from her. Possible treachery by Mabel worried her a great deal more. Mabel's deceits over the last twenty years had all been matters of concealment, not aggression, and this latest seemed unlikely; but it was for her beloved Fred. Elizabeth's faith in her own judgment was shaken. And Jennifer? Was Jennifer involved? Would she mock her mother and her fiancé to get money for Fred Greggs? Why? She would have liked to talk things over with Charles, but the whole story made her out a complete fool at the very point where she had established her autonomy from him. She arranged instead to lay her case before Ginny Pearsall and Peter Williams.

"It's my pride rather than my pocket, of course," she ended her recital by saying. "I feel that I cannot trust anyone in my own home."

They sat in Peter's bookstore in Cecil Court, a small square room piled floor to ceiling with books heavy with the smell of dust. A narrow flight of ancient wooden stairs led to an enormous cellar filled with shelves of more books, all neatly arranged so that only Peter knew where anything was. A large window and a glass door opened the view to the court itself. Two aging armchairs faced the desk, backs toward the window, like heirlooms with their cracked leather and wool cushions. Peter sat behind his desk, Ginny and Elizabeth in the armchairs. Bands of smoke from their cigarettes hung at head level between the warm air from the radiator and the outside chill. They drank tea, and thought about her suspicions.

"I think you can quite count out Jennifer," said Peter eventually. "It's such a lower-class sort of plot, isn't it? I mean to say, a hundred pounds is a lot of money, but most of us could find a chap to borrow it from. I can't see Jennifer stooping to a confidence trick, can you?"

"Does Jennifer have any money of her own?" asked Ginny.

"I should think so. She has savings. I don't know how much."

"There you are, you see," said Peter. "She could have found most of the money herself, borrowed the rest. It sounds to me like Brandon did it all himself. Greggs. God knows he could have gotten anyone to write that letter, especially theater people."

"You have only the evidence of the letter that Jennifer was involved at all, don't you, my dear?" asked Ginny.

"And what Brandon said."

"He might be lying entirely. And if he wrote the letter, then there's no evidence at all, is there?"

"He knows her. I'm sure he knows her."

"Perhaps he does know her, and got the idea all himself. I should think the best thing is to ask Jennifer," said Peter.

Elizabeth smiled. "Perhaps Ginny understands a mother's pride. If she isn't involved, then any mention at all of his name will make me look an ass. And if she is involved, we should only have a fight, and I certainly don't want that, not with her wedding in the offing."

"You don't want to know whether she is involved, then?" asked Peter, puzzled.

"Of course she does," said Ginny. "Men!"

"But let us consider the case of Mabel, then," said Peter, sitting back in his chair. "Here I should make a straight character judgment. I've known her for damn near twenty years, haven't I? Of course she's good at keeping herself to herself, as women of that class must be, but I'd be willing to bet she's straight as a die."

"I've always thought so. But this is her brother, to whom she's quite devoted."

"But think what she has to lose if she did it and was found out! Poor Mabel!" said Peter. "Imagine if her brother did all this without her knowing!"

"Either way," said Ginny sadly, "the possibilities for treachery in this little plot are stunning. So very destructive."

"Perhaps they were all in it," said Elizabeth glumly. "Do I really seem such a fool as to make people who know me think they can do this sort of thing?"

"Well, of course there would have been no way at all of your finding out if it had not been for that letter to Mabel, would there?" said Ginny. "I don't think your foolishness was the basis for the plot at all. Something a little nastier than that." There was a look of slight disgust on her face.

"How could they tell you would go see Brandon?" asked Peter. "Surely it would be more likely that you would speak to Jennifer?"

"Sooner or later I, or Charles, would have had to see Brandon. Perhaps he—they—wouldn't have waited for me to come to him. As it was, I made it easy. All he had to do was charm me. If I had spoken to Jennifer, at least I would know whether or not she was infatuated with him. I can't say she has seemed upset at his departure, which would suggest she is innocent."

"Or a good actress," laughed Peter. Ginny looked at him coldly.

"But then Mabel, if she was involved," said Elizabeth, "surely she would have been more reticent when that letter arrived. She must have known that I would guess the minute those two names were put together."

"Unless she wasn't thinking," said Ginny.

"There, you see," exclaimed Peter. "That would very much suggest that she knew nothing about it at all, which is what I suggested, and if Jennifer had been involved, surely she would have shown some sign of a broken heart, or at least pretended. We simply don't know whether she has ever met the fellow in truth, do we? Who would know? Could you ask Maureen?"

"I suppose I could write," said Elizabeth slowly.

"Again, why not simply ask Jennifer *and* Mabel?"

"Oh, Peter," said Ginny impatiently. "That simply would be breaking the eggs to make the proverbial omelet."

The trio fell silent.

"It's such a greedy little plot," said Ginny thoughtfully. "Whose the gain, one should always ask. A hundred pounds? Surely there is more to it." She fell silent, looking vaguely surprised at her own thoughts.

"But there's the point, you see. Brandon is the only one who gained."

"Yes," said Ginny unexpectedly. "And you know, the whole thing could be much more innocent than we are making out. What if it's all true, that Jennifer did have feelings for this Brandon person? That letter could have come from a real friend, you know. And as long as she's marrying Anthony, there's no harm done, is there?"

"A hundred pounds," said Peter.

"And what if that all fell out just the way it seemed to fall out, and this Brandon person merely seized the opportunity when you offered it?"

"I suppose you could be right," said Elizabeth reluctantly.

"Of course I could be. You may have misled us, Elizabeth. It's not wise to think badly of people." She seemed now suddenly ardent to convince.

"I must agree with Ginny," said Peter. "It fits in much better with Mabel's character, and with Jennifer's. She is, after all, a girl, not some demon schemer. Are you going to tell Charles?" He laughed. "I should love to see the old dear's expression, robbed of a hundred pounds."

The conversation turned to the reasons for keeping Charles ignorant, until customers began to peer in the window and rattle the handle of the door. As Elizabeth walked with Ginny down Cecil Court, Ginny offered some final advice: "I should put it all out of my head, if I were you. What have you lost, after all, but a hundred pounds? I cannot help thinking it is unwise for any of us to poke up rocks just to see what lies underneath. Lord knows, there's enough creepy-crawly lying about in plain view these days."

"Unless," replied Elizabeth, "there's more to this that I *should* know. I hate not to trust people."

Distrust fades slowly. It spoiled Elizabeth's pleasure in the preparations for her daughter's wedding, which she had expected to pull her out of the doldrums that sometimes made her cry at night over her mother's dying. Jennifer herself was gay as a sparrow, chirping through the showers, the breakfasts, the rehearsals, the shoppings. She dashed off every day to RADA and every evening to Anthony. She managed to play the lead in the Academy's production of *The Country Wife,* receiving a couple of notices from the press which, although they emphasized her beauty more than her skill, were highly gratifying. She and Anthony mixed with the theatrical crowd, supping at the Savoy Grill or the Ivy, and though girlish about her coming marriage, Jennifer quickly grew more mature and mannered under their influence. Shortly before her wedding, *Town and Country* asked her to model a gown and she appeared under the heading, "Great British Beauties." Anthony was pleased. Elizabeth found something hard in her daughter's behavior. Her carelessness was scarcely of F. Scott Fitzgerald dimensions, but it was there. Like all her generation, she seemed to want what she wanted when she wanted it, and she wanted a great deal more than had Elizabeth at her age.

That June she sat in the quiet of Brompton Oratory as her daughter's nuptials wound their solemn way over the couple's head. Charles sat comfortably in formal wear beside her. Ginny sat on the other side, wiping her eyes with a lace handkerchief, thinking of her lost sons. Mabel sniffled in the pew behind, while Peter sat further back. The couple knelt before the altar and bowed their heads beneath solemnities. Eternal love, they whispered, eternal truth, eternal us.

In fact the wedding participants were in very different degrees of innocence. Charles knew nothing. Head of the family, he was free to indulge his sentimentality about his cherished daughter. If he was guilty, it was of other deceits; Mrs. Mountjoy sat toward the rear on the side of the bride's family. Peter, never having cared much about the plot, had by now forgotten it. Anthony, elegant except for his blush, was also innocent. He had been gratified at the speeding up of their wedding, but since he and Jennifer had not spoken further of the matter between their conversation after *Cavalcade* and the announcement of her mother's change of heart, he had no occasion to be suspicious.

Other guests were less innocent. In the middle of the tribunal at Peter's bookstore, Lady Pearsall had realized that one consequence of this silly little plot—and hence its real goal—could be the removal of Elizabeth's opposition to Jennifer's early marriage. She had been appalled at the possibility of deceit in Jennifer which thereby opened up, and when Elizabeth had indeed removed her opposition, the possibility became in her mind a fact. She resolved to keep her eye on young Jennifer, but saying something to Elizabeth would only widen any breach between mother and daughter, and for no purpose. If true, what would the truth do but harm?

Mabel sniffled quietly into her handkerchief behind Elizabeth's unsheltered back. Mabel loved Jennifer, thought Elizabeth too possessive, regarded eighteen as the perfect age for a woman's marriage, wanted her lamb settled down before she got a taste for wildness, and loved the romance of weddings. Ever so lightly, she had supported Jennifer's impatience to be wed. "But your mother knows best, I'm sure," she had always said. Then, so very very lightly, she had encouraged Jennifer's interest in this Robert Brandon whom she had met by chance. But when she had told Fred that there was money somewhere in all this if he kept his eyes open, surely she had thought of no more than what fell out: his passage money to Hollywood, a fair reward for work well done. And as to the response that March breakfast which revealed the identity of Robert Brandon—that could as well have been the result of fluster as of a calculation that the truth having to come out sometime had best come out when she would look most innocent. Mabel's conscience was easy as she went about her familiar rituals in the comfort of the fashionable church. She had taken care of her own. No harm done.

And what of the bride herself? When she had arranged matters with Robert Brandon that night after *Cavalcade* at Bobby Page's, she had thought of him as a fallback just as she thought her plot no more than a jape. Her plan had been that Elizabeth would come directly to her and convince her that early marriage was better than elopement, but Elizabeth had acted more decisively than expected, and Brandon, though caught unawares, had come through with flying colors. Impulsiveness, he said, had led him to snatch at the chance brought by Elizabeth's offer of a hundred pounds.

Jennifer had laughed at this twist to her plot. "Mother can afford it," she said. "Out of the money she saved by canceling my deb ball, if need be."

To be fair, Jennifer did not realize that she was making a fool of Elizabeth. Daughters see mothers as far too powerful to be clowns. Nor did Jennifer at that time know that Robert Brandon was Fred

Greggs, neither Mabel nor Robert having seen fit to mention the matter. She had been amused when Mabel sprang that surprise and assumed that it meant no more to her mother. What, after all, is a hundred pounds? She herself had what she wanted: marriage to Anthony in June. No day in her life would be more important, she was sure, than that day of her wedding. She bowed her head now before the altar and her husband, conscience as clear as her complexion.

35

1932–1933

The Brandon incident did not undermine Elizabeth's self-confidence; it made her what she quickly came to term "realistic." It was a window on the world that she needed. By early 1933, when the mail brought Brandon's postal order for a hundred pounds, an expensive flask of perfume, and a graceful note of thanks, she was no more than mildly pleased that the fellow had proved no thief. She had found her own way of skirting the decade's despair. She was, she thought, open-eyed about human nature now. I should be grateful to him, she thought, for reminding me not to take things for granted. Her political associates noticed the change. They said: "Since Ramsay MacDonald betrayed the party . . ." Her family said: "Since Grandmother died . . ." or "Since Jennifer left home . . ." Peter lent her a new book: Howard Scott's *Science versus Chaos*. "We Technocrats," she read, "like to think of an optimist as a man who believes that everything is for the best in the best of all possible worlds, and of a pessimist as a man who agrees with him." She liked that word "technocrat."

Charles was somewhat surprised that Elizabeth kept on the bungalow in Wimbledon, but he paid its small bills uncomplainingly. He was more surprised when she announced shortly after Jennifer's wedding that she would pay those bills herself from now on, for she had taken a job. The job had come to her through a Labour Party paid organizer called Harris who had cropped up off and on through the years in various of the electorates where she operated. He was a loose, fat little man given to tight suits in the Moss Bros manner, with a cockney accent, a graying mustache, and an eye for the main chance. Standing in a dim meeting hall after a successful rally, he had complimented her: "If you ever need a job, missus, give me a ring. I'll see you right. Got a little business on the side, I have. I could use you. Brains and class. Give me a ring, why don't you?"

Eighteen months later, she had given him a ring.

"Called me at the right time, you 'ave," said Mr. Harris cheerily. "Going full-time, I am. And I've got these Yanks coming over here, want to set my little business up very nicely, thank you. Ten o'clock tomorrow. Come and see me. Forty-seven Greek Street. You know where that is? Soho? Mind you, I can't pay much right now. Cheerio!"

The little business had not been as sordid as it sounded. The new art of opinion research had come into the world, and Mr. Harris was well-placed to become its English maestro.

"Mind you," he said, "these Yanks can show us a thing or two."

He signed Elizabeth on as office manager in exchange for five and a half long days of her week, with two weeks off per year "for good behavior." Elizabeth found her Friday envelope holding five pounds and small change as great a pleasure as her mother had told her it would be. Mr. Harris' little business undertook surveys for commercial clients, exploring such matters as the number of vacuum cleaners present in a given area, the likely attitude to sliced bread, and the probability of selling white salmon meat by the slogan "Guaranteed not to turn pink in the tin." Mr. Harris dealt with the clients and with endless forms sent by America full of personal questions at which, if left unchanged, English housewives would have taken umbrage. Elizabeth was in charge of the interviewers: a still-youthful returned soldier inclined to vanish into black moods and his bed-sitter at unpredictable moments; a war widow of her own age who complained incessantly of sore feet; and various part-timers who would respond to her summons if babies, binges, and husbands permitted. They were, she said, rather a new experience.

At the end of her first month a trio of American experts arrived: smooth-faced young men with capital, know-how, ambition, and self-confidence that even Mr. Harris found astonishing. They spoke of expansion and logistics and deploying teams into districts and regions against target populations and showed her pictures of their wives and children. When they said "consumer" they meant the Labour voters of the towns and cities she had come to know so well as a political organizer. A month of their slashing through figures on income and unemployment and numbers of "indoor johns" and "radio sets" and "residents per unit" gave her more knowledge of those voters than she had ever thought or wanted to possess. She was told she would have a stable of girls. They also gave her a buck-toothed young graduate of the University of Reading to work with, a Mr. Thomas Hendricks, who had dozens of little maps and sheaves of paper covered with mathematical hieroglyphs and a chain-smoking habit which she hated, but his statistics told her where to send the girls.

At first she handled her stable with courtesy. They were mostly lower-middle-class girls who had left school at fourteen and wandered the frontiers of respectability as shop assistants, typists, or receptionists until the American adventurousness of Mr. Harris' job made its appeal. She sent them out in groups of five or six to live in provincial digs where their stockings dripped forlornly in front of the gas heater. Once on the road, there they stayed, weather, domestic crises, health, children notwithstanding. When they were new, Elizabeth went with them. Later she sat in London and took their phone calls, amazed at the illness, family disasters, and personal plumbing problems which crowded their lives. She authorized weekend excursion tickets to London until eventually Mr. Harris came to her.

"Look, luv," he said. "I didn't hire you to be a mum to these girls, you know. You wouldn't let the upstairs maid take advantage of you, would you? So why let this lot?" He grew serious, a fellow conspirator, bosses together. "Now, you've got good sense, you 'ave, but you want to toughen up a little, luv. Not too much, mind you. We're a 'uman business, we are, not a bunch of capitalist exploiters, but I do 'ave me partners to worry about."

Elizabeth became what she thought of as stiff and grim with the stable, and after a few buck-up chats from Mr. Harris the number of phone calls from the provinces dropped off. There followed a few incidents of deceit which proved Mr. Harris right. The girls, she realized, did not think of her as the friend she had tried to be. For the first time since Colombo she fired someone, a butter-wouldn't-melt-in-her-mouth type caught with her skirts up for a pipe salesman in an alleyway behind a pub.

"I wasn't doing it for money!" she protested angrily to Elizabeth, as though that excused everything.

"Better if you had been, perhaps," replied Elizabeth.

By the spring of 1933 it became clear that fraud had spread among the teams, who had formed the winter habit of filling in each other's forms beside the gas fire among copies of *True Romance, Screen Gems,* and cups of tea. An American youth called Mr. Donald Wallace materialized from across the Atlantic to represent the partners' interests. He talked of percentages and productivity and profit margins, and Elizabeth felt overwhelmed by America. He insisted on ending the women's paid trips home.

"I don't see how they'll go for that," said Mr. Harris, whose socialist past made him twitch every now and then.

"Tell 'em business is bad," said Mr. Wallace with his ready smile. "There's a depression on, after all."

Then he insisted on firing the women who earned the biggest bonuses.

"But they're the hardest workers!" protested Elizabeth.

"Yeah," he said. "So if they go, we'll be out of trouble. It's the average that counts." He flashed a white-toothed smile. "This is a democracy, you know."

"But you'll get the mediocre if you go for the average," said Elizabeth.

"We don't hire these women at half what men would cost just so we can pay them the same as men, Elizabeth." His explanation was delivered with patience and charm. She hated him, seeing him as the world's future. She also liked him: the energy, the decisiveness, the newness. He let her keep on Mrs. Moore, a widow with three children.

At night Mabel bathed her in a flow of good-humored cynicism about workers and bosses: "Them as go along get along, they say. Got to learn to take orders, you and Mrs. Moore."

Over the months Mabel managed the household, negotiated with Mrs. Hooker about the meals, scrutinized the bills, set a glass of sherry ready for Elizabeth's return home in the evening, and listened with fascination to her tales. She's more a wife to me, thought Elizabeth wryly, than I am to Charles.

Charles had reacted gracefully to her taking a job. "Some of the best people are," he said ironically. "These days."

She saw more and knew less of him. Their truce was in place again, but if they had communicated little before, now they were like old soldiers ordered to eat in the same mess for years after they have run out of things to say to each other. In the autumn of 1932 Jennifer aged them overnight by telling them they were to be grandparents in the spring. She was delighted, but Elizabeth could not help comparing Jennifer's ease at becoming pregnant with her own long struggle.

Anthony had bought an eighteenth-century house off Curzon Street that squeezed its five narrow stories between two mansions in a manner that made Americans invariably call it cute. With the money given by Charles as a wedding gift, Jennifer had turned its interior into a triumph of good Regency taste. Mabel helped out more and more often, complaining mightily about the tiny, narrow staircases, whose difficulty Jennifer began to discover with pregnancy. For her last months she retreated to a bedroom on the first floor, and Mabel, deputizing the stolid Mrs. Hooker to keep St. James's going, moved to Mayfair. Her departure gave the St. James's flat the ever-ready but never-used air of officers' quarters. On one or two occasions when Elizabeth worked late, Charles had to take his dinner out of the oven himself.

Pregnancy at first inspired Jennifer. She saw it as a special Christmas present and wrote long letters to Maureen and Jill and Fern about baby clothes and schools. Maureen wrote back about Hollywood parties and cars. Jill Knight, soon to be married herself and living in the country, sent special diet instructions. Already married Fern took to visiting every day and crying mysterious tears with sad, luminous eyes. When her belly grew distended, Jennifer's delight gave way to disgust with and distrust of her own body. The baby was pressing against her kidneys. Her ankles swelled and her face grew puffy. With Anthony she was glum, with Elizabeth petulant, with Mabel impatient. Elizabeth wanted her to move to St. James's Mansions, where she and the baby would be properly nursed, but Jennifer insisted on delivery in a hospital with the new anesthetics.

"I'm going to have gas, and in a proper place."

"It's not nearly as bad as you think, darling," said Elizabeth. "When I had you–"

"Oh, Mummy!" exclaimed Jennifer. "Don't be so old-fashioned! Nobody goes through all that these days! Good Lord, the baby will be with me the rest of my life!"

Cast as Lady Teazle in the spring RADA production of *The School for Scandal,* she had to surrender the part. "Mona Harmon-Bowman!" she cried. "She'll ruin it! That part was *written* for me. Why couldn't they postpone?"

"It's time you gave RADA a rest anyway, dear," said Anthony.

"It'll all be over soon, love, you'll see," said Mabel. "Get yourself a young 'un and you won't be worrying about plays. Don't you worry about her, Mr. Anthony, there's nothing like a baby in the house to make a woman happy."

In Mabel's experience babies made life more rather than less difficult. Anthony made a good enough husband but she couldn't see

Jennifer settling down to motherhood. Unlike Elizabeth, therefore, she was not surprised when Jennifer came out of the hospital after her ten days' confinement, put the baby in her mother's arms, and took Anthony dancing at Ciro's to celebrate Mona Harmon-Bowman's success as Lady Teazle. "Darling!" said Jennifer to Mona. "I'm devastated that I missed it. I hear you were absolutely wizard!"

"Laying it on a bit thick, weren't you?" said Anthony mildly, and as a consequence had to bring her home weak and weeping at eleven o'clock.

The elders worried about her indifference to her new daughter.

"She's going to have to learn that being a mother is a full-time job," said Elizabeth. "You can't always get what you want in this life, she can't always have it her own way."

"If you ask me," said Mabel, smoothing a pile of sun-dried nappies, "she got a bit of a scare. She was looking forward to good times. I'm sure she didn't think about what she was getting into. But then, who does?"

"And what were you doing at the same age?"

"Ah, well," said Mabel, looking solidly forty and tucking her chin into her neck. "I had to earn a living, didn't I, now?"

"She has a chance at a film part next month," said Anthony, looking moodily out of the kitchen window at the area steps, where a heavy summer rain chipped the whitewash.

"A film?"

"Something about Henry the Eighth, made by a bunch of foreigners."

"Really, Anthony," said Elizabeth, rising to clear away the supper dishes. "You ought to put your foot down."

"Some liberated woman you are!" Mabel smiled. "She'll make more money at this than she ever would as a teacher, I'll tell you."

"At the expense of her daughter and husband!" protested Elizabeth.

"Oh, yes?" said Mabel.

"I think it's better, actually," said Anthony, "that she get it out of her system."

Jennifer wrote enthusiastically to Maureen that she had landed the part of one of Henry's queens and that Alexander Korda might put her under contract for twenty-five pounds a week. Maureen wrote back: "No more costume bios for me, thank God. I'm to make something called a 'jungle flick.' You must watch and learn what real acting is. From the chimpanzee, not me."

Lady Pearsall was not reassuring. "I don't think Anthony takes her acting seriously enough, you know. If it keeps her happy, then the man thinks it's all right, but I sometimes wonder if he knows what she really has in mind. She might be more ambitious than any of us realize. You and I didn't have to deal with Hollywood at her age, did we?"

The filming of Jennifer's part in *The Private Life of Henry VIII* took all of four summer days. She was there the day King George V visited the studio and the set. In his soft Hungarian voice, Alexander Korda told the King that there were a dozen British beauties in the cast.

"*Are* there that many?" said the King.

Korda offered up Jennifer, who repeated her debut curtsy.

"Ah, yes," sighed the King.

She found Korda full of continental charm, always with time to give sympathy, but it took months for her to receive her salary. Anne Boleyn was played by Merle Oberon, who turned out to be Queenie Thompson, the dance hostess she had known at the Embassy Club. Korda and this film, everyone said, would make her a star.

"Have you met the Prince of Wales yet?" asked Merle on the set.

"Not yet," said Jennifer seriously. "But I shall."

"Better watch out." Merle smiled. "They say he has an eye for married women, you know."

"Then he's the only one who does."

To make the film, Jennifer starved and exercised herself with ruthless determination. She postponed the christening of her daughter, Meredith, called Merry, until she was fit for the photographers, and Elizabeth was angry that photos should appear in *Town and Country* and *Queen*. "Mothers should not look like Marlene Dietrich," she said to Ginny.

"How nice!" replied Ginny wryly. "A new rule, and one so easy to obey."

"Oh, I know I'm being foolish," said Elizabeth crossly. "It's only fashion. In my day we were supposed to look like milkmaids stuffed with cream. I'm sure the lounge lizards find her gorgeous."

For a change, Elizabeth was visiting Ginny in her bright little flat in St. John's Wood. She had driven over in her Austin on a Sunday morning to help Ginny complete her billings for the Season, and the table was covered with neat piles of receipts, each topped by a gold-leafed notebook embossed with a girl's name.

"What are these?" asked Elizabeth, lifting one unmarked heap.

"Discounts, dear. I've already done them."

"Discounts?"

"You might call them kickbacks," said Ginny gaily. "But for God's sake, don't. You know, I think you may be in danger of making a mistake with young Jennifer."

"Kickbacks?" Elizabeth waved the sheaf of papers in the air. "You're worse than Mr. Wallace, Ginny. What on earth have the pair of us come to? I'm sure I've made many mistakes with young Jennifer, but what is this new threat?"

"Opposing her about her career."

"I don't oppose her about her career!" said Elizabeth, startled. "What I oppose is . . . Oh, damn, I suppose it's nothing more than that her definition of what a lady is and does differs from ours so much. I worry about her. What else can a parent do?"

"Avoid nagging."

"She's a child still, and she has a daughter of her own now."

"Child or not, she has, as they say, her own row to hoe. I shouldn't get in her way if I were you. Now, tell me, shall I overcharge Mrs. Goodwin by ten percent or fifteen percent? If I make it fifteen and don't tell Inland Revenue, I'll have an extra week in Antibes."

"Oh, by all means take an extra week at Antibes, courtesy of Mrs. Goodwin."

"And what was that you said about our definition of a lady?"

The two women laughed.

The photographers enjoyed Jennifer's new glamour more than did her husband. Jennifer managed to use his ignorance of feminine medical matters to postpone her return to lovemaking for some weeks. She dressed and undressed in the bathroom and faded into fatigue when they came home late, but when in September she started a new round of agents' offices and producers' lunches, he insisted that she accompany him on his regular autumn tour of European banks. He took her up the Rhine by steamer and sat with her in the open-air cafés of Frankfurt and Zurich, letting the crisp air and autumn colors revive her soul. By Geneva she was uncurling like a kitten when the maid drew the curtains to the day. In Rome they began making love again, and though she insisted that he and she both take unromantic precautions, she was as eager in the shadows as he could have wished. At the end of their second week away, she was missing Merry, and he agreed that after Salzburg, where he had planned a surprise for her, she should go home ahead of him.

Salzburg's spires dreamed over dusty squares and colonnades and a river reduced to murmuring by September drought. When the traffic rested, one could hear the cow bells from the mountainsides. Anthony disliked the town intensely, no matter how beautiful. He called it a shrine to Austrian ignorance, offering a choice between indifferent hostility and self-righteous *gemütlichkeit.* Each year it took the money of foreigners at a festival the town never attended, of music the town never heard, by Mozart, the native son it had scorned. Each August the town put on serge and brocades and sat in the square to watch von Hofmansthal's *Everyman,* directed by the famed Max Reinhardt. The play showed them how hard it was for a rich man to enter the gates of heaven. They whispered of Reinhardt: "And who should know better than a Jew?" When this spring's last snow still covered its stones, the same cathedral square had housed the pro-Nazi rioters demonstrating against the installation of Dollfuss as chancellor of their Austria. Adolf Hitler, born a few kilometers away, had become chancellor of Germany on January 20. Who was this Dollfuss to stop their native son from uniting them with a Greater Germany? Anthony did not like Salzburg.

However, he and Jennifer wandered happily enough through the city's Saturday streets, buying apples at the market stalls and sipping beer at tables placed in the cool of the colonnade. Anthony pointed out on the mountainside the Schloss Leopoldskron, where they would be going this evening, improbably medieval, a perfect eighteenth-century fake. They were to sup there at eleven at the invitation of its owner, the great Max Reinhardt himself, founder of the Salzburg Festival, director of Berlin's Deutsche Theater, Berlin's Kammerspiele, Berlin's Grosses Schauspielhaus. Former director, corrected Anthony. In Oxford when the German National Socialists had conducted the first of their public anti-Jewish purges that winter, Reinhardt had resigned all his posts without returning to Berlin. The German papers now called him "the Jew Goldmann." Reinhardt was Anthony's surprise for Jennifer.

"But how do *you* know him?" she asked, as though he had no right.

"In the banking business, darling, one meets everyone."

After an evening of rest and lovemaking, Jennifer looked her best in an ice-blue satin gown bought in Rome and the sapphires which Anthony had given her at their engagement. Her face was a pale triangle dominated by the green of her eyes and the red of her lips and the white column of her throat. Relaxed by eroticism, she sank back into the long wolf-fur coat which had been his wedding present, letting her dark hair pool into waves against the collar, and in the horse-drawn *fiacre* to Leopoldskron she entered a dream world where the sky's stars and the mountain's black and the castle's candle-lit windows conspired with her beauty and the texture of the fur and the camellia scent of her perfume to make her feel a creature of history.

"Ah, Kultur!" murmured Anthony in her ear as they entered the high-ceilinged reception room. The air shimmered with art and taste and money. It was lit only by a huge fireplace and candelabra and sconces, shining on old wood and metal and fur rugs. It was filled with women in jewels and silks and men in white tie and tails. In a minstrel gallery overhead, a trio played Mozart.

"Who are they?" whispered Jennifer, surrendering her furs.

"Theater people, aristocrats, the rich, from all over Europe." He paused thoughtfully. "You will never see them again."

"It looks just like a movie," said Jennifer, taking a glass of champagne from a scarcely visible waiter.

"They have a story here," said Anthony. "A Hollywood producer said the same thing. They told him they were all hired extras. He believed them. Excruciatingly naive? Or by chance very shrewd, would you say?"

Unreality lent Jennifer the sensuality of a floating flower. Gentlemen were presented to her, leaned over her hand, murmured, "Ah, but you are so lovely!" Her ice-blue satin shone in the clusters of candlelight, which made the skin of her breasts and the shape of her throat things from which the men could not take their eyes.

"Then you know my friend Alex Korda!" they exclaimed delightedly. "How very pleasant! I have not seen him since . . ." And it would be Berlin or Vienna or Budapest or Paris, cities whose names had a lilt as they slipped saluted into the mist.

She was presented to the Master, an elegant world-weary man who had celebrated his sixtieth birthday two weeks before. He was gracious and enormously self-possessed, but his thirty-year career was coming to an end, and he seemed to know it.

"You should always be seen by candlelight," he said. "We should have nothing but candlelight for the ladies, is that not right, my dear?" He turned to his wife, a white-haired lady who appeared at his elbow. "We had here as a guest one night Mr. Louis B. Mayer. You know of him? A nice little man. We should not make fun of him. When he saw the candles he said, very sympathetically, 'A short circuit, Mr. Reinhardt?'"

"I had to explain what he meant to poor Max," said Mrs. Reinhardt. The Master was shaking his head sadly. "When he saw *Jedermann,* he was so very disappointed. 'You can't put that on in America!' he said to Max. 'There are too many rich people there!'"

"Ah, but he is right," said the Master. "We need the rich people."

He was about to accept refuge in Hollywood, a city he hated. Invited to stage Shakespeare's *Midsummer Night's Dream* before twenty-five thousand people in the Hollywood Bowl, he would demand that they tear down the band shell, which they did, and ask that they give him good actors for the play–Charlie Chaplin as Bottom, Greta Garbo as Titania, Clark Gable as Demetrius, Gary Cooper as Lysander, John Barrymore as Oberon, W. C. Fields as Quince, Wallace Beery as Snug, Walter Huston as Theseus, Joan Crawford as Hermia, Myrna Loy as Helena, Fred Astaire as Puck. He would not, of course, be given them. This Europe did not understand America yet, thinking money should create art rather than the other way around. "It is dark," Reinhardt had written recently to a close friend. "Around us the lights are going out. We are lost always in time. My heart is heavy from all that remains unsaid and undone."

A gentleman whose name she had not caught took Jennifer by the elbow. "But we are all so grateful to your husband!" he said in a strong Hungarian accent.

"And why is that?"

"My dear lady! Perhaps I am being indiscreet? But because of your husband we are all able to keep a little of what we have earned."

She cornered Anthony. "What did he mean? What is it that you do for these people?"

"It isn't me personally."

"But what?"

"Only a technical matter, actually. We are helping the Swiss to set up their banking system so that the German government will not be able to confiscate the holdings of those who flee. Rather a challenge, really. Sort of no names, no pack-drill operation."

"Flee whom?"

"Herr Hitler, of course."

"Oh, yes, the Jews, I suppose. I should have thought–"

"We are all Jews here tonight," said Anthony. "Don't you have that feeling?"

At two-thirty carriages arrived to take guests down to the city. An aging, elegant man with humorous eyes came to Jennifer and Anthony. "Mrs. James? After the others have gone, the Master would like you to stay. A small private party. Stay for an hour. Please."

They were conducted to a small, dusty room above the minstrel gallery, from where the Reinhardts and a few friends could look down upon the scattered glimmer of the city's lights. Servants brought drinks and a light supper. The conversation was of art and literature and the theater and never politics.

"You are very beautiful," said Reinhardt to Jennifer, tilting her chin to the side with one finger. "There have been so many beautiful women here. When I am in America, perhaps you will come to visit me?"

He spoke of the annual *Everyman.* "The nicest part of these festival summers is that each one may be the last." He paused to look at the circle of tired people who surrounded him. "You can feel the taste of transitoriness on your tongue."

They stayed until dawn began to turn the mountains into dim blue shapes and the river into a piece of silk beneath its mists. They rode back to the hotel to the clip-clop of the horse through empty streets and the first birdsong. They had to waken the night porter, grizzle-faced, to let them in through the glass doors.

"There is a telegram," he grumbled, and shuffled to the desk to hand them a folded form.

"YOUR FATHER DIED YESTERDAY. PLEASE TELEPHONE. MOTHER."

36

September 1933

The day of Charles' dying was filled with the gifts of autumn, a fine, bright day. He had spent his last evening with Julia Mountjoy, and they had made love in the manner that made Charles think of rich dark colors. He had walked home across Hyde Park with his umbrella over his shoulder and he had let himself into the St. James's flat, where a night light burned and Mabel had left a slice of cold pork pie with Major Grey's Chutney for his supper. He went happy to bed. Next morning he saw Elizabeth briefly as she pinned on her hat in front of the hallway mirror before leaving for work.

"Good morning, dear," she said, friendly enough.

"'Morning," he replied, half-awake, and went into the bathroom, from where he heard the front door close behind her.

He breakfasted with Mabel, who was all chatter about the imminent return to London of brother Fred to publicize the premiere of his second starring film at the Empire in Leicester Square. Brandon had mailed her the money for an evening dress, and she displayed its pearl satin against her plump body, reminding him of the girl she had been. He took the underground to the City, feeling tired for some reason, and he arrived in Threadneedle Street, heading for Great Swan Alley. To his left the new giant structure of the Bank of England was, as it had been for years, in process of construction behind its ancient windowless original wall. Behind him was Mansion House, official residence of the lord mayor; ahead lay the Royal Exchange, and beyond that the Stock Exchange. The walk always gave him pleasure: its names, history, wealth, the huge facades of commerce. It was to him the heart of England, that part in which one took pride. Right now it might not be in the best of shape, he thought. He worried again about the deal in Madrid which Plunkett was trying to put together at this very moment. Well, he shrugged, looking around him. She'll be right. London was still all muscle and blood and the thud of life.

The morning was bright and cool, September's sun warm on his right side, a northwest wind blowing from his left between the buildings, cleaning out the old canyons of the streets on its way down to the river and out to the sea, bringing him a freight of vague, gay childhood recollection. He looked very much the City gentleman this morning, pausing there at the curb to lean on his umbrella near the steps up to the great bank, waiting, it seemed, for a gap in the traffic. He looked east, and it seemed to him that the sun coming in bursts or in swoops like the wind had made him breathless. It dazzled his eyes, and as the first great pain hit his chest he thought briefly that something unseen had come out of the sun's center to strike him. The umbrella fell from his left hand. His right arm reached to protect his chest. When his legs gave way, it looked as though he were stooping to retrieve the umbrella, but then he fell forward onto his knees, and then onto his face, and his bowler hat tumbled and fell upside down in the gutter, leaving the sunlight to gild his thinning hair almost white.

We look so like a bundle when we fall there in public, preoccupied with owning up to frailty. Suddenly there is too much flesh, as though it were no longer needed, too many clothes hunching around us. Shoes, and then feet and legs, seem discarded belongings, and our faces take on a blank absorption with the inner self that makes others reluctant to disturb us, thinking quickly that perhaps we are doing something private and not really as odd as it looks. Should they wait till we have finished? Bystanders glance at Charles as he falls, turning from the crossing of the street to hesitate in his direction, themselves looking as preoccupied as he. One woman talks louder to her companion, as though she does not see. Charles closes his eyes to the brightness of the sun and seeks by mind alone to tear from his heart that which his hands are now too weak to grip. Someone bends over him, talks to him, rolls him about, digs at his neck. The dim memory comes that this has all happened to him before, and he sees Wilpattu's lagoons where the cranes stoop to fish their own images and their bills make circles spread from their center. The pain changes to something else, to something larger than the swoop of the wind and the burning of the sun. Someone talks to him, someone fusses with his collar stud. He is back in the bedroom of the house in Mount Lavinia.

"Elizabeth?" he says. He opens his eyes. But it is a young policeman, who does not hear him, and his hope vanishes as the officer oddly consoles him for not making it across the street.

"No," says Charles distinctly. "But I tried, didn't I?"

And then sound and light stop.

37

When they brought the news to Elizabeth—a policeman at the door, Mrs. Mountjoy later by telephone—she felt more shock than grief. The young City policeman, accepting tea while he gave and took particulars, saw her white but not weeping and mistook manners for coldness. Elizabeth stayed efficient even when sturdy Mabel crumbled into tears and had to be sent to bed, and even when Ginny offered help, one widow to another, though Ginny did notice that Elizabeth could not look her in the eye. That same afternoon the telegram was sent to Jennifer, Elizabeth feeling the need to have her family about her.

Two days later she remained composed when she stood waiting for her daughter's boat train under the great glass canopy of Victoria

Station. Pale, dressed in black, the baby Meredith in her arms, she stood among the bustle as though a spotlight held her amid the tinny thunder of loudspeakers and great shouts of steam from the engines. Jennifer, dressed in a gray wool suit and a small black hat, looked wistful as the guard helped her descend from the first-class carriage, and Elizabeth felt the urge to protect her. They embraced awkwardly till the baby between them awoke and complained and they both stood looking at her rather than each other.

"It was very quick, they say," said Elizabeth as the two women moved slowly toward the exit after the crowd had passed. "A policeman was right there. They sent him to tell me, poor thing. It must be very difficult for them." Elizabeth fussed with the baby's wrappings but remained dry-eyed. "He said your father was conscious to the last and did not seem in pain. He spoke to him."

They reached the baggage car and stopped.

"He says he chatted to him. Chatted. Consoled him for not having made it across the street." Elizabeth sounded as though the policeman should have had better manners at the moment of death, and Jennifer looked up into her mother's face to see the tears swollen in the flesh. "And Charles . . . your father said, 'No, but I tried.' Then he . . . he died. Those were his last words." She looked suddenly into Jennifer's green eyes, which were at that moment identical with her own. "Why should one pay so much attention to last words? So ambiguous, don't you think?" She seemed to imagine her daughter could explain. "I could . . . they could . . . it could . . . mean so *many* things." She looked away, shaking her head slowly.

Jennifer did not need to know her mother well in order to feel for the first time in her life the meaning of grief, the guilt of love for parents expressed too late. For once, she thought, Mother is attending to herself rather than me. Elizabeth would cope with this like everything else, but Jennifer felt for the first time that her own younger strength might be needed, and so she offered it, putting one arm around her mother's waist.

"So very *many* things," repeated Elizabeth slowly. "I think perhaps I had forgotten to admire your father *enough*."

Tears might then have come to wife and daughter, but at that instant an elegant young man who had been fussing about his luggage stepped backward and bumped into them. He turned, started at the sight of Jennifer, and let his handsome features give rise to a huge smile. "Jennifer Wingate, by God! What an amazing omen! You're just the person I wanted to see!"

"Robert!" exclaimed Jennifer, releasing her mother. "Robert Brandon!"

Few meetings could have been worse timed. Elizabeth was cool and disagreeable. Recognizing Brandon immediately, she recalled but did not feel the anger which he had inspired. "How do you do, Mr. Greggs," she said, to enjoy his discomfiture, then stepped aside to see if there was anything special in her daughter's reaction to this man whom she had once presumably loved.

Jennifer was caught between her feeling for her mother and excitement over Brandon, whom she had not heard from in ages. There were hasty explanations on both sides.

Brandon assumed a politely mournful mien. He was here to promote his new film. He thought it best that Jennifer telephone him in a few days. "At Brown's," he said, forgetting to be cheerless. "I've come up in the world." She agreed, and Jennifer sought to explain to her mother who he was as they walked away.

"We've already met," said Elizabeth blankly.

"Of course you have," said Jennifer, cursing her fluster. "I was forgetting." She cast an apprehensive sideways glance at her mother.

"So you did know?" said her mother, staring at her. "I've never had the courage to ask you directly, but it makes such a difference, you see." Then she shrugged. "Oh, for God's sake, no it doesn't. We'll talk about it later. It scarcely matters now, does it?"

She ordered the taxi to take them to Jennifer's house in Mayfair, explaining that she had invited Peter Williams and Ginny Pearsall to join them.

"We have to have a council of war, I'm afraid. Like Mr. Roosevelt's kitchen cabinet," she said, sitting back to scrutinize her daughter's face. "I'm afraid that your father's death has been followed by some very surprising news. You haven't heard yet?"

"News? What do you mean?"

"Apparently I did not know Charles Wingate as well as I thought," said Elizabeth dryly. She saw what she was about to tell her daughter as some kind of test. She wanted the companionship of a woman, not a child, and she was not quite sure of Jennifer's capability. "They telephoned me from the local police station yesterday morning. They had something to tell me, they said. I told them I was at home. They sent round an inspector, just like in a play. An agreeable man." She turned away from Jennifer to look out the window of the taxi, which was stalled in the usual traffic jam near Hyde Park.

"He needed to smoke his pipe, and he was surprised when I told him he might. I've never minded the smell of a pipe."

"But what did he have to say?"

Elizabeth looked back at her daughter for one last measurement, then nodded in the direction of the pavement near the Underground station. "One finds news in the newspapers," she said.

The usual row of placards stood in a row against the wall and screamed their crayoned headlines from behind wire. "CHARITY PRINCE DIES." "DEATH OF PEOPLE'S HERO" "MYSTERY MILLIONAIRE FOUND."

"Daddy?" said Jennifer, turning large eyes to her mother. "Daddy? Daddy is the Mystery Millionaire? Oh, don't be absurd!"

"It seems the police have known for years." Elizabeth looked steadily at her daughter. "Of course they would have to, wouldn't they? One can't just have a Mystery Millionaire wandering around giving out money to passersby without knowing what he's up to. They talked to Charles, apparently. He was frightfully keen to remain anonymous, the inspector said. But when he died, someone would tell the press, he feared. The inspector was very apologetic. He thought we should have notice."

"No. I can't believe it," said Jennifer in a daze. "Daddy? But we used to laugh about the Mystery Millionaire, all of us. When I wanted my deb ball, Daddy said perhaps I should ask the Mystery Millionaire for the money. How could he have said *that?*"

"As you see, my dear, your father had his unexpected side, it seems." She made a gesture of farewell at the placards as the taxi moved forward. "And as you see, the newspapers are turning him into some kind of hero." She turned a face with an almost childlike expression toward Jennifer. "Can you imagine? Your father as kindly capitalism personified?"

"But it's all so ridiculous!" Jennifer exploded. "Daddy?" she almost laughed out loud.

"That's exactly what I felt," said Elizabeth, animation enlivening her face. "I hoped you'd understand! To think that your father . . . wandering the streets . . . looking for poor people . . . his pockets full of pound notes." A little bubble of laughter interrupted her words. "They brought me his wallet, you know. It was stuffed, absolutely stuffed with pound notes." She looked wildly at her daughter.

"With pound notes? When he died?" For a moment the two women looked at each other, trapped in a wild surge of irreconcilable emotions. "Oh, no, I mustn't laugh!"

"I know," said Elizabeth, "it's so wrong, and it isn't funny, we mustn't laugh, but I couldn't help thinking–now, I shall have people coming to the door, asking for more!" She laughed. "It's so unfitting. It's so unexpected." The two women grew instantly serious, staring at each other. "And what did they mean, then, his last words? 'No, but I tried'?"

Elizabeth let her head slip forward so that she was staring at the hands on her lap. "Oh, Jennifer," she said. "I loved your father. But perhaps not enough. I feel as though I had missed something terribly important about him."

The afternoon's council of war had the aura of a board meeting, all the women in black gathered around the mahogany table in Jennifer's tiny Regency dining room, with Peter strangely energetic and conscious of his position as sole male present. They discussed arrangements. As Peter said, "It may be a nine-day wonder, but nine days can be a devilish long time."

They agreed quickly: Elizabeth would refuse to speak to the press and move to Wimbledon to avoid them; the funeral would be private and Ginny would attend to the details; Peter would have a special card of thanks printed for Elizabeth to sign and mail. There were some special messages: Lady Warwick had sent condolences; the prime minister's secretary had telephoned; William Morris had left a card; so had a representative from Charles' club. Alexander Korda had sent flowers. Mona Harmon-Bowman wanted Jennifer to get in touch.

"And Winston Churchill? Nothing from him yet?" inquired Elizabeth wryly.

Jennifer would attend to the VIP's. There was nothing from Colombo yet. And where was Joe Plunkett? Had no one heard from Joe? Joe must be found, told. Elizabeth telephoned Mrs. Mountjoy, who reported herself besieged by reporters and disintegrated into tears. "He's in Madrid, I think, Mrs. Wingate. Or perhaps Morocco. He and Mr. Wingate were in the middle of some terribly important negotiations." She hesitated. "I expect to hear from him anytime. He's to cable. Or telephone. But we don't expect him back for at least another fortnight."

Gradually arrangements organized themselves, and the council of war fell into talk about Charles.

Mabel provided tea and mounds of cakes and scones. "He loved my scones," she said mournfully. "Mr. Wingate did. So full of life, he was. Ah, well, an adventurous man."

Elizabeth gave her an odd look. Adventurous? By speaking of Charles, Mabel had put him behind glass, as though he were a species.

Peter went out to get the evening papers, which carried further stories about the death of the Mystery Millionaire. One had discovered that his daughter was a "film actress." Others called him merchant prince, financier, City magnate. They don't know what he did any better than I do, thought Elizabeth. Rich. Wealthy. There was a ten-year-old photograph taken in Colombo. "Did this man bless you?" read the caption.

It was when he saw that caption that Peter blew up, casting the paper from him. "Phew! The fellow's done me in at the last! I should have known he'd pull something like this!" He groaned, causing them to stare.

Ginny fixed him with her gaze, then slid her focus to somewhere over his left shoulder. "The man's adrift," she snorted. "Fame. Envy."

"It's not the damnable *fame,*" snapped Peter, glaring at her. "It's the–what else can I call it–it's the damnable *imaginativeness* of what he did. Did you suspect he had this in him, Elizabeth?"

Elizabeth looked up from reading the *Standard* and peered through her glasses at her love. "Imaginative? Charles?" She thought for a moment. "He was always interested in the theater."

"You can't see it, can you? Any of you." Peter stared in turn at each of them.

Jennifer stared at her shoes and said, "Perhaps I can."

"Ah," groaned Peter. "The whole thing is so . . . grandiloquent, can't you see it? Here the whole world is in the middle of this terrible slump, and all anyone does is argue socialism and capitalism, while good old Charles, who doesn't talk about politics, of course, quietly and *secretly* takes all that filthy capitalist lucre he makes and gives it away, simply gives it away to those who need it."

"But it's an absurd gesture," protested Elizabeth.

"Only as absurd as anything that cuts right to the heart of the matter," said Peter, subsiding gloomily. "All the fellow did was strip money of its magic. You need money? Here it is. Only the most staggering imaginativeness could have thought that one up."

The room fell into a gloomy pause. Peter resumed, a grumbling coda. "God knows we all want a memorial, and look what he's pulled off–turned himself from nobody into the people's hero overnight!"

And suddenly Ginny Pearsall spoke out, the energy of anger clipping her words. "Charles stayed anonymous precisely so that no one could make anything of it. Don't be a fool, Peter Williams. He didn't care what people thought!" Peter looked at her skeptically. "And don't look at me like that, you silly man. Charles Wingate was always more reticent than he needed to be. He refused chance after chance for honors. Fame indeed!"

"Ginny," said Elizabeth gently, shocked at the anger.

Peter rose from the table and strode to the window. "But the imagination," he said to the room in general. "The one quality I thought I had over him. . . . Ah, dammit." He looked miserably at Elizabeth, who stared back in bewilderment.

"He wasn't competing with you, darling." The endearment slipped out. Ginny nudged Elizabeth with a look which Jennifer intercepted.

"I've known about Mother and Peter for years," she said, smiling. "If that's what you're worried about."

"You have?" said Elizabeth.

"The afternoon is full of little surprises," said Peter gloomily.

"All the trouble we took to be discreet for your sake," laughed Elizabeth, rising from the table, moving to stand by and touch her daughter.

Peter shrugged his shoulders. "Didn't he care about money?"

"Charles?" Elizabeth considered the question. "I've never thought about it. He loved to work. He was always very generous."

"It wasn't money he cared about after all," muttered Peter.

"Money does not make itself," said Ginny Pearsall.

"Of course you're right," said Elizabeth, again surprised, looking thoughtfully at Ginny. "Perhaps, even these last years, Charles worked harder than I knew. It rather bothers me, you know, that I don't even now know how he made his money. Well. We shall just have to ask Joe Plunkett."

Peter had sunk into his chair and was gloomily knocking a knuckle against the table edge. "Well, he turned out to be downright whimsical," he said. "Thereby depriving me of my only claim to distinction."

Elizabeth moved soothingly toward him, and Ginny taut as wire, cast an angry look at both of them. "Your taking Elizabeth away from him was more than enough. You took the life out of him. He could have done so much more if he'd had a wife who cared."

She stopped abruptly, appalled at being led into betraying friendship, but Elizabeth turned to reveal an amused face. "I think you're quite wrong, Ginny. Charles always went his own way. Indifference is all he felt lately toward me. Not need. If he had . . . But he took so little from me, nothing that he couldn't and didn't get from other women, actually." She stared directly at Ginny. "You'll have to forgive Ginny, Peter. She has a soft spot for Charles because of something that happened years ago that she's never forgotten."

Ginny stared back at Elizabeth. "That's a very cruel remark, Elizabeth." She turned to Peter and said calmly, "Charles and I had a brief affair, perhaps too brief, many years ago, that's what Elizabeth means." Her tone was as though something bitter and treasured had at last emerged. "It meant very little to him, I suspect. Not much more than when he slept with your late wife, I suspect."

Elizabeth was angry. "Why," she said, "do Englishwomen so easily turn from sugar to spite?"

Mabel, following the growing dispute in amazement, suddenly jumped to her feet and leaned forward across the table. "What's the matter with you all? Stop this, stop it right now!" It was her nanny tone, but they ignored it.

"*I* asked Charles," said Peter, looking straight back at Ginny, "to sleep with Mary." He laughed and looked at his hands. "I thought it would cheer her up." He began to laugh softly, and so did Elizabeth.

Ginny looked at them both and then, unexpectedly, she too smiled. "We always wondered," she said. "Elizabeth and I. Your wife–she was so terribly . . . pallid!"

"But it's all so long ago, can't you see?" laughed Jennifer.

Mabel had remained tense. Now she turned on Jennifer, her face flushing with anger. "If you don't have any respect for yourself, miss, then at least have some for your father!" She turned on Peter, her composure quite gone. "And 'e was a better man than you are, Mr. Williams. And a better husband than you deserved, Mrs. Wingate! And if you can't see what a good man he was, what a *kind* man, and what a job it was for 'im–him–to take care of us all these years, then what I say is, then you'd be better just to *shut up*."

Eyes snapping, she turned on her heel and headed for the door. The group had sobered with her anger. Elizabeth sat expressionless. They all spoke of him in the past tense, she thought, this man whose body covered, entered mine, this man whom I had never thought to live without. Stony-faced, she spoke at Mabel, pulling her up at the very door with her voice. "No, Mabel," she said. "So very much better to have at the truth at last."

38

October–November 1933

Elizabeth found that widowhood made her life more simple and less important. She shook her head over what people said about her dead husband. A tired little woman humbly pushed two scrubbed children at her one afternoon. "Give me money, 'e did, mum, your 'usband," she said. "I thought it might make you feel better, like, to see their shoes. I 'ope I'm not intrudin'." Elizabeth felt overwhelmed by the kindness of it. She received letters ill-spelled on coarse paper. "Oh, no," said Elizabeth, "there's more to this than money." The pigeon lady from Trafalgar Square brought a bunch of lilies wrapped in newspaper and patted her on the arm and said her husband had been a fine man and any woman who had a fine man, even for a few months, was luckier than most. From the Haymarket Theater came an anonymous envelope containing passes. "To be used at your convenience," said the block letters on the envelope. A man in gray sidled up to her in the street. "We did not want him gone," he said, shaking his head.

She listened, marveled, and failed to recognize the Charles they offered her. She thought: They are mistaken. But doubt seeped in. How much had she misestimated him? She remembered how she had failed him when he had had such fears of death in the resthouse at Wilpattu. The sensation of sharp hollowness in her chest made her press her hand to her breast as though to massage the pain away. What if it never went away? But this is absurd, she told herself. She had loved Charles, of course; but not this much, not for years. Peter, not Charles, had her affection. So why this pain, which had no other meaning than loss, than ending, than alone?

Others did not mention her loss often. Mr. Harris had begun with sympathy, oozy. "Take a couple of days off, dear," he had said, patting her arm, flashing stained teeth and bad breath in a wince of understanding. "Be kind to yourself. We'll get Mrs. Moore in off the road for a few days. Keep the seat warm for you, like."

But a week later, the day after the funeral, he telephoned at ten o'clock. "We was expecting you, Mrs. W.," he said. "Life goes on, you know."

She went back to work, so muffled in cotton wool that no one would meet her eye until a few days or a fit of impatience enabled them to forget she was a widow. She sat looking bleakly across the room at Mrs. Moore, presumably staying on as her assistant. Really nothing had changed about her life, not really. So why did she feel so pointless? She went often to the pictures. She thought a great deal about her mother. She would not grow domestic with Peter, but she took to stopping by his Cecil Court bookery after work and walking back to his Bloomsbury rooms, where they would cook a sort of dinner together. He was patient with her form of mourning, and his lovemaking was gentle, as though it were for comfort rather than excitement. They talked a great deal.

The evening after the reading of Charles' will she sat with her feet up and shoes off in front of the fire, ignoring a plate containing the remains of a pork pie and greasy peas.

"At least you'll still have an income," said Peter. "Which is nice to know."

"I wonder."

"Wonder what?"

"If any income from Charles is a good idea for me." She smiled into the flames of the self-indulgent fire Peter had lit. "Perhaps he set me an example which I shouldn't ignore."

"He didn't do without an income. You'd find that rather difficult."

"I must admit his leaving such a large sum to Mrs. Mountjoy was a surprise. I scarcely know the woman."

"You know what it means, of course."

"I just hope he was happy with her. She seems a very pleasant sort of woman. I think she loved him very much. But what does one say? In any case, I've told Mr. Blakeley to pay her bequest as soon as possible, even if it means selling things. I just wish Joe Plunkett would show up, so that I can get clear of the whole business, let it be his worry, not mine."

"You'll shift your capital elsewhere?"

"Of course. Mr. Blakeley will take care of it." She stared at the flames. "Mr. Blakeley apparently blames Charles for having left me without cash, but I'm sure he didn't mean to. He even borrowed against his life insurance, which ties that up. Oh, well, the creditors will wait. Perhaps I should ask for contributions from all these poor people who keep appearing at my elbow?"

She yawned, letting her breasts show partially at the opening of the wool robe that had been her sole concession to her visits with Peter. It was old-fashioned by now, but still fresh.

"When does the appraiser come to the St. James's flat?"

"He was there this afternoon, I believe. They'll send an offer or a statement, and I'll take it. The publicity of an auction . . ."

They fell silent, listening to the soft crackle of the flames. Peter was somnolent, as usual after making love. He is getting fat, she thought; as solid and as dusty as his books. He ought to get more exercise. Yes, Mrs. Williams. She smiled at herself.

"Implausible," she said. "Impractical. Irresponsible. What is the word I want?"

"For what?"

"Charles. Messing up his own will. Not thinking ahead. You say he was imaginative, but I can't believe it."

Peter stirred to life. "And what else have our past fifteen years been but the gift of Charles' imagination? Have no doubt: he's the base on which our eternal triangle has rested, not you."

"I should have said his indifference."

"You know there was more to him than that."

"I suppose so." She stubbed out a cigarette and lit another. "I read somewhere that there are two dimensions we can never understand: those of the universe, and those of a man's heart. I shall never understand Charles."

"And perhaps that's the surprise."

"Do you remember telling me once that husbands and wives are no more than incidents in each other's lives?" She recalled the hot sun and wind on the long grass outside his bungalow on the hilltop, Mary's grave. Peter grunted and opened one eye to look at her. "You were wrong, I think," she continued.

He looked at her with the quizzical humor that had always given him youthfulness. "I don't see how that could be."

"How often do you think of Mary?"

He opened both eyes, and then pushed himself halfway up in his armchair. "It's been over fifteen years." He sighed. "Oh, no more than three or four times a week." He looked sideways at her with a wry and knowing expression. "As one would a sign reading, 'Danger. Crumbling cliff.' If one lived above the sea. The warning has to be there." His expression grew solemn, his face showing some of the fine Greek line that had always attracted her. "In other words, as though she were an incident, a bad incident. One remembers if one falls off a cliff. One becomes aware that an attraction to cliff edges can be fatal."

They fell silent until he resumed.

"It's terrible what we do to the dead, isn't it? Turn them into signposts. As though they had no purpose of their own. As though their lives were important only insofar as they affect ours."

He stared at her with curiosity, his bright blue eyes filled with amusement at human nature. She sat quietly, rubbing her stocking feet together, fingers tapping her teacup as though she were playing scales. He broke a prolonged silence by stretching, rubbing the back of his neck, and picking up the newspaper that rested on his knees.

"If we're going to see this *Grand Hotel,* we ought to start out. Garbo and Crawford won't wait, even for me."

For some reason the moment reminded her of Colombo and Charles. Domesticity felt as soft and heavy as a presence.

"And what about us now?" She had not even known that the future weighed on her mind.

He looked at her in surprise. "Are my intentions honorable, do you mean?"

"What are our plans?"

"We shall get married, of course. You have to make an honest man out of me."

She looked at him unamused. "Years ago, you never wanted to get married. Now I don't. Is that something that being widowed does? I know that it's time to go on to new things."

He would not believe her. Women wanted marriage. One can't be married to a man for thirty years without coming to believe him irreplaceable for a month or so. She would get over it. So he jollied her into her clothes, a taxi, and the Leicester Square Empire. Afterward, walking home through the lights and seediness of Tottenham Court Road, he said, "You're turning out to be a very decisive person, aren't you, darling? I used not to think you were. You used to be so much the lady."

"The practicality was always there," she replied, hugging his arm. "As Joan Crawford has just shown you, ladies can be surprisingly decisive even when men, shall I say, don't exactly encourage them to show it."

They turned into Bedford Square, where the leaves of oaks and beeches caused the light to fall doubtfully upon them.

"I used to nag you, if you remember. I used to say: you must choose. I thought you drifted. I still do, rather. But it turns out that your drifting gives you a kind of balance, doesn't it? You never go too far either way, do you?" He laughed suddenly, his face caught by the streetlamps. "Perhaps it is you, not me, who is the real intellectual."

"Ah, Peter," she said. "You always like to read meanings into us women. I'm not a bruised Garbo, and I'm not Crawford, all hard shell concealing hope!" She was laughing at him, but she had stumbled upon a truth about her independence.

Elizabeth's feelings for herself rather than Charles had shaped her relationship with Peter. Either age or custom seemed to have staled Peter's sensitivity about her. The cynicism that made him think of their marriage as some kind of gravitational event underestimated the strength which kept her aloof from him—as though that strength had never been more than a manifesto. He lent her that week Sylvia Pankhurst's latest book, *The Home Front.* Since the war, Sylvia had become an unwed mother by intent, and now she flaunted the lack of legal ties to her husband, made childbirth a statement of women's rights to control their own bodies, challenged the state in bed. Elizabeth found the book sad because it made her realize that her farewell to politics had been genuine. Lady Astor had been not enough the woman; Sylvia Pankhurst was too much so. Elizabeth was somewhere between.

She was amused that Peter should have lent her a book against legal marriage at the very time he expected it of her. Ambivalence, as ever, in Peter: between the notion and the deed, between revolution and custom. He came at her from a tangent. The thought gave her pause. For all the irritation between her and Charles, she had always felt that they shared a center and an orbit. And now, suddenly, she felt disloyal to Peter: his tangential, outmoded, but kindly offering up of Pankhurst. She was irritated with herself.

Sex so confuses things, she thought. Had Peter and I not slept together, would we not have remained the best of friends? What would have happened to our lives if I had not gone to his cabin that night? Such a flimsy excuse—that dreadful woman's laughter. But we enjoy making love, if only sometimes just for the kindliness of it. . . . And what if, with Charles, I had not let that tie go? If we had made love these last years instead of just being married?

We would have fought. We would have been too much together, and I couldn't take that much together anymore. Ironic, isn't it? To stay together, Charles and I, we needed to keep ourselves apart. Staying separate is as important as staying together. She would not talk further to Peter about marriage.

Therefore, by the time of her financial crisis, she was already clear as to the outlines of her future, and when Peter responded to her financial crisis with a spurt of gentlemanliness and common sense that made him point out forcefully that two could live as cheaply as one and they should get married, her refusal was impatient. Peter could not change what she wanted and did not want.

The financial crisis itself took her by surprise. The solicitor had assured her that the inheritance of real property, and especially of Charles' share in the business, should leave her very well off, but Mr. Blakeley was more cautious, waiting to talk to Joe Plunkett, who had inherited management of Elizabeth's share of the business. Available records showed, he said, that Charles had converted much of his wealth into cash during the last few years. Of course he couldn't have given it all away, but it would be better not to settle quite yet perhaps with Mrs. Mountjoy? Reluctantly he followed her instructions to sell shares and bonds and continued to worry.

Over a stand-up lunch with a colleague at the public bar of the Hoop and Grapes, surrounded by other gents in wing collars and cutaways, Blakeley admitted that Plunkett's failure to appear bothered him.

"Nine weeks overdue, you say?" said the colleague from the midst of a pint of bitter. "If he were a ship he'd be sunk, I'd say."

Mr. Blakeley tossed his chin mournfully.

"*And* had the funds, presumably, with him?" confirmed the colleague. "He's got the word and scarpered, don't you doubt it!"

"I shouldn't have thought it, not of this one," sighed Mr. Blakeley. "But then, one never does, does one?"

"All the right inquiries in hand, then? Missing persons, consuls, embassies, all that sort of thing?"

"Last seen in Tangier," admitted Mr. Blakeley, descending into gloom.

"Tangier! My God!" A touch of salaciousness. "What sort of business was the feller in, then?"

"Not that sort of thing at all," replied Mr. Blakeley indignantly. "On the contrary, very respectable. Armaments brokerage, actually, one of the best respected in the country. Plunkett knew arms, Wingate knew trade. Very successful, very prosperous."

"Still," said the colleague, pursing his lips. "Not exactly like selling Cadbury's, is it, the arms business?"

"No," admitted Mr. Blakeley, resuming sadness. "Poor wife didn't know a thing. Horrified when she found out the family fortune comes from arms dealing, you know, usual sort of womanish attitude, all morals and nonsense, didn't know how hubby made his money until I told her. We shall just have to wait until Plunkett shows up."

"Pity your chappie didn't last just a bit longer. Could have made a packet by the sounds of it. We're just about rid of this League of Nations nonsense, I should say. There's going to be good money in arms. Give Winston a year or two and he'll talk the rest of these silly blighters into rearming. Your chappie was in on the ground floor."

There was a pause, while the colleague ordered up another round of drinks.

"Your chappie, this Mystery Millionaire chap," he resumed. "Bit mad altogether, shouldn't wonder? Giving it away like that!"

"The whole family's a bit mad," said Mr. Blakeley, as though glad to relieve his feelings. "At least I'm beginning to think so. Widow doesn't seem to give a hoot about being penniless. Won't touch money made that way. As though money cares how you made it. Says *I* should have told her years ago! Me! But she'll be up against it in a month or two. *We* can't carry her on overdraft."

"Without doubt."

"And she doesn't want any publicity about Plunkett at all. Say there's been more than enough already. Mind you, she has a point. Mystery Millionaire's Widow Left Penniless. Can't you see what Fleet Street would do with that one?"

"How much do you stand to lose?"

"Us?" Mr. Blakeley was surprised. "Not a penny, of course. No, I'm doing all this out of habit, I suppose, and kindness of heart. She's a nice woman, Mrs. Wingate. I'll be sorry to lose her as a customer."

"And if she doesn't bring the law against the Plunkett feller, he'll get away scot-free?"

"Assuming he hasn't already had his throat cut by some bloody murderous Arab bastard."

Through the weeks of financial negotiation that followed, Elizabeth was intrigued to find how important the men thought money, and how infantile they thought her for not showing equal interest.

"Mr. Blakeley wanted me to go hat in hand to Mrs. Mountjoy," she complained to Mabel, "and ask her to share. Can you imagine? I'm developing a distaste for Mr. Blakeley."

"You'd go if you were poor enough," said Mabel, knitting faster.

"What do I use on this?" asked Elizabeth. She was washing iron cooking pots at the kitchen sink.

"Did you burn it? Use the steel wool. Then you'll have to size it. I'll show you how."

"They can scarcely say I'll be poor."

"Any sensible person takes money when they can get it."

"Take it from whatever source? I don't think so, Mabel."

"It was your husband's money," said Mabel indignantly, rising to seize the pot from Elizabeth's soapy hands. "That's all you need to know. Your husband made it."

"And my husband gave it away." Elizabeth refused to surrender the pot. "I know how to size a pot, Mabel. There are some things I remember from early days."

Anthony too was impatient with her.

"I do wish you wouldn't fuss at me, Anthony," she said.

"I wouldn't fuss if you were sensible about your future."

"Mr. Blakeley tells me that I shall have what he calls a modest sum, which I shall have him invest as a nest egg for my old age. I shan't be a charge on you."

"And for your living expenses?"

"I have my job. My expenses will be small."

"Jennifer—"

"—insists that I take money from you, which I have told you over and over I won't do. I don't need it."

"But you shall, you know."

"I wish you would stop treating me as though I couldn't know my own mind. I shan't take any money from you, and there's an end to it. Now, I don't want another word about the matter."

Four months after Charles' death, she responded to a summons by Mr. Blakeley. The bank's interior was huge. Six floors of office corridors rose around a vast atrium under a reinforced glass roof, the whole held up by huge brown columns. Tellers' cages made of brass gave the feeling of a very rich zoo. The bank of lifts overlooked the atrium, so that one thought of the tellers as prisoners vulnerable to one's majestic rise above them. Elizabeth entered Mr. Blakeley's office feeling slightly dizzy. "The ascent of the Mountains of Finance," she murmured in greeting. "Very alarming!"

He wanted to talk to her about the necessary legal action against Joe Plunkett.

"But I fail to see," she interrupted, "what purpose legal action would serve against a man who has disappeared and who has no assets in England! Joe's dead, Mr. Blakeley, and the money's gone—back to the kind of people it came from, I expect. And if he's not, if he has absconded, then there's an end to it too. It must mean a great deal more to him than it does to me. I don't want the money. I do want to be free of the business. You were going to tell me if you could arrange that. Can you?"

Mr. Blakeley was reluctant to the point of being surly. "Yes," he said. "But it's against my advice, as you know."

"Poor Mr. Blakeley." Elizabeth smiled. "You don't want to see me begging in the streets."

"It won't be as bad as that," he said stiffly. "You'll have enough to live on one way or the other."

"A modest income."

"A barely adequate income."

"A Kensington sort of income, like a military pension, perhaps?" Her imitation of Lady Pearsall's tone was deliberate. "I shall of course be able to afford a Pekingese?"

"A little more than that." He could not believe that she understood her loss.

"No Pekingese in bad years, then," she sighed, and smiled again. He thought how charming she looked in black. She started to gather her gloves and handbag. "Well," she continued, "I had better think in terms of taking care of myself."

As she stood to go, he rose and became voluble, as though unwilling to let things end. "I do regret all this," he said. "You do realize that there was nothing the bank could do. I thought your husband rather prodigal, but we never realized he was giving that money away. I could have saved him so much on taxes."

"Almost as though he intended to leave me poor?" she said, looking at him intently.

"No, no! I don't mean that at all!"

"Don't think I haven't wondered myself, Mr. Blakeley." She started to pull on her gloves. "But I think, you know, that it would have broken Charles' heart to know that he left me poor and his daughter nothing to inherit."

She stood looking wistful, and Mr. Blakeley blushed with the need to express more understanding. "Such changes of life," he said. "It must be very unsettling for you."

She was surprised by him, as though there had been the hint of suggestiveness in his sympathy, the whisper of an offer. Such a fat, plain man, she thought. "I suppose it will be a change," she said briskly. "Being without wealth will cause some . . . unsettlement."

"Money is so agreeable a buffer," he said, shaking his head.

"It must be very pleasant to believe in money, Mr. Blakeley. What a pity we can't all measure each other just in terms of money."

"Your husband, I thought, understood the value of money very well. We have to, he and I, men like us."

"And you think I don't."

"Forgive me. Mrs. Wingate"—he shrugged—"but if you were poor like those poor devils on the street outside, you would think differently."

"I'm sure I would. But I'm not talking about 'enough money,' you know, all of us need enough. I'm talking about more than enough, about money as a measure rather than a means." She gave a small laugh. "Perhaps it was that thought that made Charles give money away. It could have been awful for him, you know, to realize at sixty that what he'd worked to get all his life meant nothing to him. He was a good and kind man, Mr. Blakeley. Perhaps I made a socialist of him after all. Could I have a glass of water, please?"

He poured her a glass of water from a carafe on his desk and begged her to sit down, but she stood there, sipping from the glass, meditative.

"I suppose it will be unsettling to be without wealth," she said, "but then, that's not necessarily a bad thing, is it?" She looked at him very directly. "Did you know, Mr. Blakeley, that money can give you a dangerous illusion of significance? With money it is harder to feel mediocre." She continued to stare at him, making him uneasy. "But that doesn't mean it's an unmixed blessing, does it? Its very comfort, when you have it long enough to take it for granted, it muffles your imagination, doesn't it, Mr. Blakeley?" He had not the slightest idea of what she was talking about. "Perhaps that's what my husband found out. I'm told he was very imaginative. He could take the risk of doing without money even at his age. So why shouldn't I?"

"But such a risk, Mrs. Wingate!" His plump hands fluttered from the wrist.

She looked as though she were patting his hand. "No period in my life has meant *that* much to me, Mr. Blakeley. I have never, ever felt: Here I am, I've arrived, here I'll stay." She began again smoothing her gloves over her fingers, pushing firmly at the leather, a way of bullying him and herself into shape. "I've always felt as though I were just journeying through, you know, waiting for the next event to arrive, the next stage, as though I were always somehow between here and there." She shrugged her shoulders. "Perhaps everyone feels like that. As though we were all drops of squeezed water sliding between two layers of glass. Do you ever feel like that, Mr. Blakeley?"

She saw him almost gaping with alarm. "Of course you don't, how foolish of me!" She smiled as she extended her gloved hand to his. "But you have been very kind to me, Mr. Blakeley. I do appreciate your kindness, one pilgrim to another. I thank you. No, really, I can find my own way out."

She smiled still as the creaking lift descended into the world of humans and as she crossed the open spaces of the atrium between the tellers' cages. Turning left in the street toward the Underground station, she found her way barred by a small flood coming from a broken fire hydrant, so she stepped across the gutter and into the street, moving with the traffic. She was halfway along the few yards of her course when there was a sudden cry and she felt her shoulders seized roughly from behind as someone almost lifted her from her feet as a bus roared past, just brushing her right sleeve. Her savior was a pale-faced man wearing a cap and gray scarf, and he escorted her politely along the remainder of her path, tipping his cap to say farewell.

"Wait," she said, fumbling for her purse. "I must thank you."

The purse contained only a pound note and a few pennies.

"This is all I have," she said, and proffered the pound note.

The man's eyes lit up, but he remained unsmiling and said only, "Thank you, lady. I shall use this to get home."

He snatched the note from her fingers, tipped his cap again, and vanished into the crowd, leaving Elizabeth to realize that her pennies would not pay the fare all the way back to Wimbledon.

Charles would have managed the pound note better, she thought. Then: Well, I shall just have to go as far as I can with what I've got.

The ticket seller behind his bars wondered why this elegant lady should be laughing to herself as she paid her fare.

39

April 1934

To avoid publicity surrounding the burial of the Mystery Millionaire, Peter had found, some twenty miles from London, a rural graveyard in the midst of an ugly village built in the late nineteenth century for Irish factory workers, where a red-brick St. Patrick's squatted perilously close to a new highway and a filling station.

Elizabeth always thought of Charles as an outrider here, as though he had been parked temporarily among strangers, because the church gave her no sense of eternity.

One Saturday morning as she knelt to her weeding, a country Irishwoman busy at a nearby grave addressed her—an Irishwoman with the bright red cheeks of children's books and stiff reddish hair fading to white and shoes run down at the heels over darned cotton stockings and a black cotton coat too thin for the spring winds.

"Nice here, isn't it?" she said comfortably. "I like to come and think of when me and Dad were together."

Her gentle manner assumed kinship from Elizabeth, as though they were sisters there beside the elms, the cypresses, and the petrol pumps. She gave comfort as easily as she apparently took it.

"Of course," she continued, "I like to come on Fridays best, when I can get away. You know Father Dick?"

Elizabeth shook her head.

"Nice old man for a priest," said the woman with a realistic shrug. "Understands us widows. You haven't tried him, then?" A girlishly bright smile of mischief crinkled her apple cheeks. "If I need a good sin to make him take me serious, I just make one up. But I think he knows, mind you. Sometimes he forgets the penance."

Creakily she pushed herself up from her knees and stood over her husband's grave, plump hands brushing dirt from each other.

"It's better than not having a man to talk things over with, I always say. You might try him sometime."

She nodded, and smiled softly, and murmured words of farewell, and left: a compact presence with soft edges, like a Christmas parcel.

Her gentle gift for some reason stayed with Elizabeth for days, until eventually on a Friday she slipped away early from work and drove herself to the village through heavy traffic. Father Dick behind the grille was a friendly presence waiting for her grief, but after moving through the ritual's starting phrases—question, response, the smaller sins—she found no words for whatever it was she wanted from him. She left the confessional with no more than absolution.

"No more than absolution." She smiled sourly to herself. "And what more is there, then?" She sat in a pew near the rear of the church. "Understands us widows," the stranger had said. "Us widows." Understood what? That we loved our husbands? But what if we did not?

The crucifix was of brass, and its Christ had muscles, which made him seem curiously untortured by his sacrifice, as though it were no more than a decathlon. "You're dead," she told him unspeakingly. And you too, she thought, looking at St. Patrick beautiful in the glass window. Dead and useless when I'm tired. Now she rocked slightly backward and forward. A *little* grief, she thought. The widow's mite? What should I do . . . do . . . do . . . ? Light a bloody candle? Pour holy water over myself? The image flashed into her mind of that other, hideous water with which the barbaric coast had baptized her, and she smelled the stink of goat hair in her nostrils, and she felt again the life and pain flow back into her body. But she snatched herself back from the edge of mourning. "Well, whoever promised us anything else?" She straightened her back, then let it sag again with a sigh. "But I'm so tired all the time, so tired. I have forgotten," she said softly to herself, "the reason for being."

The thought lifted her to her feet, and she walked away from the pew and to the wooden door of the church, which was so quiet it seemed to be holding back, Father Dick a presence waiting still in the confessional, quiet as the church, both of them waiting for her realization. She laughed to herself and shook her head. "How can one *forget* something like that?" The door opened onto light and the graveyard. She walked through it, turned as it began to swing closed, and addressed the crucifix that gleamed still through the narrowing gap. "Don't worry," she told Jesus. "I shan't take one ready-made, not even from you." The door clicked shut, and she walked away down the gravel path to where Charles' grave waited. Elms, chestnuts, evening, birdsong, the smell of spring's earth. Her eyes blurred with tears as she stumbled across the grass verge.

The graves had not been mown, with the result that shy bright wildflowers sprouted above Charles today. She pushed aside the vision of their roots stretching for his juices of decay. Why did you go ahead, she thought, if it was only to wait? Why leave me here? Something I have to do, to know, before I'm *good* enough for you? Rocks squawked their way into ragged cypresses. Outrider, she said. It's you who are alone, not me. *I* put you here. I put *you* here because you were . . . finished. You're *finished,* don't you see? It might have made some sense when you were alive to know whether I still loved you, but not now. None at all, not now. She looked quickly around her at the tombstones waiting in the evening sun and long shadows. All of you, she thought, with nothing to do but wait. Nothing. Nothing to connect you anymore, none of you under the ground there waiting.

She stepped back involuntarily from Charles' grave, possessed by a vivid momentary sense of some great force stirring under her feet. She moved away from the grave. I don't have the time for superstition, she thought, looking at the squat red-brick church. And suddenly she cried out to the men inside the church: "Of course I loved him, you fools! Is that what you wanted to know? Is that *all* you wanted?"

With shock she realized that she had spoken aloud, in this mounded and monumented peace. She took her handkerchief and blew her nose and wiped her eyes and put on her glasses as she moved back to the car. Leaning to open its door, she gave St. Patrick's one last glance and chose to speak to it aloud: "You may think I lack grace," she said. "But I'll tell you I have courage. By God, any of us alive, we have courage."

40

1934 and 1935

Mabel Greggs had taken to watching Elizabeth Wingate closely. If she had some satisfaction in her mistress's fall, it was only that which comes from seeing again that life is real, life is earnest. Mabel wasn't a selfish person and was willing to lend a helping hand. She taught Elizabeth how to cook simple, economical meals for one and urged her to make her own sandwiches for lunch. She traveled to Wimbledon once a week to "help" clean house. Elizabeth certainly seemed cheery enough, treating the whole experience with amusement, but Mabel suspected her of putting up a front and worried about whether she should offer to lend her money, especially when the guttering collapsed and had to be replaced. She noticed that trinkets were vanishing slowly from the house and Elizabeth's jewel case, and cleverly suggested that neither the set of wedding china nor the silver that had graced the table in the St. James's flat fitted comfortably in the new house and might fetch a pretty penny—which they did. By the time Elizabeth's little Austin needed a new clutch, Mabel felt free enough not only to find a cheap mechanic but also to suggest that Mr. Williams could dispose of Mr. Wingate's books for a good price, and when Lady Pearsall expressed a wish to buy some of the jewelry that Elizabeth no longer needed, it was Mabel who negotiated the price.

Elizabeth accepted the schooling but ignored Mabel's hints that the smart thing would be to marry Mr. Williams, choosing instead the obvious alternative of raising her own income, which in late 1934 Mr. Harris permitted, if with much sucking of air between his yellow teeth. Elizabeth felt now that she swam with rather than through the people who surrounded her in the Underground, at the cinema, at the butcher's looking for the economical cuts of meat, and she was as anonymous as they. She lunched with pleasant people at the firm's expense, she had drinks at pleasant places like the Coach and Horses and developed a nodding acquaintance with a couple of the painted ladies who stood in Dean Street doorways. Her life was casual, her emotions limited. She saw more of Jennifer because Merry came to visit on Sundays, but less of Ginny because she gave up all grand occasions.

Mabel convinced her to resume going to church, for the good of Merry, but she would not go again to confession.

"Heaven and hell would be rather nice to believe in," she said mildly. "I think perhaps Mr. Rich converted me to Buddhism."

"Mr. Rich?"

"Someone you never met, Mabel." And she was possessed suddenly of one of those vivid recollections where the light, the smell, the very texture of the past vividly return. She smiled back at the little Buddha Peter had given her, which sat now on her bedside table where her father's photograph had been during her mother's widowhood.

"Well, you're not a very good Catholic," Mabel chided. "And why not? If the Church is right, then you've got everything to win. If it's wrong, then you haven't lost but the skin on your knees, have you?"

"Now, if Gandhi were a Roman Catholic!" Elizabeth laughed.

Later that same week Anthony and Jennifer sat in the small garden behind their house, still dressed in tennis clothes, drinking gin and lemon.

"Shouldn't we be seeing more of your mother?" inquired Anthony.

"It's so enormously complicated–her schedule, ours." Jennifer was abstract, caring more about throwing bread crumbs to the cheeping city sparrows at the edge of the birdbath. "We'll see her tomorrow when she comes for Merry."

"But . . . Well . . . It occurs to me she may be rather lonely."

"Lonely? Mother?" She looked at him, surprised, thinking about what he had said, and dismissing it. "I shouldn't think so. She's so independent. Anyway, she knows she doesn't need an invitation. Besides, she has Peter, darling."

"Any sign of their getting married? It's been almost a year."

"She hasn't said anything. Perhaps they don't intend to." She smiled. "They think they're so modern, and they're such old-fashioned radicals, aren't they?" She finished with a shrug. "Mabel! Turn down the wireless a little, would you, darling?" The strains of the BBC studio orchestra playing "I Only Have Eyes for You" died in the kitchen window, and Jennifer leaned forward to pluck dead chrysanthemums.

"Though you'd think they'd at least live together," resumed Anthony.

"Women's sex drive doesn't last through the change, does it? Anyway, I can't imagine Mother and Peter puffing away in the toils of passion at their age."

"I can."

"That's your dirty mind."

"Your mother's a very sexy woman!"

"Oh, Tony darling, don't be such an ass! How embarrassing to fall in love with your mother-in-law! She used to be beautiful, but she's been overweight for years. I'm sure Daddy didn't like it."

"There are those of us who prefer flesh on the bones we fondle, you know."

"And no more smart remarks about my being too thin, thank you. Blame the camera, not me." She looked genuinely irritated. "You should see Celia Johnson or Ann Todd."

"But I'm not married to them."

Jennifer picked up a piece of bread and threw it at a sparrow. "And being married gives you the right to determine what shape and size I'll be?" She was gloomy suddenly.

"Some say in the matter." He leaned forward to pat her on the shoulder, but she shook his hand away. Now he was irritated. "Though I suppose my opinion doesn't count for as much as that of Alexander Korda or Laurence Olivier or Robert Brandon."

She flew to him in a daze of giggles and kissed him and ruffled his hair, ending up sitting on his lap. "I love you to be jealous," she said. "You're so adorable!"

"Adorable, yes," he said, mollified. "But do I have grounds?"

"Oh, darling, don't be silly."

"I don't think I'm being silly. It's all right to be modern, but you see a great deal of other men, you know, even if it is on business."

She stood up from his lap, and though she distracted herself by kneeling to rearrange the stones at the edge of the little path, she cast one frown in his direction. "You shouldn't interfere with what I do about my career, pet."

"Now, don't get all in a huff!" he protested. "Your career isn't serious enough to make us fight." She said nothing, and refused to look at him. "At least it wasn't when I married you." Having met Jennifer when she was to him a child, Anthony had made the mistake of thinking her enthusiasms childish. This sunny afternoon after tennis had brought the inevitable battle closer.

For some moments there was tension between them; then Jennifer rose and dusted her hands against her skirt and came back to his lap, her hands linked around his neck. "Shall I ring up Mummy and ask her over for dinner tonight? Mabel! What are we having for dinner?"

Mabel's head appeared in the window of the kitchen. "My good barley bread," she said. "And whatever you choose to cook."

"Oh, bother," said Jennifer. "I wish I'd never been to Ravenscroft! Then we'd *have* to hire a cook."

Early in 1935 Elizabeth broached the matter of a second raise to Mr. Harris.

"What!" he exclaimed. "With unemployment worse than it's ever been! After you 'ad one last year? Ooo, no, Mrs. W. The firm can't see its way clear to that." He followed rejection with a lecture on the need for all of us to economize. "Look at Mrs. Moore," he said. "Now, you don't see her asking for more money, do you? And she can do most of your job right up, eh?" Mrs. Moore, whom Elizabeth had saved from being fired, had sealed an alliance with Harris soon after her move to headquarters as Elizabeth's deputy. "I'll tell you what, come 'n 'ave lunch on me and we'll forget you ever said anything nasty." Mr. Harris grinned. "God knows we gents are always ready to 'elp out a needy widow, eh?"

She pondered her choices for some weeks, unsure of what to do, feeling for the first time trapped. She studied the faces of the tired women hanging to the straps in the Underground carriages.

"Give it up altogether," said Ginny Pearsall without hesitation. "Come in with me, as I've said a hundred times! The income's a little less predictable, of course, but at least you'll get some good dinners."

Peter was gloomier. "If we got married," he said, "I suppose we could start a tobacconist's or something. . . . Nobody's buying old books these days."

"That whole situation," exploded Jennifer, "is simply intolerable! How can you put up with that vile Harris, Mother? You must just resign. God knows I can give you enough out of my spending money, and you can have everything from my next film, and Anthony won't have to know a thing about it. I shall simply tell him that I'm taking more taxis."

But Mabel gave her the advice she had to hear. "Sounds like it's either Mrs. Moore or you, doesn't it?" she said. "You'd better get rid of her or you'll be out on your ear. You can't afford to monkey around if she's got him by the you-know-whats, can you?"

Chance saved her; May brought the annual visit of the young American, Mr. Donald Wallace, to represent the interests of Mr. Harris' partners, and he brought surprise. Elizabeth had never quite taken Wallace seriously. He was so bland and clean, as though he were coated with a fine film of soap that made him impossible to grab. But she liked him, and he found her attractive, and this year he was more attentive—and somehow watchful—than usual, so that he brought fresh spirit to Greek Street.

At the first meeting of the senior staff, the reason for his mood became clear. "There's a guy called Gallup, George Gallup, at Princeton, which is sort of like your Cambridge I guess, and he's come up with a great idea that we plan to steal if we can."

"And what is this 'ot new idea, then?" inquired Mr. Harris genially, with a wink at Mrs. Moore. The younger man's enthusiasm made him condescending.

Wallace proceeded to sum up quickly the theory behind public-opinion polls and Gallup's methodology. Using a combination of the marketing techniques in which Harris' firm specialized, modern statistical theory, and the sense of the public mind he had developed as a journalist, Gallup planned to poll samples of the public and sell the results, especially to politicians.

"America *loves* to listen to its own heartbeat," Wallace said with the poetry of captivation. "Gallup's onto a winner."

"That's all well and good for America," said Mr. Harris jovially, "but this is England, you know. We already know what everyone else thinks, haha!"

Wallace looked at him sharply. "That's clearly not true, Harris." Wallace was abrupt. "Or why would we be in the business we're in now?"

There followed a long and sometimes heated discussion. "But we don't like to be pried at and spied upon, we British," said Mr. Harris at one point. Mrs. Moore denied all understanding of the issue. Mr. Thomas Hendricks calculated over the lighting of another cigarette, and plumped for Harris. Mrs. Wingate said what she thought: the idea was good, but she doubted that there would be much money in it.

When they adjourned for lunch, Elizabeth was surprised to find Wallace waiting for her on the narrow pavement to ask the pleasure of taking her to a restaurant. She chose a new little place called Peter Mario's on Frith Street, and over excellent *involtini* managed to be truthful without malice about Mr. Harris.

"He's not going to buy it," said Wallace. "I can tell."

"Perhaps he thinks you're a little young," said Elizabeth. "But forgive me, does he have to, as you say 'buy it'? Can you not simply go ahead?"

"Not if he doesn't want it. He has the senior partnership here." Mr. Wallace leaned back in his chair and wiped his lips with a checkered napkin. "I have a proposition, Mrs. Wingate," he said solemnly. "I anticipated we would run into a little trouble with Mr. Harris. My partners and I think the time may have come to dissolve our little partnership with him. These days you have to run to stay in the same place, and it may be he's too stick-in-the-mud."

"But wouldn't that be very costly?"

He waved away the objection. "There's always capital for the right idea, even in the middle of a business slump. God, that's when you can really score! Let me tell you what I have in mind."

What he had in mind was to establish a new company, tentatively called the Opinion Research Corporation, headed by Mr. Wallace himself. He would hire away young Mr. Thomas Hendricks to handle the statistics. And Mrs. Wingate would be his own deputy, with the eventual prospect of taking charge.

"Now, we can't put you in the top spot, obviously," he explained, "because you're a woman, but you'll get a big salary increase. You're perfect for the job, you know, with your experience in the business and your political connections. You'll get an office of your own, and not in a dump like this."

Elizabeth looked across the coffeecups and the red tablecloth at this young man. The fingers of her right hand thrummed briefly on the table. She enjoyed the sensation of power; but she knew she must not choose wrongly. "Yes," she said suddenly. "Yes. I think that would be quite suitable."

Wallace had expected much more indecision. He beamed and pushed his hand at her to be shaken. "A deal!" he said.

She raised her hand to ward off his. "But," she said, "I have a suggestion that might be attractive. Something simpler." She looked coolly at him. "Let us suppose that you have not really discussed all this with your partners and your wife. Have you?"

He looked embarrassed. "Well, no, but they–"

"Then the new company, it is for the moment only a possible eventuality?"

"You might put it that way."

"And possible eventualities can be used as threats, can't they, to make people see where their best interests lie? And if Mr. Harris could be converted, that would cause everyone much less bother?"

"Sure, I see what you mean, but Harris has gotten so goddamn obstructive the last few months, I'm not sure we want to keep dealing with him."

"Mr. Harris," she interrupted, "doesn't much understand the difference between England and America. You have to understand, Mr. Wallace, that the English are all imperialists at heart. It is hard for them to see that all the energy these days is coming from America. They've never realized that you won the war, you see. However, one should be able to make clear to Mr. Harris that he is not quite as much on top of things as he likes to think?"

"I could push him around a little, sure," said Wallace cheerily.

"Not pushing so much as puncturing, don't you think? I myself would be willing to try to make the situation clear to Mr. Harris first."

"If you think you can do it," he said doubtfully.

"I can only try," she said. "I have a card or two to play. And then, of course, you can come up trumps if need be."

"Pull it off and I'll see that your salary is twice whatever it is now."

"Then let's go back and see what we can do."

Elizabeth captured Mr. Harris in his office. Her card or two consisted of the impression that Mr. Harris liked the idea much more than he had admitted and had in mind stealing it to use with his own and Elizabeth's special political knowledge. Delicately she explained to him her understanding of her own significance to both sides, should it come to a dispute. Her own preference, she said, was to keep both her present loyalty and the American capital, but if ill will should unfortunately arise, she would feel her loyalties strained. She hoped he would understand.

"Got something up your sleeve, 'aven't you?" Mr. Harris was angry. He could not look at her, but neither could he afford to lose her favor, so he held himself in check by focusing on his paper knife.

"Up my sleeve?" Elizabeth assumed the indignation of innocence, but not so far that it would seem the truth. "But that would be a kind of blackmail, Mr. Harris. I'm sure you don't mean that. I am merely speaking as a senior member of the staff about what would make me feel comfortable!"

"I have me own political contacts," he said with defiance. "And I could use them, too." Both of them knew that hers were the better. "But I 'aven't got your class, then, have I?" His sneer was almost savage.

For a moment he vibrated with frustration. Then he tossed his knife onto the desktop and forced himself into amiability.

"But what am I getting all in a stew about, eh? Of course it's a clever idea. If that Wallace 'adn't come bursting in 'ere showing off, pushing me around, if 'e'd given me time to get used to the idea, like, well, nobody wants a fight on their 'ands, do they?" His face was red but genial, his hands open to indicate good nature. "Looks like you're a proper little peacemaker, Mrs. W! Perhaps I'll 'ave another little think. I'll 'ave a talk to 'Is Nibs and see what 'e really 'as in mind." He grumbled himself into a frown, then wiped his face with good humor again. "Well, thanks for the tipoff, Mrs. W. If things work out right, I'll see you're taken care of, eh?"

From then on Mr. Harris kept his hostility under veils and curb. Mrs. Wingate made him very nervous.

After this confrontation, Elizabeth began to use rather than serve her time at Harris and Company Pty. Ltd. The accountant who came twice a week found her suddenly attentive to understanding the books, and Mr. Thomas Hendricks, long conditioned to her indifference, found himself charmed into imparting lessons in statistics. Mrs. Moore felt hemmed in. Given clear limits to her responsibilities, she had full authority within those limits and so grew careful to anticipate Mrs. Wingate's preferences. She knew what had been done to her and admitted to her friends that it was a neat trick.

Over drinks Elizabeth showed her political friends the sample forms from America and sought their advice about redesigning them for British circumstances. Should they be interested, she inquired, precisely what would they want to know about the voters? We might just be interested, they said, and by the time Prime Minister Baldwin called that autumn for a snap election, all three major parties were armed with preliminary results on the voters' views about housing, old-age pensions, and the raising of the school-leaving age to fifteen. Success bred more respect, and respect companionship. "Married men!" sighed Elizabeth, shaking her head as she refused a weekend *à deux* with a member of Parliament.

"Well, of course, darling," said Ginny Pearsall over afternoon tea in the Oxford Street Kardomah. "Don't you see? You've become a trophy again in your old age. Look at yourself!"

Elizabeth stared at her image in the mirror. She did look chic.

"There's something vital about you," said Ginny. "You no longer need them, of course! So they are interested."

Pleased, Elizabeth laughed. This shantung suit is flattering, she thought. Later she listened to her heels click as she walked with her fatter pay envelope to the bank. That envelope solves more than just the practical difficulties, she thought. Is that what Charles knew? She tapped the envelope against her gloved thumb as she waited in the queue and studied the weary lady behind the bars of the teller's cage. And you too can be free, she thought.

41

June 1936

On a chill, sunny spring Sunday, the daffodils leaping in the wind, Elizabeth started to spade the flowerbeds next to the low wall by the street, enjoying the smell of earth and cow manure. She was just working up a mild sweat when Ginny Pearsall arrived in her modest and cautious Morris.

"My dear Elizabeth!" she exclaimed from the car window. "A wool shirt! boots! trousers! Do you want the neighbors to stone you?"

"They're Charles'," laughed Elizabeth, brushing the strands of hair blown across her face. "Come in—you give me a wonderful excuse for a tea break."

"It's so dreadful," said Ginny, once they were in the kitchen. "All my friends are becoming drab! They look like cossacks or muzhiks or whoever it is that frightful Stalin is supposed to be slaughtering."

She drew back to view Elizabeth as though by lorgnette. "Though the woman looks disgustingly healthy, one must admit." Ginny herself was as bright as a tropical bird, and as neat, sheathed in a long red coat with brass buttons and jutting shoulders, with gauntlet gloves and a crazy, tip-tilting yellow hat. She was exuberant. She had decided to give a grand party.

"It will be my last, my last after so many!" she exclaimed with joy. "I'm not sure whether it is to celebrate the ending of things . . ." She bowed her head to a photograph of King George the Fifth ringed in black crepe which stood on the shelf above the stove where Mabel had placed it on January 20, when the King had died. ". . . or the beginning of things." She nodded grimly to a brand-new little poster pinned to the wall, an illustration of a child wearing a gas mask, which gave instructions as to air-raid precautions. "In any case, things are stirring in the world again, and so am I. If we are all to be gassed in our beds, we can at least be found smiling, and at *very* least I hope my friends will be pleased to find me safely turning seventy."

"Seventy?" said Elizabeth, filling the tea kettle at the sink.

"My real friends of course"–Ginny glared–"will not be surprised at anything I tell them."

"What's a year or two between friends?" Elizabeth smiled, scratching a match against the wall to light the gas stove. "Where will you have the party, and when?"

"I thought: a theater party, so that we will not all bore each other to death. I thought: after all the Jubilee nonsense last season, and after this dreadful winter, and what with the Germans invading the Rhineland and the Italians invading Abyssinia and that dreadful Roosevelt likely to be elected again, we could all do with lots and lots of *escape* . . ."

Elizabeth was getting cups and saucers from the cupboard and placing them on a silver tray. "The Holborn Empire, then, and Max Miller?"

". . . into the country. And who better, I thought, for *escape,* than Mozart, so I rang up that agreeable greengrocer man, that Captain John Christie."

"Glyndebourne!" Elizabeth exclaimed with pleasure. "What a superb idea! But won't it cost the earth?"

"I can have twenty or more seats any Tuesday night in June at a reduced rate, he said, so I said, 'Snap!' I shall have Fortnum's do up hampers, and if it rains we can use the dining hall, and I have two cases of thirty-two champagne put down—German, but who's to complain these days?—they can sleep it off during the opera if they want, but at Glyndebourne one eats, don't you know, in little snatches—something before the show, gobs during the entr'acte, and an enormous birthday cake before they toddle off into their cars and buses to go home. I've talked already with Christie's butler, Childs, and he assures me that as long as I don't mind the orchestra and singers popping in for a share of the cake and ale, it should all go off rather well."

Elizabeth had opened a tin of shortbread and was arranging the pieces on a flowered plate.

"I know you can't get off on Tuesdays," Ginny continued brightly, "but if you can't make an excuse for yourself when you're in charge of the whole office, then you shall just either have to give up that silly job or lie. If you must, you can get the three-ten from Victoria, but if you take the whole day off, which you should, then you can join me and drive down in a Daimler."

"It does sound like the old days," said Elizabeth wistfully, lifting the kettle as it began to scream. "Even if the chauffeur is rented."

Elizabeth took off the whole day and spent the morning in the kind of grooming for which she had lost the habit, with the result that she could climb into the sweet-smelling Daimler feeling relaxed and looking as though this really were one of those distant days in hot Ceylon, all chiffon and lace and amusement. The day was perfect summer: blue, leafy, warm, a show-off breeze. They were driving early to Sussex so that Ginny might place her thirty guests where she chose among the grounds of Glyndebourne.

Set fantastically in the open countryside of the South Downs, its environs tamed since the sixteenth century, Glyndebourne manor had the air precisely of a village in the films, much too neat and clean to be real. The very idea of a private opera house was so nineteenth-century that the management provided no garbage cans; it was conceivable that any of the three hundred or so paying guests could litter. Captain John Christie, M.C., was the nephew of an earl and very rich from the proceeds of providing pipe organs for those huge movie palaces sprouting in every suburb. At least, thought Elizabeth, he doesn't give it away.

Lady Pearsall gave judicious orders to the help ("*Quite* like the old days, after all!"). She deployed rugs, hampers, and place cards to occupy lines which stretched from the fir trees through the elms to the weeping willows near the stream wherein the wine was trailed on string for cooling. She laid siege to as many wooden benches as possible ("Some of the guests, my dear–if we put them on the ground, we'd have to put them in it next"). In garden beds burgeoned snapdragons and huge hollyhocks and sweet william. Pinned to brick walls, rosebushes were like rows of bright and idle women made drunk by the sun, and the lawns were so chastened by mower and roller that they became artifact. For the hostess Elizabeth chose a bower surrounded on three sides by shoulder-high hedge, smelling of grass and lavender and honeysuckle and sheltered by an oak.

When the guests began to gather, one could not tell whether the perfumes belonged to the women or nature. One dressed artfully for Glyndebourne: black or white tie for the gentlemen, and for the ladies an evening gown not quite long enough to get filthy on the grass, slippers that grew damp when the dew arrived, a shawl or fur-trimmed cloak against the chill, and jewels to catch the sun. Against the lawns, the guests looked like actors using the three-story brick manor house as a backdrop.

Lady Pearsall offered sherry. "If you must have whiskey," she told the gentlemen, "then please, do, order it from the bar! This, my dear, is an occasion rather like me, from the time before cocktails were invented. See what I have for you!"

And she gestured them to open hampers, to unclip and flourish linen dinner napkins, silverware, crystal glasses, to shift the top layer of china and reveal the pink of Parma ham sliced to transparency, the glow of chilled artichokes shimmering with oil, the green and black glisten of fat olives. "Tuck into the antipasto, darlings," she said. "It will fortify you for *Così Fan Tutte.*" She was attuned tonight, quick as silver. Creator of this evening, she gave her guests stature, grace, moment. They had a sense that their timing was superb.

The guests came from several generations, but Ginny brusquely divided them into the Ruins and the Shards. "If the Ruins can prop themselves up, they may stay where they are," she proclaimed. "But the Shards are young enough to circulate, and circulate they shall!" The Ruins included her sole remaining close relative, her cousin the dowager duchess, whose wheelchair an ancient retainer maneuvered over the lawn. She was in her nineties.

"But not at all senile, thank God," she announced vigorously. "The legs go first, of course, and I do take the odd little catnap now and again, but if I should, just go on with whatever you were doing. I shall be back in a moment or so." Her voice was light, clear, with the accent of another age, and her gnarled fingers held the champagne glass with negligence.

"Specially invited," whispered Ginny to Elizabeth, "to remind people that I may just be around long enough for them to *have* to return the hospitality."

Among the Shards, unexpectedly, were the former Jill Knight and her husband, her two children left with their grandmother, her dress held over from her debutante season. She and Jennifer fell back into the rapport of schoolmates and told each other news of Maureen O'Flynn's recent marriage to a wealthy landowner.

"And Fern? Have you heard from Fern?" asked Jennifer with excitement.

"Nobody has heard from Fern," said Jill, looking odd. "They say she went to Switzerland to have her baby. They say her husband . . . Oh, well, we mustn't gossip. And I must help with those hampers!"

"And you, my dear," said Ginny, appearing at Jennifer's elbow, "must circulate. You are one of the *interesting* people, you see, and so you must sing for your supper by keeping your mother and some of these other wrinklies amused. But where is your husband?"

"He'll be late," replied Jennifer ungraciously. "I drove myself down."

"Oh?" said Lady Pearsall. "Such a solemn man, your husband." She grinned wickedly. "May I find you someone else?"

For a moment Jennifer did not reply. Her gaze moved over the scene, the men in black, the women soft and colorful. As though we were waiting for them to set up the next shot, she thought. There was the orchestra near the house, one man tuning a violin, the rest playing croquet. She had already mistaken their conductor Fritz Ebert for a waiter. And the program gave a credit to the head gardener, F. Harvey, and here was the producer, Rudolf Bing, as handsome and charming and at ease as any guest. Where, not when, did the play leave off? Jennifer turned to Ginny, her green eyes gleaming, the corners of her mouth turning into a smile that was half sulk.

"Perhaps," she said. "It would be a change, wouldn't it?"

"Ah!" replied Ginny, smiling, but with a shrewd look. "You have so much more spirit than your mother. From your father, perhaps?"

Jennifer felt irritable and scratchy, perhaps because her period was imminent, more likely out of frustration with Anthony. She had telephoned the bank to discover why he was late coming home to change.

"I have a meeting," he said. "I can't get away."

"You have to get away. I don't intend to be late."

"Look, Jennifer, I can't traipse around the countryside being your . . . . your accompanist when I have work to do."

"I know you don't get on with Lady Pearsall," she hissed, "but this *is* her birthday, and she *has* invited Gladys Cooper specially for me to meet. We *have* to go. Ginny's paid for our seats."

"Drive yourself down. You love your car. I can do without the Mozart: I know enough about the way women are." His voice was cold. The surliness was perhaps only carelessness, but Jennifer took it personally.

"Damn you, Tony!" she said sharply.

This in turn raised his anger. There was a pause.

"I'll get down there as soon as I can." Another pause, then the voice insinuated itself along the wire. "Save some strawberries and cream for your husband. If you can. . . ."

He had rung off before she could swear a reply, leaving her in a rage aimed equally at his sarcasm and her inability to influence his schedule. She hated that dry tone of his, light and bitter as soured wine: save some strawberries and cream for your husband, if you can! And if you asked him what he meant, he'd deny any double entendre. She felt compacted, as though her body wore a padded cover. The Molyneux copy in pale cream satin which she wore was too tight around her hips, but she wore no bra, and the dress's discreet folds cupped her breasts lightly as a hand, giving them a constant caress. Her eyes blazed with daylight green. She savaged artichoke leaves with small white teeth, so that an old gentleman standing across from her shook his head and sucked in his breath for recollection. He could almost taste the girl.

Elizabeth had chanced to see Jennifer arrive in her new Morgan, canvas top down, the thin wheels spraying the gravel of the driveway, and the sight had irritated her. The little car had enormous significance for Jennifer as the first large purchase made entirely from her own earnings, and Elizabeth understood the girl's pride, but not her ostentation. Whizzing around the countryside, hair blowing over her face, on her own–it might be very modern, but that didn't make it right. Seeing Jennifer's present expression, she chose to turn away. Another fight with Anthony, by the look of it, and she did not want to hear about it. She wore the diamonds Charles had given her for Jennifer's birth. Now she fingered them and thought how different were expectations from reality.

"Quite frankly, my dear, I'm rather tired of your complaints," she had said to Jennifer after the last bout. "Sooner or later you will have to accept Anthony as he is, not blame him for being what he isn't. That's what they mean when they say the honeymoon is over, really. You can't expect to change an older man."

Now, however, watching her daughter pluck an olive from the dish, she wondered if her lack of sympathy were quite fair. She expected too much, perhaps, from one so young. Her daughter was a splendid creature, beyond doubt. Her manners were delicate, impeccable. Her grooming was unostentatious, her voice calm and low, her attentiveness to her elders remarkable. Elizabeth still remembered a conversation with Mabel from years ago. Well, Mabel, she thought, the rules have done their work. No matter what else she is, we have made a lady of her. With mild surprise, Elizabeth realized that her daughter really could not be *instructed* anymore.

But she did not like selfishness. It was all very exciting, no doubt, to have everyone say she was a great beauty, but it didn't fit with real life. Could a wife and mother be like this, rustling with sensuality? At that moment Jennifer looked up and caught her mother's gaze. Her face was expressionless, but Elizabeth blushed and looked away as though caught staring by a stranger. How they can twist one's heart with love! she thought.

Sensing disapproval in her mother's gaze, Jennifer fell further into irritation. She gazed sullenly at her companions: the ancient dowager duchess, Lady Pearsall, a gloomy old military type who kept peeking at her breasts, her own aging mother, a middle-aged female mathematician with dyed black hair. She listened to their ridiculous conversation: gossip and stupid dirty jokes about the King and Mrs. Simpson. And suddenly she was angry with them: for being, for ruling her.

"But he really *is* a Prince Charming!" she suddenly blurted across the complacency of their humor. "And can't you see how sad his face is?" They turned to look at her, patient. "If romance will make him happier, then why should he not have it?"

"But Jennifer," responded Elizabeth quickly, unhappily, "romance is such a dangerous thing."

And the wrinkled dowager duchess leaned forward in her wheelchair to pat her hand and say, "It won't last a lifetime, you know, my dear."

She sought to hurt them: "You've all forgotten what it is to be young."

They looked away from her, but the dowager duchess would not capitulate. "There is nothing *but* romance these days," she said vehemently. "Everyone is so very impatient. People think magic will save them." She waved both hands in the air. "All those silly Nazi banners! Have you seen what they plan for the Olympics? Ridiculous! In Russia one worships Lenin's tomb, in America cinema stars. Everyone wants to leave what God gave them and have something better. The monarchy used to be a bastion. Nowadays . . ." The old face grew suddenly mournful.

"Ah, Rose," said the old military type, addressing her with sudden care and admiration, "if there were a revolution in this country, and you weren't sent before the firing squad as a decadent aristocrat, you'd die of a broken heart."

The dowager duchess did not reply: "To each her own romance." She was falling softly asleep, the wineglass depending slowly from her hand.

At that moment the sudden sound of trumpets came, the fanfare from *Fidelio* on loudspeakers.

"Good God, what's that?" exclaimed the dowager duchess, jerking awake.

"Curtain-up," announced Lady Pearsall. "We still have ten minutes. Shall we go? You may leave everything exactly as it is."

A handful of Ginny's guests were still missing when the audience moved into the theater for the first act, but to Jennifer's surprise Anthony awaited her in the auditorium, a plain rectangular room filled with seats covered in brown velour.

"They have dressing rooms here," he said. "So I changed and had a nip in the bar."

He took her by the elbow, kissed her brow, stood back to stare at her. "And how are you enjoying yourself, dear? Met anyone interesting yet?" His grin was disturbing, vaguely wolfish. She moved away from him, and this made his expression turn bland and gentlemanly as he greeted his hostess and they took their seats.

The first half of *Così Fan Tutte* contained exactly the kind of events that would keep Elizabeth's thoughts on her daughter. Jennifer and Anthony sat stiffly together to her right in front. Something was very wrong; this was more than a squabble. God knows what made her think that; this stupid opera, probably. Women are like that, says Mozart, she thought impatiently. Like what? Faithless? Vain? Foolish? But there can't be any truth in Anthony's jealousy about Jennifer's freedom.

"It's not the acting that bothers me," he had confessed to her some weeks ago. "It's the way of life, the people. What are they, after all, but a bunch of children dressing up in grown-ups' clothing?"

"Jennifer is still very young," Elizabeth had said, not without sympathy. "Are you sure you don't expect too much of her?"

"I'm not sure that I don't expect too little," he said gloomily. "I should have put a stop to this career stuff when we married. Now it seems more important to her than I or Merry. I hoped she wouldn't succeed. I didn't think she would, but I suppose I underestimate the effect of her looks. Ever since *Sweets to the Sweet* ran for six months, she has seen herself as a serious actress."

"It must be very difficult for her, Anthony. You and I have never had to deal with that beauty and that glamour."

"But she must see it can't last."

"Perhaps that's why she tries so hard."

"If you could use your influence, I'd be grateful."

"I'll talk to her, but as you know, my influence over Jennifer these days is limited."

She had needed courage to confront her daughter, which was absurd.

"I know he doesn't like my being an actress," Jennifer retorted. "But he knew I was an actress when he married me."

Jennifer's petulance had always annoyed Elizabeth.

"It's one thing when you're eighteen," she said. "Another when you're a wife and mother." Almost, she reminded Jennifer of her advice not to marry too soon.

"You don't under*stand,* Mother," snapped Jennifer. "It has nothing to do with my being an actress. You think Tony is adorable, but he isn't. You don't have to live with him."

"He makes you a good husband," said Elizabeth indignantly. "He's generous, indulgent even!"

Jennifer exploded at her: "He's indifferent and obtuse!" How did she tell her mother of Anthony's complacency: that he was a juggernaut? Night after night, no matter how she felt, no matter whether they'd had a fight or not, going to the bathroom to fiddle with all that horrible paraphernalia so that he could make love to her. "He doesn't care whether I'm me or not, just so long as I'm there."

Elizabeth was silent, her own fire paled by Jennifer's greater blaze.

Jennifer searched for some way of communication. "If I say something, he doesn't hear, he doesn't even listen. Last week, last Saturday, he asked if I'd like to go to the pictures, and I said I'd love to see Bette Davis in *Of Human Bondage,* which I'd really been looking forward to, and he came home with tickets for *The Thin Man* because he'd forgotten what picture I wanted to see. Forgotten! He might as well have bought tickets to Shirley Temple!"

Elizabeth could not help laughing. Jennifer looked at her under her eyelashes, then grinned sheepishly. "It does sound stupid, doesn't it? But little things come to mean so much, and he doesn't, he really doesn't take me seriously."

"You do seem to be making a lot of very little, darling."

Jennifer looked levelly at her mother. "I often think that myself. If I'm not, then I'm in trouble."

Looking at the stage now, Elizabeth remembered her feelings when Jennifer had said those words. They had given her pause. It had been easy to assume that her daughter did not know what she was doing; it had been so easy to learn that she did. If disillusionment had already come to Jennifer, what gift was left for a mother to offer?

But in the opera, when all this distrust and deception and testing were over, it would all end happily. The men would marry the girls, admitting the error of their ways. Youth and beauty would be enough for everybody. The theater is so very reassuring, thought Elizabeth.

42

At the intermission the guests streamed cheerfully down the lawn to refreshment, where they were joined by Gladys Cooper, who took her place at the head table amid a barrage of apologies and self-assurance. She was newly arrived from New York.

"We've come almost literally straight off the boat!" she said. She was not a large woman, but by carrying her head forward with the chin slightly up, and mostly through the intensity of her energy, she contrived to seem so. At forty-seven, she was still a great beauty in the English manner, but her manners were terribly matter-of-fact, like those of a good governess or businesswoman.

"What a superb hamper!" she exclaimed, rummaging. "Shall I carve the chicken? God knows I've enough years of experience."

Within seconds it was as though the party had joined Gladys Cooper rather than the other way around. Hers was the real self-confidence, whose lack in themselves Elizabeth remedied by reserve, Lady Pearsall by vagueness, and Jennifer by ill temper. Gladys Cooper was a self-made woman: a West End star for twenty years, the only actress to manage her own theater, soon to launch a whole new career in Hollywood.

Seated next to her, Anthony stared as though she were unreal. It was eerie, he explained, to see her in the flesh. During the war, her photographs, all those postcards—everyone seemed to have had a photograph of Gladys Cooper somewhere as though she were Blighty personified.

"Ah, those wretched postcards," she said, examining him with those candid blue eyes. "You're not flattering me by remembering them, you know. I did them to earn a living, and they became the bane of my existence. People don't take beautiful people seriously. The best notice I ever had in those days said, if I remember rightly, 'Gladys Cooper surprised us by acting.' I *was* pleased! Can I offer anyone more salad?"

"Speaking of beautiful people," said Lady Pearsall. "What have you done with your husband-to-be?" It was popular gossip. Gladys Cooper was divorcing her present husband to marry the handsome actor Philip Merivale.

"Philip has gone straight to London," replied Miss Cooper, "but I did bring another bone to fling to you lions. A rather handsome bone, in fact. He's changing now. He says he knows you. We played together in *The Painted Veil* five years ago and met again on the boat. Robert Brandon?"

Elizabeth and Jennifer exchanged glances. Elizabeth thought: This man seems to haunt my life. She did not want to touch that sore place; better to pretend it did not exist. She never encouraged Mabel to talk about Brandon, but she saw his name often enough in the papers, for he had become an international, not just a British, star, appearing in a procession of light romances and pseudo-historical dramas. She still knew nothing about his relationship with Jennifer, and now suddenly, fearing conspiracy again, she leaned across to her daughter. "Does Anthony know about you and Mr. Brandon?" she said.

No sentence could have been better calculated to alarm Jennifer.

She had been thinking: Anthony will be sure I arranged this on purpose, that it's Robert I wanted to see.

She grew still, looked to the horizon, and murmured back, "What should there be for him to know?"

Both women looked toward Anthony James. Dangling a chicken leg from his hand, one trouser leg rucked high enough to display a suspender, Anthony seemed engrossed by Gladys Cooper, but Jennifer did not trust his appearance. Too often the smooth crust concealed bitter herbs. Because she had seen Brandon several times after her father's funeral, Anthony had made him a favorite whipping boy, and whether or not she had made love to Robert Brandon, whatever she might feel for him, Jennifer felt convicted in her husband's eyes. And now by her mother too. She quietly watched Anthony and Gladys Cooper in conversation.

"What effect has your beauty had on your career, Miss Cooper?"

"Willie Maugham has always claimed my beauty is my curse," she laughed. "The only good thing about it, he says, is that it got me on the stage in the first place. He maintains that actresses with regular features can't act. He likes to pontificate about my success being due to hard work and common sense. Perhaps he's right." She smiled.

"Seriously," said Anthony. "Has your beauty given you a career, or made it more difficult?" He did not look at Jennifer, but she could hear him thinking at her: I hope you're paying attention to this.

Miss Cooper studied him this time, unsmiling. "I don't know that anyone can answer that question." The comment was wistful, with a sense of old wounds. "If you have a reputation as a beauty, it doesn't matter how desperate you are to act, most of the audience simply come to sit and stare at you. They don't even notice the play." She looked beyond the dinner guests toward the entrance of the bower. "But here is a gentleman who I'm sure has the same problem."

The group turned as one to look at the new arrival, Robert Brandon, who had been thereby handed a star entrance. He bowed. "You know I shall bear you out in anything you may say, Gladys, no matter how fanciful."

Introductions and recognitions followed, and Brandon was given the seat to Miss Cooper's right and Elizabeth's left, which brought him across the rug from Jennifer, to whom he smiled warmly. And handsome he is, thought Elizabeth. Fitter, fuller than before, as though California's good food had taken away the last of the cockney weed. He moved lightly in elegant tailoring. He was modest, tactful, charming. Another impersonation? wondered Elizabeth. Or has his assurance grown as much as his shoulders? He settled quietly to eating, leaving the limelight to Gladys Cooper, and Elizabeth thought this very clever.

Anthony all but ignored Brandon. They had never met but seemed to know each other. Anthony resumed conversation with Gladys Cooper so abruptly that he made Brandon seem an interruption. "But real actors," he said, "never think it is enough to be beautiful, do they? You yourself, for instance?"

As he spoke, he glanced at Jennifer, and Gladys Cooper, seeing that glance, sensed undercurrents. She laughed lightly. "When I'm in a long run, I change the costumes every six months and ask the fashion magazines back for another look. One uses whatever one can. One has to have an audience. But may I offer anyone some cheese? Isn't this that delightful cheese from Siena, Lady Pearsall?"

The conversation grew general, and Miss Cooper took the opportunity to lean around Anthony to speak to Jennifer. "Excuse me," she said. "But I didn't catch your name, and I'm sure you're an actress I know."

"This is my wife," said Anthony. "Mrs. James. Jennifer Wingate."

"Ah, but Robert has told me all about you! You did *Sweets to the Sweet* while I was overseas. He says you're very good indeed. You should ask your wife, Mr. James, not me, about the problems of being beauty or actress! But where did I see you, my dear?"

"I was in *Henry the Eighth,*" said Jennifer eagerly. "And in—"

"The actors were about the only English elements in our great national picture. Tell Miss Cooper about Vincent Korda giving directions in sign language, darling." Anthony had cut across Jennifer's response as clean as a knife. Jennifer flushed.

"And what else have you done, my dear?" asked Miss Cooper kindly. "What are you doing at the moment?"

Again Anthony cut across Jennifer's response. "Or tell about Binnie Barnes eating too much when they were filming the banquet scene. It seems that when she complained to Alexander Korda, he . . ." And to everyone's embarrassment, Anthony proceeded to tell the not-so-amusing anecdote himself. Jennifer, visibly annoyed, sank into silence. Anthony finished his tale apparently unaware that he had made a fool of himself.

"I do suggest," said Lady Pearsall, "that we *circulate*. If you have finished eating, Anthony, would you be so kind as to accompany me while I see if all the other guests are still living? Would you excuse us, everyone? I know that these two actresses would like to share a little shop talk."

The general movement left Jennifer with Gladys Cooper on one side of the rug, and Elizabeth and Robert Brandon to decide whether they would talk to one another opposite. The fortuitous conjunction of Anthony's boorishness and Gladys Cooper's remarks about beauty and acting had had an inappropriately powerful effect on Elizabeth, one which unexpectedly brought her into full sympathy with her daughter. She had always agreed with Anthony's view that Jennifer was not a "real" actress, and she had never imagined that her daughter's beauty was anything but the main reason for her success. Abruptly she turned to Brandon and asked, "Is my daughter a serious actress?"

She took him by surprise. He thought, then replied in a voice as soft as hers, "I'm tempted to say I don't know Jennifer well enough. I haven't seen enough of her work."

"Then there is some doubt."

He studied her this time, as though wondering how much of the truth she could take. "It seems a very serious question to you."

"Suddenly it is."

He nodded, then spoke. "Anyone who catches Gladys Cooper's eye, or Alexander Korda's, has something." He paused and plucked grass. "Acting is almost all technique, and she's very good at that, there's no doubt. And of course she's very beautiful."

"But."

He smiled at her, the shrewd and rough self-knowledge in his eyes reminding her of Mabel.

"I've tried to get her to Hollywood as my leading lady," he said, then stopped smiling. "But that tells you something, if you look at it hard, and we're a hard lot, we actors. I don't think she'll get much further than me." He laughed at himself. "I think she could. I doubt she will."

Elizabeth said nothing.

"We don't know what turns a good professional into a serious actor," he said. "Mostly hard work, I think. Commitment, perhaps. And something inside, something dredged up out of experience. You would know better than I which of those it is that she lacks, wouldn't you?" He laughed again at his seriousness. "I think you can safely put your daughter on the stage, Mrs. Worthington. She'll have a respectable career."

When he had used that tone to her before, it had made her angry, and it did again. "Don't patronize me," she flared, though her voice was still low.

"Far be it from me! After all you have done for my family!"

The sun slanting across the hedge cast Brandon's face in shadow and Jennifer's in golden profile. Birdsong floated, and the voices of guests gave Elizabeth a wave on which to plunge ahead. "Really?" she said coldly. "Then I have the right to be told something I have never known. When I gave you the hundred pounds–was that a scheme cooked up by Jennifer and you?"

She resisted the urge to explain, to justify, to force him to understand why it was so important to her. She was powerless as only a parent can be powerless before strangers.

At last he replied. "Jennifer has the impression that you don't trust me."

"We've never discussed you," she said hastily. Then: "Why should I trust you? Just how well do you know my daughter?"

He raised a hand to ward off her intensity. "And if you don't trust me, then what is the use of my giving you an answer one way or the other, assuming I could?" He now looked at her directly, his face open and candid.

"But . . ."

"But what? No words are going to make you trust me. I could lie, Jennifer could lie, we could contradict each other, we could say the same thing by chance or concert–how would you know where the truth lay? I paid you back your hundred pounds. Isn't that all that matters? Something concrete?"

"But you lied to me! You said you were a parson's son!"

He looked at her with irony. "The Wingates were rich then, and I was poor. The difference between the rich and the poor is that the rich lie voluntarily."

The statement was so full of possibilities about Jennifer and guilts for Elizabeth that she could think of nothing more to say. And the thought came to her: If I am deprived of knowledge, then I am left only with parenthood's sacramental act. I will believe Jennifer.

"To tell the truth," Gladys Cooper said to Jennifer, "I really hate acting. But one has no choice. I have to do what I can to the best of my ability, and acting is the only thing I know how to do. I don't think of it in terms of great art. An actress just goes on, and is: that's all there is to acting, as to life. If you have to do something, you'll do it."

An act of nature, thought Elizabeth. If I am to be on Jennifer's side, it will be an act of love and faith. It need have nothing to do with worth.

43

Lady Pearsall had been engaged in tense conversation with one of Glyndebourne's staff. Now she clambered onto the wooden seat near the bower and raised hands and voice to attract attention. "Listen, everybody!" she called. "Listen! May I have your attention, please!"

Heads turned, and her guests gave her a scattering of mock applause, which pleased and flustered her.

"I have an announcement," she continued. "I am informed that the curtain will be delayed for twenty minutes." Groans went up. "There is an event which Captain Christie believes we may be eager to see. He has learned that we are to be flown over–quite peaceably, he assures me–by the *Hindenburg*."

A hubbub of conversation arose. This was the first season of the *Hindenburg,* the largest dirigible built and successor to the *Graf Zeppelin* built in the days before Hitler. The German dirigibles had made some 150 Atlantic crossings, carrying about thirteen thousand passengers between Frankfurt and the United States. This spring and summer the *Hindenburg* had been flying over portions of England on its transatlantic route, the first zeppelin to do so since the wartime bombings. Because of the winds, said the Deutsche-Zeppelin-Reederei Company. To frighten us, said the English. Now Glyndebourne's guests formed excited groups to stare at the horizon north of the lowering sun, where the sky was still a bright pale blue, and there was much chatter of air-raid precautions and rearmament and the League of Nations.

Anthony came to stand by Jennifer, taking her arm. The old military type spoke to him quietly. "Lot of nonsense these civilians talk, eh?" To Jennifer's surprise, Anthony nodded solemnly in assent. "Spot of war might do this generation no harm at all," continued the military type, encouraged. "Hate to quote a fascist, but that feller Mussolini's right, you know: 'War is to man what maternity is to a woman.' Certainly take care of all those dole-bashers, wouldn't it?"

He got his comeuppance from the black-haired mathematician. Muttering about warmongers, she burrowed into her handbag to pull out a frayed newspaper clipping. "Read this!" she insisted, thrusting the clipping under his nose. "I always carry it to warn people like you."

The old military type shied away as though she offered a scorpion. "Haven't me spectacles with me!" he demurred.

"Then I'll read it to you," she insisted. "Listen, listen to this!" She seized his arm, using her voice to seize others. "This is a speech by Baldwin, your prime minister, everyone! Hear what he says! 'I think it is well for the man in the street to realize that there is now no power on earth that can prevent him from being bombed. Whatever people may tell you–' "

Suddenly the cry was raised, "There she is! Oh, look!"

Against the light sky to the northwest a black shape had appeared, much larger and lower than one expected, close enough already for the gleam of silver to shine along the side presented to the sun. The people turned and raised their eyes, shading them with their hands, taking small steps toward that black shape. The *Hindenburg* was a monster: eight hundred feet long, rising ten stories high. It was a shark, foraging with quiet and sudden purpose over the checkerboard of English fields.

The mathematician with black hair kept reading, and as the crowd fell silent to awe, her voice rang clear across the evening lawns. " 'Whatever people may tell you the bomber will always get through. The only defense is offense, which means that you have to kill more women and children more quickly than the enemy, if you are to save yourselves.' " Her tone was awestruck as she finished reading. "Our own prime minister! Telling us what war will mean!"

They stood about the tamed and ancient grounds, among the oaks and swans, the glow of old brick and the gleam of flowers by sunset. The audience, the orchestra, the waiters, beyond them the kitchen staff, the chauffeurs, the ticket seller, the ushers, the management, the performers in costume–standing in little clumps and rows, staring to where the sun declined in the west and there arose in its place that great silent shape chasing its shadow over the hills and pasture before it, over the car park, the manor house, the grounds. They could see the giant swastikas black and bold against its flanks, the number Z-129. They could see faces, uniforms–up there in the observation lounge, fifty passengers dined in evening dress, late so that they might view England. Someone waved and called out, and on the ground below, one person raised an arm halfway as though a child responding to a passing train, then hesitated and withdrew the link.

Quite clearly they could see a crewman on the outside of the vessel's bulk, attached by ropes, a paintbrush in hand. He stood, and knocked a paint can with his foot, and the can rolled down and over, falling and tumbling slowly down to the ground on the other side of the manor house. Someone cried out and others flinched as though for the explosion. As the giant craft hurtled toward them, its shadow darkening them in their evening costumes as though each in turn were snuffed out, they saw the crewman leaning over, his face aghast, or just amazed at what he saw beneath him.

The craft passed, and by its passing released Glyndebourne. The mathematician had tears in her eyes. Lady Pearsall, caught with one foot still on the bench, looked wild and ragged. Anthony stood frozen, his fingers digging painfully into Jennifer's arm. Elizabeth stood with her hands clasped and face down. Gladys Cooper waved a piece of celery with vague rudeness in the air, her face scornful. They began to form into an audience again, moving slowly toward the theater. The dowager duchess summoned Lady Pearsall. Her cousin must forgive her. She was tired, it was late, the airship, very upsetting. Jill Knight and her husband approached–if she didn't mind, the children, they could not be late home.

Mozart's second act gave everyone time and tempo to pull themselves together, and by the time they had applauded and wandered forth again for the birthday cake and toasts, they were chatting politely again of Mozart's artifice. A search by the staff had discovered the paint can burst open in the middle of the car park, its contents splashed black upon the grasses, and now the sticky trophy was passed from hand to hand, as though it were to be disarmed. They gathered for the blowing out of candles, but Lady Pearsall's very amusing speech of thanks was short because it was time to board the buses which met the last train from Lewes. Elizabeth noticed that Robert rather than Anthony was accompanying Jennifer.

"Champers, anyone?" said Lady Pearsall breathlessly, stooping to draw the last two bottles by their strings from the stream. "We must finish it. The staff has consumed quite enough at my expense."

Brandon filled two glasses and took one to Jennifer, toying with her strawberries and cream in the bower.

"Care for a stroll?" he said.

She rose, and Elizabeth watched them walk down through the garden, where hedges and walls channeled them tactfully toward an ornamental lake sparkling with blue irises, reddened by the evening light, split by the paths of mallards. Elizabeth saw them seated on a bench under a weeping willow tree, their heads leaning toward each other in earnest conversation. They seemed only friends. She set about stacking the remains of the picnic into the single remaining hamper.

"Have you seen Robert?" asked Miss Cooper, suddenly appearing at her elbow. "He's terrified of my driving, but then, so is everyone, and I must have company. He is so very pleasant. I do like handsome men."

Elizabeth pointed out where Robert sat and watched her walk toward the couple. She returned with Jennifer to say her good-byes, while Brandon hastened on some errand in the direction of the parking lot. The women were strolling slowly up the lawn before he rejoined them–Ginny and Elizabeth quiet, Jennifer and Gladys Cooper in intense conversation. In his hand was a thick book with a dust jacket striped in orange and cream, and he gave it to Jennifer as though by arrangement.

"What is the book?" asked Lady Pearsall as the group congealed in the middle of the lawn. A handful of guests remained. The staff had gathered up the last hampers and were carrying them to a waiting van.

"The hit of the season," said Brandon. "I bought it in New York and it struck me Jennifer should read it. A publishing phenomenon, as they say in America. Came out last month and it's already selling faster than *Anthony Adverse* and the Bible together."

"Robert says the heroine reminds him of me," said Jennifer, dimpling. She was in good humor now.

"I can't imagine an actress better, when they make the movie." He smiled at Elizabeth rather than Jennifer.

"What is the name?" said Lady Pearsall, peering shortsightedly at the book. *"Gone With the Wind?* Oh? Is it about us?"

For some reason nobody responded to what she had intended as a joke. Something in her tone–or perhaps simply the memory of the airship–had twisted her intent.

Gladys Cooper wriggled her shoulders and stood more upright. "All too much like *Heartbreak House,* isn't it?"

She took Robert by the arm, and they said their farewells and strode off ahead of Jennifer, Elizabeth, and Ginny, who now engaged in a taut and puzzled discussion as to the whereabouts of Anthony, whom none of them had seen since the auditorium.

"I'm sure he's gone ahead," concluded Jennifer, suspiciously unconcerned. "We brought two cars. Though I should think he would have stayed for the strawberries and cream."

Suddenly Gladys Cooper turned back and rejoined them all haste.

"I've just remembered something apropos to our conversation," she said to Jennifer. "Something Edith Evans told me a year or so ago. She was a milliner, you know, and had no intention of becoming a serious actress, but after the run of her first play she went back to making hats and found she couldn't anymore. 'I couldn't make my hats,' she said. 'So I had to become an actress.' I know exactly what she means. I suspect you may too." She placed her hand briefly on Jennifer's arm. "Now I must dash!"

She hastened to rejoin Robert Brandon and find her car.

"It's very pleasant to be taken seriously," said Jennifer. Her face was suddenly petulant again, but Elizabeth realized that what she saw as petulance might more likely be thoughtfulness. She was embarrassed. Gladys Cooper took her daughter more seriously than did she.

"She seems a very vital woman, very competent," she said cautiously.

"That's funny," said Jennifer, coming to a stop and looking at her mother. "She said almost the same thing about you."

Elizabeth was pleased, but she protested, "I have no idea why! We scarcely talked."

"You have this talent for earning people's respect without really deserving it."

Lady Pearsall laughed. "Jennifer! That's very rude!"

"I mean without really trying."

"What can I say," laughed Elizabeth, "other than that Miss Cooper is very astute?" Though she was used to her daughter underestimating her, it still hurt. "Did she have any concrete suggestions about your future?"

"She thought I ought to think of Hollywood."

"Now, there's the place to become a glamour girl, if you like that sort of thing," said Ginny.

"Yes, but I can't sign any kind of contract when Anthony won't let me, and besides, I should be trapped in exactly the way she was talking about. They might come to look at me rather than my acting." She gave a small and rueful smile.

"Does it matter?" said Ginny with fatigue. "It *is* an income."

"Ah, no, Ginny!" contradicted Elizabeth, again mildly surprising her daughter. "I see exactly what Jennifer means. If you are serious about a profession, it would be terrible not to be taken seriously."

"It is not very pleasant," said Jennifer, resuming their stroll up the lawn, "to be valued only for the way you look." She spoke so fiercely that Elizabeth knew there was personal rather than just professional dissatisfaction behind it.

"Someday *I* shall go to America," Elizabeth said sympathetically. "Just to see for myself what it's like."

"Good Lord, my dear," said Ginny. "I've never had the slightest inclination! Does this have something to do with your Mr. Wallace?"

She was teasing, but Elizabeth chose to take her seriously. "I have come to know him," she said judiciously. "And I begin to think we are not fair to the Americans. And sometimes I get restless with all of this." With a gesture she indicated the carpeted grounds, the predictability of the lawn, the restraint of English nature. "When something like that dirigible happens, then I think that somehow we lack the energy here for another fight, and I think America has it."

"Must we discuss war on my birthday?" Lady Pearsall had cracked the words out. Elizabeth raised one hand to touch her shoulder gently, and she said quietly, "I know, Ginny. I understand. I was there."

Jennifer did not understand the exchange between the two older women, who stood immobile together for a moment, miles away. "You shan't have to worry about it this time," she said sulkily. "It'll be my generation this time."

The two others looked at her—briefly, as though from another planet, then softly.

Ginny patted Elizabeth's hand before speaking to Jennifer in an amused tone. "And you think therefore that we don't have to worry?"

In silence and the last light of the sun the three women finished the crossing of the lawn, where Jennifer said good-bye to the others and left them waiting for the Daimler near the driveway while she went to search the theater and house for Anthony.

In the gloaming, faces took on luminosity. Lingering members of the audience waited for their chauffeurs nearby, and they spoke of the Pankhurst family. Christabel, now an immigrant to California, had just been made Dame Commander of the British Empire either in apology to her dead mother or in recognition of her newfound evangelism for the Second Coming of Christ. Adela, the youngest and quietest daughter, had immigrated to Australia. Sylvia now battled on behalf of Abyssinia, even though this cause too was clearly lost. It was as though the family's time had passed, and both Ginny and Elizabeth felt a moment of regret, remembering the war and the Mothers' Union.

"God," said Ginny lightly. "Whoever thought that one would become an aging, childless widow?" The Daimler appeared on the driveway, and they moved toward it, Elizabeth silent. "That wretched dirigible!" continued Ginny. "I should have known better than to celebrate a birthday. Now we start it all over again."

They climbed into the great car.

"But there is still a chance," said Elizabeth, settling herself, "that Jennifer's generation will know better than did we what to do about it all."

"Ha!" exploded Ginny with scorn.

Jennifer searched for Anthony among the buildings and the bar, but she had not the patience for a long search, suspecting that he was punishing her for Brandon, so she walked down to the parking lot, where few cars remained. Her Morgan was some distance away, and the grasses swished under her evening slippers. Though it was dark now, the day's shapes blurred and unknown, there was enough afterlight for her to see the great splash of paint on the grass where the paint can had fallen. She was quite alone in the meadow, fumbling in her embroidered evening bag for her keys, juggling *Gone With the Wind*. She reached the little sports car and leaned over to throw her book into the passenger seat, then recoiled with a cry of alarm. It seemed to her for a brief moment that something black and horrid crouched and spread tentacles over her car, and she felt fright until she realized it was a substance, not an entity. She stretched out a hand to touch it. Black paint had splashed over the side of the car, the bonnet, the windscreen, some of the interior, as though someone had stood to the side and thrown. She realized at once that it came from the dirigible's paint can. At such a distance? Distressed, she took a chamois from the glove box and cleaned the seat and windscreen, then a rug from the back and spread it across the driver's seat. From the steering wheel, the brake, the gear lever, paint attached itself to her hands and gown. She started the car with a roar of its small engine, and it jerked forward to bounce in a tight circle over the meadow grass. At the main road, she hesitated, looking back at Glyndebourne, wiping paint from her hands onto the rug.

"Damn it all," she cried, drumming her hands in exasperation against the steering wheel. "Damn you all to *hell!*"

Almost in tears, she forced the car into gear and spun off onto the London road, the snarl of her engine like a claim against the downs and the dusk.

She was not the only person at Glyndebourne plagued by black paint. A watcher in the dark had found another splotch on the heel of his hand and stood idly rubbing it with his handkerchief. He wore evening dress and had been noticed earlier by one of the kitchen hands standing quietly in the gloom near the kitchen wall which overlooked the car park, but the youth had shrugged his shoulders, emptied his garbage, and gone back to work. As Jennifer's car snarled off into the hills, the watcher carefully placed a champagne glass on top of the wall, folded his handkerchief and then dropped it, as if in insolence, on the ground, and walked—or sauntered—to his Hillman parked under an oak tree at the edge of the meadow.

44

February 1937

On her Wednesday half-day Mabel liked to take afternoon tea in the manner she enjoyed, in a nice place with her gentleman friend, Mr. Charlie Phipps, with whom for more than ten years now she had been "walking out," as she put it—walking out, she thought smugly, so carefully that not a single soul suspected them of more than a little hand-holding in the back stalls. Charlie Phipps was a shiny little man in his early fifties, with hair which tufted boyishly, a tendency to bulge out of his shirts, and an unfortunate taste in tie clips and wristwatches given him by his clients, but he was a man who had done very well, thank you, as an independent accountant with an office on Theobald's Road and a semidetached at Maida Vale. Charlie was a cheerful soul, much given to the practical and the comfortable, and happy enough on this bleak day to accompany Mabel to the warm insides of Madame Tussaud's Wax Museum.

Mabel liked Madame Tussaud's. She found it cultural without being boring, economical without being cheap, and above all genteel. One had the sense of hobnobbing with the famous, and the guards—unlike those at the Victoria and Albert—were ready with a bit of gossip when you wanted it. Like being part of the family, it was, standing there in front of those wax figurines and chatting about their funny ways. They were that lifelike, you thought they'd join in. This visit had a particular object: a figure not in the official catalog but advertised modestly in the newspapers: "Dly. Sun. (10–10). Portrait

Model. Mrs. Simpson." Her, as the Londoners said, her as caused all the trouble.

Mabel Greggs and Charlie Phipps now stood in the elegant room on the second floor in front of the specially lit niche where the lady stood alone, her only protectors a crimson rope and a hirsute guard given to balancing backward and forward on the balls of his feet to show that he was real.

"Scarlet, that gown, wouldn't you say?" commented Charlie. "Very *fitting,* heh?" He laughed at his wit, but Mabel frowned.

"I wouldn't rush to judgment, myself," she said.

"Look at that fancy evening bag they've given her, then. Of course, those initials, they wouldn't be real diamonds. Mind you, they say the real one scarpered with half the Crown Jewels that 'Is Nibs had given 'er."

"They say a lot of things," said Mabel, bridling. "Just because she's got what they wanted."

"I say," resumed Charlie. "Do you think they could 'ave shrunk her? Never knew she was such a little bit of a thing. Skinny, isn't she?" he asked, his hand lightly brushing Mabel's ample rump in its sensible tweed. "Hard eyes."

"Hard my foot," snapped Mabel. "Take her for the very worst she is, and all she's done is take care of her future by getting the man she wanted. There's thousands of women do that. Because they have to."

A little boy pushed between them to read the plaque aloud and turn to his parents. "Who was Mrs. Simpson, then?" he demanded.

"Never you mind that," said his mother, snatching him away.

"Middle-class morality," sniffed Mabel.

"Where's her husband-to-be, I wonder?" asked Charlie.

"With the rest of the royal family, I should imagine." She turned to the guard. "When are they going to put them together?" It was as though she held the guard personally responsible not just for the space that parted the wax figures but also for that which plagued the real lovers while they waited cautiously for her divorce decree to become absolute, he pacing the chill corridors of a castle in Austria, she imprisoned in a villa near Cannes, thumbing envelopes addressed "King Edward's Whore."

"Not till he puts on the old ball and chain, I should think." The guard grinned behind his mustache. "Up here all the time, they are, on about where to put them. Go see what they did to His Former Majesty, you want to see problems. Other side of the Famous Soldiers."

Under a great scarlet canopy stood a high dais fronted by a flight of steps. On the dais stood King George the Sixth and Queen Elizabeth, their daughters next to them, the rest of the family in descending order of precedence on the steps. One figure stood alone except for his placard: "HRH the Duke of Windsor." He alone stood at floor level, as though offered up to scavengers, his blue eyes slightly agoggle above the scarlet tunic frogged with gold, but otherwise the charm, the air of derring-do still clinging like the blond shine in the hair. His neck was just on a level with the boot of the Duke of Wellington, who seemed to disregard the opportunity only by unnatural restraint.

"Put him there the day after the abdication," said the guard. "See what I mean."

Mabel addressed the Duke of Windsor face to face. "Jennifer's on your side, anyway," she said, consolingly. "Though, mind you, I don't think she knows any better than you what it'll cost to get what she wants. Romance!" She sniffed, and tipped her chin, and turned to stare at Charlie. "I wonder what *you'd* do if you had to choose between me and the wife and kids?"

"All for love and the world well lost," said Charlie breezily.

"You only say that because you don't think I'm serious," persisted Mabel. "What would you think if I said I meant it?"

She brushed away the hand with which he was trying to pinch her tweed, and he looked uncomfortable. "Now, I thought we'd settled all of that long ago," he said uneasily. "Me and you being Catholics and everything."

"That's as may be," Mabel replied doggedly. "But when push comes to shove . . . *I* think Mrs. Simpson's lucky to have found a man she can trust."

"How about my cup of tea?" said Charlie Phipps plaintively, finding it important to change the subject, and the couple walked out into the rain to a favorite little ABC on Marylebone Road, where the waitresses knew to warm the pot first.

That same afternoon Jennifer sat in the private office of Alexander Korda at London Film Productions in the mews off Grosvenor Street, sipping from a gold-rimmed cup the coffee which Korda had brewed for her.

"But you must, Alex darling," she said intensely. "You simply must. Even if you don't think it will work. I've never asked for a favor before, have I?" She laughed throatily in the manner of the trained actress. "At least not in the last six months. God, if a partner in United Artists can't help, who can? And if a friend won't help, who will?"

She looked delectable. Too thin, he thought, but delectable, almost as perfect as Merle and Vivien. He sighed, enjoying himself. The halo-brimmed hat gave her away. Effective but out of season; therefore a device. He sipped his coffee and studied her from behind thick lenses and settled to the game.

"Am I everybody's father, then?" he sighed, and made the Hungarian gesture of impossible burden with his shoulders and arms.

You look the part, she thought. That gray hair, the wise look, the Sulka shirt, the beautiful suit, the Knize tie, the Lobb shoes that always shine as though they had never touched anything grosser than the carpeting in the Rolls. God how I wish just for once someone *would* act like a father to me.

"Darling, I know it's the most awful favor I'm asking, but you don't even have to put a good word in for me. Just get me in the door." Her eyelashes slowly shuttered her eyes as she looked at the floor and lowered her voice. "You of all people should understand why I need help."

She was beautiful. She had talent. She was well-connected. She helped Merle with hairdressers. So she didn't have a clue about careers, this should make a difference? To gain time, he took a cigar from his pocket, clipped it, and lit it with the desk lighter. He'd promised her Messalina in *I, Claudius* because Laughton liked her, then given it to Merle instead. If it were only just a matter of money . . .

"We have offered you a contract, yes?" His voice was soft, the Hungarian accent charming.

"Many times."

"And you have said no, yes?"

"Many times." She looked at him, and he saw genuine regret and gratitude in her face.

"What have we offered you, eh? No–don't tell me. Whatever it is, double it."

"So you can keep me *not* making any films at all, like you have Vivien Leigh and Ann Todd?" She was briefly hard, then gave it up. "Oh, Alex, it isn't a matter of money." For a moment she felt despair. "Besides, with you in the headlines for losing money–making everybody at London Films take a pay cut–how could you pay me that much?"

Korda's eyebrows rose, and he laughed. "I think that's why I love you, my dear! Money doesn't matter, eh? But you know more about it than me?" He became serious and leaned over the desk. "We could give you a lead. What we have is this Queen Elizabeth story, this *Fire Over England* with Larry Olivier. Sign a contract, and it's yours."

She shook her head but smiled. "I'll take the part anyway."

He threw up his hands and stood up to begin pacing the lush carpet slowly, as though he were measuring it.

"There has to be something in it for the studio!" he protested. "We make you a star, then you go off to make films for someone else, no? Me, Mayer, Selznick–it's the same with all of us."

"For Selznick I'll sign a contract. May I have some more coffee, please?"

"For Selznick you'll have to." He moved to the sideboard, where the coffeemaker stood. "And what does that do to your marriage?"

"I'll break the contract *after Gone With the Wind.*"

Korda's eyebrows went up again, and he made a sudden gesture, spilling a jug of water slightly. "And for this you want me to send you to Selznick? I didn't hear you say it." He turned his back on her for a moment, he who knew that the first person to get away with breaking a promise was always the winner.

She studied his back, then rose to carry her coffeecup to him. "I've told you I'm deadly serious about this, Alex." She placed her hand on his sleeve, so that he turned half toward her. "I'll take the consequences," she said. "With Anthony, with Selznick, with everybody. Just get him to take me seriously. Please?"

She spoke with such intensity that Korda abandoned the game. He put the coffee brewer down and moved back to his desk, staring at her on the other side of the room, her face shaded under the halo of the hat against the light from the windows. "Selznick wants an unknown opposite Gable," he said.

"You know as well as I do that Scarlett's going to be in every foot of that film. He can't afford an unknown who can't hit her marks and doesn't know what a key light is." She leaned on the edge of his desk with her hands. "He wants someone who isn't well-known in America but who knows the business. I've done seven films without a single leading role. You know I'd be perfect." She spun away from the desk and turned to face him, fists clenched by her sides. "You know I'd be perfect for that part. It's me. I'm her."

Korda picked up the cigar from his ashtray and started lighting it again with great puffs. He stared at her over the top of his glasses. "So if I get him interested, what next?"

"What do you mean, what next?" The anticipation of triumph gave an edge to her voice. "I'll go to America. I've saved the money. Anthony won't have to give me a penny."

Carefully he ashed the cigar. He had already promised Vivien Leigh, who was under contract to him, to do what he could to get the role of Scarlett O'Hara for her. He raised his eyebrows and heaved a sigh. "I'll do what I can."

A smile burst across her face. "Oh, Alex!" she said. "You don't know what this means to me!" She sat down abruptly on the couch and burst into tears that ruined her mascara in an instant.

45

March 1937

When the hospital telephoned her at work to tell her that Peter was asking for her, Elizabeth was stunned. In hospital? Of course he was ill, ever since he had turned sixty and old at the same time, even though, as she had once acerbically reminded him, he had now lived longer than Charles. In hospital? The sudden fear was great enough that she wished they had not telephoned.

She walked to the sprawling hospital across Westminster Bridge, whipped by bursts of cold wind off the Thames. The smoke from chimneys hung low and gritty in the March wind, and the many windows of St. Thomas's pavilions looked blank because of reflections of the western light. She snapped at the sister in her smart gray uniform, and the sister in sweet retaliation deposited her at the door of the ward without instructions. She wandered its white and linoleum length past all the beds where old men lay, and she did not see him, but upon her slow return she found that it was not that the sister had made a mistake. She had walked past without recognizing him.

She was glad that his eyes were closed. It had been his hands, not his face, that she recognized, even though they lay pale and still upon the coverlet, as though set aside. They had wet his hair and combed it back on the wrong side. It looked faintly ludicrous like that, baring his high forehead, and so silver, like an old man, like her father. His face was a flat white, tinged faintly with gray around the eyes and mouth. His lips were puffed and chapped as though he had not drunk for days, and she fled in search of the ward sister.

"What's wrong with him?" she demanded. "What has happened?"

The sister was busy with her metal cart. "Are you the next of kin?" she demanded in reply.

"No. He has no next of kin. I'm a friend."

"Well, we have to find the next of kin. Do you know the next of kin?"

"We are . . ." Elizabeth hesitated. ". . . engaged to be married."

The sister looked at her in sharp doubt, her age, her clothes. "*I* can't know that," she said. "You'll have to speak to the next of kin." She turned to bustle away.

Elizabeth, furious, seized her by the upper arm and half-turned her to face her. "There *are* no next of kin, I tell you," she said softly but with fierce intensity. "I'm all he has in the world."

"*I* can't know that," repeated the sister. Her eyes would not meet Elizabeth's. "There's so many of you, always wanting to know. *I* can't tell you anything." She wrested her upper arm from Elizabeth's clutch.

Elizabeth went back to the bedside. His eyes were open, and as she had known they would, they had that flat and wandering look by which the very ill quest to understand the little out-of-focus world about them.

"Well, darling," she said cheerily, "you seem to have gotten yourself in a bit of a fix, don't you?"

Peter's eyes settled solemnly on her face. His voice was wet-throated, but he spoke with complete rationality. "Come to join the party?"

She laughed and replied in a confused manner, her head simply not able to clear itself, "The party, yes, yes. But what's wrong, Peter, what are you here *for?*"

His cracked lips parted, and his eyes smiled, blue as ever. He began to cough, the phlegm choking in his throat and rattling in his chest. Pneumonia, she thought. He has pneumonia.

"Nurse, nurse!" she called. A little nurse, a girl, came and pushed her aside and held the expectorant bowl to his mouth as the drool tumbled from his lips and the coughing racked his body, leaving him to fall back gray and at the edge of sleep or unconsciousness. His hand crept forward to take Elizabeth's as she resumed her seat, and while the nurse fussed with thermometer, she felt the slightest pressure from his fingers.

"You might help," hissed the nurse suddenly at Elizabeth. "We only let you here because he's you-know."

Elizabeth looked at her gap-mouthed. "No," she said quietly. "He's not."

The nurse shrugged and went away with the bowl.

"He's not," repeated Elizabeth softly to her back. She wet her handkerchief in the glass of water that stood on the bedside table and wiped Peter's dry lips with it. He was so hot, she thought. If she had some cologne. If they could get his fever down. He was dozing now, the breath rattling in his chest, the handsome nose become a beak.

"The pneumonia started last night." The voice of the ward sister came from behind her. "He was quite all right till then. Very weak but all right. He came here on Tuesday."

The woman's face was still red between her dark gray cap and stiff white collar. "I'm sorry," she said, looking very vulnerable. She waved a form at Elizabeth in search of understanding. "He wouldn't put down a next of kin, you see. Some of them won't. And it makes things very difficult for us. By the time we got your name and phone number out of him, it was too late to do any good. Wasn't it?" Her last sentence was a demand.

"I want him moved to a room," said Elizabeth.

"There are no rooms," said the sister. "And besides, he's very weak. We wouldn't have bathed him today if we hadn't wanted to get that temperature down."

"What's wrong with him?"

"You'll have to speak to doctor, when he makes his rounds."

"Who is his doctor?"

"Whoever makes the rounds. He said he doesn't have a doctor of his own."

"But that's nonsense!" exclaimed Elizabeth. "He was being treated by Dr. Mallert on Half Moon Street–for his arthritis."

Suddenly Elizabeth found herself weeping, the tears pouring out of her eyes as she tried to keep her face turned to the sister with whom she was doing battle for Peter's life, it seemed. "Oh God," she sobbed, "will no one help me? Will no one tell me what is happening?"

She felt the sister's hand firm on her shoulder. "We'll put the screens around," she said. Then she leaned close and whispered in Elizabeth's ear, "He doesn't have arthritis. He has . . . It is a blood disease. He must have known for months."

She left, and Elizabeth buried her face in one of the towels she had placed on the foot of Peter's bed and listened to the screens creak into place, their wheels squeaking on the waxed linoleum.

She spent the rest of the afternoon and evening behind those screens. When the nurses came to bother him with pills or thermometers or fob watches, hand on wrist, Peter squirmed uncomfortably. They brought a bowl of ice water and she herself swabbed his face, his neck, under the armpits. His genitals were a tiny bud under the covers, all gathered in, when she helped with his water bottle. He was sweating heavily, and one of the nurses said that was a good sign. But he moved less now, only an occasional fitful protest of his limbs or head, and the breath was heavy with liquid in his chest, and coughs no longer shaking his eyes open. Elizabeth doubted that he knew she was there.

She would not stay the night. She would not wait until those small dark hours that had taken her mother. She would leave early enough to get the last Underground home. But she could not leave him alone, not now. I shall not feel guilty for living, she told herself. If *you* go beneath the ground with those waiting others, she said to Peter in her mind, it will be because you went there of your own accord, not because I wasn't there to help.

The lights came on. Those who could eat were given meals. Those who could receive visitors kept their joy quiet. When they turned out the overhead lights, a young nurse came to look.

"When do they make their rounds?" demanded Elizabeth.

"Oh," said the nurse, blushing under cheery brown curls, holding Peter's limp hand as though it were a fish. "They made their rounds ages ago, simply ages ago. Not till tomorrow morning again."

Had they made their rounds before she came? Had she slept, forehead on the edge of Peter's mattress, when the doctor came and sighed with relief at seeing her sleeping and slipped away, another squeak on the linoleum?

At midnight they brought her a blanket and urged her to lie down on the next bed, surrounding them both now with screens. She fell asleep, and at some time in the darkness felt someone take her pulse, but she did not wake until the clatter of bedpans accompanied the dawn. Her eyes fled to Peter. They had not taken him away. He had not died. Under the acrid carbolic she could smell her own body. Her dark dress was a wreck. Her legs were sore where she had not undone her garter belt, the fasteners stabbing into her flesh. She was exhausted, vile.

A little gray-haired lady brought her hot sweet tea from her cart. She said, "Why not go home and wash up and 'ave a bit of a rest, luv. I'll keep my eye on 'im while you're gone. On the wards till eleven, I am. Keep me eye on the nurses, if you like."

At seven they told her they needed the bed now, and rather than retreat again into that narrowing confine of Peter's dying, she fled to her home, where she bathed and forced herself to eat an absurd breakfast and telephoned the office to say she wouldn't be in that day.

She drove the Austin back to the hospital and found Peter not only alive but better, his fever broken for a while. Too weak to raise his head, he looked at her quite brightly, and when she moistened his lips, he croaked words at her in pattern with his breath, like a man who has just run a mile at top speed. She could not understand what he said. She had missed nothing but the doctor, the ward sister told her—this nurse softer than the other, but no more cooperative in the way of answers.

"Is he getting better?" demanded Elizabeth.

The ward sister looked away from her. Why did they all look away from her?

"He's very weak, you know," said the sister. "It's not just the pneumonia."

"How long does he have?" said Elizabeth.

"You can't tell, really," said the ward sister, not realizing that no one had yet officially told Elizabeth her patient was dying. "Some of them hang on . . . well, you wouldn't think they could."

She sat beside the bed again, where Peter mumbled at her, eyes dull but focusing on her face.

"It's no good, Peter darling," she said sadly, holding his hand. "I can't understand a word you are saying."

Suddenly he spoke very clearly. "I feel so dozy," he said with one breath. "But I don't want to miss anything," he said with the next. His eyes closed again and he slept.

"Oh, yes, my darling," said Elizabeth softly, the tears flooding again. "I forgot, didn't I? You're still here, aren't you? It may not look like you, but you're still here."

From that moment she felt a numbness come upon her, a numbness that had the edge of exaltation to it, as though she were rising to meet some moment for which she needed her last strength. Later they came with a needle and gave Peter a shot which made him grimace with pain.

"Why do you do that?" protested Elizabeth. "Can't you leave him in peace? What is that?"

"It'll make him comfortable," said the nurse, forcing him to swallow water.

And he did seem to relax a few minutes later, the lines of battle fading from his face, which now took on a look of grotesque youth, as though some young man had been shocked into white hair. He was slipping away, she knew, slipping away with all those years, all those happenings that brought one a face, all those memories that were theirs.

His eyes opened: blue, clear, focused on her face as though they had been in the middle of a conversation. "What is," he panted, "our schedule?"

"What do you mean, darling?" He panted at her but said nothing. "Do you mean, how long will I be here?"

He nodded.

"As long as you want me," she said firmly, speaking up as though he were a little deaf. "I shan't go home till later."

"What is," he panted, "my schedule?" Another pant. "When can I," he panted, "go home?"

"Oh, my darling, whenever you like, you can go home whenever you like."

Merely he nodded, his face solemn as a child, believing, as a child would, whatever she told him.

She wiped his lips again with the damp cloth. "Would you like some water?" she asked gently.

"Remember?" He tried to smile, looking at her. "Wanted . . . to be a . . . railway guard. . . ."

She nodded, scarcely understanding, some dim recollection of twenty years ago, clearer in his fading mind than in hers.

"Laughed," he panted. "On the Brighton line . . . we said . . . you and I . . . laughed . . ." He was smiling now, the lips turned upward, the eyes merry, his fingers touching her hand with what must have been all their remaining strength. "Never made it . . ." he panted. "Doesn't matter . . . You and I." His voice did not trail away. It ended on an upward note, and he ended with it, no change of expression, just his eyes slowly closing halfway, as though they would not give up the sight of her, while death changed smile into rictus.

She was quite composed. She summoned a nurse, who brought the ward sister, who led her away, asking if she was all right. It was the one who had been angry because she was not the next of kin, who had talked to her a hundred years before, when she had not understood.

"You'll need to talk to the almoner," said the ward sister now. "I'll take you to the office now."

She led her to the ground floor, where she sat quietly for a long time in a hard chair. The bill for Peter's dying, she thought. When she came out of the hospital, it was, she found, early afternoon, scarcely lunchtime. On her car was an official ticket for overtime parking, which she screwed up and dropped into the gutter. She knew where she wanted to go, and through the heavy afternoon traffic she proceeded to drive there as calmly as though she were early for a luncheon date at Simpson's.

St. Patrick's was as ugly and squat as ever under the sunlight of early spring. It did not care that Peter Williams was no Roman Catholic. She walked first into the graveyard and stood at Charles' feet.

"There's space enough," she said. "You won't mind. It will bring me a bit nearer to you when the time comes, you there waiting."

Father Dick, to whom she had spoken just that once in the confessional, turned out to be as silver-haired and unctuous and Irish as she had feared: sternly consolatory.

"He is my brother," she lied simply. "We were very close. My husband and he were very close."

Father Dick had to consult with the gravedigger, who took some time to allow as how there would be room for the three of them if they didn't mind squeezing up a little. She asked Father Dick to recommend an undertaker, and he–kindly enough for all she didn't like him–volunteered to arrange the whole thing, and the funeral tomorrow, for there would be only her, no, that was the way her brother had wanted it, he and I, together. "On the Brighton line," she said as a bright non sequitur which Father Dick was too experienced to query.

The next morning was suitably filled with soft spring rain, and the cypresses dripped noisily as she stood under her big umbrella at the foot of the grave, listening to the rites that were all too familiar. She was appalled to find that the earth stank under the rain–this place where she would rest–but it would not matter to her when the time came, and she shoved out of her mind the thought of the sources of that stench that would accompany her while she waited, here between her men, for the Resurrection and the Life.

Not trusting herself to drive that day, she had come by train. For the trip back she had a whole first-class compartment to herself, and a copy of the *Daily Telegraph* to tell her in handsome black and white the news of the world. She calmly turned and folded the newspaper's big pages, and the countryside fled at her elbow. Of course she had Jennifer. And Genevieve Pearsall. She should have telephoned them. Jennifer, who had come for a visit ten days ago white-faced and distraught to announce that she was exhausted, that she had to have a holiday, that she was taking Merry and Mabel to the south of France. "PETER DIES," said the newspaper headlines. "ELIZABETH LEFT ALONE IN WORLD." Nonsense, she said to herself, I can telegraph Ginny in Juan-les-Pins. I wanted it this way, to be alone. Asserting, she punched the *Telegraph* straight to rustle terror away. Oh, Maman, where are you?

A week off for Charles, they gave me, she thought. How much for Peter, two days? God, I'm so tired. Mrs. Wingate regrets that due to the death of the two Mr. Wingates. Prevents me, Mr. Harris, from fulfilling all my future engagements.

Today's *Telegraph* had many headlines. Good, bold headlines. The Spanish Loyalists have defeated the Italian troops at Brihuega and captured large stores of equipment. How very interesting. The Moscow trials continue. What the hell does one more dead man matter? Herr Hitler, said the editorial, seems serious in his intentions of bringing about a union between Germany and Austria. There was much in his personal background to explain why. Prime Minister Baldwin should pay attention. The independence of Austria under Schuschnigg, after Germany's expansionary territorialism in the Rhineland. A buffer between the fascists and the communists. A buffer between, a buffer between, sang the rails to her nodding head, a buffer between, Peter and Charles, buffer between, Peter and Charles. The American Medical Association has announced its unqualified support for contraception as a method of birth control. President Roosevelt's attempt to pack the Supreme Court is costing him heavily in terms of political support. All those justices in their wigs and gowns, lying neatly side by side in a suitcase. Buffer between.

"I need a new life," she said aloud to the railway compartment. "If I can't go on with this one, I shall need a new one."

The newspaper had gotten crushed between her heavy hands and her lap. Her gaze traveled out the window past the streams of raindrops forming and running on the pane. The suburbs filed past. They were far too wet in the rain, these Englishmen's castles, their damp courses rotting and stinking, their outdoor dunnies rotting and stinking, their tiled roofs so carelessly patched that water leaked into sweating walls and chilled the babies to the bone, rotting and stinking, rotting and stinking, the whole structure undermined and dying behind the neat facade of painted steps, rosebushes, garden, fish pond, hedge.

A-MER-ica, A-MER-ica, A-MER-ica, A-MER-ica, sang the rails. IshallneedaNEWone.

When her train reached Paddington, she had a mug of tea alone in the crowded buffet. "I'm not exactly looking for anonymity," she told the cashier. "Actually, I like men." The *Daily Telegraph* told her what to do next. She went to the Odeon. Ginger Rogers and Fred Astaire in *Swing Time*. "A fine romance," she muttered, agreeing with them up there. "That's what *this* was. A fine romance. . . ." She found she could cry here in the dark when she wanted to, and was surprised. And she could eat jelly beans as if she were a little girl again.

"You're not that young," she said aloud to the lovers on the screen. "And I can buy you for a hundred pounds." In the darkness heads turned in alarm and someone hushed her. She giggled. "You're not that young anymore," she shouted at the top of her voice. "None of us is that young anymore!" And suddenly she was sobbing, crouched helplessly into the seat over her handbag and jelly beans, watching the figures on the screen.

The usherette came with a torch and led her away quickly to the manager's office, where they gave her smelling salts left over from the publicity for *King Kong*. "No," she said, "there's no one you can telephone." They put her in a taxi.

They were a roomful of widows. Elizabeth: lying on her bed weak and ill, as she had when they had carried her back to the resthouse after the gray and dry peninsula had crumbled and given her over to the evil of water, except that this time there was no Charles for her to await. Genevieve Pearsall: sped back from the Riviera on the first train after Elizabeth's feeble telephone call on the evening of Peter's funeral, since patiently nursing, sitting now staring into the fireplace's flames in the chair from which Henriette Malloy's stroke had tumbled her. And Henriette herself: her chair, her clock, her photograph of her dead husband, her wardrobe, her soft old lady's scent. Ginny's blue eyes shone amid the tan of Juan-les-Pins, and with memories and regrets. Her head had the slightest persistent tremble.

"It is the first time in my life that I have been without a man," said Elizabeth feebly from the bed. She had not, as she had feared, lost her mind, but she had the habit of making these wandering statements now and again, as though they helped her look listlessly for something. "I don't know what to do with the rest of my life."

She stirred restlessly in the bed, and Ginny looked at her, at the cold teapot, at the crumbled soda biscuits.

"When someone we love dies," said Ginny thoughtfully, "what they take with them is *really* irreplaceable." She paused to stare at the flames. "When my mother died, there was no one left to remember me as a girl. I didn't know what I was anymore, as a girl. There was no one to tell me. And my boys? When my boys died? It wasn't just that I was no longer a mother. It was as though I never had been one."

The room was dark with silence and old wood.

"These last years," said Elizabeth from the bed, "have been nothing but loss after loss for me." Her voice was full of self-pity that she did not hear because she felt so utterly miserable.

Ginny shook herself and sighed, then raised her eyebrows and spoke dryly. "My dear Elizabeth! The story of growing old! Perhaps, as some say, the story of life." She stood up slowly and smoothed her dress. "But one goes on, you know. I do not quite know why, but there it is."

Tears came into Elizabeth's eyes, but as Ginny moved more briskly to the bed and began to straighten the remains of afternoon tea, she did not notice.

"When my boys were killed, I was almost the same age as you now," she said. "Do you remember?" She looked at Elizabeth.

"Of course."

"And what was I like then? How was I different after?"

Elizabeth shook her head plaintively and almost whined her reply. "You pulled yourself together. You didn't change."

"Didn't change? My dear Elizabeth, what rubbish! In what did I *not* change?" She leaned over Elizabeth to straighten the pillow, and in doing so, sat her up and looked her directly in the eye. "You know me better than that," she said brusquely.

Elizabeth looked at her uneasily, then spoke tentatively. "You felt less?"

"Indeed," said Ginny dryly. "I felt less. I allowed myself to feel very little at all. I became, as they say, superficial. Ever since, I have taken great care to stay on the surface of life." She straightened and stood over Elizabeth, who looked at her dumbly, and when she spoke again, her voice had become distant. "She thinks she's unfortunate, doesn't she?" she mocked. "Loses a husband, a lover, and thinks she's lost everything?" She paused. "You still have a daughter."

"A daughter too busy even to come back from holiday when I ask her," she complained.

Ginny picked up the teacup from the bedside table, then banged it down again sharply, so that Elizabeth flinched. When she spoke, her voice was hard and almost cruel. "You have a daughter. You know how to earn a living. You have years ahead of you. Survival is a fact, Mrs. Wingate, not a game. I used to think when you were young that you were too weak, but the simp in you faded away a long time ago. I find nothing so repellent as self-pity." Suddenly she leaned over the bed as if she would hit Elizabeth, who started back, but she instead grabbed the top of the sheet and blanket and stripped them back as far as Elizabeth's feet in one grand gesture. "Now, get up!" she said, filled with anger. "Get up and stop feeling sorry for yourself. Get up and get dressed. You've had a soft life. Now, see if you can live a hard one."

For moments the two glared at each other, one standing, the other lying. Then Ginny spun and strode to fling open the wardrobe to reveal a waterfall of dresses. "What will you wear?" she said. "The polka-dot? This gray? Or shall I look for a little something in *black* so you can make sure everyone knows how badly off you are?"

Elizabeth, disordered with hurt and rage, clutched the blanket in front of her but sat up on the edge of the bed. Ginny snatched the polka-dot dress from the hanger and threw it at her across the room so that she had to seize it.

"Come on out and fight, widow woman," she said mockingly. "Let's see if you can live without a man and not feel sorry for yourself."

46

May 1937

Because she intended it that way and had always kept herself to herself, people thought of Mabel Greggs as having lived her life secondhand, through others. She was quiet, and chunky, and forty-five, and so modest that not even Ginny Pearsall could produce a good reason for disliking her. But as Ginny somehow suspected, the truth about Mabel was, as it had always been, rather different.

By the end of Coronation Week, Mabel felt that she had been on her feet for a month, and she was glad to put them up before Charlie came home and after Mrs. Prosser had gone back downstairs with the special coronation tea set because it would save the energy of doing the washing up. Dulcimer Street, in Pimlico, is one of those many anonymous gifts which nineteenth-century London bequeathed to the twentieth-century poor after the wrappings came apart. The west side of the street had gone commercial, its neat facades peeling and spotted with "To Rent" signs. The east side, Mabel's side, still kept up the pretense, even though it had long since become all flats and bed-sitters. Mabel had rented her two rooms at Number 10, first-floor back, about five years previous, the very week that brother Fred had sent his first little supplement from Hollywood. Here she was known as Mrs. Phipps. Mrs. Prosser, the lady who occupied the ground-floor front with her husband and daughter, thought it sad that her husband had to travel so much and nice that his wife traveled with him, though how she managed, Mrs. Prosser couldn't imagine, having to do her shopping and housework twice a week like lightning and never getting a day to properly rest up.

"Never mind," she said to her husband. "He makes a good living, it seems, and in this day and age, that's what counts."

Mabel sighed and rose to her feet. Like it or not, she couldn't postpone her little talk with Charlie any longer. Better to get it done tonight and they'd have the whole holiday to talk it over. "Whole holiday!" she mocked. Half a day sneaked from his family! When he got home, they kissed and she put his tea of sausage and tomato in front of him and listened to his usual complaint about the smell of kipper drifting down the two pairs of stairs from the landing where Mr. Puddy cooked. It had been a good week, but tiring. Up all night, just because the police said you had to be in place by five to see the procession, even though it had been worth it. By arrangement, she had even spotted Charlie with his family, but they hadn't talked much about the procession itself, afterward.

"He has a nice face, doesn't he?" had been Mabel's major comment on the new king.

Then next night, after a bit of sleep, going out late and walking miles to see the illuminations! Daft, that had been, but more fun than they'd had in years, going out together. All the way from the Tower of London, lit up for the first time in history, as far as the flowers in St. James's Park and the great facade of the palace, with Queen Victoria in front. They'd sung "God Save the King" with thousands of others, hoping they'd come out on the balcony again. Then up to Piccadilly Circus, where the crowds had been so huge that they had spilled over the barricades and special traffic signs. The police had been saying over the loudspeaker, "Pedestrians! Do not pass before moving vehicles. The traffic will shortly be held up for you." Then they had given up. "Ladies and gentlemen," the loudspeaker had intoned, "the Circus is yours!" And after the cheer had subsided, Charlie had gotten in a good one. "What about the bread, then!" he had called out, and raised a good laugh. Then back to the local pub, open till midnight for the first time since the war, singing "Land of Hope and Glory" and a lot of swing songs with the people from Dulcimer Street. A good time, that, thought Mabel. Best we've ever had, perhaps. She looked at Charlie, wiping his plate clean with a slice of bread.

"Ah, this is what marriage ought to be," said Charlie, sitting back with a smothered belch and offering up his cup for filling. "Always makes me relax, this place."

Charlie liked to complain that the real Mrs. Phipps was always on at him about the house and the little Phippses (not so little now, either), though Mabel never said anything in reply and privately thought it all a bit of my eye. Nonetheless she pulled out last week's *Sunday Times* and prepared to read it aloud to him, for it was from that stately vehicle that Mr. Phipps drew the points which Mr. Phipps told Mrs. Phipps he had made as a member of the South London Debating Society which he attended every Friday night and which ended, unfortunately, far too late for him to get the last bus back to Maida Vale.

After the reading, Mabel took out her knitting while Charlie scanned the pages for the financial notes.

He's a comfortable man, Charlie Phipps, she was thinking. I shall miss him.

Eventually Charlie reached that point where his digestion would allow him to pay attention to his mistress. He pushed away the paper, poured himself a last cup of lukewarm tea, and said, "So what have we got on for the weekend, then?"

Mabel held out her knitting in front of her–a nice plum sweater, it was, just the color of that one she'd seen in Marks and Sparks–and counted stitches for a while, looking over the top of her glasses to do it. Mr. Phipps realized that something was up.

"Well," she said eventually, "I think my time has come at last."

For a split second Mr. Phipps felt mortality in his flesh, but he was used to her orphic ways and waited for her to explain.

"I've about made up my mind to leave the Jameses," she said.

"Well, that's a bit of a turn-up," he said.

He was surprised, because she had been with Jennifer or her mother forever, and her grumbling had always seemed enough to let off her head of steam. But he wasn't worried. Mabel had always been a good earner, and the little something she got from her pretty-boy brother stood her in good stead. She's never taken a penny from *him.*

"I hate to say it about someone I as good as brought up," she said eventually. The needles clicked. "But there are things a lady does, and things a lady doesn't," she concluded.

"What's that, then?" he asked. "That husband been giving her trouble again? He's a nasty piece of work if there ever was one."

"It's not him this time. At least, not directly. It's her."

"Your precious Jennifer?"

"Precious is as precious does."

"Well, what is it, then?" he queried impatiently.

"You know that trip we took to Cannes?" she said.

"How could I forget it?" he leered. "A whole month without you?"

"You know what she did, like I told you, two years ago without telling anyone? Well, she went and did it again."

"What? You mean she . . . ? She didn't!"

"She *did.* Knew the whole routine, she did. Went off for a couple of days, came back right as rain. I wouldn't have known anything if she hadn't told me. Thought I wouldn't mind, and I was that shocked I didn't set her straight."

"Seems to me you'd better teach her a thing or two about avoiding it," he leered.

"It's not that," she said, disgusted. "I've my standards, you know."

"Well," he said judiciously. "Whose was it, then?"

"Her husband's. No doubt about that." Charlie wondered if she wasn't a bit quick off the blocks with that answer. Brother Fred had been in town till after New Year's, and though Mabel denied there was ever anything between those two, Charlie had his own opinion. But it wasn't any of his business, was it?

"Then I don't see what you're on about," he said. "What do you expect from a film star?"

"Lot of nonsense they talk about film stars," said Mabel, starting to wrap up her knitting. "You shouldn't believe what you read in the papers."

"Well, it is their business, isn't it? Hubbie know?"

"Not unless I tell him."

"I'd stay well out of it if I were you."

"There are some things that are just a bit much. Besides, I don't like being *used* like that, specially not by a whipper-snapper I as good as brought up. What her father would say, I can't imagine."

They mulled over this intriguing subject for some time, and it wasn't until they were both almost ready for bed that Charlie thought to ask her of the future: "What will you do, then?"

"Changes," said Mabel, unclipping her stockings from her corset. "Big changes." She turned directly to look at him. "I'm thinking you and I ought to either settle down or end it, I am." She stood one hand on a hip, making her casualness defiance.

He was goggle-eyed, leaning back on the bed in his underpants and singlet. "You mean get married?" he said incredulously.

"I don't care how we do it," she said quietly, for this was an answer she had long studied. "You can keep Mrs. Phipps as far as I'm concerned. I'll not take the bread out of the mouths of women and children, and she's put up with you longer than I have. But if you keep her, then I've got to keep myself, haven't I? That's the long and the short of it."

The long of it was so unchallengeably the same length as the short of it that Charlie Phipps swallowed it all at once. "What will you do, then?" he said dazedly.

"Fred," said Mabel.

"Fred what?"

"My brother Fred. He wants me to come to America. To be his housekeeper."

"You'll never go *there!*"

"Always wanted to have a bit of a look at America," said Mabel, modestly turning her back to remove the last of her underwear and don a pink flannelette nightgown. "Ever since I was a girl. Fred says he'll buy me a ticket. First class. On the *Queen Mary,* if I like."

"Sounds like you've got it all arranged then, you do." Charlie was still stunned. "Je-e-e-sus!"

"Now, none of that, thank you," said Mabel sharply, sitting on the edge of the bed. "And there's no good in your getting all upset about it before the time comes. It won't be for a few months yet." She nudged his shoulder gently. " 'Less you're too tired, of course."

Charlie grinned, took her by the shoulders, and tipped her over backward onto the bed. "When I'm too tired for a bit of slap-and-tickle," he said, leaning over her, "then you can go to America with knobs on, far as I care."

"Oh, you!" she said, and rolled over to embrace him fully.

The week after Whitsun, Mabel behaved in her own judgment more than fairly to Jennifer: she gave three months' notice and no reason for leaving.

"You've got to talk to her," cried a distraught Jennifer over the telephone to her mother at the office. "I can't manage without her, but she won't listen to me. She says she's leaving on the *Queen Mary* in August, and neither hell nor high water will budge her. You've got to talk to her. He can't let her do this to me. He knows how important she is to me!"

Elizabeth was almost as surprised as Jennifer. They had been together, after all, for almost twenty-five years. But she thought she could anticipate Mabel's reasons for leaving: she was forty-five, after Merry she had no future with Jennifer, and she had always been very attached to her brother. She certainly had a right to do whatever she wanted, which seemed not to have occurred to Jennifer.

Summoned to the telephone, Anthony was calm to the point of sounding callous. "After all," he said, "Merry is four. She'll need a governess, not a nurse, soon, and women like Mabel are two a penny these days."

After she and Mabel had gone to church next Sunday, Elizabeth sat them both down to the kind of good cold lunch that Mabel liked and proceeded to talk over the situation with her. Basically she was on Mabel's side, she said. She was sure there were very good reasons. It was just a pity . . .

"You don't know the half of it," said Mabel abruptly, skewering a rollmop of herring and eel.

Given this invitation, Elizabeth was able to squeeze the story out with little more than the pressure of those twenty-three years of living together. At first Mabel emphasized only the growing unpleasantness of living in the James household, so vaguely that Elizabeth thought she was complaining of no more than lack of space.

"You can't get away from it," said Mabel. "And it's not right."

When Elizabeth learned that "it" applied more to Anthony than to anything else, she was shocked.

"I wouldn't say it to anyone but you," said Mabel dourly. "And I wouldn't say it to anyone at all if I wasn't leaving and someone on the outside ought to know about it, but there's something I don't like about that gentleman. No, he never lays a rough hand on her, or I would have said something of course. I sometimes think he just doesn't like women very much. Got a nasty tongue, has that gentleman, and he uses it on Jennifer or me or whoever happens to be handy—excepting Merry, of course. I'm not one to stick my nose in, but if I were you I'd keep a sharp lookout after I'm gone."

Deeply disturbed by news that was a clear call to accept a mother's responsibility in some way, Elizabeth frowned over different courses of action while Mabel grumbled her way through the better half of a tin of chilled asparagus.

"And there's another matter," said Mabel eventually, "which I feel it is my responsibility to tell you about, even though I promised not to."

Elizabeth looked at her questioningly. Mabel seemed very uneasy, like a schoolmistress equally scared of parents and duty, and it was in a schoolmistress's prim tones and circumlocutions that she proceeded to tell Elizabeth that her daughter had undergone at least two abortions.

Macaulay's dictum is well-known: "We know nothing so ridiculous as the British public in one of its periodical fits of morality." At Glyndebourne just a few months previous, Elizabeth had vowed to have faith in her daughter come what may, but while faith may move mountains, it has difficulty with molehills, which are likely to trip us up at any moment. Having long since discarded most of the rules provided by her religious upbringing, Elizabeth liked to say that she agreed with Dean Inge, who pointed out that the Church's rules are based on the law of Christ and that "what this is, is by no means clear." Now, however, she was possessed by a disgust for her daughter's deed that overthrew both faith and reason in favor of a rule. Sitting over lunch in her own sunny kitchen, she felt revulsion for her daughter.

Perhaps if she had had a little time to regain her balance, all would have been well, but Jennifer was impatient to find out the result of her mother's interview with Mabel, so that Mabel had scarcely broken the news to Elizabeth when they were interrupted by a knock at the front door, which opened to reveal an anxiously smiling Jennifer—her little sports car at the curb, Merry at her knee, all hope that her mother would have been able to keep her nanny for her.

"Mabel has told me," said her mother, hanging on to the door, "what you were doing in Cannes this March while I was alone with Peter. It's the most terrible thing you have done. I *cannot* forgive it."

Her words froze Jennifer's terrible guilt in a blaze of frigid light. Her only hope of forgiving herself had been the deed's privacy. Made in a press of speed and anxiety, Jennifer could justify her decision to abort only if she saw it as courageous. Now she felt disemboweled, and loathsome. There might have been a slender chance of better understanding if Merry's presence had not prevented rage and tears, if guilt and grief and pain had emerged and been assuaged. But standing in that narrow hall with the child big-eyed at their fury, the women could only hiss at each other. Left only with arrogant defensiveness, Jennifer evoked every bit of self-righteous coldness her mother could muster. The dreadful words sparked between them as they stood in the hall's Victorian darkness, Mabel standing appalled at the kitchen door.

Within minutes, a red-faced Jennifer was headed back down the corridor toward the little sports car, dragging a frightened Merry behind her. As she stood in the front door, she had the rage of the persecuted to arm her. "I should be glad," she said, standing there against the light, "if you, Mabel, come back to Curzon Street only to remove your belongings." She turned her blazing green eyes on her mother. "And I should be just as glad if I never hear from *you* again."

She left the door open wide so that her mother had to watch the two surviving members of her family walk from her life. It was almost evening, and the light had taken on the same golden tone it had had last year at Glyndebourne. Elizabeth's eyes fastened on the splash of black paint that had dried on the mudguard of Jennifer's car that night, curving out of the evening sky from that tumbling can. It reminded her instantly of her child's vulnerability to chance and therefore brought her a fierce spasm of fear and regret. She had a sense of isolation that was the mirror image of what her daughter felt.

"Oh, Nanny," Elizabeth said. "What have we done to our girl?"

Mabel looked at her grimly. "She brought it on her own self," she said.

In the weeks that followed the fight between Jennifer and Elizabeth, Jennifer declared her mother worthless because she believed her mother thought her worthless, and Elizabeth, though grieving for her daughter and grandchild and feeling desperately alone, did not pick up the telephone to dial, to say, "Jennifer?" Instead she fell into trust with the man she knew better than to trust. She accepted Anthony's invitations to take tea once a week. Jennifer, having been told of the meetings, believed with cold despair that her husband and her mother had formed an alliance against her.

47

July 1937

"So what's she on her high horse for?" sniffed Mrs. Moore. Elizabeth had just snapped at her over some piece of missing paperwork. "Been like this all day, and I've just about had enough."

The day was damp and steamy, one of those in which July alternates shower and sun. The entire staff was irritable, dreaming of August holidays to come.

"She's turning into a bear, an absolute bear!" concluded Mrs. Moore, who had the habit of using complaints to Mr. Thomas Hendricks in order to settle her ruffled feathers.

"I dunno," said Mr. Thomas Hendricks wearily, inking himself in his impatience with a bent nib. "There's been something going on all day between her and old Harris. I'm keeping my nose out of it."

Mrs. Moore glanced at Mr. Harris' closed door. "I wonder what they're up to in there," she speculated. "In and out of his office all day. There's something afoot, mark my words."

"So she's gone out, why not ask Harris himself?" Mr. Thomas Hendricks knew that Mrs. Moore rarely needed urging. "She'll not tell you till she wants to, you know that."

She pursed her lips to express the unpleasantness of duty. "Perhaps I will just ask Mr. Harris." She picked up a little pile of forms and headed for his office door.

Mr. Thomas Hendricks yawned, lit another cigarette from the end of the one he was smoking, and abandoned the purer world of mathematical calculation. Old Moore thought Wingate was after Harris, but that was a lot of my-eye-and-a-bicycle. If Mrs. W. was interested in anyone, it was that Donald Wallace chap, the Yank. Thick as thieves, they were. Well, after all, her being a widow, him away from home months on end: what did you expect? He daydreamed until Mrs. Moore sailed out of Mr. Harris' office round with news.

"So what do you think of *that!*" she said triumphantly, crossing her arms under her breasts in the soft red dress which Mr. Harris had gotten on the cheap.

"That what?" he said blearily, scratching an eye full of smoke.

"Off to America, would you believe it? She's off to America!"

"Come off it," he said.

Surprise had made Mrs. Moore incoherent, and it took him time to assemble the story. According to Mr. Harris, she said, Mrs. Wingate that morning had asked for a year's leave of absence starting in the autumn. She'd had an offer from Mr. Wallace and his partners to come to America for some special job. According to Mr. Harris, he'd put her straight right smart.

"I told 'er it's not on, that's what I told 'er," he had said to Mrs. Moore. "Us or them, I told 'er. You can't have both. You can't go traipsin' around the world and expect us just to keep the seat warm for you, I told 'er."

She had not, it seemed, quite made up her mind yet.

"Be a nice step up for you, wouldn't it?" Mr. Thomas Hendricks grinned at the flushed Mrs. Moore. "Old Moore ruling the roost, eh? We'd have to watch our P's and Q's then, wouldn't we? My word!"

"And I certainly wouldn't put up with any more of *your* impertinence," she snapped.

Wallace had made the offer during one of their now usual luncheons toward the end of his annual visit. He knew it would come as a surprise, and he took great pleasure in it. The American partners, it seemed, were to open an office in Los Angeles, now almost large enough to become a major market and of special importance because of what he called "the entertainment industry."

"Normally we wouldn't think of having either a woman or a foreigner involved in an operation like this," he said solemnly. "But I'm telling you, that town is different. You gotta have a gimmick, they say." He grinned widely, arms apart. "And you–you're our gimmick! With that accent, that goddamn class! They love you Brits out there. You'd be a smash. And you'd be working right under me, if you'll excuse the expression."

Should she accept, she would spend two weeks in New York at "headquarters," during which time she could stay all expenses paid at "the Waldorf," or with the Wallaces themselves "in Connecticut." Then on to Chicago for a week to look at a "branch operation."

Then on to L.A., where an "advance team" was already checking out "space availability."

"You'd be doing just what you do here, Elizabeth," Wallace had said excitedly. "P.R. stuff and sales. Only you'd be working for me instead of that crud Harris, and you'd be making twice the money. I tell you with all due respect to Their Majesties, London ain't got half as much to offer as L.A. That is one town!"

So there it was. The offer of a future. What she had wanted, perhaps even before Peter's death. All she had to do was say yes. It took her six weeks to make up her mind.

For several years loss had been the theme of Elizabeth's life: her mother, Charles, money, Peter, finally Jennifer and Merry. It sometimes seemed to her that in coming to London in 1919 she had made the biggest mistake of her life. This center of the world had given her no center. What was to stop her trying somewhere else? This was not Home. She had no Home. And though she might be fifty-six, she could give the mirror the lie, telling that face she didn't feel half as old as it looked. How old had Maman been when she had set off to work in a munitions factory, for God's sake? If one could do something, one should do it. Either she was too old to do it, or she was too old not to do it. In early adulthood we think the things around us trap us, but by middle age we know that we have trapped ourselves. The thought made Elizabeth nervous. What did she really want? She had told Don Wallace that she would let him know by September.

"What should I do?" she demanded of Peter's Buddha.

The habit of bouncing off men made Elizabeth discuss her problem with Anthony. He had telephoned her the night after her fight with Jennifer, who in tears had confessed the true cause of Mabel's departure. The news had not upset him as Elizabeth would have expected. She had the impression that his main regret was that another baby would have kept Jennifer at home. But he had offered himself as a conduit for news, a confidential source, and Elizabeth could not refuse, even though she no longer really trusted him.

Their weekly teas were taken at the Savoy, which pleased her for its view of the Thames and its memories of wealthier days. He professed concern at Jennifer's thinness. She blamed overwork. He worried about the frequency of Merry's tears. "Does Jennifer know?" she asked. Her bearing made the waiters deferential, which he liked. Gloves and handbag were not really top-drawer, he noted, but the hairdo upswept to emphasize her graying temples was very flattering.

It was not until they had left the hotel and were walking up the alley to the Strand between the Grill and the theater that she chose to surprise him. "There's one thing you should know," she said as they rounded the shoulder of a backing taxi. "I'm thinking of going to America."

"How very pleasant," he said. "You must let me give you some names, some letters of introduction." He was wondering where she got the money. "How long a visit?"

"Thank you," she said as they passed the theater, which brought them both memories of one of Jennifer's successes. "I'm not sure one can call it a visit." She paused to straighten her gloves unnecessarily, then looked up at him with eyes candid but slightly apprehensive. "I'm thinking of going there to live."

"Good God!" he exclaimed. "At your age?"

"Anthony!" she laughed. "Where is your tact?"

He apologized offhandedly, for his surprise was great. "It's just that you are so very English, Elizabeth. All your ties—they're here."

She reassured him as they turned the corner toward Charing Cross and the Underground, the pedestrians buffeting them, "Don't worry. I shan't give up all my ties yet. I shall only lease out the Wimbledon house for now."

He grabbed her elbow and pulled her into the doorway of a men's shirt shop, from whose interior two middle-aged clerks gazed with equal indifference at them, the pedestrians, and the red buses roaring and smoking down the street.

"Forgive me for prying," he said. "But how can you think of doing this without . . . well, without a man? What will you do for money? Have you *work* there?" He made the word sound like a disease, and she mocked his accent in reply.

"Yes," she laughed, "I have *work* there. With Mr. Wallace, one of our American partners. A new office. They seem to think I will be useful as well as decorative."

"Good God!" said Anthony again. "I say . . . Look, I can't see what possible amusement you can find in going to live in a land filled with gangsters, and away from your family."

"At the moment, my family, as you so nicely put it, seems to have very little use for me. I do have a life of my own, you know."

"But they may need you. At any moment! My God, how can you

tell? Really, Elizabeth, this is the most absurd idea. Tell me you are not serious about it!"

"Nothing's settled," she admitted reluctantly, wondering at how shaken he seemed. "But surely you make too much of this, Anthony? Good heavens, if Jennifer's plans work out, we shall all see each other over there."

"Never, I assure you." His reply cracked like a whip. "It is here that Jennifer needs you—that Merry needs you. Not wandering the world like the ancient mariner!"

She was offended and stepped back into the stream of pedestrians on the pavement. They walked on at the pace of the worn crowd, staying obediently to the left of the yellow line.

"I had not really planned just to drop this on you, Anthony, and I do apologize for startling you. Quite frankly, I hadn't thought it would make that much difference. You do see that I can't just hang around on the off chance that I might be useful as a grandmother someday?"

He would not agree, and he spoke sternly in reply. "You will at least give me the opportunity to talk you out of it."

"All the opportunity you wish!" she said, surprised. "It's not a final decision, as I said. I shan't go until autumn. They call it 'the fall.' Isn't that beautiful?"

He stood and watched her walking away from him, flickering among the crowd. If she were only uncharming or unclever, he was thinking. He would as soon she fell under a bus, damn her.

He used their weekly meetings to press her to stay in London.

"What does Jennifer think?" she asked.

"I'm sorry to say she seems completely indifferent," he replied, "but I really don't think she means it."

"I'm not just a winter coat, you know, to be kept in cold storage."

He himself, he said, had come to value her support so very much. He would miss her greatly. She was the only person he could talk to about his domestic troubles. Merry would need her in years to come. Elizabeth could not say why, but the forcefulness of his appeals to her sense of family duty had the very opposite effect from what he had intended.

"I cannot imagine that whatever I contribute is really very important either to your happiness or to Merry's. I simply can't. I won't be a fringe for the rest of my life. I will not become some self-pitying old woman waiting for crumbs. I have to start a new life of my own."

She did not understand his reactions. He seemed likely to swear at her, he was so furious under that cool exterior. Elizabeth had not forgotten Mabel's warning about Anthony's home life, merely set it aside on the grounds that there was absolutely nothing she could do about it if Jennifer would not speak to her, and his demeanor in this present dispute made her suspicious. She really knew very little about him, she realized, and God knows you cannot judge men by the way they seem in public.

"I really can't see exactly why you are so determined that I not go, Anthony," she said. "It seems a trifle . . . forgive me, but a trifle exaggerated."

The reason for his opposition was not that complicated, but it was of a nature that Elizabeth would never have suspected. Quite simply, she had thwarted his plans to use her. At the moment his wife was at home, "resting," as one said, between engagements, but he knew what she had in mind. Another film, as soon as the offer came along. And then another film. And another. She would not stop, she was quite mad on the subject, as stubborn as her mother about America. A streak, he said. A streak in the Wingate women. He had succeeded in losing his wife at least one job, he knew, by knowing the chap who was putting up the money and warning him that he hoped he knew what he was doing because his wife's health, well, you know, she's rather frail for all her courage, and it wasn't a risk he'd care to take himself if any large sum were involved, just between friends, thought I owed it to you.

But he had a larger scheme. Sooner or later her big chance would come: a heavy commitment, weeks of shooting and postproduction. It was for that time that he was keeping Elizabeth in reserve. She would do very well then as a grandmother, with her Wimbledon house, big enough to take in a granddaughter and a nurse-governess, take them in on the grounds that the child *had* to have stability, could *not* go through the turmoil of another film. And her child gone, her mother in league with her husband–that would bring Jennifer to heel as nothing else would. But now even the mother was causing trouble! These damned Wingate women–both of them rotten as mothers, uncaring to the point of being unnatural. No wonder he felt bitter, and rightly so, too! If Wingate hadn't packed it in, he'd at least have someone to share the family burden.

When Anthony's appeal to Elizabeth's family feelings failed to work, he sought new arguments, and as they met week by week, Elizabeth discovered that they were involved in a kind of chess game which she actively enjoyed. She got clearer and clearer about what she wanted.

"America's economic situation," he said, his pale banker's hands fiddling with the salt cellar. "An absolute disaster! You'll be impoverished if things go wrong, you know, and I may be unable to help."

"But I thought you so admired capitalism?" she said brightly.

"Precisely," he said, thinking fast. "Capitalism and Roosevelt are very different matters. He's much closer to communism, you realize."

"But, Anthony dear, you know my political sympathies." She smiled. "You can scarcely expect me to agree with you."

"There will be the most frightful bill to pay, you know, and America is the most violent country in the world."

"Violent?" she said sharply. "And what of the war dear Europe is about to have? In America I shan't wait for a bomb to fall on my head, and there won't even be any lists of names in the newspapers for me to look at." Her face was bleak with recollection. "Your safe little English island won't be so safe this time," she said nastily, "and I don't intend to be with you."

"But that is rank cowardice!"

"Of course," she said calmly. "Cowardice is the only refuge of sane people. I'm a woman, so I don't have to be ashamed of it."

But at their next meeting he was back with more arguments: "The Americans have no sense of station, you know. They have no discipline.

"You won't find the Negroes amusing, I assure you." He spoke of the riots in Chicago and Detroit, of the Ku Klux Klan and the Lindbergh kidnapping, of Upton Sinclair and Father Coughlin and Huey Long and Earl Browder and Americans' lack of table manners. She listened with patience and a polite smile.

"Then let me appeal to your common sense, Elizabeth," he said solemnly, swilling brandy in his glass and leaning slightly backward. "I wouldn't say this to most people, darling, but my experience in working on the Swiss Bank Secrecy Act in thirty-three opened my eyes to something we all should realize, no matter how unpleasant it is. I don't at all agree with what Hitler is doing to the Jews, of course, but I understand his point of view. Wherever the Jews go—and they are flooding into America these days—wherever they go, trouble follows. I'm sure it's not all their fault, of course, some of them are very likable, but let me recommend that you think about what's happening—if they go to America, do you really think they'll let the country stay out of a war against Germany? Really? You'll find they practically run the place already, you know."

She was exasperated. "Anthony, really!" she protested. "You sound like a real Colonel Blimp. You can't mean it. You sound as though you despise Americans."

He flushed with anger. "I despise a great many people, and for good reason. My judgments are based on experience."

His arrogance made her withdraw physically, an unconscious recognition of what she could not comprehend: that among those Anthony despised were women. Anthony had gone to war a youth. He now looked on that youth clinically, as someone who had swallowed anything anyone had told him about life and men, so bloody naive that all one could say for him was that he had learned fast: Life is survival; competition with other males is a man's only proper function. What could a woman know about that, without war? How would a woman learn it anyway, since she couldn't by her very nature share those things that males shared, that keen joy in each other's being that was all the keener for having no smell of sex about it. To Anthony, competition was the only avenue to love.

He had fallen in love with manliness one night on the battlefield. Sent out on useless patrol, they had met Germans on a similar mission, poking quietly about no-man's-land, and the two groups had mingled in the darkness with all the sounds of lust—the grunts and panting and thumps—each side terrified for the quiet. It had been not lust but murder. He had grappled with a youth his own age, a grotesque partner in a dance of staggering and tumbling among the shell holes, their breaths mingling as the stubble on their cheeks rasped. Anthony had finally freed his knife arm, pulled back his elbow, thrust the blade home, into the groin, into the belly, again, and he had felt the other youth's erection filled with blood spring against him where their bellies strained together even as his grip weakened, and he had looked so pale, so blond, so young in that half-light of a far-off flare drifting to earth—like a lover swooning to the ground as he left Anthony standing there above him, splay-legged, knife dark with blood, panting, exalted. Each, Anthony knew, had gratitude for the other. He had never since felt gratitude for a woman.

Now he glared at Elizabeth, unsure whether he wanted her to surrender or to fight, watching half-admiringly her attempt to conceal her shock at his roughness. She was as stubborn as her daughter.

She looked away from him but lifted her chin and spoke. "Your judgments," she said, "contain too much hatred for my taste."

He grinned, sensing submission. But he was an English gentleman and therefore used to disguising his hatreds as opinions. He would be seen to compete fairly. So he tried another argument: America's terrible climate, tornadoes, hurricanes, snowstorms, dust storms, droughts, blizzards. It was a mistake; she laughed, having had time to recover.

"You'll have the Red Indians scalping me next, I believe," she said calmly. "But I'm told on the contrary that the California climate is very agreeable."

"California?" He had not known her destination was California, and it gave him fresh energy: earthquakes, fires, Mexicans; the cults for strange religions; the total absence of culture, the sheer mad primitivism of the place stuck there on the other side of desert at the fringe of ocean. "California?" he said. "But that's where people go when there's nowhere else for them to fit!"

She paid him the compliment of taking him seriously. "Has it ever occurred to you that perhaps I would fit there very well, and for that very reason, Anthony?"

"But you can't be serious," he said as though thunderstruck. "It's the frontier without the hope."

"On the contrary," she checked. "It would seem to me that hope is exactly what California offers to people–people like me."

For a few moments, each studied their hands, playing with the forks and spoons and wrecked sandwiches that lay between them.

Elizabeth sought normality by a lighter tone. "You are so eager to convince me," she said, "that I'm surprised you don't try a bribe." She laughed lightly as she spoke, meaning to be witty.

His reply was so savage in tone that she recoiled. "If I thought you were smart enough to take it, I would," he said.

Though Elizabeth used Anthony in order to firm up her decision for America, the fine dust of madness that sifted from his arguments made the decision difficult in another way. Her son-in-law stood revealed as a man of uncertain temper and much force. She herself could handle him, but could her daughter? And if not, was her own obligation to stay and protect Jennifer? However, because there were ill feelings between them, her daughter's marriage seemed an institution that had no doors, no windows at all. Elizabeth cared, but not enough to know what to do.

In the end she went to Ginny rather than to Jennifer, to sit before the small windows of that lady's tiny chrome-and-pressed-wood flat in St. John's Wood, where the scent of August's rose gardens blew back and forth with the curtains.

"Are you in touch with Jennifer?" asked Elizabeth.

Lady Pearsall was faintly embarrassed at being detected in disloyalty. "We do ring each other now and again," she admitted.

"What does she say about my going to America?"

"She hasn't said. I rather think she approves."

"If I do go to America, I should like you to ring her rather more often, if you would."

"What is this nonsense—*if* you go to America?"

Elizabeth gave a quick smile. "I haven't actually said yes as yet. Do you approve? You've never said a word."

"My dear, I should be the last person to advise you not to voyage to a colony! Perhaps you can do them some good. Perhaps they might like to borrow a king from us, since we have one scarcely used to spare. One would think they would be ready to admit their little mistake by now, no?" They paused to listen to the sound of children playing in the garden at the center of the square. Ginny resumed in a tone of weariness. "I can understand so well your being tired of Empire. The fun has gone out of it rather, hasn't it? I should probably go myself if I were your age. The rules one used to live by—they've all gone smash. As Aldous Huxley says, one might be better off among the savages than among the ruins of civilization." She rubbed her eyes, which had been troubling her. "Dash off to America like a good girl and enjoy yourself. I shall quite look forward to having something useful to do, keeping an eye on Jennifer."

"I rather used Anthony, you know," Elizabeth said with modest guilt. "I mean, he was very good as a sounding board to help me make up my mind about America."

"I had always thought that Jennifer would make him miserable," said Ginny thoughtfully. "But when men grow miserable, they seem to think they have the right to do anything at all, especially to women, don't they?"

Elizabeth did not reply, and soon Ginny spoke again. "Of course, you are already at least half American, are you not?"

"I?"

"You have this terribly naive belief that life has a *purpose,* that *you* should have a purpose, as though we were all always headed *toward* something."

Elizabeth was amused. "You make me sound like one of those

tourists one sees wandering around the ruins with a guidebook in hand, intent on self-improvement!"

"A happy image!" Ginny heaved herself with arthritic pain out of her chair. "Never mind. At least you shall be able to tell me who is the more interesting ruin, this side of the Atlantic or that."

For years Elizabeth had used habit, motherhood, and men to define herself, and now, making her solitary decision to give up everything she had been, she felt like a refugee. Next morning she sent a cable to Don Wallace in New York: "ACCEPT YOUR KIND OFFER STOP ARRIVE LATE SEPTEMBER STOP PLEASE INFORM ARRANGEMENTS." She signed it "Elizabeth Wingate," leaving off the "Mrs."

PART V

Before the Second War

48

August 1937–May 1938

In the space of ten months, Mabel, Jennifer, and Elizabeth all set sail for America and the future, each taking only the baggage she had to carry. Mabel was the first, in the middle of August 1937, on the *Queen Mary,* second class, pocketing the cash difference from the first-class fare sent by brother Fred on the grounds she'd be uncomfortable among the rich. Though she arranged with her downstairs neighbor Mrs. Prosser to sell the furniture from the apartment at number 10 Dulcimer Street, she still had more baggage than either Jennifer or Elizabeth, for she was going for good. Elizabeth gave her a mohair traveling-rug and promised to see her soon, but only Charlie Phipps was there to see her off at the boat train, unexpectedly teary-eyed.

When Elizabeth went a month later, also on the *Queen Mary,* her sole fareweller amid the smoke and steam of Victoria Station was Lady Pearsall, trembly with nostalgia, brave with excitement. Elizabeth took only two suitcases, one large, one small, no steamer trunk. Don Wallace's firm paid for her first-class cabin. The Wimbledon bungalow was leased to strangers who let her lock the personal bric-a-brac in what had been the maid's room. In the process of packing she found a small cache of souvenirs from Colombo days in a neglected drawer. Newspaper photos of dead soldiers and children, which she threw out. Two letters from Anthony James as a young soldier, which she read with wonder and decided to save for Jennifer later, when they were speaking again. And a list of her own qualities which she dimly remembered to have created out of some vagrancy of Victorian orderliness when she had set sail that other time to find a future overseas. She looked at the list, smiled at the girl within, and threw it away. The only superfluous items she packed, knowing she still needed them, were the clay Buddha Peter had given her years ago, and the diamonds given by Charles to reward Jennifer's birth.

Jennifer sat through those two departures, of which she was told by both Anthony and Ginny Pearsall. The packet of clippings and photographs had gone off from Korda to David O. Selznick that spring, and Jennifer lived in a vivacity of rumors about the search for a Scarlett O'Hara, agonized each time an inside story announced her discovery. She was waiting that autumn and winter of 1937, waiting into 1938. She made two movies, turned down the offer to do *Peter Pan* at Christmas because she had to be with her family, and tried to avoid fighting with Anthony. When at last she sailed in May—also on the *Queen Mary*—it was like the snapping of a stretched rubber band. She took two suitcases and a cabin trunk and hand luggage including her jewelry case and two hatboxes. She paid her own fare, first class. Ginny Pearsall was there to see her off, and she had no idea how long she planned to stay, for her departure approached the melodramatic; she left a letter for Anthony on the mantelpiece.

That winter Myron Selznick had come to town in search of stars, and in three frantic minutes at a cocktail party Jennifer's agent got across to him that there was a woman called Jennifer Wingate, that she'd be perfect for Scarlett O'Hara, that she'd just finished making the first British film in Technicolor, that Twentieth Century-Fox thought she was terrific. Myron Selznick was already Hollywood's most aggressive agent, and he was David O. Selznick's brother. Now he became Jennifer Wingate's target.

Charles Wingate's love and money had made Jennifer believe that if she pleased men, men would please her. She had pleased her father, her directors, and even her husband, just by being what she was. She had gotten what she wanted. Wanting now to star in *Gone With the Wind,* at first she waited: for Korda, for Selznick, for anyone with the power to give. She lived those months with nerves grated by the thin high whine of frustration. That year was the driest since 1785. To save the greens, St. Andrew's golf course closed. All through England, little old ladies used steaming kettles to swell organ pipes in the churches back into pitch, and in the shallow riverbeds the salmon died unspawned. And Jennifer, parched for success shriveled into an inevitable decision.

She called her agent twice a week.

"I can get you plays," he said. "I can get you other films." Later, less patient: "I can't get it for you, and Korda won't try further unless your bloody husband lets you sign a long-term contract. We're all flesh peddlers. You included. So peddle." And in dry, dusty May: "I've got you Myron. The rest is up to you. Give my regards to Hollywood and Vine."

In her elegant drawing room Jennifer slid the receiver back into its cradle. She could hear Merry laughing upstairs with the nurse-governess. She looked at her wedding photo taken on the steps of the Brompton Oratory, her dress and veil blown by wind, her eyes filled with stars. She picked up the telephone again gingerly and turned her address book to the right page: C for Cunard White Star Steamship Line, the number written there months ago for purposes of magic. She listened to the squirrel-squeak as the number rang.

Bugger Alex Korda, she thought. Even if I won't sign his bloody contract, he could have done more for me. The telephone rang in that steamship office. It's not that I won't. I can't. Why won't they understand?

Someone answered the telephone line.

"I want the next sailing of the *Queen Mary,* please," she said. "Two tickets to New York; one adult with accompanying five-year-old. No, one way, please. First class. But not expensive, thank you. Thursday? This Thursday? But I can't . . . Yes, this Thursday will be fine, thank you." She sank back into the armchair and wondered what she had done.

When she had made the bargain with Anthony–his assent not to interfere with her career in exchange for her promise never to sign a long-term contract–she had believed herself businesslike and fair. She realized that a bargain which required her to choose husband over self was like those bargains made by her mother and grandmother, but she was also determined to do better than they had. She would not, like Henriette Malloy, grow bitter at having chosen duty. She would not, like Elizabeth Wingate, wander between choices, never fully discovering who she was. Her decision made, she was not greatly worried about Anthony. She had chosen to be secretive only to avoid fuss. She wouldn't sign a contract, or if she had to, she'd get out of it after *Gone With the Wind,* so going to Hollywood wasn't really breaking their bargain. Neither Anthony nor David Selznick would, she believed, really punish her.

And yet now in that elegant living room, staring at the telephone by which she had made her decision real, she felt utterly miserable. In that quiet room an enormous but not unexpected feeling of guilt swept over her. She felt that she had betrayed not just Anthony, not just Merry, but herself. She had won action; she had lost the balance she had fought to preserve.

She sensed in those moments in the quiet room that not just her life but her character had taken some decisive turn. She knew she had to be a wife and mother. That was her foundation and her capstone, without which the structure of her self was no structure at all. But it was not enough, to be just a woman. She had always been special. I'm an *actress,* she had told herself. For months she had thought about what Gladys Cooper had said at Glyndebourne. I *have* to be an actress, she had told herself—so often and so loud that she knew she did not really believe it, so that she damned her own restlessness. She did not blame Anthony; she blamed herself, for wanting too much, for not settling for what she had. But she still believed that she could have it all.

Her choice to try for everything she wanted now made at last, she sat there among the Regency restraint of her drawing room—the lines orderly, the colors clear—and briefly glimpsed the kind of person she might now become: deceitful, vain, all the other adjectives that Ravenscroft and her mother had taught her to despise. Old guilts renewed themselves, and she responded. She *would* not give in. She had faced down those adjectives over the abortion: her mother's face, eyes, words; Mabel's pursed and condemnatory lips; Anthony's stillness when she told him. She would *not* throw all that away now. And suddenly she was exhausted, feeling the bleakness of the need to build alone.

Abruptly she stood up and lit another cigarette, staring at the photograph of herself on her wedding day.

I shall not think about consequences until I have to, she promised the photograph. She smiled ironically. I'll think about that tomorrow.

She went upstairs to start packing. She knew only that to do nothing would be to lose. She was willing to pull herself apart rather than that.

Anthony, who saw Jennifer as willful and himself as her bridle, believed that her search for Scarlett was almost over, and he was reasonably content when he accompanied her the next Thursday night to see Maurice Chevalier at the Café de Paris. She seemed nervous and inattentive to their friends, but whenever she got depressed like this he had learned just to leave her alone. He was not surprised when she excused herself to go to the ladies' cloakroom and sent a note by the cigarette girl to say she had gone home early because of a migraine. He intended not to let her spoil his evening.

She left the nightclub quickly. The doorman summoned the limousine she had booked, and she stood there in the cool wind, holding the collar of her silver wolf-fur coat—Anthony's wedding present—tight at her neck, the emeralds at her ears glittering in the doorway's bright lights. "I want you to drive fast," she murmured to the Daimler's driver. For one moment she hesitated as though it were not too late to go back, descend the stairs, sit down next to Anthony, allow a great moment of life to pass like the flutter of a bat's wing. But she had paused only for inventory. The luggage already on board ship. Her passport in her evening bag. The note leaning against the clock on the mantelpiece. She shook her head and climbed into the back of the car. The doorman slammed the door behind her and tipped his cap lightly.

They were in Southampton well before midnight, the Daimler pulling quietly up at the nearest entrance to the departure shed on the wooden dock. She could not see the ship, just the entrance to the single gangway that remained in place for late arrivals, clotted by officials, crew, and a few passengers. She looked frozen, white face an orchid in a slant of moon-colored neon light that shone through the window. It was not too late. She could change her mind. The thought of suffering for duty had its own grim appeal.

Her fist clenched over the peacock-green evening bag bright with diamantés. Then she opened the car door, said good night to the chauffeur, and began to walk toward the gangway, the heels of her evening slippers hitting the ground as though she were pinning herself to decisiveness. As the Daimler made the dock's wood ties rumble with its departure, her steps slowed and stopped until she stood staring at the people a hundred yards in front of her with fright on her face. He had found out already. He would be there. He had telephoned the police. She could see police there, in front of her. She slipped sideways to a small door in the wall, and as she clicked it shut behind her back, her native theatricality made her lean against it. The interior of the departure shed was huge, neon-lit, and open on the opposite side to the giant black-and-white glisten of the *Queen Mary*'s flank, its portholes all alight, random streams of water hiccuping from mysterious vents. Between her and the ship lay a shoulder-high wall of new sandbags, placed there to protect against the blast of coming war. The shed was empty here, and she afraid; she walked toward the people cautiously as in a weekend warehouse, her face as triangular and wary as that of a Sunday cat.

Ginny Pearsall saw her approach: a young woman in white evening dress, the gray of fur and the green flash of emeralds, the dark hair tumbling shoulder-length, the face terrified. The child looked exactly like a refugee. To Jennifer, Ginny Pearsall looked like rescue. She too was in evening dress, sitting on an upturned box in a circle of dock workers, a smile from the talk with them still on her face as her eyes met Jennifer's. She rose a little unsteadily. They spoke on top of each other's words:

"One might have known the girl would find a *different* way in."

"Thank God you are here!"

Embarrassed by the girl's astonishing beauty, the longshoremen tipped their caps and moved away as Jennifer walked quickly forward to embrace Ginny.

"Is everything all right?" she said, glancing over Ginny's shoulder.

"What should be wrong?" said Ginny. "Merry's sound asleep in your cabin with the stewardess on watch. I came ashore to wait, and I made some friends, most *amusing* friends. Did everything go smoothly at your end?"

"Yes, everything's fine. It's just . . . Oh, nothing, a stupid worry." Jennifer's fear had collapsed.

"Anthony?"

"Not really. He stayed at the restaurant, as I told you he would. They'll go on somewhere else. He won't get my letter for another hour at the soonest."

"By that time you'll be on the high seas. They have already sounded the gong. Everything went as planned at my end. Your luggage is in the cabin, and I ordered champagne."

"There was no trouble?" She spoke as though that were impossible, and Ginny, noting her glance at the ship's and government officers who had gathered in a wedding party of braid and badges, was amused.

"A few air-raid precautions, only," she said with a gesture at the sandbags. "But no special search for German spies or others with a guilty conscience. A small price for the freedom of Czechoslovakia, one would think." She was contemplative. "As long as we are ready to pay it." She studied Jennifer shrewdly, fingers tapping the back of her hand, but Jennifer ignored her undermeaning.

"Shall we board, then?" she said brightly.

Ginny paused, unmoving.

"Not yet," she said, bringing Jennifer up short. "We have to talk where we will not disturb Merry."

She allowed Jennifer no choice, her gesture turning the packing cases into thrones. Jennifer pulled out her cigarette-case. "A Sobranie?"

"We haven't had the time to talk," said Ginny firmly. "I have done everything you asked without question or argument, have I not?"

"I'm very grateful."

"As a matter of fact, I have rather enjoyed it." The two women with straw at their feet looked like actors in some odd French drama. "But that's not the point, is it?"

Jennifer used the lighting of her gold-tipped cigarette to avoid Ginny's eyes.

"What is the point, I wonder?" Ginny asked herself. She did not know daughters, but she did know rules. "I shan't give you a lecture, my dear, not about your relationship with your husband, because I long since stopped being able to understand marriage. But I cannot allow you simply to launch yourself into the unknown all alone. You must let your mother know."

Jennifer sparked instantly. "I don't need *her,*" she said.

Ginny stifled a word or two on the subject of young people's thoughtlessness, knowing that Elizabeth's need would not influence Jennifer. "But Merry," she said. "Merry does. It would be wanton to keep them apart when you will be in the same city."

She was startled by the response of Jennifer's face, which flashed with fatigue and tearfulness like a knife seen from the corner of the eye. "She has to come to me," she replied. "It was what she said, not what I did, that was wrong."

Ginny was weary with years and the memory of fights. "Your mother has always maintained that you want everything and will settle for nothing less." Jennifer flung her a startled look. "It's so unwise, my darling, so *unkind* to others."

Jennifer responded with anger and self-pity. "I have *always* done what others want. I can get *nothing* that I really want. When just once I do something that Mummy doesn't approve, she turned on me as though I were *scum.*" She had spoken childishly and was embarrassed. Now she shrugged and spoke normally, as an adult, and it was this sentence that shocked Ginny with its bitter closeness to the truth: "My mother envies me. She envies me because I do what she only dreams about."

"If you intend to leave Anthony—"

"I am not leaving Anthony," interrupted Jennifer. "I am taking

Merry for a trip without his permission. You may not believe it, but he will understand why I did it without fighting about it. It's the sort of thing he does all the time. He will probably admire me for doing it this way."

Ginny put her hand on Jennifer's knee.

"I may have helped you scheme against your husband, God forgive me, but I shall not scheme against your mother. I shall tell her quite simply what has happened, and I shall give her your address. I shall also rely on your good sense returning when you get some rest on board ship, so I shall tell her that I believe that you, having due regard for the welfare of your daughter, will telephone her soon after you arrive."

Because the last three days of adventure had exhausted her, Ginny had nothing left but disapproval. "It is very fashionable for your generation to be what you call psychological about mothers and daughters these days. Common decency would be of more use."

From the deck above came the sound of chimes and a steward's call: "All visitors ashore. Last call. All visitors ashore. Last call." Under the canvas cover of the gangway there was a gaggle of activity as officials rounded up belated passengers. People were gathering at the railings above, and the longshoremen had dispersed.

"You must go," said Ginny.

Jennifer was inured to disapproval. Hardened by Anthony, she would have responded better to almost anything else, so she did not speak or relent. She took her passport and ticket slip out, and the two women stood, not yet capable of a farewell embrace.

"At least," said Jennifer miserably, "I shall have my chance to be a star."

"Oh, Jennifer," said Ginny. "Oh, Jennifer." The weight of her years and others' folly crumbled her face, and her head throbbed with fatigue. "We don't care if you're a star. We want you happy, only happy."

The farewell embrace shimmered in the air between them, but Jennifer held it off by a stare so steely with isolation that not the greatest compassion could have broken it, let alone the confusion of loyalties that possessed Ginny.

"Good-bye," she said, a thin-lipped half-smile making her face grim.

Ginny lifted her right hand a few inches toward the younger woman. It was brown with age spots, and it trembled, speaking for her. Then she starched herself into propriety.

"Good-bye, my dear," she said lightly. "Good luck. My best love to your mother, of course."

The nervous glances of the officials summoned Jennifer, and she walked toward the gangway straight and alone, alone as her mother and nanny had been those months ago, setting off for their Americas.

49

The day after Jennifer's departure, Ginny sent her letter to Elizabeth, who was now nine months away from England and a year from the break with her daughter. Because Elizabeth had discovered the new life for which she had hoped, that old life had faded; she thought of Jennifer quite often, but of her having had an abortion never, and if she regretted their dispute, it was out of the sense that rebellion seemed to have become necessary to young people these days. She read Ginny's letter sitting in an old rattan garden chair next to a moribund swimming pool in the dappled shade provided by eucalyptus, and her reading was much interrupted by the comfortable business of social life in the hour at which one returns from work.

In coming to America in September of 1937, she had good timing. A week later and the trip would have been canceled by a letter from Don Wallace, telling her that the new crash of the New York stock market in August–all the way down again to its 1929 levels–had wiped out his partners' capital and her job. As it was, the immigration officials had received her as calmly as she had received the pink-gray dawn over the Statue of Liberty, none of them expecting yet what the press would call "Depression II."

But at the Waldorf-Astoria, tickets and a letter awaited her. No visit to headquarters, no Connecticut with Mrs. Wallace and the kids, no time to discover more than that New York, as filthy and poor as Naples, was redeemed by something magnificent called a chocolate malted, no companion on the overnight *Twentieth Century Limited* to Chicago. Wallace had gone ahead. She should follow immediately. In Chicago at the Blackstone she had a call from the regional office. Mr. Wallace had gone ahead again to L.A. and would call. She should await him in Chicago, a week at most: "At our expense, of course." They showed her the office and had her to dinner at home in a lavish house on a tree-lined street near a university. She couldn't get a word in edgeways because of the kids. The grown-ups were very nice to her, but preoccupied. "Caught us at a bad moment," said the regional manager with silver hair and a pudgy face. "We're having to let some people go."

Chicago baked under a steaming heat, and as the first week of waiting passed she watched the elms turn yellow and brown with exhaustion, but the gritty city was too exciting for her to stay in the air-cooled hotel. She was fascinated by an employment agency with a shop window on State Street placarded with job offerings and besieged by job applicants: 300 jobs, 5,000 applicants. She talked to a tubercular woman with two young children hanging on to her torn coat and a southern accent so strong she could scarcely understand her. "I come up," said the woman. "Down in Tennessee I worked from can-see to can't-see, and we'd still be eatin' wild greens since January. Ain't got no man no more. He jest couldn't take it no more and he up and went I don't know where. It's hard on the chilrun. Seems like a worker's got no rights to have no chilrun anymore." Elizabeth gave her five dollars, and the woman wept and laughed. There were strikes all over town: the barbers were sitting in the chairs of nonunion shops to keep them free of customers; the hotel workers were sitting on the cold stoves of their kitchens to keep them free of food. In the sunshine on the edge of the canal, a hearth worker fired by Republic Steel for striking sat next to a Pinkerton goon laid off for strikebreaking, and the two men, rueful about the need to do anything for money, told her about the Memorial Day Massacre earlier that year, when the police killed ten strikers and wounded a hundred more, including women. Elizabeth thought of Amritsar; all massacres are the same. Then she went to a State Street picture palace to see Fred Astaire in *Damsel in Distress,* sighing when he sang "A Foggy Day in London Town."

At last Don Wallace's voice came echoing across the wires threading the great empty spaces of the map. News not good but she should come ahead anyway. Thursday's *Chief.* To Pasadena, not L.A. He would meet her in Pasadena. How did she like America? Everyone asked her how she liked America. It was not politeness; they needed to be reassured. So did she.

The first night out on the Santa Fe *Chief,* Elizabeth sat in her Pullman and read deep into the night. Sometime around two o'clock the train pulled into a small station in the middle of the plains at a town which showed only as a glimmer of yellow light across the tracks. The train sank into stillness as though for rest, and the porter said they had a half-hour stop while the engine took on coal and water.

She might descend, he said, unhooking the door and putting the footstool in place.

The air was colder than anything she had ever known, and dry, so that the moisture in her nostrils froze. Giant white moon, giant black bowl of sky, giant white flatness of snow-covered earth stretching forever from the curve of the black train that frightened her by making now one sudden pant. The snow was crisp and just thick enough that one could not tell shadow from substance, a delusionary landscape where the human soul quivered and the human body asserted itself by a cough into the emptiness. She pulled the fur tippet close around her chin and stepped toward the platform and buildings of the station, the first to stir the earth's white cover. She tucked her gloved hands into her coat pockets, and her high heels stumbled over hidden lumps. The train's innards ticked and cracked as they cooled. Far ahead the two engines steamed, and every few minutes one or the other gave a roar like the yawn of a beast primordially squatting, and its breath made clouds of ice that hung tight to the ground. Delusion grew close to hallucination. She seemed to be making a journey out of time.

The platform had been blown clear of snow. Three high lamps threw yellow cones upon it. A single guard balanced her presence at the other end, as though they were on a seesaw. She thought of Peter and the Brighton line. She strolled, looking at notice boards, schedules, a faded map, a machine for the dispensing of gum, an empty paper rack, a luggage cart veiled by tarpaulin. From the chipped brick building a dim light glimmered, and when the train startled her with another hiss of steam and threat, she took hold of the doorknob beneath a sign that said "Waiting Room."

The room behind the door was full of bodies. Two dim overhead lights shone on a wounded wooden floor, on walls discarding the skin of their paint, on an empty fireplace with a huge mantel solid as shoulders, on the dark eyes of ticket windows shuttered with wire. A heap of clothing that she recognized as a child lay on the mantel. On the benches were bodies wrapped in the rags of blankets and the wreckage of coats. On the floor at the other side of the room lay other bodies covered by newspapers. She stood still in the door with shock, cast back into the sweat of childhood nightmare, holding the doorknob like a parent's hand.

Then the cold thin draft whining at her ankles reached someone on the floor, and they stirred to rearrange their rags, and someone else coughed, and a woman covered her child. There was a moment of stillness as they looked at the woman bringing in the cold, and it was as though danger had come in with her like a cloud of ice particles and turned to face her, hanging in the chill room.

The voice of the guard made her jump. "They bother you any, lady? Gimme the say-so and I'll move 'em on. You wanna use the place?" The voice was weary of passengers, roughened by contact with the rich, but ready to do the duty expressed by the silver-and-red badges of office. He took the doorknob from her. "You wannit, lady?"

"Oh, no! Oh, no!" she almost yelped at him. She put her hands in her pockets and her head down and stepped backward as he closed the door. "Who are they?" she said softly.

"Okies, miss, just a bunch of Okies. On their way to California from who the Christ knows where. Bums mostly, from the Hooverville down by the bridge. Railroad wants 'em off, but what are you gonna do, cold like this? Mayor says, don't want the town to get a bad name. Last winter, used to find them stiff as a board down by the bridge, so the mayor says let 'em use the waiting room, let 'em use the toilets, for Christ sake." The man shrugged, glaring up at her from the depths of a gray muffler, his red lantern as still at his side as a weapon. "Ain't anyone else ever uses this room at night. Never anyone get off at this hour!" He shrugged as though to indicate that was the end of her punishment, small good it would do. "You got five minutes," he said over his shoulder, dismissing her back to the world of warm roomettes and tablecloths and nice Negro porters with rich chuckles.

Elizabeth stumbled back along the train. She had been a rich woman in the doorway, her mouth open in surprise, her lips bright red in that yellow light, the silver fur around her neck, the warm coat of black wool, the little pixie hat with a single pheasant feather stuck above her ear, the red high-heeled shoes. She was back again briefly at Jennifer's debutante presentation when she had watched from the window as the drunken man struck and kicked at his woman. She fled back along the track, frightened that something from the waiting room might reach out to seize her, some terrible want filled with animus toward her. The gulf between her and those shadowed figures was enormous. It was not wide enough. Everyone is at risk in this country, she thought. And I know nobody. Anthony was right after all.

The porter pulled her aboard, shivering in the chill, and she told him to leave the step down for a moment, please. She flung back the sliding door to her Pullman and pulled first one, then the other suitcase up from the floor and began to rummage with frantic speed. Frilly underwear, open-toed shoes, her good skirts, her blouses, her only sweater and cardigan set, her toiletry bag, books—oh, God, she had so little with her. The engine sent a long, high whistle curling across the emptiness of the white plain, up to the glittering stars.

"Oh, God," she muttered, and she began to pull her coat off as though it were burning her, wrestling with the little foxes around her neck. As the first jerk from the engine ricocheted down the train's snake-length, she threw herself into the seat and began to force the window open. A blast of cold air dispelled the roomette's warm fog of cigarette smoke and perfume. The coat came loose at last, and just as the door marked "Waiting Room" drew abreast of her carriage, she flung it through the window, where it splayed black and flat on the platform under the yellow light. She reached back into her suitcases and began to fling clothes out: sweater, cardigan, blouses in the wind like leaves, balls of silk stockings falling and rolling, her gloves separating, and as the train pulled her abreast of the lone and red-lanterned guard hunched against the cold, his face an amazement, she shouted at him, "They should have warm coats. Give them the coat, the clothes!"

He stared at her in shock, and she watched him retreat like a cutout against the yellow lights of the platform. She fell back into her seat, letting the wind blow cold on her, feeling the silver-fox fur chill against her cheek. She was wondering how foolish she had been. She was wondering what more she could have done.

Next morning she rose to fences drifted feet deep with dust rather than snow and to breakfast under silver chafing dishes. This country is not real to me, she told herself. When I became a refugee I did what Mother said: I took my warm coat. But I do not need it. It was as though nothing bad could happen to her here, as though she were free to risk whatever she wished: the cold, the night, the poverty, her foreignness, her age, her aloneness. That night she was caught eating a steak when the carriage pulled up beside a shantytown, and she looked down on the gray figures that turned hollow eyes away and shambled off, and she felt no need to act. She let a stranger in the club car buy her a whiskey and soda and show her the photographs of the family in his wallet, and when he asked if she would like to come back to his room for another drink, she declined and made the mistake of laughing. He grew morose, then surly about her accent.

"You foreigners think this country's a midway, don't you? Come here, take our money, go off home when the party's over, eh?" He leaned and breathed on her, mean-eyed. "Let me tell you, lady, this great country ain't for sale!"

A gentleman from Omaha led him away eventually, arm over his shoulders, swaying with the train and liquor, and the gentleman's middle-aged wife with sausage curls and a print frock patted her hand and said, "I'm real sorry, honey. Don't you pay him no mind."

But he hadn't bothered her. She traveled in a bubble through whose transparent shell nothing might touch her. I know nobody, she told herself. I am free. The wife from Omaha asked her name. "Mona," she replied. "Mona Harmon-Bowman." She wondered if Charles had felt this way when he gave away pound notes.

Having no goal is, for a pilgrim, having no anxiety. Having no country is, for a fresh expatriate, having no obligations except to oneself.

Next morning she awoke to the movie world of sunshine and saguaros and orange groves, with a palm tree ragged against the straight skyline. As she snapped shut the locks on her half-empty suitcases, the platform appeared and there was Don Wallace, his pink face all expectation, and she laughed with glee. He took her hand to help her down the steps, and she leaned up to kiss him on the cheek.

Donald Wallace was relieved to find that Elizabeth's pleasure in watching them squeeze juice from fresh oranges at the station buffet vastly exceeded her alarm at his not having the promised job for her.

"But of course I shall stay," she said calmly. "I have a permit. One must be able to find some job."

"Anyway, you've got a month's pay coming to you." He was doing what he could, and brightened with a new thought. "If you don't use the return ticket we'd planned for you, maybe I can wangle a bit extra."

"Could I have it now?" She actually giggled. "I have to buy some clothes."

She found him nervous, preoccupied with personally finding the customers that would get the business on its feet. Here he somehow looked more ordinary than in London; less rather than more American. She was getting used to them already. He took her to Coulter's and Bullock's, where she laughed and buried her face in a heap of beautiful pastel shirts and had her hair shampooed and set and came out wearing a new pair of slacks to ask shyly, "Now, do I look like a proper American?" He did not recognize this new Mrs. Wingate; away from London she was somehow more individual, younger.

She would not go to a hotel because of cost, so they decided to find an apartment in the cheap residential district of Hollywood just south of Sunset Boulevard, where overbuilding and the Depression had nurtured groves of vacancy signs. She chose an apartment court called Olde Englande on Seward Avenue within a few blocks of Hollywood and Vine, consisting of sixteen two-story Mexican-style apartments arranged in groups of four around flagstone yards and a small central swimming pool spotted with the leaves of eucalyptus and loquat trees and crumbling at the rim. She took a furnished studio apartment on the first floor: a Murphy bed which soon she was to take to folding unmade into the wall; a bathroom whose tiny shelves she was to fill with the seeds of avocados sprouting on toothpicks in glasses of water; an efficiency kitchen which in a moment of delight at a cut-price store she filled with pots, pans, and more china than she could use; and weekly maid service from a meticulous and sour-smelling Hungarian woman whom, once Elizabeth had found a job, she never saw.

All this cost forty dollars a month, and in a gesture of optimism, Elizabeth spent another $4.50 a month on a telephone which had the immediate effect of making her popular with the other tenants, who had no such luxury. California life was lavishly cheap. She lived only two blocks from the supermarket at the world's first shopping mall, Crossroads of the World, whose tower with the lighted, turning globe was visible from her doorstep, and the prices were half what she had paid in London. She lusted after the pinks and reds and yellows of fruit, and buried her hands in the mounds of fresh greens. There seemed no seasons here. When they sang that the best things in life were free, one could believe them.

She plunged into residence. Wimbledon's predictable rows of houses had sought to show as little difference from each other as modesty demanded, as if individuality were a matter for flirtation rather than passion, but here in Los Angeles it advertised itself. In America, if one doesn't shout one isn't heard, the architecture taught Elizabeth. A few blocks to the west past Hollywood High School lay Grauman's Chinese Theater, in whose courtyard she knelt to test the size of her hands against the concrete image of Joan Crawford's. A few blocks to the east was the Pantages Theater, its great floodlights hooded like hunting birds during daylight. Due north lay the small stores of Hollywood Boulevard, where she went often to an automat to prove to herself that she was at last in the land of marvels: a three-course meal for twenty cents, and no visible servants.

Her eyes slowly began to lose their freshness. The sunshine and the palm trees and the blue sky and the huge cars and the light clothes and the shrill neon and the sound of music blasting into the open air and the cups of coffee at diner counters became things she was accustomed to, until there came a day when she decided not to buy another avocado. She bought a newspaper for the first time in a month, but there was no news of England, just land-use squabbles, and a water-rights scandal, and plans for taking over the big ranch at Malibu from the widow Rindge. That would be a hem to the country's west, she thought. In California, the news taught her, we have gone as far as we can go.

Earlier in her life Elizabeth had never found initiative easy, but in America she acted as though she could do anything she wanted. When she found that unmarried women could not get credit at Bullock's, she even lied, giving her husband Don Wallace's occupation and business address. Her world was anything but narrow, and the job she soon found made it diverse. She used some of the money from her return-ticket allowance to take a real-estate course at a fly-by-night school on Santa Monica Boulevard and the rest of it to buy an old Ford coupé. On graduation evening she drove out Sunset Boulevard to the heights along the bridle path and pulled off into the dry grasses somewhere near Hillcrest, from where, as she leaned against the fender and smoked a cigarette, she could see the glittering carpet that was Beverly Hills, Hollywood, Los Angeles. She felt as though it belonged to her.

Next day she landed a job first try at a realtor's on Hollywood Boulevard. They liked her age, her manners, her appearance, her accent. She had a diploma and a car. She would earn only commission, and only part of that. She would start work after Christmas. I have, she told herself, stopped limiting myself. She went on a new fad diet of grapefruit, and forgot to fear old age. She roamed the wide boulevards and flat little streets like a landlord. She did not see Los Angeles as an American would. She saw it as America: as a vast froth spreading on the desert convinced that it was taming the wilderness. She liked to drive to where its streets petered out into empty lots where the huge cylinders of sewage pipes lay as still as dinosaur bones or the bulldozers roared and ground away at the orange groves as though there were no dust and no end to man.

It was the impermanence that pleased her. People moved as often as refugees before an alien army, and other people fleeing other alien armies moved into their place. Los Angeles had been hurt less by the Depression and recovered faster than any other metropolitan area in the country, and Elizabeth knew why the Okies in the waiting room froze in order to get here. They were boosters at the real-estate school. With the Hoover Dam finished in 1935, they told her, we already got the cheap electricity last year. Next year it'll be water from the Colorado—two hundred and forty-two (rolled over the tongue like magic incantation) miles of aqueduct pouring money into our hands. Business? You want business? Hell, L.A. already makes more cars than everywhere but Detroit, and if we go to war, she'll be fantastic for the aircraft industry out in the Valley. Three million people in the Basin, they said, as though it were the miracle of manna to the desert, and a million goddamn cars. Wait till they open those freeways—nine miles of double lanes on the Arroyo Seco to Pasadena just about ready to go, and they've started work on Cahuenga through the mountains. Eight lanes, you'd better believe it! You—you're in a trade that just won't quit!

Poor old England, laughed Elizabeth. Poor old cow. One never owned a piece of England. One rented it from generations past and future and pretended ownership. But when the Americans said this land was their land, they meant it. Mine, said the giant machines to the red earth. Mine, said the mailboxes with names on them that sprouted like wildflowers after rain. And then when you were tired of your land, you went somewhere else, carrying home with you, leaving house to others who put their name on the mailbox. Mine, said the moving vans, mine from sea to shining sea. Poor old England, laughed Elizabeth, wheeling her Ford with the top down through the wide streets under the endless sun. I shall never go back.

The realtor for whom she worked had branch offices in Westwood and the Valley, and after she had made her first sale (which came with what she considered ludicrous ease), she had her choice of domain. She wouldn't touch Beverly Hills, not just because she knew she would be intruding on the other employees' most profitable territory but also because someone told her that it was the only decent-sized community in the country to have voted for Alf Landon in 1936, and she couldn't imagine she would like Republicans. Or film stars, she thought with a moment's unease. She had not telephoned Mabel even after all these months. She would have nothing to do with Robert Brandon.

"It's absurd," she told Don Wallace that spring. "They build everything here in one or two stories and put miles of ground around it. The boss says the county has forty percent of its area under single-family houses. Everybody except me lives in a single-family house!"

"So buy one!" said Don with a grin. "Be part of the world's first linear city."

"I don't want a house!" she protested. "I can't afford a house! Besides, that's exactly what I left behind in Wimbledon."

She liked to drive at night with Don in his big Hudson Terraplane, drives that lasted hours just in search of a restaurant, along the strips lined with neon that boasted, beckoned, coaxed, demanded like Mexican jumping beans.

"Anyway," she concluded, "the turnover is terrific."

"You're even beginning to sound like an American," he said.

She had learned to forget what ownership meant. Escape gives rest. But hope makes dupes.

50

June 1938

"From the midst of chaos and calumny," wrote Ginny in that letter received at the beginning of June, "I bring good news."

Elizabeth had gotten home early, cherished the opening of the letter through the process of changing into slacks, blouse, and bandanna, and taken it with a tall tequila and lime to the chair by Olde Englande's pool, where she could greet her fellow tenants as they trailed in from work. It had become a ritual, this. Whoever got home first started a social process that wound casually through everyone's separate drinks and dinners and on into the evening's murmured confidences. The only person not allowed to start the ball was she or he at the moment unemployed, who right now was the large gray-haired widow in number four, Mrs. Arlen. She'd been the wife of a returned serviceman, a Pennsylvania farmer wiped out during the agricultural depression of the late twenties. Now she had two goals in life: to write a letter to Eleanor Roosevelt, all of whose "My Day" columns she kept, and to have the money to pay for a visit from her teenage sons, who worked on a farm back home. She seemed never to make progress to either goal. Elizabeth could hear her upstairs now, singing away at "When the Moon Comes Over the Mountain" like the Kate Smith she resembled in size if not voice.

"From the midst of chaos and calumny," wrote Ginny, "I bring good news. The chaos, of course, is our Czechoslovakian policy. I remain unsure whom to dislike more: Herr Hitler, the mystic with the curiously practical mind; or our own Herr Chamberlain, who, finding that he cannot restrain our enemies, has determined to restrain our allies, on the grounds that he must be seen to restrain somebody. They say we shall have war, and though I think not, I have dutifully this weekend attended a special class for the residents of our block of flats in how to don a gas mask, and how to help others, especially those with beards, don a gas mask. I personally have no intention of interrupting my race to the basement in order to help a bearded man don his mask. For me, he had better shave."

Elizabeth laughed out loud and took a long sip of tequila and lime juice. Mr. Albert Roth, carrying his violin wearily home from his work with Warner Brothers' studio orchestra, asked what the joke was, but even though the courtly and gentle Mr. Roth was Elizabeth's favorite, she declined the opportunity to share. Mr. Roth had family in Europe, and he saved every penny to bring yet one more to America. He was out many evenings, either as a fill-in in the Hollywood Bowl Orchestra or as a member of the "Cavaliers," who were hired by rich and drunken celebrities to accompany them and keep them safe when they boozed it up.

If you want to be an expatriate, pick a country where they speak the same language; it will give you the comfortable illusion that the natives mean the same thing as you because you use the same words, that you understand each other.

Elizabeth had written to Ginny earlier in the year: "I have no need to go further than my own courtyard to understand that all the myths about American diversity are true. They think they can be what they want. They all tell you quite openly all about themselves and ask you quite naturally all about you, as though they didn't have time to waste in going about the job of getting personal. I have more friends here than I've had since Mount Lavinia. Are new friendships less trustworthy than old? What else is there in a country where everyone seems like a refugee?"

Ginny's letter continued: "The calumny of which I spoke comes directly from the chaos. Since the Czechoslovakian crisis, we have taken to calling each other names, and we are all apparently either fascists or communists. Among those named as fascists, you will be amused to know, are your friend Nancy Astor and Jennifer's admired, the Duke of Windsor, which all seems rather unlikely if not undeserved. Shopping has already become political, just like the last time. If one buys a strudel at Selfridge's, one had jolly well better buy caviar at the same time."

Elizabeth left the letter while she returned to her apartment to get another drink and to warm last night's casserole in the oven. She was not expecting Don tonight, so she gave up the bother of a salad. By the time she got back, other residents had gathered, and for a while the letter flapped idly under an ashtray. Warley Starbuck was very amusing on the subject of objects labeled "Made in Japan." He had bought a can opener, very cheap, and it had fallen to pieces in his hand the first time he tried to use it. "My dear," he said, "it's all those earthquakes, and besides, what do they know about cans? They probably misread the instructions and thought they were building a *car.*" Warley Starbuck was a cowboy from Montana who looked nothing like Gary Cooper. He was slight and effeminate and very, very tough. When introduced, he took you firmly by the hand and said, "Hi! I'm Warley Starbuck and I'm a fruit," and you had the feeling you had better not laugh.

Irene Steppels, who lived next door to him and did not like his bringing so many strange young men into Olde Englande, nonetheless enjoyed his point of view on life. Nobody knew what Irene did for a living. She was a fat woman stuffed into expensive dresses, with startlingly black hair of the kind that took a marcel badly. She liked to number the days until, sometime in 1940, the Social Security Act would make her one of the first to be paid retirement benefits, but she still worked sometimes at night, on a job she never explained, and Elizabeth found her suspiciously worldly-wise.

"He can sleep with goats as far as I care," she had once said of Warley Starbuck. "God knows, if you worry about what men still stick their little thing into you'll never sleep nights. But I don't want the cops coming here and disturbing my peace, not me."

Elizabeth was fascinated by the wash of psychological and economic opportunism in which these people floated. They accepted her for what she was, and she could have said she was anyone. Frank Lloyd Wright despised the people of Los Angeles. It is as though, he said, they tilted the whole country and all the common people fell into one corner. Elizabeth saw things differently. "There are no common people here," she had written to Ginny. "Here at Olde Englande we all class as poor, but we don't think of ourselves as *des-*

tined. Common today, perhaps, but tomorrow everything could change for any of us, and that gives everyone hope, which I personally find an exhilarating change from home. Don't you?"

It had taken Elizabeth less than six months to make herself comfortable with the transient, the slogan, the improvisation. She had made her strangers into family, and she laughed at poolside over booze as though she and they had always been here, as though forever were this evening. She had convinced herself that the right emotions were pleasure for today and hope for the future.

Tonight Irene Steppels was busily depleting her inexhaustible store of gossip about the sex lives of male movie stars. Gary Cooper, she said, was hung like a horse and had made his career being ridden by older women. Clark Gable went for older women too, more's the hope, but he'd just as soon stay out of bed altogether, and according to those who knew best, might just as well do so.

"What about Robert Brandon?" asked Elizabeth.

"Haven't heard a word about him," replied Irene. "Funny, that. Been very quiet since his divorce."

She seemed uneasy because she had nothing scornful to say about him, but cheered up at the thought of Cary Grant getting it up only for rich women. Something scabrous about Irene made her illusion of inside knowledge utterly convincing, and Jim Schockgrieb in number three claimed that she was the one who'd stolen Mary Astor's diary and sold bits of it to whoever would pay. Elizabeth wondered about Brandon's divorce. She had not even known he was married.

Elizabeth returned to her dry-edged casserole a little tight, and it was only when she had splatted a reluctant portion onto a plate that she continued Ginny's letter. "Enough of chaos and calumny," wrote Ginny. "I promised you good news. Jennifer–yes, your daughter–will arrive in Los Angeles perhaps by the same train as this!"

Elizabeth almost dropped the letter with excitement, then let go her fork instead, and had to wipe up the splash on the tabletop before continuing to read.

"I have not broken the news well, have I?" continued Ginny. "But I see no way of overcoming the surprise we both feel at the suddenness of her decision. Merry is of course with her, and she will be staying at a hotel called, rather Americanly, 'The Garden of Allah.' It is, I believe, in Hollywood." It was within a good walk of Elizabeth's apartment. By car she could be there in five minutes, by telephone in thirty seconds. Her hand reached for the telephone even as she read on.

"But before you dash off there madly, I have a delicate matter to mention," continued Ginny. "Your daughter's departure from England was not only sudden but secret. The exact circumstances are now history, so I shall declare them no longer pertinent. Suffice it to say that she left a letter for Anthony and that Anthony, upon receiving it, did not favor its news. Indeed, so little did he favor it that, upon learning of my slight involvement in the plot, he assured me in no uncertain terms that I was no longer welcome to be at the other end of the telephone when he answered it. There is worse—but, I hasten to say, not much worse! Jennifer wished her departure kept secret even from you. Despite my urgings, she rather forcefully stated that she would not let you know of her arrival, whereupon I informed her that I would. Which I have now done.

"I am unwilling to embroil myself further in disputes between either wife and husband or daughter and mother, but I do have an observation or two. Anthony's anger at Jennifer's departure seemed to me exaggerated. As to degree of emotion, it was surpassed only by that which caused Jennifer to leave—I almost wrote 'to flee.' While aware that the prospect of the leading role in *Gone With the Wind* is an important attraction, I could not help but think the power which drives her *from Anthony* to be of equal force. Quite frankly, were I Jennifer's mother, my first step would be to find out more about her relationship with her husband.

"My dear, you have a busy time ahead of you! I can see that your return—for which I long as much as ever—will be yet further postponed. We in England can wait. We have had our Chelsea Flower Show, but there is Wimbledon to come, and the planting of the penny hedge at Whitby should we choose to be rural. The Test matches begin soon, and I shall of course attend with my gels—I to see, they to be seen, though how one is to explain cricket to Americans I cannot imagine. Then of course there is the annual cart-horse parade in Regent's Park, practically outside my window, when I shall as usual feed as many docked and decked dobbins as much sugar as they can consume. Life goes on, my dear, even with us under the shadow of war. I hope you will remember this profound piece of philosophy, since it is perhaps one's only sustenance in the face of children who imagine they are quite grown. Do not, I beg you, act impetuously!"

Elizabeth might have felt a deeper response to Ginny's news if she had been left alone, but she had barely finished the letter when there was a knock at the screen door and Albert Roth stuck his head in, bearing a slab of hot tart which he had baked with the year's first peaches, and she had scarcely settled him in the single armchair with a Jack Daniel's when Jim Schockgrieb knocked at the door and asked to use the telephone. A piano tuner in his thirties, he was newly divorced, and he liked to call the kids every night before they were put to bed, muttering anger over his shoulder about that bitch, my wife. They had both settled in when Mrs. Arlen arrived trailing clouds of gin and flimsy excuses for seeking company, and there might have been a sort of party if they had not all been rousted by the unexpected arrival of Don Wallace, just finishing work for the day.

"Honey, you take good care of that man, you hear?" advised Mrs. Arlen with a pat on the arm as they went out the door. Elizabeth's relationship with Don was popular in Olde Englande. He was a nice man, and a woman needed a man. Mrs. Arlen used to lie awake nights listening for the bang of the screen door as he left in the early hours for the Hudson he always parked discreetly on the street.

Tonight he was tired, and what with the fixing of some leftover casserole and a can of baked beans, and the listening to his chatter about a highly promising day of work, Jennifer's arrival went clean out of Elizabeth's mind until she was dozing off after they had made love, and then it appeared only among the list of problems she must think about tomorrow. The truth was she did not want the bother that it sounded as though Jennifer would bring.

She and Don had started sleeping together calmly, as though it came at the right time. They had always liked each other, and with them both alone in the City of the Angels, lovemaking had always been a possibility. It had been Christmas Eve and Olde Englande was partying it up around the pool. Don had acted as bartender, slogging backward and forward to chip ice from people's iceboxes. Elizabeth had celebrated with one too many tequilas, so that the general sense of dislocation given by Santa Clauses in the hot sun had made her dizzy, and she saw the remnant and relic residents of the apartments as gay and witty society. Back in her apartment for some grilled cheese sandwiches, Don lay sprawled on the couch with his shoes off and grew maudlin about his wife, whom he hadn't seen in months, and he complained that the thought made him horny. Elizabeth brought the grilled cheese in from the kitchen and put it on the coffee table, standing over him as she thought briefly of Charles and Peter. Then she leaned forward and rested her hand lightly on the front of his seersucker trousers. They had made love there on the couch that first time, and their affection had been gently but passionately expressed, Elizabeth suddenly and with surprise discovering the enormous, overwhelming thirst in her own body.

It was not a friendship, this, and not a grand passion either. Privacies kept them separate. Finding that he assumed her experienced, she did not tell him that he was only the third man she had ever slept with. She had never before seen a hairless man, and the bareness of his body ever so slightly repulsed her. His penis, too, elevated and drooped with a speed she found astonishing, as though like everything else in America it had to move fast, and once or twice he climaxed even before entering her. She had never before had to restore a man's bravado. In return he brought her a book called *Woman's Coming of Age,* which encouraged her to know enough to bring herself to orgasm, and he looked proudly at her, as though he had been helpful. But he was a kind and generous man, a good man she thought, and their lovemaking was a rest from loneliness, and they liked each other and shared stories about the trials of work. The affair was like her whole life now: pleasant, but without real attachment. They had grown more familiar without growing closer. Anyway, she thought that night while smoking a last cigarette in bed after he had gone, I know him better than I know my own daughter. And he's a lot less bother.

51

July 1938

In movies, reconciliation results in great moments, but Elizabeth and Jennifer remained just free enough of art to follow the plainer course of reality. Their first meeting took place on an afternoon at the counter of Schwab's Drugstore at the eastern end of Sunset Strip, chosen because it felt neutral. As Elizabeth came through the glass doors, her eyes met those of Jennifer perched on a stool, avoiding the ogle of a man in a gray business suit. Their great moment was the shock of recognition, that they had both changed. Jennifer stood up to greet her mother at arm's length with a kiss on the cheek, and their how-are-you, it's-so-good-to-see-you criss-crossed.

"What will you have?" said Jennifer, sliding back onto her seat and pulling her skirt down over her crossed knees.

"The usual for you, Mrs. Wingate?" intervened Jack Schwab, who was washing sundae glasses with flair and splash.

"Chocolate malted, Jack, thanks," nodded Elizabeth. "And this is my daughter Jennifer, who is an actress."

"Seen ya round," said Jack, lending her a wet hand to shake. "What'll it be?"

"Lemonade, please, I have to watch my figure! I didn't know you were known at this place, Mother."

"Oh, Jack's customers are my best source of who's leaving what house. If I don't make much money, it isn't the fault of the four Schwab brothers, is it, Jack?"

He smiled, and slapped a chocolate malted on the counter, then went to grind lemons and sugar.

"And your hair, Mother!" exclaimed Jennifer, who was surprised to find her mother capable of modernization. "It looks marvelous that way! And you've lost so much weight!"

"Not on chocolate malteds, I haven't!" And they both laughed, and they chatted, in that metallic manner of intelligent women wisely keeping themselves in public view, each guarding her own rightnesses. They had both chosen to wear tailored suits and solid little round hats that perched over their foreheads, and as they bent their heads over straws, the man in the gray business suit saw the family likeness and turned to look out the window, wondering if Schwab would let him run up his tab as far as a hamburger and Coke.

When Elizabeth had telephoned almost a full month after getting Ginny's letter, they had both been stiff, brief. Elizabeth had toyed for a long time with the idea of telling Jennifer only that she wanted to see Merry, but she knew her pride would wound, so she set it aside as parents will. Besides, it wasn't true; it was her daughter she wanted to see.

"And how do you like America? Hollywood?" she asked now. She had been here long enough to need the answer, like a native.

"Oh, it's divine, Mother!" gushed Jennifer nervously. "Fabulous! I have to tell you all my good news! I've got my first part."

Elizabeth seemed to listen enthusiastically to the chatter that followed, of Jennifer and Myron Selznick, of Jennifer and a screen test at Fox, of Jennifer and how they snapped her up for the part of Isabella in *Wuthering Heights* with, "can you guess who? Merle! Merle Oberon, whom I've known for years, I'm sure she helped me get the part, and Larry! Larry Olivier, he'll make the most marvelous Heathcliff, and it's a Goldwyn film, Samuel Goldwyn, you can't get much better here, directed by William Wyler, he made *Jezebel*?" Elizabeth was wondering: What is she trying to prove to me? "And I have more news for you," said Jennifer, growing confidential. "But let's move to a booth, where we can be more private."

They took their beaded glasses to a booth distant from the busy telephone boxes and the noisy pinball machines in the back room. Myron Selznick had seen her and agreed to act as her agent. She was perfect for Technicolor, he said. And she was to test for Scarlett O'Hara.

Elizabeth forgave her daughter for not having yet asked a single question about her: "And what about you? What's been happening to you?" Her answer would be of little interest to either of them. The last concern of girls her age was mother's destiny or day. She herself had not felt that same excitement for years, but she remembered and would never spoil it. And as she thought this, Elizabeth experienced a sudden jolt in the pit of her stomach, as though she had been caught doing something very foolish. Somehow being back with maternal feelings for Jennifer made her colored hair and new glasses frames and slim figure feel like a costume.

They decided to sit in comfort and privacy at Jennifer's cottage in the Garden of Allah, which was linked to Schwab's by the parking lot, so they went out into the heat and glare. The Garden of Allah consisted of a main house and twenty-five bungalows arranged around a kidney-shaped swimming pool. Once the private home of the silent star Alla Nazimova, who had turned it into a hotel by building the bungalows in 1927, it had become one of Hollywood's fashionable places, along with the older Beverly Hills Hotel and the Ambassador on Wilshire, and its guests and visitors included every famous film star from the decade.

"It's a ridiculous expense for me," admitted Jennifer, confessing that she paid $250 a month for her two-bedroom villa, "but I had so little time, and I couldn't take Merry to an ordinary hotel. Clara Bow used to live here, and Garbo, and Ronnie Colman, and Alex Korda said it was very nice. When I heard about it, it somehow seemed more glamorous than it is."

"You could say that about life as a whole!" laughed Elizabeth. "Everything in America seems to fall to pieces very quickly." It wasn't at all what she had intended to say, and in recompense she gave too much praise to the lush garden, and ignored the gloom of Jennifer's bungalow to praise the comfort of its Moderne furnishings.

"The place seems to be full of drunken writers," said Jennifer, heading for the kitchen to put on hot water. "There's a little fat man from New York who . . . Oh, well, it's not really suitable for Merry, even though she has her own room. The parties go on till all hours, and the fights! My God! I shall move soon. To a house."

"Could I help you find one?"

"I shan't be able to buy. I thought you didn't handle rentals." The safety net at work, thought Elizabeth. The first offer of help. Not yet, quite, the first rejection.

"One can always find a way," she said mildly, without pressing.

"I think I have a line on something already. A sublease on a place down on the beach near a place called Malibu. It would be good for Merry if I could ever be sure of finding it! All the roads seem to go on straight forever, and then if you miss your turn you're miles away in the middle of the hills." Jennifer was still very nervous. Elizabeth felt rejected, absurdly. She would not offer to help again.

"Fortunately Merry's at play-school from eleven to four. Then she has her nap, and she sleeps at night like an absolute log. We have a Swedish woman come in to cook the evening meal, take care of her if I have to go out. She's really very nice. Merry adores the pool, she's learning to swim."

"Well," Elizabeth said. "I'm sure it will all be very much easier when you have your own place again." She felt that her tact was resolute.

There was an awkward silence. Elizabeth had many questions which she was afraid to ask.

"Would you like a cup of tea?" said Jennifer with hostess charm.

"Thank you, but I can't stay long. . . ."

A second awkward silence. They sped simultaneously to fill the gap.

"Merry must be . . ." began Elizabeth.

"Mother, there is something . . ." began Jennifer.

Elizabeth won this polite contest, forcing Jennifer to proceed.

"I was just going to say that there is something you could do for me, if you wouldn't mind."

"Of course!"

"When I start this picture—we start costumes in a month or so—I'm worried about Merry. I shall have to leave the house before she's awake, and I shan't get back until seven at night, and we work Saturdays, and—"

"You will have to find a nanny, of course."

Elizabeth was surprised by the relief that this innocuous remark brought to Jennifer's face. She did not know that Jennifer, propagandized by Anthony, had steeled herself for a lecture on motherhood versus career.

"I should have brought her new governess from London with us, but . . ." Here was the area for questions. Anthony. Jennifer herself. The marriage. Jennifer slid quickly away. "I thought I'd find one here easily, but I haven't, and I thought that perhaps you . . . ?"

"I'd be glad to make inquiries," said Elizabeth. "I'm sure someone I know will know someone. Everyone survives over here by what they call 'contacts.' Very amusing, really."

"But I thought," said Jennifer, again quick and nervous, "I mean, I know your real-estate work is only part-time, and I wondered if you yourself–it would only be for six weeks–if you could take care of Merry for me, perhaps she could live with you, mornings. She misses you most dreadfully, and I know you miss her."

"Not particularly," Elizabeth said thoughtfully, as though surprised into the realization. "I love her dearly, of course, but I think, you know, that grandparents don't *miss* children."

"But you will take care of her? You will help me?"

It would seem inevitable for Elizabeth to say yes, but the reconciliation had not extended so far that she was ready to be used in ways she did not choose. In the back of her mind was wisdom for the future: what if we disagreed over Merry?

"I think not," she said decisively. "I'd love to be able to help, but I have to earn a living, and my hours aren't my own."

"I'd be glad to pay you."

Elizabeth looked at her ironically, then laughed. "I'd make a terribly expensive baby-sitter if you were to keep me in the manner to which I am accustomed."

Jennifer looked sullen, or was it simply disappointed?

"Had you thought of Mabel?" asked her mother.

Jennifer's face clouded, and Elizabeth realized that she had led them onto thin ice.

"I don't intend to see Mabel again, ever," said Jennifer. "Have you?"

"As a matter of fact, no." Then the reciprocal challenge. "Have you seen Robert Brandon?"

The ice crackled all around them. Their eyes were intent on reactions.

"He took me to dinner last week," said Jennifer with some defiance. "He's invited us to stay at *his* house in Malibu, but–"

"Impossible, of course, darling." (The first endearment slipped by unremarked but not unnoticed by either woman.) "But aren't we both putting ourselves in a kettle of fish over nothing or whatever the wretched cliché is? I should like to see Mabel, but I don't call her because I simply can't bring myself to trust Mr. Brandon. You'd like to see him, but you can't because you are angry with Mabel."

Had Elizabeth planned, she would have said none of these words, but her quick glissade over the sensitive skin of their relationship was perhaps the best route to healing, if healing was to come. Jennifer had wit enough to pick the right dispute for response. "If you knew Robert better, you would like him."

"I expect so," said Elizabeth. "You're quite probably right."

Concession brought concession: "For Merry's sake, so long as you saw Mabel instead of I . . ."

"I'm sure we could arrange something, especially if you both live at Malibu. Why don't I call Mabel and break the ice? Shall we get together in a couple of days? I should like to see Merry too."

"You can't stay? I'd thought that you would still be here when she came home from play-school."

Elizabeth looked at her watch. "I've an appointment on the other side of Beverly Hills. It would rush things too much. Let me give you a call."

As she picked her way back across the crazy-paving to the parking lot, Elizabeth was well-satisfied. She felt she had stood her ground without being rigid. She was going to have trouble with her tendency to disapprove, but it wasn't more than she could handle. America had reminded her of survival by tolerance. The parking lot baked under the sunshine, and she took her sunglasses from the glove compartment, but then, instead of driving off, she walked back to Schwab's and picked out a stuffed pea-green sea serpent and two small note cards. On one she printed: "From Grandmother, with all my love." On the other she wrote quickly: "Darling, it was so very good to see you. I love you very much. Mother."

"Would you deliver these?" she said to the woman behind the cash register.

As she walked finally to her coupé, its metal too hot to the touch, her satisfaction was spoiled by a random thought: She would only really appreciate Merry or me if we were to die. That's what missing someone is all about.

52

"Oh, I'm not sure I could do *that*. I'm not sure at all."

Mabel looked vaguely over Elizabeth's shoulder, and Elizabeth suffered another of the succession of surprises with which her former employee had presented her today. She had expected no opposition, but this was a new Mabel, sitting on the chaise longue in this fern-filled lanai, a drink in her hand, a snappy expression on her features.

"I don't think I could go back to those days."

When she had called Mabel the day after meeting Jennifer, Mabel had sounded a little miffed that she hadn't called sooner, and she had been too busy to see her until after the weekend. "How about Tuesday for lunch?" she had said. "When Mr. Brandon's safely out of the way at the stoodio." American pronunciations stuck like raisins in the dough of her London speech.

Obediently, Elizabeth had driven over the following Tuesday. She took U.S. 101A past the rolling hills and empty beaches of Rancho Malibu, where sheets of cardboard on the tall wire fence lining the road flapped in the wind to announce the federal court order removing control of all this land from the doughty Mrs. Rindge, past the waters of the lagoon with seals sunning on the rocks at its entrance, as far as the sand spit where again there was a wire fence, and a sign saying "Malibu Beach Colony," and guards with emblems reading "Malibu Seashore Patrol." Brandon's single-story house stood behind shrubs and a brown stucco fence, but its other side faced west onto the beach and was open to the full energy of the undeferential sky. Its roof was wooden shingle, its walls the color of sand, and she could not resist appraising its worth as she rang the door chimes.

She was surprised by the Mabel who opened the door and welcomed her. Mabel did not look beautiful. Just rich. London pallor had given way to the walnut tan seen only in Southern California on skins well-nourished by expensive lotions and ready for the camera anytime. Her lightly hennaed hairstyle came from Max Factor's salon, the sleek afternoon dress of floral silk from Saks Fifth Avenue, and the pearl earrings and necklace from brother Fred, as she volunteered while showing Elizabeth into the living room.

"Or shall we go straight onto the lanai?" she asked politely. The architect had given Brandon a long, porticoed veranda that curved to fit the horizon, and the strong sea breeze fluttered everything with the smell of brine and kelp.

They toured the house. Lanai and living room were huge and bare in the modern manner, unimpeded by the soft, streamlined furniture from the Paul Laszlo showroom on Rodeo Drive. The huge kitchen and pantry gleamed in wood and aluminum. There were four bathrooms, and four bedrooms including Mabel's separate suite that looked like something out of *House Beautiful*. But Elizabeth was not truly impressed until she came to the library at the south end of the house with huge plate-glass windows stained by salt and colored by the view up the coast and out to sea.

"Books, books, and more books!" Elizabeth exclaimed, a twinge in her heart for Peter. Books towered on shelves to the ceiling on two walls and had overflowed into boxes and stacks on the floor. A half-dozen lay open around one of the armchairs.

"He won't let me touch them," said Mabel, "let alone the maid. He's a great reader, my brother."

Elizabeth looked at new books on a table near the door: *The Basic Writings of Freud,* Cronin's *The Citadel,* Lin Yutang's *The Wisdom of Living,* Arnold's *The Folklore of Capitalism.* She did not want to improve her opinion of Brandon, so she thought: A bit Book of the Month. She picked up Evelyn Waugh's brand-new *Scoop,* whose flyleaf was autographed.

"He visited here," said Mabel. "Didn't like him one bit, I didn't." A flash of her London humor returned. "Came with a pair I call the long and the short of it–Aldous Huxley, who writes those science-fiction novels, and that little bitty woman that wrote *Gentlemen Prefer Blondes,* which is more like it, I should think, in the way of stories."

"I had no idea," said Elizabeth. "I didn't know."

"How would you?" said Mabel matter-of-factly, as she resumed her show on the lanai by unveiling a table of cold meats, salad, fruits, and expensive place settings. "So," she said, surveying the table with satisfaction, offering dishes in a ladylike fashion. "I must say they eat well here." And her "they" brought the first sign of linkage between the two women, so that they could start a conversation as other than strangers.

"I love it here, I really do," said Mabel. "In America, I mean. I'm not as keen on this Malibu as Fred is, bit isolated for my taste, though I do like the beach. I'm taking out my papers soon as they'll let me. No more Blighty for me, all that cold, no thank you."

Elizabeth broached the subject of Jennifer fairly easily.

Mabel was philosophical. "I suppose she and me had to have a bit of a row sometimes. To tell the truth, what she did, well, I just don't like it."

"I don't think her marriage is very happy."

"I always thought she would have been better off marrying someone like my brother, to tell you the truth," said Mabel expansively. She had gone to the refrigerator for a huge pitcher of fruit juice jammed with whole fruit and added gin to it. Long glasses clinking with ice and beaded with condensation had been refilled, so that the edges of the afternoon blurred pleasantly. Mabel did not seem to care if she shocked Elizabeth; the rules were different out here.

"Why?" asked Elizabeth.

"Jennifer needs a man who'll let her have a long rope, is my opinion. That Mr. Anthony always tugging on her leash, he's more like to strangle her."

"I think you exaggerate." Elizabeth was stiff.

"Needs must if the devil urges," said Mabel cryptically. "I used to like him myself once. My opinion is: he changed. Couldn't cope with a woman has as much spirit as Jennifer." She sniffed.

The liquor, the afternoon, the egalitarian Mabel had dislocated Elizabeth, and she had chosen without forethought this moment to make her–Jennifer's–request that Mabel take charge of Merry.

"Oh, I'm not sure I could do *that*. I'm not sure at all," Mabel said. "I don't think I could go back to those days."

Elizabeth found herself explaining the reason for Jennifer's need, pleading temporariness, offering Merry as reward and sacrifice. She felt impossibly awkward, and she had the impression that Mabel, who would say neither a straight yes nor a straight no, enjoyed the reversal in their relationship.

Eventually Brandon himself straightened out the situation. He startled the women to their feet by appearing at the glass doors, and while he explained that they'd finished shooting a bit early today and gave Mabel a brotherly kiss and one-armed hug, Elizabeth had a chance to study him. A new Mabel; now a new Fred. He had grown up. Rapid calculation placed his age at about thirty-five, and he was solid, with creases at the corners of his mouth and eyes that had not been there when she had last seen him two years ago at Glyndebourne. He wore thin California clothes, and his body moved gracefully in them. He was still not exactly handsome, but his features had gathered strength, as though he grew handsome through confidence. He was relaxed, easy, friendly, quiet, attentive, gentle with his sister and his guest.

Quite suddenly a feeling that had not flooded her since the first years of marriage to Charles came over her. She could relax with this man. He would take care of her. Long forgotten, the sensation took from under her whatever pins the liquor had left, and she became flustered with a girlishness she had not shown for decades. Good God, she thought in acute embarrassment, surely it's not his sex appeal! She told him the reason for her visit.

"Mabel will enjoy that," he said quietly. "She gets lonely here when I'm working. We have no guests then, of course." And the matter was settled. Later, when she announced that she really must go, he fussed at her just enough to determine whether the alcohol had worn off enough for her to drive safely.

She was halfway along Wilshire on the way home when she realized that her attitudes to four people important in her life had changed for God knows what reason. Mabel: for the first time Elizabeth had seen her as a woman. Had Mabel changed, or had Elizabeth started to see? Jennifer had not changed. Elizabeth herself had ended some phase of motherhood and begun another. I don't know what to think of Jennifer right now, she thought. Perhaps it's just as well we will see little of each other. I don't approve of what she is doing. That grief made her pause too long when a traffic light changed, so that the car behind her hooted. But I am the only person who will ever be her mother, and she is the only person who will ever be my daughter. And it is up to me to adjust. She turned off the main road onto her own street. And precisely what is Jennifer's relationship with Robert Brandon? And was I angry with Brandon precisely because I always found him so attractive? And with that question came a thought which jostled her into a new blaze of perception. I wish, she thought, that he were my son. I would be proud of him.

That her son-in-law should choose that very evening to call her, was one of Anthony's poorer pieces of timing. He could not get hold of Jennifer at the Garden of Allah, he shouted from London. They were all drunk there. Would Elizabeth get Jennifer and Merry out of that place immediately? (It was an order, not a request.) He had decided to come to Hollywood as soon as possible. He had to visit New York on bank business. He would take his holidays in California.

Elizabeth hung up the phone that tied her to her old life and went back to bed, where Don lay a hump under the blanket. She snipped off the bedside lamp and tucked herself under his arm, which hugged around her, then lay still, her eyes adjusting to the dim light from lamps outside.

"I no longer know what to think," she said to Don after explaining the call. "I've always liked Anthony, but perhaps that was just because he is respectable and my son-in-law. Perhaps I've never really looked at him, or perhaps he's changed. Mabel and Ginny think so."

"Men change. We age."

"I've just discovered that I like Robert Brandon. I don't know whether he's changed or I have. I still don't trust him, but today he reminded me of my husband, which is odd."

Don rolled over to fetch them cigarettes from the bedside table, and they half-sat, smoking in the dark.

"You liked your husband."

"But I forgot that for a long time while he was still alive. Oh, God!" she sighed, and pushed herself from the bed to go to the bathroom. "I wish one didn't *reassess* things so often. I've had so many different opinions about Charles." She spoke to him through the half-open door, the light above the mirror shining into the bedroom. "The more that happens to me, the more I seem to understand why other people are the way they are and why they can't be different. Like Jennifer, I married for love."

"Romance makes the world go round."

"Round and round and round. There has to be something more . . . progressive."

"There are good men, you know," he said. She had come back to the bedside. She stood above him, so that her face was hidden by backlight. "But you're pretty hard to match. You're not exactly your conventional English lady."

"I know," she sighed. "Looking back, I don't know when I changed, or even why. It just happened. Perhaps everybody changed."

"Would you like to make love?" He took her hand, but she took it back.

"No. I have to think. I'm going to make some coffee. Want some?"

"I think I'll take off," he said, slipping his feet to the floor and reaching for his shirt. "It's late."

After he had gone, she sat over coffee and cigarettes at the kitchen table, worrying about Jennifer and Anthony and Charles and Robert and Mabel and even Peter. She could do with Peter's company now. They were all coming back into her life, as though she had come home from vacation. It was like playing some strange kind of chess in which more and more pieces were placed on the board instead of being taken from it.

53

September 1938

"Mrs. Wingate? Elizabeth Wingate? Would you hold the phone, please, for Mr. Myron Selznick?"

"Mrs. Wingate? Myron Selznick here. It's a pleasure to speak with you. You know who I am?"

"I believe so, Mr. Selznick." He had caught her in the middle of mashing tomatoes for a spaghetti sauce, and her glasses were spotty with juice. "You are Jennifer's agent."

"My firm represents Miss Wingate, yes, and I need your help."

"How extraordinary." She took the tomatoes off the stove and started washing a scattering of plates and cutlery, the receiver tucked under her chin. "What can I do for you, Mr. Selznick?"

"We got a few problems, Mrs. Wingate. I need your advice."

"That's very flattering, but I know nothing about Jennifer's career." She picked up the big spoon and resumed mashing tomatoes. She had seen little of Jennifer since she had taken the lease on a cottage in the tacky part of Malibu, an old two-story frame house with rented furniture situated on the row of dunes immediately off the two-lane highway, a mile north of Brandon's. All Jennifer had to do was drop Merry off with Mabel on her way to work, and on the two occasions on which Elizabeth had visited, they had spent more time at Brandon's than at Jennifer's.

"Trust me, you can help!" he said. The voice was eastern, cultured, with a vaguely European touch. Myron was the eldest of three brothers, four years older than David. Their father had been Lewis J. Selznick, one of the silent era's most successful studio heads. "But this isn't something we can talk about over the telephone. I should be honored if you would give me the pleasure of accompanying me to dinner."

"Tonight?"

"Tonight or any night, Mrs. Wingate. I understand you're a working lady."

"But I don't see that there is anything useful I could do. I do not interfere with my daughter's career in any way, Mr. Selznick. She tells me what she is doing, but we never discuss plans. I'm sure you would do better to talk to Jennifer."

"Mrs. Wingate, you should know I wouldn't go behind a client's back! You want me to tell Jennifer after we talk, then I tell her, but I want that you should listen first. I need a mother's advice, eh? Now, tell me, where would you like to eat: La Rue? Players? You like a good steak—how about the Toad-in-the-Hole, it's near you? No, I'll tell you what, you been to Romanoff's yet? I've got a table I practically own. Let's make it Romanoff's." Flattery and forcefulness so bombarded Elizabeth that she poured too much salt into the tomatoes. Every one of the places he had named, she knew, cost more than five dollars a meal, and she had been to none of them.

"Romanoff's would be fine, Mr. Selznick, but tomorrow night, not tonight."

"I know, you gotta get your hair done!" He laughed. "I'll send a car for you. Seven o'clock?"

"I'll meet you at the restaurant. That's on Rodeo Drive?"

"I'm looking forward to it, Mrs. Wingate, I'm looking forward to it."

"And I too, Mr. Selznick."

After she hung up, she laughed. She had met Hollywood hustlers in the course of business; she had never before been their target. She ignored the cooling tomato paste and dialed the hairdresser's.

She had not realized that Romanoff's was designed to be the most public place in town. One entered through a cocktail bar lined by stars and celebrities arranged according to the judgment of Kurt Nicklas, the maître d'hôtel. If you were a celebrity, the mustachioed Prince Michael Romanoff (the title phony, the talents real) would himself escort you down the short flight of stairs into the main restaurant so that everyone could have a good look at the new arrival. Elizabeth experienced the embarrassment rather than the power that the entrance brought, her black cocktail dress feeling immediately shabby and out of date as the waiter led her across a portion of the dance floor to Selznick's table, third on the left. Tourists stared at her, but it was too early for the place to be crowded.

"A pleasure, Mrs. Wingate, a great pleasure!" Selznick rose to greet her, his strong-featured face shining. He was taller and younger than she had imagined, and beautifully tailored. He bowed her into her seat, beaming pleasantries. He had a very intelligent, very Jewish face, and the gold studs and watch and cufflinks were only decorations for self-assurance. There was a tall, dark drink on the red-checked tablecloth in front of him, which he disposed of in one long swallow before ordering them both martinis, and a telephone which he commanded taken away. He ordered for her.

"Borscht to start with, eh? And quails, you like quails? Well done, eh? Crisp. With wild rice. Yes. And you got any of that fresh asparagus today?"

They chattered their preliminaries: how she liked America; what a terrible thing this war situation is, her prime minister flying off to Berchtesgaden and Munich.

"Bad move, bad move. If you're not going to bully, make the other man come to you. That Hitler, he knows how to bully."

For a moment his eyes gleamed sadly behind the horn-rimmed spectacles. He would not talk business until she had finished spearing the crisp little birds on the plate. His martinis were rapidly emptied, hers lined up like dewy chorus girls, but she showed the effects of her liquor more than he.

"With the cherries jubilee we talk business!" he said, ordering coffee as well. She was aware of strangers trying to catch his eye, but he flattered her by ignoring all of them except Myrna Loy, whom he excused himself from the table to address briefly.

"A client," he apologized. "Gable the King, Loy the Queen. They crowned them last year! Nothing's too good for a client, right?"

Eventually he could not wait for the cherries jubilee. "You say you don't know much about movies, Mrs. Wingate, but I hear from Jennifer you're a businesswoman, right? You understand what it is to do business?"

Elizabeth nodded, holding her coffeecup between her hands.

"Well, I'm about to tell you something that *nobody* knows. And I'm taking a risk, because it could cause a lot of trouble for me if this gets out, so I want you to tell me that I can trust you, because if not, then I'll say it's been a very pleasant evening and thank you very much."

He stared at her intently. She found it beneath her to give the reassurance he wanted and merely looked back at him with an expression ever so slightly tinged with amusement. He seemed to like this response, and leaned forward to confide. "Your daughter, I can get her signed for the biggest role in film history."

"Scarlett O'Hara?"

"I told you you were smart."

She felt a thrill of pleasure. The role that Jennifer had always wanted, that had made her leave her husband (she believed) and come to America.

"You want her to have it, right? I don't think Jennifer thinks you do."

"I don't care one way or the other, Mr. Selznick. Jennifer is my daughter, and I want whatever would make her happy. Sometimes I suspect she does not know what that is. Like the rest of us." She smiled.

"Well, we have a little problem. I've got my brother to the water, and I'm ninety-eight percent sure he'll drink." He threw up his hands and drew back. "Sure he wants Goddard, but he's not going to take her for a role this big because of this business about the phony marriage to Chaplin, so he's looking at Jennifer, and she looks like Scarlett, and she did an amazing test, a fantastic test. He needs to get someone cheap, and I'm willing to sell him Jennifer cheap. It's not the money that counts now, you understand that? She gets this role, I'll get her five thousand a week, then, from now on."

"I've learned not to believe what the newspapers say about the movie business," said Elizabeth coolly, "but I thought your brother had signed Norma Shearer?"

"Gable, yes. Shearer, no. She's too old. The public don't want her. The public wanted Sonja Henie to play the goddamn part, he'd announce he was making the movie on skates, set in Alaska. He's late, Mrs. Wingate, he's a whole year late, and he's got backers and a drop-dead December date to start shooting and he hasn't even got a script or a star, so we come up with what he needs and we've got him."

"And Jennifer is what he needs."

"But we got a problem." He sat theatrically back against the leather of the banquette, as though exhausted, then took another drink. "This no-contract thing that Jennifer insists on."

"I—"

"I know, I know, you can't do a thing. Nobody can do a thing except that husband of hers, he's due out here, but he's stuck in London, she says, because of this scare about war, and I don't want to talk to the man over the phone, first time, about a delicate matter like this. But David isn't going to be the horse that drinks the water unless she signs a contract." He leaned forward to peer intently at her. "It hasn't even occurred to him she wouldn't sign a contract.

The moment he learns that, scratch one, he'll give the part to his secretary for Chrissake, if he has to." He threw up his hands.

"But I don't see what I can do, Mr. Selznick. My daughter and son-in-law run their own lives."

At that moment they brought the cherries jubilee aflame, and he was the excited host for the minutes it took to serve them.

"I tell you frankly, Mrs. Wingate," he said suddenly, "I thought maybe a mother-in-law could make that phone call for me. That's the favor."

He did not look for her reaction but returned to the dessert with enjoyment and ordered a brandy from the hovering waiter.

Elizabeth used the excuse of eating to think, then replaced the spoon carefully and spoke in a measured voice. "We British, Mr. Selznick, don't interfere between our children and their spouses. I understand from my daughter that Anthony was not in favor of her coming to Hollywood and that there was quite a drama concerning her departure. You'll agree it might be unwise for me to say anything to either of them?" He started to protest, but she held up her hand. "But I shan't offer family reasons for not interfering, since you've probably had more than enough of family reasons in this matter." She smiled sympathetically, and he grew watchful. "I told you earlier that I didn't care one way or the other about Jennifer's being cast in the biggest role in film history." She paused to dab her lips with the napkin, wary lest her lipstick smear. "That's not quite true. If she gets the part, I shall enjoy her pleasure and success. She has very much wanted it." She reached for her small handbag to find a cigarette, but the waiter anticipated her with a silver box of assorted brands and a lighter. She blew out a stream of smoke and looked directly at Selznick. "But my daughter wants a great many things from life, and not all her wants are sensible or even reasonable. She tends to want whatever she wants, rather than what is best for her."

"As if we ever knew the difference!" he interpolated.

"Hollywood doesn't impress me quite the same way as it does those who are in the business." She was looking steadily at him. "I see a great many very handsome, very young people working extremely hard to become very rich, very famous. Forgive me, but there are other goals in life."

"You don't like movies?" Selznick was surprised.

"Oh, it's not that. Like all the world, I'm a moviegoer." She smiled, thinking of her breakdown after Peter's funeral in the cozy familiarity of the Odeon. "Perhaps it's just a matter of age, Mr. Selznick. I think when one is young one can become totally involved in the films. But as one gets older, you know, pleasure comes from familiarity rather than novelty." Her own words briefly surprised her. They were true, but would she have said them six months ago, before Jennifer made her a mother once more? She continued: "Most films these days–they offer miserable people escape, poor people riches, which I'm sure they need in such bad times, but I'm not miserable and I'm not poor, and after one reaches a certain age, all young people look beautiful."

Selznick was a little daunted and thinking quickly. "You're an intelligent woman, Mrs. Wingate."

"Thank you, but it's not very smart to point out that older people tend to choose reality over romance whether they prefer it or not." She paused, then spoke very steadily to be sure he understood. "Your real problem with me, Mr. Selznick, is that I think Jennifer should–indeed must–choose reality too. Her family."

He nodded slowly, and this time he paid her the compliment of not paying her a compliment.

"Let me tell you a story, Mrs. Wingate," he said slowly. "You maybe have heard of my father? Lewis J. Selznick, huh? He practically started the business, him, Zukor, Mayer, Laemmle. Nineteen-twenty, we had an eighteen-thousand-a-year apartment on Park Avenue full of paintings, music, good food. I went to school in a Rolls-Royce, for Chrissake." The eyes behind glasses were filled with nostalgia. "Early twenties, he was worth what? Twenty-five million? I started working with him, president of a goddamn film company at twenty." He leaned his elbows on the table and looked at his hands, cuffed expensively. "So in 1923 they broke him, bankrupted him. Laemmle, Mayer, Zukor. They brought the whole show down. We were a happy family, and they wrecked it, the bastards, and they kept on pushing him down so he couldn't get up again, and they pushed down me and David too, like the name Selznick was poison."

The waiter brought him another drink, and this time Elizabeth asked for one too, a light brandy, and only then did the waiter clear away the row of martinis that sat limp and untasted in front of her.

"So that, Mrs. Wingate," resumed Selznick, "is why my brother became a producer and I became an agent. David figures to beat them by making the best pictures ever made, and he'll do it, goddammit, as an independent. And me? Every time I get a client they want, I screw them to the wall. Money's the only thing those bastards understand, so that's where I hurt them, and I'll tell you something else,

Mrs. Wingate, what I've got over them is that I don't give a damn about money. What I do give a damn about is *family!*"

He finished triumphantly, as though he had just won an argument.

"What is all this leading up to?" asked Elizabeth quietly.

"Look, Mrs. Wingate, Jennifer's your daughter. She's *your* family!"

Elizabeth stared at him, thinking, then she shook her head slowly. "I'm sorry, Mr. Selznick, but that's not enough to convince me to interfere. Jennifer has her own way to make in life now. She always has."

"So that means you don't care about her happiness?"

"You know that's not true. I simply don't think that playing the biggest role in film history is going to make her happy."

Now Selznick shook his head. "And you think not playing it is going to make her happy?" He leaned across the table. "Look, Mrs. Wingate, you can let this son-of-a-bitch husband keep her from making it as a big star, but you can't ever stop her from knowing that he did."

"What do you mean?"

"I mean when Jennifer realizes what she's given up because of him, who's going to get it in the neck? Me? Who's going to be miserable? You?"

He sat back with hands splayed, his case made. Elizabeth saw his point immediately, and just as immediately she agreed with it. If Anthony won, he lost. If the marriage was preserved at the expense of Jennifer's career, it would be wrecked. Right or wrong, Anthony had to give way. For one single moment she regretted that she should emerge as the only person who could rescue her daughter. Then she spoke, and without reluctance, her decision cleanly made. "Actress or not, I shall always see Jennifer as my daughter."

Selznick beamed. "You'll make that call?"

"I'll interfere on two conditions. First, whatever salary you had in mind for Jennifer, get your brother to double it."

He roared with laughter. "Done!" he said.

"Second, I won't speak to Anthony by telephone, for the same reasons you won't. Bring him to Hollywood, however, and I will talk to him. How much time do we have?"

He seesawed his hand. "I'll work on it," he said. "If need be, I'll have them postpone the goddamn war to get him over here!" He grinned wickedly and offered his hand. "A deal?"

She took his hand and shook it. "A deal."

* * *

Elizabeth drove home excited by Myron Selznick, by Myrna Loy and Romanoff's, by making a deal and finding a task for motherhood. Not until she was in the middle of undressing–unsnapping her garter belt to roll down her stockings–did she fully realize that she had agreed to do what she had never willingly done: interfere in her daughter's marriage and in her career. Americanism had briefly blinded her: glamour, money, deals. Back in Olde Englande on the side of the Murphy bed, sight returned. Family? Under no circumstances, under no circumstances should she get involved in Jennifer's life.

She was suddenly furious at Selznick for hustling her. She was angry with Jennifer for needing her. She was angrier still at herself, a stupid bystander caught by an unexpected wave. Selznick and Anthony and Jennifer revivified the webs and networks from which she had escaped, but they had not snared her. She had trapped herself.

Anger became misery. She poured a glass of orange juice, and as she kicked shut the icebox door she caught sight of her face in the mirror above the kitchen sink. Tired and ugly. Not just a fool, but an old fool. Folly's pain made her twist her shoulders. She stood at the screen door. Olde Englande sagged outside, a cracked spotlight making the shrubbery orange.

"How did I end up *here?*" she muttered.

A burst of laughter came from another apartment, and she slammed the door closed.

"Oh, shut up!" she said, gritting teeth.

54

October 1938

Maureen O'Flynn was getting tired as the evening and, Elizabeth feared, life wore on. She and Jennifer seemed to be trying to outsmoke each other, and the grass was littered with the stubbed butts of Lucky Strikes and Camels. Elizabeth did not like them when they behaved like this.

The Hollywood Bowl had been Jennifer's idea, along with the picnic beforehand, as though Glyndebourne had inspired her. They had driven up into the hills in Maureen's Buick and looked down from the parking lot at the lights of Los Angeles and up at the forty-foot wooden letters of the Hollywoodland sign, but the Bowl's grounds had been crowded, so they had wandered down over coarse grass until they found a small glade among the shrubbery. Evening was drawing on now, their delicatessen sandwiches reduced to crusts, the wine bottles empty, the concert by Artie Shaw and his orchestra about to start, but the women still talked. The girls had proved too metallic, and their laughter left the taste of irritation on Elizabeth's tongue.

She had been startled by Maureen's appearance, which showed no relic of the Ravenscroft debutante. She was thin, painfully thin, so that her flesh seemed only the strands which held her joints together. She wore a bare-backed summer frock with straps and a full skirt, its illusion of youthfulness spoiled by the eczema that festered on her back and shoulders, caused, she explained offhandedly, by too many years of body makeup. She was blond now, platinum blond in the Harlow manner, with a Harlow mouth and her eyebrows plucked and replaced by pencil, so that she looked harsh and manufactured. Her soul had hardened too.

"Shit!" she had laughed, to explain the hair color. "I'm far too old to play dewy-eyed anymore! Harry Cohn wants his sex in more ways than one, and he swears he'll help me make the transition to comedy, the little creep. If he doesn't, I'll screw him in ways he hasn't even thought of, you bet I will."

Fortunately the expression on Elizabeth's face moderated her language, but she did not really know she was coarse; she thought herself realistic. She was twenty-seven, and eight years in the movie business, and she drank too much. Elizabeth had watched her take a single bite from each of three sandwiches, and she had resisted the urge to make her eat up. She was grateful when the conversation at last turned to a subject that interested her.

"An English girl playing Scarlett O'Hara?" Maureen laughed. "Darling, you don't know those southerners, believe me! They'll burn your effigy in Mississippi and Alabama, and in Atlanta they'll lynch you in person. Surely it's not up your alley, that of all parts?"

"I think you're wrong there," intervened Elizabeth. "Ever since she read the book, Jennifer's seen herself as the incarnation of Scarlett."

"A Ravenscroft girl as Scarlett O'Hara? Oh, no!" Maureen laughed with light scorn.

"Scarlett goes for what she wants," said Jennifer with unexpected seriousness. "So do I. She gets it. So will I."

"Well, you shouldn't want that part, my dear, the whole thing's a white elephant. Even if Civil War pictures are making a comeback thanks to Bette and *Jezebel,* it won't be this monster."

"Why not?"

"It's been oversold. How can anyone live up to the expectations? Everyone thinks they know Scarlett *personally*. Can't you see all those fans throwing popcorn at the screen because you're not the Scarlett they wanted? Anyway, the talk is that it'll never be made at all after all these delays. They say Selznick's waiting for Shirley Temple to grow up so that he can cast her as Scarlett!"

That light, hard laugh is really irritating, thought Elizabeth, but she saw that Maureen was serious underneath, darting quick glances in search of their reactions. Could she be jealous?

"Anyway, darling, let's not kid around," continued Maureen. "You've made up your mind to take that part, and what you want us to tell you is that everything will be all right if you do. Am I right?"

Jennifer managed to look simultaneously imperial and embarrassed. "There *are* a few problems," she admitted. "I shall have to sign a long-term contract, and Anthony—"

"Anthony will be mad as hell, poor little man," said Maureen. "Though why should one care?"

"He is my husband."

"So? I'm on my third. They all care if their convenience is ruffled. You really can't pay attention." Apart from the offense given by the sentiment, Elizabeth wondered what had become of Maureen's religious principles. People were trailing up the hill past them. They would have to leave soon. She began picking up papers and cigarette butts.

Suddenly Maureen collapsed into another mood. "I shouldn't be glib," she said. "A career isn't worth a marriage." Elizabeth and Jennifer both looked at her in surprise.

"Well, it's not," she said defensively, looking at them under her lashes. "For God's sake, what does a career give you?" She had instantly become a sad blond: dyed, metaled, miserable.

It took a little time for Jennifer to say, "That's not really my choice, you know. Anthony won't leave me, he'll just be very angry."

Elizabeth's thoughts had gone on another track. "Must one choose? Surely there are many people who do both. How long does one spend on a part? Didn't you say six weeks, Jennifer?"

"This'll be more like six months, Mother. It's going to be the longest movie ever made, they say, and Scarlett is in every scene. It may be Gable's picture, but it's Scarlett's story." She was very subdued.

"Well, surely Anthony will understand that you have to work hard for six months. He himself is away from home on work often enough. If you make special arrangements for Merry, I'm positive he'll understand."

"It's not just the six months, Mrs. Wingate," said Maureen. "It's everything that goes with it. There's preproduction and postproduction, that's another six months, and then there's promotion—premieres in Hollywood and New York, that kind of stuff."

"And in Atlanta," interrupted Jennifer.

"And Atlanta, and tours in all those godawful cities in the Midwest, and photographs and autographs and theater openings and God knows what. And what if the movie *is* a success? Oh, God, you can't *imagine* what that's like!"

Elizabeth having finished cleaning up, Maureen rose to her feet and brushed crumbs and grass from her dress. "Do you think we'd be able to have a picnic here if that movie made you famous? God, even me, I'm sure we haven't been bothered only because they don't recognize me with blond hair."

The other two women rose to their feet to survey the world above the shrubbery. Suddenly the head of a three-year-old boy appeared through the bushes at the height of their knees. "Hi!" he said.

They laughed at his timing, and he thought they laughed at him and fled embarrassed.

"That's about the last age at which they don't ask for an autograph," said Maureen grimly as they stared up the hillside track. "The fans—they look so harmless, don't they?" She waved at the cheerful shirtsleeved and summer-frocked people crowding toward the entrance, and stood still. "Let them go ahead, please. They're *animals. Animals.*"

Her intensity made them silent, and they waited minutes staring half at the view, half at the image of fame.

"It doesn't have to be like that," said Jennifer quietly. "You don't have to let fame do that to you."

Maureen looked at her bitterly. "You can't know what fame will do to you until you've experienced it." She had grown very bitter. "Or tried to experience it and failed."

Elizabeth touched her arm lightly. "But one has to try, dear. It would be worse not to." She was surprised by her own sentiment.

"Would it?" said Maureen. "It's so very hard to tell when it's too late to *stop* trying. I never thought that I . . . Well, let's take our seats and enjoy the pretty music, shall we?"

They reached the steps leading into the auditorium itself. The smooth concrete balustrade curved down toward them with all the streamline one could wish, and soft lights illuminated the gentle lapping of water flowing down from pool to pool, which they could faintly hear beneath the crowd and the first brassy strains of "Where or When." Above them stood the giant and hieratic figure of a muse in stone, and high above her shoulder the brightly lit cross on the hilltop which announced that Los Angeles belonged to Christ. Beside them stood a large concrete kettle covered with chicken wire and filled with coins. Elizabeth threw a silver dollar in as their entrance donation, more than she could afford, but Jennifer chose to ignore the wail of the trombones and saxophones within. "Would you mind?" she said at the foot of the steps. "I'd like to sit here awhile."

Maureen and Jennifer chattered while Elizabeth stared at them seated on the wall, their full skirts bunching around them, the soft light flattering their hair and eyes. The young are so intense, she thought. As though these choices mattered.

"Is all this really necessary to get what you want out of life?" she said when they paused. "Aren't you going the long way round? There are other things in life, aren't there? Than success?"

They ignored her because they did not understand her. They were too focused for her, too intent, too *narrow*. She gave up: the cure was age, not advice. She settled back and listened to Maureen interrogate Jennifer about Anthony's reaction if she signed the contract.

"Well, of course he'll be angry," said Jennifer. "But what can he do?" Her eyes slanted green and mischievous. "It will be six months since he's seen me. I think I'll be able to get him to do what I want rather easily, as a matter of fact. He'll come round. Men are such fools."

Maureen looked sharply at her. "I don't agree," she said.

"Not at all," murmured Elizabeth.

When Maureen then inquired precisely how Anthony did treat her, Elizabeth was privileged to learn something of Jennifer's perceptions of Anthony as husband.

"It's never anything so obvious as a beating," said Jennifer dryly. "Sometimes I wish it were. It isn't so much what he does as what he says, and what he doesn't do." She tossed her hair back and started to repin it. The saxophones and a woman singer throbbed in the air. "He thinks of my work as something I'll get over. Because he doesn't like the kind of women who are attracted to the theater, he thinks I can't really be one of them. It's not that he wants anything special, you know. I can make him quite content with the old pipe-and-slippers and I'm-going-up-to-bed-now-darling routine." She gave a knowing laugh that made Elizabeth cringe inside. "I think he married someone young and pretty who would just be there, and as long as I'm adoring, everything in the garden is lovely, and when I'm not, I think he just doesn't believe it."

She stuck a hairpin between her lips and stopped talking. Maureen had been tracing patterns with a twig in the dust. Now she snapped the twig. "I know exactly what you mean."

Elizabeth understood, but at a greater distance. Charles had always faced and accepted her reality, even if it took him time to understand it, and Peter had sometimes understood her faster than she understood herself.

"It's as though he doesn't see *me,*" said Jennifer sadly, the hairpin in her fingers. "He has some picture in his mind of the ideal woman, and if I don't fit that picture, then he'll cut me and shape me till I do." She shrugged and rose to her feet. "But I'm sure I can handle him. What will he do, after all? Let's catch the rest of the concert, shall we?"

They walked slowly up the steps, where the usher seated them near the back, but their mood had changed and the music lost its appeal, so they slipped out before the interval began.

They were driving down Highland when Jennifer spoke again as though she had not been interrupted: "What really bothers me, I suppose, is that I don't really exist for him. He tells me I said something when I didn't say it. He tells me that when I said something I meant something else." She gave a sideways smile. "He's even worse than you at that, Mother."

"Oh, well," said Maureen, and Elizabeth saw that her face had become a mask. "One can survive that, I suppose."

But one shouldn't have to, thought Elizabeth savagely. I never had to. What do these two know about men and marriage that I don't? But she did not speak.

"There were four of us at school," continued Maureen slowly. "The four Beauties, we liked to be called. Would you rather be Jill Knight or Fern Hardacre? Jill popping out babies like some rotten

Coke dispenser and getting older and poorer by the day? Fern, falling in love with a wifebeater, then leaving him for a married man who wouldn't even pay the bill for a Swiss abortion? Would you really rather be them?"

Jennifer did not respond. The big dark car flashed along the concrete road, its tires swishing like rain.

"What will you do if you don't get this part?" Elizabeth broke their silence as they turned onto Hollywood Boulevard.

"Scarlett O'Hara?" Jennifer started to smile. "I'll think about that tomorrow," she quoted, with a gesture at a southern accent. "Tomorrow is another day."

55

November 1938

Elizabeth swiftly painted her lips in front of the mirror and blotted them against each other, then powdered her nose lightly. It was an old trick, this, leaving the husband and wife a few minutes alone before you discussed whether they liked the house. If one of them did, she or he would convince the other and you'd have an impulse sale, which was very nice. Not that she expected much from this couple, looking, out of curiosity and dreams, at places way above their means, but curiosity had also driven her to show them this house because she wanted to see its wealth. It was the first of eight developed by speculation on the very summit of the Santa Monica mountains. Strung out below it was a series of sites in various stages of completion, islands of bare red earth in the gray-green chaparral. It occupied the spur, while the others were on the saddle of the ridge, with the result that while its formal entrance looked back down to Beverly Hills, its private face was turned northwest to sea and sky and a view of peaceful coastline north of Malibu Beach. Though the house was left unfurnished, the tank of gas had already been installed, the electricity and water were on, a temporary field telephone had been connected, and the grounds had been fully turfed, so that here was an island of brilliant green rather than red, looking like the oasis to which the steep concrete roadway led.

Elizabeth finished her makeup and studied her seams in the full-length mirrors. Her hair needed another tinting, but she looked . . .

well, yes, elegant. She had worn her one good suit of ivory shantung with matching shoes, and the alligator bag sent last Christmas by Ginny, and her seedpearl necklace and earrings. The boss had lent her the Cadillac. One could pretend one owned places like this. She put her compact back in her handbag and snapped the clasp shut, then walked confidently out to where the clients were now waiting in the timber-beamed entryway, the front door already open. No sale, then.

"It's very nice," they said. "Beautiful. But beyond our means. We'll let you know. Thank you so much for showing it to us."

God knows she'd heard those words often enough, and at least they weren't rude. She smilingly watched them swing their Chevrolet past her Cadillac and vanish down the driveway and the half-finished road between the builders' sites past a bright yellow tractor parked at random like a beast dead in its tracks, its mouth full of earth. She had plenty of time, the rest of the afternoon to pretend in if she wished. The living-room windows looked out onto the pool, which stretched almost to the edge of the bluff, shielded from the drop by a cantilevered wooden deck topped by a sixty-foot length of glass panes in wooden frames.

She walked outside to look at the two-story redwood house. The very best America can build, she thought. Sorry, Mr. and Mrs. Midwest. Only movie stars need apply. Her heels cut deeply into the turf until she came to the fringe of loose earth that divided it from the chaparral, then turned to look at the house against the sky. The mountains stretched back flat and dry, living bones. The earth at her feet was dry and friable, crumbling through her fingers, and the wild grasses were stiff and brown with the long heat of summer. She felt the sweat on her forehead and upper lip dry under the stiff breeze coming up the hill. She felt as though she were in a flat bowl of silent sky and unspeaking earth, stranded at the edge of this oasis in the mountain's wasteland where no roar of traffic came, no other human soul was visible.

She had to think more about last night's conversation with Anthony. She had followed through with her promise to Myron Selznick and taken Anthony aside on the first occasion they met, in Jennifer's cottage at Malibu, where he looked pale and too well-dressed. She had learned quickly that Jennifer had been right. He understood, he had said, the motives that led his wife to America. He admired, he said, her feistiness. It must have been very difficult for her. He worried only about the effect on Merry, who was having too much unsettlement. Genially he had agreed to a private meeting.

As she walked back to the house and sat in one of the director's chairs by the pool to drink her beer, she wondered if that attitude had rung quite true. Well, perhaps, in the light of what he had said to her last night during their private meeting at the Coconut Grove. He had chosen that grotesque locale because it would amuse him, he said, to see what the Americans could really do in the way of fake coco palms and real chorus girls.

"They say the palms were left over from *The Sheik,* and the owner bought them directly from Valentino," he said in amusement. "It seems suitably unreal for this town, doesn't it?"

Though it was a Friday night, he had managed to get them a diminutive table at the top of the stairs on a balcony facing the orchestra, where the spectacle of glamour rumbled beneath them like an ocean. The room was huge, seating perhaps four hundred, with a large dance floor presided over by the bandstand on the left as one entered. The decor–balustrades, stairs, chairs, false interior walls–was Moroccan, the palms and electric-eyed monkeys lewd, the people in evening dress around the individually lit tables exquisitely groomed, the huge silver moon and desert panorama on the rear wall a suitable exaggeration.

Awkward at first in this new environment, they had talked of the Munich crisis, which had delayed Anthony's departure from England in September, when all the lesser members of the British financial delegation to Washington had had their cabin space requisitioned for panicky Americans.

"*Utter* panic," Anthony said condescendingly. "Millionaires slept in corridors, they say. They even brought a liner into the roads at Gravesend, presumably expecting to take aboard poor Yankees fleeing by canoe down the Thames after London burned in a German air raid. One can't help doubting Americans' nerve."

"There is some hope that it will never be tested," she replied.

"My dear Elizabeth," he protested, "it is not a matter of whether we go to war, but of when. And perhaps against whom."

He smiled without parting his teeth, which gave him a peculiar air of unused malice, but he looked distinguished: the hair graying at the temples, the rosiness of a week spent at Malibu. She could trace no connection between him and the boy who had written those sensitive letters to her from the front twenty-odd years ago. She had worn her sole evening dress and it clung comfortably to her figure, and she had worn the diamonds that Charles had given her when Jennifer was born—now the sole relic of her past wealth.

"My own personal opinion," he said, inspecting a fork for cleanliness, "is that we would be much wiser to ally ourselves with Germany and let them fight the communists for us."

"You will find many friends here," she concurred. "Though you must know I find such an idea cynical."

"Cynical?" He arched his eyebrows to indicate surprise. "Only if you think of war as something other than an extension of politics. Herr Hitler can't be expected to last long, and we would presumably be wise to use the time to have him knock out the real enemy."

She fiddled with her napkin. "I fail to see why we should 'knock out' any enemy, real or imagined."

"But then, you have never understood economics, have you?"

She flushed at the idea and his tone. "I understand what it is like to be poor and powerless."

"You? Really? You who have had a life that most people would call privileged?" He seemed almost to regard her as an enemy.

"Privileged but not isolated, I think," she said, leaning forward for him to light her cigarette. "Certainly not enough for me to think I have no common ground with those less fortunate." She looked at him, letting smoke drift from her nostrils, certain she could handle him.

"How admirable," he murmured.

"I really dislike it when you condescend to me, Anthony." She spoke very levelly, merely conveying the information to him.

"And you are perfectly right," he replied, throwing down the fork with which he had been fiddling. "I do apologize. It is just that in England we are growing tired of this sort of argument. The ideas seem vital, but they're not really. It's all been decided, so why bother? The Americans stand to make a great deal of money from war, whoever wins, just like last time."

The waiter brought their drinks, vast tropical concoctions with straws that made her feel childish, and she searched Anthony's eyes for some haunt of conscience, some memento of the youth who had written her those letters during the war. Disillusionment then, she thought, but cynicism now. And there is a world of difference between the two.

"I should think after all," he said, staring at her, "that women even more than men have discovered the advantages of war. You got the vote out of the last one. I wonder what it will be this time."

Antagonism flared from him, but she could not afford to let herself get irritated. She did not like him, but if she showed her feelings, then she would fail in her promise to Myron Selznick and Jennifer.

"I suppose you can see war as a way of speeding things up," she said uneasily. "At least you don't romanticize it, as do most men."

"My dear Elizabeth," he said genially, "it's no good protesting that men romanticize war. Women are much better than men at romanticism."

This remark stung her, perhaps because she believed it true. "I do wish you could be less arrogant about your opinions, Anthony."

He was unrepentant. "If arrogance means someone thinks that what he knows is truer than what most people believe, then I plead guilty."

"You are insufferable," she said mildly.

"Would you like to dance?" he asked with a wolfish grin. They danced to a medley of fox-trot ballads, "Two Sleepy People" and "You Go to My Head" and "September Song," and she enjoyed the firm way he led her, reminding her of Charles and the sweaty excitements of Colombo ballrooms. He was a very sexy man, she thought, but when the band swung into a samba they left the floor to younger people, not knowing the steps. They talked spasmodically of Jennifer's long hours and his unfortunate timing in arriving just as she started preparations for the long-awaited *Wuthering Heights*. She found him studiously bland and neutral, so that she had to seize on his brief mention that Jennifer was one of the final candidates for Scarlett O'Hara.

"It's that that I wanted to talk to you about," she said, concentrating on spooning the last of her soup. As she laid out the matter for discussion, he concentrated on his oysters.

"I wouldn't bring up the subject at all if Myron Selznick had not thought it would be more tactful for me to do so than him."

Anthony's eyebrows rose, and the toothed smile shone. "How very convenient for Mr. Selznick."

"I hope you won't approach the matter by arguing against me. I understand all your arguments. I have talked to Jennifer."

"And Jennifer, you think, represents my views fairly?" He spoke seriously, as though he really wanted to know.

"Like you, she feels a drastic conflict between being a proper wife and mother and being an actress. She doesn't know how to resolve it. She is anxious to please you."

"That's good to hear."

"I want to ask only one question, really. If Jennifer gives up her career for the sake of her marriage, have you thought what effect that is likely to have on you both?"

This was a sentence over whose structure and vocabulary she had so long and earnestly labored, the whole intended to look at feelings objectively. Elizabeth was proud of it.

"Yes," he said. She waited, but he spoke no further.

"And?" she asked eventually. He looked at her and paused long enough to light a cigarette. The pause made her feel as though she had asked a banker for a loan; all of a sudden she was dependent, without knowing how it had happened.

"You do realize that if I answer your question, you are interfering in our marriage."

She was embarrassed. The district attorney was using her guilt against her. "Yes," she said modestly, eyes on the table, angry at humiliation.

The waiter appeared beside the table and involved them in the ceremony of the main course. During the interruption Anthony relaxed, quite suddenly, and he could scarcely await the waiter's departure before busting out, "I'm not proud of what I'm doing, you know. It's not ever what I wanted to do as a husband."

She looked up at him in amazement, and she saw his face was miserable. He hacked at his steak as though it were yet to be killed.

"But I thought–" she began.

"You thought I had become a villain, just as Jennifer does. Perhaps it's because I'm so much older, Jennifer tends to think I have no feelings. It's very easy under those circumstances to seem something out of a Gothic novel."

Elizabeth was stunned. That character was precisely what she had been on the way to writing.

"You tell me what I should do, Elizabeth." He placed his knife and fork on the plate. "You tell me. Of course I can let us break this bargain we made, or Jennifer herself can. I see what a big chance this role is for her. I don't want her to take it, but it's obvious that if I cause her not to, then of course I'm going to be the loser, and I do love her, you know." He stared across the table, intent that she believe. Elizabeth almost gaped. It was as though a facade had collapsed.

"But you tell me what I ought to do. If she goes through with this and becomes a famous star, what will be left of our marriage that I like? Was I wrong to want an ordinary wife and mother when I married? And what will I have if she becomes a public personality? It's bad enough already, without Scarlett O'Hara. But you tell me what to do, if her success makes me miserable for the rest of my days. If she goes ahead with this contract, what do you think the effect will be on *my* feelings for *her?* What is she telling me but that her marriage doesn't mean anything to her?"

There was silence between them, Anthony fiddling with his fork.

"One movie," he said quietly. "It doesn't sound much, does it? And if it's a flop, we have no problems. But what if it's a success? And it's not one movie, but movie after movie after movie, and living in Beverly Hills behind a five-foot brick wall—what happens to London and my career then? Do I become the husband who's in *banking?* Or lose her to another man? The marriage wouldn't survive."

On a nearby palm, a monkey blinked at her with pink eyes. The orchestra played the theme from *Snow White*. Suddenly Elizabeth's eyes filled with tears. "I don't know what to do about marriage," she said. "Has it become im*pos*sible? Why doesn't it work anymore?"

"Your own didn't work very well, did it? This is not exactly a new problem."

She flared up. "My own marriage worked beautifully. Charles did not object to . . ." She trailed off.

"Exactly. He did, didn't he? But he did the same thing I've done for years, the reasonable thing, let you have as much rope as you seemed to want, relied on you to preserve the marriage because it was important to you. And what happened? Peter Williams happened."

He spoke so calmly, offering up her life on a platter, a life she'd never seen.

"It wasn't like that. It wasn't like that at all!"

"I don't mean to pry in your personal life," he said with a shrug. "I just ask you to look at it from my viewpoint instead of just your daughter's. You tell me: what am I to do?"

"Surely there must be some midway point, surely you can compromise."

"On what? If Jennifer signs this contract, then we've gone the whole route that I don't want for the future. *She* chose this sticking point, I didn't. *She* chose to want everything. I'd already given her everything I could, but she wants more. I only want what we already had. Where's the compromise there?"

Elizabeth felt as miserable as he looked. She pushed her half-finished meal away, laying knife and fork so neatly that a waiter immediately removed her plate. "Can't you talk to her, explain it to her?"

"Ha!" he said in sad exhaustion. "We've talked endlessly about it. We've yelled and screamed about it until I thought we were both insane. I never thought marriage would be like that. Not my marriage. You tell me: what's my alternative?"

"What alternative do you see?"

"I don't see that I have any at all."

"What do you mean?"

"I mean that I've thought this thing over and I can't come up with anything other than what I'm doing now. I've taken leave of absence from my job at very great difficulty, but I'm going to stay here until this matter is settled. I shan't argue until it's necessary. I may not argue at all. If they do offer her the role, I shall continue to refuse to agree to her signing a long-term contract. She can go ahead and sign anyway if she wants. But I have to find out whether she really cares about me and Merry or just . . . just fits us in. I've already bent over backwards, much further than I ever thought I would. I have to say: I can go this far and no further. You women want everything. There's nothing wrong with that. We men want it too. But men learn you can't have it all. We settle for less. You have to learn to do the same."

"I hadn't thought of it that way," mumbled Elizabeth.

"Of course you hadn't. Why should you?"

The implication she read was: Like mother, like daughter. She scanned her mind for something to say, and then chose the fairest words she could find: "I've certainly learned my lesson about not interfering, haven't I?" She gathered up her gloves. "I shall have to think about this. Right or wrong, I will admit, I hadn't looked at it from your viewpoint. I'm sorry."

He dismissed her apology and her dilemma with a shrug of shoulders and face, murmuring something like, "It can't be helped." Then he reached for his wallet, and as he took dollar bills out of it, he said, "You want to leave?"

She nodded and picked up her handbag, ruffling within for the claim check for her battered car. They left the grotto just as the MC announced the beginning of the floor show, but Anthony, frowning and preoccupied, had not even memory of chorus girls. They were both equally upset, eager to part. As they waited in the driveway of the hotel for the attendant to bring both cars, she said, "I think there are some problems which are insoluble. Marriage, these days, seems to be one of them. Perhaps if men and women did not expect so much from each other, we would all be happier."

Now, in the hot sun on the high hill by the new house and its sun-glared swimming pool, Elizabeth was no clearer about her ideas than she had been in the artificial pink light of the Coconut Grove. She had started as her daughter's flag-bearer, and though she hadn't gone over to the enemy, she had ended up somewhere in between on the battlefield. Jennifer had always been so selfish, so foolish. But Anthony: should she still know better than to trust him? She sipped at her glass of beer, which was making her sleepy, and decided to stretch out on the grassy slope above the pool's walkway, smoothing her ivory skirt so that it would not wrinkle, taking off her jacket to lie upon. The sun shone against her eyelids, and she watched the sunfish swim, listening to the sounds around her: a bird calling alone, distant roar of traffic, the buzz of an aircraft heading for Burbank. They could pick up their own pieces. His. Hers. Theirs. But her daughter, there must be something she could do to help her own daughter. . . . She drifted off into a sound sleep, her last sensation that of the grass soft and lumpy under her back.

56

Perhaps an hour later, the sun having moved substantially toward afternoon, she woke with a mild headache. Tasting the dryness of her mouth, she looked straight ahead at the sky above the glass wall of the swimming pool and thought how amazingly hot the afternoons up here must be, because the air rising from the canyon shimmered and refracted the light like water. Then with a start she realized that a thin vapor of pale white smoke was also rising, and she smelled a faint odor of burning wood. Dear Lord, she said, there's a fire in the canyon. I must report it.

Feeling mild alarm, she pushed herself to her feet, patting her hair and skirt back in place, leaving her jacket where it lay, and walked quickly along the pavement by the pool to look down through the deck's glass wall at the upper end of the canyon. A few heavy trails of smoke nudged their way through the scrub. Some five hundred yards down the canyon the smoke was heavier, and she could see flashes of flame crimson and yellow at its base. Only one side of the canyon was as yet on fire, the chaparral and pepper trees and live oaks on the other side flustered only by the stiff breeze that flowed from the northwest up the canyon, but one glance was enough to show the danger. Nothing separated the fire from the deck on which she stood but yards of combustibility. She turned and walked quickly back along the length of the pool to the steps, where a very long red rubber hose began its stretch across the lawn. She turned the tap on full. Pierced with holes to water the grass, the hose quickly produced along its length a fine spray that drifted softly over the new turf. That might do some good, she thought.

She crossed the patio and clacked quickly across the wooden floor of the beamed living room to the entrance hall, where a field telephone lay in its webbing on the red tiles. She knew how to work these things, she thought gratefully, and rang energetically away at its handle. There was no sound at all from the instrument. Damn, she thought. I don't know how to work it. I shall just have to drive down and tell somebody. She was terribly thirsty and went to the kitchen to draw a glass of water. The great appliances hummed quietly to themselves, boasting cleanliness and newness. She rinsed the glass out and set it upside down on the stainless-steel sink, picked up her alligator handbag from the bench where she had left it, and walked back into the entrance hall and out the teak double doors that led to the driveway where the boss's Cadillac sat, rummaging for car keys, wondering whether she should lock up before she left.

The sight that greeted her from the stone porch of the front doorway stopped all thought of getting out by car. Heavy gray smoke rolling from the north was flowing right over the saddle that separated the house from the main slope of the nearest mountain, and the north side of that far slope was already aflame. She could hear it crackle. Already the furthest of the other building sites that lay between her and Topanga Road were invisible, and even if the road itself were still free of fire, she would be unable to see to drive. She felt her first spasm of real alarm. The smell of smoke was very strong now, and she heard the call of a fleeing bird.

She stood on the porch for a moment, measuring the scene, a well-dressed matron pausing as though to remember whether she had forgotten anything before leaving for her bridge party. In case of fire, she was thinking. There's always glass to break or numbers to dial, and people rush to help you while you stand and wait to see which side will win, because it is not really personal. She turned back into the hall, and when she closed the big door, the house felt safe and solid and rich despite the slight smell of smoke.

But it will burn. Fireproof shingles, said the write-up in her handbag. The external cladding–redwood, impregnated, fire-resistant? The pool, then. I can get in the pool. Back into the placid living room to where the glass doors onto the patio stood open. There she felt her first wave of fear, for she could see smoke now rushing up past the swimming pool's glass fence in a solid wall which rose into a tower that blew away across the other side of the house or billowed down to cloud the pool, which was already dotted and specked with blackened fragments. Sweet Jesus, everything is happening so fast, she thought. It won't even notice this house as it eats it!

The smoke, they said, the smoke kills most people. It clung to the surface of the water greasily, dimming its blue green. Hadn't she read about firestorms using up all the oxygen, somewhere in the fright literature about the coming war? A sheet of plate glass in the fence exploded as though it had been struck, and a great whoof of smoke and hot air rushed through the gap. The sound of roaring flames was instantly loud, and Elizabeth slammed shut the glass doors.

She stood there for a moment, thinking, the house quiet behind her, tapping the glass with the fingernails of one hand, the other clasping the huge drapes of loosely woven brown linen that could be drawn to shut out danger and chill. Suddenly she looked at the pelmet holding the drapes, and then tugged at the material experimentally. She had to exert her full strength to get them loose, discarding her high heels and handbag as she did so, but once loose they were not too difficult to gather into her arms. She forced the patio doors open, and, stooping, raced to the nearest edge of the pool and threw her armful of drapery in.

The first smoke entered her lungs and made her eyes water, and the heat stunned her as she knelt, poking air pockets out of the fabric, forcing it to get wet. Dear God, it is worse, this heat is fantastic. Quickly she slipped over the side of the pool into water that was warmer on top than further down, and she immediately realized that her plan to stay under the protection of the linen would not work. She was in the deep end, where she could not stand, and the material was so heavy with water that it would drown her.

Still she did not panic. She pulled herself along the pool to the steps tugging one of the half-sunk drapes with her. Her forearm registered her first burn as one of the many live cinders fell on it, and hastily she ducked her hair under the water, rising up streaming water and minus one pearl earring. Suddenly there was a loud popping sound, then a huge roar, and a blast of heat that made her shield her face, and the smoke at the other end of the pool lifted like a theater curtain replaced by a solid sheet of flame. The entire wooden deck had caught fire at once, and it burned with a black and stinking smoke that billowed right above her head. So much for fire resistance, she thought grimly, coughing, standing to stumble up the steps, dragging the weight of the wet drape behind her.

Though barely able to see the ground in front of her, her nose as well as her eyes streaming now with mucus, she could still follow the line of the red hose. Staggering around the corner of the house, she faced a stretch of turf completely clear of smoke, lying under the south lee of the house, shining green and dewy with spray. She could breathe again. Hastily she dragged the cloth with her, keeping it in the spray from the hose, her skirt dank against her thighs, heading as far away from the house as the hose would permit; then she stood straddle-legged in the center of the line of spray, reeling the long yards of linen in toward her, thinking that if the water pipes buckled under the heat, well . . . She unfolded the drape and laid it next to the hose so that the water played on its full length.

On the other side of the hose, where the wind blew the spray of water away, the grass was wilting and she could feel the oven-air like the breath inside a beast's mouth. On three sides of her, smoke rushed past just feet away. The side wall of the house stood some eighty feet away, and even as she bent over the cloth she saw the shingles of the roof over that immaculate kitchen begin to melt under a flame so hot it could not be seen. Dammit, she thought, I left Ginny's handbag inside. She was exhausted, her breath coming in coughing gasps, her face and blouse filthy with mucus, her heart beating madly, her head telling her she was far, far too old for this sort of thing.

She sat on top of the cloth and began to wrap it loosely around the lower part of her body, then over her shoulders with a double-layered cowl for her head. Inside her a voice was stating: I don't want to die, I don't want to die, I don't want to die. Before she wrapped the cloth around her head, she took one last hopeful look. The roof of the house was one mass of dancing flames, like a bonfire, the shingles curling in agony and vanishing into blackness. "Now I lay me down to sleep," she said distinctly. Now I lay me down to sleep, now I lay me down to sleep. Mind and heart blanked by fear, she covered herself and lay down.

Around that still lump of brown linen slowly drying, the sparkle of the hose fell like a baptism. Smoke clung to the ground as though searching for her. Inside the cloth it was almost dark, and so stifling that she had to poke for an air hole. She lay very still, eyes shut, knees folded up, feeling the heat. Let me faint before I burn. Let me not feel it, Oh God, let me not feel my flesh burn, let me not die in pain, Oh Lord, not the burning, not the burning of my flesh. A loud explosion outside flicked her back into consciousness. The gas tank of the Cadillac in the driveway exploded, though no flame had touched it, and the whole car went up with a great whoosh, and almost immediately afterward came a sound as though an artillery shell had exploded. The house's silver propane-gas tank had split one side and sent out a fifty-foot sheet of pure flame which, though Elizabeth did not know it, quivered briefly into the air right above her and incinerated the nearest wall of the house.

But she did not hear the next great roar, produced as the roof of the house collapsed into its beautiful interior, sending sparks and solid pieces of wood gaily spiraling into the air, and she did not feel the single piece of burning wood that tumbled through the sky to fall hard on her shoulder and lie smoldering on the drying linen, for God and her terror had let her slip into unconsciousness. Her body lay there very small and very still, as though it had never been useful to anybody.

Elizabeth's fight for life had been glimpsed through the smoke by a team of twelve firefighters frantically working to cut a firebreak on the mountainside above the development. Seeing the solitary house with the rich car in front, they had shaken their heads and declared its doom. One of them, gazing with a clumsy sense of poetry at the smug mansion with its placid pool, had happened to see Elizabeth appear at the front door to look down the slope at the smoke that veiled the roadway. He gave a shout of alarm, and the fire boss sent two men leaping and galloping down the steep hillside to Topanga Road, where a headquarters had formed an hour ago to take charge of the defense against the line of fire marching from the north.

Headquarters could do nothing in the face of that holocaust. They managed to get a truck up the road later, when the fire had burned on up the mountainside. The concrete of the new road was still hot and covered with ashes, and they feared for the tires, but the newsmen wanted to try. They could see the ruins of the house clearly: one wall, a chimney, smoke and an occasional flame rising above charred wreckage. Who had that woman been? A star? Too new even for mailboxes. If she'd made it down the hill to one of these construction sites, she might have made it safely. They hung from the sides of the truck as it growled up the last bit of hill and churned across the curb and the dead grass to where the heap of brown linen lay. They raced each other the last few yards to see who could be first to pluck at its dry folds pocked with small black holes.

But there was no body within, and they gaped and poked ludicrously, as though they did not know what to do without death, until a shout came from the other side of the ruined house: "Here! She's here!" They rounded the corner of the ruins, which still radiated heat, and there, instead of a charred corpse, they saw a woman with matted hair sitting on the steps of a swimming pool filled with gray water. She was so filthy that a clean string of pearls around her neck was the only recognizable reality. "Son of a *bitch!*" one of them cried out. "It's a goddamn miracle!" They rushed at her with flasks and blankets and cameras and questions, looking into her green eyes as though she knew something they did not.

Elizabeth refused to give her name, refused the stretcher, refused the help of their hands in walking back to the ambulance that had followed the fire truck up the hill, then refused the ambulance itself.

"I'm quite all right," she said calmly. "I can take care of myself, thank you."

They noted her accent and tried to recognize her through the filth on her face, thinking that, so rich, she must have been a star. They saw tears tracing lines down her cheeks through the filth and could not imagine they came from the joy of being alive, so they insisted that she be taken to the hospital. To get away from the reporters, she succumbed to the ambulance and the hospital's insistence on a bed for the night, but she managed to keep her name from the reporters, with the result that the Sunday papers turned her into an eerie echo of Charles by printing photographs of her in various stages of disrepair with the label "MYSTERY WOMAN ESCAPES DEATH IN FIRE." Looking at them when she was clean and refreshed by a night's sleep, she felt like a gangster's moll. Her skin was sore, and they said it might peel, but she was unharmed except for a very rough throat that made it hard to talk to Don when, informed by her boss lamenting his Cadillac, he tracked her down. He brought her clothes, then stayed until they released her after lunch.

"It's nice to know they would have identified me quickly if I had burned," she said.

On Don's advice that they might as well get it over with, she gave her name to one of the reporters.

"Then you're a nobody after all," he said, disappointed of his story, taking few notes.

"Exactly," she replied, amused. "I'm a nobody. No story at all." And as he left, she lifted her hands for Don to look at the small red burns. "But I have never felt more myself," she murmured, smiling at him, briefly radiant.

"I'm sure Jennifer will want you to have told them you're her mother," Don said smilingly. "Those movie stars—they love the publicity."

But she was savage. "I will not be an appendage to my daughter."

57

December 1938–January 1939

David O. Selznick sat in his comfortable office in the antebellum mansion at 9499 Washington Boulevard, Culver City, and drummed his fingers on the desktop. He was a tall and burly man, given to fistfights when he had drunk too much, no matter the expensive suit, the neatly wavy hair, the gold-rimmed glasses. He was thirty-six, and since Irving Thalberg's death, he had had no rival as Hollywood's boy wonder. Selznick had a string of distinguished films behind him, and the best, he believed, yet to come. Restless, impatient, creative, he was used to defeating frustration by bulldozing it. But this time? The fingers drummed a last violent rhythm, and he pushed himself up from the chair and walked to the window overlooking the back lot, where his name stood out in black on the tall silver water tower. He looked at it and grinned. Sure, he only leased the place from RKO, but Louis B. Mayer, his father-in-law, had to look at that tower every morning on his way to his office a mile away at MGM.

Selznick turned from the window and grew serious. In leaving, George Cukor had not quite closed the door, and he could hear the clack-clack of a couple of typists working late on his memos. He could handle Hitchcock for *Rebecca.* He could gamble on that Swedish woman for *Intermezzo* even though she wouldn't sign a contract. He could even stall Whitney again over the financing for *Gone With the Wind*. But if he didn't have a Scarlett? If what Cukor had said was right? He sighed and turned back to his desk.

Selznick's search for the right woman to play Margaret Mitchell's

Scarlett O'Hara had backfired; thirty months after purchasing the rights and eight days before the date on which his backers demanded he at last start shooting, he still did not have her. The search had begun like many others of the time, part for publicity, part because he needed to stall until he had completed distribution commitments to United Artists. It had been great publicity. The story had won more space in the papers than the romance of Edward and Mrs. Simpson, the debate over the Neutrality Act, and the story of what Germany was doing to its Jews. But by now, December 1938, it had become a nightmare for Selznick–less his search than the nation's, as though citizens hag-ridden by Depression sought to find Scarlett's savagely surviving soul in their own bosoms.

Clark Gable was right, Selznick liked to say, to fight being assigned to play Rhett Butler. Like he said, in these roles, what actor could match the audience's dreams? Every time he had Russell Birdwell announce someone for Scarlett, he stirred a hornet's nest of complaints. The search had offered the women of America hope, and that was a force more powerful than any producer could control.

They had said *Gone With the Wind* was a novel too long and too expensive for Macmillan to make its money back, and since other magnolias-and-moonlight sagas had died at the box office, he had not at first wanted it himself. But when it sold a million copies within six months of publication and kept outselling everything else for two years, he knew the best-selling novel of all time had to become the best movie he had ever made.

Nobody except George Cukor pretended to know why the book was so popular. "That bitch heroine," Cukor liked to say, and as the best women's director in Hollywood, he ought to know.

"For God's sake, George," said Selznick, "what does that tell us about the women of America?"

"That times are bad," said Cukor.

Selznick looked down at the list of names which he and Cukor had been studying. It included almost every female star in Hollywood, and a score of unknowns, and every one of them had been discarded as a candidate.

"Fourteen hundred women all across the country interviewed," Cukor had said that night, slumping exhausted on the couch. "Ninety screen tests. One hundred and forty-two thousand feet of black-and-white. Thirteen thousand feet of Technicolor. Ninety-two thousand dollars spent so far–more than the whole budget for some of my movies. You have to make up your mind, David."

So what had they agreed? Selznick sat at the desk and picked up his gold fountain pen and looked at the notes he had made.

"Number one," he had said, "she's got to look perfect."

Cukor agreed, and there sat the single word on the page: Beauty, underlined. No matter the novel's first line, no matter Margaret Mitchell telling the press that she didn't know anyone in the movies who looked like Scarlett. A square jaw and thick eyebrows? Not at the box office.

"Number two," said Cukor. "Birdwell said it in that memo about Goddard: 'the girl who gets the part must be prepared to have her life laid bare in cold black print.' "

And on the notepad, there it was: Legion of Decency.

"And three?" said Selznick morosely. "An unknown who can do the job."

They were both unhappy with that one. Cukor still held out for Katharine Hepburn.

"Number four," he said. "This month." So they agreed to keep Hepburn in reserve.

Underneath that list lay the names they had agreed upon: the final candidates. Paulette Goddard, twenty-seven, did well in *Modern Times* and *Young in Heart,* the favorite of insiders, his own favorite. Except. Except that he could not risk Louella Parsons and the rest being scandalized by her relationship with Chaplin. Married by a ship's captain, my ass. Jean Arthur, thirty-three. Too old, and too well-known. He had promised them—he had promised himself—a new star. Joan Bennett, then, twenty-eight, with her hair newly dyed black, a last-minute addition. But was she good enough? Vivien Leigh and Jennifer Wingate. Both twenty-five, both English, both gorgeous, both of them unknown enough to rank as discoveries.

Selznick took off his glasses and rubbed his eyes. He and George didn't agree on those two, and it had been another of the endless wranglings. George wanted Leigh because he thought she was the better actress, but George did not have to haggle with Alex Korda over her contract, and Korda wanted an arm and a leg. And if the press found out she and Olivier were living together while still married to other people? Worse scandal than Goddard!

"Where does Myron stand?" Cukor asked.

Selznick shrugged. "He won't say."

"It's your decision, David." Cukor threw up his hands. "More tests?"

"For my money, it's Wingate," Selznick had replied. "No ties, no contract with Korda, lots of morality, ambitious as hell."

But Selznick had agreed to wait until Leigh got into town next week and they would get a test in Technicolor.

Now he eased his tired shoulders and twisted his chair around to look out the window at the gleaming silver water tower. For this I spend my life in screening rooms staring at the millimeters of flesh that are measured in millions of dollars? For this I alone have to find that one form, face, and voice that those eighty-five million people will plunk down a quarter to see? He took out his gold fountain pen again, and reluctantly unscrewing its top, turned back to the list of names that stared at him under the desk lamp. Then he leaned forward and placed a neat check mark next to the name Wingate.

That same night, Jennifer lay in their big bed with her legs apart and her knees raised, Anthony between them, making love to her and his own nature. Inside her, he was not moving. He fondled her breasts to make her nipples register excitement. He was never clumsy or specially selfish; it was the routine of it that numbed her.

Feeling her body respond, but as though it were some other part of her, she thought of work: next morning's fifty-mile drive to location in the Conejo Hills, the bad feelings between Wyler and Goldwyn, Olivier and Merle at each other's throats, the damned imported heather growing under the California sun till it looked like a wheatfield.

She hated his locking the door between them and Merry.

Laying his full weight on her, he began to move inside her, his slow thrust evoking her body's dream, forcing her response. If she thought of Olivier, it was because he was so vital. If she fantasied Niven, it was because he was so kind. She moved restlessly, mind and body in conflict. Damn Anthony's jealousy. She placed her arms around him, and her mouth sought his. She thought of Brandon in the house a mile further down the beach. Her heartbeat increased, her body moving with Anthony's, his smell warm in her nostrils. She lay with her head back, excitement increasing.

"Mummy?"

She scarcely heard that first tentative request, was not sure of it, but stopped the movement of her hips.

"Mummy?"

She was instantly alert, lowering her knees, raising her hands to clasp Anthony's back and stop him from moving, a thrill of guilt making her heart race.

"It's Merry," she said.

He stayed where he was, relaxing on top of her, within her. "Ignore her, she'll settle down," he said.

"Let me up, darling," she said softly. "She's having a bad dream."

Instead of moving aside, he started again his slow thrust, trying to kiss her.

She moved her mouth crossly away to the side and pushed up with one hip. "Darling," she said more firmly, "let me up."

"Mummy?" The voice was louder now, and there was a five-year-old's soft unrhythmed knock on the door. "Mummy?" A note of anxiousness.

"Yes, darling?" she called out. "What is it?" Her face was to the door, her neck strained away from Anthony, who was pushing her thighs apart with his, as though he had begun the progress to climax.

"Hadders, Mummy, hadders," came the voice.

"What shadows, darling? They can't hurt you." She pushed against him with her hands and glared at his ear next to her face. "Anthony," she whispered fiercely. "Let me up."

"Hadders, Mummy, hadders." There was a touch of sob in the voice.

"I'll be right there, darling," she called. "Anthony!"

"The door's locked," murmured Anthony. "Leave her alone, she has to learn to deal with this."

"Let me up!" She was angry.

"Hadders, Mummy, hadders. . . . I'm scared, Mummy." There was a sob now to accompany the soft fumbling at the handle, the little thumping on the door.

Anthony began to move faster, his thrust deepening, pushing her against the bed. She lay passive, thinking: Just get it over, hurry up, just get it over, hurry up, hurry up, hurry up.

"Mummy!" Anthony came to urgent climax with a moan and a fierce clutching; the child began to weep.

"Just a minute, darling," called Jennifer, cooing, as Anthony let his full weight collapse on her, breathing heavily.

"Mummy, there's hadders!" The words had a tinge of panic.

"Yes, darling, Anthony, let me go, I have to go, she's frightened!"

"Let her alone," panted Anthony.

Now she scorned him, and moved her body under his, angrily pushing him away.

"Mummy!" The wail rose, and this time there was only fear.

That was when the struggle in the bedroom began, the nightmare of love and hatred. Outside the door Merry's sobs quickly changed to a loud, panicked weeping, and her daughter's panic bred rage in Jennifer. She pushed up against Anthony, hard and fierce. He pushed down against her and held her still, his legs twined around hers, his pelvis pinning her, his arms clamped around hers and joined behind her back, so that she could only twist and gasp. She felt his penis begin to swell inside her again, excited by their grappling, and when she threshed her head for freedom he bit down on her mouth, hurting her.

"She has to *learn,*" he panted softly in her ear. "I won't have her *babied,* you have to *learn.*"

She froze herself: rigid, resisting, her chest heaving for air, until he lay there motionless but holding her still. Her senses alone reached out: the smell of the sea air through the open window, the lights of passing automobiles flicking across the ceiling, the long, lonely sobs of her daughter. His penis at last sank again until she could feel the trickle of liquids on the inside of her thigh. Their breathing slowed, and there was a stink of fighting about them. She stared at the doorway. She was icy.

"Let me up," she said once, but he tightened his grip, and they lay there listening to their daughter's terror until the sobbing became silence and there was no more thumping against the door. Only then did he slide off her and head for the bathroom without a word, and for a minute she lay unmoving, feeling the circulation return to painful limbs.

"You see?" he said from the bathroom. "She's gone back to bed. You have to learn to be firm. You can't baby her."

She rose from the bed and let her gown fall over her hips and knees. In the light from the bathroom she walked to the bedroom door and opened it. Merry lay curled outside on the floor, sound asleep, thumb in mouth, face tearstained. Jennifer knelt down to her child and began to weep.

On December 7, Vivien Leigh arrived in California by plane for what she had told everyone would be a five-day visit. Laurence Olivier, limping from the athlete's foot that made the filming of *Wuthering Heights* agony, was there to meet her. Fellow actors, he told the press. Vivien and her husband were his good friends. She moved into his house at 520 North Crescent Drive, and Russell Birdwell told

Selznick that if Parsons or Hopper found out about it then she could whistle "Dixie" because she'd sure never play it.

On December 10 they started filming *Gone With the Wind.* They needed the back lot for new sets, so they killed two birds with one stone by turning the village wall from *King Kong* and the remains of De Mille's *King of Kings* into the facades of Atlanta's munitions warehouses, then ran oil lines through the whole mess and rented every Technicolor camera in existence to film the flight of Scarlett and Rhett from burning Atlanta. David Selznick invited several hundred guests to watch the spectacle, which was delayed because his brother Myron was late.

When Myron showed up at last, he brought Olivier and Leigh with him onto the platform where David fiddled with the console that controlled the flames.

"David"–Myron grinned–"let me introduce you to your Scarlett." Vivien Leigh's green eyes shone in the dying glow of the flames. Corny, thought David, but what a story it would make.

During the next two weeks Cukor made one last round of tests: Jean Arthur, Joan Bennett, Paulette Goddard, Vivien Leigh, and Jennifer Wingate. Cukor filmed three of them in color: Goddard, Leigh, Wingate. David had huge stills of all five actresses made up and set around his office. He had the five tests spliced a dozen different ways and sat in his private screening room watching them run and rerun, cigar smoke drifting into the projector's light, his shoulders hunched. Cukor came and watched with him, overweight from months of overwork. His lawyer, Danny O'Shea, slid into the seat next to him. Korda had arrived in town, he said, and would not stand in Leigh's way. Later, alone, as Scarlett after Scarlett confronted Ashley in the library at Twelve Oaks, Selznick took his golden fountain pen out of his pocket and looked at the five names on the yellow pad in front of him. He drew a line through Arthur, through Bennett. Both of them personal friends, he thought. How was he going to handle that, for Chrissake?

Myron joined him next day, the family resemblance clear in the way they slouched. He'd moved Olivier out of the house, he said, and he'd put Sunny Alexander, his own goddamn secretary, in. Let Hopper make something of that!

"Yeah," said David, "but Will Price says Wingate can do the accent better. Leigh thinks it's just a matter of saying 'foah-doah Foahd.' And with both Gable and Howard refusing even to try?"

Myron shrugged.

"And Lee Garmes says Leigh's neck is so long he'll have to use shadows every scene. I'm not going to ask Walter Plunkett to redesign her dresses."

"Look," said Russell Birdwell. "Wingate's a publicist's dream—husband, daughter. She's clean. Isn't that enough to at least knock out Goddard?"

That night, slowly, the gold pen scratched a line through Goddard.

"One thing," said Birdwell. "I don't think she'll give a damn. That lady's got other things going for her."

On Christmas Eve, a dark limousine slid through the gates in front of Selznick International's antebellum mansion, swung along the driveway past leafless oaks and pruned shrubs, and pulled up at the broad flight of steps that led to the main entrance behind the columns. A curt flunky greeted the man who descended from the car and led him quickly to the darkened screening room where Selznick sat wreathed in smoke and indecision. The producer rose to shake his guest's hand and his shadow blocked the image on the screen of Jennifer Wingate slapping Ashley Wilkes's face.

"Nice to meet you," said Selznick. "What can I do for you, Mr. James?"

The following day Santa Claus rode a fire truck one last time down Hollywood Boulevard and George Cukor gave a Christmas lunch at his elegant home on Cordell Street in Beverly Hills. Elegant cars discharged elegant guests, among them Olivia de Havilland, Leslie Howard, Laurence Olivier and Vivien Leigh, Charlie Chaplin and Paulette Goddard, Jennifer Wingate and Anthony James. Cukor served mint juleps as well as eggnog, and everyone was very nervous. The house was huge, its effects circular, its windows open to the sunshine shimmering on a blue-green swimming pool and pink flagstones and white statuary. Cukor waited until Leigh and Olivier had tired of admiring the Rouault, the Picasso, the Augustus John, the Braque. Leigh went outside alone, to sit among the statuary for fresh air and cigarettes. Cukor followed her, and he bent over her, his face solemn. "Well, it's finally settled, Vivien," he said. "David has made his choice." They both enjoyed in different ways the next moment of suspense. Then he beamed. "I guess we're stuck with you," he said.

Later that afternoon, everyone went to the party Merle Oberon was giving in honor of Myron Selznick. Korda was there, of course; everyone knew he and Merle were getting married. Korda told David Selznick that he had wanted Leigh for the princess in *The Thief of*

Bagdad, but he saw no reason why they couldn't come to an arrangement, though he still didn't think the part fit her English-rose image. No announcement yet. No gossip even.

On New Year's Eve Myron Selznick bused everyone through the orange groves of San Bernardino and up into the pine-clad mountains and the thin snow surrounding Hillhaven, his lodge on Lake Arrowhead. Anthony charmed them all, and Jennifer at last took the opportunity to introduce him to David Selznick. The tension made them all artificial, but Jennifer looked very composed and was careful not to drink too much. On January 4 Chaplin told Paulette Goddard that Vivien Leigh was reporting at the studio for fittings and makeup tests, and on January 5 the *Hollywood Reporter* identified Leigh as the final choice, but there was no official word.

On Thursday, January 12, Jennifer and Anthony stayed at Don the Beachcomber's long after hours, with the result that Jennifer slept late on Friday. Merry was with Mabel for the night. Anthony rose early to take a run on the beach. He had just gotten back when the messenger arrived with a personal note for Jennifer from Selznick, and a bowl of mauve orchids. The announcement had been released in Atlanta late last night, said the note. As Ashley Wilkes, Leslie Howard. As Melanie Wilkes, Olivia de Havilland. As Scarlett O'Hara, Vivien Leigh.

Anthony, wearing shorts and with a towel around his neck, carried the bowl of mauve orchids up the stairs to the bedroom, where he roused Jennifer from under the covers. His face curiously intent, he sat on the edge of the bed and handed her the note. Setting the bowl of orchids on the bed, he watched her expression of sleepy anticipation turn blank, the freshness of her face turn gaunt as she read. He lifted a hand to stop her words.

"Before you cry," he said, "there's something I think it only fair to tell you." She looked at him, bewildered. "*I* told Selznick that if you signed a contract with him it would be against my wishes. I also told him that if you did, I would immediately file for divorce on the grounds of your adultery with Robert Brandon. I want you to know, because I want you to realize that I am at last taking charge of this marriage."

Elizabeth had a busy schedule planned for Saturday, January 14. The season was terrible for house sales, she was almost broke again, and she was eating a quick lunch at home in Olde Englande before showing a house in Brentwood, when there was a knock on her screen door and she looked up to see two policemen standing there. Her first thought was that Irene Steppels would be livid with her for bringing this on them, but she forgot Irene as soon as the officers asked if she was Jennifer Wingate's mother. Yes, she said, feeling the rush of blood to her head. No need to be alarmed, ma'am, they said, and can we come in?

Miss Wingate had given them her name. A patrol car had spotted her daughter on the beach near Malibu early this morning. She'd been sitting in her car, staring out to sea, and the car was over its hubcaps in water. They didn't tell her how eerie it had been—the opalescent fog surrounding them with a cage that made their voices echo, the car riding the ripples of the water through which they'd had to splash, this beautiful dame in her nightie, ignoring them. Yeah, she'd been . . . well, she'd had a couple too many, but sure she was all right, except for a bad bruise on her cheek. They just couldn't get much out of her, only her mother's name and address. They had her in the station now, but the press hadn't got onto it, and there being no harm done, would Mrs. Wingate like to come with them and bring some clothes?

The station house stank of carbolic and urine and stale cigarette smoke, and its floors were damp and sandy. Jennifer was chain-smoking in the captain's office, huddled in a gray blanket. Against the flat white of her face, the bruise on her left cheek stood out black and red, centered by a small cut. Her feet were bare, and she wore a nightgown wet at the hem. Her eyes recognized her mother, and she stood up to leave, but she would not speak, would not answer questions.

"Just get me out of here. Please."

She wouldn't go back to her own cottage, shaking her head without words, the hair falling over her face, so Elizabeth drove her to Brandon's house in the Malibu Beach Colony and handed her over to Mabel, who regressed instantly to Nanny and fussed her into bed with a hot-water bottle.

"Anthony picked up Merry yesterday, didn't he?" asked Jennifer.

"Yes, dear, Merry's in good hands," replied Mabel, fluffing up the pillows. "Now, you just get yourself some nice sleep."

Jennifer looked up at her and laughed sourly.

Elizabeth and Brandon drove to Jennifer's cottage, where the screen door flapped in the wind. The house was silent; no neglect, no bodies on the carpet, just unmade beds and the signs of hasty packing. In the main bedroom a bowl spilled dead mauve orchids in a patch of wetness on the bedclothes. In the hall Brandon found a note on a scrap of kitchen paper blown under a table near the front door.

Merry and I are flying to New York, said the note. *We will expect to see you in London as soon as you have come to your senses.* No signature; just a period that had broken through the paper like a stab wound.

Later in January Selznick went to Wardrobe to help them drape Vivien Leigh, and he spent the better part of a day fussing about the way her breasts looked. She modeled bra after bra for him. "More pointed!" he demanded, waving his cigar in the hot and dusty room smelling of cloth and sweat. "Now, lower the left nipple!" he ordered. "Hell, no, not that far." She was getting hot, tired. "Tape," he said. "Use the tape to push up her cleavage."

At last they got it right.

"That's perfect!" he exclaimed with joy. "How'd you do it?"

She smiled sweetly. "It's just plain me, David," she said.

Well, maybe Selznick wasn't to blame. Women's real selves are not the stuff of most men's dreams.

That same evening, Elizabeth was packing a suitcase in her apartment at Olde Englande, sympathetically watched by Don Wallace.

"But I don't see how you can be so angry with *Jennifer,*" he was saying.

"I need to earn a living," she replied. "I have my own life to live."

"But when your daughter needs you!" he said. "She is ill, you know."

Pale and withdrawn the first few days after her drama, Jennifer had become rosy with fever that threatened pneumonia. She had asked Elizabeth to nurse her, and Robert Brandon had offered his last spare bedroom.

Rummaging among shoes at the bottom of the wardrobe, Elizabeth spoke sarcastically. "A mother is something you pull out of the closet when you think you need her?" She straightened and looked at Don. "I'm tired of my daughter's dramas. I have my own."

"Now, Elizabeth, you know you don't really mean that." Don was assured, paternal. He was amazed when she blazed out at him.

"Don't tell me what I mean!"

He raised his eyebrows, and she tossed a pair of shoes into the suitcase beside him, then spoke more quietly in apology. "I don't even know whether I like my daughter. I never have known. She has a long history, you know, not just of willfulness but of judgments that are just plain silly. She should have known how Anthony would react. I may have been taken in by his charm, his damnable . . . reasonability. But she is his wife!"

"Then why bother with her at all?"

Folding underwear, she smiled wistfully. "I'm still her mother. I do have all the ordinary decent human feelings." She laughed grimly. "I bring it on myself. I said years ago that I would always be my daughter's safety net. I suppose I meant it."

Don shook his head in bewilderment, having retreated long since. She looked at him for a moment, seeing that he was a decent man, and her face grew sad. Very softly she said, "When you have nothing in common with your only daughter, can you imagine the grief you feel?" Then she smiled and touched him. "Can we make love before I leave for Malibu? I don't know when I'll see you next."

He reached up and pulled her down to him with kindness.

Dark had fallen when he carried her suitcase out to the old Ford coupé. Before she locked the door, she looked over the cheap improvisations that were her home and found herself suddenly thinking again of the waiting room at the railway station in the middle of the winter plains, when she had felt the peril of being a foreigner in a strange land. This room was as ugly as that. She was quickly, enormously depressed and closed the door sharply.

The swimming pool was filthy. Bottles and overflowing tin ashtrays sat on the swaybacked chairs. Someone came out of Warley Starbuck's apartment upstairs opposite, and she and Don glimpsed a roughneck being kissed good-bye by a Warley Starbuck naked as a jay. She shuddered, and when at her car she kissed Don good-bye, she said angrily, "Sometimes I hate this place, this whole bloody country. The whole damn thing is an illusion. Like freedom."

58

January–March 1939

"You know," said Mabel, looking over the top of her glasses and her knitting, "you're beginning to pick up an American accent, Mrs. Wingate."

"I wish you would call me Elizabeth."

Mabel smiled, her lap domestically full of colored wools. "That's the sort of thing America does to you, isn't it?" She sighed. "Which is one good reason for me never going back Home, if you won't take me wrong."

They had laughed together at Fibber McGee and Molly. They listened now to Kay Kyser and his orchestra. They would wait for H. V. Kaltenborn's oracular anxieties about alliances and threats before making a cup of milk-coffee and going to bed. The last weeks had brought Elizabeth closer to Mabel and to Robert Brandon, but not to her daughter. In a house of family, she had come to sense her loneliness.

Ill, Jennifer had become a child again, mopish and querulous for days on end. How could Elizabeth say, "I have only the money that I earn"? With the routines of the house at Malibu Beach Colony centered on this drama's star, she could not say: "I need to be with my man." They would laugh: at her age!

Day after day the sound of the radio filled Jennifer's bedroom. At breakfast, *One Man's Family* and *Our Gal Sunday;* at lunch, swing music; at dinner *Amos 'n Andy* and the news with Fulton Lewis, Jr., and George McCall's *Hollywood Screen Scoops,* which told them one night that Jennifer Wingate was recovering well. After dinner, Elizabeth and Mabel would sit in the living room knitting or reading or waiting for Robert to emerge from the study where he usually spent an hour or so in conversation with Jennifer before she went to sleep.

Jennifer talked very little at first. When she was allowed up, they had trouble dragging her out of the house. Walking on the sun-filled beach, she would hug her thin arms against the breeze, wandering apart and head down. She had Elizabeth read her Anthony's regular letters: brief, cool, like report cards from school or Charles' letters from Mount Lavinia in 1920. She asked Elizabeth to handle her business. Elizabeth did not tell her that Anthony had closed their joint bank account two days before he had left with Merry for London, removing even Jennifer's earnings from *Wuthering Heights.* At first she drew upon her own slender funds. Later she took the diamond necklace and earrings which Charles had given her at Jennifer's birth and sold them to a jeweler, not knowing whether or not she got a good price. The last of Charles' protection vanished with the diamonds. When Jennifer grew well enough to make shopping excursions, the proceeds evaporated quickly. Elizabeth said nothing to Jennifer. She wrote to Anthony asking him to send money, but he did not reply. She could have borrowed from Robert or Don but could not bring herself to do so.

Eventually she had to tell Jennifer that there was no money. Jennifer laughed. "How typical of my husband!"

She immediately asked Robert for a loan but forgot to repay her mother. Proximity was pushing them apart rather than together.

I have only one daughter, Elizabeth told herself again and again. What if we never get on better? I never thought I would live out my life alone.

She asked Jennifer several times what she planned for the future.

"I'll think about that tomorrow," Jennifer laughed with theatrical bitterness. Elizabeth felt like shaking her.

She asked Jennifer what had happened between her and Anthony. There had been a fight, Jennifer admitted. The bruise on her cheek? A book flung by her husband.

"But he didn't mean it to hit me. And I'd already hit him."

She seemed to hold nothing against him. Indeed, Elizabeth thought sometimes, she seems to like him the better.

"You don't think I care about his taking Merry?" Jennifer said once. "She's just as well off with him as with me. He did to me only what I'd done to him."

"Merry is your daughter. You have rights, responsibilities."

"Who was it wanted to send me off to school when I was exactly Merry's age?"

Hearing her mother's silence, she looked up and saw that she had hurt, and grew sullenly defensive. "Anthony and I have had one of our squabbles, that's all," she said. "You shouldn't worry about it. I don't even want him back right now, and he's going to have to get over his guilt about losing me Scarlett O'Hara before he can face me again. Things are better this way, don't you see?"

The daughter's hardness made the mother stiff. "You're speaking of your *marriage!*"

"Oh, Mother!" Cooperativeness vanished. "You don't understand."

"Don't be rude to me!"

A long silence lasted until both decided that they did not want it.

"Anyway," resumed Jennifer, "I shall have the chance now to stay on for a couple of pictures, and Anthony won't be able to blame me for it." She pushed herself up from the armchair and spoke brightly. "He acted wrongly, and I intend to take full advantage of it before I take him back."

"Is a part in a film more important . . . ?" began Elizabeth, but Jennifer had walked outside.

By the middle of March, Jennifer was well enough to spend half the day on the telephone and to go out with Myron Selznick for dinner, and Elizabeth immediately announced that she would return to Olde Englande and work the following weekend. One evening that last week, she and Mabel and Robert had played a game of Monopoly with much laughter. Now Mabel sat knitting by the fire while he read. Elizabeth had grown very comfortable with Robert. He was a quiet, good-tempered man who reminded her of Peter Williams because he loved books and took her seriously. He leaned forward to poke the fire into orderliness, and the driftwood crackled and sparked, turning his face ruddy.

Fire inside, fog outside, whitely alive against the glass doors to the lanai. The room had its own soft, warm life, so that the three people were as though inside an oyster shell. By daylight the house itself, crouched against the sand, seemed to surge forward while the waves and wind and clouds stayed still, and tonight, because she was leaving it, Elizabeth felt that they were all suspended between the past and future. She glanced at Mabel: no longer Nanny, no longer English. She watched Robert: a man, neither actor nor enemy. The house seemed a thing imagined, an act of the human imagination to create escape, a fantasy to deny time, impertinent, perhaps unwise.

Robert looked up from the *New Statesman*. "There's a nice quotation here," he said to her. "Churchill supposedly said that politics are almost as exciting as war and quite as dangerous. From your experience, is he right?"

"Churchill is a brilliant man," said Elizabeth, "who is intensely stupid." But in this mood she could not feel anger with her old demons. "I used to hate him, but I shall probably cheer when they trot him out to fight the next war for us."

Robert removed his glasses to stare into the fire. "Uncommon men never understand us common people," he said.

Elizabeth had a lightning vision of herself as Mrs. Arlen, fired from Bullock's linens department for stealing towels. The vision faded in the fire's flames, which she and Mabel also now studied, caught by something in Robert's tone and posture.

"The Wingate family does not consist of common people," Robert continued. His eyes were vulnerable without spectacles, and Mabel looked at him sharply. He glanced at Elizabeth. "When we were young and poor, Mabel and I, and she used to come home to Wapping with tales of your doings, I found you enormously exciting. When you came to visit me at the theater, I found you frightening. And you lent me money."

He bent forward to lift a tumbling log, then stayed staring into the shift of flames and sparks. "Jennifer was never just another deb. She was my princess in a golden tower."

"She was the same thing to her father," Elizabeth responded quietly.

"I'm glad I've gotten over that," he said, straightening. "Even if I had to get rich to do so." He smiled at her gently. His voice was soft and melodic. "I shouldn't think it did me any harm at all, you know, having the Wingate family as idols. It gave my life its dream, and there are times when one needs dreams."

Elizabeth could think of nothing to say, and eventually he resumed. "At various times I've had a vision of myself moving through life completely untouched, protected inside a pleasant place. I suppose that's the reason I had this house built this way." He gestured at the great windows, where the white fog shuffled. "Of course I've always known that my protection was very slight. A bubble, really. A veil."

The sound of the ocean seemed suddenly clear and close. Elizabeth looked at him and spoke quietly. "And what do you think lies behind that veil?"

He looked sharply at her. "You've had that vision yourself, haven't you? I used to think, the Wingates, they're immune. But you know as well as I do what is behind that veil."

They stared at each other, linked by mind and fear, and Elizabeth's vision now was of the people behind the door marked "Waiting Room" in the nameless railway station on the faceless winter plain.

"Don't you?" he challenged abruptly, then gave the answer: "Whatever one most fears."

She shuddered slightly but responded to his stare. "And eventually death."

"And eventually death." He nodded.

The moment could go no further, and Mabel's sudden words were a splash of cold water. "Comes from being poor when you're a child, that kind of thinking does," she said brusquely, cutting magic, resuming knitting.

Her brother turned to stare at her. "I think not," he said politely. "I think money has nothing to do with it. It is something that all of us feel but few of us admit, even to ourselves."

Memory again tricked Elizabeth. She was back at Wilpattu when Charles had told her of his visions of his dying, and she had refused them.

Even Mabel's knitting stilled as the three fell to listening again to the silence, until she looked up at her brother and spoke as gently as had he. "Are you still in love with her, then?"

"Yes," he said very softly. Now Elizabeth became the watcher, Mabel the interrogator.

"As much as back in thirty-one?"

"More, I think." He had grown very still. "Differently anyway."

Elizabeth could not see his face. Suddenly she drew a deep breath and expelled it. "I wish," she said, "that she could have married you."

She was shocked at her own statement. She had not known she had thought it. Now thought, it seemed that wish had been hers as long as she could remember. She grew flustered and stood up, reaching to pick up a cup and saucer from the table at her side. "I mean," she said, trying to avoid folly, "that you would at least have parallel careers."

Brandon's face remained obscure.

"Of course," said Mabel, and rose to help with the coffeecups and lead her to safety in the kitchen. Once there, Mabel gave her no time to compose herself. "I asked that question," she said in measured tones, " 'cause I thought you ought to know. He'll never talk about it, not Fred, but I've known from the beginning. Kind of complicates things for you, doesn't it? Not that she has the least idea, if you ask me, she's always seen him as just her nanny's brother. But I've always said that she'd be better off with Fred than with Mr. James, if someone could make her see what's right in front of her nose."

Elizabeth had been rinsing the cups. Now she stopped and looked directly at the woman who had been Jennifer's nanny. "You helped Anthony, didn't you? When he came here to pick up Merry that morning–you already knew what he had in mind, didn't you?"

Mabel continued to dry cups, her lips pursing, her face a little flushed. "And what if I had known?" she said crisply. "Which I'm not saying I did, mind, but what if I *had* helped? Would it have been so stupid, then?" Her defensiveness became defiance, and she looked at Elizabeth. "She has to make up her mind, doesn't she? You know that. Mr. James is right about pushing her to the point. She has to choose, you know. Family or career. She shan't have both."

"And you thought," continued Elizabeth as though Mabel had not spoken, "that with Anthony and Merry gone, and Robert here, then Jennifer would give Robert his chance." She spoke with wonder rather than disapproval, thinking that if she was right, how long and how secret a dream Mabel must have had.

"That's as may be," replied Mabel curtly. "But choosing either one once and for all, she'll be better off, make no mistake about it. You have to make your bed and then lie on it in this life. Unlike some others we know, she can't spend her life mucking about somewhere in between men, can she?"

Elizabeth was bewildered and started rinsing the cups again. "I don't know," she said finally. "But it's her business, you know, not ours."

"Huh!" sniffed Mabel. "Those who don't know their own minds will have 'em made up for them by someone else."

That night Elizabeth had a dream. She saw herself as though from a distance standing in the middle of a chessboard, the squares around her stretching black and white as answers. Sometimes in the dream she was herself, sometimes Jennifer. At the edge of the board against a backdrop of darkness stood dim, giant figures like a Christ, a Buddha, a Churchill, but she knew they were unimportant compared to the four males who stood on the board, one to each corner square. Robert Brandon. Anthony James. Donald Wallace. Charles Wingate. The four men stood still and calm, hands loose at their sides, facing her, and she knew they were waiting for her to move. She also knew that she must stay exactly where she was or court some terrible danger. And she also knew that she had to move, could not stay where she was. They would not wait for her much longer. They would walk from the board and into the gloom where the dim great figures stood, and she could hear Mrs. Arlen, weeping in her widow's weeds, call a warning to her. It was a terrible dream, from which she woke shaking.

The next morning she spoke to Jennifer while the girl was still in her robe, drinking her tea on the lanai. "There's something I must know."

"What?" said Jennifer, puzzled.

"About you and Robert Brandon." Jennifer's expression remained unchanged, but Elizabeth felt that its blankness was wary, not innocent. "In 1931, when you wanted to get married to Anthony sooner than your father and I thought proper, I received an anonymous letter telling me that you were planning to elope with Robert Brandon. Were you?"

"Oh, that!" said Jennifer, relaxing. "No." She picked up a piece of toast and started to spread jam on it.

"Who wrote that letter?"

"I did." She looked at her mother with a puzzled expression, as though she could not imagine what the fuss was about.

"What was your intention?"

"I wanted you and Daddy to let me marry Anthony," said Jennifer with a shrug. "I thought that it would scare you into it. It did, didn't it?"

"Did you know that as a result of that letter I went to see Robert and gave him the money to get to Hollywood?"

"Yes," said Jennifer. "He's always been very grateful."

"Were you both blackmailing me, then?"

Jennifer looked shocked, and the shock seemed genuine. "Blackmailing you? Mother! You have the most awful mind." She bit into her toast and looked out to the beach. "Good Lord, what do you think both of us are?"

Elizabeth looked steadily at her daughter. "On that subject," she said eventually, "I seem to change my mind rather frequently."

So it became easier for her to leave her daughter that weekend to return to Olde Englande, and if she missed anyone from that house of dreams on the beach at Malibu, it was Robert Brandon, with whom she felt uneasily she had rather too much in common.

Olde Englande had changed in her absence. Mr. Roth came down to see her as soon as he noticed her return, bringing with him a thin eight-year-old nephew with huge eyes and greasy locks of hair who spoke no English and sat terrified in her armchair.

"We don't know where his mother and father are," said Mr. Roth. "But he likes Sears, Roebuck, don't you, Johnny? Sears, Roebuck, eh?"

Irene Steppels arrived soon after, full of gossip. Warley Starbuck had gone to live with a man he had met in the record store. Miss Jerzinsky in number eleven had gone back to Boise. Mrs. Arlen had flown the coop, done a moonlight flit because she couldn't pay the rent, left her canary on her doorstep one morning, no note, nothing, not a word to anyone. She herself wasn't as well as she might be. Had a lump in her right breast. "*They* want to put me in the hospital," she confided. "But who can afford that? I know how to fix it for myself."

"She's rubbing meat tenderizer into it," whispered Mr. Roth later, shaking his head.

Elizabeth watched the trio depart, standing by her screen door to look out at the unusable pool and the ashtray overflowing onto the broken rattan table. *"Bloody* California," she said aloud. *"Nothing* but stucco. Why don't they ever *mend* anything?"

But she telephoned Don that afternoon and was very glad to see him, even though he brought his own beer and pretzels so that he could listen to the broadcast of the game. She basted a roast in the hot little kitchen, then stood in the doorway wiping her hands on a towel to watch his enthusiasm, comfortable with domesticity of her own again.

"They say," she commented good-humoredly over the yelling from the radio, "that a woman who respects herself makes men out of boys and an adult out of herself. But it doesn't always work out that way."

He had proposed to her after Christmas dinner, when they had both been a little weepy with liquor and homesickness, and she had turned him down.

"You have a family already," she had said, "and I'm old enough to be your mother."

"In California, who cares?" he had said. "I'm serious, you know. I love you."

"A man loves any woman who keeps his stomach well filled," she had said with resolute flippancy. "Propose again in . . . let me see . . . 1950? By that time I'll need someone to push my wheelchair, and you should still be reasonably fit."

She liked him very much, but she didn't love him, and she had been firm when he insisted she take him seriously. "I don't want to be coaxed," she said. "You have to believe me. You have a wife and children, and you mustn't let your loyalties entirely follow your affections, you know. I have absolutely no desire to marry again. It took me years to learn to live alone happily. Now I like it, and I won't give it up."

She had been flattered rather than surprised at his proposal, for he was a sentimental, decent man who saw his wife and family too rarely, and tonight after eating the meal and dancing to swing music they made love, he lingering over her body as though to reassure her that he forgave her absence, her rejection. Afterward they lay beside each other to smoke and talk. His business was booming, he said, the clients sidling into his tent, pouring money into his lap in exchange for his reading of the winds to which they might trim their ethics.

"What about taking that job now that wasn't here when you arrived? Another couple of months, we could use you."

She was silent for a few moments. "I don't think so. No."

"Because of us, you mean?"

She let his misinterpretation stand. She was not ready to discuss her plans.

"Well perhaps it's for the best," he sighed eventually. "I have to tell you something. I've bought a new house. I'm bringing Joanie and the kids out."

"At last!" she said, rising to lean on an elbow and look at him. "I've told you for months they should be here with you."

"But what about us?" he said plaintively.

"We'll survive." She laughed, and led him to make love again.

Much later, after she had given him one last kiss to speed him out the door, she again lay in bed smoking in the dark, listening to the sound of car tires swish, the sound that always deceived her into thinking of good, solid English rain. She wondered whether she was foolish. At her age she couldn't expect to find another man she could share her bed with. She found herself thinking back to that moment after the great fire when she had looked up from cooling her legs in the filthy swimming pool of the burned-out house and seen her rescuers approach. She had seen them as aliens rather than just strangers.

"I can do even without intimacy if I have to," she said aloud. "Better to be lonely on my own terms than have company on someone else's." She thought of Jennifer and Anthony. I don't think I could stand all that again, not again. She sat up to stub out her cigarette. We waste so much of our lives on love, she thought. But what else is there?

"It's almost the second anniversary of Peter's death," she said aloud to the darkness. "And I wish I could see him."

A car roaring by on the street sent light running across the ceiling.

"My daughter *may* need me," she said. "So what?" She smiled. "And they say that people who talk to themselves are crazy. Well. I'll think about that tomorrow." Again she smiled, lay back, and pulled up the covers. "Tomorrow is another day," she said, and closed her eyes.

Expatriates and older women have something in common. Sooner or later they come to a crossroads which has no other signpost than a clock, and the clock tells them only that they must now go home or stay where they are forever. It takes courage to go home.

59

April–August 1939

The art of planning for the future has two styles, one used by those who feel the need for more power, the other by those more eager to maintain than to acquire. Jennifer as yet had developed no sense of the power that flows naturally from a clear sense of self. She was still caught between images of herself, and her power came from others: Charles, Anthony, other men, the audience, all that is meant by Success. Elizabeth, having survived war, marriage, widowhood, and even youth, had developed a sense of self so strong that only her daughter could damage it. As their two styles of planning caused them to drift further apart, distaste was the natural result. They would have something in common only if Jennifer decided that her mother had the power which Jennifer needed.

Early in April, Jennifer smiled into the telephone in her bedroom at Brandon's house as though it were a person.

"So are you filing against that prick of a husband?" asked the voice of Myron Selznick.

"Good Lord, no!" She laughed and reached for another cigarette. "You're as bad as the columnists–making mountains out of molehills. For heaven's sake, Myron, it was no more than a spat. Poorly timed, I will admit, but just a spat between husband and wife."

"You got it in writing he won't make more trouble?"

"Myron! We love each other! It was only Scarlett he didn't want me to play, and frankly, with what I hear about the troubles David is having filming that monster, perhaps Anthony was right. Besides, with the war coming, everything's changing. Anthony understands now that this may be my last chance to make good. He writes to me twice a week, you know, and you don't think they could all be business letters, do you?"

When Jennifer said these things, part of her believed everything she said. Things, she thought, had to be said in a way that men would understand properly.

"Get it in writing," he replied gloomily. But he was used to actresses fighting to stay ahead of the game, so he went on to a grumble rather than a confrontation. "Threatening grounds of adultery against you, yet! Those divorce laws of yours must have been written by the Legion of Decency. What about you and Brandon? Are you two really a hot number or is that all your husband's nightmare and Warner's publicity?"

"We never have been a hot number, darling. It's all fantasy. Robert and I have known each other since we were children. His sister was my nanny, you know, and we never appear in public together since the rumors started."

"You English," he sighed. "So at least the stories will stop the public from thinking he's gone queer since his divorce. You moved out on him yet?"

"Darling, don't you see my new telephone number? Though why anyone should think there is anything between us! Anthony and I have been married for seven years, and after this I suspect things are going to get better, much better. There will be no problems with either Robert or Anthony, I promise you, and that's why I want to know if you have any work for me. I really am *desperate* to go back to work."

"A ton of it, sweetheart, a ton of it. What with the war coming, you Brits are top of the market this year!" She could hear him grin. "If you're really ready to sign a seven-year contract at last, I'll get you the moon–they'll take anything with an English accent and nice tits."

"What about your brother?"

"Ouch, you don't want much! Don't you think you burned him badly enough?" But he was still grinning, liking the game. "He's got some piece of schmaltz in production with some huge Swedish broad for the lead, along with Howard when he's finished work on *GWTW*, but I don't think you want it. I was thinking about this English mystery story, this Du Maurier thing. Leland's pushing our clients for that. Hang on a minute, I'll get the file."

She heard him yelling to his secretary. "You read this thing yet?"

"I even know the author personally."

"*Rebecca,* that's it, but it isn't the heroine's name. She hasn't got a name for some dumb reason, but Leland says my brother's going to have another of his godalmighty searches for a new star. Real reason? He can't afford a star, for Chrissake, until some money comes in from *GWTW*. So Leland's notes say a mousy type who gets glamorous. Glamour you can do. How about mousy?"

"Look at a print of *Devon Dawn.* I played a thirty-three-year-old housewife and I was only twenty. The other woman got the man."

"So this list of possibilities, you're not on it yet but I can fix that. Fontaine and De Havilland? Jesus, either Leland or David's mad. They'd kill each other. Maggie Sullavan–that's all right, he puts her name down for everything. Loretta Young? David puts *her* in for everything. You know an Anne Baxter? Never heard of her. Forget it, he's going to need someone with a name for this, and now you got a name. So long as Leigh doesn't want it, which she probably will. Olivier's down for the lead if he can't get Colman. Leigh mousy? My brother's out of his mind." There was a thrumming pause. "So we'll offer him Colman and Wingate, I think we got a chance."

"Is Hitchcock directing?"

"So you already know about it, huh?"

"Just gossip," she laughed. "You forget I worked once with Hitchcock."

"I hope he still likes you. I'll talk to David this weekend, but I tell you he's going to want something ironclad about that marriage of yours. You had Scarlett until that prick of a husband did you in, and you louse up this time, that'll be it for you in Hollywood, you know." His tone had darkened to a point of seriousness that alarmed her.

"Darling!" she protested gaily. "What, as you so elegantly put it, is to louse up?" She would face that ironclad something later.

"So I'll call you back Monday. You keep your legs crossed, you hear?"

Jennifer lowered the telephone, disgruntled. She was having to take so many damn risks, but she couldn't afford her own apartment. So what if David Selznick's beach house was only a few hundred yards away? What could be more respectable than living with her old *nanny,* for God's sake. She would write to Anthony to ask for money. She would move out as soon as she got it. Myron was right. She would even tell Anthony honestly that she was going to sign a seven-year contract and explain that she had not the slightest intention of adhering to it and they couldn't do a thing to hold her to it because by the beginning of next year she would be back home where she wanted to be. With him and Merry, she would tell him. *Rebecca?* She'd seen a copy somewhere. Robert must have a copy. She took her hand off the telephone and headed for Robert's study with no more than a glance into the mirror. Mousy! Like hell she'd be mousy!

* * *

Elizabeth believed that her decision to return to England was both foolish and right, so she questioned its wisdom even as she made her plans. She saw only two problems: money and war. Hitler dismembered and occupied Czechoslovakia on March 15, and on March 21 he demanded the return of the Danzig Corridor to Germany. On March 28 the Fascists won the Spanish Civil War by conquering Madrid, and on April 7 Italy invaded Albania. On April 26 Prime Minister Chamberlain announced England's first peacetime conscription. Though occasionally the evening news gave Elizabeth a feeling very much like nausea, she was unafraid. War would not make her choices this time.

Everyone thought she was crazy.

"Go back to London now?" said Mabel, looking offended. "Why on earth would anyone want to do that? What bee have you got in your bonnet this time, I wonder?"

"It must be a bee," laughed Elizabeth. "I don't really know that I could put it into words, anyway, though it is a bit more than a buzz."

"Wait a minute, I'll muck up this hollandaise if I don't pay mind to it," said Mabel, whipping away with her fork in the pot, giving herself time to think. "My goodness, this is nice asparagus. How you'll ever give up the food here, I can't imagine."

"Nor can I," said Elizabeth.

"Or the sun!" Mabel peered suspiciously into her pot. "Well, I don't know about that, but it'll have to do," and she started ladling the sauce onto the asparagus. "You and Fred, you've got bitten by the same bug. I told him, I said if he's such a *bloody* fool as to go back, he can't count on me being with him." She was angry, but a moment more of banging with pots made her philosophical. "Well," she sighed, "it seems barmy to me, but there's no arguing about tastes, is there?"

She picked up two laden plates and headed for the dining room. "Bring those with you when you come, will you, love?" She bumped the swinging door open with a generous hip. "Mind you," she said, looking back over her shoulder, "you'll be able to visit their graves after all this while, and that'll be nice, won't it? Mr. Charles and Mr. Williams, I mean."

Elizabeth picked up the other two plates, then stepped back to avoid the backswing of the door. She thought she heard Mabel say, "I shall quite miss you, you know."

She tackled Robert Brandon after dinner. He had started filming *Raffles,* and work made him both tired and good-humored.

"There is a kind of tug, isn't there?" he said. "War has its charms."

"Mabel says you may go back yourself. Enlist."

The setting sun tipped the waves with gold and made him look very brown, very handsome in swim trunks and wet-combed hair. He stood on the lanai with a drink in his hand, and she could see the outline of his genitals.

"I haven't made up my mind," he said slowly. "Like the rest of us, I expect I'll wait till the last minute. Niven is liable for the call-up, of course, but the rest of us exports seem to be waiting for some alarm clock to go off." He turned abruptly, his face worried. "What use anyone would have for a four-eyed actor my age I can't imagine, but probably there'll be something useful I can do."

"What about your career?"

"I imagine that whatever you are doing feels trivial when war starts. I missed the last one by a hair, and I've never felt quite right about that. God knows I've got enough money to last me to the end of my years, and," he said with a smile, "we dreamboats don't age as fast as the love goddesses." He moved to the drink tray. "Another?"

She accepted, and he fussed with ice and fresh fruit and gin.

"I must admit I'm a little surprised that you would want to go back," he continued, handing her the glass. "You have no ties there except perhaps Merry, and you fit so very well in America."

She laughed, rather pleased. "Everyone fits well in America," she said. "I thought that was why they invented the place!" She sipped from the cool glass and moved to the entrance of the lanai, where the breeze blew back her hair to reveal the gray. "Or at least one misfit more isn't so noticeable where nobody is sure where or even who they might be tomorrow."

"You like it here, though."

"I like it very much," she said, her eyes on the luxury of the beach. "But it isn't my home and never will be." She turned toward him. "Do you understand?" The side light of the sun showed her at her most attractive. At last she had found the right answer to the question Americans always asked.

"Home is where the heart is." He shrugged. "I carry mine on my back."

"I think one has to be greedier than I to be really happy in America. Greedy for things, not just money. Greedy to succeed." She put her glass down on the railing and gestured around her. "I can think of no fate worse than to be old and poor in America."

"What about Jennifer?"

"She has her own life to live, and who knows where that will be? I have a small nest egg back in England that Charles left for my old age, and it's been growing because of the rent on my house—but it's more than money I worry about. I would just feel safer there. Ever since the fire . . ." She shuddered violently, then picked up her glass and drank. "One is so anonymous here. Either famous or anonymous. It is hard just to belong."

He moved to stand beside her, and it was almost as though he would put his arms around her. Instead he said, "I do hope you won't become one of those instant experts on America."

She laughed. "I shan't blame my retreat on America." Conscious of his bare flesh and the scent of salt on his body, she moved away to light a cigarette. "Our opinions about places tell a great deal about us and very little about the place."

"I must go and change," he said, toweling his hair. Then he paused. "If I stay here, it will be because both America and I are good at the business of encouraging illusions. I realize illusions are very dangerous, but we can't live without them."

He looked boyish. She felt maternal.

"Illusions are something we all have," she said. "But we can each choose whether or not we want them."

"Which is as good an explanation of going back to face England and war as any *I* can think of!" he laughed.

Don Wallace still stopped by Olde Englande for a drink once or twice a week, though his family had arrived in May, and she chose to tell him her plans during the regular after-work gathering around the pool.

"Well, that's fine," he said cheerfully enough. "I shall be over as usual next spring to put the bite on old Harris. We'll see each other then, won't we? This war stuff'll all blow over, you can bet on it. Our polls show nobody wants a war!"

"With the whole of Europe wanting to come here," said Mr. Roth incredulously, "you should want to be going back there? You should thank God you're not a Jew, Elizabeth!"

"So what's the matter with it here, you don't like it?" said Irene Steppels coldly.

"No, no!" protested Elizabeth. "You know that's not true!"

Late in June Jennifer visited Olde Englande to tell her, full of glee, that she had signed a seven-year contract with David O. Selznick and her first role was the lead in *Rebecca* with, they expected, Laurence Olivier.

"But what about your agreement with Anthony?" Work on a picture or two was one thing, a seven-year contract another. "What about Merry? How long will you stay here?"

"Oh, I can come and go as I like," Jennifer said airily. "I've written to Anthony that I shall be home next spring. If he chooses to think that means I'll stay, well and good. We'll sort out everything else when I talk to him. I tell you, Mother, he is being very nice in his letters. Everything is going to be fine between us."

"You have to make your own judgments, child," said Elizabeth skeptically, "and I'm not going to try to interfere, but I think you will hurt Anthony badly. Though I suppose if he's willing now to let you sign that contract—well, he must have thought things over."

"Obviously if we go to war Merry will come and live with me here, and I don't see any reason why Anthony couldn't give up his job in England and get one with, I don't know, the Bank of California or somewhere. He's been through one war, you know, and he's not going to want another."

"You do know I'm going back at the end of August?"

"Yes, Mabel told me. I meant to tell you you are quite insane." Jennifer laughed charmingly and hugged her mother fondly. "But I have trust in your good sense, dear. You'll be back as soon as you see what it is really like."

"Do you want me to see Merry?"

"Of course! And I have all sorts of presents for you to take her!"

Later that night Elizabeth told Peter's Buddha, impassive on the kitchen windowsill, that she was taking him home. His smile did not change.

"I know," she said to him. "You see even my reality as illusion, so it doesn't matter to you where you are. But thank you all the same, I'll make up my own mind."

Elizabeth had almost asked Jennifer for the return of the money she had expended on her behalf, but pride stopped her—pride and the suspicion that it would be Robert's money Jennifer gave her. She had again written to Anthony about Jennifer's money from their joint account, and again she had received no reply. She needed to save a hundred dollars a month to pay for her train fare across country and her passage on the *Aquitania,* sailing August 25, and she enjoyed the challenge more than she minded the effort. It was the first time she had ever earned with a special, selfish purpose in mind. By the beginning of August she had enough for a Pullman across the country, and with one last lucky house sale for which the boss generously gave her full commission, plus the price she got for the old Ford, she upgraded her sea passage to first class just the day before she left Los Angeles.

Of all Elizabeth's departures over the years, never had she been accompanied by so many people. They gathered in the south patio of the huge Los Angeles Union Passenger Terminal which had opened for business the previous May and still looked as California should. Those last minutes in the bright station made Elizabeth realize what she would miss most: the golden sun shining on orderly gardens arranged around pepper trees, palms, and olive trees; the warmth of the stucco walls hung with trumpet vines and cup-of-gold; the breeze smelling more of flowers than of smoke; the people casual, friendly, as open as their climate. Those who had gathered made her feel nostalgic: Jennifer, Robert, Mabel. My family, she thought, feeling settled and pleased. I think Mabel is right. They will marry. The courtly Mr. Roth skittered around the edges of the group looking rather sad. "I understand why you are going back," he said quietly in an accent more Jewish than usual. "Though I would not even if I could. This country is too kind to us. It deserves the best we can give it."

"You're right," she said gently, and he gestured helplessly with his fine musician's hands and faded so quietly into the background that she never formally said good-bye to him. In the flurry of loading her suitcases into Robert's big Cord, she had forgotten to leave farewell notes for the shabby, familiar residents of Olde Englande. Two years here, she thought. Did I make no friends?

But just as they all started to move into the reception hall which led to the departure lobby, a pink-faced Don Wallace appeared bearing flowers and a box of chocolates, so that it was he to whom she chatted brightly on that last long walk through the tunnel giving access to the *Chief*. She had called his office to say good-bye, and he had said he would be there, she should have had more faith. Once beside her Pullman, the others discovered sudden missions to the bookstall. Thrust into intimacy, Don grew moist-eyed. "I'm sorry things didn't work out," he said quietly. "Real sorry."

"You're very sweet," she said, resisting the impulse to pat his arm. "But things did work out, you know. Whatever I came for, I got. I'm ready to go home now, just as I was ready to leave it forever then."

"Come off it, Elizabeth!" Don protested, as though angry at her condescension. "I had such different plans for us."

His anger shocked her into seeing him as an individual rather than an American, so she complimented him by refusing to hide behind clichés. "I think I've given up planning," she said simply. "I want to be somewhere where I don't have to plan quite so much."

"Plans are what I live by," he said wonderingly. "We all need something to protect ourselves against the future. How can you live without them? You are much braver than me."

"Braver?" she laughed in surprise. "Most people would think I'm foolish."

"That too," he said. Then Jennifer and Mabel returned with fruit and magazines and a silly copper ashtray in the shape of a cowboy hat with the green enamel emblem "California, Here I Come." By the time she had gone to her compartment and lowered the window to say farewell to those standing beneath her on the platform, Don had vanished as quietly as Mr. Roth, into her past.

Rocking steadily eastward behind the column of smoke emitted by the engine, Elizabeth had a sense of winding up that which had unwound two years before: the deserts, the mountains, the plains, the farms, the small towns, the industrial cities, all in the right order. She carried in her handbag a long letter from Ginny Pearsall which she had often reread since its arrival in June. It was her future, and now she studied it once more.

"My dearest Elizabeth," it began. "In response to your dreadful question, let me answer this way. I cannot speak of the purlieus of Wimbledon, which may be as immune from firestorms and poison gas as they are from my ken, but since your tenants' lease does not expire for another year or so, I assume you may stay at Anthony's house on Curzon Street, and I should warn you that the only shelter offered Mayfair by the government is a crumbling series of trenches in Green Park. Since these have been marked with large signs reading 'These Trenches Are Dangerous,' they bring gloom to the faces of those regarding them from the windows of the Ritz. One considers alternatives eagerly. I could get you an efficiency in my building quite easily, since the general opinion is that the mere whistle of a bomb would be enough to cause it to fall down. There are of course the government-supplied Anderson air-raid-shelter cabins which one can place in the garden like some kind of super compost heap, but most people believe that is just what they will become and do not care to grow roses with their own bones."

Elizabeth had written back: "Please do get me a flat in your block if you can! I shall find the money somewhere. And please, please do meet me at the boat train if you are free."

The letter continued: "But come by all means! I should adore to have us face this war together. The city should be more livable than in years. Conscription promises to remove some 50,000 pimply and noisy youths from our midst immediately, all the wretched children are to be evacuated, and even the government promises to remove itself to Bath. God save Bath! Since Their Majesties ruined the Season (and my income) by visiting your domains, I am having a jolly good rest, interrupted only by minor excursions to my beloved Chelsea Flower Show and to our Ming, the new giant panda at Regent's Park Zoo, who, upon being presented to Winston Churchill, pronounced him acceptable–thereby reflecting precisely the public mood.

"To reply seriously to your request to know what you could do, should you be so foolish as to return–war of course makes women invaluable. Do you not remember our little meetings back in Colombo, my dear, which we both so much enjoyed? There is the Women's Army, of course, though you may be a little long in the tooth for that. There are the Women's Voluntary Services for Civil Defense, run by the Dowager Marchioness of Reading, or the Women's Auxiliary Territorial Service, run by Mrs. Montagu Norman, wife of the head of the Bank of England, with whom I am sure Anthony would be glad to intervene on your behalf. I recommend the St. John's Ambulance Corps. Their uniforms are definitely chic: blue trimmed with red, and they would suit your coloring well. Otherwise, just think of what men do now; women will be doing it shortly."

Elizabeth wanted work which had some meaning other than that one manufactured for it. In the dining car that night she was enveloped by a sense of Voyage Home parallel to that which she had felt during the return from Colombo in 1919, but this time she had no nostalgia for things ended and begun.

"Of course," continued Ginny's letter, "the crisis is really grave, though 'grave' is not a word at my age that I care to use. Really, you know, though our jokes make the Americans think us unserious and unready, we have used the time well. Every precaution has been taken, every plan made. War is something familiar to us now, isn't it? A difficult relative one cannot avoid. Why, they have even manufactured and stored hundreds of thousands of coffins for the casualties they expect in the first few weeks of bombing! Very comforting, I must say.

"Yes, I shall definitely stay in London, even though I am classified by the press as a 'useless mouth.' Frankly, I would not miss what is coming for worlds! Does that sentiment surprise you? Of course I think of my sons, but I have learned that there is nothing one can do to stop a war, and this time I shall not be trapped by doubt. I shall be *glad* when it starts, and I shall try to get it over with just as quickly as possible."

The womblike rocking of her Pullman, so very private; the neat routines of porters, mealtimes; making up and stripping down the bunk; managing her fruits and magazines and fading flowers—everything gave Elizabeth a sense of readiness. Heading west on the voyage out, she had not known what she would face. Heading east, she knew she was going to face war. If it looked as though she were retreating from her furthest bastion, this was only because she must withdraw to the citadel. She felt that she was heading not from but toward safety. I am gathering myself in upon myself, she thought, and there I *am* safe.

"So, my dear, come home!" wrote Ginny. "If you want conscription and shortages and rationing and hiding in Selfridge's basement to avoid bombs and queuing up for everything, if you want no new fashions and crowded trains and looking at casualty lists for the names of people one knows, then come home and I shall be there at the station to greet you. As the great banner presently draped over that confoundedly inconvenient Marble Arch proclaims, 'Be prepared! National service! Have You Offered Yours?' If I read you right, my dear Elizabeth, you must come home. How would you feel if you stayed away?"

To save money, Elizabeth skipped the chance to say farewell to Chicago by taking a taxi from the *Chief* directly to the connecting *Twentieth Century*. The porter on the new train left her complimentary copy of the Chicago *Tribune* on the seat, and from its raucous headlines she learned that the USSR and Germany had announced the signing of a mutual nonaggression treaty.

"I don't see anything to worry about," said a cowboy type in the club car that evening. "It's peace, ain't it?"

She threw up her hands and shook her head and laughed. "Politics!" she replied to the cowboy type. "I really don't understand politics. It's not as though anything you or I might do makes any difference to anything, is it?" And she thought: How happy Churchill will be, to be proved right.

On the trip westward two years before she had felt light, as a refugee feels light. Returning eastward now, she was light as is a soldier, his burden of complexities behind him, the great simplicity in front. She knew which illusions still wrapped her; she allowed herself to keep them on the grounds of need. As the train snaked slow and rattling through the forever suburbs of New York City, she took Ginny's letter from her handbag to reassure herself with its last paragraph:

"Do come home! The weather has been frightfully wet and chilly, but they say September will be superb, and a spirit grows here such as I have never known before. One no longer feels alone. One is not lonely. One has the feeling that everyone is on the same side and will *help*. One meets fools still, but no enemies, not even Chamberlain or Churchill. One belongs. Even you, my Irishwoman, will be English. It is agreeable to imagine that, once more before I die, there might be something important for me to do."

Elizabeth took a taxi straight from Grand Central to the West Side Pier 90, where the grand old four-funneled *Aquitania* floated on the Hudson opposite the sleek giant *Normandie*. When the ship sailed quietly after dark, it was less than a third full. The few American tourists felt foolhardy and were sheepish, but the British calmly gossiped about the latest news in the lounge. They were due to berth at Southampton on August 31, and already someone had started a pool to choose which day of their voyage would bring the declaration of war. One did not dress for dinner the first night out, and when the gong sounded to announce the single sitting, Elizabeth immediately took her assigned place at the purser's table. She was already looking at the heavy menu when a second person came to the table and made her presence felt at her elbow.

"Mother?"

Elizabeth looked up from the menu, eyes blank behind her spectacles. "Jennifer," she sighed. "What on earth are you doing here?"

PART VI

The Second War Begins

60

August 1939

If Jennifer's unexpected appearance made Elizabeth feel outmaneuvered, her tale—first murmured in snatches between polite war gossip at the dinner table, then told over and over again during the days and evenings of the voyage—brought Elizabeth near despair. Driven by nerves, wrapped against the Atlantic wind, walking by passengers mummified in deck chairs and rugs, Jennifer talked. Elizabeth listened, trying to find out how she might act as a mother when she wished she was not.

Having seen Elizabeth off on the train at Union Station, Robert had driven Jennifer and Mabel back to the house at Malibu Beach Colony, and almost immediately a mailman had arrived to demand Jennifer's signature in exchange for a large envelope bearing English stamps. It came from a firm of London solicitors. It informed her that Anthony had filed suit for divorce on the grounds of her adultery with Robert Brandon, who was formally named as corespondent. Anthony also requested the court to give him custody of Merry.

Speaking of the moment she had first read that document, Jennifer still narrowed her face with pain, and her green eyes darkened. "I cried," she said helplessly. "I didn't understand. I still don't."

The world of the ship seemed not to exist for her. She stood at the railing looking for the horizon in the swelling gray seas. She ate little and smoked endlessly and was rude to fellow passengers.

The day after the arrival of the official envelope, she had received a call from a stringer for Hedda Hopper. "Would she deny the rumors?" An hour later Selznick International called: "What about these rumors?" Hedda Hopper broke the story on the radio that same night—just one among the smaller items, of more interest because of Brandon than Jennifer.

Warner's called Robert within the hour. "Get her the hell out of there," they said. "For Chrissake!"

At three A.M. Myron Selznick called Jennifer, who had not yet gone to bed. "You blew it," he said. "They want you out of *Rebecca.*"

"But they can't!"

"I can't hold them to the picture. I can't even hold them to the contract if they want out. They can break it through the moral-turpitude clause anytime they want now. You didn't act so smart, Jennifer."

"I didn't do anything. It's all a misunderstanding!"

"Cut and run, Jennifer. Get your ass out of Malibu before the photographers find you, and maybe we can save something. Make like a refugee, sweetheart, and we'll see how much of this shit will blow over and how much will stick to that pretty face."

She had turned to Robert for help. "I can put a stop to all this if I get to England and see Anthony. Can you lend me the money? It's all a terrible mistake. Anthony only wants to frighten me."

Robert drove her through the dawn to the Beverly Wilshire and paid for her room, then paid for her fare home. Two days later he put her on the plane at Burbank airport, with the result that she arrived at the *Aquitania* just minutes before its sailing, bringing only one small suitcase, a hatbox, and her jewel case.

Now on the windswept deck she said crossly, "Of course I never had any idea Anthony would do this, and no he does not really mean it. He wants me to give up my career, and this is how he thinks he'll do it. He wants me back home. He loves me. I know him so very well." A small smile crossed her face. "I must admit there is a certain thrill about being wanted so much by a man, even if he is your husband."

Jennifer avoided doubt, but Elizabeth did not. She blamed Jennifer. She blamed Anthony. She blamed herself. It was not fair of her, she thought, to grow exasperated just because Jennifer had no experience and had not listened. It was not fair, she told herself, to blame Jennifer for being trapped between career and wifedom when she herself had spent her life caught between things which she could not control. Guiltily she remembered Charles' long-restrained accusation that she had failed as wife and mother, and memory made her more tender toward Anthony than she might have been. The process of dispensing blame exhausted her.

She tried to help Jennifer think more purposefully, but Jennifer did not really want to hear her mother's opinion, no matter how often she asked for it. Eventually Elizabeth gave up trying to give advice, then trying not to give advice. Finally she gave up feeling almost anything other than the relief of being alone at last in her cabin at night, where she could retrieve some sense of her own future.

The atmosphere on board ship was as tense as Jennifer. Copies of the ship's newspaper vanished every morning with amazing speed as people sought to understand the cryptic summaries of diplomatic maneuvers and guessed at Hitler's state of mind. The purser began pinning up fluttering hourly bulletins typed out by the radio officer. As the hours passed, more and more people were losers in the pool to choose the time of war's start, and the hope began to grow that war might just be avoided. A new poll taken in London showed only one out of five Londoners expecting war, and on the *Aquitania* an agitated camaraderie sprouted. They drank champagne to the strains of "Moonlight Serenade" and "A Tisket, a Tasket," and when the band-leader dared a medley of songs from the Great War, he was surprised to find that they all remembered the words.

"You don't forget the songs you learn when you're a kid," said the philosophical saxophone player.

On the third night at sea, they screened *Beau Geste,* starring Gary Cooper and Robert Brandon, and the ambivalent heroism of the movie's ending left everyone subdued. Elizabeth and Jennifer went to take their evening stroll and found the doors to the deck impeded by heavy canvas curtains. The young seaman guarding them was polite and ruthless: "They're a light trap, ladies. Careful not to show a light now for the U-boats, if you please!"

It was absurd–the decks themselves were brightly lit, and the portholes shone upon the dark waters–but it gave one a sense of threat, and Elizabeth and Jennifer stayed on the lee side of the promenade deck.

"What will Robert do when war is declared, do you think?" asked Elizabeth.

"I don't know," replied Jennifer offhandedly. "He said something about enlisting, but he's far too old for them to be interested in him as a soldier, and he's smart enough to stay out of it."

They strolled past the windows of the salon, dimly hearing the strains of "There'll Always Be an England."

"I wish they'd stick to 'Three Little Fishes,'" said Jennifer.

"Then perhaps he'll be there when you get back to Malibu."

"And the Nazis won't shift Mabel either!" laughed Jennifer.

She was wrong. Robert that week had made inquiries at the British consulate in Los Angeles about joining up, and Mabel, though dour and grumbling, had privately decided she would go wherever her brother went.

Elizabeth wanted to tell Jennifer to give up on Anthony, partly because she suspected that he was more serious than Jennifer suspected, partly because by her standards the marriage had become intolerably sour, and mostly because it would all be so very much simpler if Jennifer would choose Robert. But she could not make Jennifer feel the way she thought she ought to feel.

"Have you made up your mind yet how long it will be before you get back to Hollywood?" asked Elizabeth.

"Mother, we've been through this before." Jennifer's face was sulky. "I can't tell you anything until I talk to Anthony, and all I can say is just what I said before, that I'll get back as soon as I can. I'm *not* going to stay and face a war, and Anthony simply can't make his wife and child do that, that's all there is to it. They won't be making any films in England, and once this scandal is taken care of, I'll be all right again in Hollywood. The publicity might even help."

"What if Anthony does mean it about the divorce?" Jennifer started to turn on her. "I'm only asking *if,*" continued Elizabeth quickly. "What will you do? What if you can't get work in Hollywood because of it?"

"There's no need even to think about that, Mother." Jennifer, exasperated, was shrill. "Anthony doesn't want a divorce any more than I do. He may be angry with me, but it would be too humiliating for him to have people think another man had taken me away. And besides, if I'm living with my daughter and my nanny, who can say that I'm *immoral?*"

Elizabeth dared: "Does he have any real grounds to be jealous of Robert?"

Jennifer threw back her head and laughed with dramatic bitterness. "You always think the worst of me, don't you?" She stopped walking and turned to face her mother, her hands thrust forward in the pockets of her fur coat, Anthony's emeralds gleaming at her ears. "What good would it do to tell you that I've never slept with anyone but Anthony, that I've never wanted to and never shall? I love Anthony, and I have as long as I can remember."

She was at that moment as much like her mother as she had ever been, her voice low, her manner resolute, and it was that image of herself that made Elizabeth finally realize that her daughter was her own woman for good or ill. Did it even matter whether she was telling the truth? Abashed at her own attempt to interfere, Elizabeth looked down at the deck.

The morning of the next day, Wednesday August 30, members of the crew suddenly appeared in odd regions of the ship carrying cans of black paint which reminded Elizabeth and Jennifer ominously of the can that had fallen from the *Hindenburg* at Glyndebourne. They were blacking the portholes, inside and out, of all occupied cabins. That day the news circulated that they would arrive late at Southampton. The ship would be changing speeds and zigzagging.

"Just a precaution," said the purser.

"Some precaution!" mocked the well-informed. "They want to make the run down the Channel at night. Better sleep with the old life jacket on tonight, dear."

The next night, when the dawdling liner like an animal pursued suddenly surged straight ahead, its bow wave foaming white and high, the atmosphere became tense and close. Even Jennifer ceased her preoccupation with her own troubles and joined in the gossip in the bar. Elizabeth was left alone for once, and, attending to her own mood, found that she was still unafraid. Jennifer had her own problems, but she herself would simply *not* be involved. She made herself think of her own plans: Ginny, a new flat, a new job. The feeling of buoyancy came back. She had stayed on the periphery of the last war, and she would not make the same mistake twice. At the very center of war she would find the center of her self. On her journey to America she had sought escape; at the end of the journey home she would no longer need escape.

The *Aquitania* berthed at the Cunard-White Star dock in the first light of a calm and beautiful summer morning. The skies were blue, the hills green and serene above cliffs and ocean, the city all neat rows of chimneys and red tiles. Nobody quite believed that they had made it, and embarrassment at previous fear hastened the separation of shipboard friends. Despite sandbags and barbed wire, everything ashore looked absurdly normal, but the officials examining papers were very stern, and the news came that since this was the first of the long-planned three days of evacuation for children from large cities, there would be a slight delay for the boat train. They were given tea in the lounge. Over the loudspeaker at ten-thirty suddenly came the signature tune before the morning news from the BBC, and then the sepulchral voice of the announcer, giving not the weather forecast as he should, but saying, as one sat suddenly still and terrified: "There is grave news this morning." Germany had invaded Poland.

Elizabeth and Jennifer lunched on the train. On this first day of September, England was at its most beautiful. Elizabeth, with American eyes, had never seen anywhere so green and lush. Traffic seemed no heavier than on the usual holiday weekend. The trip had its moment of excitement–a bombing plane began to follow the train as though on a strafing run. Elizabeth realized quickly, of course, that it had RAF markings, but there was that feeling in the stomach, and afterward the wondering: If that had been an enemy plane . . . ?

Arriving at London's endless suburbs, the train slowed. Those rows of houses were still there. Their chimneys still saluted. Their neat and orderly doors stood all in rows, and women put washing on the line, and flowers bloomed everywhere–lupins and delphiniums and stocks and great heavy dahlias and asters and zinnias and, everywhere, England's roses heavy-headed in the sunlight. The guard came through to put signs reading "Special" in the window. The train was to be used for evacuating children. And at last here came the children–hordes of them on the platform, most in school uniform and hat, cheerful and noisy and orderly. Placards and harried teachers and a very few mothers chivied them into groups, and each carried some small cardboard suitcase or string-tied parcel, and each had a tag bearing name and address tied to a buttonhole or neck. God, thought Elizabeth, they are London's cockney heart and soul. Most of them carried or wore coats despite the hot day, and she smiled to find herself thinking the English were smarter than the Belgians.

Amid that sea of shining faces, Lady Pearsall stood out like a beacon near the barriers to the station proper. She wore a cotton suit of sapphire blue and a hat crazy with bright little flowers, and she leaned negligently on a tightly furled parrot-green umbrella with a pleased expression on her thin features. Thin, old, frail, and well, thought Elizabeth.

"I didn't think I could be so pleased to see anyone!" Elizabeth exclaimed to Jennifer, and waved as frantically as the schoolchildren through whom they had to push their way.

Ginny caught sight of them and stirred with pleasure, and then they were together, embracing wordlessly amid the noise and confusion.

"I was thinking while I waited," murmured Ginny into Elizabeth's ear. "Thirty years! More than thirty years we have known each other."

Elizabeth felt at last that she had come home.

61

September 1, 1939

The station was full of children and mothers and young soldiers with kit bags. Both groups reporting for duty, thought Elizabeth. Ginny took the surprise of Jennifer calmly after Elizabeth's promise to explain later. They put her into a taxi to find her own way home to Mayfair and went to bully Elizabeth's suitcases into Ginny's new baby Austin, which stood imperiously in a zone clearly marked "No Parking."

"I shall have to get myself some sort of official sign to put in the window," said Ginny. "Simply everyone has one, it seems. Now, shall we go straight back to your new flat? Or would you like a cup of tea first?"

"If you don't think me quite mad," said Elizabeth, "I should like to drive out to St. Patrick's, to the cemetery."

"God knows if we'll make it through all this wretched evacuation traffic," said Ginny, clambering awkwardly into the driver's seat of the little car and looping spectacles around her ears. "But heigh, ho, it's off to the boneyard we go!"

She beamed and started the engine under the very nose of a policeman, who tilted his helmet back on his forehead as she ground the gears and jerked straight off into the jammed traffic lane without looking.

London smelled the same as ever. It also looked festive, the people's faces calm.

"We're all hoping Chamberlain won't lose his nerve a second time," explained Ginny. "I mean, one has to do something about those Nazis. We wouldn't have waited so long in my day, I can tell you."

"Time now to wheel out Winston Churchill, would you say?" asked Elizabeth only half-ironically.

"I'm sure Winston thinks so," said Ginny, amused.

"The manly types have their uses."

Giant steam shovels were digging up the green in front of Knightsbridge Barracks where lapdogs used to whiddle. "Earth for sandbags," explained Ginny. On the skyline beyond Parliament a squad of silver antiaircraft balloons waddled against the blue like overfed elephants. "You will need a gas mask immediately," said Ginny, pointing out the knapsacks or cardboard boxes which everyone carried over their shoulders. His Majesty's pillar boxes, all scarlet and tubby, bore squares of greenish-yellow paint above the letter slots. "Detector paint," said Ginny. "For poison gases. One is supposed to recognize all their different smells, but one wonders–if one can smell it, is one not already dead?" She beamed. The streets were filled with uniforms. "There's St. John's Ambulance," said Ginny, pointing out a lady crossing in front of them as they waited for the light at Oxford Circus. "Didn't I tell you that uniform is by far the smartest?"

Traffic was not as heavy as expected, and they made good time, so that before leaving the suburbs they stopped at a flyblown fish-and-chips café for strong tea in thick china mugs. There, Elizabeth told Ginny Jennifer's tale and experienced the comforts of friendship–there was so much that she did not have to explain.

"Bother the girl!" said Ginny. "It really is most wretched of her to dump all this in your lap just as you have so many more important things to do. Does she not know there is a war on? She should have the sense to settle in and enjoy it."

Elizabeth laughed. "I came home to enjoy living, not war," she said. "And we should be fair–she has a war of her own on at the moment."

"Are you expected to do anything?"

"Nothing, I most profoundly hope. There should be no need if Anthony is simply playing some dreadful game with her, and she should know whether he is or not."

"I shall admire her if she wins this one, but I cannot see how she will," said Ginny frowning. "I should not, myself, call it a win even if she does get Anthony back."

"Exactly," said Elizabeth. "I wish she would choose Robert Brandon instead."

Ginny's eyes glazed slightly, and in her old manner she spoke to the air over Elizabeth's shoulder. "The woman doesn't know what faces her," she said.

Elizabeth did not know precisely whether she referred to Jennifer or to Elizabeth herself.

St. Patrick's was not to be moved by threats of war. It sat in the afternoon sunlight under its sheltering elm trees, and its brief steeple rose stubbornly against a sky marked by the contrails of aircraft. To the north a mass of dark thunderclouds rose high, black edged with white.

"It won't rain yet," said Ginny. It had grown very humid, the air heavy, and she fanned herself as she got out of the car. Elizabeth remembered that her friend was no longer young, to drive so far. "It's been thundery all week." She straightened from the side of the car, easing her feet in her smart shoes. "Actually, it has been rather amusing. Every time there is a distant roll of thunder, everyone jumps and then looks embarrassed. Nobody seems to remember what a stick of bombs really sounds like."

They walked stiffly along the gravel path. Marble and granite monuments surrounded them, and the grass was soft and brilliant green. The birds were those of the city–chirpy sparrows and cooing pigeons and one or two starlings–but the feeling was of the country, the soft rustling of the line of poplars, the scent of mown grass, the rattling of a mower interrupted by the bleating of sheep. War had not reached here, and though the northern thunderclouds gave an edge of oppressiveness to peace, to enter the graveyard was to cross the line into some other world where death was for meditation, not fear.

They came to a stone bench and Ginny sank gratefully upon it, loosening one foot from its shoe. "I shall just sit here and rest a moment. Do go on," she said.

Elizabeth walked on alone over the few yards that brought her to the place where Peter and Charles lay buried. She came at last to a stop at the foot of the two graves, precisely between them. For a moment she closed her eyes and listened to the sounds of life. The grass had not been allowed to cover the graves, and tiny plots of forget-me-nots grew at the foot of each. She turned toward Ginny and in her low voice called out softly across the monuments which separated them, "Was it you who tended them for me?"

"Of course," called out Ginny. She made a small offertory gesture with her gloved hands. "One should have more than one grave to tend by my age. But I didn't do the flowers. I don't know who did the flowers."

She laughed, and their voices across the graves deepened the sense of strangeness, as though they had been defiant. Now Ginny pulled herself to her feet and walked to join Elizabeth.

"Doesn't it worry you to be here?" asked Elizabeth quietly after a moment. She herself felt very old; but not yet tired.

"No, it doesn't worry me," replied Ginny slowly. "I feel much more sorry for them."

The two women stood silent and still graceful, only their brightly colored clothing linking them to the life of the trees and sky and grass rather than to the graves' gray.

Elizabeth moved the tip of one expensive shoe and prodded the grass directly in front of her. "I shall lie precisely here," she said, her slight smile an exact repetition of Ginny's. "It will be very fitting. I never could really choose when they were alive."

"You always expected too much of both of them," said Ginny.

"Did I really?" Elizabeth was surprised and sharp and looked sideways at her friend. "Well, perhaps." She thought a moment. "Perhaps in my own way I have been just as romantic as Jennifer, wanting more of men than they can reasonably be expected to give."

"Ah, men!" laughed Ginny.

"There's nothing wrong with men," said Elizabeth seriously. "Or at least nothing more wrong with them than there is with us. We each have our own romance: Hollywood for us, war for them. It would be nice if they didn't think they had to bully people in order to survive. I know one or two of them who don't think that way."

"If that is really true, marry them at once."

Elizabeth smiled. "Peter once said years ago that spouses are no more than incidents in each other's lives. Later he came to think he was wrong about that, because he never forgot Mary. Looking at it from here, I'd say he was right both times. We go on without each other, but we are never truly alone again."

"Marriage is a temporary rental," agreed Ginny crisply, thinking of Sir Reginald, "which death makes a permanent vacancy."

The clouds to the north sent out a long and very distant roll of thunder. A puff of humid air made the row of nearby poplars stir. They could hear the small drone of an airplane engine, and against the backdrop of the dark clouds there was the machine itself, quicksilver in the sunlight. The moment had its tension between action and inaction. The women seemed static, but under the stillness, their minds hummed like telephone wires in a rising wind, filled with the past.

Elizabeth spoke out of meditation. "We women all spend our lives between, don't we? Between then and now, between here and there, between memories and plans." She spoke very softly, her low voice in naturally musical rhythm. "There are so many obligations, so many complications. So very many rights and wrongs."

Ginny's response was almost liturgical. "We are always on the way somewhere, never arrived. Somewhere between war and peace, between doing and thinking, between being and becoming. Never wholly one thing, never wholly the other."

"Less than we hope," responded Elizabeth slowly. "More than we know. Never as important as we would be, always more important than others would have it."

Elizabeth took in a deep breath and turned away from the graves of men, looking toward the sky, gesturing at the airplane droning beneath the thunderclouds.

"There have been so many generations, and no matter what this war brings, there will be so many more." She shivered, as though the afternoon had turned chill, and looked at the red-brick church. "I do not like to think of God. I wish I could be just me. But that will never happen, will it? That still point at the center that the poets write about? I shall never be just myself."

Now Ginny, sighing, bristled into activity. She straightened her back against fatigue and looked at her friend. "I certainly do not think that I am simply one moment's drop of sweat," she said, emphasizing this last crude word deliberately, "upon the face of the Buddha on a single hot day of eternity. You make our pilgrimage have no meaning, and it cannot be so. You have been a daughter. You have been a wife, a mistress, a lover. You are a mother. You have been a perfect friend." She rested one hand commandingly on Elizabeth's arm, and her face was tired. "And somewhere in between all that, you have managed to survive as your self. That, my dear," she ended softly, "is the eternal individual miracle."

The magic bond still held these moments in place, and Elizabeth smiled. "Then I should forgive both God and men?"

"Then you should forgive both gods, men, and yourself." Ginny rearranged her umbrella, dusted her skirt. "As for daughters, I cannot say." She rummaged in her handbag. "And while you are doing all that, would you please kindly take these car keys and drive me somewhere a little more cheerful? There is a war on, you know."

As Elizabeth learned to orient herself to driving on what only gradually became the right side of the road again, the present quickly enwrapped them. Traffic from the city was now very heavy, laced with military lorries and other government vehicles, and many private cars were loaded with belongings. It looked less like holiday than flight, and it brought expectancy and mild alarm.

"I wonder," said Elizabeth, "if the Prime Minister has declared war yet."

"One would hope so," said Ginny cheerfully, "but I fear not. Look at the placards."

The news agents still advertised the invasion of Poland. Men stood about while women crowded the food shops.

"Wait till you see *our* stocks of supplies," said Ginny proudly. "I have purchased exactly the number of tins that enables me to feel safe without getting me accused of being a hoarder. Your larder–if something so ridiculously tiny can be called a larder–overflows. And I had Swan and Edgar's run up special blackout curtains for us, with floral linings! Most people are using plain brown paper because they think it will all be over by Christmas, but I remember the last time. Do you think we shall have raids tonight? Never mind, we shall be all set for the blackout. The wardens do shout at one so if there is so much as the tiniest chink of light showing. Very impertinent, the working classes have become!"

"There is to be blackout tonight? Even though we are not at war?"

"My dear, you must learn to read the posters."

White posters festooned hoardings and windows and lampposts. "BY THE KING, A PROCLAMATION," began some in august black print. "LIGHTING RESTRICTIONS," headlined others in more democratic type.

"At seven-forty-seven P.M. British Summer Time precisely," said Ginny smugly, "we shall do our bit to sink ourselves into gloom." She smiled cheerily. "I have a stirrup pump for each of us, and a spade and shovel for putting out incendiaries. I took classes in how to do it. And I stocked up on long white gloves this time." She grinned, looking with bright eyes at Elizabeth. "And on elastic. For our knickers!"

So they arrived laughing at the block of flats in St. John's Wood, which Elizabeth's American eyes saw as less modern than it had been. The hall porter turned out to help them with her baggage, and as he puffed ahead of them up the staircase with glass-brick walls which he had been patiently painting black, he said over his shoulder, "There's a young lady, Lady Pearsall. Mrs. Wingate's daughter, she said, but I took her to your flat. I didn't think you'd mind. She seemed a bit upset like, so I took her a cuppa."

Elizabeth came to an abrupt stop on the stairs. "Damn and blast," she said. "What has gone wrong now?"

Ginny opened her own door but stood aside for Elizabeth, who could at once see Jennifer on the window seat of the living room across the little hallway. She sat hugging her knees and looking out the window, cigarette smoke drifting from an ashtray, an untouched cup of tea beside her. She turned her head reluctantly as though she were ill and essayed a placating sort of smile, that of a child who has hurt herself on the forbidden swing. "I lost," she said softly. "I lost everything."

When Jennifer had left the railway station in a taxi, the crowds of children, the uniforms, the teams of men building walls of sandbags around important buildings had scarcely registered on her. The smaller rather than the larger war absorbed her as one last time she ran over her plans for apologizing to Anthony, for admitting that he had his rights even while she fought to preserve hers. The thought of Merry brightened her into anticipation, and as the taxi drove along Curzon Street she sat forward, suddenly eager to see that gray door with its brass knocker and letter slot leading to husband and daughter. A crew of men repairing gas mains worked noisily with jackhammers at the side of the roadway, so that the taxi had to skirt a barricade of earth, but the street and the house were unchanged. She paid off the taxi and managed her suitcase, her hatbox, her jewel case, and her handbag up the steps, setting them down outside the door. As she had so many times before, she slipped her brass key into the lock, turned it, and entered her home.

It was the same as ever: immaculate, subdued but shining in the afternoon sunlight. Anthony would be at the office, of course, but Merry would be here, Merry and the governess and the housekeeper and the maid. But the house was very quiet.

"Merry!" she called out. "Merry darling!"

The hallway shone in front of her as she lifted her belongings inside, kicking the door shut behind her as of old: the shine of waxed wood, the deep red Turkish runner, the Queen Anne table she had found in Hammersmith, the crystal vase bought during their Austrian honeymoon and filled with great roses whose perfume had scented the air.

"Merry! Where are you, darling?"

The narrow stairs faced her, curving upward toward the bedrooms and nursery. They would have heard her if they'd been down in the kitchen. They had to be in by now; it was almost teatime. She started up the first steps and thereby seemed to trigger a response—a woman's voice calling out above her.

"Who is that? Who's there?"

Jennifer smiled gladly. She must have alarmed the governess by using her own key.

"It's Mrs. James," she called out cheerily, pausing on the stairs, looking up. "I'm just back from America. Is my precious daughter up there?"

She smiled—eager, polite. There was no reply, so she started again up the stairs to make herself visible.

"It's perfectly all right," she said reassuringly. "Don't be alarmed. We don't know each other, but I'm Meredith's mother, and . . ."

She had rounded the curve of the staircase and saw the woman who had called out to her, standing there at the top of the stairs with one hand on the wall as though to bar the way.

"Fern?" said Jennifer. "Fern Hardacre? What on *earth* are *you* doing here?" Through her mind flashed the wild thought that her old school friend had fallen so far as to become a governess, but Fern wore a dressing gown which Jennifer recognized as her own, and Fern had bare feet and loose hair. Slowly Jennifer mounted another step.

Fern's soft, silly face looked frightened, and the pale flesh of her throat was mottled with the flush of blood. Her eyes were wide, and she suddenly clutched the robe across her breast, as though she were about to be attacked. "Jennifer," she said flatly. "What are *you* doing here?"

"This is my house," said Jennifer in a sensible tone, mounting another stair. "When did you get here? Are you in trouble with that wretched brute of a husband? Did Anthony take you in?"

But as Jennifer slowly advanced, Fern steadily retreated down the hallway, looking more and more frightened, until as Jennifer's last words brought her to the top step she buried her face in her hands and started to sob, thus loosing the front of the gown and showing herself, under it, to be naked except for panties, her blue-veined flesh intensely erotic. Jennifer had a sudden vision of Fern during that last week at school, lying on her back in the field, talking of sex and stroking with one fingertip the bare skin between her stocking top and knickers.

"Are you ill?" she said. "What's the matter?"

Fern the helpless, she thought, Fern the masochist, Fern the abandoned mistress, Fern the beaten wife.

And then, over Fern's bowed shoulders, she saw Anthony. He was coming from their bedroom, closing the door behind him, clad in his own dressing gown and slippers, his face flushed but his expression resolute as he stepped forward and placed his hands around Fern's upper arms to support her.

Jennifer sprang suddenly as a cat, realization instantaneous. She sprang not toward the couple but to the right, where the curve of the staircase continued upward to the nursery and Merry's bedroom.

"Where is Merry?" she called out. "I want my daughter! Where is my daughter?"

She was two or three stairs up before Anthony's measured reply reached her. "She's not here," he said. "She has left."

Jennifer backed down the steps and turned—as if under water—to look at her husband and her friend. If she had wanted to look beautiful enough to seduce her husband, she would have been pleased at her appearance now. Her eyes were a bright green, and her cheeks pink, and her chest panted with emotion. "What do you mean, she has left? What do you mean?" Her voice was rough now. "I want my daughter."

Anthony moved in front of Fern, placing the woman behind him as though for protection. Fern gave a sob and peeked childishly at Jennifer between her hands.

"She's been evacuated, of course," said Anthony. "You must have seen the children on your way here." His tone was calm and censorious, as though Jennifer were an ill-informed schoolgirl.

"And why," said Jennifer with a gesture at Fern, "is *she* here?"

"I don't see that that is any concern of yours."

"This *is* my house. You *are* my husband."

"It will not be your house again."

"I see." Jennifer lowered her head and walked past him and started down the stairs. "We had better discuss this in private," she said. She would not scream at him. She wanted him back.

He stayed above her. "There is nothing to discuss anymore," he said.

Jennifer continued slowly down the stairs, thinking only that she must not make another mistake with him. "I shall want to see Merry immediately. Where have you evacuated her to?"

He stayed silent, drifting down the top flight of stairs as she reluctantly reached the foot and stood with her back to him looking down the hallway at her luggage.

"Where have you sent her?" she repeated.

Behind her at the turn of the stairs he came to a stop, and a small smile appeared on his features. It was not a pleasant smile. "Where would you want her to go, my dear?" His voice held a touch of malice, of triumph. "Eh? Where would you want me to send her but the place you like so much and where she will be perfectly safe?"

She turned slowly to look at him, amazement growing on her face. "America?" she breathed.

"She's on her way to Canada at this moment, my dear," he said, and his eyes were alight with a mean pleasure. "She sails tomorrow from Liverpool, on the *Athenia.* If only you had known, you could have met her in Montreal." She stood still, amazed, the color draining from her face. "If you had ever shown the slightest sign of motherly concern for her well-being, then you would have known, wouldn't you? Wouldn't you?"

Jennifer's body seemed to collapse in upon itself, her face losing now tone as well as color. Her mind could focus only on a single task: I have to get them back.

Anthony–gifted with cruelty at this moment–read her mind. "You are thinking that you will be able to get me back," he said, face composed into ice. He stood with one hand on the rail, the other in the pocket of his dressing gown. "And I want you to be very clear, Jennifer, that the moment you signed that contract you ended our marriage, just as I had warned you. *You* chose to end our marriage, Jennifer, not I. You knew what you were doing. And it is done for good. I should tell you that Fern and I plan to marry."

He seemed very eager to say that, as though he had planned those words, treasured them up.

"You couldn't do this," said Jennifer in a murmur. "I love Merry. I love you. I *need* you. You *couldn't* be so unfair."

"I shall be in my office tomorrow morning." He seemed to burn with cold. "And I expect to see you there, for indeed we do have business to discuss. Fern and I go to the country in the afternoon." His calm was eerie, as though this were any old appointment. "And I expect you also to remove your remaining belongings from this house before we return on Monday. And to leave your key when you have done."

She stood beneath him, whipped. For a moment they looked at each other. Then there was a tumble of steps down the stairs above him and Fern's head appeared, peering over his shoulder, her face pale and anxious, her hands clutching the gown together at her neck. "I never meant any harm, Jennifer," she said desperately. "You must understand that. Anthony and I didn't mean to fall in love, did we, Anthony? You understand that, don't you, Jennifer? Love?"

Jennifer looked at Fern briefly; then she turned as though her body were a mass of pain and walked the length of the hallway toward the front door. They did not speak, staring at her. She lifted her luggage outside item by item. She turned to look at the couple motionless on the stairs, then spoke directly to Fern in a voice dry as winter grasses under snow. "I would have thought you would already know what love brings us women to," she said. "If not, then stay with Anthony. He will be glad to teach you."

Holding her head high, even now a trifle theatrical, she left the house. She closed the door as she always had, softly. She checked as she always had to make sure that it latched. She picked up her suitcase and hatbox and jewel case and faced the steps and the street where workmen labored. There were no taxis at the corner stand. There was, she thought, no future.

As Jennifer told them what happened, Ginny made them all strong gin-and-lemons instead of breaking out the bottle of champagne. Later she boiled eggs and burned toast for an early supper, saying that it was probably better not to go out in the blackout anyway. They ate their supper listening to the six-o'clock news read by Stuart Hibberd, who sounded shaken by the need to announce calmly the Nazi attack on Poland, the mobilization of Great Britain's Civil Defense, and the amalgamation, starting tomorrow, of the BBC's national and regional services. It was still very warm and airless despite intermittent rain, so rather than pull the heavy sateen blackout curtains they drank coffee by the light of candles placed well away from open windows.

Jennifer spoke little. She did not weep, but she looked puffy and pasty. She loved Anthony, she said many times. She loved Merry, she kept saying. How could she have acted so foolishly? She had no plans.

Ginny tried to respond rationally until she found out that the girl was not rational, but Elizabeth spoke even less than Jennifer, and one could not tell what she thought, only that she was thinking. A curious atmosphere came to be in that room. The women made small movements which the candlelight enhanced. Occasionally a puff of wet air from the open windows sent shadows scuttling into new positions on their faces. Outside there was total darkness. No reflected glow lit up the bellies of the rain clouds. Masking had reduced the traffic lights to glimmering red or green crosses. The flashlights of pedestrians made tiny flickers of light in the street below, but there were few cars and they drove with only parking lights, or with one hooded headlight. Buses lit only upstairs by dim blue lights looked like ghost ships. Occasionally a sound of loud knocking would come dimly from a nearby street, or a shout: "Light! Put out that light there!" Only the smell of wet earth reminded that there was a garden, houses, a city, for they could not see even the rain, just hear it chuckling in the gutters.

They had sat in silence for a long time before Elizabeth finally spoke. "Before we get a night's rest," she said, "we had better decide what you are going to say to Anthony when you see him tomorrow."

Jennifer looked up at her with dull eyes. "It's no use," she said. "You didn't hear how he said it. He meant it. I can't see him again." She seemed to resent being disturbed and put her chin back down on the hands clasped over her knees, staring out the window at the invisible.

"Well, you cannot just do nothing," said Ginny abruptly.

"I'll think about that tomorrow," Jennifer said in a girlishly high voice.

Elizabeth regarded her daughter coldly, the soft light not kind enough to her face to erase the day's fatigue and tension, and then she spoke contemptuously. "You really did think you were Scarlett O'Hara, didn't you? Now you have a real war on your hands." Suddenly she stood up. "And if you are going to fight, then you had better learn one thing. Tomorrow is *not* another day, no matter how much we wish it to be." She spoke crisply now, the candlelight making her expression unreadable. Ginny had grown very still, her face arranged as though she were listening to distant music. "Tomorrow is today. Tomorrow is yesterday. Tomorrow started when we were born, and it comes about because of all the choices that we have made, all that we have and have not become." Her voice was low and hauntingly musical, and she stood still, hands clasped in front of her. "'We have left undone those things which we ought to have done,'" she quoted, staring at her daughter, perhaps addressing herself. "'And we have done those things which we ought not to have done.'"

The rhythms of the ancient familiar words of the General Confession held them all still a moment longer. Then Jennifer rose from the window seat and crossed the room. "I have to go to the bathroom," she said.

Ginny stirred as soon as she had closed the bathroom door. "She cannot see Anthony in this mood," she said. "She will plead; therefore she will lose. She is a liar, therefore she will not be able to tell the truth when she needs to."

"Young people's lies are so inconsequential to them that they do not even remember them. She has harmed Anthony as much as he has harmed her. They are equally romantics. They would both rather kill than give up the dreams with which they married."

"You cannot *excuse* Anthony."

Elizabeth studied Ginny in the dim light and spoke with careful thought. "My daughter is a fool. She deceives herself. She is totally self-centered. I cannot excuse either of them."

She walked to the windows and pulled the curtains shut, closing out the sound and smell of rain. Then she crossed the room to switch on the standard lamp and the overhead light, so that the room's chrome-and-glass-and-bentwood sterility leaped back into presence.

"And she is my daughter," she said. "You know the saying that responsibility is the other side of freedom. But I am learning that the only freedom is that of choosing which responsibility one wants."

Jennifer emerged from the bathroom, and Elizabeth turned to her. "If you can't face Anthony," she said flatly, "I most certainly can. I shall keep your appointment with him tomorrow."

62

September 2, 1939

Whenever she entered a London bank, Elizabeth would think of plump, helpful Mr. Blakeley, whom she had so much bewildered at their last meeting. Banks are the haunts of men: stiffly buttoned-up importances behind tall closed doors, women going to and fro with bunches of papers in their hands. On this last Saturday before war, the City had been much busier than usual, but the long corridors of Anthony's bank retained their calm. The floors were antique and simple mosaic, and at their edges the wax had built up until it looked like a brown weld, making the whole corridor a single unalterable vault. Elizabeth rearranged her parcels and clasped the new alligator bag with which Ginny had presented her that morning on the grounds that she needed it more today than she would at Christmas, and listened to the click of her heels echo through the dim silence.

Jennifer had been indifferent over the morning's cup of tea. "Whatever you arrange, whatever he wants," she had said listlessly.

Anthony's name and title appeared on his oak door in gold lettering, and Elizabeth paused to look at it, her hand on the knob. "If and only if," she repeated to herself, "Jennifer were willing to end this marriage." She took one deep breath, forcing out of herself her anger at this man, and pushed open the door.

In front of her stood a waiting room, a typical private secretary's office, all leather chairs and filing cabinets and a solid desk with a typewriter and three telephones. Elizabeth's entrance surprised not just the secretary but also Elizabeth, for the secretary, when last she had seen her, had belonged to Charles. Mrs. Mountjoy.

"Mrs. Wingate!" exclaimed Mrs. Mountjoy, rising from her chair behind the desk. "What are you doing in England?"

"Mrs. Mountjoy!" exclaimed Elizabeth simultaneously. "What are you doing here?"

The two women knew each other very well, though they scarcely knew each other at all. Their mutual surprise made them laugh, which put them at ease.

"Please, do come in and make yourself comfortable," said Mrs. Mountjoy, moving around the desk to indicate a chair in front of a low table covered with magazines. They had a moment for reciprocal survey. She's aged very little, thought Mrs. Mountjoy. She looks so very English and proper, thought Elizabeth, glancing quickly at the twin-set, the tweed skirt even in summer, the gray hair demurely styled. But she has a pleasant face. Elizabeth pulled off her gloves and offered her hand.

"Perhaps you didn't know," said Mrs. Mountjoy. "I've been with Mr. James since 1934, since . . ."

She blushed brilliantly, recollecting only now that they had shared Charles Wingate. She looked down at her hands, and Elizabeth, recognizing the source of her embarrassment, could not help her out.

"Anthony never mentioned it," she said.

"But . . ." Mrs. Mountjoy looked confused.

"But I'm so glad for you," continued Elizabeth. "Charles always said that you were an excellent secretary."

And now she blushed, feeling she had made a gaffe, and there was a moment of silence as both women thought the situation impossible.

Elizabeth decided to break through. "It seems a very long time ago, doesn't it?" she said, touching the other woman's arm. Mrs.

Mountjoy remained tongue-tied. "All we have in common now—and it is a great deal, perhaps—is our memories."

When Mrs. Mountjoy looked up, her eyes were filmed with tears. She spoke softly and rapidly. "I have a confession to make. After you went to America, I . . . I started taking care of Mr. Wingate's grave. And Mr. Williams'."

"The forget-me-nots," said Elizabeth wonderingly.

"I hope you don't mind. It's very impertinent of me. But I thought . . . Mr. James said that you would never be back."

"Thank you," said Elizabeth quietly. "He was a man worth our care."

Each had given to the same man, each had taken from him. They had never been rivals.

Elizabeth took a seat and arranged her bag and gloves. "I'm back for good, now," she said. "At least, I think so."

"And of course you want to see Mr. James. But was he expecting you? He tells me very little of his private life, of course, but there's nothing on his calendar this morning."

"No,"—Elizabeth smiled—"Mr. James does not yet know that I have returned."

"I'm sure he will be absolutely delighted, but you are lucky to have found him in. He's in a meeting this moment—this war business, you know—but I'll let him know you are here the moment he is free."

"Thank you, Mrs. Mountjoy."

"I wish you would call me Julia."

"And I am Elizabeth."

Mrs. Mountjoy shook her head and blushed again. "You will always be Mrs. Wingate to me, I'm afraid." She smiled. "America has made you democratic."

Elizabeth laughed and decided that she liked Julia Mountjoy and would try to make her an ally if she could. "I do need to see my son-in-law as soon as possible, if you can manage it," she said. "We Americans are always in a hurry."

There followed a conventional discussion, Mrs. Mountjoy perching on the edge of a matching chair. How Elizabeth liked America; how were Mrs. Mountjoy's sons; how had the crossing been; how absurd it was to come back to a country facing war; how much extra work it had all been. It was only the second conversation the two had ever held, and they did well. They found they had more in common than memories—as one might have known, each thought privately. They got on very well indeed, and Mrs. Mountjoy made them both a cup of tea, then took her own cup to sit behind the desk as though nervous about presuming.

"Where are you staying?" she asked. "The Savoy?"

Elizabeth laughed. "Obviously you don't know that my financial circumstances have rather changed," she said without embarrassment. She still felt no ill will about the inheritance that Mrs. Mountjoy had received from Charles. "A friend has found me a tiny flat in St. John's Wood, and I shan't be able to keep even that on for long if I don't find a decent job fairly quickly."

Mrs. Mountjoy looked at her oddly. "Really?" she said with polite incredulity. "But . . ." Then she snapped the coming sentence shut on that one word, giving Elizabeth the impression that she was genuinely taken aback, having assumed that Elizabeth in some way still lived on Charles' money.

Elizabeth was vaguely amused. There was a long silence during which she sipped tea while Mrs. Mountjoy fiddled with papers, as though she had been offended, until suddenly she came to a decision and set the papers down firmly. She had a frown of puzzlement when she spoke. "Forgive me for intruding upon your personal affairs, Mrs. Wingate. But it has been less than a year since . . . Well, it was such a large sum that, frankly, I don't see how you could have spent it so quickly." She now looked confused by her own impertinence and retreated behind more fiddling with papers.

"I don't understand what you mean," replied Elizabeth. She was completely puzzled. Surely the woman didn't assume that the amount she had received from Charles' estate was large, even if her way of life was more modest than Elizabeth's.

Unfortunately her puzzlement made her sound chilly, and this drove Mrs. Mountjoy back into embarrassment. "I'm sorry," she said hastily. "I do apologize. I don't mean to intrude."

There fell an awkward silence during which, by banging file drawers and zipping paper into the typewriter, Mrs. Mountjoy forced Elizabeth to seek refuge in a financial magazine. After some minutes, she rose from her desk with a ring of keys in her hand. "Would you excuse me a moment?" she said, moving toward the door to the inner office. "I just want to check something in Mr. James' personal files."

Elizabeth nodded, thinking the woman a little strange to make unneeded explanations. She thumbed through the magazine and thought of her coming interview. She was resolved to be as direct as possible with Anthony. She would not hide her disdain for his conduct. What other weapon than disapproval did she have to bring him back to his wife? Damn the man.

Julia Mountjoy was gone a good five minutes. When she reappeared, she had a very different air. She seems, thought Elizabeth, indignant.

"I think it much better that you wait in here," said Julia Mountjoy stiffly, standing aside with a gesture at the entrance to the sanctum. "I have left something on Mr. James' desk which I think you ought to read."

Slightly bewildered, Elizabeth picked up handbag and parcels and followed the invitation. Mrs. Mountjoy closed the door firmly behind her. She faced a large and handsome office with windows looking out across the City's rooftops toward the Thames and the Tower. The office was very masculine: dark oak paneling, watercolors of English country life, a huge wooden desk with a glass top bare of all but essentials. She moved toward the desk, on whose shining expanse lay a long envelope, presumably containing what Julia Mountjoy wanted her to read. She picked it up and held it at arm's length, then fumbled hastily for her spectacles.

Her surprise came from recognizing not just her name on the envelope but Charles' handwriting. Her glasses on, she turned the envelope in her hands for a moment, then slowly, dread in her heart, she slipped one red fingernail under the flap and moved around the desk to catch the light.

At the head of the first page was a date which she could place precisely: October 20, 1931, a week after her mother's death, when Charles had come home from Rome to attend to all the details of her mother's will. The letter now grew so heavy with memories that her hand dropped with its weight. She sat in Anthony's great chair, which almost coffined her in leather, and began to read.

"My dearest Elizabeth," it began. "I find the greatest difficulty in writing this letter, and if it is ill-phrased, I ask you to remember that difficulty. I ask you too to remember that we have known each other a very long time—twenty-seven years—and that our life together has shown that we respect each other. The contents of this letter will not please you, but I hope you will understand."

Her dread increased.

"I think I have not made a bad husband. I have tried to be a good husband, and if I have not succeeded, that is only because I am a man like other men. I hope that by the time you read this you will have forgiven me my minor sins and that there were no major sins which you could not forgive after my death.

"Those are strange words to write: 'after my death.' I have never admired those who leave letters behind them, but now I understand them better because there will be unfinished business between us after I am gone, things that cannot be said between us while I am still on the face of this earth."

Elizabeth was scanning the words by now, the image of Charles speaking and writing vivid in her mind. It gave her the strangest feeling, this message from the dead.

"The doctors gave me a time limit almost a year ago. A year or so at most, they said, and your mother's funeral has reminded me that I cannot safely delay this writing. I have not told you this news because anything you might feel impelled to do about it would distort our lives in ways which would not be fair to either of us."

The letter fell again into her lap as tears came to her eyes. Charles had always secretly been so afraid of death, yet he had faced a long dying all alone.

"We have had a long life together, my dear wife, one more complicated than either you or I expected. We have loved each other, and we have felt so many other emotions toward each other that I can find no single word or string of words to sum them up. That is the way of marriage, is it not? You understand what I mean. I have come to admire your intelligence.

"Indeed, I have admired most things about you during our life together, and it saddens me to think that this letter leads us both to think about where we disagreed, but when I tried to speak to you a few days ago, you shut me out. You would not listen, and it is important that you listen."

She could not think for a moment what he was talking about, and then she connected the dates. He had written only days after they had had the single bitter dispute of all their married years. The cause and substance of that dispute were much more ghostly than he, but she still remembered the gist of it, that she was a poor wife and mother, his saying, "I loathe you. I really loathe you." Recollection stiffened her, so that she read on with less sentimentality.

"Money seems such a trivial matter for dispute, and yet perhaps it is not, certainly to me. Some months ago I established a trust in your name, and since you are reading this letter, you must be with someone who can give you all the necessary financial and legal details. You will not have to worry about money again, and I am sure that will come as a relief to you following the last three years, when you must for the first time in your life have had to earn your own money to support yourself. You will be angry to think that I have deprived you intentionally of money that you have a right to, especially when I tell you that I have recently been giving large sums away."

The paragraph made no sense at all. She had to reread it, then reread again. Dimly she recalled now the subject of their dispute. He had said, hadn't he, that their marriage was awry because she never gave him credit for his compulsion to earn? Oh Charles, she thought, it is all so very long ago. Was he about to tell her that he had been the Mystery Millionaire?

"But in your case, I believe the temporary absence of funds will be best. It will give you the chance you deserve to survive in the world entirely by your own individual efforts, as you seem to think you want. I suppose I hope that this will lead you to understand, not money so much, but me. If you understand, you will forgive."

At this point in the letter, she thought him, frankly, deranged. It had always been so very important to him, this money business. He had never understood that money simply was not as important to her as to him.

"My darling, I hope that the past three years have not been hard for you. I feel even at this moment the desire, the obligation to protect you. You say that such protection is not something you either need or want. I have therefore withdrawn it for as long as I am able. But I cannot think of you as suffering from want, and I hope you enjoy the money that has now come to you. When we married, I undertook to love, to honor, and to cherish you. You wanted freedom and I gave you as much freedom as I could. If I failed, it was not for want of trying. I tried."

His signature unadorned sprawled at the bottom of the page. Twice now they had been his last words: "I tried." She had believed him the first time. She had always believed that he tried.

"Oh Charles," she murmured to the dark oak room. "How can you be such a fool? If only you had said it instead of writing it to me!"

She was briefly possessed by an enormous sense of time lost, a feeling much too huge to be that merely of regret. Her hand slightly crumpled the pages in her hand, and her chin fell to her chest and her eyes filled with tears for him, for herself. She laid the pages of handwriting and their envelope neatly on the desk.

"This was all so unnecessary," she said aloud. "I already understood whatever it was you wanted to teach me. What I did not understand, obviously, was you."

She took a handkerchief from her purse, and a compact to repair her makeup, and then she picked up the letter again and crossed the office and opened the door. Julia Mountjoy sat at her desk, doing nothing. Her linked fingers rested lightly on the edge of the desk in front of a large green accordion file. She looked up at Elizabeth calmly enough, as though she knew what she felt.

"Do you know anything about this . . . this 'trust' of which my husband writes?" Elizabeth spoke practically, unemotionally, and despite the sympathy in her eyes, Julia Mountjoy was equally businesslike.

"The details of the trust are all in here," she said. She lifted the green accordion file and held it to her chest as though it were a child. "But perhaps you would prefer me just to tell you."

Elizabeth nodded. They both moved to the conclave of leather chairs and table for visitors, where Julia Mountjoy set down the file and the two stood looking at each other.

"I have not of course read Mr. Wingate's letter. I did not know it existed until I came here. I did not know the trust existed until Mr. James gave me access to his papers. I knew that Clarkson and Son had no cash, but I thought that Colonel Plunkett had taken it all with him to make a business deal."

Elizabeth nodded again, and Julia Mountjoy continued, "Charles apparently established a trust in 1931 and added to it regularly. I knew his health was not good, and I'm afraid I nagged him about it, but Mr. James told me after I came here that Charles knew for some time before he passed away that there was no hope."

"*Anthony* knew?"

"I'm afraid that Mr. James knew a great deal more than you realize." Her face looked briefly grim. "The idea of the trust, I later learned, was that you would have a minimal income from Charles' will but the bulk of the money would not come to you for three years to the day after Charles' death." She looked intently at Elizabeth. "I ask you to believe that I did not approve of this idea. But once I became an employee of this bank, I was sworn to silence. One wonders if perhaps that is why I became an employee of this bank." Again she looked grim, almost angry. "No matter. The trust contains almost all of his personal holdings. What he left me was only odds and ends. Everything else was to come to you. As trustees Charles named Colonel Joseph Plunkett and your son-in-law, Mr. Anthony James."

There was a definite edge of contempt in those last words, and Elizabeth stirred uneasily in her chair.

"That," continued Julia Mountjoy, "proved to be a mistake in more ways than one. When Colonel Plunkett vanished—I should say, failed to return—there were legal difficulties. Had he died, Mr. James would have become sole trustee." She took a deep breath and let it heavily out. "The sum in the trust is very large now, very large indeed. The bank has done well by you in that respect. The three years expired, of course, in September 1936. At that time the legal difficulties remained." Another deep breath. "Mr. James then decided that it would be wiser not to tell you until they were solved. I disagreed."

"You mean that Anthony decided to keep control over money intended for me?"

Julia Mountjoy nodded. "The legal problems," she continued, "were solved some two years ago. Shortly after you left for America. Mr. James delayed for some time. Eventually I asked him. He told me that he would write to you and hand over the bequest. I assumed he had. I have not since had occasion to look at the file." She pushed the file toward Elizabeth. "It's all in here. You are a rich woman again."

Elizabeth stared at the file wonderingly, then stared again at Julia Mountjoy. She had no curiosity to know the sum.

"I'm sorry," said Julia Mountjoy simply. "I should have acted differently. The bank has not done well by you. Mr. James has behaved disgracefully."

Elizabeth knew at this moment precisely what emotions filled her. They were not gibbering monsters fleeing down the corridors of her mind, but familiars solid as tombstones. Grief, surprise, a sense of contempt for Anthony, and anger—anger at Anthony and at Charles. She did not care about the money. It would be useful, but not magical. She was furious that Anthony should cooperate with Charles' attempt to reach out beyond the grave to control her.

She opened her mouth to make some comment, but at that moment the door to the corridor opened and there, in formal banker's uniform of wing collar and striped pants, stood her son-in-law. He looked very distinguished, his fair hair graying nicely at his temples, the still-youthful face preoccupied. He came to an abrupt stop as he saw the tableau in front of him. "Elizabeth!" he said.

His eyes left her face to move to the letter she held in her hands, then to Julia Mountjoy, then to the green accordion file. His face became suddenly expressionless.

"I think," said Elizabeth, rising slowly to her feet, "that it is time for you and me to have the last of our little talks, Anthony."

Ignoring Julia Mountjoy, Anthony ushered Elizabeth into his office and seated himself opposite her in the high-backed leather chair. He offered her a cigarette, which she refused. She placed the envelope from Charles on the desk between them, and he glanced at it ruefully.

"I suppose you think I'm a complete cad," he said.

"You put it mildly."

"I knew you would. May I explain?"

"Please do."

"I take it Julia has explained the trust to you? And you have your husband's letter—which, by the way, I have of course not read, though Charles told me the gist of it himself. I have been acting according to his wishes throughout, you understand."

Her face wore the smallest of smiles, whose meaning she did not want to interpret. His face was serious but open.

"I hope you see that I have been in a difficult position," he continued.

"I'm rather tired of your difficulties, Anthony. You seem to have the habit of resolving them at others' expense. If I were you, I should avoid any appeal to my sympathy."

"I can't expect you to understand."

"Oh, I understand quite well," she said. "You have been acting very responsibly, the head of the family taking care of the Wingate women."

He looked nonplussed. "I do not feel that I have acted wrongly."

"Of course not."

Abruptly he swung his chair half away as though he would look out the window. "Do you want to talk about Jennifer?"

She took cigarettes from her handbag and lit one before she replied. "I don't think so."

He was surprised. "You care more about the money?" He swung his chair back to look at her.

"There is only one thing to be said about you and Jennifer. Do you intend to pursue this divorce?"

He nodded, looking grim.

She smiled. "Then be aware," she said, "that I shall use this money to fight you all the way. And Jennifer will have Merry whether you like it or not."

He looked instantly angry and started to speak, but she talked over him. "And if you fight back, then I shall see what action I can take to have your conduct over Charles' trust investigated."

He forced his anger to become stiff propriety. "My conduct has been unimpugnable. I was trustee with sole discretion. Your husband's instructions to me were perfectly clear. You should have the money only when you needed it, not when you wanted it. If you remember, I repeatedly inquired to determine your financial status."

She merely smiled, and when he resumed, his tone was very different. "Elizabeth, you must believe that I did what I thought was for the best."

"I'm sure you did. I'm sure you always do what is for the best. I'm sure you are quite incapable of understanding when you have done anything wrong. Let me explain it to you, Anthony. To try to divorce your wife at all, let alone on the ruinous grounds of adultery, is not righteousness. It is revenge. You are trying to reduce my daughter to the status of a thing. You did the same to me over Charles' money. But it doesn't work, Anthony, and what earns you my contempt is that you act not villainously, but stupidly. You cannot reduce us. You are a fool."

The scathing contempt of her tone stung but did not change him. "I have always acted responsibly," he said.

She studied him for a moment, thinking that they were words which Charles might have used—an explanation that was to men a full defense.

"I could almost feel sorry for you, Anthony. You are divided into two halves, and you can't make them match up. When you feel at your most reasonable, you are acting out of pure emotion, and you cannot tell the difference." She stubbed out the cigarette. "The difference between you and my husband is that you don't try to." She shrugged. "I am not interested in filling up the gaps in you. If Jennifer is, then she will have to deal with you herself. Now, shall we talk business?"

The signatures, the contents of the green accordion file, took no more than half an hour. When they had finished, Elizabeth picked up one of the parcels she had carried. "I have a little gift for you," she said, and pushed it across the desk toward him, amused at something private.

"A gift?" He looked at the parcel as though it contained snakes.

"Open it," she said.

He took off the string and wrappings, and from the box within emerged the clay figure of the Buddha, chipped, faded, but not much older than when it had come to Elizabeth. Anthony looked from it to her, bewildered.

"Peter gave it to me years ago. The idea is that it should go to the person who most needs it." She rose to her feet. "It's yours now, with my blessing." She turned to the door. "If I may make a recommendation, study its smile. Try to discover what it means."

As he opened the door for her exit, he thought that it was the expression of satisfaction on her face that he would like to understand.

63

"Has the man no conscience?" asked Ginny indignantly.

She sat that evening in her own armchair, knitting industriously.

"Conscience?" said Elizabeth. She gave the mound of dough on the table in front of her a healthy punch. She wore an apron over a cotton dress, and her face was slightly sweaty from the heat of a room closed off on a warm evening by heavy blackout curtains. She straightened from the table, which was covered with mixing bowls, bags of flour, jugs of water, a large bread board, a rolling pin, and a worn edition of Mrs. Beeton's *Household Cookery*.

"Why should he have a bad conscience? According to his own lights, he had done nothing wrong. Everything he did was justified." She laughed briefly. "I'm sure he believes he was put into this world with the duty of keeping order and reason. He happens to regard both myself and Jennifer as representatives of disorder and unreason, so how could he believe himself unjustified?"

She gave another single-fisted punch to the dough, then started kneading it energetically.

"I still don't see how you could have got *nothing* out of him," said Jennifer with a touch of querulousness. She sat in a straight-backed chair near the window, working spasmodically at a piece of embroidery which Ginny had found for her. Elizabeth had forced her to prepare their light evening meal. She had done a good job with omelet and vegetables, and effort and success had strengthened her.

"I got *that* out of him," said Elizabeth, bowing her head sideways to indicate the green accordion file which sat on a chair next to the table.

"And according to my reading of that," said Ginny, "it was no mean victory. You have made yourself rich, which is not a bad effort for a single day's work."

Elizabeth stood back from her kneading. "I suppose he had to give up that," she said thoughtfully, "so it wasn't much of a victory, really. It was mine to begin with."

"As Merry is mine," flashed Jennifer.

Elizabeth looked ironically at her daughter, wiping her hands on the apron. "I've said before. You have precisely as much right to decide Merry's future as does he. You can fly to New York by the *Dixie Clipper* tomorrow if you want, and you can meet Merry at the dock in Montreal and you can take her with you back to Hollywood."

They had spent most of the afternoon talking about what they could do next, and Jennifer had refused to decide, refused even to comment, as though one part of her were paralyzed with misery.

The radio filled the silence with Sandy Macpherson at the theater organ vamping through "Roll Out the Barrel" in endless choruses. He had played most of the day, interrupted by bulletins. Parliament had been called into session, and a declaration of war was expected any moment. Outside it was almost dark, and heavy thunderstorms had been predicted.

Elizabeth stared for a moment at her daughter, shrugged, went back to gentler kneading.

"I did not make much of a dent in him, I expect," she said meditatively. "But, really, what dent is there to be made? He knows what he wants. He is reasonably happy with the choice he has made." She cast a quick glance at her daughter. "Anthony came of age in the war. He does not think just that fighting is sometimes necessary. He thinks it is right."

"By your own admission, you didn't even really try," said Jennifer.

"I won't have that, young lady," snapped Ginny unexpectedly. "If your mother could not change his mind, his mind is not to be changed."

"I think Julia Mountjoy made a dent." Elizabeth smiled, again kneading the dough. "I shall never forget the look on his face. There she was when we came out, sitting very quietly at the desk with her hat and coat on, and when she handed me that file and dropped the keys on her desk right in front of him, and simply went, I think that got to him. I think it was the keys. Keys are so important to men, particularly when they delegate them to us to take care of."

"All men want is to control us," said Jennifer. "I hate them for that."

Elizabeth continued kneading, sprinkling more flour. "I think you are quite wrong," she said. "And I think generalizations about men are very harmful to us. Anthony is not all men. Peter was not like that. Charles was not like that. More important to you at the moment, Robert Brandon is not like that."

"How can you say Father was not like that," sparked Jennifer, "when you have just learned that he tried to control you even from the grave?"

"Charles was wrong," replied Elizabeth. "But he was not cruel. He tried." She kneaded the dough briskly. "And you and I must accept our own part in their failure. Anthony's logic, like your father's, is impeccable to him. If it was not visible to us, that is our responsibility."

A sudden rattle of rain hit the windows, and Jennifer started nervously and reached for the drapes to look out.

"Don't open them!" said Ginny hastily. "You'll get us yelled at. One forgets so easily." She stretched her knitting as a crash of thunder sounded close by and the radio let out a burst of static. "Though why they should require us to have a blackout when the wireless says that the bombing planes can't possibly fly while we are covered with clouds, I cannot imagine."

"Oh," smiled Elizabeth. "They will want us all very orderly and reasonable for the duration. They will want us to do as we are told."

"I would be much more ready to do what they told me if they followed through with their part of the bargain," grumbled Ginny. "As long as the men were all in the front line and we were safe at home, then it was all very reasonable to cooperate. But when they make this the front line, then I totally fail to see why we should go along with them."

Again Elizabeth smiled. "A good moral for life as a whole," she said. "But you know as well as I do you won't live up to your threats. We'll go along with them."

"When they yell at one so, I don't see what choice there is," said Ginny acerbically. "I'm tired of this wretched blackout already." For a moment her face looked gray with fatigue in the face of a future endlessly ordered and reasonable.

"Yell back," said Elizabeth quietly.

"It's the same problem with Anthony," said Jennifer sulkily. "And with Father."

"Your father did not seek to control me, Jennifer," said Elizabeth firmly. "He may have made other mistakes, but even with the money I think he was trying to give me—both of us—freedom. You've read his letter. You've seen how torn the poor man was."

"Anthony isn't torn," said Jennifer, but Elizabeth ignored her. "The mistake Charles made," she said, looking at the green accordion file, "was to think I valued things as much as did he, and I never have. Money was what he, not I, used to control the world."

She lifted the breaking lump of dough from the board and pushed it into a mixing bowl, then read the cookbook. "Good Lord," she said. "Now we let it sit for another hour! I had no idea baking bread was such a complicated process."

She sat down in the chair, wiping her hands on her apron. "He may have made a second mistake—thinking you can give anyone freedom. People aren't given freedom. They take it. They either have it or they don't."

She pulled a packet of cigarettes from her apron pocket, took one, and sat banging its tip slowly against the table, looking with kindly eyes at her daughter. "I have to point out," she said, "that you chose to marry Anthony. You could have chosen differently. If we'd known him better at the time, you could have chosen Robert. You still could. If you must have a man, he would be by far the most sensible choice."

Ginny looked up at her with surprise, thinking she spoke more boldly to Jennifer than usual.

"I don't love Robert," said Jennifer sulkily. "I do love Anthony. And I still believe that Anthony loves me."

"Even setting aside Fern," replied Elizabeth abruptly, "who you say is trivial—though I think she is what you might become if you are not very careful indeed—even setting Fern aside, how can you say Anthony loves you? Of course he does not. Good Lord, girl, he blames you for having changed! He says you caused the whole failure of your marriage! Love doesn't *flinch* like that. Love allows for change, as your father allowed for my changes and his own. Love welcomes change. Love rejoices in change. Love *loves* change, and it changes with change. You have to face up to it, Jennifer. Anthony does not love you. He doesn't even know the meaning of the word. I just hope you do."

She had stared at her daughter intently through this speech, as though she would make the matter-of-fact passionate. Now she sat back and lit her cigarette. "I think," she said in a quieter tone, "that you still have a romantic attachment to Anthony, which is very different from love. It's exactly the same as your wanting to play Scarlett O'Hara. You started off to be an actress, but somewhere along the way you got sidetracked into wanting to be a star, which is a very different matter. It brought you to disaster, didn't it?"

Jennifer looked up at her with the expression of a wounded animal. "How can you be so cruel?"

A clap of thunder ended her sentence, and a flash of lightning illuminated the blackout curtains, and suddenly the electricity outside seemed to have entered the room, so that as Jennifer and her mother stared at each other, some energy rose to unite them.

"I don't think now is the time to play the poor little thing, Jennifer," Elizabeth said steadily. "I think it is time to give up all that. You are going to have to think now, and think directly and honestly for once. You've always preferred merely to go according to what you thought you wanted, and that has led you into folly and deceitfulness."

Jennifer flinched.

Ginny put down her knitting and said, "Listen to your mother, child. She's telling you the truth, and one should always listen to the truth. One hears it so rarely."

Jennifer looked with bewilderment at the two older women, conveying a sense of betrayal, but Elizabeth, rising to her feet, continued with resolution. "I can only suggest what you might do. I can't control you. And nor can Anthony *unless* you want him to. He's rubbish. Clever rubbish. Why should I have argued with him today? The moment I discovered that he had kept Charles' money from me I knew that I didn't want him in the family. There was no choice for me. Apparently there still is for you. You should be asking yourself: what is it in me that makes me want to keep a piece of clever rubbish?"

She stubbed out her cigarette and crossed the room to the light switch. Jennifer looked angry, hurt.

"What Anthony wants to give you, after all," said Elizabeth, standing with her hand on the light switches, "is your freedom." She smiled again, with more irony than compassion. "Why are you so uncomfortable with that idea? It is not very different from that which Ginny and I faced when our husbands died."

"It is not very different," said Ginny unexpectedly, "from that which your mother and I faced while our husbands lived."

"It would be better if—" began Jennifer.

"It's not a matter of what would be better," interrupted Elizabeth. "It's a matter of what *is*. You have to find out what the world is and deal with it as it is. Romance is always *better* than reality. You have to learn to tell the difference between them. Only then is it safe to enjoy both."

One can hear the truth, recognize it, but not admit that one has heard, especially when one is a parent and child.

"That's all right for you to say," said Jennifer. "You have the courage for it. And I don't live in a fantasy. All I tried to do was have everything I wanted. What is so wrong about that? Why should I have to end up with *nothing?*"

Elizabeth sighed to hear her daughter's sullen anger. "I don't know," she said. She felt, in a sense, that her admission of ignorance was the last offering a mother could make. Mother and daughter now looked at each other across a space that neither could bridge.

"I'm going to turn out the lights," said Elizabeth, and did so. The room became completely black. "Let's look at the storm, shall we?"

She crossed the room and twitched back the blackout curtains. Outside the lightning flashed almost continuously, and when Elizabeth opened the windows the sound of rain and thunder took on enormous volume. Ginny rose to stand with her at the open window, Jennifer remaining in her seat next to them, facing the room. The only light was that of the lightning, but it was enough to show the great city's houses crouched in astonishment at the barrage which nature inflicted on them.

"All you have to do, my dear," said Elizabeth, looking out the window rather than at her silent daughter, "is imitate Julia Mountjoy. Just put the keys on the desk in front of him and say, 'I shall not be needing these any further, thank you. I shall not be coming back. Good-bye, Mr. James.'" She laughed softly with the memory. "Is that really so very hard?"

64

September 3, 1939

The West End was very quiet that Sunday morning on which war was to be declared. The baby Austin wheeled through empty streets. It was a perfect sunny day, refreshed by the storms which had come and gone during the night, taking dirt and humidity with them. Soldiers no longer littered the bus stops with their kit bags, and the workmen piling sandbags had taken the morning off to be with their families and listen to the radio. More police than usual stood about on empty corners, looking odd because their tall headgear had already given way to flat and shiny new steel helmets. Otherwise great London was at her best that morning, her streets clean, her buildings looking spruce as well as dignified.

The women had agreed to divide responsibilities: Ginny to do the driving, Elizabeth to help Jennifer pack her belongings. Rather too much, thought Elizabeth, depended on whether Jennifer would accept that responsibility or not.

Nervous, Jennifer began with resolve, but when they found the turn from Curzon Street blocked to vehicles by earthworks abandoned from the repair of gas mains, the extra obstacle was too much for her. "It's no use," she said. "I can't do it. I just can't."

Elizabeth buried her exasperation. "I'll do it for you," she said calmly. "One last time."

Jennifer wanted her to bring only clothes and other personal belongings–no photos, no knickknacks, no souvenirs, no valuables. Cheered by this small showing of independence from the material and sentimental, Elizabeth acceded without agreeing and set off down the street alone, holding the brass house key in her fingers. Ginny and Jennifer would return for her at eleven-thirty.

Elizabeth felt the crossing of the threshold as an event. The hallway stretched before her calm and still, slightly perfumed, a few petals falling from roses in a vase on the table as the current of air stirred them. She went quickly down the stairs to the kitchen to find the battery-powered radio, which she switched on as she climbed the stairs to the main bedroom where, Jennifer had promised, she would find all her belongings except her coats. Prime Minister Chamberlain, announced the radio, would address the nation at eleven-fifteen.

So that, at last, will be it, thought Elizabeth.

The BBC began playing selections from *Princess Ida,* and Elizabeth did not have to search for suitcases. They stood in a neat blue trio outside the door to the master bedroom. The next hour was to bring other signs of Anthony's cooperativeness. The only traces of Fern's presence were a spill of powder in the bathroom and the scent of expensive perfume in the air. Tact? More likely prudence. The perfume irritated her.

It took an hour to pack up her daughter's marriage, including the mementos and photographs. Wrapped in tissue in a bottom drawer was her daughter's wedding veil. She left it, and as she shut the drawer upon it she knew that she was deeply, passionately angry, with an anger as far from rage as from despair, an anger that filled her very much the way she filled the suitcases, an anger made solid with indignation, disappointment, righteousness. The radio gave up on Parry Jones singing "The Passionate Shepherd" and played a recorded talk on "Making the Most with Tinned Foods." She closed the suitcases and carried them one by one to the front door, then returned for one last check.

In the bedroom the radio introduced the Prime Minister, Mr. Chamberlain, and she gave it a contemptuous look as his mournful, nasal, old man's voice began: "I am speaking to you from the Cabinet Room at Ten Downing Street."

She turned up the volume, then walked into the bathroom for a final survey. As he spoke heavily on, she found herself staring at Anthony's bottle of after-shave: Lilac Végétal.

"This morning the British ambassador in Berlin handed the German government a final note, stating that unless the British government heard from them by eleven o'clock that they were prepared at once to withdraw their troops from Poland, a state of war would exist between us."

And now she felt the burden of responsibility. She could not tell, in that moment, whether she wanted it or not, only that she resented that it had been given to her. She picked up the bottle of Lilac Végétal and walked back into the bedroom, where Jennifer and Anthony's marriage bed was placid, smoothed.

"I have to tell you now," said the Prime Minister intimately, "that no such undertaking has been received, and that consequently this country is at war with Germany."

She stooped. She seized the counterpane on the bed and pulled it off as though stripping the shirt from someone's back. Then she did the same to the blankets and sheets, letting them fall in a heap behind her.

The clear voice on the radio continued: "The situation in which no word given by Germany's ruler could be trusted and no people or country could feel itself safe, has become intolerable. Now we have resolved to finish it."

The dislodging of pillows revealed nightwear: his, hers. They lay defenseless and frivolous before her. Slowly she removed the top from the bottle of Lilac Végétal, loosing its sharp-sweet smell into the room.

"May God bless you all. May he defend the right, for it is evil things that we shall be fighting against."

She lifted the bottle above the bed.

"Brute force," said the Prime Minister. "Bad faith. Injustice."

She tipped the bottle, and the liquid began to pour upon the nightgown and pajamas. The glug-glug was voluptuous.

"Oppression. And persecution."

Wet, the nightclothes shriveled.

"And against them I am certain the right will prevail," His Majesty's Prime Minister assured her.

A small, bitter smile curved Elizabeth's lips. "So anger," she said, "at last becomes determination." She dropped the empty bottle onto the bare mattress.

Silent for a moment, the radio now crashed forth with the opening notes of "God Save the King," and she leaned forward and clicked it off in mid-chord.

It took a handful of minutes to carry the radio back to the kitchen, to open the hall closet and add Jennifer's winter coats to the three blue suitcases, to place the luggage at the top of the steps. The street had become utterly quiet; no sound even of traffic.

Ginny and Jennifer appeared at the corner, the one injured by age, the other by youth. She watched them walk toward her, and when they reached the bottom of the steps, she said, "You've heard? We are at war?"

Ginny gave her a bleak smile with lifted eyebrows. "My dear," she said softly. "When are we not?"

Jennifer's face was filled with utter misery, and Elizabeth offered action as the only comfort she could bring. "Help me carry these things, will you, darling?" she asked softly.

They each carried a suitcase down the steps, then placed the pile of coats on top. Jennifer's face was soft with grief. Elizabeth handed her the house key, and when she refused it with a shake of her head, she persisted. "You have to," she said. "Put it on the hall table."

Jennifer slid the brass key onto the shining table next to the roses as though replacing a thing stolen, then hastened back to her mother.

"Oh, well," said Elizabeth. "You are not quite Julia Mountjoy, yet."

Briefly she put her arm around her daughter's waist and smiled at her. Jennifer walked down the steps with her head bent, so that it was Elizabeth who closed the door and checked that it had latched.

"That's done," she said to them cheerfully enough. "Now we can start working on our future."

Descending the steps, she was caught halfway by the beginning of a sound from the sky, a sound so unfamiliar that all three women looked up to see what it was. A siren had started up in the distance, and others joined it, and the great haunting sound drove closer to them until a monster almost right above their heads awoke to batter at them in waves, as though the house itself expressed its rage.

"Dear God!" shouted Ginny. "The Germans haven't wasted any time!"

Her face had shown alarm, but as she looked up at Elizabeth, confusion was replaced by a smile that had in it the light of pure mischief, and Elizabeth, unexpectedly, felt herself exhilarated. Ginny, as always, had courage. But Jennifer's face had gone white and her eyes wide, and she stared desperately at her mother. "We have to get inside, quickly," she demanded. "To get away from the poison gas. Quickly." And as she ran up the stairs, she pushed aside her mother's restraining hand. "The gas masks! We don't have gas masks!"

Heated by Jennifer's panic, Elizabeth shouted at her over the siren, "You can't go back! We just locked ourselves out!"

Jennifer turned from the door, her face a mask of fear as the great wailing of the sirens sank, then began to rise again. "Oh, God," she said wildly, looking about. "Where is the shelter?" She began to shout at her mother. "We have to have shelter, don't you understand?" Coat flying, she stumbled down the steps in high heels, dragging her mother with her. "Leave all this," she said with a desperate glance at the luggage. "None of it matters. We can get to the car at least. Quickly!"

She begged, but Ginny and Elizabeth stood. The siren rained blows on them, and Jennifer looked up at the sky, face expressionless with shock, until slowly she crumpled onto the steps sobbing, "Oh, God save us, God save us."

The street seemed suddenly full of people. Householders, wild-eyed and staring at the sky as had Jennifer, had run from the radio to the street, becoming neither reasonable nor orderly. Out of nowhere cycled a policeman, head down and pedaling madly. On his back and front were printed signs reading "Take Cover!"

Elizabeth glanced at the confusion, then moved decisively toward Jennifer. "We won't get anywhere except on our own two feet!" she shouted. "Get up! Ginny, take her other arm!" She grasped her daughter under the armpit and dragged her to her feet. Beneath the siren, she muttered in her daughter's ear with rage, "Don't make me despise you for a coward."

But Jennifer sagged, and tears streaked mascara onto her cheeks. "Merry!" she sobbed. "I must find Merry! Where is my daughter? I want my daughter!"

And as she spoke, the siren gave them a sudden silence more unexpected than its noise, and, embarrassed, the people in the street stood still, then began to move back inside, and Elizabeth looked up at the sky and let her daughter's arm fall. The silence was filled with a tension almost tangible, waiting to splinter.

An observer might have found Elizabeth comic now, as she was, for one last time, irresolute. She walked away a few steps from her daughter, then turned to look at her, opening her mouth to speak. Then she walked back and bent to pick up a suitcase, then changed her mind again and stood to stare at her daughter. When she spoke into the electric silence, her voice was low with exasperation. "I know I've had enough," she said. She stepped closer, and her voice rose. "Enough, do you hear?" And suddenly she seized Jennifer by the shoulders and began to shake her. "Enough of all your wants, your must-haves, your whining for other people to fix things for you! Do you understand?"

"Leave me alone," sobbed Jennifer, rag doll between her mother's hands.

As she spoke, the siren resumed and steadily rose to screaming pitch, so that Elizabeth had to thrust her face into her daughter's in order to be heard. "No I will *not* leave you alone. You want your daughter back? You're stupid enough to want your husband back? You want everything you can get? Then you can fight, damn you, fight like I had to!"

She took her hands away from Jennifer's arms, and the two stood looking at each other.

"Fight?" questioned Jennifer, the word scarcely audible.

Elizabeth's voice now rose to beat the siren. *"We* are going to fight, do you understand? You and I together. They cannot beat us *both!"* And she turned away, disgusted, giving up. "God, there is nothing that I envy you anymore."

"Fight?" repeated Jennifer.

There was the glimmer of some spirit in her face, and Ginny Pearsall saw it. She reached to take the girl by the hand. "It's what the government wants of us," she said with as much irony as a shout would allow. She stooped to pick up a suitcase. "Why don't you take these coats? And why don't we go to find a nice cup of tea?"

Elizabeth turned, so that mother and daughter faced each other across the luggage. As the long sound of the siren sank, Elizabeth spoke to Jennifer almost imploringly. "Don't you see? If they make us fight, we *have* to fight." Her low voice was intense, as though she would pour knowledge of the future into her daughter. "And if we have to fight, we have to *win,* we will *win.*"

Jennifer looked down at the suitcase at her feet. "Win?" she said, as though the idea were a newborn.

The siren rose again, and then again began its falling wail, and Jennifer looked at Ginny and Elizabeth and stooped to pick up the suitcase. And she smiled.

"If you two can manage," said Ginny matter-of-factly, "I think we should drive down Piccadilly to the Ritz, which has the best cup of tea in our vicinity. And the most comfortable cellars."

And Elizabeth, looking at her daughter, laughed.

Each carrying a suitcase and coats, the three women stepped into the roadway toward the barriers of earth around the gas mains. They had almost reached them when a coarse shout came to them over the siren's wail: "Hey, you! What the bloody hell do you think you are doing!"

They turned to look back down the street, in which the sole remaining figure was that of a stout and sturdy little man coming toward them at a jog. He wore big boots and brown overalls and a flat tin helmet, all clearly marked with ARP. Equipment flapped and clattered all around him, and he carried a whistle in his hand.

"Oh, Lord," muttered Ginny. "I warned you about the working classes."

His face was red, and he was shouting. "Take cover, you idiots! Take cover!" He stopped yards away to blow his whistle at them. "I'm to arrest anyone who disobeys the whistle," he shouted. "Off the street! Now!"

He was covered with badges of office, but it wasn't hard to see that underneath the uniform was a fat and nervous little man frightened equally by his job, the prospect of death, and the need to face down three well-dressed women in Mayfair. He had expected to bully nothing more than a delivery boy on a bicycle or a taxi driver being greedy.

"You must be bloody mad!" he said at them. "Don't you hear the bloody siren?" They merely looked at him. "Don't you know I'm here to take care of you? That you got to do what I say?"

"My good man," Lady Pearsall said firmly. "We do not require your help. We do not need you to take care of us." She advanced slowly upon him. "We most certainly do not *want* you to take care of us."

She had arrived immediately in front of the man, who began to retreat reluctantly toward the earthworks. She raised a forefinger and poked him on his puffed chest with its badges of authority. "Now, run away, little man, and find someone else to do what you say." Ginny was on the verge of laughter. "These are *our* lives, not yours," she said with a poke. "And if we choose to risk them, then that is *not* your responsibility, but ours." She stuck her chin forward and glared at him, undeniable. "Do you understand?" she shouted over the siren. "Ours? To do with what we wish, now and always?"

She gave him one last prod, and he stepped backward once more, and stumbled over the pile of earth left by the workmen, falling onto his back in the hole at the edge of the road, head lower than his heels, struggling like a beetle to right his portliness and authority from the smelly dirt.

Ginny looked down at him and started to laugh, an old woman's throaty cackle. Then Jennifer, looking at Ginny, at the little man on his back, at Elizabeth, began to smile, and the color flooded back into her face, and as though she had been freed, she too began to laugh. And finally Elizabeth, watching her daughter, catching her smile, tilted her head to send her own laughter into the cloudless, empty blue sky that stretched above the great calm city.

So that in that neat and narrow street in the heart of the city that was the center of the world, nothing could be heard as war began but the high, pulsing wail of the sirens and the mightier, further sound of high, human, women's laughter.